WHY ARE THEY CHEERING THIS MAN?

"The Cowardly Lion of the British Empire . . . Flashman's back, the Sioux and Apaches have got him, and we're all the richer for it."
—*Chicago Tribune*

"Flashman—scoundrel, cheat, bully, cad, lecher—and the best entertainment going! Villainy triumphant!"   —*Houston Chronicle*

"A deplorable seducer of women of all sizes, shapes, rank and country of origin . . . and a marvelous storyteller."
—*Pittsburgh Post-Gazette*

"Defenders of decency, disciples of honor, students of courage— take heed! Bolt your doors, lock your windows, hide your daughters . . . and prepare to be royally entertained. . . . Take our word for it, the West has never been so wild!"—*Cleveland Plain Dealer*

FLASHMAN
— and —
THE REDSKINS

GEORGE MACDONALD FRASER was born in England, schooled in Scotland, and now lives with his family on the Isle of Man. He is the author of *Flashman, Royal Flash, Flash for Freedom! Flashman at the Charge, Flashman in the Great Game,* and *Flashman's Lady*—the first six volumes of The Flashman Papers, to which *Flashman and the Redskins* is the latest highly acclaimed edition.

SCALE OF MILES

0   100   200

UTAH

ROCKY

Green River

Colorado River

COLOR

SANGRE DE CRISTO MOUNTAINS

SOUTH

Colorado River

ARIZONA

MTS.

Eagle Nest

Taos
Santa Fe

Rayado

Las Vegas

Rio Grande del Norte

Albuquerque

NEW MEXICO

Socorro

Gila River

GILA FOREST

San Marcial

JORNADA
DEL MUERTO

Santa Rita
City of Rocks

Frontier of 1848

Donna Ana

Frontier of 1853

El Paso

MEXICO

Rio Grande

SONORA

CHIHUAHUA

Freda Tuford

Cheyer

Pu

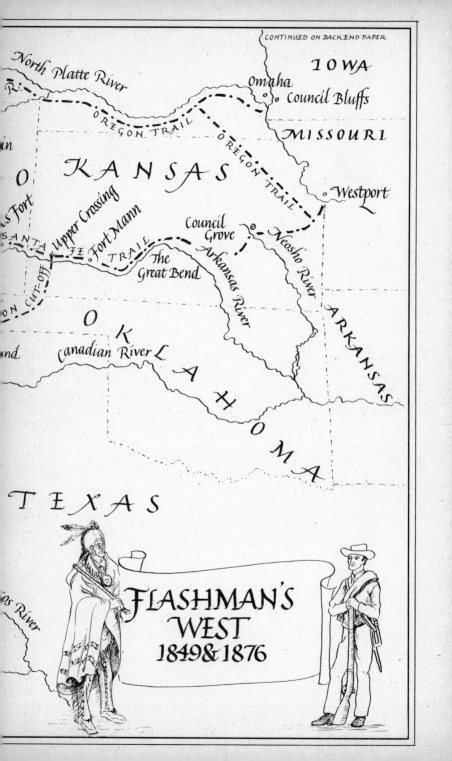

CONTINUED ON BACK END PAPER

IOWA

North Platte River

Omaha

Council Bluffs

OREGON TRAIL

MISSOURI

KANSAS

OREGON TRAIL

Westport

Fort

Upper Crossing

SANTA

Fort Mann

Council Grove

The Great Bend

Arkansas River

Neosho River

ARKANSAS

CUT-OFF

TRAIL

FE

OKLAHOMA

Canadian River

TEXAS

os River

FLASHMAN'S WEST
1849 & 1876

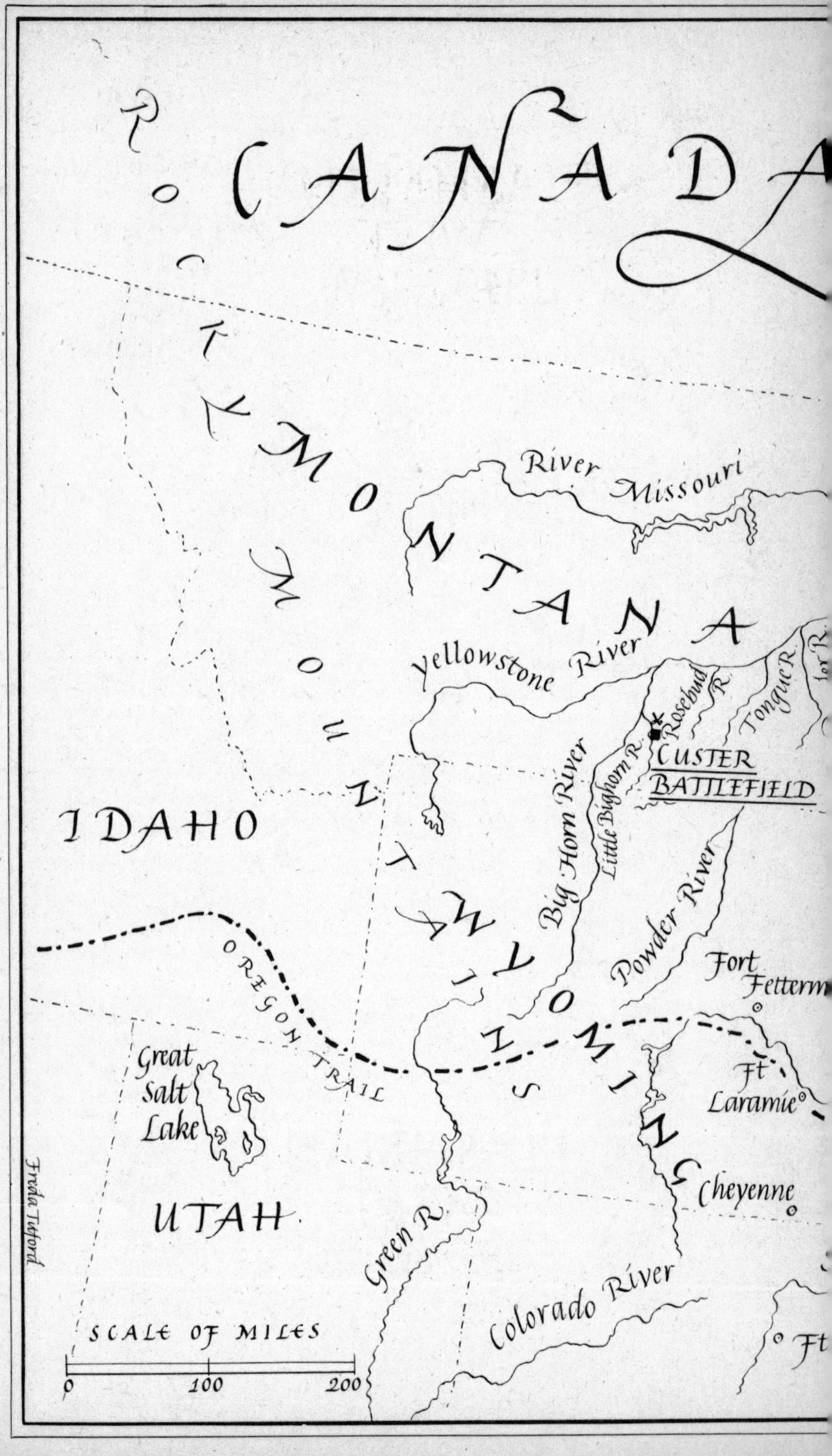
CANADA
ROCKY MOUNTAINS
MONTANA
River Missouri
Yellowstone River
Rosebud R.
Tongue R.
CUSTER
BATTLEFIELD
Big Horn River
Little Bighorn R.
Powder River
IDAHO
WYOMING
OREGON TRAIL
Fort
Fetterm
Ft
Laramie
Great
Salt
Lake
UTAH
Cheyenne
Green R.
Colorado River
SCALE OF MILES
0
100
200
Freda Tufford

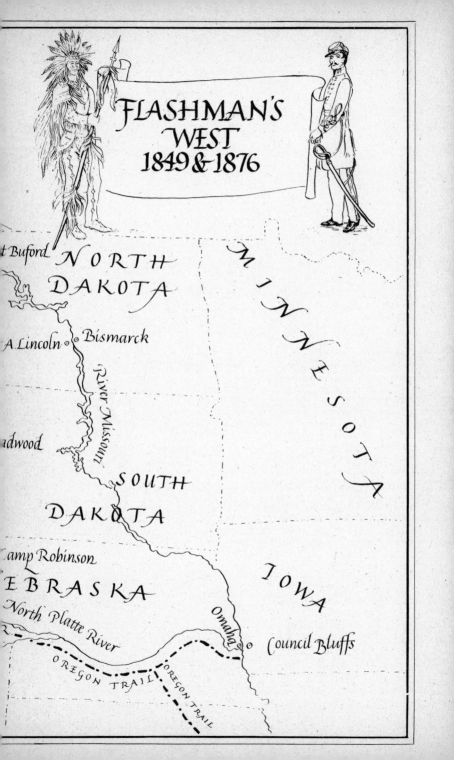

FLASHMAN'S
WEST
1849 & 1876

t Buford

NORTH
DAKOTA

A. Lincoln Bismarck

River Missouri

adwood

SOUTH
DAKOTA

amp Robinson

EBRASKA

North Platte River

MINNESOTA

IOWA

Omaha Council Bluffs

OREGON TRAIL

OREGON TRAIL

FLASHMAN

and

THE REDSKINS

George MacDonald Fraser

A PLUME BOOK

NEW AMERICAN LIBRARY

TIMES MIRROR

For
Icimanipi-Wihopawin
"Travels-Beautiful-Woman"
from Bent's and the Santa Fe Trail
to the Black Hills

NAL BOOKS ARE AVAILABLE AT QUANTITY DISCOUNTS WHEN USED TO PROMOTE PRODUCTS OR SERVICES. FOR INFORMATION PLEASE WRITE TO PREMIUM MARKETING DIVISION, THE NEW AMERICAN LIBRARY, INC., 1633 BROADWAY, NEW YORK, NEW YORK 10019.

 PLUME TRADEMARK REG. U.S. PAT. OFF. AND FOREIGN COUNTRIES
REGISTERED TRADEMARK—MARCA REGISTRADA
HECHO EN FAIRFIELD, PA., U.S.A.

SIGNET, SIGNET CLASSIC, MENTOR, PLUME, MERIDIAN and NAL BOOKS are published by The New American Library, Inc., 1633 Broadway, New York, New York 10019

First Plume Printing, September, 1983

1 2 3 4 5 6 7 8 9

PRINTED IN THE UNITED STATES OF AMERICA

Explanatory Note

A singular feature of the Flashman Papers, the memoirs of the notorious bully of *Tom Brown's Schooldays,* which were discovered in a Leicestershire saleroom in 1966, is that their author wrote them in self-contained instalments, describing his background and setting the scene anew each time. This has been of great assistance to me in editing the Papers entrusted to me by Mr Paget Morrison of Durban, Flashman's closest legitimate relative; it has meant that as I opened each new packet of manuscript I could expect the contents to be a complete and self-explanatory book, needing only a brief preface and foot-notes. Six volumes have followed this pattern.

The seventh volume has proved to be an exception; it follows chronologically (to the very minute) on to the third packet,* with only the briefest preamble by its aged author. I have therefore felt it necessary to append a resumé of the third packet at the end of this note, so that new readers will understand the events leading up to Flashman's seventh adventure.

It was obvious from the early Papers that Flashman, in the intervals of his distinguished and scandalous service in the British Army, visited America more than once; this seventh volume is his Western odyssey. I believe it is unique. Others may have taken part in both the '49 gold rush and the Battle of the Little Bighorn, but they have not left records of these events, nor did they have Flashman's close, if reluctant, acquaintance with three of the most famous Indian chiefs, as well as with leading American soldiers, frontiersman, and statesmen of the time, of whom he has left vivid and, it may be, revealing portraits.

*Published in 1971 under the title *Flash for Freedom!*

As with his previous memoirs, I believe his truthfulness is not in question. As students of those volumes will be aware, his personal character was deplorable, his conduct abandoned, and his talent for mischief apparently inexhaustible; indeed, his one redeeming feature was his unblushing veracity as a memorialist. As I hope the foot-notes and appendices will show, I have been at pains to check his statements wherever possible, and I am indebted to librarians, custodians, and many members of the great and kindly American public at Santa Fe, Albuquerque, Minneapolis, Fort Laramie, the Custer battlefield, the Yellowstone and Arkansas rivers, and Bent's Fort.

G.M.F.

Introduction

In May, 1848, Flashman was forced to flee England after a card scandal, and sailed for Africa on the *Balliol College*, a ship owned by his father-in-law, John Morrison of Paisley, and commanded by Captain John Charity Spring, M.A., late Fellow of Oriel College. Only too late did Flashman discover that the ship was an illegal slave-trader and her captain, despite his academic antecedents, a homicidal eccentric. After taking aboard a cargo of slaves in Dahomey, the *Balliol College* crossed the Atlantic, but was captured by the American Navy; Flashman managed to escape in New Orleans, and took temporary refuge in a bawdy-house whose proprietress, a susceptible English matron named Susan Willinck, was captivated by his picaresque charm.

Thereafter Flashman spent several eventful months in the Mississippi Valley, frequently in headlong flight. For a time he impersonated (among many other figures) a Royal Navy officer; he was also a reluctant agent of the Underground Railroad which smuggled escaped slaves to Canada, but unfortunately the fugitive entrusted to his care was recognised by a vindictive planter named Omohundro, and Flashman abandoned his charge and beat a hasty retreat over the rail of a steamboat. He next obtained employment as a plantation slave-driver, but lost his position on being found in compromising circumstances with his master's wife. He subsequently stole a beautiful octoroon slave, Cassy, sold her under a false name, assisted her subsequent evasion, and with the proceeds of the sale fled with her across the ice-floes of the Ohio river, pursued by slave-catchers who shot him in the buttock; however, he succeeded in effecting his escape, and Cassy's, with the timely assistance of the then Congressman Abraham Lincoln.

With charges of slave-trading, slave-stealing, false pretences, and even murder hanging over his head, Flashman was now anxious to return to England. Instead, mischance brought him again to New Orleans, and he was driven in desperation to seek the help of his former commander, Captain Spring, who had been cleared of slave-trading by a corrupt American court and was about to sail. Flashman, who throughout his misfortunes had clung tenaciously to certain documents from the *Balliol College*—documents proving the ship's slaving activities with which Flashman had hoped to blackmail his detested father-in-law—now offered them as the price of his passage home; Captain Spring, his habitual malevolence tempered by his eagerness to secure papers so dangerous to himself, agreed.

At this point, with our exhausted narrator quaking between the Scylla of United States justice and Charybdis in the person of the diabolic Spring, the third packet of the Flashman Papers ended—and the next chapter of his American adventure begins.

The Forty-Niner

1

I never did learn to speak Apache properly. Mind you, it ain't easy, mainly because the red brutes seldom stand still long enough—and if you've any sense, you don't either, or you're liable to find yourself studying their system of vowel pronunciation (which is unique, by the way) while hanging head-down over a slow fire or riding for dear life across the Jornada del Muerto with them howling at your heels and trying to stick lances in your liver. Both of which predicaments I've experienced in my time, and you may keep 'em.

Still, it's odd that I never got my tongue round it, for apart from fleeing and fornication, slinging the bat* is my strongest suit; well, I speak nine languages better than the natives, and can rub along in another dozen or so. And I knew the 'Paches well enough, God help me; I was even married to one for a spell, banns, beads, buffalo-dance and all, and a spanking little wild beast she was, too, with her peach-brown satin skin and hot black eyes, and those white doeskin leggings up to her thighs with the tiny silver bells all down the sides . . . I can close my eyes and hear them tinkling yet, sixty years after, and feel the pine-needles under my knees, and smell the wood smoke mingling with the musky perfume of her hair and the scent of the wild flowers outside her bower . . . the soft lips teasing my ear, murmuring "Make my bells ring again, *pinda-lickoyee*†. . ." Aye, me, it's a long time ago. But that's the way to learn a language, if you like, in between the sighs and squeals, and if it didn't happen in this case the reason is that my buxom savage was not only a great chief's daughter but

---

*Speaking the local language (Brit. Army slang).
†Literally, "white-eye"; a white man.

Mexican hidalga on her mother's side, and inclined to put on airs something peculiar, such as speaking only Spanish in preference to the tribal dialect of the common herd. They can be just as pert and hoity-toity in a Mimbreno wickiup as they can in a Belgravia drawing-room, believe me. Fortunately, there's a cure.

But that's beside the point for the moment. Even if my Apache never progressed far beyond *"Nuetsche-shee, eet-zan"*, which may be loosely translated as "Come here, girl", and is all you need to know (apart from a few fawning protestations of friendship and whines for mercy, and much good they'll do you), I still recognise the diabolical lingo when I hear it. That guttural, hissing mumble, with all its "Tz" and "zl" and "rr" noises, like a drunk Scotch-Jew having trouble with his false teeth, is something you don't forget in a hurry. So when I heard it in the Travellers' a few weeks ago, and had mastered an instinctive impulse to dive for the door bawling " 'Pash! Ride for it, you fellows, and save your hair!", I took stock, and saw that it was coming in a great spate from a pasty-looking specimen with a lordly academic voice and some three-ha'penny order on his shirt front, who was enthralling a group of toadies in a corner of the smoking-room. I demanded to know what the devil he meant by it, and he turned out to be some distinguished anthropologist or other who had been lecturing to the Royal Geographic on North American Indians.

"And what d'you know about them, apart from that beastly chatter?" says I, pretty warm, for he had given me quite a start, and I could see at a glance that he was one of these snoopopathic meddlers who strut about with a fly-whisk and notebook, prodding lies out of the niggers and over-tipping the dragoman on college funds. He looked taken aback, until they told him who I was, and that I had a fair acquaintance with North American Indians myself, to say nothing of other various aborigines; at that he gave me a distant flabby hand, and condescended to ask me an uneasy question or two about my American travels. I told him I'd been out with Terry and Custer in '76—and that was as far as I got before he said: "Oh, indeed?" down his nose, damned chilly, showed me his shoulder, and began the most infernal prose you ever heard to the rest of the company, all about the Yankees' barbarous treatment of the Plains tribes after the Uprising, and their iniquitous Indian policy in general, the abominations of the reservation system, and the cruelties practised in the name of civilisation on helpless nomads who desired only to be left alone to pursue their traditional way of life as peaceful herdsmen, fostering their simple culture, honouring their ancient gods, and generally prancing about like fauns in Arcady. Mercifully, I hadn't had dinner.

"Noble savages, eh?" says I, when he'd paused for breath, and he gave me a look full of sentimental spite.

"I might call them that," snaps he. "Do I take it that you would disagree?"

"Depends which ones you're talking about," says I. "Now, Spotted Tail was a gentleman. Chico Velasquez, on the other hand, was an evil vicious brute. But you probably never met either of 'em. Care for a brandy, then?"

He went pink. "I thank you, no. By gentleman, I suppose," he went on, bristling, "you mean one who has despaired to the point of submission, while brute would no doubt describe any sturdy independent patriot who resisted the injustice of an alien rule, or revolted against broken treaties—"

"If sturdy independence consists of cutting off women's fingers and fringing your buckskins with them, then Chico was a patriot, no error," says I. "Mind you, that was the soft end of his behaviour. Hey, waiter, another one, and keep your thumb out of it, d'ye hear?"

My new acquaintance was going still pinker, and taking in breath; he wasn't used to the *argumentum ad Chico Velasquez*, and it was plainly getting his goat, as I intended it should.

"Barbarism is to be expected from a barbarian—especially when he has been provoked beyond endurance!" He snorted and sneered. "Really, sir—will you seriously compare errant brutality committed by this . . . this Velasquez, as you call him—who by his name I take it sprang from that unhappy Pueblo stock who had been brutalised by centuries of Spanish atrocity—will you compare it, I say, with a calculated policy of suppression—nay, extermination—devised by a modern, Christian government? You talk of an Indian's savagery? Yet you boast acquaintance with General Custer, and doubtless you have heard of Chivington? Sand Creek, sir! Wounded Knee! Washita! Ah, you see," cries he in triumph, "I can quote your own lexicon to you! In face of that, will you dare condone Washington's treatment of the American Indian?"

"I don't condone it," says I, holding my temper. "And I don't condemn it, either. It happened, just as the tide comes in, and since I saw it happen, I know better than to jump to the damfool sentimental conclusions that are fashionable in college cloisters, let me tell you—"

There were cries of protest, and my anthropologist began to gobble. "Fashionable indeed! Have you read Mrs Jackson,[1] sir? Are you ignorant of the miserable condition to which a proud and worthy people have been reduced? Since you served in the Sioux campaign, you cannot be unaware of the callous and vindictive zeal with which it and subsequent expeditions were conducted! Against a resistless foe! Can you defend the extirpation of the Modocs, or the Apaches, or a dozen others I could mention? For shame, sir!" He was getting the bit between his teeth now, and I was warming just a trifle myself. "And all this at a time when the resources of a vast modern state might have been employed in a policy of humanity, restraint, and enlightenment! But no—all the dark old prejudices and hatreds must be given full and fearful rein, and the despised 'hostile' annihilated or reduced to virtual serfdom." He gestured contemptuously. "And all you can say is that 'it happened'. Tush, sir! So might Pilate have said: 'It happened'." He was pleased with that, so he enlarged on it. "The Procurator of Judea would have made a fit aide–de–camp to your General Terry, I daresay. I wish you a very good night, General Flashman."

Which would have enabled him to stalk off with the honours, but I don't abandon an argument when reasoned persuasion may prevail.

"Now see here, you mealy little pimp!" says I. "I've had just about a bellyful of your pious hypocritical maundering. Take a look at this!" And while he gobbled again, and his sycophants uttered shocked cries, I dropped my head and pulled apart my top hair for his inspection. "See that bald patch? That, my industrious researcher, was done by a Brulé scalping knife, in the hand of a peaceful herdsman, to a man who'd done his damnedest to see that the Brulés and everyone else in the Dacotah nation got a fair shake." Which was a gross exaggeration, but never mind that. "So much for humanity and restraint . . ."

"Good God!" cries he, blenching. "Very well, sir—you may flaunt a wound. It does not prove your case. Rather, it explains your partiality—"

"It proves that at least I know what I'm talking about! Which is more than you can say. As to Custer, he's receipted and filed for the idiot he was, and for Chivington, he was a murderous maniac, and what's worse, an amateur. But if you think they were a whit more guilty than your darling redskins, you're an even bigger bloody fool than you look. What bleating breast-beaters like you can't comprehend," I went on at the top of my voice, while the toadies pawed at me and yapped for the porters, "is that when selfish frightened men—in other words, *any* men, red or white, civilised or savage—come face to face in the middle of a wilderness that both of 'em want, the Lord alone knows why, then war breaks out, and the weaker goes under. Policies don't matter a spent piss—it's the men in fear and rage and uncertainty watching the woods and skyline, d'you see, you purblind bookworm, you! And you burble about enlightenment, by God—"

"Catch hold of his other arm, Fred!" says the porter, heaving away. "Come along now, general, *if* you please."

"—try to enlighten a Cumanche war party, why don't you? Suggest humanity and restraint to the Jicarillas who carved up Mrs White and her baby on Rock Creek! Have

19

you ever seen a Del Norte rancho after the Mimbrenos have left their calling cards? No, not you, you plush-bottomed bastard, you! All right, steward, I'm going, damn you . . . but let me tell you," I concluded, and I dare say I may have shaken my finger at the academic squirt, who had got behind a chair and was looking ready to bolt, "that I've a damned sight more use for the Indian than you have—as much as I have for the rest of humanity, at all events—and I don't make 'em an excuse for parading my own virtue while not caring a fig for them, as you do, so there! I know your sort! Broken treaties, you vain blot—why, Chico Velasquez wouldn't have recognised a treaty if he'd fallen over it in the dark . . ." But by that time I was out in Pall Mall, addressing the vault of heaven.

"Who the hell ever said the Washington government was Christian, anyway?" I demanded, but the porter said he really couldn't say, and did I want a cab?

You may wonder that I got in such a taking over one pompous windbag spouting claptrap; usually I just sit and sneer when the know-alls start prating on behalf of the poor oppressed heathen, sticking a barb in 'em as opportunity serves—why, I've absolutely heard 'em lauding the sepoy mutineers as honest patriots, and I haven't even bothered to break wind by way of dissent. I know the heathen, and their oppressors, pretty well, you see, and the folly of sitting smug in judgment years after, stuffed with piety and ignorance and book-learned bias. Humanity is beastly and stupid, aye, and helpless, and there's an end to it. And that's as true for Crazy Horse as it was for Custer—and they're both long gone, thank God. But I draw the line at the likes of my anthropological half-truther; oh, there's a deal in what he says, right enough—but it's only one side of the tale, and when I hear it puffed out with all that righteous certainty, as though every white man was a villain and every redskin a saint, and the fools swallow it and feel suitably guilty . . . well, it can get my goat, especially if I've got a drink in me and my kidneys are creaking. So I'm slung out of the Travellers' for ungentlemanly conduct. Much I care; I wasn't a member, anyway.

20

A waste of good passion, of course. The thing is, I suppose, that while I spent most of my time in the West skulking and running and praying to God I'd come out with a whole skin, I have a strange sentiment for the place, even now. That may surprise you, if you know my history—old Flashy, the decorated hero and cowardly venal scoundrel who never had a decent feeling in all his scandalous, lecherous life. Aye, but there's a reason, as you shall see.

Besides, when you've seen the West almost *from the beginning*, as I did—trader, wagon-captain, bounty-hunter, irregular soldier, whoremaster, gambler, scout, Indian fighter (well, being armed in the presence of the enemy qualifies you, even if you don't tarry long), and reluctant deputy marshal to J. B. Hickok, Esq., no less—you're bound to retain an interest, even in your eighty-ninth year.[2] And it takes just a little thing—a drift of wood smoke, a certain sunset, the taste of maple syrup on a pancake, or a few words of Apache spoken unexpected—and I can see the wagons creaking down to the Arkansas crossing, and the piano stuck fast on a mudbank, with everyone laughing while Susie played "Banjo on my knee" . . . Old Glory fluttering above the gate at Bent's . . . the hideous zeep of Navajo war-arrows through canvas . . . the great bison herds in the distance spreading like oil on the yellow plain . . . the crash and stamp of fandango with the poblanas' heels clicking and their silk skirts whirling above their knees . . . the bearded faces of Gallantin's riders in the fire glow . . . the air like nectar when we rode in the spring from the high glory of Eagle Nest, up under the towering white peaks to Fort St Vrain and Laramie . . . the incredible stink of those dark dripping forms in the Apache sweatbath at Santa Rita . . . the great scarred Cheyenne braves with their slanting feathers, riding stately, like kings to council . . . the round firm flesh beneath my hands in the Gila forest, the sweet sullen lips whispering . . . "Make my bells ring again . . ." oh, yes indeed, ma'am . . . and the nightmare—the screams and shots and war-whoops as Gall's Hunkpapa horde came surging through the dust, and George Custer squatting on his heels, his cropped head in his hands as he

21

coughed out his life, and the red-and-yellow devil's face screaming at me from beneath the buffalo-scalp helmet as the hatchet drove down at my brow . . .

"Well, boys, they killed me," as Wild Bill used to say—only it wasn't permanent, and today I sit at home in Berkeley Square staring out at the trees beyond the railings in the rain, damning the cramp in my penhand and remembering where it all began, on a street in New Orleans in 1849, with your humble obedient trotting anxiously at the heels of John Charity Spring, M.A., Oriel man, slaver, and homicidal lunatic, who was stamping his way down to the quay in a fury, jacket buttoned tight and hat jammed down, alternately blaspheming and quoting Horace . . .

"I should have dropped you overboard off Finisterre!" snarls he. "It would have been the price of you, by God! Aye, well, I missed my chance—*quandoque bonus dormitat Homerus.**" He wheeled on me suddenly, and those dreadful pale eyes would have frozen brandy. "But Homer won't nod again, *Mister* Flashman, and you can lay to that. One false step out of you this trip, and you'll wish the Amazons had got you!"

"Captain," says I earnestly, "I'm as anxious to get out of this as you are—and you've said it yourself, how can I play you false?"

"If I knew that I'd be as dirty a little Judas as you are." He considered me balefully. "The more I think of it, the more I like the notion of having those papers of Comber's before we go a step farther."

Now, those papers—which implicated both Spring himself and my miserly Scotch father-in-law up to their necks in the illegal slave trade—were the only card in my hand. Once Spring had them, he could drop me overboard indeed. Terrified as I was, I shook my head, and he showed his teeth in a sneering grin.

"What are you scared of, you worm? I've said I'll carry you home, and I keep my word. By God," he growled, and

---

*Even good Homer nods sometimes (i.e., even the cleverest can make mistakes).

22

the scar on his brow started to swell crimson, a sure sign that he was preparing to howl at the moon, "will you dare say I don't, you quaking offal? Will you? No, you'd better not! Why, you fool—I'll have 'em within five minutes of your setting foot on my deck, in any event. Because you're carrying them, aren't you? You wouldn't dare leave 'em out of your sight. I know you." He grinned again, nastily. *"Omnia mea mecum porto**" is your style. Where are they—in your coat-lining or under your boot-sole?

It was no consolation that they were in neither, but sewn in the waistband of my pants. He had me, and if I didn't want to be abandoned there and then to the mercy of the Yankee law—which was after me for murder, slave-stealing, impersonating a Naval officer, false pretences, theft of a wagon and horses, perjury, and issuing false bills of sale (Christ, just about everything except bigamy)—I had no choice but to fork out and hope to heaven he'd keep faith with me. He saw it in my face and sneered.

"As I thought. You're as easy to read as an open book—and a vile publication, too. We'll have them now, if you please." He jerked his thumb at a tavern across the street. "Come on!"

"Captain—for God's sake let it wait till we're aboard! The Yankee Navy traps'll be scouring the town for me by now . . . please, Captain, I swear you'll have 'em—"

"Do as you're damned well told!" he rasped, and seizing my arm in an iron hand he almost ran me into the pub, and thrust me into a corner seat farthest from the bar; it was middling dim, with only one or two swells lounging at the tables, and a few of the merchant and trader sort talking at the bar, but just the kind of respectable ken that my legal and Navy acquaintances might frequent. I pointed this out, whining.

"Five minutes more or less won't hurt you," says Spring, "and they'll satisfy me whether or not you're breaking the habit of a lifetime by telling the truth for once." So while he bawled for juleps and kicked the black waiter for being

*I carry all my things with me.

dilatory—I wished to God he wouldn't attract attention with his high table manners—I kept my back to the room and began surreptitiously picking stitches out of my flies with a penknife.

He drummed impatiently, growling, while I got the packet out—that precious sheaf of flimsy, closely-written papers that Comber had died for—and he pawed through it, grinding his teeth as he read. "That ingrate sanctimonious reptile! He should have lingered for a year! I was like a father to the bastard, and see how he repaid my benevolence, by God—skulking and spying like a rat at a scuttle! But you're all alike, you shabby-genteel vermin! Aye, Master Comber, Phaedrus limned your epitaph: *saepe intereunt aliis meditantes necem**, and serve the bastard right!" He stuffed the papers into his pocket, drank, and brooded at me with that crazy glint in his eyes that I remembered so well from the *Balliol College*. "And you—you held on to them—why? To steer me into Execution Dock, you—"

"Never!" I protested. "Why, if I'd wanted to I could have done it back in the court—but I didn't, did I?"

"And put your own foul neck in a noose? Not you." He gave his barking laugh. "No . . . I'll make a shrewd guess that you were keeping 'em to squeeze an income out of that Scotch miser Morrison—that was it, wasn't it?" Mad he might be, but his wits were sharp enough. "Filial piety, you leper! Well, if that was your game, you're out of luck. He's dead—and certainly damned. I had word from our New York agent three weeks ago. That takes you flat aback, doesn't it, my bucko?"

And it did, but only for a moment. For if I couldn't turn the screw on a corpse—well, I didn't need to, did I? The little villain's fortune would descend to his daughters, of whom my lovely simpleton wife Elspeth was the favourite—by George, I was rich! He'd been worth a cool two million, they reckoned, and at least a quarter would come to her, and me . . . unless the wily old skinflint had cooked up some legal flummery to keep my paws off it, as he'd done

---

*Those who plot the destruction of others often destroy themselves.

these ten years past. But he couldn't—Elspeth *must* inherit, and I could twist her round my little finger . . . couldn't I? She'd always doted on me, although I had a suspicion that she sampled the marriage mutton elsewhere when my back was turned—I couldn't be sure, though, and anyway, an occasional unwifely romp was no great matter, while she'd been dependent on Papa. But now, when she was rolling in blunt, she might be off whoring with all hands and the cook, and too much of that might well damp her ardour for an absent husband. Who could say how she would greet the returning Odysseus, now that she was filthy rich and spoiled for choice? That apart, if I knew my fair feather-brain, she'd be spending the dibs—*my* dibs—like a drunk duke on his birthday. The sooner I was home the better—but Morrison kicking the bucket was capital news, just the same.

Spring was watching me as he watched the weather, shrewd and sour, and knowing what a stickler he could be for proper form, murderous pirate though he was, I tried to put on a solemn front, and muttered about this unexpected blow, shocking calamity, irreplaceable loss, and all the rest of it.

"I can see that," he scoffed. "Stricken with grief, I daresay. I know the signs—a face like a Tyneside winter and a damned inheriting gleam in your eye. Bah, why don't you blubber, you hypocritical pup? *Nulli jactantius moerent, quam qui loetantur**, or to give Tacitus a free translation, you're reckoning up the bloody dollars already! Well, you haven't got 'em yet, cully, and if you want to see London Bridge again—" and he bared his teeth at me "—you'll tread mighty delicate, like Agag, and keep on the weather side of John Charity Spring."

"What d'you mean? I've given you the papers—you're bound to see me safe—"

"Oh, I'll do that, never fear." There was a cunning shift in those awful empty eyes. "*Me duce tutus eris†*, and d'ye

---

*None mourn with more affectation of sorrow than those who are inwardly rejoiced.
†With me for your leader you will be safe.—Ovid.

know why? Because when you reach England, and you and
the rest of Morrison's carrion brood have got your claws on
his fortune, you'll discover that you need an experienced
director for his extensive maritime concerns—lawful and
otherwise." He grinned at me triumphantly. "You'll pay
through the nose for him, too, but you'll be getting a safe,
scholarly man of affairs who'll not only manage a fleet, but
can be trusted to see that no indiscreet inquiries are ever
directed at your recent American activities, or the fact that
your signature as supercargo is to be found on the articles
of a slave-trader—"

"Christ, look who's talking!" I exclaimed. "I was shanghaied, kidnapped—and what about you—"

"Damn your eyes, will you take that tone with me?" he
roared, and a few heads at the nearest table turned, so he
dropped his voice to its normal snarl. "English law holds no
terrors for me; I'll be in Brest or Calais, taking my money
in francs and guilders. Thanks to those misbegotten scum
of ushers at Oxford, who cast me into the gutter out of
spite, who robbed me of dignity and the fruits of scholarship
. . ." His scar was crimsoning again, as it always did when
Oxford was mentioned; Oriel had kicked him out, you see,
no doubt for purloining the College plate or strangling the
Dean, but *he* always claimed it was academic jealousy. He
writhed and growled and settled down. "England holds
nothing for me now. But your whole future lies there—and
there'll be damned little future if the truth about this past
year comes out. The Army? Disgrace. Your newfound fortune? Ruin. You might even swing," says he, smacking his
lips. "And your lady wife would certainly find the social
entrée more difficult to come by. On which score," he added
malevolently, "I wonder how she would take the news that
her husband is a whoremongering rake who covered everything that moved aboard the *Balliol College*. By and large,
mutual discretion will be in both our interests, don't you
think?"

And the evil lunatic grinned at me sardonically and
drained his glass. "We'll have leisure to discuss business on
the voyage home—and to resume your classical education,

whose interruption by those meddling Yankee Navy bastards I'm sure you deplore as much as I do. *Hiatus valde deflendus**, as I seem to remember telling you before. Now get that drink into you and we'll be off."

As I've said, he was really mad. If he thought he could blackmail me with his ridiculous threats—and him a discredited don turned pirate who'd be clapped into Bedlam as soon as he opened his mouth in civilised company—he was well out of court. But I knew better than to say so, just then; raving or not, he was my one hope of getting out of that beastly country. And if I had to endure his interminable proses about Horace and Ovid all across the Atlantic, so be it; I drank up meekly, pushed back my chair, turned to the room—and walked slap into a nightmare.

It was the most ordinary, trivial thing, and it changed the course of my life, as such things do. Perhaps it killed Custer; I don't know. As I took my first step from the table a tall man standing at the bar roared with laughter, and stepped back, just catching me with his shoulder. Another instant and I'd have been past him, unseen—but he jostled me, and turned to apologise.

"Your pardon, suh," says he, and then his eyes met mine, and stared, and for full three seconds we stood frozen in mutual recognition. For I knew that face: the coarse whiskers, the scarred cheek, the prominent nose and chin, and the close-set eyes. I knew it before I remembered his name: Peter Omohundro.

*A want greatly to be deplored.

2

You all know these embarrassing little encounters, of course—the man you've borrowed money off, or the chap whose wife has flirted with you, or the people whose invitation you've forgotten, or the vulgarian who accosts you in public. Omohundro wasn't quite like these, exactly—the last time we'd met I'd been stealing one of his slaves, and shots had been flying, and he'd been roaring after me with murder in his eye, while I'd been striking out for the Mississippi shore. But the principle was the same, and so, I flatter myself, was my immediate behaviour.

I closed my mouth, murmured an apology, nodded off-hand, and made to pass on. I've known it work, but not with this indelicate bastard. He let out an appalling oath and seized my collar with both hands.

"Prescott!" he bawled. "By God—Prescott!"

"I beg your pardon, sir," says I, damned stiff. "I haven't the honour of your acquaintance."

"Haven't you, though, you nigger-stealin' son-of-a-bitch! I sure as hell got the honour o' yores! Jim—git a constable—quick, dammit! Why, you thievin' varmint!" And while they gaped in astonishment, he thrust me by main strength against the wall, pinning me there and roaring to his friends.

"It's Prescott—Underground Railroader that stole away George Randolph on the *Sultana* last year! Hold still, god-dam you! It's him, I say! Here, Will, ketch hold t'other arm—now, you dog, you, hold still there!"

"You're wrong!" I cried. "I'm someone else—you've got the wrong man, I say! My name's not Prescott! Get your confounded hands off me!"

"He's English!" bawled Omohundro. "You all hear that? The bastard's English, an' so was Prescott! Well, you dam' slave-stealer, I got you fast, and you're goin' to jail till I can get you 'dentified, and then by golly they gonna hang you!"

As luck had it, there weren't above a dozen men in the place, and while those who'd been with Omohundro crowded round, the others stared but kept their distance. They were a fairly genteel bunch, and Omohundro and I were both big strapping fellows, which can't have encouraged them to interfere. The man addressed as Jim was hanging irresolute halfway to the door, and Will, a burly buffer in a beard and stove-pipe hat, while he laid a hand on my arm, wasn't too sure.

"Hold on a shake, Pete," says he. "You certain this is the feller?"

"Course I'm sartin, you dummy! Jim, will you git the goddam constable? He's Prescott, I tell you, an' he stole the nigger Randolph—got him clear to Canada, too!"

At this two of the others were convinced, and came to lend a hand, seizing my wrists while Omohundro took a breather and stepped back, glowering at me. "I'd know the sneakin' blackguard anywhere—an' his dadblasted fancy accent—"

"It's a lie!" I protested. "A fearful mistake, gentlemen, I assure you . . . the fellow's drunk . . . I never saw him in my life—or his beastly nigger! Let me loose, I say!"

"Drunk, am I?" shouts Omohundro, shaking his fist. "Why, you brass-bollocked impident hawg, you!"

"Tarnation, shet up, can't ye?" cries Will, plainly bewildered. "Why, he sure don't *talk* like a slave-stealer, an' that's a fact—but, see here, mister, jes' you rest easy, we git this business looked to. And you hold off, Pete; Jim can git the constable while we study this thing. You, suh!" This was to Spring, who hadn't moved a muscle, and was standing four-square, his hands jammed in his pockets, watching like a lynx. "You was settin' with this feller—can you vouch for him, suh?"

They all looked to Spring, who glanced at me bleakly and then away. "I never set eyes on him before," says he deliberately. "He came to my table uninvited and begged for drink." And on that he turned towards the door, the perfidious wretch, while I was stricken speechless, not only at the brute's brazen treachery, but at his folly. For:

"But you was talkin' with him a good ten minutes," says Will, frowning. "Talkin' an' laughin'—why, I seen you my own self."

"They come in together," says another voice. "Arm in arm, too," and at this Omohundro moved nimbly into Spring's path.

"Now, jes' you hold on there, mister!" cries he suspiciously. "You English, too, ain't you? An' you settin' all cosy-like with this 'bolitionist skunk Prescott—'cos I swear on a ton o' Bibles, Will, that Prescott agin' the wall there. I reckon we keep a grip o' both o' you, till the constable come."

"Stand out of my way," growls Spring, and although he didn't raise his voice, it rasped like a file. Will gave back a step.

"You min' your mouth!" says Omohundro, and braced himself. "Mebbe you clear, maybe you ain't, but I warnin' you—don' stir another step. You gonna stay here—so now!"

I wouldn't feel sorry for Omohundro at any time, least of all with two of his bullies pinioning me and blowing baccy juice in my face, but I confess to a momentary pang just then, as though he'd passed port to the right. For giving orders to J. C. Spring is simply one of the things that are never done; you'd be better teasing a mating gorilla. For a moment he stood motionless, while the scar on his brow turned purple, and that unholy mad spark came into his eyes. His hands came slowly from his pockets, clenched.

"You infernal Yankee pipsqueak!" says he. "Stand aside or, by heaven, it will be the worse for you!"

"Yankee?" roars Omohundro. "Why, you goddam—" But before his fist was half-raised, Spring was on him. I'd seen it before, of course, when he'd almost battered a great hulking seaman to death aboard ship; I'd been in the way of his fist myself, and it had been like being hit with a hammer. You'd barely credit it; here was this sober-looking, middle-aged bargee, with the grey streaks in his trim beard and the solid spread to his middle, burly but by no means tall, as proper a citizen as ever spouted Catullus or graced a corporation—and suddenly it was Attila gone berserk. One short step he took, and sank his fists left and right in Omohundro's midriff; the planter squawked like a burst football, and went flying over a table, but before he had even reached the ground, Spring had seized the dumfounded Will by the collar and hurled him with sickening force against the wall.

"And be damned to all of you!" roars he, jerking down his hat-brim, which was unwise, for it gave the fellow Jim time to wallop him with a chair. Spring turned bellowing, but before Jim could reap the consequences of his folly, one of the coves holding me had let loose, and collared Spring from behind. If I'd been wise I'd have stayed still, but with only one captor I tried to struggle free, and he and I went down wrestling together; he wasn't my weight, and after some noisy panting and clawing I got atop of him and pounded him till he hollered. Given time, I'd have enjoyed myself for a minute or two pulping his figurehead, but flight was top of the menu just then, so I rolled off him and came up looking frantically for the best way to bolt.

Hell's delight was taking place a yard away; Omohundro was on his feet again, clutching his belly—which must have been made of cast-iron—and retching for breath; the fellow Will was on the floor but had a hold on Spring's ankle, which I thought uncommon game of him, while my other captor had Spring round the neck. Even as I looked, Spring sent him flying and turned to stamp on Will's face—those evenings in the Oriel combination room weren't wasted, thinks I—and then a willowy cove among the onlookers took a hand, shrieking in French and trying to brain my gallant captain with an ebony cane.

Spring grabbed it and jerked—and the cane came away in his hand, leaving the Frog holding two feet of naked, glittering steel, which he flourished feebly, with Gallic squeals. Poor fool, there was a sudden flurry, the snap of a breaking bone, the Frog was screaming on the floor, and Spring had the sword-stick in his hand. I heard Omohundro's shout as he flung himself at Spring, hauling a pistol

31

from beneath his coat; Spring leaped to meet him, bawling "Habet!"—and, by God, he had. Before my horrified gaze Omohundro was swaying on tiptoe, staring down at that awful steel that transfixed him; he flopped to his knees, the pistol clattering to the floor, and fell forward on his face with a dreadful groan.

There was a dead silence, broken only by the scraping of Omohundro's nails at the boards—and presently by a wild scramble of feet as one of the principal parties withdrew from the scene. If there's one thing I know, it's when to leave; I was over the counter and through the door behind it like a shot, into a store-room with an open window, and then tearing pell-mell up an alley, blind to all but the need to escape.

How far I ran, I don't know, doubling through alleys, over fences, across backyards, stopping only when I was utterly blown and there was no sound of pursuit behind. By the grace of God it was coming on to evening, and the light was fading fast; I staggered into an empty lane and panted my soul out, and then I took stock.

That was escape to England dished, anyway; Spring's passage out was going to be at the end of a rope, and unless I shifted I'd be dancing alongside him. Once the traps had me the whole business of the slavers Cassy had killed would be laid at my door—hadn't I seen the reward bill naming me murderer?—and the Randolph affair and Omohundro would be a mere side-dish. I had to fly—but where? There wasn't a safe hole for me in the whole damned U.S.A.; I forced down my panic, and tried to think. I couldn't run, I had to hide, but there was nowhere—wait, though, there might be. Susie Willinck had sheltered me before, when she'd thought I was an American Navy deserter—but would she do it now, when they were after me for the capital act? But *I* hadn't killed Omohundro—she needn't even know about him, or Spring. And she'd been besotted with me, the fond old strumpet, piping her eye when I left her—aye, a little touch of Harry in the night and she'd be ready to hide me till the next election.

But the fix was, I'd no notion of where in New Orleans

I might be, or where Susie's place lay, except that it was in the Vieux Carré. I daren't strike off at random, with the Navy's bulldogs—and the civil police, too, by now—on the lookout for me. So I set off cautiously, keeping to the alleys, until I came on an old nigger sitting on a doorstep, and he put me on the right road.

The Vieux Carré, you must know, is the old French heart of New Orleans, and one gigantic fleshpot—fine houses and walks, excellent eating-places and gardens, brilliantly lit by night, with music and gaiety and colour everywhere, and every second establishment a knocking-shop. Susie's bawdy-house was among the finest in New Orleans, standing in its own tree-shaded grounds, which suited me, for I intended to sneak in through the shrubbery and seek out my protectress with the least possible ado. Keeping away from the main streets, I found my way to that very side-alley where months earlier the Underground Railroad boys had got the drop on me; it was empty now, and the side-gate was open, so I slipped in and went to ground in the bushes where I could watch the front of the house. It was then I realised that something was far amiss.

It was one of these massive French colonial mansions, all fancy ironwork and balustrades and slatted screens, just as I remembered it, but what was missing now was signs of life—real life, at any rate. The great front door and windows should have been wide to the warm night, with nigger music and laughter pouring out, and the chandeliers a-glitter, and the half-naked yellow tarts strutting in the big hall, or taking their ease on the verandah like tawny cats on the chaise-longues, their eyes glowing like fireflies out of the shadows. There should have been dancing and merriment and drunken dandies taking their pick of the languid beáuties, with the upper storeys shaking to the exertions of happy fornicators. Instead—silence. The great door was fast, and while there were lights at several of the shuttered windows, it was plain that if this was still a brothel, it must be run by the Band of Hope.

A chill came over me that was not of the night air. All of a sudden the dark garden was eerie and full of dread. Faint music came from another house beyond the trees; a carriage clopped past the distant gates; overhead a nightbird moaned dolefully; I could hear my own knees creaking as I crouched there, scratching the newly-healed bullet-wound in my backside and wondering what the deuce was wrong. Could Susie have gone away? Terror came over me like a cold drench, for I had no other hope.

"Oh, Christ!" I whispered half-aloud. "She must be here!"

"Who must be?" grated a voice at my ear, a hand like a vice clamped on my neck, and with a yap of utter horror I found myself staring into the livid, bearded face of John Charity Spring.

"Shut your trap or I'll shut it forever!" he hissed. "Now then—what house is that, and why were you creeping to it? Quick—and keep your voice down!"

He needn't have fretted; the shock of that awful moment had almost carried me off, and for a spell I couldn't find my voice at all. He shook me, growling, while I absorbed the dreadful realisation that he must have been dogging me all the way—first in my headlong flight, then on the streets, unseen. It was horrifying, the thought of that maniac prowling and watching my every move, but not as horrifying as his presence now, those pale eyes glaring round as he scanned the house and garden. And knowing him, I answered to the point, in a hoarse croak.

"It . . . it belongs to a friend . . . of mine. A . . . an Englishwoman. But I don't know . . . if she's there now."

"Then we'll find out," says he. "Is she safe?"

"I . . . I don't know. She . . . she took me in once before . . ."

"What is she—a whore?"

"No . . . yes . . . she owns the place—or did."

"A bawd, eh?" says he, and bared his teeth. "Trust you to make for a brothel. *Plura faciunt homines e consuetudine, quam e ratione**, you dirty little rip. Now then, see here. Thanks to you, I'm in a plight; can I lie up in that ken for

*Men do more from habit than from reason.

34

a spell? And I'm asking your opinion, not your bloody permission."

My answer was true enough. "I don't know. Christ, you killed a man back there—she may . . . may not . . ."

"Self-defence!" snarls he. "But we agree, a New Orleans jury may take a less enlightened view. Now then—this strumpet . . . she's English, you say. Good-natured? Tolerant? A woman of sense?"

"Why . . . why, yes . . . she's a decent sort . . ." I sought for words to describe Susie. "She's a Cockney . . . a common woman, but—"

"She must be, if she took you in," says this charmer. "And we have no course but to try. Now then," and he tightened his grip until I thought my neck would break, "see here. If I go under, you go under with me, d'ye see? So this bitch had better harbour us, for if she doesn't . . ." He shook me, growling like a mastiff. "So you'd better persuade her. And mind what Seneca says: *Qui timide rogat, docet negare*."

"Eh?"

"Jesus, did Arnold teach you nothing? Who asks in fear is asking for a refusal. Right—march!"

I remember thinking as I tapped on the front door, with him at my elbow, brushing his hat on his sleeve: how many poor devils have ever had a mad murderer teaching 'em Latin in the environs of a leaping-academy in the middle of the night—and why me, of all men? Then the door opened, and an ancient nigger porter stuck his head out, and I asked for the lady of the house.

"Miz Willinck, suh? Ah sorry, suh, Miz Willinck goin' 'way."

"She isn't here?"

"Oh, no, suh—she here—but she goin' 'way pooty soon. Our 'stablishment, suh, is closed, pummanent. But if you goin' next doah, to Miz Rivers, she be 'commodatin' you gennamen—"

Spring elbowed me aside. "Go and tell your mistress that two English gentlemen wish to see her at her earliest convenience," says he, damned formal. "And present our compliments and our apologies for intruding upon her at this untimely hour." As the darkie goggled and tottered away, Spring rounded on me. "You're in my company," he snaps, "so mind your bloody manners."

I was looking about me, astonished. The spacious hall was shrouded in dust-sheets, packages were stacked everywhere, bound and labelled as for a journey; it looked like a wholesale flitting. Then from the landing I heard a female voice, shrill and puzzled, and the nigger butler came shambling into view, followed by a stately figure that I knew well, clad in a fine embroidered silk dressing-gown.

As always, she was garnished like Pompadour, her hennaed hair piled high above that plump handsome face, jewels glistening in her ears and at her wrists and on that splendid bosom that I remembered so fondly; even in my anxious state, it did me good just to watch 'em bounce as she swayed down the stairs—as usual in the evening, she plainly had a pint or two of port inside her. She descended grand as a duchess, peering towards us in the hall's dim light, and then she checked with a sudden scream of "Beauchamp!" and came hurrying down the last few steps and across the hall, her face alight.

"Beauchamp! You've come back! Well, I never! Wherever 'ave you been, you rascal! I declare—let's 'ave a look at you!"

For a moment I was taken aback, until I recalled that she knew me as Beauchamp Millward Comber—God knew how many names I'd passed under in America: Arnold, Prescott, Fitz-something-or-other. But at least she was glad to see me, glowing like Soul's Awakening and holding out her hands; I believed I'd have been enveloped if she hadn't checked modestly at the sight of Spring, who was bowing stiffly from the waist with his hat across his guts.

"Susie," says I, "this is my . . . my friend, Captain John Charity Spring."

"Ow, indeed," says she, and beamed at him, up and down, and blow me if he didn't take her hand and bow over it. "Most honoured to make your acquaintance, marm," says he. "Your humble obedient."

36

"I never!" says Susie, and gave him a roving look. "A distinguished pleasure, I'm sure. Oh, stuff, Beauchamp—d'you think I'm goin' to do the polite with you, too? Come 'ere, an' give us a kiss!"

Which I did, and a hearty slobber she made of it, while Spring looked on, wearing what for him passed as an indulgent smile. "An' wherever 'ave you been, then?—I thought you was back in England months ago, an' me wishin' I was there an' all! Now, come up, both of you, an' tell me wot brings you back—my, I almost 'ad apoplexy, seeing you sudden like that . . ." And then she stopped, uncertain, and the laughter went out of her fine green eyes, as she looked quickly from one to other of us. She might be soft where well-set-up men were concerned, but she was no fool, and had a nose for mischief that a peeler would have envied.

"Wot's the matter?" she said sharply. Then: "It's trouble—am I right?"

"Susie," says I, "it's as bad as can be."

She said nothing for a moment, and when she did it was to tell the butler, Brutus, to bar the door and admit no one without her leave. Then she led the way up to her private room and asked me, quite composed, what was up.

It was only when I began to tell it that the enormity of what I was saying, and the risk I was running in saying it, came home to me. I confined it to the events of that day, saying nothing of my own adventures since I'd last seen her—all she had known of me then was that I was an Englishman running from the Yankee Navy, a yarn I'd spun on the spur of the moment. As I talked, she sat upright on her chair in the silk-hung salon, her jolly, handsome face serious for once, and Spring was mum beside me on the couch, holding his hat on his knees, prim as a banker, although I could feel the crouched force in him. I prayed Susie would play up, because God knew what the lunatic would do if she decided to shop us. I needn't have worried; when I'd done, she sat for a moment, fingering the tassels on her gaudy bedgown, and then says:

"No one knows you're 'ere? Well, then, we can take our time, an' not do anythin' sudden or stupid." She took a long thoughtful look at Spring. "You're Spring the slaver, aren't you?" Oh, Moses, I thought, that's torn it, but he said he was, and she nodded.

"I've bought some of your Havana fancies," says she. "Prime gels, good quality." Then she rang for her butler, and ordered up food and wine, and in the silence that followed Spring suddenly spoke up.

"Madam," says he, "our fate is in your hands," which seemed damned obvious to me, but Susie just nodded again and sat back, toying with her long earring.

"An' you say it was self-defence? 'E barred your way, an' there was a ruckus, an' 'e drew a pistol on you?" Spring said that was it exactly, and she pulled a face.

"Much good that'd do you in court. I daresay 'is pals would tell a different tale . . . if they're anythin' like 'e was. Oh, I've 'ad 'im 'ere, this Omo'undro, but not above once, I can tell you. Nasty brute." She wrinkled her nose in distaste. "What they call a floggin' cully—not that 'e was alone in that, but 'e was a real vile 'un, know wot I mean? Near killed one o' my gels, an' I showed him the door. So I shan't weep for 'im. An' if it was 'ow you say it was—an' I'll know that inside the hour, though I believe you—then you can stay 'ere till the row dies down, or—" and she seemed to glance quickly at me, and I'll swear she went a shade pinker "—we can think o' somethin' else. There's only me an' the gels and the servants, so all's bowmon. We don't 'ave no customers these days."

At that moment Brutus brought in a tray, and Susie went to see rooms prepared for us. When we were alone Spring slapped his fist in triumph and made for the victuals.

"Safe as the Bank. We could not have fallen better."

Well, I thought so, too, but I couldn't see why he was so sure and trusting, and said so; after all, he didn't know her.

"Do I not?" scoffs he. "As to trust, she'll be no better than any other tearsheet—we notice she don't bilk at abetting manslaughter when it suits her whim. No, Flashman— I see our security in that full lip and gooseberry eye, which tell me she's a sensualist, a voluptuary, a profligate wanton," growls he, tearing a chicken leg in his teeth, "a great licentious fleshtrap! That's why I'll sleep sound—and you won't."

"How d'you mean?"

"She can't betray me without betraying you, blockhead!" He grinned at me savagely. "And we know she won't do that, don't we? What—she never took her eyes off you! She's infatuated, the poor bitch. I supposed you stallioned her out of her wits last time. Aye, well, you'd best fortify yourself, for *soevit amor ferri**, or I'm no judge; the lady is working up an appetite this minute, and for our safety's sake you'd best satisfy it."

Well, I knew *that*, but if I hadn't, our hostess's behaviour might have given me a hint, just. When she came back, having plainly repainted, she was flushed and breathless, which I guessed was the result of having laced herself into a fancy corset under her gown—that told me what was on her mind, all right; I knew her style. It was in her restless eye, too, and the cheerful way she chattered when she obviously couldn't wait to be alone with me. Spring presently begged to be excused, and bowed solemnly over her hand again, thanking her for her kindness and loyalty to two distressed fellow-countrymen; when Brutus had led him off, Susie remarked that he was a real gent and a regular caution, but there was something hard and spooky about him that made her all a-tremble.

"But then, I can say the exact same about you, lovey, can't I?" she chuckled, and plunged at me, with one hand in my curls and the other fondling elsewhere. "Ooh, my stars! Give it here! Ah, you 'aven't changed, 'ave you—an', oh, but I've missed you so, you great lovely villain!" Shrinking little violet, you see; she munched away at my lips with that big red mouth, panting names in my ear that I blush to think of; it made me feel right at home, though, the artful way she got every stitch off me without apparently taking her tongue out of my throat once. I've known greater beauties, and a few that were just as partial to pork, but none

*The passions are in arms.—Virgil.

more skilled at stoking what Arnold called the deadly fires of lust; when she knelt above me on the couch and licked her lips, with one silken knee caressing me to distraction while she slowly scooped those wondrous poonts out of her corset and smothered me with 'em—well, I didn't mind a bit.

"I'll distress you, my fellow-countryman," says she, all husky-like. "I'm goin' to tease you an' squeeze you an' eat you alive, an' by the time I've done, if the coppers come for you, you'll just 'ave to 'ide, 'cos you won't be fit to run a step!"

I believed her, for I'd enjoyed her attentions for five solid days last time, and she'd damned near killed me. She was one of those greedy animals who can never have enough—rather like me, only worse—and she went to work now like Messalina drunk on hasheesh. About two hours it took, as near as I could judge, before she gave a last wailing sigh and rolled off on to the floor, where she lay moaning that never, never, never had she known the like, and never could again. That was her usual form; any moment and she would start to weep—sure enough, I heard a great sniff, and presently a blubber, and then the gurgle as she consoled herself with a large port.

As a rule I'd have sunk into a ruined sleep; for one thing, a bout with La Willinck would have unmanned Goliath. But after a while, pondering Spring's advice, I began to wonder if it mightn't be politic to give her another run—proof of boundless devotion, I mean to say; she'd be flattered sweet. It must have been my weeks of abstinence, or else I was flown with relief at the end of a deuced difficult day, but when I turned over and watched her repair her paint at the glass, all bare and bouncy in her fine clocked stockings—d'you know, it began to seem a not half bad notion for its own sake? And when she stretched, and began to powder her tits with a rabbit's foot—I hopped out on the instant and grappled her, while she squealed in alarm, no, no, Beauchamp, she couldn't, not again, honest, and you can't mean it, you wicked beast, not yet, please, but I was adamant, if you know what I mean, and bulled her all over the shop until she pleaded with me to leave off—which by that time, of course, meant pray continue. I can't think where I got the energy, for I'd never have thought to be still up in arms when Susie, of all women, was hollering uncle, but there it was—and I truly believe it was the cause of all that followed.

When we'd done, and she'd had a restorative draught of gin, with her head on the fender, heaving her breath back, she looked up at me with eyes that were moist once they'd stopped rolling, and whimpers:

"Oh, Gawd—why did you 'ave to come back? Jus' when I was gettin' over you, too." And she started to snuffle again.

"Sorry I did, are you?" says I, tweaking her rump.

"Bloomin' well you know I'm not!" she mumps. "More fool me. I *knew* I was gettin' a sight too fond of you, last year . . . but . . . but it was on'y when you'd gone that I . . . that I . . ." Here she began to bawl in earnest, and it took several great sighs of gin to set her right. "An' then . . . when I saw you in the 'all tonight, I felt . . . such a joy . . . an' I . . . Oh, it's ridiklus, at my age, carryin' on like a sixteen-year-old!"

"I doubt if any sixteen-year-old *knows* how to carry on like that," says I, and she gulped and giggled and slapped me, and then came over all maudlin again.

"Wot I mean is . . . like I once said . . . I know you're jus' like the rest of 'em, an' all you want is a good bang, an' I'm just an old . . . a middle-aged fool, to feel for you the way I do . . . 'cos I know full well you don't love me . . . not the way I . . . I . . ." She was blubbering like the Ouse in spate by now, tears forty per cent proof. "Oh . . . if I thought you liked rogerin' me, even, more than . . . than others . . ." She looked at me with her lip quivering and those big green eyes a-swim. "Say that you . . . you *really* like it . . . with me . . . more . . . don't you? Honest, when I caught you lookin' at me in the mirror . . . you looked as though you . . . well, cared for me."

Tight as Dick's hatband, of course, but it proved how right I'd been to give her an encore. If a thing's worth doing, it's worth doing well, and if Susie wants to go with you a mile, gallop with her twain. I improved the shining hour by telling her I was mad for her, and had never known a ride to compare—which wasn't all that much of a lie—and murmured particulars until she quite cheered up again, kissed me long and fondly, and said I was a dear bonny boy. I told her that I'd been itching for her all these months, but at that she gave me a quizzy look.

"I bet you didn't itch long," says she, sniffing. "Not with all them saucy black tails about. Gammon!"

"One or two," says I, for I know how to play my hand. "For want of better. And don't tell me," I added, with a sniff of my own, "that some lucky men haven't been playing hopscotch with you."

Do you know, she absolutely blushed, and cried no such thing, the very idea! But I could see she was pleased, so I gave her a slantendicular look, and said, not even one? at which she blushed even pinker, and wriggled, and said, well, it wasn't her fault, was it, if some very valued and important clients insisted on the personal attention of Madame? Oh, says I, and who might they be?

"Never you mind, sauce-box!" giggles she, tossing her head, so I kept mum till she turned to look at me, and then I frowned and asked, quite hard:

"Who, Susie?"

She blinked, and slowly all the playfulness went out of that plump, pretty face. "'Ere," says she, uncertain. "Why you lookin' at me like that? You're not . . . not cross, are you? I thought you was just funnin' me . . ."

I said nothing, but gave an angry little shrug, looking quickly away, and she gasped in bewilderment and caught my arm.

"'Ere! Beauchamp! You mean . . . you mind? But I . . . I . . . lovey, I never knew . . . 'Ere, wot's the matter—?"

"No matter at all," says I, very cool, and set my jaw tight. "You're right—it's no concern of mine." But I bit my lip and looked stuffed and all Prince Albert, and when I made to get up she took fright in earnest, throwing her arms round my neck and crying that she'd never dreamed I would care, and then starting to blubber bucketsful, sobbing that she'd never thought to see me again, or she'd never have . . . but it was nothing, honest, ow, Gawd, please, Beauchamp—just one or two occasional, like this rich ole Creole planter who paid a hundred dollars to take a bath with her, but she'd have flung the ole goat's money in his face if she'd known that I . . . and if I'd heard gossip about her and Count Vaudrian, it was bleedin' lies, 'cos it wasn't him, it was only his fourteen-year-old nephew that the Count had engaged her to give lessons to . . .

If I'd played her along I daresay I could have got enough bizarre material for a book, but I didn't want to push my little charade of jealousy too far. I'd tickled the old trollop's vanity, fed her infatuation for me, scared her horrid, and discovered what a stout leash I'd got her on—and had the capital fun of watching her grovel and squirm. It was time to be magnanimous and soulful, so I gave her bouncers a forgiving squeeze at last, and she near swooned with relief.

"It was jus' business, Beauchamp—not like with you—oh, never like with you! If I'd known you was comin' back, an' that you *cared*!" That was the great thing, apparently; she was full of it. "'Cos, you *really* care, don't you? Oh, say you do, darlin'—an' please, you're not angry with me no more?"

That was my cue to change from stern sorrow to fond devotion, as though I couldn't help myself. "Oh, Susie, my sweet," says I, giving her bum a fervent clutch, "as if I could ever be angry with you!" This, and a glass of gin, fully restored her, and she basked in the sunshine of her lover's favour and said I was the dearest, kindest big ram, honest I was.

Her talk of business, though, had reminded me of something that had slipped my mind during all our frenzied exertions; as we climbed into her four-poster presently, I asked why the place was closed up and under dust-sheets.

"Course—I never told you! You 'aven't given me much chance, 'ave you, you great bully?" She snuggled up contentedly. "Well—I'm leavin' Orleans next week, for good, an' what d'you think of that? Fact is, trade's gone down that bad, what with my partikler market bein' overcrowded, and half the menfolk off to the gold diggin's to try their luck—why, we're lucky to get any young customers nowadays. So I thinks, Susie my gel, you'd better try California yourself, an' do a little diggin' of your own, an' if you can't make a bigger fortune than any prospector, you're not the woman—"

"Hold on, though—what'll you do in California?"

"Why, what I've always done—manage an establishment for the recreation of affluent gentlemen! Don't you see—there must be a million hearty young chaps out there already, workin' like blacks, the lucky ones with pockets full of gold dust, an' never a sporty female to bless themselves with, 'cept for common drabs. Well, where there's muck, there's money—an' you can bet that in a year or two Sacramento an' San Francisco are goin' to make Orleans look like the parish pump. It may be rough livin' just now, but before long they're goin' to want all the luxuries of London an' Paris out there—an' they'll be able to pay for 'em, too! Wines, fashions, theatres, the best restaurants, the smartest salons, the richest shops—an' the crackiest whores. Mark my words, whoever gets there first, with the quality merchandise, can make a million, easy."

It sounded reasonable, I said, but a bit wild to establish a place like hers, and she chuckled confidently.

"I'm goin' ready-made, don't you fret. I've got a place marked down in Sacramento, through an agent, an' I'm movin' the whole kit caboodle up the river to Westport next Monday—furnishin's, crockery, my cellar an' silver . . . an' the livestock, which is the main thing. I've got twenty o' the primest yellow gels under this roof right now, all experienced an' broke in—so don't you start walkin' in your sleep, will you, you scoundrel? 'Ere, let's 'ave a look at you—"

"But hold on—how are you going to get there?" says I, cuddling obediently.

"Why, up to Westport an' across by carriage to—where is it?—Santa Fe, an' then to San Diego. It only takes a few weeks, an' there's thousands goin' every day, in carts an' wagons an' on horseback—even on foot. You can go round by sea, but it's no quicker or cheaper in the end, an' I don't want my delicate young ladies gettin' seasick, do I?"

"Isn't it dangerous? I mean, Indians and ruffians and so on?"

"Not if you've got guards, an' proper guides. That's all arranged, don't you see, an' I 'aven't stinted, neither. I'm a business woman, in case you 'adn't noticed, an' I know it pays to pay for the best. That's why I'll 'ave the finest slap-up bagnio on the west coast goin' full steam before the year's out—an' I'll still have a tidy parcel over in the bank. If you got money, you can't 'elp makin' more, provided you use common sense."

From what I knew of her she had plenty of that—except where active young men were concerned—and she was a deuced competent manager. But if she had her future planned, I hadn't; I remarked that it didn't leave much time to arrange my safe passage—and Spring's, for what that was worth—out of New Orleans.

"Don't you worry about that," says she, comfortably. "I've been thinkin' about it, an' when we see what kind of a hue an' cry there is in the town tomorrow, we can decide what's best. You're safe 'ere meantime—an' snug an' warm an' cosy," she added, "so let's 'ave another chorus o' John Peel, shall we?"

You can guess that I was sufficiently pale and wan next morning to satisfy Spring that he could continue to rest easy chez Willinck. One look at me, and at Susie languid and yawning, and he gave me a sour grin and muttered: "Christ, *non equidem invideo, miror magis**," which if you ask me was just plain jealousy, and if I'd known enough Latin myself I'd have retorted, "*Ver non semper viret†*, eh? Too bad," which would have had the virtue of being witty, although he'd probably not have appreciated it.

Pleasantries would have been out of season, anyway, for the news was bad. Susie had had inquiries made in town, and reported that Omohundro's death was causing a fine

---

*Indeed, I don't envy—I am rather inclined to wonder.—Virgil.
†The spring does not always flourish.

stir, there was a great manhunt afoot, and our descriptions were posted at every corner. There was no quick way out of New Orleans, that was certain, and when I reminded Susie that something would have to be done in the next few days, she just patted my hand and said she would manage, never fear. Spring said nothing, but watched us with those pale eyes.

You may think it's just nuts, being confined to a brothel for four solid days—which we were—but when you can't get at the tarts, and a mad murderer is biting his nails and muttering dirty remarks from Ovid, and the law may thunder at the door any minute, it can be damned eerie. There we were in that great echoing mansion, not able to stir outside for fear someone would see us from the road, or to leave our rooms, hardly, for although the sluts' quarters were in a side-wing, they were about the place most of the time, and Susie said it would be risky to let them see us— or me to see them, she probably thought. Not that I'd have had the inclination to do more than wave at them; when you have to pile in to Mrs Willinck every night, other women take on a pale, spectral appearance, and you start to think that there's something to be said for monasteries after all.

Not that I minded that part of it at all; she was an uncommon inventive amorist, and when you've been chief stud and bath attendant to Queen Ranavalona of Madagascar, with the threat of boiling alive or impalement hanging over you if you fail to satisfy the customer, then keeping pace even with Susie is gammon and peas. She seemed to thrive on it—but it was an odd thing—even when we were in the throes, I'd a notion that her mind was on more than passing joys, if you follow me; she was thinking at the same time, which wasn't like her. I'd catch her watching me, too, with what I can only call an anxious expression—if I'd guessed what it was, I'd have been anxious myself.

It was the fourth evening when I found out. We were in her salon before supper, and I'd reminded her yet again that New Orleans was still as unsafe for me as ever, and her own departure up-river a scant couple of days away. What, says I, am I to do when you're gone? She was brushing her hair before her mirror, and she stopped and looked at my reflection in the glass.

"Why don't you come with me to California?" says she, rather breathless, and started brushing her hair again. "You could get a ship from San Francisco . . . if you wanted."

It took my breath away. I'd been racking my brains about getting out of the States, but it had never crossed my mind to think beyond New Orleans or the eastern ports—all my fleeing, you'll understand, had been done in the direction of the Northern states; west had never occurred to me. Well, God knows how many thousand miles it was . . . but, by George, it wasn't as far-fetched as it sounded. You may not agree—but you haven't been on the run from slave-catchers and abolitionists and Navy traps and outraged husbands and Congressman Lincoln, damn his eyes, with a gallows waiting if they catch you. I was in that state of funk where any loophole looks fine—and when I came to weigh it, travelling incog in Susie's caravan looked a sight safer than anything else. The trip up-river would be the risky part; once west of the Mississippi I'd be clear . . . I'd be in San Francisco in three months, perhaps . . .

"Would you take me?" was the first thing that came to my tongue, before I'd given more than a couple of seconds' thought to the thing, and her brush clattered on the table and she was staring at me with a light in her eyes that made my blood run cold.

"Would I take you?" says she. " 'Course I'd take you! I . . . I didn't know if . . . if you'd want to come, though. But it's the safest way, Beauchamp—I know it is!" She had turned from her mirror, and she seemed to be gasping for breath, and laughing at the same time. "You . . . you wouldn't mind . . . I mean, bein' with me for—for a bit longer?" Her bosom was heaving fit to overbalance her, and her mouth was trembling. "I mean . . . you ain't tired of me, or . . . I mean—you care about me enough to . . . well, to keep me company to California?" God help me, that was the phrase she used. "You do care about me—don't you? You said you did—an' I think you do . . . ."

Mechanically I said that of course I cared about her; a

fearful suspicion was forming in my mind, and sure enough, her next words confirmed it.

"I dunno if you . . . like me as much as I—oh, you can't, I know you can't!" She was crying now, and trying to smile at the same time, dabbing at her eyes. "I can't help it—I know I'm just a fool, but I love you—an' I'd do anythin' to make you love me, too! An' I'd do anythin' to keep you with me . . . an' I thought—well, I thought that if we went together, an' all that—when we got to California, you might not want to catch a ship at San Francisco, d'you see?" She looked at me with a truly terrifying yearning; I'd seen nothing like it since the doctors were putting the strait-jacket on my guvnor and whisking the brandy beyond his reach. "An' we could . . . stay together always. Could you . . . would you marry me, Beauchamp?"

3

If half the art of survival is running, the other half is keeping a straight face. I can't count the number of times my fate has depended on my response to some unexpected and abominable proposal—like the night Yakub Beg suggested I join a suicidal attempt to scupper some Russian ammunition ships, or Sapten's jolly notion about swimming naked into a Gothic castle full of Bismarck's thugs, or Brooke's command to me to lead a charge against a head-hunters' stockade. Jesu, the times that we have seen. (Queer, though, the one that lives in memory is from my days as a snivelling fag at Rugby when Bully Dawson was tossing the new bugs in blankets, and grabbed me, gloating, and I just hopped on to the blanket, cool as you please for all my bowels were heaving in panic, and the brute was so put out that he turfed me off in fury, as I'd guessed he would, and I was spared the anguish of being tossed while the other fags were put through it, howling.)

At all events—and young folk with their way to make in the world should mark this—you must never suppose that a poker face is sufficient. That shows you're thinking, and sometimes the appearance of thought ain't called for. It would have been fatal now, with Susie; I had to show willing quick, but not too much—if I cried aloud for joy and swept her into my arms, she'd smell a large whiskered rat. It all went through my mind in an instant, more or less as follows: 1, I'm married already; 2, she don't know that; 3, if I don't accept there's a distinct risk she'll show me the door, although she might not; 4, if she does, I'll get hung; 5, on balance, best to cast myself gratefully at her feet for the moment, and think about it afterwards.

All in a split second, as I say—just time for me to stare uncomprehending for two heart-beats, and then let a great light of joy dawn in my eyes for an instant, gradually fading to a kind of ruptured awe as I took a hesitant step forward, dropped on one knee beside her, took her hand gently, and said in husky disbelief:

"Susie . . . do you really mean that?"

Whatever she'd expected, it hadn't been that—she was watching me like a hawk, between hope and mistrust. She knew me, you see, and what a damned scoundrel I was—at the same time, she was bursting to believe that I cared for her, and I knew just how to trade on that. Before she could reply, I smiled, and shook my head sadly, and said very manly:

"Dear Susie, you're wrong, you know. I ain't worth it."

She thought different, of course, and said so, and a pretty little debate ensued, in which I was slightly hampered by the fact that she had clamped my face between her udders and was ecstatically contradicting me at the top of her voice; I acted up with nice calculation, as though masking gallons of ardour beneath honest doubt—I didn't know, I said, because no woman had ever—well, honoured me with true love before, and rake that I'd been, I'd grown to care for her too much to let her do something she might repent . . . you may imagine this punctuated by loving babble from her until the point where I thought, now for the coup de grâce, and with a muffled, despairing groan of "Ah, my darling!" as though I couldn't contain myself any longer, gave her the business for all I was worth on top of her dressing-stool. God knows how it stood the strain, for we must have scaled twenty-two stone between us, easy.

Even when it was done, I still did a deal of head-shaking, an unworthy soul torn between self-knowledge and the dawning hope that the love of a good woman might be just what he needed. I didn't do it too strong; I didn't need to; she was over the main hurdle and ready to convince herself against all reason. That's what love does to you, I suppose, although I don't speak from personal experience.

"I know I'm foolish," says she, all earnest and sentimental, "an' that you're the kind of rascal that could break my 'eart . . . but I'll take my chance o' that. I reckon you like me, an' I 'ope you'll like me more. Love grows," says the demented biddy, "an' while I'm forty-two—" she was pushing fifty, I may say "— an' a bit older than you, that don't 'ave to signify. An' I reckon—please don't mind me sayin' this, dearest—that even at worst, you might settle for me bein' well-off, which I am, an' able to give you a comfortable life, as well as all the love that's in me. It's no use sayin' practical things don't matter, 'cos they do—an' I wouldn't expect you to have me if I was penniless. But you know me, an' that when I say I can make a million, its a fact. You can be a rich man, with me, an' ave' everythin' you could wish for, an' if you was to say 'aye' on those terms, I'd understand. But I reckon—" she couldn't keep the tears back, as she held my chin and stroked my whiskers and I looked like Galahad on his vigil "— I reckon you care for me enough, anyway—an' we can be happy together."

I knew better than to be fervent. I just nodded, and ran a pin from her dressing-table into my leg surreptitiously to start a tear. "Thank you, Susie," says I quietly and kissed her gently. "Now don't cry. I don't know about love, but I know . . ." I took a fairish sigh ". . . I know that I can't say no."

That was the God's truth, too, as I explained to Spring half an hour later, for while he wasn't the man you'd seek out to discuss your affairs of the heart, it was our necks that were concerned here, and he had to be kept au fait. He gaped at me like a landed shark.

"But you're married!" cries he.

"Tut-tut," says I, "not so loud. She doesn't know that."

He glared horribly. "It's bigamy! Lord God Almighty, have you no respect for the sacraments?"

"To be sure—which is why I don't intend our union to last any farther than California, when I'll—"

"I won't have it!" snarls he, and that wild glitter came into his pale eyes. "Is there no indecency beneath you? Have you no fear of God, you animal? Will you fly in the face of His sacred law, damn your eyes?"

I might have expected this, when I came to think of it. Not the least of Captain Spring's eccentricities was that while he'd got crimes on his conscience that Nero would have bilked at, he was a fanatic for the proprieties, like Sunday observance and afternoon tea—he'd drop manacled niggers overboard at a sight of the white duster, but he was a stickler when it came to lining out the hymns while his equally demented wife pumped her accordion and his crew of brigands sang "Let us with a gladsome mind". All the result of boning up the Thirty-nine Articles, I don't doubt.

"What else could I do?" I pleaded, while he swore and stamped about the room, snarling about blasphemy and the corruption of the public school system. "The old faggot as good as promised that if I didn't take her, she'd whistle up the pigs[3]. Don't you see—if I jolly her along, it's a safe passage out, and then, goodbye Mrs Willinck. Or Comber, as the case may be. But if I jilt her, it's both our necks!" I near as told him I'd done it before, with Duchess Irma in Strackenz, but from the look of him he'd have burst a blood vessel, with luck.

"Why in God's name did I ever ship you aboard the *College*?" cries he, clenching his hands in fury. "You're a walking mass of decay, *porcus ex grege diaboli*!*" But he wasn't too far gone to see reason, and calmed down eventually. "Well," says he, giving me his most baleful glower, "if your forehead is brazen enough for this—God have mercy on your soul. Which he won't. Bah! Why the hell should I care? I can say with Ovid, *video meliora proboque, deteriora sequor†*. Now, get out of my sight!"

He'd given me a scare, though, I can tell you. Even now, I couldn't be sure that some quirk of that diseased mind wouldn't make him blurt out to Susie that her intended was already a husband and father. So I was doubly uneasy, and puzzled, when Susie bade the pair of us that night to a supper party à trois in her salon—we'd had our meals on trays in our rooms since our arrival, and besides, I knew Susie's first good opinion of Spring had worn thin. I'd given

*A swine from the devil's herd.
†I see and approve better things, but follow the worse which I condemn.

her a fair notion of the kind of swine he was, and since he could never conceal his delightful nature for long, she'd been able to judge for herself.

"A small celebration," was how she described it when we sat down in her salon. "I daresay, captain, that Beauchamp 'as given you our happy news." And she beamed on me; she was dressed to her peak, which was dazzlingly vulgar, but I have to say that she didn't look a year more than her pretended age, and deuced handsome. To my relief, Spring played up, and pledged her happiness; he didn't include me, and he wasn't quite Pickwick, yet, but at least his tone was civil and he didn't smash the crockery.

Mind you, I've been at dinners I've enjoyed more. Susie, for once, seemed nervous, which I put down to girlish excitement; she prattled about slave prices, and the cost of high-bred yellows, and how the Cuban market was sky-high these days, and the delicacy of octoroon fancies, who didn't seem to be able to stand the pace in her trade at all; Spring answered her, more or less, and they had a brief discussion on the breeding of sturdier stock by mating black Africans with mulattos, which is a capital topic over the pudding. But by and by he said less and less, and that none too clearly; I was just beginning to wonder if the drink had got to him for once when he suddenly gave a great sigh, and a staring yawn, caught at his chair arms as though to rise, and then fell face foremost into the blancmange.

Susie glanced at me, lifting a warning finger. Then she got up, pulled his face out of the mess, and pushed up one eyelid. He was slumped like a sawdust doll, his face purple.

"That's all right," says she. "Brutus!" And before my astonished eyes the butler went out, and presently in came two likely big coves in reefer jackets. At a nod from Susie, they hefted Spring out of his chair, and without a word bore him from the room. Susie sauntered back to her place, took a sip of wine, and smiled at my amazement.

"Well," says she, "we wouldn't 'ave wanted 'im along on our 'oneymoon, would we?"

For a moment I was appalled. "You're not letting the

bogies have him? He'll peach! For God's sake, Susie, he'll—"

"If he does any peachin', it'll be in Cape Town," says she. "You don't think I'd be as silly as that, do you—or serve 'im such a mean turn?" She laughed and patted my hand. "'E don't deserve that—anyone who put out Peter Omo'undro's light must 'ave some good in 'im. Anyway, if it wasn't for the likes o' your Captain Spring, where'd I get my wenches? But I didn't fancy 'im above 'alf, from the first—mostly 'cos 'e didn't mean you no good. I seen 'im watchin' you, an' mutterin' 'is Italian or wotever it was. So," says she lightly, "I just passed the word to some good friends 'o mine—you need 'em in my business, believe me—an' by the time 'e wakes up 'e'll 'ave the prospect of a nice long voyage to cure 'is poor achin' 'ead. Well, don't looked so shocked, dearie—'e's not the first to be shanghaied from this 'ouse, I can tell you!"

Well, it was capital—in its way, but it was also food for thought. Offhand, I couldn't think of a better place for J. C. Spring than a long-hauler bound for South Africa, with a bucko mate kicking his arse while he holystoned the deck (although knowing the bastard, by the time they made Table Bay he would probably *be* the mate, if not more). He'd have been better fed to the fish, of course, but we must just take what benevolent Providence sends us, and be thankful. On the other hand, it was a mite disturbing to discover that my bride-to-be was a lady of such ruthless resource. There she was, all pink and plump and pretty, selecting a grape, dusting it with sherbert, and popping it into my mouth with a fond smirk and a loving kiss that was like being hit in the face by a handful of liver—and not two minutes earlier she'd had a dinner guest trepanned before he'd even had his coffee. It occurred to me that severing our marriage tie in California would call for tactful management; hell hath no fury, and so forth, and I didn't want to find myself bound for Sydney on a hellship, or dropped into Frisco Bay with my legs broken.

No, it bore thinking on. I'd always known that although Susie was a perfect fool for any chap with a big knocker, she was also a woman of character—she managed her slave-whores with a rod of iron, kindly enough but standing no nonsense, and the cool way she'd taken Omohundro's demise, and seen Spring outward bound with a bellyful of puggle just because he was in the way, showed that she could be even harder than I'd have believed. But I was committed now—it was California or bust with a vengeance, and the only safe way when all was said. If I played my cards cleverly, I might even come out with a neat profit which should see me home in style, there to enjoy the fruits of the late unlamented Morrison's labours. With luck I'd be back with my loving Elspeth after a total absence of about eighteen months—just nice time for the Bryant scandal to have died down. And there was no possibility that Susie would ever be able to trace her absconding spouse; she knew I was English, but nothing more, for Spring had naturally backed up my imposture as Beauchamp Millward Comber. I was clear there.

So now, once I'd put behind me the uncomfortable recollection of Spring with his beard soaked in custard being whisked off by the crimps, I gave my full attention to my betrothed, congratulating her on the smart way she'd recruited him back to the merchant marine, and regarding her with an admiration and respect which were by no means assumed.

"You're sure you don't mind?" says she. "I know it was a bit sudden-like, but I couldn't 'ave abided 'avin' 'im along, with that ugly phiz of 'is, an' those awful creepy eyes. Fair gave me the shakes. An' Jake an' Captain Roger, they'll see 'im well away, an' never a word about it. An' we can be just the two of us, can't we?" She subsided on to my lap, slipped her arms round my neck, pecked me gently on the lips, and gazed adoringly into my eyes. "Ow, Beachy, I'm that 'appy with you! Now, 'ave you 'ad enough to eat? Wouldn't fancy a nice piece of fruit for dessert? I think you would," she giggles, and she took a peach, teased me with it, and then pushed it down the front of her dress between her breasts. "Go on, now—eat it all up, like a good boy."

* * *

We started up-river two days later, and if you haven't seen

a bawdy house flitting you've missed an unusual sight. The entire contents of the house were shipped down to the levee on about a dozen carts, and then Susie's twenty sluts were paraded with their baggage in the hall, under the stern eye of their mistress. I hadn't been invited to be on hand, but I watched through the crack of the salon door, and you never saw anything so pretty. They were all dressed in the most modest of crinolines, with their bonnets tied under their chins, like a Sunday school treat, chattering away and only falling silent and bobbing a respectful curtsey as Susie came opposite each one, checking her name and that she'd got all her possessions.

"Claudia . . . got your portmanteau an' your bandbox? . . . good . . . brushed your teeth, 'ave you? Very well . . . let's see, Marie . . . are those your best gloves? No, I'll lay they're not, so just you change 'em this minute—no, not your black velvet ones, you goose, you're goin' on a steamboat! Now, then, Cleonie . . . oh, I declare white does suit you best of anythin' . . . why, you look proper virginal . . . wot are you now—thirty dollars, isn't it? Well, I must be goin' simple, you're a fifty if ever I saw one. Ne'er mind . . . no, Aphrodite, you don't wear your bonnet on the back of your 'ead . . . I know it shows you off, but that's not what we want, dear, is it? You're a young lady on your travels, not summat in a shop window . . . that's better . . . stand up straight, Stephanie, there's nothin' becomes a female less than a slouch . . . Josephine, your dress is too short by a mile, you'll lengthen it the minute we're aboard. Don't pout at me, miss, your ankles won't get fat just 'cos they're covered. Now, then, shoulders back, all of you, duck your heads just a little, hands folded, that's right . . . eyes down . . . very pretty indeed. Good."

She walked back along the line, well satisfied, and then addressed them.

"Now, I want you gels to pay careful heed to me. On the boat, and indeed all the way to California, you'll behave yourselves like young ladies—an' I mean real ladies, not the kind of young ladies we talk about 'ere for the benefit of gentlemen, you hear? You'll go always two an' two, an' you will not encourage or countenance the attention of any men you chance to meet—an' there'll be plenty of 'em, so take care. You won't heed any man if he addresses you, you won't talk to 'em, you won't look at 'em. Is that clear?"

"Yes, Miz Susie, ma'am." It was like a chorus of singing birds, soft and clear.

"Nor you won't stand nor look nor even *think* so's to attract a man's attention. *You* know what I mean. An' bear in mind, I've forgotten more about takin' a man's eye than you'll ever know, an' if I catch you at it, it's six of the cane, so there! You're not workin' till we get to California, none of you—an' you're not flirtin' private, neither. Well?"

"Yes, Miz Susie, ma'am," very subdued this time.

"Now, you're all good gels, I know that. It's why you're 'ere." Susie smiled as she looked along the line, for all the world like a head mistress at prize-giving. "An' I'm pleased an' proud of all of you. But none of you've been outside Awlins in your lives—yes, Medea, I know you an' Eugenie bin to 'Avana, but you didn't get outdoors much, did you? But where you're goin' now is very different, an' I daresay there'll be trials an' temptations along the way. Well, you must just bear with 'em an' resist 'em, an' I promise you this—when we get to California you'll 'ave nothin' but the best gentlemen to accommodate, an' if you're good an' do well, I'll see each one of you settled comfortable for life, an' you know I mean it." She paused and drew herself up. "But any saucy miss that's wilful or disobedient or *won't* be told . . . I'll sell 'er down the river quicker than look—an' you know I mean that, too. Some of you remember Poppaea, do you?—well, *that* contrary piece is bein' whipped to hoe cotton on the Tombigbee this very minute, an' ruin' the day. So take heed."

"Yes, Miz Susie, ma'am," in a whisper, with one little sob.

"Well, we'll say no more about that . . . now, don't cry, Marie—I know *you're* a good gel, dear." Susie clapped her hands sharply. "Into the carriages with you—don't run, an' don't chatter, an' Brutus'll see your bags on to the wagon."

No doubt it was the vision of all that enchanting tail lined up in the hall below that had drawn me through the salon door during Susie's address; one of the sluts, Aphrodite, I think, a jet-black houri with sinful eyes, had caught sight of me and nudged her neighbour, and they had both looked away and tried not to giggle; it wouldn't do to draw back, so I sauntered down the stairs and Susie saw me just as she was dismissing them.

"Wait, gels!" She beamed and held out a hand to me. "You should know—this is your new master . . . or will be very soon. Make your curtsies to Mister Beauchamp Comber, gels—there, that's elegant!" As she passed her arm through mine I nodded offhand and said, "Ladies" as twenty bonneted heads ducked in my direction, and twenty graceful figures bobbed—by George, I daren't stare or I'd have started to drool. Every colour from ebony and coffee brown to cream and all but pure white—and every size and shape: tall and petite, statuesque and slender, lissom and plump, and all of 'em fit to illustrate the Arabian Nights. They fluttered out, whispering, and Susie squeezed my hand.

"Ain't they sweet, though? That's our fortune, my love."

One of them lingered a moment, telling Brutus to mind how he carried her parrot's cage "—for he does not like to be shaken, do you, my little pet-pigeon?" She had a soft Creole accent, well-spoken, and just the way she posed, tapping the cage, and the little limp gesture she made to Brutus, told me that she was showing off for the new boss: she was a creamy high-yaller, all in snowy crinoline, with her bonnet far enough back to show an unusual coiffure, sleek black and parted in the centre; a face like a wayward saint, but with a slow, soft-footed walk to the door that spoke a rare conceit.

"M'm," says Susie. "That's Cleonie—if she 'adn't turned back I'd ha' thought she was sickenin' for somethin'. I may 'ave to think about takin' the cane to 'er—yet you can't blame 'er for doin' wot makes 'er valuable, can you? Know wot she can make for us in a year?—fifteen thousand dollars an' more—an' that's workin' 'er easy. Now then . . ." She pecked me and winked. "Let's be off—we don't want to keep a very important gentleman waitin', do we?"

Who that gentleman was I discovered when we boarded the *Choctaw Queen* at the levee just as dusk was falling—for we'd agreed I must run no risk of being recognised, and that I'd keep out of public view in daylight until we reached Westport. Susie had bespoken the entire texas deck on the steamboat, which was one of the smaller stern-wheelers, and when we'd made our way through the bustling waterfront and its confusion of cargo and passengers milling under the flares (me with my collar well up and my hat pulled down), up the gangway past the saluting conductor, to the texas and its little private saloon—there in the sudden light of chandeliers was a table spread with crystal and silver, and nigger waiters in livery, and a band of fiddlers scraping away, and the big red-faced skipper himself, all consequence and whiskers, bowing over Susie's hand and clasping mine heartily, while a little clergyman bustled up, solemnly a-smirk, and a couple of sober coves behind looked wise and made play with pens and certificates.

"Well, now, that's just fine!" cries the skipper. "Welcome 'board, Miz Willinck, ma'am, an' you too, suh, kindly welcome! All ready, ma'am, as you see—Revn'd Hootkins, an' heah Mistah Grace the magistrate, an' clerk an' all!" He waved a great hand, and I realised that the crafty bitch had brought me up to scratch all unawares—she was smiling at me, wide-eyed and eager, and the skipper was clapping my back, and the magistrate inquiring that I was Beauchamp Comber, bachelor of sound mind and good standing, wasn't that so, while the clerk scribbled away and blotted the page in haste, and had to start again, and we both wrote our names, Susie's hand shaking as she held the quill—and then we stood side by side while the little sky-pilot fumbled his book and cleared his throat and said shet the doah, there, an' keep them fiddlers quiet, till we do this thing solemn an' fittin', now then . . . Susan Willinck, widder . . . an' Bo-chump, how you say that? Bee-chum, that a fact? . . . we bein' gathered in the sight o' God an' these heah witnesses . . . holy matrimony . . . procreation, yeah, well . . . long as ye both shall live . . . you got the ring, suh? . . . you hain't? . . . *lady* has the ring, well, that's a new one, but pass it over to him, anyhow, an' you, suh, lay a-holt the bride's hand, that's it now . . .

I heard the bells boom over Strackenz Cathedral, and smelt the musk of incense, and felt the weight of the crown jewels and Irma's hand cold in mine . . . and then it was Elspeth's warm and holding firm, with little Abercrombie watching that I didn't make a bolt for the abbey door, and Morrison's irritable mutter that if there wisnae suffeeshent carriages for the aunts and cousins they could dam' weel walk tae the weddin' breakfast . . . and I was at the peephole looking down on Ranavalona's massive black nakedness while her handmaidens administered the ceremonial bath—not that there'd been any wedding ceremonial there, but it had been a ritual preliminary, in its way, to my union with that ghastly nigger monster . . . Irma's face turning, icy and proud, her lips barely brushing my cheek . . . Elspeth glowingly lovely, golden curls under her bridal veil, red lips open under mine . . . that mad black female gorilla grunting as she flung off her robe and grabbed my essentials . . . I don't know what conjured up these visions of my previous nuptials, really; I suppose I'm just a sentimental chap at bottom. And now it was Susie's plump face upturned to mine, and the fiddlers were striking up while the skipper and magistrate applauded and cried congratulations, the nigger waiters passed the plates with mirthful beams, with corks popping and Susie squealing with laughter as the skipper gallantly claimed the privilege of kissing the bride, and the little clergyman said, well, just a touch o' the rye, thank-'ee, no, nothin' with it, an' keep it comin' . . .

But what I remember best is not that brief unexpected ceremony, or the obligatory ecstatic thrashings on the bed of our plushy-gilt stateroom under the picture of Pan leering down appropriately while fleshy nymphs sported about him, or Susie's imprisoning embrace as she murmured drowsily: "Mrs Comber . . . Mrs Beauchamp *Millward* Comber," over and over—none of these things. What I remember is slipping out when she was asleep, to stand by the breezy texas rail in the velvet dark and smoke a cheroot, looking out over the oily waters as we ploughed up past Baton Rouge. The great stern wheel was flickering like a magic lantern in the starshine; far over on the east shore were the town lights, and from the main saloon on the boiler deck beneath me came the sound of muffled music and laughter; I paced astern and looked down at the uncovered main deck—and that's what I can see and hear now, clear across the years, as though it were last night.

From rail to rail the great deck was packed with gear and people, all shadowy under the flares like one of those Dutch night paintings: here a couple of darkies crooning softly as they squatted in the scuppers, there a couple of drummers comparing carpetbags, yonder some rivermen lounging at the gangway and telling stretchers—but they were just the few. The many, and there were hundreds of them, were either groups of young men who gossipped eagerly and laughted a mite too loud, or obvious families—Ma wrapped in her shawl beside the children huddled in sleep among the bales and bundles and tied wagons; Pa sitting silent, deep in thought, or rummaging for the hundredth time through the family goods, or listening doubtfully near the groups of the noisy single men. Nothing out of the way—except for a strange, nervous excitement that rose from that crowded deck like an electric wave; even I sensed it, without understanding, for I didn't know then that these ordinary folk were anything but—that they were the emigrants, the vanguard of that huge tide that would pour into the wilderness and make America, the fearful, hopeful, ignorant ones who were going to look for El Dorado and couldn't for the life of them have told you why, exactly, except that Pa was restless and Jack and Jim were full of ginger. And Ma was tired—but they were all going to see the elephant.

He was crowded two deep along the port rail, was Pa, soberly looking west as though trying to see across the thousands of miles to where he hoped they were going, wondering what it would be like, and why hadn't he stayed in Pittsburgh? The single fellows had no such doubts (much); beneath me a bunch in slouch hats and jeans were

passing the jug around boisterously, and one with a melo-
deon was striking up:

> Oh, say, have ye got a drink of rum?
> Doodah, doodah!
> I'd give ye a taste if I had some,
> Doo-doodah-day!

and his mates clapped and stamped as they roared the
chorus:

> For it's—blow, bully-boys, blow!
> For Californeye-o!
> There's plenty of gold as I've been told
> On the banks of the Sacramento!

You never hear it now, except maybe on a sailing ship
when she's upping anchor, and I doubt if it would have the
same note of reckless hope that I heard off Baton Rouge—
it wasn't too well received then, either, with cries of shet-
up-cain't-ye? from the sleepers, and damn-yer-eyes-I-
reckon-we-kin-sing-if-we-want-to from the optimists, and
then a baby began to wail, and they piped down, laughing
and grumbling. But whenever I remember it, I have an odd
thought: I never suspected that night that I—or Susie and
the sluts, for that matter—had the least thing in common
with those folk down on the main deck, but in fact we all
belonged to a damned exclusive company without knowing
it, with a title that's a piece of folklore nowadays. Millions
came after, but we were the Forty-Niners.

That claim to immortality lay ahead in the unseen future;
as I pitched my cheroot into the river I was reflecting that
wherever the rest might be going, I was bound for home,
admittedly the long way about, and they could keep
Californeye-o for me. If there were pickings to be got along
the way, especially from the overfed trollop snoring and
sated in the stateroom, so much the better; she owed me
something for the amount of tup I'd given her, and no doubt
would give her again before the journey's end. There were
worse ways of crossing America—or so I thought in my
innocence. If I'd had any sense I'd have followed my cheroot
and taken my chance among the enemies hunting me along
the Mississippi valley.

4

Fifteen dollars a bottle they were charging for claret at the Planters' Hotel in St Louis that year, and it was like drinking swamp-water when the mules have been by; I've tasted better in a London ladies' club. But you daren't drink anything else because of the cholera; the good folk of St Louis were keeling over like flies, the whole town stank of camphor and burning bitumen, you could even find bodies lying in the street, and the only place more crowded than the Planters' must have been the cemetery—which was probably as comfortable.

It wasn't only the plague that worried me, either; St Louis was the town where a few weeks earlier they'd been posting rewards of a hundred dollars for my apprehension, describing me to a T and warning the citizenry that I had Genteel Manners and spoke with a Foreign Accent, damn their impudence. But the *Choctaw Queen* went no farther, and we had to wait a day for a vessel to carry us up the Missouri to Westport, so there was nothing for it but to venture ashore, which I managed in safety by purchasing one of the new "genuine cholera masks, guaranteed to prevent infection" for two bits, and sneaking into the Planters' looking like a road-agent.

There I had further proof, if I'd needed it, of my new wife's strength of character, and also of the length of her purse. Would you believe it—she had bespoken half a dozen rooms, and when the manager discovered that four of them were to be occupied by twenty nigger wenches, he had the conniptions; by thunder, he'd swim in blood before any black slaves stank up his rooms, no matter their airs and refinements. Unfortunately for him, Susie had the girls settled in and their doorkeys in her reticule before he realised it; he and she had a fine set-to in our parlour, while I kept

63

safely out of view in the bedroom, and she told him that since her "young ladies" were on no account going to be herded in the pens with fieldhands and such trash, nor in quarantine neither, he'd better put a hundred dollars in his pocket and forget it. I'd have let 'em go to the pens myself, but it was her money, and after some hem-haw he took it, and retired with a grovelling request that the "young ladies" keep to their rooms, for his reputation's sake.

But what with the din of the overcrowded hotel, the stink of sulphur smouldering in the fireplace, and the fear that some sharp might discover Mr Comber was the notorious slave-stealer Tom Arnold, I was mightily relieved when we boarded the Missouri packet next evening, and I felt it safe to drop my cholera mask over the side—the passengers included sufficient tall dark strangers with every kind of accent, whether their manners were genteel or not. She was a smaller and much dirtier vessel than the *Choctaw Queen,* and the girls had to make do in steerage among all the roughs and roustabouts and gamblers and frontier riff-raff; Susie just singled out the four biggest and ugliest and paid them handsomely to keep the wenches safe in a corner— which to my astonishment they did, for four days up to Kanzas Landing. The first drunk who tried to paw a crino- line was tipped over the side without ceremony, and the gamblers haw-hawed and laid bets whether he'd float or sink. After that our Magdalenes were left alone, but they had a miserable passage of it, even under the lean-to which the toughs rigged up to keep out the fog and drizzle, and they were a doleful and bedraggled jam of tarts by the time we tied up. Susie and I shared a cramped and stuffy saloon on the texas with about seventeen snoring merchants and dowagers with bad breath, but for once I didn't mind the lack of privacy; I needed the rest.

They tell me that Kansas City nowadays covers the whole section, but in those days the landing and Westport and Independence were separated by woodland and meadow. And I wonder if today's city contains more people than were crowded along the ten miles from Independence to the river when I first saw it in '49: there were thousands of them, in tents and lean-tos and houses and log shacks and under the trees and in the few taverns and lodging-places; they were in the stables and sheds and shops and storehouses, a great swarming hive of humanity of every kind you can imagine—well, I remember the Singapore river in the earlies, and it was nothing to Westport-Independence. The whole stretch was jammed with wagons and carts and carriages, churning the spaces between the buildings into a sea of mud after the recent rain, and through it went the mules and oxen and horses, with the steam rising from them and the stench of hides and dung and smoke filling the air— but even that was nothing to the noise.

Every other building seemed to be a forge or a stable or a warehouse, a-clang with hundreds of hammers and the rasp of saws and the crack of axes and the creak of wheels and the thump and scrape of boxes and bales being loaded or unloaded; teamsters snapped their whips with a "Way-hay, whoa!", foremen bellowed, children shrilled, the voices of thousands of men and women blended with it all in a great eager busy din that echoed among the buildings and floated off to be lost in the surrounding forest.

I daresay it was nothing to what it must have looked like a year or two later, when the gold-fever was at its height and half Europe came pouring to America in search of fortune. But in that spring every human specimen in North America seemed to have assembled at Kanzas Landing for the great trek west—labourers white and black and olive, bronzed hunters and pale clerks, sober emigrants and raffish adventurers, harassed women with aprons and baskets prodding at vegetables set out before the store-fronts and slapping the children who bawled round their skirts; red-faced traders in stove-pipe hats and thumbs hooked in fancy weskits, spitting juice; soldiers in long boots and blue breeches, their sabres on the table among the beer-mugs; Mexicans in serapes and huge-brimmed sombreros leading a file of mules; farmers in straw hats and faded overalls; skinners with coiled whips, lounging on their rigs; bearded ruffians in greasy buckskins bright with beadwork, two-foot Bowies gleaming on their hips, chattering through their noses in a language which I recognised to my amazement as Scotch Gaelic; bright-eyed harpies watchful in shack doorways; Spanish riders in ponchos and feathered bonnets, their sashes stuffed with flintlock pistols; a party of Indians beneath the trees, faces grotesquely painted, hatchets at their belts and lances stacked; silent plainsmen in fur caps and long fringed skirts, carrying buffalo guns and powder horns; a coach guard with two six-shooters at his hips, two five-shooters in his waistband, a slung revolving rifle, a broadsword, and a knife in his boot—oh, and he was gnawing a toothpick, too; an incredibly lean and ancient hunter, white-bearded to the waist, dressed in ragged deerskin and billycock hat, his "nail-driver" rifle across the crupper of his mule, staring ahead like a fakir in a trance as he rode slowly up the street, his slovenly Indian squaw at his stirrup, through the crowds of loafers and porters and barefoot boys scuffling under the wagons, the swaggering French voyageurs, gaudy and noisy, the drummers and counter-jumpers and sharp-faced Yankees, planters and crooks and rivermen, trappers and miners and plain honest folk wondering how they'd strayed into this Babel—and those are only the ones I noticed in the first mile or so.

But soft! who is this stalwart figure with the dashing whiskers so admirably set off by his wideawake hat and fringed deerskin shirt, a new patent Colt repeater strapped to his manly rump, his well-turned shanks encased in new boots which are pinching the bejeezus out of him? Can it be other than Arapaho Harry, scourge of the plains?—that alert and smouldering eye must oft have hardened at the sound of the shrill war-whoop, or narrowed behind the sights as he nailed the rampant grizzly—now it is soft and genial as he chivvies the dusky whores into the back of the cart, an indulgent smile playing across his noble features. Mark the grace with which he vaults nimbly into the driver's seat beside the bedizened trot in the feathered bonnet—his aunt, doubtless—and with an expert chuck on the reins sets the team in motion and bogs the whole contraption axel-deep in the gumbo. The whores squeak in alarm, the aunt—

his *wife,* you say?—rails and adjusts her finery, but the gallant frontiersman, unperturbed save for a blistering oath which mantles the cheeks of his fair companions in blushes, is equal to the emergency; for two bits he gets a gang of loafers to haul them out. The western journey is not without its trials; it is going to be a long trek to California.

But at least it looked as though we were going to make it in some style. Once we'd got the rig out of the stew, and rattled through Westport and the great sea of emigrant tents and wagons to Independence—which was a pretty little place then with a couple of spires and a town hall with a belfry, of which the inhabitants were immensely proud—we were greeted by the celebrated Colonel Owens, a breezy old file with check trousers full of belly and a knowing eye; he was the leading merchant, and had been commissioned to outfit Susie's caravan. He and the boys made us welcome at the store, pressed sherry cobblers on me, bowed and leered gallantly at Susie, and assured us that a trip across the plains was a glorified picnic.

"You'll find, ma'am," says the Colonel, ankle cocked and cigar a-flourish, "that everything's in real prime train. Indeedy—your health, sir. Yes, ma'am, six Pittsburgh wagons, spanking new, thirty yoke of good oxen, a dozen mules, and a real bang-up travelling carriage—the very best Hiram Young[4] can furnish, patent springs, hand-painted, cushioned seats, watertight for fording streams, seats half a dozen comfortable. Fact is," with a broad wink, "it's one of the new mail company coaches, but Hiram procured it as a personal favour. Indeedy—you won't find a more elegant conveyance outside Boston—am I right, boys?"

The boys agreed that he was, and added in hushed tones that the mail company intended to charge $250 a head for the three-week non-stop run to Santa Fe, and how about that?

"We're goin' to take three months," says Susie, "an' ten cents a pound for freight is quite dear enough, thank you. To say nothin' of fifty dollars a month for guards an' drivers, who'll eat like wolves if I know anythin'."

"Well, now, ma'am, I see you've a proper head for business," chuckles the Colonel. "An' a real pretty head it is, too, if I may say. But good men don't come cheap—eh, boys?"

The boys swore it was true; why, a good stockman could make two hundred *a week,* without going west of Big Blue.

"I'm not hirin' stockmen," snaps Susie. "I'm payin' high for reliable men who can look after theirselves, and me."

"And you shall have the best, ma'am!" cries the Colonel. "Say, I like your style, though! Your health again, Mr Comber! Indeedy—eight outriders, each with a revolving rifle and a brace of patent pistols—why, that's a hundred shots without reloading! A regiment couldn't afford better protection! A regiment, did I say? Why, three of these men rode with Kearny in the Mexican War—seasoned veterans, ma'am, every one. Isn't that so, boys?"

The boys couldn't fault him; dogged if they knew how the Army would have managed without those three. I remarked that so much firepower was impressive, and seemed to argue necessity—I'd been noting a bill on the store wall advertising:

Ho! Hist! Attention!

Californians! Why not take, among other necessaries, your own monuments and tombstones? A great saving can be effected by having their inscriptions cut in New York beforehand!!![5]

The Colonel looked serious and called for more cobblers. "Indian depredations this past ten years, sir, have been serious and multiplying," says he solemnly. "Indeedy—red sons-o'-bitches wherever you look—oh, beg pardon, ma'am, that runaway tongue of mine! However, with such vast convoys of emigrants now moving west, I foresee no cause for apprehension. Safety in numbers, Mr Comber, hey? Besides, the tribes are unusually peaceful at present—eh, boys?"

The boys couldn't remember such tranquility; it was Sunday afternoon the whole way to the Rockies, with all the Indians retired or gone into farming or catching the cholera. (That last was true enough, by the way.)

Susie inquired about a guide, reminding the Colonel she had asked for the best, and he smacked his thigh and beamed. "Now, ma'am, you can set your mind to rest *there*—yes, indeedy, I reckon you can, just about," and the boys grinned approval without even being asked.

"Is it Mr Williams?" says Susie. "I was told to ask for him, special."

"Well, now ma'am, I'm afraid Old Bill doesn't come out of the mountains much, these days." The boys confirmed that indeed Old Bill was out west with Fremont. "No, I'm afraid Fitzpatrick and Beckwourth aren't available, either— but they're no loss, believe me, when you see who I've engaged—subject to his meeting you and agreeing to take the command, of course." And he nodded to one of the boys, who went out on the stoop and bawled: "Richey!"

"Command!" says Susie, bridling. "Any commandin' that's to be done, my 'usband'll do!" Which gave me a nasty start, I can tell you. "He's in charge of our caravan, and the guide'll take 'is pay an' do what he's told! The idea!"

The Colonel looked at the boys, and the boys looked at the Colonel, and they all looked at me. "Well, now, ma-'am," says Owens doubtfully, "I'm sure Mr Comber is a gentleman of great ability, but—"

"'E's an' officer of the Royal Navy," snaps Susie, "an' quite accustomed to command—aren't you, my love?"

I agreed, but remarked that leading a caravan must be specialised work, and doubtless there were many better qualified than I . . . which was stark truth, apart from which I'd no wish to be badgering roughriders and arguing with drunk teamsters when I could be rolling in a hand-painted, watertight coach. Seeing my diffidence, she rounded on me, demanding if I was going to take orders from some grubby little carter? I said, well, ah . . . while the Colonel called loudly for cobblers and the boys looked tactfully at the ceiling, and just then a burly scarecrow came into the store—or rather, he seemed to drift in, silently, and the Colonel introduced him as Mr Wootton, our guide.

I heard Susie sniff in astonishment—well, he *was* grubby, no error, and hadn't shaved in a while, and his clothes looked as though he'd taken them off a dead buckskin man and then slept in them for a year. He seemed diffident, too, fiddling with his hat and looking at the floor. When the Colonel told him about my commanding the caravan he thought for a bit, and then said in a gentle, husky voice: "Gennelman bin wagon-captain afore?"

No, said the Colonel, and the boys looked askance and coughed. The clodpole scratched his head and asks:

"Gennelman bin in Injun country?"

No, they said, I hadn't. He stood a full minute, still not looking up, and then says:

"Gennelman got no 'sperience?"

At this one of the boys laughed, and I sensed Susie ready to burst—and I was about fed up being ridiculed by these blasted chawbacons. God knows I didn't want to command her caravan, but enough's enough.

"I've had some experience, Mr Wootton," says I. "I was once an army chief of staff—" Sergeant-General to the nigger rabble of Madagascar, but there you are "—and have known service in India, Afghanistan, and Borneo. But I've no special desire—"

At this Wootton lifted his unkempt head and looked at me, and I stopped dead. He was a ragged nobody—with eyes like clear blue lights, straight and steady. Then he glanced away—and I thought, don't let this one go. It may be a picnic on the plains, but you'll be none the worse with him along.

"My dear," says I to Susie, "perhaps you and the Colonel will excuse Mr Wootton and myself." I went out, and presently Wootton drifts on to the stoop, not looking at me.

"Mr. Wootton," says I, "my wife wants me to command the caravan, and what she wants she gets. Now, I'm not your Old Bill Williams, but I'm not a greenhorn, exactly. I don't mind being *called* wagon-captain—but you're the guide, and what you say goes. You can say it to me, quietly, and I'll say it to everyone else, and you'll get an extra hundred a month. What d'you say?"

It was her money, after all. He said nothing, so I went on:

"If you're concerned that your friends'll think poorly of you for serving under a tenderfoot . . ." At this he turned the blue eyes on me, and kept them there. Deuced uncomfortable. Still he was silent, but presently looked about, as though considering, and then says after a while:

"Gotta study, I reckon. Care to likker with me?"

I accepted, and he led the way to where a couple of mules were tethered, watching me sidelong as I mounted. Well, I'd forgotten more about backing a beast than he'd ever know, so I was all right there; we cantered down the street, and out through the tents and wagons towards Westport, and presently came to a big lodge with "Last Chance" painted in gold leaf on its signboard, which was doing a roaring trade. Richey got a jug, and we rode off towards some trees, and all the time he was deep in thought, occasionally glancing at me but not saying a word. I didn't mind; it was a warm day, I was enjoying the ride, and there was plenty to see—over by the wood some hunters were popping their rifles at an invisible target; when we got closer I saw they were "driving the nail", which is shooting from fifty paces or so at a broad-headed nail stuck in a tree, the aim being to drive it full into the wood, which with a ball the size of a small pea is fancy shooting anywhere.

Richey gave a grunt when he saw them, and we rode near to where a group of them were standing near the nail-tree, whooping and cat-calling at every shot. Richey dismounted.

"Kindly cyare to set a whiles?" says he, and indicated a tree-stump with all the grace of a Versailles courtier; he even put the jug down beside it. So I sat, and waited, and took a pull at the jug, which was first-run rum, and no mistake, while Richey went over and talked to the hunters—fellows in moccasins and fringed tunics, for the most part, burned brown and bearded all over. It was only when some of them turned to look at me, and chortled in their barbarous "plug-a-plew" dialect which is barely recognisable as English, that I realised the brute was absolutely *consulting* them—about *me*, if you please! Well, by God, I wasn't having that, and I was on the point of storming off when the group came over, all a-grin—and by George, didn't they

71

stink, just! I was on my feet, ready to leave—and then I stopped, thunderstruck. For the first of them, a tall grizzled mountaineer, in a waterproof hat and leggings, was wearing an undoubted *Life Guards tunic,* threadbare but well-kept. I blinked: yes, it was Tin Belly gear, no error.

"Hooraw, hoss, howyar!" cries this apparition.

"Where the devil did you get that coat?" says I.

"You're English," says he, grinning. "Waal, I tell ye—this yar garmint wuz give me by one o' your folks. Scotch feller—sure 'nuff baronite, which is kind of a lord, don't ye know? Name o' Stooart. Say, wasn't he the prime coon, though? He could ha' druv thet nail thar with his eyes shut." He considered me, scratching his chin, and I found myself wishing my buckskin coat wasn't so infernally new. "Richey hyar sez he's onsartin if you'll make a wagon-captain."

"Is he, by God? Well, you can tell Richey—"

"Mister," says he, "you know this?" And he held up a short stick of what looked like twisted leather.

"Certainly. It's cured beef—biltong. Now what—"

"Don't mind me, hoss," says he, and winked like a ten-year-old as he stepped closer. "We're a-humourin' ole Richey thar. Now then—how long a hobble you put on a pony?"

I almost told him to go to the devil, but he winked again, and I'll say it for him, he was a hard man to refuse. Besides, what was I to do? If I'd turned my back on that group of bearded grinning mountebanks they'd have split their sides laughing.

"That depends on the pony," says I. "And the grazing, and how far you've ridden, and where you are, and how much sense you've got. Two feet, perhaps . . . three."

He cackled with laughter and slapped his thigh, and the buckskin men haw-hawed and looked at Richey, who was standing head down, listening. My interrogator said:

"Hyar's a catechism, sure 'nuff," and he was so pleased with himself, and so plainly intent on making game of Richey that I decided to enter into the spirit of the thing. "Next question, please," says I, and he clapped his hands.

"Now, let's calkerlate. Haw, hyar's a good 'un! Hyar's a

72

night camp; I'm a gyuard. What you spose I'm a-doin'?" He looked at a bush about twenty yards away, walked a few paces aside, and looked at it again, then came back to me. "Actin' pee-koolyar, hoss—you reckon?"

"No such thing. You're taking a sight on that bush. You'll take a sight on all the bushes. After dark, if a bush isn't where it should be, you'll fire on it. Because it'll be an Indian, won't it?" We'd done the same thing in Afghanistan; any fool of a soldier knows the dodge.

"Wah!" shouts he, delighted, and thumped Richey on the back. "Thar, boyee! This chile hyar'll tickle ye, see iffn he doan't. Now, whut?"

Richey was watching me in silence, very thoughtful. Presently he nodded, slowly, while the buckskin men nudged each other and my questioner beamed his satisfaction. Then Richey tapped my pistol butt, and pulling a scrap of cloth from his pocket, drifted over to the tree and began to snag it on the half-driven nail. My tall companion chuckled and shook his head; well, I saw what was wanted, and I thought to blazes with it. I'd taken as much examination from these clowns as I wanted, so I decided to put Master Richey in his place.

The tall chap had a knife in his waistband, and without by your leave I plucked it out. It was a Green River, which is the best knife in the world, and just the article to practise the trick that Ilderim Khan had taught me, with infinite patience, on the Kabul Road almost ten years before. As Richey adjusted his target, I threw the knife overhand; my eye was well out, for I was nowhere near the mark, but I damned near took his ear off. He looked at the blade quivering in the trunk beside his face, while the tall buffoon cackled with laughter, and the buckskin men doubled up and haw-hawed—if I'd put it through the back of his head, I daresay that would have been a *real* joke.

Richey pulled the knife free, while his pals rolled about, and drifted over to me. He looked at me for a moment with those steady blue eyes, glanced at the tall chap,[6] and then said in that gentle husky voice:

"I'm Uncle Dick. An extra hunnerd, ye said—cap'n?"

The men hoorawed and shouted, "Good ole Virginny! How's yer ha'r, Dick?" I nodded and said I would see him at sunrise, sharp, bade them a courteous good-day and rode back to Independence without more ado—I know when to play the man of few words myself, you see. But I didn't delude myself that I had proved my fitness to be a wagon-captain, or any rot of that sort; all I had shown, through the eccentric good office of our friend in the Tin-Belly coat, was that I wasn't a know-nothing, and Wootton could take service under me without losing face. They were an odd lot, those frontiersmen, simple and shrewd enough, and as easy—and as difficult—to impose upon as children are. But I was glad Wootton would be our guide; being a true-bred rascal and coward myself, I know a good man when I see one—and he was the best.[7]

* * *

We started west three days later, but I am not going to take up your time with wordy descriptions of the journey, which you can get from Parkman or Gregg if you want them—or from volume II of my own great work, *Dawns and Departures of a Soldier's Life,* although it ain't worth the price, in my opinion, and all the good scandal about D'Israeli and Lady Cardigan is in the third volume, anyway.

But what I shall try to do, looking back in a way that Parkman and the others didn't, is to try to tell you what it meant to "go West" in the earlies[8]—and that was something none of us understood at the time, or the chances are we'd never have gone. You look at a map of America nowadays, and there she is, civilised (give or take the population) from sea to sea; you can board a train in New York City and get off in Frisco without ever stepping outside, let alone get your feet wet; you can even do what I've done—look out from your Pullman on the Atchison Topeka as you cross Walnut Creek, and see the very ruts your wagon made fifty years before, and pass through great cities that were bald-head prairie the first time you went by, and vast wheatfields where you remember the buffalo herds two miles from wing to wing. Why, I had coffee on a verandah in a little town in Colorado just last year—fine place, church with a steeple, schoolhouse, grain warehouse, and even a motor car at the front gate. First time I saw that place it consisted of a burning wagon. Its population was a scalped family.

Now, you must look at the map of America. See the Mississippi River, and just left of it, Kansas City? West of that, in '49, there was—nothing. And it was an *unknown* nothing, that's the point. You can say *now* that ahead of the Forty-Niners stretched more than two thousand miles of empty prairie and forest and mountain and great rivers—but we didn't know that, in so many words. Oh, everyone knew that the Rockies were a thousand miles off, and the general lie of the country—but take a look at what is now North Texas and Oklahoma. In '49, it was believed that there was a vast range of mountains there, blocking the way west, when it fact the whole stretch is as flat as your hat. Somewhere around the same region, it was believed, was "the great American Desert"—which didn't exist. Oh, there's desert, plenty of it, farther west; nobody knew much about that either.

I say it was unknown; certainly, the mountain men and hunters had walked over plenty of it; that crazy bastard Fremont was exploring away in a great frenzy and getting thoroughly lost by all accounts. But when you consider, that in '49 it was less that 60 years since some crazy Scotch trapper[9] had crossed North America *for the first time*—well, you will understand that its geography was not entirely familiar, west of the Miss'.

Look at the map again—and remember that beyond Westport there was no such thing as a road. There were two trails, to all intents, and they were just wagon-tracks—the Santa Fe and the Oregon. You didn't think of roads then; you thought of rivers, and passes. Arkansas, Cimarron, Del Norte, Platte, Picketwire, Colorado, Canadian—those were the magic river names; Glorieta, Raton, South Pass—those were the passes. There were no settlements worth a dam, even—Santa Fe was a *town*, sure enough, if you ever got there, and after that you had nothing until San Diego and

Frisco and the rest of the cities of the west coast. But in between, the best you could hope for were a few scattered forts and trading posts: Bent's, Taos, Laramie, Bridger, St Vrain, and a few more. Hell's bells, I rode across Denver when the damned place wasn't even there.

No, it was the unknown then, to us at least; millions of square miles of emptiness which would have been hard enough to cross even if it had truly been empty, what with dust-storms, drought, floods, fire, mountains, snow-drifts that could be seventy feet deep, cyclones, and the like. But it wasn't empty, of course; there were several thousand well-established inhabitants—named Cheyenne, Kiowa, Ute, Sioux, Navajo, Pawnee, Shoshoni, Blackfeet, Cumanche . . . and Apache. Especially, Apache. But even they were hardly even names to us, and the belief—I give you only my own impression—in the East was that their nuisance had been greatly exaggerated.

So you see, we started in fairly blissful ignorance, but before we do, take one last look at the map before Professor Flashy endeth the lesson. See the Arkansas river and the Rockies? Until the 1840s, they had been virtually the western and south-western limits of the U.S.A.; then came the war with Mexico, and the Yankees won the whole shooting-match that they own today. So when we jumped off for California, we were heading into country three-quarters of which had been Mexican until a few months before, and still was in everything but name.[10] Some of it was called Indian Territory, and that was no lie, either.

That was what lay ahead of us, gullible asses that we were, and if you think it was tough you should have seen the Comber caravan loading up in the meadow at Westport. I've squared away, and ridden herd upon, most kind of convoys in my time, but shipping a brothel was a new one on me. Visiting 'em *in situ,* you don't realise how elaborately furnished they are; when I saw the pile of gear that had come ashore off the steamboat, I didn't credit it; a stevedore would have taken to drink.

For one thing, the sluts all had their dressing-tables and mirrors and wardrobes, stuffed with silks and satins and gowns and underclothes and hats and stockings and shoes and garters and ribbons and jewellery and cosmetics and wigs and masks and gloves and God knows what beside— there were several enormous chests which Susie called "equipment", and which, if they'd burst open in public, would have led to the intervention of the police. Gauzy trousers and silk whips were the least of it; there was even a red plush swing and an "electrical mattress", so help me.

"Susie," says I, "I ain't old enough to take responsibility for this cargo. Dear God, Caligula wouldn't know what to do with it! You've had some damned odd customers in Orleans, haven't you?"

"We won't be able to buy it in Sacramento," says she.

"You couldn't buy it in Babylon!" says I. "See here; two of the wagons must be given over to food—we need enough flour, tea, dried fruit, beans, corn, sugar, and all the rest of it to feed forty folk for three months—at this rate we'll finish up eating lace drawers and frilly corsets!" She told me not to be indelicate, and it would all have to go aboard; she wasn't running an establishment that wasn't altogether tip-top. So in went the fancy bed-linen and tasselled curtains and carpets and chairs and chaise-longues and hip-baths, and the piano with candlesticks and a case of music—oh, yes, and four chandeliers and crystal lampshades and incense and bath salts and perfumes and snuff and cigars and forty cases of burgundy (I told the demented bitch it wouldn't travel) and oil paintings of an indecent nature in gilt frames and sealed boxes of cheese and rahat lakoum and soap and pomade, and to crown all, a box of opium— with Cleonie's parrot in its cage to top everything off. In the end we had to hire two extra wagons.

"It's worth it," says Susie to my protests. "It's all investment, darlin', an' we'll reap the benefit, you'll see."

"Provided the goldfields are manned entirely by decadent Frog poets, we'll make a bloody fortune," says I. "Thank God we shan't have to go through Customs."

The whores were another anxiety, for while Susie had them thoroughly chastened, and kept them dressed like charity girls, they wouldn't have fooled an infant. They were all coloured, and stunners, and they didn't walk, or even sit, like nuns, exactly. You just had to look at the stately black Aphrodite, regarding herself in a hand-mirror while the pert creamy Claudia dressed her hair, or Josephine perched languidly on a box, contemplating her shapely little feet with satisfaction, or Medea and Cleonie sauntering among the wildflowers with their parasols, or the voluptuous Eugenie reclining in a wagon, sultry-eyed and toying with her fan—no, you could tell they weren't choir-girls. I took one look at the score of drivers and guards that Owens had hired for us, and concluded that we'd have been a sight safer carrying gold bullion.

They were decent men enough, as hard cases go, half of them bearded buckskineers, a few in faded Army blues, and all well-mounted and armed to the teeth with revolving pistols and rifles. Their top spark was a rangy, well-knit Ulsterman with sandy whiskers and a soft-spoken honey-comb voice; his name, he informed me, was Grattan Nugent-Hare, "with the hyphen, sir—which is a bit of a pose, don't ye know, but I'm attached to it." There was a dark patch on his sleeve where chevrons had been; when he dismounted, it was like a seal sliding off a rock. Gentleman-ranker, thinks I, bog-Irish gentry, village school, seen inside Dublin Castle, no doubt, but no rhino for a commission. A very easy, likely lad, with a lazy smile and a long nose.

"You were with Kearny," says I. "And before that?"

"Tenth Hussars," says he, and I couldn't help exclaiming: "Chainy Tenth!" at which he opened his sleepy eyes a little wider. I could have bitten my fool tongue out.

"Why, so it was. And you're a naval gentleman, they tell me, Mr Comber—your pardon . . . captain, I should say." He nodded amiably. "Well, well—d'ye know, I'd ha' put you down for cavalry yourself, by the set of the whiskers? I'd ha' been adrift there, though, right enough."

It gave me a turn; this was a sharp one. The last thing I wanted just then was an old British Army acquaintance—but I'd never known the Tenth except by name, which was a relief.

"And how far west did you go with Kearny?" I asked.

"Gila River, thereabout . . . that was after Santa Fe, d'ye see? So it's not new country to me, altogether. But I apprehend you're all the way for California—with the ladies." And he glanced past me to where Susie was chivvying the tarts out of sight into the wagons. He grinned. "My stars, but they're as bonny as fluffy little doe rabbits on the green, so they are."

"And that's the way they'll stay, Mr Nugent-Hare—"

"Call me Grattan," says he, and grinned as he patted his pony's muzzle. "I'm up the road ahead of you, Mr Comber. You were about to say, I think, that after a few weeks those boys of mine might feel the fever, and those charming little maids—if ye'll forgive the term—would prove a temptation? Not at all, at all. They'll be as safe as if they were in St Ursula's." He tilted his hat back, not smiling now. "Believe me, if I didn't know how to manage rascals like these—I wouldn't be here, would I now?"

He was a cocksure one, this—but probably, I reflected, not without cause; the Army had left its stamp on him, all right. I reminded him that military discipline was one thing, and these were civilians, out on the plains.

He laughed pleasantly. "Military discipline be damned," says he. "It's simple as shelling peas. If one of 'em so much as tips his tile to your young ladies, I'll blow the bastard's head off. And now, sir . . . the order of march . . . what would ye say to a point rider, a rearguard, two to a flank, and myself riding loose? If that would be agreeable . . . And you'll be riding herd yourself? Quite so . . . "

If his nose hadn't been quite so long, and his smile so open, it would have been a pleasure to do business with him. Still, he knew his work, and he was being well paid; captain or no captain, it struck me I might spend most of the trip lounging in the carriage after all.

However, when the great moment of starting came I was in the saddle, in full buckskin fig, for one has to show willing. With Wootton silent alongside, I led the way down the meadow and into the trees, and after us trundled the carriage, with Susie fanning herself like Cleopatra, and her nigger maid and cook perched behind, and then the eight big schooners, flanked by Nugent-Hare's riders; their canvas covers were rolled up like furled sails in the spring sunshine, with the tarts sitting primly two by two; in the rear came the mules, with a couple of Mexican *savaneros,* the three-hundred-pound loads piled incredibly high and swaying perilously. It was a well-rutted trail, and the schooners rolled now and then, which caused some flutter and squeak among the girls, but I noticed that the guards—who might have taken the opportunity to render gallant assistance—barely glanced in their direction; perhaps Grattan was as strong a straw-boss as he made out, after all.

Once through the timber, we came out on the prairie itself, all bright with with the early summer flowers, and I galloped ahead to a little hillock for a look-see. That's a moment I remember still: behind lay the woods with the smoke haze rising from Westport; left and right, and as far ahead as the eye could see, was limitless rolling plain, dotted with clumps of oaks and bushes, the grass blowing gently in the breeze, and fleecy clouds against a blue sky that seemed to stretch forever. Below, the wagons crawled along the trail, its furrows running clear and straight to the far horizon, where you could just see the last wagon of the caravan ahead. And I absolutely laughed aloud—why, I can't tell, except that in that moment I felt free and contented and full of hope, with my spirits bubbling as high as they've ever done in my life. Others, I know, have felt the same thing about starting on the trail west; there's an exhilaration, a sense of leaving the old, ugly world behind, and that there's something splendid waiting for you to go and find it, far out yonder. I wonder if I'd feel it now, or if it happens only when you're young, and have no thought for the ill things that may lie along the way.

For it's an illusion, you know—the start of the trail. Those first ten days lull you to sleep, as you roll gently down over that changeless plain, through the well-used camp-places to Council Grove, which is the great assembly point where little caravans like ours form themselves into regular wagon-trains for the long haul to the mountains—there! I'm

80

writing in the present tense, as though it were all in front of me again. Well, it ain't, thank God.

But it soon becomes dull; the only notable thing happened about the third day, when we came to a little stream and copse where there was a fairish assembly of wagons, and the trail divided—our fork continuing south-west, while the northern trail branched up towards the Kanzas River, and then to the North Platte, and eventually to Oregon. As we were breaking camp, with several other California-bound parties, the Oregon folk were already setting out, and there was great badinage and cheering and singing as they got under way.

They were a serious lot, those Oregoners, being mostly farm folk intent on honest work—not like us California scamps off to the gold-fields. We were a raffish crew, but they were sober men and grim women, with never a tin pan or a rope out of place, everything lashed down hard and the kids peeping solemnly over the tailboards. They had an American flag on their lead wagon, and their captain was a bearded Nemesis in a tail coat, his harsh voice echoing down the mule-lines: "One train, are ye set? Two train, are ye set?" and every *arriero* sang out in turn, "All set! All set!", which was the signal to go, for you don't loaf about with a laden mule, and you don't stop for a noon halt, either, or the brute will never start off again. So now it was "All set!" and the whips cracked and the skinners yelled and the wheels groaned, and the great train rolled away and the mules plodded forward with their bells jingling, and all the California people yelled and waved their hats and hurrawed and fluttered their handkerchieves and cried: "Good luck! Oregon or bust! Take care, and God bless you!" and the like, and the Oregon folk waved back and began to sing a song that I've forgotten now, except that it went to the tune of "Greensleeves" and was all about how the Lord would have a land of milk and honey flowing for His children, over there—and the women from the California wagons began to cry, and some of them hurried after the Oregoners, with their aprons kilted up, offering 'em last gifts of pies and cakes, and the children went scampering along after the wagons, whooping and cheering, except for the little ones, who stood with their fingers in their mouths staring at an old minister who sat astride a mule beside the trail and blessed the Oregon people, with his Bible held above his head. And the caravan wound over the ridge and out of sight, and there was a sudden stillness in the camp-site under the trees, and then someone said, well, better git started ourselves; come on, mother . . .

And they cheered up, for they were a jolly, carefree lot that went to California that year, with their wagons piled any old how with all sorts of rubbish that they thought might prove useful at the diggings, like patent tents and mackintosh boats ("Gold-seekers, take heed! Our rubber boats and shelters are unsurpassed!! You cannot face the chill of the gold rivers without a rubber suit!!!") and water-purifiers and amazingly-fangled machinery for washing gold dust. And they didn't sing any hymns about milk and honey and Canaan, either; no, sir, it was a very different anthem, plunked out on a banjo by a young chap in a striped vest, with his girl dancing impromptu on a packing-case, and everyone thumping the tailboards—I daresay you know the tune well enough, although it was new then, but I'll be bound you don't know the words the Forty-Niners sang:

> I'll scrape the mountains clean, my boys,
> I'll drain the rivers dry,
> A pocketful of rocks bring home,
> Susannah, don't you cry!
> Oh, Californey!
> That's the land for me,
> I'm off to Sacramento
> With my wash-bowl on my knee!
> (*omnes, fortissimo*)
> Oh, Susannah, don't you cry for me,
> I'm off to Sacramento
> With my wash-bowl on my knee!

It was a raucous, ranting thing, but when I hear it now in imagination it's just a ghostly drift down the wind, fading into a whisper. But it was hearty enough then, and we sang it all the way down to Council Grove.

I promised not to do a Gregg or Parkman, but I ought to tell you something of how we travelled.[11] When we camped at night, we set guards; Wootton insisted, but I was all for it anyway, for you must do things right from the start. Susie and I slept in the carriage, which was as comfortable as Owens had promised, and the tarts slept in two of the wagons close at hand. The drivers and guards had a couple of tents, although some preferred to doss down in the open. At breakfast and supper, and at the noon halt, Susie and I were waited on by her nigger servant, the tarts ate in their own wagons, and the guards messed at a discreet distance— oh, we were a proper little democracy, I can tell you. I suggested that we might have Grattan over for supper one night, since he was a bit of a gentleman, or had been, but Susie wouldn't hear of it.

"They're our work-folk," says she, holding a chicken leg with her pinkie cocked, and guzzling down the burgundy (now I saw why we'd brought such an unconscionable lot of it). "If we encourage familiarity, they'll just presume, an' you know where that leads—you finish up 'avin' to call in the militia to put 'em in their place, like New York.[12] Anyway, that Nugent-Thingummy looks a right sly smart-aleck to me; whatever 'e may say about lookin' after my wenches, an' keepin' them randy guards at arm's length, I'm glad I've got Marie an' Stephanie on the cue vee."

"What's this?" says I, for I took a fatherly interest in the welfare of our fair charges.

"Marie an' Stephanie," says Susie, "would rat on their own mothers, an' the other little trollops know it. So there'll be no 'anky-panky—or if there is, I'll soon 'ear of it. An' Gawd 'elp the backslider; she won't be able to sit down between 'ere an' Sacramento, I promise you that."

So two of the tarts were Susie's pet spies, were they? That was useful to know—and lucky I'd found out before I'd done anything indiscreet. I could foresee circumstances where that knowledge might be useful.

One acquaintance that I did cultivate, though, on the quiet trek to Council Grove, was Uncle Dick Wootton. He was a strange case; after our first meeting he'd hardly said a word to me for days, and I wondered was he sulking, but I soon discovered it was just a pensive shyness; he kept very much to himself with new acquaintances, although he could be genial and even garrulous when he got to know you. He was younger that I'd thought, and quite presentable when he'd shaved. However, down to Council Grove he had no proper duties anyway; Grattan and I set the guards, and halts and starts seemed to determine themselves; when anything out of the way happened, like a river-crossing, the teamsters and guards saw to it, and since there were good fords and the weather was dry, all went smoothly enough.

So Wootton had no guiding to do, and he spent the time riding far out to flank, or some way ahead; he had a habit of vanishing for hours at a time, and once or twice I know he slipped out of camp at dusk only to reappear at dawn. He ate all on his own, looking out across the prairie with his back to camp; sometimes he would sit on a hill for hours at a time, looking about him, or wander silent round the wagons, checking a wheel or examining the mule-loads. I would catch his eye on me, occasionally, but he would turn aside and go off again, humming quietly to himself, for another prowl over the prairie.

Then one day just after a noon-halt he trotted up to me and said: "Buffler, cap'n", and I rode out with him a couple of miles to where a small herd of the beasts were grazing—the first I'd ever seen. I was for taking a shot at once, but he bade me hold on.

"Got to pick a tender cow. Bull meat tough enough to build a shack, this time o' summer. Now, see thar; you take a sight a half finger width down from the hump, an' a finger from the nose, or she'll cairry your lead away for ye. Gotta hit hyart or lungs. Now, cap'n; you blaze away."

So I did, and the cow took off like a rocket, and ran quarter of a mile before she suddenly tumbled over, stone dead. "Gone under," says Wootton. "You shoot sweet", and as he skinned the hump very expertly, and removed the choicest meat, he explained to me that a buffalo was damnably hard to kill, unless you hit it in a vital spot; I gathered I had gone up in his estimation.

I thought we would drag the carcase back to the caravan, but he shook his head, and set to roasting hump steaks over a fire. I've never tasted meat like that first buffalo-hump; there's no beef to compare to it, and you can eat it without bread or vegetable, so delicious it is. Wootton also removed the intestines, and to my disgust grilled them gently by pulling them through the embers, whereafter he swallowed them in a great long string, like some huge piece of spaghetti. I watched him in horror—or rather, I didn't watch him, for I couldn't bear the grisly spectacle. Instead, I turned my head aside, and saw something infinitely worse.

Not twenty yards away, on the lip of a little grassy ridge looking down on the hollow where we'd built our fire, three Indians were sitting their ponies, watching us. I hadn't heard them or had the least intimation of their approach; suddenly, there they were—and I realised that the wretched dirty creatures I'd seen at Westport, and scavenging round our train on the way down, were mere cartoon. These were the real thing, and my heart froze. The foremost was naked to the waist, with braided hair hanging to his belt, and what looked like a tail of coonskin round his brows; the face beneath it was a nightmare of hooked nose and rat-trap mouth crossed by stripes of yellow paint. There were painted signs on his naked chest, and his only clothing was a white breech-clout and fringed leggings that came to his knees. He had a rifle across his saddle and carried a long lance tufted with buffalo hair—at least, I hoped it was buffalo hair. The other two were no better; they had feathers in their hair, and their faces were painted half red and white; they carried bows and hatchets, and like their leader they were big, active, vicious-looking sons-of-bitches. But what truly scared me stiff was their sudden apparition, and the silent dreadful menace in the still figures as they watched.

I suppose it took me a couple of seconds to recover—but as my hand went to my pistol Wootton's fingers closed on my wrist.

"Set froze, cap'n," says he softly. "Brulé Sioux. Friendly . . . kind of."

A fine reassurance, but Wootton seemed untroubled—

85

you'll notice that even with his back turned he knew they were there, and *what* they were. Now he turned his head and called out to them, and after a moment they dismounted and came slowly down to us. They looked even wickeder at close quarters, but they squatted down, and the leader raised a hand to Wootton and grunted something that sounded like a mortal insult, but was presumably a greeting. Wootton responded, while I sat stone still and kept my hand close to my pistol-butt, nonchalant-like—which ain't easy with the fiend incarnate hunkered down a yard away, glaring with basilisk eyes out of a mask of paint, and you're uncomfortably aware that he's a muscular six feet of oiled and smelly savagery, with a hatchet like a polished razor on his hip.

He and Wootton grunted some more at each other, and presently Wootton introduced us. "This hyar Spotted Tail," says he. "Big brave." How-de-do, says I, and to my surprise he shook hands, and made a noise between a snarl and a belch which I took for civility. While he and Wootton talked, I studied the other two—if I'd known that the red dots on their feathers signified enemies killed, and the notches stood for cut throats, I'd have been even uneasier than I was. For that matter, Spotted Tail himself had five eagle feathers slanted through his pigtail; each one, I learned later, stood for a scalp taken.[13]

Wootton was plainly asking questions, and the Indian answered with his slow grunts, accompanied by much deliberate gesture—mighty graceful it was, too, and expressive. Even I could tell when he was talking of buffalo, just by the rippling motion of his hand, so like a bison herd seen from far off; a gesture which I noticed he repeated more than once was a quick cutting motion with his right fingers across his left wrist, which I later learned meant "Cheyenne", whose nickname is "Cut Arms".[14] Then Wootton invited them to join him in his awful mess of buffalo guts, and much to the amusement of the other two, he and Spotted Tail had a nauseating contest in which each took an end of an immensely long intestine and gobbled away to see who could down the most of it. The Indian won—I spare you a close description, observing only that they swallowed whole, without chewing, and Spotted Tail, by suddenly jerking his head back, *regained* a fair amount that Wootton had already eaten![15]

There being no dessert, I gave each of the three a cigar, at Wootton's prompting. They ate them, and presently went off, taking the remains of our buffalo carcase without a by-your-leave; I've never been happier to get rid of dinner guests, and said so.

"I seen thar sign last night, an' figgered they'd show today. Huntin' party—fust time I ever see Brulés east o' the Neosho," says Wootton. "In course, they dog the buffler— but since they say tharselves that thar's heap big herds all along th'Arkansas, my guess is thar takin' a lick at the Pawnees. That a powerful lather o' vermillion thar wearin', fer hunters—an' I read sign o' fifty ponies last evenin'. Yup. I rackon thar be a few Pawnees talkin' to th'old gennelman 'fore long."

Which meant the Pawnees would be dead and in hell. But were the Sioux liable to attack us? Wootton considered this long enough to give me the shudders.

"Cain't say, prezackly. Spotted Tail has a straight tongue; then agin, Sioux kin be mean varmints—'thout I wuz here, they'd ha' had yore hoss an' traps for sho', mebbe yore ha'r, too. But I guess tha'r peaceable 'nuff. Uh-huh. Mebbe."

Now, this had me in a rare sweat. I don't suppose until that day I'd given Indians a thought, not seriously—it had been such a pleasant jaunt so far, and everyone in Westport had been so jolly and confident, and we still weren't more than a few days away from civilisation, with its steamboats and stores and soldiers. And then, suddenly, those three painted devils had been there—and they were the *peaceable* ones, Wootton reckoned—and there were a thousand miles of wilderness between us and Santa Fe, crawling with tribes of the dangerous bastards who might be anything but peaceable. Stories and rumours and tall tales—you can take those with a pinch of salt, and remind yourself that your caravan is well-armed and guarded. And then you *see* the living peril, in its hideous paint and feathers, and your dozen rifles and revolvers and eight frail wagons seem like a cork bobbing out on a raging ocean.

So I put it to him straight—what were our chances of winning as far as Santa Fe without serious . . . interference? Not that it could make a dam' bit of difference to me now—I was launched, and I daren't have headed back to be hunted in the Mississippi valley. He scratched his head, and asked me if I had my map.

"Look thar," says he. "Clar across to th'Arkansas we kin rest pretty easy—Spotted Tail sez thar plenty Cheyenne an' 'Rapaho lodges at Great Bend, an' thar not hostile, fer sartin. But he talk of Navajo, Cumanche, Kiowa war-parties in the Cimarron country to th' west—sez thar be 'Pashes up as fur as th' Canadian, an Utes on the Picketwire. Even talk o' Bent an' St Vrain leavin' the Big Lodge. I b'leeve *thet* when I see it. But it's all onsartin; we cain't tell hyar."

Jesus, thinks I, so much for our picnic on the Plains. But he cheered me up by remarking that Spotted Tail might be lying, it being well known that no Indian told the truth unless he couldn't avoid it;[16] also, we would be part of a much larger caravan from Council Grove onwards, and too powerful for any but a very large and reckless war party.

"We see when we git ter the sojers' new place, at Fort Mann. Then we tek a sniff at the wind, an' decide whether we go across the Cimarron Road ter Sand Crik an' th' Canadian, or cairry on west fer Bent's and down th' Ratone." He raised the blue eyes and suddenly smiled. "Made the trip ter Santy Fee more times'n he recollects, this chile has. An' ev'y time he got thar—an' cum back. If he cain't make it agin this time, cap'n, he kin slide!"[17]

5

There were three caravans waiting when we reached Council Grove, which proved to be simply a wood with a few shacks and a stable for the new stagecoach line. One of the caravans was a twenty-wagon affair of young fellows, Eastern clerks and labourers, calling themselves the Pittsburgh Pirates; another was a train of some thirty mules and half a dozen emigrant families, also bound for the diggings; the third—and you may not believe this, but it's gospel true—consisted of two ancient travelling carriages and a dozen middle-aged and elderly valetudinarians from Cincinnati who were making a trip across the Plains *for their health*. They had weak chests, and the pure air of the prairies would do them good, they said, clinging to their hot water bottles and mufflers and throat sprays as they said it.[18] Well, thinks I, captaining a brothel on wheels may be eccentric, but this beats all.

Wootton thought that among us we made a pretty fair train—not as many guns as he would have liked, for the young fellows had set off in the crazy, thoughtless spirit that so many seemed to be possessed by in '49, and had only about a score of weapons among them, and the emigrant families, although well-armed and with four guards, were few in numbers. The invalids had one fat drunkard of a driver with a flintlock musket; if attacked, they presumably intended to beat off the enemy by hurling steam kettles and medicine bottles at them. Our own caravan had more firepower and discipline and general good order than all the rest put together, so they hailed us as they might salvation—and elected me captain of the whole frightful mess. My own fault for being so damned dashing in my buckskin shirt and whiskers, no doubt; look the part, and you'll be cast in it. I demurred, modestly, but there was no competition, and one of the Pittsburgh Pirates settled the thing by haranguing his fellows from a tailboard, crying that weren't they in luck, just, for here was Captain Comber, by cracky, who'd commanded a battleship in Her Majesty's English Navy, and fought the Ayrabs in India, and was just the man whose unrivalled experience and cool judgment would get everyone safe to California, wasn't that so? So I was elected by acclamation—none of your undignified running for office[19]—and I read them a stern lecture about trail discipline and obeying orders and digging latrines and keeping up and all the rest of it, and they shook their heads because they could see I was just the man for the job.

Susie, of course, was well-pleased; it was fitting, she said. Wootton knew perfectly well that he was going to see the caravan through, anyway, and Grattan and our crew were all for it, since it meant we could take the van, and wouldn't have to eat the others' dust. So that was how we headed into the blue, Flashy's caravan of whores and optimists and bronchial patients and frontiersmen and plain honest-to-goodness fortune-seekers—I don't say we were a typical wagon-train of '49, but I shouldn't be surprised.

Now, I promised to skip the tedious bits, so I'll say only of the prairie trek in general that it takes more weeks than I can remember, is damnably dull, and falls into two distinct parts in my memory—the first bit, when you haven't reached the Arkansas River, and just trudge on, fifteen miles a day or thereabouts, over a sea of grass and bushes and prairie weeds, and the second bit, when you *have* reached the Arkansas, and trudge on exactly as before, the only difference being that now you have one of the ugliest rivers in the world on your left flank, broad and muddy and sluggish. Mind you, it's a welcome sight, in a dry summer, and you're thankful to stay close by it; thirst and hunger have probably killed more emigrants than any other cause.

There's little to enliven the journey, though. River-crossings are said to be the worst part, but with the water low in the creeks we had little trouble; apart from that we sighted occasional Indian bands, and a few of them approached us in search of whatever they could mooch; there were a couple of scares when they tried to run off our beasts, but Grattan's fellows shot a couple of them—Pawnees, according to Wootton—and I began to feel that perhaps my earlier fears were groundless. Once the mail-coach passed us, bound for Santa Fe, and a troop of dragoons came by from Fort Mann, which was being built at that time; for the rest, the most interesting thing was the litter of gear from trains that had passed ahead of us—it was like all the left-luggage offices in the world strewn out for hundreds of miles. Broken wagons, traces, wheels, bones of dead beasts, household gear and empty bottles were the least of it; I also remember a printing-press, a ship's figurehead of a crowned mermaid, a grand piano (that was the one stuck on a mudbank at the Middle Crossings, which Susie played to the delight of the company, who held an impromptu barn-dance on the bank), a kilt, and twelve identical plaster statues of the Venus de Milo. You think I'm making it up?—check the diaries and journals of the folk who crossed the Plains, and you'll see that this isn't the half of it.

But it was always too hot or too wet or too dusty or too cold (especially at nights), and before long I was heartily sick of it. I rode a good deal of the time, but often I would sit in the carriage with Susie, and her chatter drove me to distraction. Not that she moped, or was ill-tempered; in fact, the old trot was too damned bright and breezy for me, and I longed for Sacramento and good-bye, my dear. And in one respect, she didn't travel well; we beat the mattress regularly as far as Council Grove and a bit beyond, but after that her appetite for Adam's Arsenal seemed to jade a trifle; nothing was said, but what she didn't demand she didn't get, and when I took to sleeping outside—for the coach could be damned stuffy—she raised no objection, and that became my general rule. I gave her a gallop every so often, to keep her in trim, but as you will readily believe, my thoughts had long since turned elsewhere—viz., to the splendid selection of fresh black batter that was going to waste in our two lead wagons. Indeed, I'd thought of little else since we left Orleans; the question was how to come at it.

You've learned enough of our travel arrangements to see how difficult it was; indeed, if I had to choose the most inconvenient place I've ever struck for conducting an illicit amour in privacy and comfort, a prairie wagon-train would come second on my list, no question. An elephant howdah during a tiger-hunt is middling tough; centre stage during amateur theatricals would probably strike you as out of court altogether, in Gloucestershire, anyway, but it's astonishing what you can do in a pantomime horse. No, the one that licked me was a lifeboat—after a shipwreck, that is. But a wagon-train ain't easy; however, when you've committed the capital act, as I have, in the middle of a battle with Borneo head-hunters, you learn to have faith in your star, and persevere until you win through.

My first chance came by pure luck, somewhere between Council Grove and the Little Arkansas. We'd made an evening halt and laagered, as usual, and I had wandered out a little piece for a smoke in the dusk, when who should come tripping across the meadow but Aphrodite, humming to herself, as usual—she was the big shiny black one who'd spotted me that day back in New Orleans; I'd thought then that she was one of those to whom business is always a pleasure, and I was right. What she was doing so far from the wagons unchaperoned by one of her sisters in shame, I didn't inquire; you don't look a gift horse in the mouth, or a gift mare, either.

She stopped short at sight of me, and I saw the eyes widen in that fine ebony face; she glanced quickly towards the distant wagons, where the fires were flickering, and then stood head down, shooting me little glances sidelong, scared at first, and then smoky, as she realised that, however terrible Susie might be, it might be no bad thing to satisfy the lovelight in Massa's eye. I nodded to a dry buffalo wallow under some nearby bushes, and without a word she began to undo her bonnet strings, very slow, biting her lip and shaking out her hair. Then she sauntered down into the wallow, and when I came ravening after her, pushed me off, playful-like, murmuring: "Wait, Mistah Beachy; jus' you *wait*, now." So I did, while she slipped off her dress

92

and stood there naked, hands on hips, turning this way and that, and pouting over her shoulder. She was well-named Aphrodite, with those long black, tapering legs and rounded rump and lissom waist, and when she turned to face me, wriggling her torso—well, I've never looked at a pumpkin since without thinking: buffalo wallow. Pretty teeth she had, too, gleaming in that dusky face—and she knew how to use them. I drew her down and we went to work sidestroke-like, while she nibbled and bit at my ears and chin and lips, gasping and shuddering like the expert trollop she was; I remember thinking, as she gave her final practised heave and sob, Susie was right: with another nineteen like this we'll be able to *buy* California after a year or two; maybe I'll stay about for a while.

She was too much the whore for me, though; once was enough, and although she shot me a few soulful-sullen looks in the weeks that followed, I didn't use her again. I'm not just an indiscriminate rake, you see; I like to be interested in a woman in a way that is not merely carnal, to find out new fascinations in her with each encounter, those enchant-ing, mysterious, indefinable qualities, like the shape of her tits. And having studied the other nineteen, as opportunity served, weighing this attraction against that, considering such vital matters as which ones would be liable to run squealing to Susie, and which were probably the randiest, I found my mind and eye returning invariably to the same delectable person. There wasn't one among 'em that wouldn't have turned the head of the most jaded roué— trust Susie for that—but there was only one who could have brought me back for a twentieth helping, and that was Cleonie.

For one thing, she had style, in the way that Montez and Alice Keppel and Ko Dali's daughter and Cassy and Laksh-mibai, and perhaps three others that I could name, had it— it's the thing which, allied with ambition and sense, can give a woman dominion over kings and countries. (Thank God my Elspeth never had the latter qualities; she'd not have married *me*, for one thing. But Elspeth is different, and always will be.)

Also, Cleonie was a lady—and if you think a whore can't be that, you're wrong. She was educated—convent-bred, possibly—and spoke perfect English and better French, her manners were impeccable, and she was as beautiful as only a high-bred octoroon fancy can be, with a figurehead like St Cecilia and a body that would have brought a stone idol howling off its pedestal. Altogether fetching—and intelligent enough to be persuadable, in case she had any doubts about accommodating de massa wid de muffstash on his face. But I would have to go to work subtly and delicately; Spring's pal Agag would have nothing on me.

So I bided my time, and established a habit of occasionally talking, offhand, to various of the tarts, in full view of everyone, so that if I were seen having a few words with Cleonie, no one would think it out of the way. I did it pretty stiff and formal, very much the Master, and even remarked to Susie how this one or that was looking, and how Claudia would be the better of a tonic, or Eugenie was eating too much. She didn't seem to mind; in fact, I gathered she was pleased that I was taking a proprietorial interest in the livestock. Then I waited until one noon halt, when Cleonie went down to the river by herself—she was perhaps the least gregarious of them all, which was all to the good—and loafed along to where she was breaking twigs and tossing them idly into the stream.

When she saw me she straightened up and dropped me a little curtsey, preparing to withdraw. We were screened by the bushes, so I took her by the arm as she went past; she gave a little start, and then turned that lovely nun's face towards me, without fear, or any emotion at all that I could see. I took her gently by the two braids of hair that depended from that oddly attractive centre parting, and kissed her on the lips. She didn't move, so I kept my mouth there and slipped a hand on to her breast, to give her the idea. Then I stepped back, to gauge her reaction; she stood looking at me, one slim hand up to her lips where mine had been, and then turned her head in that languid duchess fashion and said the last thing I'd have expected.

"And Aphrodite?"

I almost jumped out of my skin. I gargled some intelligent inquiry, and she smiled and looked up at me from under her lids.

"Has Master tired of her? She will be disappointed. She—"

"Aphrodite," says I, distraught, "had better shut her big black gob, hadn't she? What's she been saying, the lying slut?"

"Why, that Master took her, and made much of her."

"Christ! Look here—do Marie and Stephanie know?"

"We all know—that is, if Aphrodite is to be believed." She gave me an inquiring look, still with that tiny smile. "I, myself, would have thought she was rather . . . black . . . and heavy, for Master's taste. But some men prefer it, I know." She gave a little shrug. "Others . . ." She left it there, waiting.

I was taken all aback, but one thing was foremost. "What about Stephanie and Marie? I thought—"

"That they were Mistress's sneaks?" She nodded. "They are . . . little tell-tales! And if it had been anyone but Master, they would have told her right away. But they would not readily offend you . . . none of us would," and she lowered her lids; her lips quivered in amusement. "Stephanie is very jealous—even more than the rest of us . . . if that is possible." And she gave me a look that was pure whore; by George, I tingled as if I'd been stung. "But I should not stay here," and she was making past me when I caught her arm again.

"Now look here, Cleonie," says I. "You're a good girl, I see . . . so at the evening halt, you follow me down to the river—carefully, mind—and we'll . . . have a little talk. And you tell the others that . . . that if anyone blabs, it will be the worse for them, d'you hear?" I almost added the threat I'd prepared in case she'd been difficult: that if she didn't play pretty I'd tell Susie she'd made advances to me. But I guessed it wasn't necessary.

"Yes, Master Beauchamp," says she, very demure, and turned her head languidly. "And Aphrodite?"

"The hell with Aphrodite!" says I, and took hold of her, nuzzling. She gave a little laugh and whispered: "She smells

95

so! Does she not?" And then she slipped out of my grasp and was away.

Well, here was capital news, and no mistake. Jealous of Aphrodite, were they? And why not, the dear creatures? Mark you, while I've never been modest about my manly charms, I could see now what it was: they were a sight more concerned to be in my good books than in Susie's—being green wenches, they supposed that I would be calling the tune henceforth, and no doubt they figured it was worth the risk of her displeasure to keep in with me. That was all they knew. In the meantime, Miss Cleonie was obviously more than willing, and they'd never dare to peach . . . on that score, would it be a good notion to scare 'em sick by telling Susie that Aphrodite had tried to seduce me? Susie would flog the arse off her, which would be fine encouragement pour les autres to keep their traps shut. On t'other hand, Aphrodite would certainly tell the truth of it, and Susie just *might* believe her; it would sow a seed for sure. No, best leave it, and make hay with my high-yaller fancy while the sun shone.

And I did. She was a smart girl, and since I was sleeping out most of the time, it was the simplest thing for her to slip over the tailboard in the small hours, creep into my little tent, and roger the middle watch away. We were very discreet—not more than twice a week, which was just as well, for she was an exhausting creature, probably because I was more than a mite infatuated with her. The plague was, it all had be in the dark, and I do like to see the materials when I'm working; she had a skin like velvet, and poonts as firm as footballs with which she would play the most astonishing tricks; it was a deuced shame that we couldn't risk a light.

But her most endearing trait was that while we performed, she would sing—in the softest of whispers, of course, with her mouth to my ear as we surged up and down. This was a new one to me, I'll own: Lola and her hairbrush, Mrs Mandeville and her spurs, Ranavalona swinging uppercuts and right crosses—I'd experienced a variety of bizarre behaviour from females in the throes of passion. (My darling

Elspeth, now, gossipped incessantly.) With Cleonie, it was singing; a lullaby to begin with, perhaps, followed by a waltz, and the "Marche Lorraine", and finishing with the "Marsellaise"—or, if she was feeling mischievous, "Swanee River".[20] Thank God she didn't know any Irish jigs.

She was an excellent conversationalist, by the way, and I learned things (in whispers) which explained a good deal. One was that the whores were by no means in mortal dread of Susie, who had never caned one of 'em in her life, for all her stern talk. (The one who'd been sold down-river had been a habitual thief.) Indeed, they held her in deep respect and affection, and I gathered that being bought for her bordello was a matter of close competition among the Orleans fancies, and about as difficult as getting into the Household Brigade. No, the one they were in terror of, apparently, was—me. "You look so fierce and stern," Cleonie told me, "and talk so . . . so shortly to the other girls. Aphrodite says you used her most brutally. Me, I said, *mais naturellement*, how else would Master use an animal?—with females of refinement, I told her, he is of an exquisite gentleness and tender passion." She sighed contentedly. "Ah, but they are jealous of me, those others—and yet they cannot hear enough about you. What? But of course I tell them! What would you? Scholars talk about books, bankers about money, soldiers about war—what else should our profession talk about?"

Never thought of that; still, even if she was delivering a series of lectures on Flashy et Ars Amatoria to her colleagues, I can say that I had an enchanting affair with Cleonie, grew extremely fond of her, and place her about seventh or eighth in my list of eligible females—which ain't bad, out of several hundreds.

But it wasn't all recreation along the Arkansas that year. I beguiled the long hours of trekking with Wootton, whose lore included a fair fluency in the Sioux language, and the Mexican *savaneros*[21] who had charge of our mules, and naturally spoke Spanish. As I've already said, I'm a good linguist—Burton, who was no slouch himself, said that I could dip a toe in a language and walk away soaked—and since I had some Spanish already, I got pretty fluent. But Siouxan, although it's a lovely, liquid language, is best learned from a native Indian, and Wootton taught me only a little. Thank heaven for the gift of tongues, for a few words can mean the difference between life and death— especially out West.

Of course, things were going far too well to last. Aside from our first alarming meeting with the Brulés, and the night scare with the Pawnees—which I slept through—we'd had nothing worse than broken axles by the time we got to Fort Mann, the new military post which lay in the middle of nowhere on the Arkansas, about half-way to Santa Fe by the shortest route. That was where the trouble started.

For the past week we had become aware of increasing numbers of Indians along our line of march. There had been, as Wootton predicted, villages of Cheyenne and Arapaho near the Great Bend, but they'd mostly been on the southern bank, and we had kept clear of them, although they were reputedly friendly. We would see parties of them on the sky-line, and once we met a whole tribe on the move, heading south across our line of march. We halted to let them go by, a huge disorderly company, the men on horses, the women trudging along, all their gear dragged on the travois poles which churned up the dust in a choking cloud, a herd of mangy ponies behind being urged on by half-naked boys, and cur dogs yapping on the flanks. They were a poor, ugly-looking lot, and their rank stench carried a good half-mile.

There were more camped about Fort Mann, and Wootton went out to talk to them when we laagered. He came back looking grim, and took me aside; it seemed that the party he'd talked to were Cheyenne from a great camp some miles beyond the river; there was a terrible sickness among them, and they had come to the fort for help. But there was no doctor at the fort, and in despair they had asked Wootton, whom they knew, for assistance.

"We can't do anything," says I. "What, doctor a lot of sick Indians? We've nothing but jallup and sulphur, and it'd be poor business wasting it on a pack of savages. Anyway,

God knows what foul infection they've got—it might be plague!"

"'Pears it's a big gripe in thar innards," says he. "No festerin' sores, nuthin' thataway. But thar keelin' over in windrows, the chief say. En he rackons we got med'cine men in our train who cud—"

"Who, in God's name? Not our party of invalids? Christ, they couldn't cure a chillblain—they can't even look after themselves! They've been wheezing and hawking all the way from Council Grove!"

"Cheyenne don't know that—but they see th' gear en implements on the coaches. See them coons doctorin' tharselves wi' them squirt-machines. They want 'em doctor thar people, too."

"Well, tell 'em we can't, dammit! We've got to get on; we can't afford to mess with sick Indians!"

He gave me the full stare of those blue eyes. "Cap'n—we cain't 'fford *not* to. See, hyar's the way on't. Cheyenne 'bout the only *real* friendlies on these yar Plains—'thout them, ifn they die or go 'way, we get bad Injun trouble. That the best side on't. At wust—we give 'em the go-by, they don't fergit. Could be we even hev 'em ki-yickin' roun' our wagons wi' paint on—en thar's three thousand on 'em 'cross the river, en Osage an' 'Rapaho ter boot. That a pow'ful heap o' Injun, cap'n."

"But we can't help them! We're not doctors, man!"

"They kin see us *tryin*'," says he.

There was no arguing with him, and I'd have been a fool to try; he knew Indians and I didn't. But I was adamant against going down to their camp, which would be reeking with their bloody germs—let them bring one of their sick to the far bank of the river, and if it would placate them for one of our invalids to look at him, or put up a prayer, or spray him with carbolic, or dance in circles round him, so be it. But I told him to impress on them that we were not doctors, and could promise no cure.

"They best hyar it f'm you," says he. "You big chief, wagon-captain." And he was in dead earnest, too.

So now you see Big Chief Wagon-Captain, standing before a party of assorted nomads, palavering away with a few halting Sioux phrases, but Wootton translating most of the time, while I nodded, stern but compassionate. And I wasn't acting, either; one look at this collection and I took Wootton's point. They were the first Cheyenne I'd ever seen close to, and if the Brulé Sioux had been alarming, these would have put the fear of God up Wellington. On average, they were the biggest Indians I ever saw, as big as I am—great massive-shouldered brutes with long braided hair and faces like Roman senators, and even in their distress, proud as grandees. We went with them to the river bank, taking the Major commanding the fort in tow, and the most active and intelligent of our invalids—he was a hobbling idiot, but all for it; let him at the suffering heathen, and if it was asthma or bronchitis (which it plainly wasn't) he'd have them skipping like goats in no time. Then we waited, and presently a travois was dragged up on the far bank, and Wootton and I and the invalid, with the Cheyenne guiding the way, crossed the ford and mud-flats, and the invalid took a look at the young Indian who was lying twitching on the travois, feebly clutching at his midriff. Then he raised a scared face to me.

"I don't know," says he. "It looks as though he has food poisoning, but I fear . . . they had an epidemic back East, you know. Perhaps it's . . . cholera."

That was enough for me. I ordered the whole party back to our side of the river and told Wootton that right, reason or none, we weren't meddling any further.

"Tell them it's a sickness we know, but we can't cure it. Tell them it's . . . oh, Christ, tell 'em it's from the Great Spirit or something! Tell them to get every well person away from their camp—that there's nothing they can do. Tell 'em to go south, and to boil their water, and . . . and, I don't know, Uncle Dick. There's nothing we can do for them—except get as far away from them as we can."

He told them, while I racked my brain for a suitable gesture. They heard him in silence, those half-dozen Cheyenne elders, their faces like stone, and then they looked at me, and I did my best to look full of manly sympathy, while

I was thinking, Jesus, don't let it spread to us, for I'd seen it in India, and I knew what it could do. And we had no doctors, and no medicines.

"I told 'em our hearts are on the ground," says Wootton.

"Good for you," says I, and then I faced them and spread my arms wide, palms up, and the only thing I could think of was "For what we are about to receive may the Lord make us truly thankful, for Christ's sake, amen." Well, their tribe was dying, so what the hell was there to say?[22]

It seemed to be the right thing. Their chief, a splendid old file with silver dollars in his braids, and a war-bonnet of feathers trailing to his heels, raised his head to me; he had a chin and nose like the prow of a cruiser, and furrows in his cheeks you could have planted crops in. Two great tears rolled down his cheeks, and then he lifted a hand in salute and turned away in silence, and the others with him. I heaved a great sigh of relief, and Wootton scratched his head and said:

"They satisfied, I rackon. We done the best thing."

We hadn't. Two days later, as we were rolling up to the crossing at Chouteau's Island, four people in the caravan came down with cholera. Two of them were young men in the Pittsburgh Pirates company; a third was a woman among the emigrant families. The fourth was Wootton.

6

I'm well aware that, as the poet says, every man's death diminishes us; I would add only that some diminish us a damned sight more than others, and they're usually the fellows we took for granted, without ever realising how desperately we depended on them. One moment they're about, as merry as grigs, and all's as well as could be, and the next they've rolled over and started drumming their heels. And it hits you like a thunderbolt: this ain't any ordinary misfortune, it's utter catastrophe. That's when you learn the true meaning of grief—not for the dear departed, but for yourself.

Wootton didn't actually depart, thank heaven, but I've never seen a human being so close to the edge. He hovered for three days, by which time he was wasted as a corpse, and as I gazed down at him shivering in his buffalo robe after he'd vomited out his innards for the twentieth time, it seemed he might as well have gone over, for all the use he would be to us. The spark was flickering so low that we didn't dare even move him, and it would plainly be weeks before he could sit a pony, assuming he didn't pop off in the meantime. And we daren't wait; already we had barely enough grub to take us to Bent's, or the big cache on the Cimarron; there wasn't a sign of another caravan coming up behind, and to crown all, the game had vanished from the prairie, as it does, unaccountably, from time to time. We hadn't seen a buffalo since Fort Mann.

But grub wasn't the half of our misfortunes; the stark truth was that without Wootton we were lost souls, and the dread sank into me as I realised it.

Without him, we didn't have a brain; we were lacking something even more vital than rations or ammunition: knowledge. Twice, for example, we might have had Indian mischief but for him; his presence had been enough to make the Brulés let us alone, and his wisdom had placated the Cheyenne when I might have turned 'em hostile. Without Wootton, we couldn't even *talk* properly to Indians, for Grattan's guards and the teamsters, who'd looked so useful back at Westport, were just gun-toters and mule-skinning louts with no more real understanding of the Plains than I had; Grattan himself had made the trip before, but *under* orders, not giving 'em, and with seasoned guides showing the way. Half a dozen times, when grazing had been bad, Wootton had known where to find it; without him, our beasts could perish because we wouldn't know there was good grass just over the next hill. If we hit a two-day dust-storm and lost the trail; if we missed the springs on the south road; if we lost time in torrential rain; if hostiles crossed our path—Wootton could have found the trail again, wouldn't have missed the springs, would have known where there was a cache, or the likelihood of game, would have sniffed the hostiles two days ahead and either avoided them or known how to manage them. There wasn't a man in the caravan, now, who could do any of these things.

He had lucid moments, on the third day, though he was still in shocking pain and entirely feeble. He would hole up where he was, he whispered, but we must push on, and if he got better he would make after us. I told him the other sick would stay with him—for one thing, we daren't risk infection by carrying them with us—and the stricken woman's husband and brothers would take care of them. We would leave a wagon and beasts and sufficient food. I don't know if he understood; he had only one thing in his mind, and croaked it out painfully, his skin waxen and his eyes like piss-holes in the snow.

"Make fer Bent's . . . week, ten days mebbe. Don't . . . take . . . Cimarron road . . . lose trail . . . You make Bent's. St Vrain . . . see you . . . pretty good. 'Member . . . not Cimarron. Poor bull[23] . . . thataways . . ." He closed his eyes for several minutes, and then looked at me again. "You git . . . train . . . through. You . . . wagon-cap'n . . ."

Then he lost consciousness, and began to babble—none of it more nonsensical than the last three words he'd said while fully conscious. Wagon-captain! And it was no consolation at all to look about me at our pathetic rabble of greenhorns and realise that there wasn't another man as fit for the job. So I gave the order to yoke up and break out, and within the hour we were creaking on up the trail, and as I looked back at the great desolation behind us, and the tiny figures beside the sick wagon by the river's edge, I felt such a chill loneliness and helplessness as I've seldom felt in my life.

Now you'll understand that these were not emotions shared by my companions. None of them had seen as much of Wootton as I had, or appreciated how vitally we relied on him; Grattan probably knew how great a loss he was, but to the rest I had always been the wagon-captain, and they trusted me to see them through. That's one of the disadvantages of being big and bluff and full of swagger—folk tend to believe you're as good a man as you look. Mind you, I've been trading on it all my life, with some success, so I can't complain, but there's no denying that it can be an embarrassment sometimes, when you're expected to live up to your appearance.

So there was nothing for it now but to play the commander to the hilt, and it was all the easier because most of them were in a great sweat to get on—the farther they could leave the cholera behind them, the better they'd like it. And it was simple enough so long as all went well; I had taken a good inventory of our supplies during the three days of waiting to see whether Wootton would live or die, and reckoned that by going to three-quarter rations we should make Bent's Fort with a little to spare. By the map it couldn't be much over 120 miles, and we couldn't go adrift so long as we kept to the river . . . provided nothing unforeseen happened—such as the grazing disappearing, or a serious change in the weather, or further cases of cholera, or distemper among the animals. Or Indians.

For two days it went smooth as silk—indeed, we made better than the usual dozen to fifteen miles a day, partly because it never rained and the going was easy, partly because I pushed them on for all I was worth. I was never out of the saddle, from one end of the train to the other, badgering them to keep up, seeing to the welfare of the beasts, bullyragging the guards to keep their positions on the flanks—and all the time with my guts churning as I watched the skyline, dreading the sight of mounted figures, or the tiny dust-cloud far across the plain that would herald approaching enemies. Even at night I was on the prowl, in nervous terror as I stalked round the wagons—and keeping mighty close to them, you may be sure—before returning to my tent to rattle my fears away with Cleonie. She earned her corn, no error—for there's nothing like it for distracting the attention from other cares, you know; I even had a romp with Susie, for my comfort more than hers.

Aye, it went too well, for the rest of the train never noticed the difference of Wootton's absence, and since it had been an easy passage from Council Grove, they never understood what a parlous state we would be in if anything untoward arose now. The only thing they had to grumble at was the shorter commons, and when we came to the Upper Crossing on the third day, the damfools were so drugged with their false sense of security that they made my reduction in rations an excuse for changing course. As though having to make do with an ounce or two less of corn and meat each day mattered a curse against the safety of the entire expedition. Yet that is what happened; on the fourth morning I was confronted by a deputation of the Pittsburgh Pirates. Their spokesman was a brash young card in a cutaway coat with his thumbs hooked in his galluses.

"See here, captain," says he, "it's near a hundred miles to Bent's Fort—why, that's another week with empty bellies! Now, we know that if we cross the river on the Cimarron road, there's the big cache that Mr Wootton spoke of—and it's less than thirty miles away. Well, me and the boys are for heading for it; it'll mean only two more days of going short, and then we can replenish with all the grub we want! And everyone knows it's the short way to Santa Fe—what d'you say, captain?"

"I say we're going to Bent's."

"Why so? What's the point in five days o' discomfort?"

"You ain't in discomfort," says I. "And your bellies aren't empty—but they would be if we went the Cimarron road. We're going to Bent's as agreed; for one thing, it's safer."

"Who says that, now?" cries this barrack-room lawyer, and his mates muttered and swore; other folk began to cluster round, and I saw I must scotch this matter on the spot.

"I say it, and I'll tell you why. If we were fool enough to leave the river, we could be astray in no time. It's desert over yonder, and if you lose the trail you'll die miserably—"

"Ain't no reason ter lose the trail," cries a voice, and to my fury I saw it was one of Grattan's guards, a buckskinned brute called Skate. "I bin thataways on the cut-off; trail's as plain as yer hand." At which the Pittsburgh oafs hurrahed and clamoured at me.

"We're going to Bent's!" I barked, and they gave back. "Now, mark this—suppose the trail was as good as this fellow says—which I doubt—does anyone know where Wootton's cache is? No, and you'd never find it; they don't make 'em with finger-posts, you know. And if you did, you'd discover it contained precious little but jerked meat and beans—well, if that's your notion of all the grub you want, it ain't mine. At Bent's you'll find every luxury you can imagine, as good as St Louis." They still looked surly, so I capped the argument. "There's also more likelihood of encountering hostile tribes along the Cimarron. That's why Wootton insisted we make for Bent's—so you can yoke up and prepare to break out."

"Not so fast, there!" says the cutaway coat. "We got a word to say to that, if you please—"

I turned my back. "Mr Nugent-Hare, you can saddle up," I was saying, when Skate pushed forward.

"This ain't good enough fer me!" cries he. "You don't know a dam' thing more'n we do, mister. Fact, yore jest a tenderfoot, when all's said—"

"What's this, Mr Nugent-Hare?" cries I. "Have you no control of your rascals?"

"Easy, now, captain," says he, pulling his long Irish nose. "You'll mind I said we weren't in the army."

"I say we take a vote!" bawls Skate, and I noted that most of the guards were at back of him. "We all got a say hyar, jest as much as any high-an'-mighty lime-juice sailor—oh, beg pardon, *Captain* Comber!" And the scoundrel leered and swept off his cap in an elaborate bow; the Pittsburgh clowns held on to each other, guffawing. "En I kin tell yuh," continued Skate, "thet Dick Wootton wuz jest as consarned 'bout Ute war-parties up on the Picketwire, as 'bout any other Injuns by Cimarron. Well, Picketwire's nigh on Bent's, ain't it? So I'm fer the cut-off, en I say let's see a show o' hands!"

Of course the Pirates yelled acclaim, sticking both hands up, and Skate glared round at his mates until most of them followed suit. Grattan turned aside, whistling softly between his teeth; the fathers of the emigrant families were looking troubled, and our invalids were looking scared. I know I was red in the face with rage, but I was holding it in while I considered quickly what to do—I was long past the age when I thought I could bluster my way out of a position like this. In the background I saw Susie looking towards me; behind her the sluts were already seated in the wagons. I shook my head imperceptibly at Susie; the last thing I wanted was her railing at the mutineers.

The Pittsburgh Pirates made up about half our population, so a bare majority was voting for Cimarron. This wasn't enough for Skate.

"Come on, you farmers!" roars he. "You gonna let milord hyar tell you whut you kin en cain't do? Let's see yer hands up!"

A number of them complied, and the cutaway coat darted about, counting, and turned beaming on me. "I reckon we got a democratic majority, captain! Hooraw, boys! Ho for Cimarron!" And they all cheered like anything, and as it died down they looked at me.

"By all means," says I, very cool. "Good day to you." And I turned away to tighten the girths on my pony. They stared in silence. Then:

"What you mean?" cries Skate. "We got a majority! Caravan goes to Cimarron, then!"

"It's going to Bent's," says I, quietly. "At least, the part of it that I command does. Any deserters—" I tugged at a strap "—can go to Cimarron, or to hell, as they please."

I was counting on my composure to swing them round, you see; they were used to me as wagon-captain, and I reckoned if I played cool and business-like it would sway them. And indeed, a great babble broke out at once; Skate looked as though he was ready to do murder, but even some of the Pirates looked doubtful and fell to wrangling among themselves. And I believe all would have been well if Susie, who was fairly bursting with fury, hadn't cut loose at them, abusing Skate in Aldgate language, and even turning on the sober emigrants, insisting that they obey me.

"You're bound on oath!" she shrilled. "Why, I'll have the law on you—you treacherous scallawags, you! You'll do as you're bidden, so there!"

I could have kicked her fat satin backside; it was the worst line she could have taken. The leader of the emigrant families, who'd been muttering about how the wagon-captain was the boss, wasn't he, went dark crimson at Susie's railing, and drew himself up. He was a fine, respectable-looking elder and his beard fairly bristled at her.

"Ain't no hoor-mistress gonna order me aroun'!" says he, and stalked off; most of the emigrants reluctantly followed him, and the Pittsburgh boys hoorawed anew, and began to make for their wagons. So you see the wagon-captain with his bluff called—and not a thing to be done about it.

One thing I knew, I was not crossing the river. I could see Wootton's face now. "Not Cimarron . . . poor bull." The thought of that desert, and losing the trail, was enough for me. It was all very well for Skate and his pals: if they got lost, they could in desperation ride back to the Arkansas for water, and struggle down to Fort Mann—but the folk in the wagons would be done for. And our own little party was in an appalling fix; we had our eight wagons and the carriage, with their drivers, but we faced a week's trip to Bent's without guards. If we met marauding Indians . . . we would have my guns and those of the teamsters and *savaneros*.

But I was wrong—we also had the invalids. They approached me with some hesitation and said they would prefer to continue to Bent's; the air on the north bank of the river was purer, they were sure of that—and they didn't approve of Skate and those Pittsburgh rapscallions, no, indeed. "We, sir, have some notions of loyalty and good behaviour, I hope," says the one whose diagnosis of the Cheyenne had proved so accurate. His pals cried bravo and hear, hear! and flourished their sprays and steam-kettles in approval; dear God, thinks I, whores and invalids; at least they were both well-disciplined.

"I'd better see to the rations, or friend Skate'll be leaving us the scrapings of the barrel," says Nugent-Hare.

"You're not going with them?" says I, astonished.

"Why would I do that?" says he. "I hired for the trip to California, and I keep my engagements." D'ye know, even then, when I should have been grateful at the thought of another good pair of hands, I didn't believe a word of it. "Besides," says he, with a gallant inclination to Susie, who was now standing alarmed and woebegone, "Grattan's never the boy to desert a lady in time of trouble, so he's not." And he sauntered off, humming, while my fond spouse assailed me with lamentations and self-reproaches—for she was sharp enough to see that her folly had tipped the balance. If I'd had less on my mind I'd probably have given vent to my feelings, full tilt; as it was I just told her, pretty short, to get into the coach and make sure Skate's bullies didn't try to run off any of our crinoline herd.

There was a pretty debate going on round our supply-wagons; Skate was claiming that he and his mates were entitled to food since they had been part of our caravan; Grattan was taking the line that when they stopped working for us, they stopped eating, and if they tried to pilfer he'd drop the first man in his tracks. He pushed back his coat and hooked a thumb in his belt beside his Colt as he said it; Skate bawled and gnashed a bit, but gave way, and I judged the time right to remind the emigrants that if any wished to change their mind, they'd be welcome. None did, and I believe it was simply that they clung to the larger party, and to the firepower of Skate's fellows.

They were just starting to struggle over the crossing when our depleted party rolled off up the Arkansas, and I scouted to a ridge to see what lay ahead. As usual, it was just rolling plain as far as you could see, with the muddy line of the Arkansas and its fringe of cottonwoods and willows; nothing moved out on that vastness, not even a bird; I sat with my heart sinking as our little train passed me and pitched and rolled slowly down the slope; Susie's carriage with its skinner, and the servants perched behind; the four wagons whose oxen had been exchanged for mules, and the other four with the cattle teams, all with their drivers. The covers were up on the trulls' wagons, and there they were in their bonnets against the early sun, sitting demurely side by side. The Cincinnati Health Improvement Society came last in their two carriages, with their paraphernalia on top; you could hear them comparing symptoms at a quarter of a mile.

We made four days up the river without seeing a living thing, and I couldn't believe our luck; then it rained, such blinding sheets of water as you've never seen, sending cataracts across the trail and turning it into a hideous, glue-like mud from which one wagon had to be dragged free by the teams of four others. We took to what higher ground there was, and pushed on through a day that was as dark as late evening, with great blue forks of lightning flickering round the sky and thunder booming incessantly overhead. It died away at nightfall, and we made camp in a little hollow near the water's edge and dried out. After the raging of the storm everything fell deathly still; we even talked in undertones, and you could feel a great oppression weighing down on you, as though the air itself was heavy. It was dank and drear, without wind, a silence so absolute that you could almost listen to it.

Grattan and I were having a last smoke by the fire, our spirits in our boots, when he came suddenly to his feet and stood, head cocked, while I whinnied in alarm and demanded to know what the devil he was doing. For answer he upended the cooking pot on to the fire with a great hiss and sputter of sparks and steam, and then he was running from wagon to wagon calling softly; "Lights out! Lights out!" while I gave birth and glared about me. Here he was back, dropping a hand on my shoulder, and stifling my inquiries with: "Quiet! Listen!"

I did, and there wasn't a damned thing except my own belly rumbling. I strained my ears . . . and then I heard it, so soft that it was hardly a noise at all, more a vibration on the night air. My flesh prickled at the thought of horsemen— no, it might be buffalo on the move . . . too regular for that . . . and then my mouth went dry as I realised what it must be. Somewhere, out in that enveloping blackness, there was a soft, steady sound of drums.

"Jesus!" I breathed.

"I doubt it," whispered Grattan. "Say Lucifer, and ye'll be nearer the mark."

He jerked his head, and before I knew what I was properly doing I was following him up the slope to the west of our hollow; there was a little thicket of bushes, and we crawled under it and wormed our way forward until we could part the grass on the crest and see ahead. It was black as the earl of hell's weskit, but there, miles ahead in the distance, were five or six flaring points of light—Indian camp-fires, without a doubt, along the river bank. Which meant, when you thought about it, that they lay slap on our line of march.

We watched for several minutes in silence, and then I said, in a hoarse croak: "Maybe they'll be friendlies." Grattan said nothing, which was in itself an adequate answer.

You may guess how much we slept that night. Grattan and I were on the watch as dawn broke, when their fires had disappeared with the light and instead we could see columns of smoke, perhaps five miles away, along the river; it looked like a mighty camp to me, but at such a distance you couldn't tell.

There was no question of our stirring, of course. We must just lie up and hope they would move, and sure enough, about noon we realised that the dark strip which had been the camp was shifting—down-river, in our direction. Grattan cursed beneath his breath, but there was nothing for it but to lie there and watch the long column snaking inexorably towards us past the cottonwood groves. It wasn't more than a mile away, and I was all but soiling myself in fear, when the head of the column veered away from the river, and I recollected with a surge of hope that our hollow lay in a wide bow of the river; if they held their march along the bowstring, they might pass us by, damnably close, but unless one of them scouted the bank they would never realise we were there.

We scurried down and had the teamsters stand by their beasts, enjoining utter silence; my chief anxiety was the invalids, who were such a feckless lot that they might easily blunder about and make a noise, so I ordered them into their carriages with instructions to sit still. Then Grattan and I wormed back to the crest, and took a look.

That was a horrible sight, I can tell you. The head of the column wasn't above three hundred yards away, moving slowly past our hiding-place. There was a great murmur rising from it, but not much dust after the rain, and we had a clear view. There were warriors riding in front, some with braided hair and coloured blankets round their shoulders, others with the lower part of their skulls shaved and top-knots that bristled up, whether of hair or feathers I couldn't tell. Then came what was either a chief or a medicine man, almost naked, on a horse caparisoned in coloured cloth to the ground; he carried a great staff like a shepherd's crook, ribboned and feathered, and behind walked two men carrying little tom-toms that they beat in a throbbing rhythm. Then more warriors, with feathers in their hair, some in blankets, others bare except for breech-clouts or leggings; all were garishly painted—red, black and white as I recall. Almost all were mounted on mustangs, but behind came the usual disorderly mess of travois and draught animals and walking families and cattle and dogs and general Indian foulness and confusion. Then the rearguard, after what seemed an interminable wait; more mounted warriors, with bows and lances, and as they drew level with us I found myself starting to breathe again: we were going to escape.

Whether that thought travelled through the air, I don't know, but suddenly one of the riders wheeled away from the others and put his pony to the gentle slope running up to our position. He came at a trot, straight for us, and we watched, frozen. Then Grattan's hand came out from under his body, and I saw he had his Bowie turned in his fist; I clapped a hand over it, and he turned to stare at me: his eyes were wild, and I though, by gum, Flashy, you ain't the only nervous one on the Plains this day. I shook my head; if the savage saw us, we must try to talk our way out—not that there'd be much hope of that, from what we'd seen.

The Indian came breasting up the hill, checked, and looked back the way they had come, towards the camp-ground, and I realised he was taking a last look-see. He wasn't twenty yards away, close enough to make out every hideous detail of the buffalo-horn headdress, embroidered breech clout, beaded garters wound round his legs above the moccasins, the oiled and muscular limbs. He had a lance, a little round shield on his arm, and a war-club hung from his belt. He sat at gaze a full minute, and then rode slowly along just beneath our hide, with never an upward glance; he paused, leaning down to clear a tangle of weed from his foot—and in the hollow behind us some fool dropped a vessel with a resounding clatter.

The Indian's head lifted, the painted face staring directly at our bush; he straightened in his seat, head turning from side to side like a questing dog's. He looked after his party, then back towards us. Go away, you awful red bastard, go away, I was screaming inwardly, it's only a kettle or a piss-pot dropped by those infernal hypochondriacs; Christ, it's a wonder you can't hear the buggers wheezing . . . and then he trotted down the hill after the retreating column.

We waited until the last of them were well out on the plain and vanishing into the haze before we even stirred— and then I made the terrifying discovery that while Grattan and I had been lying too scared to breathe, and Susie had been sitting tight-lipped in her coach with her eyes shut,

three of the sluts—Cleonie, black Aphrodite, and another—
had crawled up to a point on the crest to watch the passing
show! Giggling and sizing up the bucks, I don't doubt; how
they hadn't been spotted . . .

We moved out in some haste. You ain't seen galloping
oxen? Within the hour we had passed through the appalling
filth and litter of the deserted Indian camp, and it seemed
reasonable to hope that a band of such size would be the
only one in the vicinity. I asked Grattan who they were; he
thought, from the bright-coloured blankets and the
buffalo-scalp cap, that they might be Cumanches, but wasn't
sure—I may tell you now, from a fairish experience of Indians, that they're a sight harder to identify by appearance
than, say, Zulu regiments or civilised soldiers; they ain't
consistent in their dress or ornament. I remember Charley
Reynolds, who was as good a scout as ever lived, telling me
how he'd marked down a band as Arapaho by an arrow
they'd fired at him—he found out later they'd been Oglala
Sioux, and the arrow had been pinched from a Crow. That
by the way; Grattan didn't cheer me up much by remarking
that the Cumanche are cannibals.

We pushed on, and towards evening I smelled smoke. We
went to ground at once, and camped without fires, and in
the morning moved ahead cautiously until we caught the
scent of charred wood. Sure enough, there it was, a little
way off the trail—the blackened shell of a wagon, with little
drifts of smoke still coming from it. There were three white
corpses sprawled among the wreck, two men and a woman;
all had been shot with arrows, scalped, and foully mutilated.
Grattan went round the wagon, and cursed; I went to look
and wished I hadn't. On the other side were two more
bodies, a man's and a young girl's, though it wasn't easy to
tell; they had been spreadeagled and fires lit on top of them.
If that Indian in the buffalo cap had ridden a few yards
farther, we would have been served the same way.

We buried them in a cold sweat, and pressed on quickly;
oddly enough, though, the knowledge of our escape raised
our spirits, and it was with cries and hurrahs that afternoon
that we passed the mouth of the Picketwire,[24] which joins

the Arkansas about fifteen miles below Bent's. One or two of the *savaneros* were uneasy that there was still no sign of civilised life so close to the fort; there were normally bands of trappers and traders to be seen, and friendly Indians camped on the Picketwire, they said. But Grattan pointed out that with so large a band of hostiles on the prowl, the normal traffic wasn't to be expected; they'd be staying snug behind the wall at Bent's.

We were all eager to see this famous citadel of the plains, and in camp that night Grattan entertained Susie with a recital of its wonders; to hear him it was like finding Piccadilly in the middle of the Sahara.

"You'll be wonderstruck, ma'am," laughs he. "You haven't seen a building worth the name since we left Westport, have you? Well, tomorrow, after a thousand miles of desolation, you'll see a veritable castle on the prairie, with towers and ramparts—oh, and shops, too! It's a fact, and all as busy as Stephen's Green. This time tomorrow you'll be watching the captain here playing skittle pool in the billiard room, with a wee man in a white coat skipping in with refreshment, and you'll sleep on a down mattress after a hot bath and the best dinner west of St Louis, so you will."

We were off at dawn of a brisk, bright day with the breeze fluttering the cottonwoods as we rolled along by the river at our best pace. We nooned without incident; just an hour or two, thinks I, and we'll be through this horror and can lie up until other trains appear, and then head for Santa Fe in safety, with some other idiot riding wagon-boss. We were all in spirits; Susie was laughing and listening to Grattan as he rode by the carriage, the tarts had their wagon-covers up and were chattering like magpies in the sunshine, and even the invalids had perked up and were telling each other that this was more bracing than Maine, by George; I caught Cleonie's demure glance as I rode by her wagon, and reflected that Bent's must be big enough to find a more comfortable private nook than a prairie tent. And then I saw the smoke.

It was a single puff, above the gentle crest to our right, floating up into the clear sky, and while I was still gaping in consternation, there they were—four mounted Indians on the skyline, trotting down the slope towards us. Grattan swore softly and shaded his eyes, and then swung to the coach driver.

"Keep going—brisk, but not too fast! Easy, now, captain—that smoke means there'll be others coming lickety-split; you'll note we're only worth a single puff, bad cess to 'em!'[25] So we must keep 'em at a distance till we get within cry of Bent's; it can't be above a couple of miles now!"

My instinct was to turn and ride for it, but he was right. The four Indians were coming on at a brisk canter now, so with Grattan leading we rode out to head them away, me with my sweat flowing freely—the sight of those oily copper forms, the painted faces, the feathers, and the practised ease with which they managed ponies and lances, would have turned your stomach. They rode along easily, edging only gradually closer.

"They won't show fight till the regiment arrives," says Grattan. "Watch in case they try to side-slip us and scare the wagon-beasts—ah, you bastard, that's the trick! See, captain!"

Sure enough, they had their blankets ready in their hands; their leader, riding parallel with us about twenty yards off, raised his and shouted "Tread!", which I took to mean "trade"—a likely story.

"Give 'em a hail," says Grattan, so I shouted "Bugger off!" and made gestures of dismissal. The brave shouted something back, in apparent disappointment, turned his pony slightly aside—and then without warning wheeled sharply and, with his mates following suit as smart as guardsmen, made a dart across our rear towards the wagon-train.

"Donnybrook!" yells Grattan, and I heard his Colt bang at my elbow. An Indian twisted and fell shrieking, and as the leader's horse sped past me I gave it a barrel in the neck—in a mêlée you shoot at what you're sure to hit—and then my heels went in and my head down as I thundered for the wagons.

The two remaining braves were making for the rear wagon, swooping in, flapping their blankets at the beasts. I

116

roared to the teamsters to whip up; they shouted and swung their snakes, and the wagons lurched and bounced in the ruts as the beasts surged forward. Grattan fired and missed one of the Indians; a teamster, reins in his teeth, let fly a shot that went nowhere, and then the two had wheeled past us and were racing out and away.

I galloped up the train, all eyes to see where the next danger was coming from. By God, I didn't have to look far—on the crest to our right there was a round score of the brutes, swerving down towards us. They were perhaps two furlongs off, for the crest had swung away from the river, which was inclining in a big loop to the left, so that as the wagons veered to follow its course, they were also turning away from our pursuers. But in less than three minutes they would close the gap with the lumbering train.

Ahead of me, Grattan was swinging himself from his saddle over the tailboard of a wagon, and farther ahead the *savaneros* of the mule-train were doing likewise, their mules running free. In among them came the two braves with blankets, screeching and trying to drive the leaderless brutes in among the wagons; Grattan's rifle boomed and one of the braves went down; the other tried to throw himself at one of the wagon-teams, but must have missed his hold, for as I galloped by he was losing an argument with a wagon-wheel, and being deuced noisy about it.

The *savaneros* were firing now; Grattan yelled to me, pointing forward, and I was in solid agreement, for up yonder somewhere was Bent's, and I didn't mind a bit if I was first past the post. Half a dozen revolving rifles were letting go as I thundered up the train, which is just the kind of broadside you need when twenty painted devils are closing in; they weren't more than two hundred paces off our rear flank now, whooping like be-damned and firing as they came. I was abreast the leading wagon, with only the two invalid carriages and Susie's coach leaping along ahead; at my elbow the sluts were squealing and cowering behind the wagon-side; I saw a shaft quivering in the timber, and another hissed over my head; it's time to get off this pony and under cover, thinks I—and in that moment the brute stum-

117

bled, and I had only a split second to kick my feet clear and roll before she went headlong.

It's odd, what sticks in your mind. There was a grey-bearded face peering from the window of the nearest carriage, absolutely adjusting its spectacles—then earth and sky whirled crazily as I hit the ground with a bone-shaking crash. I hadn't time to wonder if aught was broken; I grabbed at a trailing rope as a wagon-wheel whirled by close to my face, and managed to get the bight round my elbow; it was almost dislocated as I was hauled half-upright, clawing for a hold. Female voices screamed as I was dragged staggering along, hands clutched at my arms and collar, and I was pulled bodily against the tailboard with my legs going like pistons in mid-air.

If I've a soft spot for harlots, d'you wonder? Somehow they kept me aloft long enough to get an arm round a stanchion and a leg over the tailboard. I gathered my strength to heave, and the whole pack of them screamed in unison and fell back in a panic of crinoline as an Indian leaped from nowhere, hatchet in hand, and clung to the tailboard not a yard away.

I may forget that painted, feathered face and screaming mouth one of these days, but I doubt it. I was hanging helpless, the prairie flying along two yards below, as he swung up the hatchet—and then there were squeals of rage, and black Aphrodite was thrashing at him with a parasol, God bless her. He clung like a leech with one hand, stubbornly determined to disembowel me with the other, but the clever, beautiful, resourceful pearl of African womanhood abandoned edge for point, and gave him the ferrule in the groin; he shrieked and tumbled off under the hooves of the team behind, and I hauled myself inboard and looked about to see what fresh horror was offering itself.

It was a battle royal. The Indians were strung out along the train, firing bows and pieces, and the *savaneros* were giving 'em volley for volley. But some of the bolder spirits, like the chap who'd experienced Aphrodite's caress, were riding in among the wagons, sliding down the offside of their ponies for protection, trying to get close enough to scupper our teams. I saw men and ponies go down; an arrow zipped into the furled canvas overhead, and when I emerged from the trollops for another peep, there was a wicked little red bastard in a war-bonnet alongside the lead mule of the wagon behind, driving his lance into its flank. The poor brute screamed and went down, bringing the others with him in a kicking tangle, the wagon lurched crazily, hung for a sickening moment, and then crashed down, scattering cases of claret all over the trail. Then our own wagon bucked like fury, and I was thrown headlong and fetched up against the sideboard with all the breath driven out of me.

I scrambled up, and if it isn't one damned thing it's another. There was an Indian on our driver's seat now, disputing the reins with the teamster; the reins fell free as they grappled, and it was a stone certainty that we'd be over in two seconds if steps were not taken. I never join in unless I must, but now there was nothing for it but to fight my way through a press of hysterical whores, of whom there now seemed to be about fifty, rolling underfoot, striking out blindly, or swooning in my path. I lurched over the front-board and got a fist into the Indian's braids and hauled; the teamster slashed at him with a Bowie, and as he dropped away, howling, I grabbed the reins and flung my weight on to steady the team. The teamster took hold—and I looked ahead and almost lost my balance in sheer astonishment.

We were on open plain, with the three carriages flying along before us, and beyond them was one of the most beautiful and unbelievable sights I ever beheld. It *was* a castle, just as Grattan had said, with two great round towers, massive walls of what looked like brown stone, and a beetling gateway—with the Stars and Stripes fluttering in the breeze. I yelled with joy and amazement as we lumbered down towards it, and then became aware that the shots and yells were dying away behind; I looked back, and there were five wagons spread out across the plain—which meant that two were goners—and in their wake the Indians were slackening in their pursuit, waving their weapons and whooping. I could see some of them clustered round the wrecked wagon, no doubt preparing to sample the claret as soon as the chief had swilled the first glassful round his palate.

Susie's carriage was making for the open gateway, and as the invalids' vehicles slowed my teamster reined in almost to a walk. I jumped down, watching the remaining wagons trundling in; one had smoke rising from its smouldering canvas; another was rolling drunkenly with a displaced axle, but at least they were safe, and Grattan and two of the *savaneros* were on foot, rifles at the ready, acting as a rearguard.

The carriages were inside, and as the first wagon followed with its wailing occupants—all but Aphrodite, who was thrashing the tailboard with the remains of her gamp, in a fine berserk fury still—I hurried through the gates. I had a fleeting impression of a great courtyard surrounded by two storeys of buildings, and then I was up a flight of steps to the parapet above the main gate. Just beneath me the last four wagons were crowded in about the gateway; Grattan, his rifle cradled, gave me a wave. Beyond lay the empty plain for quarter of a mile to the bend of the river, where about a dozen Indians were milling to and fro, but making no move towards the fort; behind them I could see the wrecked wagon beside the cottonwoods fringing the river— and then I sank down, in nervous exhaustion, by the wall; my shoulder was skinned and throbbing from my tumble; there was caked blood on the back of my hand; God knew whose it was.

Feet were running up the steps, and Grattan appeared, his faced grimed and grinning. "Will ye have nuts or a cigar, sir?" says he, and I hauled myself up. Beneath us I could hear the great gates being hauled to, and the *savaneros*' and teamsters' voices raised in oaths of relief; down in the court-yard the wagons were any old how, and the beasts were braying and roaring, with the wails of the sluts added to the din; the invalids were climbing out, shaken and bewildered; I saw Susie with her face pale and her hair awry. Then Grattan says: "Jesus Christ!", and I saw he was staring round in wonder; I stared too—at the crowded courtyard and our dazed following, at the huddle of wagons and

120

beasts, at the silent buildings, the great round towers, the broad upper walks and parapets, at Old Glory over our heads. And I realised why Grattan, that soft-spoken man, had blasphemed.

There wasn't a soul in Bent's Fort but ourselves.

7

I know now, of course, why it was so—that William Bent was crazy, and had abandoned his wonderful fortress to fate and the death-watch beetle, or whatever bugs they have out there—but at the time it was a mystery beyond belief. Here we were, winded and terrified after a chase by those infernal savages, home by the skin of our teeth—and the place that should have been swarming with people was empty, but with its flag flying and not a chair out of place. For while the teamsters and *savaneros* mounted guard and saw to the beasts, and the rest occupied the ground-floor rooms and prepared food and tended our two or three injured, Grattan and I went over the whole place from attic to cellar. And there wasn't so much as a mouse.

It was an incredible citadel, though, deserted as it was.

I suppose it would be about a hundred paces square, but I can't be sure from memory, with adobe walls twenty feet high and stout enough to resist a battering-ram. There were two huge towers, like martellos, at opposite corners; against the north wall were two storeys of buildings, with fine cool rooms, and opposite them, across the square, a shaded arcade of shops and trade-rooms; inside the gate-wall were chambers for guards and servants, with stoves and fireplaces, and on the west end were a cooper's and joiner's shops, a forge, and storehouses. The roofs of all these buildings formed broad walks running inside the upper ramparts; on this level, at the west end, there was even a little house with a porch, for the commandant, and a billiard-room, dammit—which Gratton had sworn to, and I hadn't believed—with the pills still lying on the baize. I was so astounded that I picked up a cue and slapped the red away—

and not ten minutes earlier I'd been hanging upside down from a wagon tail trying to avoid being tomahawked!

"I don't *believe* this bloody place," says I, while Grattan replaced the balls and blazed away (he made nothing of it). "Where the dooce have they gone?" For that was the eerie thing—the only thing absent was the people themselves. Wherever we went all was in order: a dining-room, with oak furniture and a linen cloth on the table, presses bursting with china and glass, a wine-cooler with bottles of '42 Burgundy, captain's biscuits in a barrel, a piece of cheese kicking up a hell of a row in the sideboard, and a portrait of Andrew Jackson on the wall.

It was the same in the shops—the blacksmith's tools were there, and the carpenter's gear; the trade-rooms were stuffed with pelts, buffalo robes, blankets, axes, nails, candles, God knows what—as I live, there was even sealing-wax and writing paper. The store-rooms had provisions for an army, and hogsheads of wine and spirits; in the sleeping-quarters some of the beds were made, there was a posy of withered flowers in a vase on the commandant's desk, and a neatly-torn newspaper in the privy.

"Whoever it was," says Grattan, "cleared out in a hell of a hurry."

"But why haven't the Indians looted the place?"

"They don't *know*," says he. "Chances are that Bent—or St Vrain, or whoever was here—left within the last couple of days . . . don't ask me why. The Injuns can't know that; I daresay the crowd that chased us are the only ones hereabouts, and new arrivals at that. If they'd known it was deserted, they'd never have left off chasing us."

That was reasonable, but provoked a disquieting thought. "D'you suppose . . . they'll come back? The Indians, I mean."

"Depends," says he. "There weren't above thirty of the dear fellows, and we sank nigh on a dozen of those. Maybe more'll come in, maybe not. One thing's certain; with our drivers and *savaneros* we muster about fifteen rifles—and it would take fifty to make this place good against an attack.

So we'd best hope that our red friends don't receive any reinforcements."

That had me flying up the ramparts again, to make sure the guards were on the look-out. The Indians were still in view, over by the cottonwoods, but no new members so far as I could see. There was a moon due that night, so they couldn't surprise us after dark. I took stock; at least we were inside, and the chances were that a caravan, or a party of traders, would heave in sight before enough Indians arrived to make the place too hot to hold. An unfortunate choice of expression, that, as you'll come to appreciate.

In the meantime, we were in residence, and once I'd heard Susie's exclamations of pleasure at the amenities, and the enthusiasm of the trollops as they settled themselves into quarters, and started washing their clothes and chattering in the well-stocked kitchen where our black cook had pans on the boil, I began to feel better. We didn't make use of the big corral outside the walls, but stabled the beasts in a wagon park off the main square; the teamsters had their own fires going in no time, and were breaking out supplies from the store-rooms; there was laughter and singing, and the great empty place echoed with our noise; the invalids took the air on the walls, and one four-eyed idiot even proposed an evening stroll down to the river; I dissuaded him by pointing out that the locals might be taking their hatchets for a walk at the same time. D'you know, he hadn't thought of that; I suppose he imagined that the brutes who'd pursued us had been just rather persistent native hawkers trying to interest us in beads and pottery.

We had the best hot meal we'd eaten in months, in the dining-room, with a pair of the tarts to wait on us, and some tolerable port and a decent cigar afterwards. I took my turn at guard that night with only middling apprehension; there wasn't a sign of Indians, the moonlit prairie was empty as far as one could see, and I was well used to the plaintive howl of the white wolves by now. I turned in shortly before dawn feeling not half bad; it was snug and jolly to see Susie snoring away in the dim candle-light, with one fine tit peeping out among the frills; I nibbled away until she squirmed into wakefulness, whereafter we set to partners, celebrating the first civilised bed we'd occupied since the Planter's Hotel, if you like. It was comforting afterwards to sip punch and glance round the high white-washed walls in the knowledge that they were about six feet thick, with sharp eyes aloft, and the Indians could prowl about outside to their hearts' content.

That's what they were doing, too, next morning, and there must have been a trip in from somewhere during the night, for I counted above sixty of the scoundrels circling their ponies just out of range, whooping and working up a head of steam. I had every spare man up to the east rampart above the gate; with the revolving rifles and six-shooters as well as our high walls we should be safe enough, unless they assembled in greater numbers than were visible now. So I remarked to Grattan, and he went off to the armoury in one of the corner towers to see what was available.

Just then there was a shout; the Indians had decided to warm us up a little. They charged in, well spread out like good light cavalry, letting fly a few shots and arrows, but plainly bent on testing our fire. I detailed three men only, and we downed one of their ponies; the dismounted brave capered and jeered and showed us his arse, and the rest drew off to reconsider. There was a chief in a war-bonnet who seemed to be haranguing them; presently he lifted his lance and howled, and the whole crowd came in like banshees, stirrup to stirrup, straight for the gate.

"Hold your fire!" bawls I. "Wait for the word!" And I was just about to give it when the cunning bastards wheeled right and left, making for the corners of the fort. We let fly just the same, and I dispatched three-quarters of our force around the other ramparts; even spread thin, we could put up enough fire to keep them at a distance, and a merry, useless little fight ensued, the Indians darting in and out, our fellows blazing away from cover and knocking one or two over, while the chief circled with a group of followers, for all the world like a general with his staff, looking to spot the best place for a concerted rush. I was taking my time with a Colt rifle, trying long pots at him and damning the

125

sights, when Grattan was at my elbow again. Just at that moment a fire-arrow came whistling over and stuck smouldering in the parapet behind us; a teamster stamped it out, but it gave point to what Grattan had to say.

"Are ye ready for bad news?" says he, and for all he tried to keep the jaunty note in his voice, there was a wild glint in his eye. "Because I'm the one that's got it, bigod! That armoury in the nor'-west tower, there—aye, well, some clever feller has laid a powder-train to the magazine, and there's enough loose powder lying about to give an artilleryman the trots—with a burned-out slow fuse in the middle of it! Not only that, in the opposite tower there's eighty kegs of the stuff, and *another* train to *them*! Which means," says he, and the sweat on his face wasn't from heat or exertion, "that whoever abandoned this fort intended to blow it sky-high, and would ha' done, but for that faulty fuse!" By this time, you will understand, I had left off shooting and was giving the man my most earnest attention, palsied with fright.

"You follow me, captain?" says he. "We're sitting in the middle of a powder-keg, and one spark'll blow the whole place to kingdom come!"

Now you may not be aware, gentle reader, in these civilised days of manufactured cartridges and cased shells, precisely what a powder-train was. Skilful sappers used to make them by piercing large cartridges with a bodkin, and carrying the cartridge rapidly away so that the powder trickled out in a stream no thicker than a pencil lead, which they ran to the charge to be detonated—in the case of Bent's Fort, I gathered, several tons of high explosive, with a similar confection in the opposite tower, just for luck. At the start of the powder-train you placed a slow-burning fuse, to enable you to get over the skyline before November the Fifth. Such a train is hard to see, even by daylight, since it is just a thin line of dust, and Grattan and I had barely glanced into the towers, and hadn't been looking for trains or loose powder, anyway. But there they were, waiting for a spark—and hostile Indians had just started shooting fire-arrows at us.

I said: "What do you advise?" or words to that effect,

126

and he didn't know, so we had a brief discussion, the fruit of which was one of the rottenest ideas I've ever heard. My own first thought was to get over the wall, but with the Upper Arkansas Hairdressers' Association on hand that wouldn't answer, and when Grattan proposed that the sluts should set to work carefully to sweep up the powder-trains, I was fool enough to agree. He must have been as panic-fevered as I was, for he had six of them lined up at the north-west tower before the suicidal folly of it came home to me. Loose powder is as vicious an article as the plague germ; the friction of a foot can set it off, and the thought of those handless harlots scraping among it brought me down from the parapet like a stung ferret.

"It won't do!" I bawled. "Water! From the well! Can you douse the trains?"

"If I could, there's still the magazine, and another pile of kegs yonder big enough to blow us to Mexico!" says Grattan. "We'll never soak them all," and at that moment another fire-arrow came winging into the square and stuck blazing in Susie's coach. Cleonie screamed, and the girls beat it out with cloths; I absolutely tore my hair in fear and consternation.

"Get the invalids!" I shouted. "Buckets of water! Post the doddering buggers about the place with as many buckets as you can find—the girls can make a chain from the well! We'll need 'em on the parapets, too—hurry, for Christ's sake! And make sure the tower doors are fast, and soaked in water!"

It was the only thing to be done; the invalids and girls must douse every burning missile the moment it struck; the mines were in stout-walled buildings, and short of a general fire they'd be harmless enough. Once we had beaten off our feathered friends we could set to work cautiously to remove the trains and kegs—in the meantime, it was back to the wall and try to sicken our attackers.

They were still full of sin and impudence, though, and had mounted a determined rush against the west wall from the corral, but the *savaneros* had made cool practice, and there were half a dozen painted corpses under the wall to prove it. Our fellows had discovered that the best field of fire was from the towers, which projected sufficiently to enfilade two walls at once. We had thinned our attackers out a little, anyway, and no others had appeared; all told there were perhaps fifty, mostly on the north side, where there were no battlements but only upper bedrooms with flat unparapeted roofs. So far I don't believe we'd taken even a flesh-wound on our side.

Suddenly they charged, again, and the 11th Hussars couldn't have done it better. They came singly and in little packs, all along the north and east sides, converging at the last minute at the north-east angle, where there were windows in the upper floor and our range was the greatest. We blazed down the wall for dear life, some of the *savaneros* exposing themselves recklessly, for if just one of the bastards got inside we might well be done for; we hadn't the men to go hunting through the fort. They surged under the wall, scrambling up on their ponies' backs and leaping for the sill; we were firing into the brown and doing fearful execution, but a Colt revolving rifle takes time to reload, and if they hadn't desisted when they did, I believe they might have got a man in. They rode off, howling, leaving dead and dying under the wall, and then screams of alarm from the court-yard brought us round to meet an even deadlier menace.

While we were engaged on the wall, a few fire-arrows had come over and been promptly stifled by the invalids, who were in tremendous trim, bawling orders to each other and striding about like Nelson on the quarterdeck. But bowmen firing from behind the corral had put a couple of burning shafts into the roof of the stable against the west wall; it was wattle and went up like a muslin curtain with a great whoosh! It only burned for a few minutes, but sparks must have reached the roof of the billiard-room, for presently it began to flame, and the invalids had to beat a retreat, roaring for more water.

If the Indians had come in then, in one spot, neck or nothing, we'd have been done for. But they circled at a distance still, yelling, apparently content to let the fire do the work for a while. Which meant that we had a respite,

128

and I was able to gibber in futile anguish. The girls at the well were running with buckets for the west steps, but I could see with half an eye that the billiard room was beyond hope, and from that the fire must spread across the whole west end of the fort, consuming the beams on which the adobe was plastered, raging out of control—until it reached the north-west tower with its tons of powder. That explosion would set the whole place alight, and the other tower would go up as well—but we'd be past caring by then. We'd all be blown to atoms or roasted in the burning ruins.

At such times, when hope is dead and there's nowhere to hide, it's astonishing how the mind clears, and you see with an icy brilliance of logic that there's nothing for it but to run like hell. Fortunately, another man who'd considered that possibility, about ten minutes before I had, was Grattan Nugent-Hare, late of the Chainy Tenth and U.S. Dragoons. In the brief space between organising the bucket brigade, and the Indians' attack on the north-east angle, he had been sending down every other *savanero* and teamster to put to the mule teams on the three coaches, and on a couple of the wagons in the little park behind the shops on the southern side. When I came bounding down from the north-west tower he met me at the steps, and nodded at the blaze that was spreading across the west roof; the heat was like a furnace.

"We'll have to break out!" he shouted. "We've maybe got ten minutes before yon tower goes up. If we throw open the gates we can make a run for it with the wagons!"

"Where the hell to?" I demanded.

"The river—it's barely a furlong from the south wall. If we can get the coaches and a couple of wagons that far we can corral and hold them off! It's that or be blown to blazes!"

Now, beastly funk I may be, but show me the ghost of a loophole and I can think as smart as the next man—and be through it first, too, with luck. The three coaches were hitched up in the square, and a teamster was leading a wagon-team from the park. Black smoke was swirling across from the west side, and the beasts shied and bellowed with fear. From the two towers a couple of *savaneros* were firing occasional shots; evidently the Indians were still content to hold off. Grattan's voice was hoarse.

"The women in the three coaches, with the three best drivers, and a rifleman to each coach—aye, and the invalids with a few revolvers. That'll leave six or seven of us to man the south-east tower and cover 'em as they drive for the river. If a savage gets within touch of them, we should be ashamed of our shooting!"

"What then?"

"When they've made the river, we'll break out with a couple of wagons. The redskins'll be ready, but there ain't above fifty of 'em. With luck we'll maul 'em bad enough to leave us alone!"

You may imagine this conversation punctuated by the crackle of burning timber, wenches wailing and coughing, shots banging overhead, and the bespectacled invalid coming to attention crying: "We are at your disposal, sir! Cincinnati shall not fail! Name our task and it shall be done, yea, even unto the end!" I gave him a revolver and shoved him into the first coach, along with a brave but tearful Susie, who gave me a hasty slobber, and four terrified prostitutes. Grattan made for the gates while the coach-drivers hustled the other tarts and invalids into their vehicles, packing them like herring. I took a quick glance at the west wall; the blacksmith's shop was ablaze now, and the flames were licking towards the catwalk leading to the north-west tower—dear God, would the heat set off the loose powder even before the flames got close? I went up the steps to the south-east tower four at a time.

Outside the fort our attackers were still keeping their distance, most of them on the north side, which was all to the good. I looked across to the north-west tower; there were two *savaneros* there, and I waved them across—if any Indian wanted to attack through the fire that was now shooting above the west wall, good luck to him. Down in the courtyard the drivers were in their places; a teamster with a rifle was at a window of the first coach; on the second, a *savanero* was sitting on the roof reloading his Colt.

130

With all the din I never heard the gates open; suddenly the lead driver was yahooing and whipping up, and we rushed to the parapet of the tower, rifles at the ready. As we looked down, the first coach shot out and wheeled right for the river, and a tremendous yell burst from the startled Indians, who came tearing in at the unexpected sally. Then the second coach, and we were firing as fast as we could, picking our men pretty neatly, I like to think. The main pursuit had to come close to the gate wall, and we fairly shot them flat; they must have lost a dozen riders in their first mad rush, and the three coaches were careering down for the river, with the redsticks yelling in fury, circling out to get at them, losing distance in their attempt to get away from our fire.

The first coach reached the river and wheeled among the cottonwoods, and then the second, lurching and bouncing on the rough prairie, lost a wheel with about twenty yards to go, but the driver must have cut the traces, for the mules ran loose, and there wasn't an Indian close enough, thanks to our shooting and the rifle in the first coach, to do any damage as the girls and their guard scrambled out and reached the safety of the trees. The third coach, with its *savanero* performing like Deadwood Dick, came to rest beside the first one, and a tremendous cheer broke from our bastion. Grattan was down in the courtyard, yelling to us, and our fellows fairly tumbled down the steps to the wagons. I took a shot of the eye around; the Indians had pulled off on the east side, milling about two hundred yards or so from the fort gate; on the south side, between the fort and the coaches at the river, there wasn't a savage to be seen.

"Come on!" bawls Grattan; he and the fellows were piling into the two wagons, preparing to make the run.

"Out you go!" roars the gallant Flashy. "I'll cover you!"

He stared, but didn't hesitate above a second. He sprang up beside the teamster, and the wagon lumbered into the gateway.

Now, you may be staring, too. For you will have concluded that it ain't quite my style to be the last man out of the beleaguered garrison, and right you are. But if I have to fly from a fight, I prefer to do it my own way—and for the past five minutes at least I'd been reflecting that my way was certainly not in one of those crazy wagons. As I saw it, there were at least forty Indians out yonder, and they weren't going to be taken by surprise a second time. Those wagons were going to have their beasts hamstrung before they got near the river, and then it would be every man for himself on foot. Odds on a man from the wagons getting to the river? About evens—and that ain't good enough when there's a safer way out.

One thing was certain, you see; with all the fun and frolic to the south and east of the fort, there wouldn't be a brave left on the north side. And during our defence of the walls I'd noticed an interesting thing—whenever an Indian fell, more often than not his pony stayed by the body. Now, that's nothing new, as any cavalryman knows; why, at Balaclava, in the hell of that Russian battery, I recall at least two of our mounts nuzzling at fallen troopers, and these redskins and their horses are close as lovers. After the attack on the north-east angle, there had been three or four ponies standing, heads hanging and lost, beside the Indian dead at the foot of the wall, and I was certain sure they'd still be there. I could drop from a window on the north side, climb aboard, and be off and away round the fort, coming down to the carriages at the river by the west side, while Grattan and the lads occupied the Indians to the east, and stopped any arrows that might be going.

One last glance to be sure the north-west tower was still unscathed, and as the second wagon surged out of the gate and the Indian yelling redoubled, I was scuttling nimbly along the east parapet above the gateway and into the end upper-storey room on the north wall. I sped across to the window and took a cautious peep—not a soul in sight as far as the eye could see, and there below, beside the tangle of red corpses, were two Indian ponies! Your luck's in again, old Flash, thinks I, chuckling as I gripped the frame to climb—and the room was shuddering like a match-box in a giant's hand, a most appalling blast of thunder filled my

132

ears, the floor gave way beneath me, and I was falling, falling through dense clouds of dust or smoke, crashing down with a shock that drove the breath out of me, and with a ghastly pain stabbing through my left ankle.

I believe it was that pain that kept me conscious. I was in clouds of swirling dust, choking as I tried to scramble on all fours; for seconds I was too dizzy to see, and then there was light before me from an open doorway, and I lunged towards it. I knew I must be in the ground-floor room; above me the ceiling had gone, and there were beams and broken timbers all about me. I reached the doorway and fell through it.

To my right the west end of the fort was an inferno. I knew the magazine had gone, and most of the north-west angle with it, but the northern rooms were blazing too, and the thatched arcade across the square was beginning to burn. The gate wall was unscathed, but there were eighty kegs of powder in the tower at the far end of it, and with flaming wreckage all over the courtyard they might blow any instant. I plunged forward and fell with the sickening pain in my ankle, but I crawled feebly on, through the fiery reek, coughing and swearing and, I don't doubt, praying; the roar of burning seemed to be everywhere, but not twenty yards ahead was the yawning gateway, if I could only scramble to it before the mine went up, and didn't lose consciousness on the way.

I learned something that day. If you've a sprained or broken leg, and want to make haste, don't crawl—roll. Your leg will give you gip at every turn, especially if your way is strewn with flaming rubble, but if you're lucky, you'll get there. I don't know how long it took; perhaps a minute, though it seemed an eternity, through which I babbled in terror and shrieked with agony. My clothes were smouldering, but now I could see, with my eyes streaming, through the gateway to the prairie beyond. I half-got to my feet and fairly threw myself under the arch, rolling for dear life; I remember a massive iron hinge at which I clutched, dragging myself along by sheer main force of my arms, and rolled again; I must be beyond the gates, but even then I struggled ahead, my face in the dust, inching on to try to escape the horror behind me.

Perhaps I fainted, more than once; I can't tell. I thought I heard a muffled crash from behind, but I didn't mind it. I dug in my finger-nails and pulled, and pulled, until I could no more. I rested my face on one side, and above the scrubby grass in my line of sight there were the legs of a pony, and I hardly had time to think, oh, dear Jesus, the Indians! when a hand took me by the shoulder and rolled me over, and I was blinking up into a monstrously-bearded face under a fur cap, and I pawed feebly at a fringed buckskin shirt that was slick with wear, and then the beard split into a huge grin of white teeth, and a voice said:

"Waal, ole hoss, what fettle? How your symptoms segashooatin'? Say, ifn thar wuz jest a spoonful o' gravy to go with ye, I rackon yore baked jest 'bout good enough to eat!"

8

It's a curious distinction, on which I have dined out in Yankee clubs more than once, that I was the last man in Bent's Fort, for it's never been rebuilt, and when I saw it a few years ago it was just a heap of ruins, with the white wolves prowling through it. What caused me to reflect, though, on the damnable unfairness of things, was that I could have been last out in perfect safety, if I hadn't been so set on preserving my own skin. There's a moral there, I suppose, but not one I've ever paid the least heed to.

What had happened was this. Just as the second wagon emerged, and the Indians were preparing to give it toco, who should heave in view down the trail but a party of Mountain Men, drawn by the smoke and sound of general uproar. They don't stand on ceremony, those fellows; one swift survey and they were charging in like the Heavy Brigade, and since there were two score of them, the Indians had lost no time in making tracks, leaving a fair few of their number on the grass. So our chaps in the wagons, whom I'd supposed were going to likely death or capture, had enjoyed a grandstand seat in perfect safety, while poor old Flashy had been browning nicely, and damned lucky not to be overdone.

Mind you, there were compensations. As the one serious casualty on our side—for it's a remarkable thing that out of all who'd been in the fort, only one of the *savaneros* had taken an arrow in the leg, and Claudia had broken her wrist when the second carriage foundered—I was the centre of attention. Susie, who had borne up like Grace Darling all through, went into floods at the sight of my poor singed carcase, and the invalids bustled about with hot fomentations and bread poultices and sound advice which I daresay

135

would have carried me off if the Mountain Men hadn't patiently lifted them aside, bandaged my sprained ankle, and soothed my burns with a most disgusting mixture of herbs and bear's grease.

The most signal behaviour, though, had been Cleonie's. She had gone into hysterics when I was borne down to the carriages, still smoking gently, and had had to be restrained from flinging herself on me. Well, I hadn't known the wench cared that much; it wasn't like the cool Cleonie's style at all, and gave me some pause. Susie seemed too distraught about me to notice this signal display of concern for Massa by his handmaiden, which was just as well. My burns were trivial enough, by the way, but my ankle kept me coach-bound for a fortnight, by which time we were on our way again.

With the Mountain Men was one Fitzpatrick, who was a big man in those parts,[26] and on his advice we waited until a caravan arrived from the east, which he and the Mountain Men joined for Santa Fe. There was every kind of Indian trouble to the south, apparently, but in a train that was eventually a hundred wagons strong we had no fears. We learned from Fitzpatrick that the big tribe of Indians we had seen on our way to Bent's were Cumanches, who were celebrated both as bitter enemies of the Cheyenne and for their medical skill; whether they were out to take their foes at a disadvantage or study the cholera epidemic was a moot point. The fellows who had besieged us at Bent's were a mixed band of Utes (who hated everybody), and Chief Dog Kiowas (who were reckoned friendly but had not been able to resist the temptation of our small caravan). But from now on, whenever Indians were mentioned, we began to hear a new and ominous name: 'Pashes; even the sound of it was vicious, and the Mountain Men would growl and shake their heads.

I didn't care if I never saw a red hide again, but in fact Fitzpatrick swore that we'd been lucky. We'd lost three teamsters and two wagons on the mad career into Bent's, but nothing except a little gear in the destruction of the fort itself. By a freak of the explosion the south wall had collapsed, exposing the wagon park, and the Mountain Men and *savaneros* had taken advantage of a change in the wind to haul our last four wagons clear. So apart from one load of claret and another of food, our goods were fairly intact, much to Susie's relief.

But Bent's was a sorry sight. The explosion had razed a third of it, and the fire eventually destroyed the rest, including the south-east tower and its powder-kegs, which oddly enough never blew up, but burned like an enormous roman candle that I'm told was seen by the soldiers at Fort Mann, more than 150 miles away. The Mountain Men were fearfully cut up about it; to them it was as great a thing as the destruction of St Paul's or the Tower would be to us; perhaps even greater.[27] I remember three of them talking softly near the coach at sundown, the night before we pulled out for Santa Fe, smoking their pipes as they watched the ruins silhouetted against the purple sky as the last of the light faded.

"'Member when I fust see Bent's—cummin' down wi' the Green River boys f'm South Park nigh on fifteen years ago. Didn't rightly b'lieve my eyes—'speckted a giant ter cum out on't hollerin' 'Fee-fye-fo!' Didn't think nuthin' cud tumble it down."

"Goin' ter be right lonely, 'thout th' Big Lodge."

"Lonely? Why, ye jackass, how you talk! How kin ye be lonely fer a *place*? Lonely is fer folks."

A long pause. "Mebbe so. All this coon know, ifn you scrapin' fer beaver on th' Powder, or bogged in a Blackfeet village in the Tetons come winter, you kin git right desolated—jes' a-wishin' you could walk in under thet gate, see St Vrain en Maxwell laughin' on th' verandie en smokin' them big seegurs, en th' Little White Man hisself a-settin' by th' hide-press countin' the pelts jealous-like, or Ole Bill cussin' en yarnin' wi' th' smith."

"Or feel the taste o' Black Sue's punkin pie, ye mean!"

"Shore 'nuff. This chile cud swaller a buffler bull, horns, tail, en snout, en still hev room fer thet pie."

"Thet's whut I'm a-sayin', though—tain't th' *place* yore hankerin' fer—it's the *folks*. En the pie, seemin'ly. Waal, th' folks is still around, ain't they?"

"Rackon. Howsumever they cain't cum t' Bent's no more, cuz tain't hyar. En . . . they won't *be*, seems like, 'thout Bent's."

"In course they will, ye durned ole fool! They *be* until they *die*, leastways. Cain't *be* any longer'n thet!"

"They cud *be*," insists the Prairie Plato, "if Big Lodge *wuz*. Now it gone, an' soon nobody 'member it—like not many 'member th' ole Rondayvoos up on th' Green en Big Horn, back afore th' Santy Fee traders cum."

"Why, I 'member those! Whut special 'bout them?"

"Nuthin'—'ceptin' they *ain't*, nowadays. En this ole hoss kin git lonely fer them, too. *Thet*'s my p'int."

"I rackon you cud git lonely fer th' ole price o' beaver!"

"Kin thet, en hev done since '36." They all laughed. "Git lonely fer all th' things thet's a-changin'. Why, it gittin' so a cuss cain't walk fifty mile 'thout seein' a sojer or a him-migrant. But makes me feel right skeery hyaraways—" tapping his breast "—ter think o' Big Lodge gone. Place *en* folks. Seems it wuz kind o' . . . like home."

"Home! Why, yore home wuz in Kaintuck'—till you bust the minister's winder en had ter vamoose! Since when home's bin wherever ye found a fat squaw en a good fire!"

"Them's th' places I used ter start yearnin' fer Bent's!" cries the old chap. "Thet proves it! Thet's my p'int! Thet's why I'm grievin' ter see it all broke down like thet."

"Waal, so'm I. But the way you talk, you'd ha' bin happier ifn Big Lodge'd never bin builded in the fust place."

"No! Don't ye see? Then, why—there'd be nuthin' to . . . to remember not to fergit!"

The grass was beginning to brown when our reinforced train rolled down the Timpas towards the distant mountains. It was a shame that our invalids, having had as much of the West's health-giving properties as they could stand, had turned back from Bent's, for there's no air in the world as invigorating as New Mexico's. We journeyed across prairie bright with flowers, and it was bliss to lie in the coach

138

watching the girls running and laughing among them like muslin butterflies, gathering them in great armfuls and filling our coach with their fragrance. Even when we began to climb into the craggy forest hills that lead up to the Raton Pass, and the going got slower, the land was still beautiful, with its winding wooded valleys; there's a fine toll road now, I believe, but in my time there was hardly a visible trail, and once or twice the wagons had to be carried bodily over rocky barriers.

Then it was prairie again, to the heel of the Sangre de Cristo mountains, and since all this had recently been Mexican territory, there were more olive faces than white in the little settlements, and that unwashed languor inseperable from dagoes began to pervade the scene. There were other branches of the trail now, and other caravans were commonplace; at Wagon Mound, a great grassy bottom surrounded by trees, we found more than three hundred vehicles assembled, some of which had come down the Cimarron route—and with them, hollow-cheeked from illness but laconic as ever, was Wootton. He had forced himself into the saddle and come on a week behind us, but a friendly Indian had misled him into thinking our whole train had crossed the river to the cut-off. He had followed and made a dreadful discovery: our deserters had lost the trail, sure enough, and split into two parties after a violent quarrel; Wootton came on one group, more dead than alive, and had brought them safe to the Candian river, but the other party, including Skate and many of the Pittsburgh Pirates, had been less lucky. "'Pashes catched 'em on th' Cimarron. Buffler hunter seen the wagons all burned, our folks massacred.''

It was a sobering reminder of what might lie over the next hill, but it would have taken every Indian in America to make an impression on the vast stream of wagons and immigrants now converging below Wagon Mound. It was an endless procession, and at Las Vegas* we met some of the trains which had been pouring across the southern plains

*Not to be confused with the better-known Las Vegas, Nevada.

all summer from Fort Smith. Spirits were sky-high now as we passed over rolling downland covered with trees and bushes and dwarf cedars sprung from earth that was red and rich, and one afternoon there was a great whooping and cheering as we sighted conical hills ahead, and the cry of "Santy Fee! Santy Fee!" re-echoed along the line. Sure enough, as we passed the great scrubby cones, there lay a vast plain, and before it, the little city that was the first in all western America, built by the conquistadores, and God bless 'em, says I. There are bigger, finer, richer towns in the world, but precious few that so many weary folk have been so glad to see.

On Wootton's advice we camped near the soldiers' fort on the slope just north of the city, and that evening Susie and I drove in to take a long slant at the place, for we must break our journey here and take order for the final stage to the coast.

It was like Calcutta in fair week. The town itself was no size at all, some adobe houses and one or two fairly decent courtyards all grouped round a fine plaza containing the governor's palace, which was a long, low colonnaded building, and the bishop's house, and dozens of stores and posadas. But to get to this you had to pass through a positive forest of wagons and shanties and huts, and the paths through, like the streets of the town itself, were swarming with people. We were told that the usual population was about a thousand; in the fall of '49 I'd wager it was ten times that, most of them emigrants who, for one reason or another, found themselves stranded in the place, with no notion of how they were going to get out.

The truth was, they couldn't afford it. They had swallowed the gold bait back east, listened to the rosy lies of those who made a fortune from outfitting and transporting them, and then discovered after a journey far slower and longer and more expensive than they'd expected (five hundred miles to Santa Fe, the Fort Smith sharps had told them; it was *eight hundred*) that they were out of cash, out of provisions, and out of luck. What little money they had left was swallowed by prices that were plain foolish—flour

140

at $1 for ten pounds, sugar at 25 cents a pound, corn at $2.50 a bushel, firewood at 25 cents—even *grass* was being offered in the streets by peasant hawkers at 20 cents the bunch, for there wasn't a mouthful of grazing for miles, and something like 6000 cattle to feed.

So the poor emigrants were reduced to selling even their rigs to buy food and shelter—and lo! a wagon that had cost them $200 now brought $50 if they were lucky, their horses and oxen they could hardly give away, and the household goods and mining gear they offered in desperation fetched only cents. Many were plain destitute, unable to go forward or back—for now they learned that it would take another six months at least to California, that the routes (which no one was clear about) lay through terrible desert alive with hostiles, and that no military escorts could be provided.

This alarming news we learned from an earnest young subaltern of dragoons called Harrison with whom we dined in the best of the plaza's restaurants—for with the press of customers it was six to a small table even there, and a handsome bribe to the *jefe* at that.

"I doubt if one in ten of these poor souls will ever see California," says he. "Even if they had the money, and sure guides on good, well-guarded trails, it would be bad enough; as it is . . ." He shrugged, and recommended wine of El Paso (which was excellent), and a fricassee of tender buffalo hump with fiery peppers, called chile colorado (also first-rate, if your belly happens to be lined with copper; if I'd eaten it at Bent's Fort I could have blown the place up without gunpowder). I asked him why no escorts, when the town was filled with soldiers, and he laughed.

"You hardly saw an Indian south of the Raton, I'll be bound? No, because the trails were full. Well, in Santa Fe you're living in an armed camp, with hostiles all around you—Cumanches and Kiowas to the east, Utes to the north, Navajos to the west, and—worst of all—Apaches to the south. The reason we can't spare a single sabre for escort is that we're never done just holding the brutes at bay, protecting the Del Norte settlements, and punishing their raids—when we can find 'em. Yesterday I came back from

141

the Galinas, where we lost two troopers in a skirmish with the Black Legs; in three hours' time I'll be riding out again with fifty men because there's word of a big band of Mescaleros coming up the Pecos. No, sir—there isn't much time for escorts."

"Well!" says Susie. "That's fine, I must say! An' wots's the . . . the government doin' about it, may I ask?"

Harrison shook his head. "If by the government, ma'am, you mean the governor, Colonel Washington—well, he came back to town yesterday, having spent five weeks chasing Navajos.[28] With four hundred infantry and troops of artillery. That's what the government spends its time doing, in these parts."

As Susie had said, this was fine. "Some trains must be reaching California, surely?" says I.

"Oh, certainly, they have been. Those that are large, and well-armed, and properly planned; why, this summer they've been pouring down the Del Norte in thousands, floating across the Rio Grande on rafts and flatboats, taking any route west they can find—and getting there, I don't doubt. But there's no question Indian trouble's becoming worse, and I wouldn't advise anyone right now to try any but two roads: Kearny's trail down to Socorro and west, but . . ." he glanced at Susie ". . . that's a man's road, if you'll forgive my saying so, ma'am. The other is down the Del Norte valley beyond Socorro to Donna Ana, and west to the Gila and San Diego. It's a long, hard haul, and I'd hate for my family to have to travel it. But if you provision for the desert, and arm for the Indians, and don't mind heat and dust, you'll get there."

Susie wondered, thoughtfully, if it wasn't possible to *hire* a military escort, and Harrison smiled patiently.

"One escort did go out last month, to convoy the new Collector of San Francisco—but even he had to wait quite a time. I'm sorry, Mrs Comber, there just aren't enough soldiers to go around."

The truth was, it became plain, that in taking over the vast Mexican territory, the Yanks had bitten off more than they could comfortably chew, and like all governments,

142

were trying to run things at the cheapest rate—which was why this lad at table with us had lines on his face that shouldn't have been there for another twenty years, and was punishing the El Paso vintage as though it were water, without visible effect. Far from pacifying the land, American occupation had made it worse, especially now that the great immigrant incursions were making the redskins sit up and take notice—not that they needed much encouragement. They had been ripping the country to shreds for centuries during the Spanish and Mexican rules, murdering and plundering at will, exacting blackmail, inflicting frightful tortures on prisoners, carrying off the peons as slaves and concubines, breaking treaties when it suited, and the dagoes had been powerless to stop them.

They'd tried military action, and been cut to bits; they'd paid danegeld without avail. Some Mexican officials had even been hand in glove with the tribes, abetting their raids, and the Mexican government had become callous about atrocities it couldn't prevent anyway. The war with America had made matters worse; with the land in confusion, the Indians had had a field day, and now when America couldn't, or wouldn't, put in enough troops, the Indians treated them with contempt, and became more insolent than ever. In effect, they ruled New Mexico except for the civilised strip down the Del Norte, which they ravaged systematically, just as much as it would bear.[29] It was enough, says Harrison, almost to make him sympathise with the old Mexican *proyecto de guerra*.

"What's that?" says I. "War project?"

"So they called it—a polite name for scalp-hunting. Back in the '30s, the Chihuahua Mexicans were so hard-pressed they paid a bounty for Apache scalps—$100 for a brave, $50 for a female . . ." he grimaced ". . . and $25 for a child. I'm afraid there was no lack of degenerates eager to earn the blood-money. The worst was a fellow-countryman of yours, I regret to say—a scoundrel called Johnson who wiped out one of the few peaceful Apache bands and sold their scalps to the Mexicans. Some say it was his massacre that turned the Apaches from regarding white men as allies against Mexico, and made them our bitterest enemies. I doubt it, personally; in my experience Apaches are the most evil, inhuman creatures on earth—if their hostility to Americans is recent, it's because their acquaintance with us barely goes back a generation. The truth is they hate all mankind. In any event, the scalp bounty brought the foulest kind of white cut-throat to this country; they're still here, living by murder and banditry—and in Mexico, which doesn't make our work any easier. No—I couldn't countenance a revival of the *proyecto* under American law[30] . . . but when I think of the horrors I've seen perpetrated by these red savages—"

He'd been talking grim-lipped, staring at his glass, a young man riding his hobby-horse as only a young man can, but now he broke off in confusion, and blushed his apologies to Susie for offending her ears with such talk. "What must you think of me?" he stammered. "Inexcusable . . . do beg pardon—gracious, is that the time?" He was just a boy, when all was said, bowing over her hand, and courteously disputing the bill with me. "You are too kind, sir," says he, all West Point. "When I return I shall insist on repaying your most enjoyable hospitality. Sir—Mrs Comber." *If* you return, thinks I; I'd seen too many gallant pups just like him, on the Afghan frontier, and I'd no doubt the Mescaleros, whoever they might be, were just as adroit at subaltern-eating as the Afridis.

"Isn't he the sweetest little thing?" says Susie, looking after him with dewy-eyed lust. "Honest, sometimes I wish I was just startin' in at the game again. I wouldn't charge 'im a cent." Fine talk before her lawful wedded, you'll agree; Master Harrison wasn't the only one who'd been overdoing the El Paso. "Let's 'ave a look at the town, then."

So we took a turn through the bustling, excited streets in the mellow dusk, admiring the magnificent New Mexican sunset and the colourful crowds in the Plaza. Every posada and place of amusement seemed to be at full steam, and packed with pleasure-seekers, for it was abundantly evident that if many of the immigrants out in the wagons and shanties were on their beam-ends, there was a multitude in Santa Fe with money to burn. I'd seen nothing like it since New Orleans; the booze was flowing like buttermilk, there was laughter and music wherever you turned, and enough gold and silver and jewellery in sight to start a Mint. The fashions were brilliant, in the Spanish style: tall caballeros in fancy shirts and bright *mangas**, their flared *calzonero* pantaloons slashed from hip to ankle and held with silver buttons, *puros*† clenched between their teeth and embroidered sombreros hanging from their shoulders by silver cords; they sauntered arrogantly by, or lounged on the corners with the gaudy *poblana*‡ wenches, or watched as the slim senoritas of the better class swirled past on high Spanish heels, their silks of every colour dazzling in the lamplight. By jove, it was the place for wanton black eyes and sleek black hair and creamy skin and heady perfume, wasn't it, though, with a great flirting of silken ankles and gracefully-held fans and fringed *rebosos*§—not a buckskin man, or Yankee trader, or vaquero but had a slender hand on his arm, and a pretty dark head nestling against his shoulder as he strode, or reeled, from posada to dance-hall, roaring and singing as he went. There were plenty of wealthy Americans of good class, local ranchers and merchants, as well as Mountain Men, trappers, and miners from the Albuquerque diggings, all getting rid of their pelf as though it was Judgement Day tomorrow; noisy, insistent peasant men and women who hawked Indian trinkets or shrilled and quarrelled round the lighted booths; young emigrant men who still had some cash left and were eager for the flesh-pots—and in the shadows, the beggars and *leperos*, squatting against the walls, and the Indians. Not just your verminous *Indios manzos*‖, but tall, silent figures in their blankets and serapes, own brothers to

*Mexican cloak.
†Cigars.
‡Working-class beauty.
§Fringed scarf worn round the head.
‖Tame Indians, as opposed to 'bravos'.

the fighting braves we'd seen on the prairies, who simply watched with blank faces, or passed without word or glance through the boisterous throng.

We looked in at a *fandango*, one of the famous public dances held in the *sala*, or ballroom, at one side of the Plaza—it was simply a great hall, bare as a riding school, with benches against either wall, one side for men, t'other for women, and a dais at one end for the musicians, a demented group of grinning greasers who thrashed away on bandolins, guitars, tambourines and drums. It was mostly that gay, heady Spanish stuff, which I like; I'm not a dancer, much, but I love to watch experts at work, especially female ones, and the sight of those bright-eyed, laughing *poblanas*, in their polka jackets and short skirts, whirling as they stamped and clattered their heels, would have done you good to see. They wheeled, graceful as gulls, whoever their partners—elegant, hatchet-faced dagoes in *mangas*, red-faced sports sodden on Taos whisky or vino, bearded miners in slouch hats and red shirts, or great clumsy buckskin brigadeers who whooped and yelled and capered like Indians. It says a lot for the band—or the liquor—that there was a Latin *sarabando* in progress at one end of the hall while an obstreperous bunch of trappers were performing a Virginia reel at the other, to the satisfaction of all. But even the drunkest gave room when a fat little chap in belled sleeves and sash took the floor with a tall, crazy-eyed virago in a scarlet silk manga and flounced skirt; they weren't the bonniest couple there (her moustache was a shade thinner than mine), but she clacked her castanets and surged like a stately galleon, and the little chap, perspiring buckets, clapped and twirled and fairly rattled round her; as the pace increased, everyone yelled and stamped, "Viva! Vaya! Olé! Hoe en toe, little greaser! Hooraw, bella manola! Bueno!" and when they danced side by side from one end of the long sala to the other, both bolt upright and progressing at a snail's pace although their heels drummed the floor too fast for the eye to follow, and concluded with a great flourish and stamp, the roof was like to come off. They bowed, panting, to the storm of applause, and the spectators showered them with gold and silver and even jewels: I saw one beauty undo her earrings and toss them, crying "Brava!", on to the boards, and the stout *ranchero* with her flung his diamond pin.

"Well, now," says Susie, tapping my arm, "let's see what else they do for recreation," and we visited one of the many gaming-houses off the Plaza, where the punters crowded round tables heavy with doubloons, pesos, and dollars, staking on faro, vingt-et-un and every other fool's game you could think of. I'd gathered Santa Fe was an extravagant, wide-open community, but even I was astonished at the amounts I saw change hands that night; the gamblers of Santa Fe, whether they were drunk traders, flash greasers, desperate immigrants, cold-eyed swells with pistols prominently displayed in their waistbands, or even the couple of tonsured priests who had an apparently bottomless satchel of coin and crossed themselves before every cast of the dice, were evidently no pikers. They were artfully encouraged by the croupiers, many of whom were Mexican belles in low-cut bodices who took care to bend low over the table when gathering in the stakes, which always makes the loss seem lighter. Presiding was the celebrated Dona Tules, a Juno with long dark-red hair and splendid shoulders who smoked a cigarro and lounged among the tables with a court of admirers in tow.

"Cheap an' showy," sniffs Susie, "an' her paddin' shows, too. Well, that only leaves one other entertainment, doesn't it?" So to my embarrassment we sought out the best bordello in town.

"You want me to go in?" says I, taken aback. "What, you're coming, too? Here, they'll charge me corkage!" But she told me not to be lewd, and shoved me inside. It was a poor enough place, with a slatternly madame who eyed Susie suspiciously, but drummed up her tarts on request, and an indifferent lot they were.

"I see," says Susie. "No, thank you, dear, the gentleman's not stayin'; 'e's a clergyman, seein' the world."

When we were back in the coach and rolling out to camp, she said suddenly: "Well, that settles it! They can keep Sacramento—for the present, anyway. Why, there's more

147

loose money an' good custom in this town than ever I hoped to see in California—an' I'm about sick of wagons an' Indians an' travellin', aren't you? A million, did I say? With gels like ours, an' the kind o' style we can show 'em, it'll be like pickin' it off the trees. I think we'll just settle down for a spell," says she to my consternation; she patted my knee with a plump hand and settled back contentedly. "I think we're goin' to like Santa Fe, dearie."

9

There was no sense in arguing, so I didn't; for one thing, I had no wish to plunge ahead into the kind of horror we'd experienced on the plains, and the prospect of a brief rest in Santa Fe was welcome. On the other hand, I'd no wish to linger in America, and was determined to get out of Susie's fond embrace as soon as the chance arose. One pressing need would be money; like so many of my women (including my dear Elspeth, I regret to say), she seemed devilish reluctant to let me get my paws on the purse-strings—they're a mean sex, you know. So I had to take stock, and see what offered, while pretending a great interest in the establishment of our brothel.

Susie got her eye on a likely place just off the Plaza, a fine, one-storey house with plenty of rooms and a good-sized courtyard, all enclosed by high adobe walls. It belonged to the church, so she paid a rare price, "but never fear," says she, "we'll make four hundred per cent on this when we come to sell." Then she hired labour to make it habitable, engaged servants and porters, and furnished it with the gear from New Orleans which had survived our journey. My respect for her increased when I saw all the stuffs, carpets, curtains, china and crockery, tables, chairs and beds—including the famous "electrical mattress", too—and realised that she'd never have come by anything half so fine west of St Louis; up went the mirrors, chandeliers, and pictures, and out came the girls' assorted finery; Susie saw to the very last detail of their personal apartments, and to the appointment of the public rooms, which included a large reception chamber where the wenches could be on view between engagements, so to speak, flirting with the customers while they made their selections; a buffet, and a gaming-room which I undertook to supervise—for there's no call, you know, for a man about the bawdy-house, apart from the porter-bullies, and I didn't care to be seen as a mere jack-gagger;* also it occurred to me that I'd be able to accumulate some private funds, with careful management.

We opened for business, with Susie dressed like a dog's dinner queening it in the hall, her cashier in an office to one side, and a broken-down medico in a little room on the other—"for the only thing they're goin' to leave here is cash," says she, "an' if they don't like bein' looked at by the pox-spotter, they can take themselves off, double-quick." The girls were all got up in their most alluring finery, lounging artlessly in the reception on their couches under the shaded lamps, while Flashy, resplendent in new coat and pants and silk cravat, shuffled the decks in the gaming-room and waited for the gulls—and I'm here to tell you that I did a damned thin trade. You see, they could gamble anywhere in Santa Fe, but they couldn't fornicate in the style to which Susie's charmers quickly accustomed them; it was like a madhouse out yonder for a couple of hours, until she closed the doors, having made appointments for clients who kept us busy until four in the morning, and when I joined her at dawn and saw the pile of rhino on her office table—well, there was a cool four thousand dollars if there was a cent. "Mind you, I won't 'ave the gels workin' at this pace other nights," says she. "It's important to make a good impression at first; the word'll spread, an' we'll attract good custom, but then we can pick an' choose the real genteel—an' put the prices up. I'm not 'avin' those dirty buckskin brutes in 'ere again, though; they're just savages! Pore little Marie 'ad to call the porters twice, she was that terrified, an' Jeanette might 'ave been 'urt bad if she 'adn't 'ad 'er pistol 'andy."

I saw there was more to this business than I'd imagined—but, by George, wasn't it a paying spec, though? Better than stock-jobbing or Army contracts, and just as respectable, really.

*One who lives off immoral earnings.

We throve astonishingly in that first week, just as Susie had predicted; our fame spread, and the dago quality began to come in, not only from Santa Fe but from the valley below Albuquerque even, and the *rancherias* in the country round. We had a rare platoon of bullies on the gate, and took no riff-raff; even so, there was no lack of customers, and since they weren't the kind to haggle, she was able to exact prices that she confessed she wouldn't have dreamed of charging in Orleans. Oh, she knew her business; taste and refinement, says she, are what we're after, and she got it; I've known rowdier drawing-rooms in Belgravia. The tarts seemed to thrive on it, too; you've never seen such airs.

One thing that alarmed us both, though, was the amount of cash that piled up in Susie's strong-box in that first week; it would have given you the frights anywhere, never mind in a town awash with sharps and slicks who'd have cut a throat for twenty cents. In New Orleans she'd have banked it, but here there wasn't a strong-room worth the name. Trust Susie, though: in no time she'd reached an arrangement with one of the governor's aides, and every second or third day the box was hefted across the Plaza by a couple of bluecoats and the blunt stowed under military guard at headquarters—I fancy the aide's fee was free use of Eugenie every Friday, but I'm not certain; Susie was close about business arrangements. But she confided that she still wasn't happy about keeping large sums on the premises between times, and perhaps we ought to hire a reliable guard. I remarked that I was on hand, and she went slightly pink and said, yes, love, but I couldn't be awake *all* the time, could I?

"I was thinkin' we might employ Nugent-Hare," she added.

I didn't care for this. He and Uncle Dick Wootton had been paid off with the *arrieros* and teamsters on Susie's resolve to settle in Santa Fe, but while Wootton had gone off with a hunting party, the bold Grattan was still about the town. I was against taking him back, I said; I didn't care for him.

" 'E's been a loyal servant to us, you can't deny! Wot's wrong with 'im, then?"

"He's Irish, and his nose is too long. And I've never trusted him above half."

"Not trust 'im—'cos 'is nose is too long? Wotever d'you mean?" Suddenly she burst out laughing, catching my hand. " 'Ere, I do believe you're jealous! Why, you silly big thing—come 'ere! You are, aren't you?" She was bubbling with delight at the idea, and kissed me warmly. "As if I could ever think of anyone but you!" She was all sentimental in a moment, her arms round my neck. "Oh, Beachie, I do love you so! Now, then, let's chase them blue-devils away . . ."

The result was that Grattan was sought out and offered the post of chief of the knocking-shop police, which he accepted, pulling his long nose and bland as you please. I was surprised—because while I'll do anything, myself, he didn't strike me as the sort who'd lower himself to being a whore's ruffian, which is what it amounted to. We discovered why he'd been so ready, two days later, when the son-of-a-bitch slipped his cable with two thousand dollars, which fortunately was all that had been in the office desk. Susie was distraught, damning his eyes and bewailing her foolishness in not heeding me; I was quite pleased myself, and comforted her by saying we'd have the scoundrel by the heels in no time, but at this she clutched my hand and begged me not to.

"Why the hell not?" cries I, dumfounded.

"Oh, it wouldn't do! Honest, I know it wouldn't! Let the thievin' little bastard go, an' good riddance! Ow, the swine, if I could lay 'ands on 'im! No, no, darlin', let it be! It'll be cheaper in the long run—it gets a place like ours such a bad name, you see, if there's any commotion with the law! Really, it does—I know! Anyway, Gawd knows where he's gone by this! No, please, Beachie love—take my word on it! Let it go!"

"Two thousand dollars? Damned if I do!"

"Oh, darlin', I know—but it ain't worth it! We'd lose by it in the end! Please—I know it's my fault, an' I should 'ave listened to you an' not trusted the long red snake that 'e is! But I'm soft an' silly—please, let it alone for my sake?''

She was so insistent that in the end I shrugged it away—it wasn't my pelf, anyway. But I kept my thoughts to myself, and she calmed down presently and promised that we would make it back a hundredfold in no time at all.

Which I could well believe, seeing how business was in the second week. Our clients were more numerous than ever, and their enthusiasm showed itself in an entirely unexpected way—to me, at any rate, although Susie said it had been common enough in New Orleans, and was regarded as a great compliment to the establishment. For now we began to receive repeated offers from the wealthier patrons who wanted to *buy* one or other of the girls outright; I recall one enormously fat greaser with an oiled moustache and rings sparkling on his pudgy hands, sweating all over his lecherous moon face as he made Susie a bid for Marie—she was the delicate little mulatto with soulful eyes whose prime trick, I gathered, was to burst into tears beforehand.

"She ees so frail and sweet, like a fresh flower!" cries this disgusting bag of lard. "She must be mine—the price, I do not care! Name eet, and I pay. Only I must have her for my own, to protect and cherish; she consumes me, the little *helado negro*!"

Susie smiled and shook her head. "But I couldn't do that, Senor Cascara de los Pantalunas, even for you! Why, I'd soon 'ave no gels left, an' then where'd I be? They're not for sale—''

"But I must have her! I weel care for her like . . . like my most precious brood mare! She shall have an apartment in my hacienda, with perfumed crystals for her bath, and bon-bons, and a silk coverlet, and a pet dog from Chihuahua—''

"I'm shore she would," says Susie firmly, " 'cos you're a real gentleman, I know—but there's the law, too, isn't there? This ain't slave territory, an' I'd be in a real fix if word got out.''

"Ah, the Americano law! Who cares? Would eet be known—who should hear of it?" He grimaced like a sow in labour, and wheedled horrid. "Are there not t'ousands of slaves? What are the peons, but chattels? Do not los Indios own many slaves, stolen and bought, and what does the law know about them? Pleez, Mees' Comber, I beg of you . . . t'ree, four t'ousan' dollar, even—what you will, por Dios! so I may possess my pure, my delicious angelic Marie!"

But she wouldn't have it for all his groans and entreaties, and he went off lamenting to console himself on rented terms with his little black ice-cream, as he'd called her. Susie sent all other would-be buyers the same road, including one I'd not have credited if I hadn't been present as translator. Believe it or not, he was a priest! Aye, from the mission just up the Santa Fe Trail, a spruce little runt of impeccable address who came in secrecy after dark, and hastened to explain that he wasn't a customer, personally, but acting on behalf of an important client.

"He has heard, as who has not, of the beauty and refinement of the young ladies who are . . . ah, under the señora's care," says he, and from his very smoothness I scented a wrong 'un from the start. "I must make it clear immediately that my patron's intentions are of the most honourable, otherwise it is unthinkable that I should act as his intermediary. But he is of consequence, and wishes to take the young lady to wife. He understands the señora's position, and is prepared to pay substantial ah . . . compensation."

When I'd recovered, and translated for Susie, she was so took aback that she didn't offer her usual polite refusal, but asked who the patron was, and which gal did he want, for Gawd's sake? I passed it back, and the Pimping Padre shook his head.

"I should not divulge his name. As to his his choice . . . he knows of your ladies only by report, and is indifferent. He would prefer, however, that she is not too black."

Susie, hearing this, said she was prepared to wager it was his bloody bishop; staunch Church of England, was Susie. "Tell 'im we regret our gals ain't for sale, wotever name 'e gives it," says she. "Compensation, indeed. An' marriage! A likely tale!"

154

He was a persistent little terrier, though, and urged the importance of his patron, the unspecified amount he would cough up, and as a last resort, the desirability of giving a poor whore the chance to go straight in wedlock—he didn't put it like that, quite. Susie shook her head grimly, and repeated her line about the law being the law, and the girls not being in the market anyway. He took himself off poker-faced, and Susie was remarking that it was all this celibacy that made 'em randy as stoats, when I voiced a doubt that had occurred to me before.

"Hold on," says I. "If it's true what you've been telling them . . . is this free territory? Because, if it is, what's to hinder one of the girls from marrying a suitor—or little Marie going off with old Pantalunas or whatever he's called? I mean, maybe they'd rather jolly a single party, with all home comforts as wives or mistresses, than be thumped by four different randies every night. And if slave law don't run here—why, the whole pack of 'em could walk out and leave you flat!"

"You think I'm simple, don't you?" says she. "Why, I knew all o' that afore I left Orleans. Leave me flat? Why should they do that—and where'd they go, silly little sluts that don't know nothink except 'ow to prop a man up? Trust 'emselves to some oily villain like ole Cascara-chops, who'd turn 'em out as soon as 'e'd tired of 'em? That much they *do* know, now. An' they 'aven't the wit to work their own lay, unprotected—they wouldn't last a week. Wi' me, they're well-off, well-fed, an' I treat 'em fair; they're never driven or ill-used, an' they know that when they're past their prime I'll see 'em set up proper—yes, or married, to some steady feller that *I* approve of. 'Ow many 'ores d'you know, in England, wi' prospects as good as my gels? That's another thing; they are *my* gels, an' they'd not leave me— no, not for twenty Pantalunasses. You see, law or no law, they're still slaves, in 'ere," and she tapped her forehead. "An' I'm Miz Susie, an' always will be."[31]

Well, she was the best judge, but I had doubts. I could think of one at least of her houris who was not a silly little slut, and who could see horizons wider than those visible in the ceiling mirrors of Susie's private salons. One Cleonie, to wit, who'd been more passionately attentive to me than ever since our arrival in Santa Fe. There was a little summer-house hidden deep in the pines near the back gate, and when occasion offered she and I would repair to it for field exercises; since I was preparing to bid Susie adieu I didn't heed the risk, but Cleonie's eagerness astonished me. I'd have thought she'd have enough of men to sicken her, but apparently not. I discovered why one afternoon when everyone else was at siesta, and I was sitting meditating in the dim, stuffy little summer-house with Cleonie astride my lap going like a drunk jockey and humming "Il était une bergère"; when she'd panted her soul out, and I'd got a cheroot going, she suddenly says:

"How much do you love me, chéri?"

I told her, oceans, and hadn't I just proved it, but she kept asking me, teasing at me with her lips, her eyes alight in the shadows, so I reassured her that she was the only girl for me, no error. She considered a moment, with a little smile.

"You do not love Miz Susie. And soon you will be leaving her, will you not?"

I started so hard I nearly unseated her, and she gave a little laugh and kissed me again. "There is no need to be alarmed. Only I know it—and that because I had a Haitian mother, and we can *see*. I see it in the way you look at her—just as I see what is in your eyes when you look at me—aahh!" And she shivered against me. "Why should you love her—she is fat and old, and I am young and beautiful, n'est-ce pas?"

If when you're fifty you can light my fire half as well as Susie can, thinks I, you'll be doing damned well, my conceited little fancy—but of course I told her different; she'd given me a turn with her prophecy, and I guessed what was coming next.

"When you go," she whispers, "why do you not take me with you? Where will you go—Mexico? We could be very happy in Mexico—for a while. I could make money for us there, and on the way, with you to protect me. If you love me as you say you do—why do we not go together?"

156

"Who says I'm going, though? I haven't—and if Miz Susie heard one word of this, and what you've said about her—well, I'd think caning was the least you could expect; she'd sell you down the river, my girl."

"Pouf! She cannot sell me—this is free soil! You think we don't know—and that she has said as much, to those who came to buy us? Oh, yes, we know that, too—already black Aphrodite is listening to that fat man—what is his name, Pantaloon? He who wished to buy Marie, only Marie is silly and timid. Aphrodite is not timid—she is of a force, as I am, even if she is black and rank and lacks education. I think she will go."

So much for loyalty to the dear old brothel, thinks I. "What about the others?"

She shrugged. "Stupid little 'ores, what do they know? They would be lost without the fat Miz Susie to waddle after them like a foolish old hen." She giggled and arched that superb body. "I shall go, whether she like or not. With you—because even if you do not love me as you say, you enjoy me . . . and I enjoy you as I have never enjoyed any man before. So I think we will march well together . . . to Mexico, hein? And there, if you please, I shall make an establishment, even as Fat Susie has done—or, if I wish, I may find a wealthy man and marry him. When will you go?"

It wasn't such a bad notion, when I thought of it—not unlike my flight with Cassy along the Mississippi. But this one, while she might lack Cassy's iron will and resource—and I wouldn't have bet on that—had advantages Cassy had lacked. She was educated, highly intelligent, a linguist, a lady when she chose, and was ready to work her passage—that would see me right for cash, which had been vexing me. And she could keep me warm at nights, too, even better than Cassy, who'd been a cool fish when all was said. And when we decamped, dear Susie could do nothing about it; Cleonie was free as air. We could travel by easy stages down the Del Norte valley, which was safe enough, to El Paso, and once in Mexico I could let her make sufficient to buy me a passage to England. I couldn't see a hole in it, and I was chafing to be away.

The long and short of it was that we discussed it until the end of the siesta, and I couldn't for the life of me see why it shouldn't be put in train at once. She was a smart wench, and had it well figured out; I must procure a couple of mounts for the journey, which could be done in the morning, and assemble what packages we needed; I had enough ready money for that, and she had almost a hundred dollars of her own—*tippique* from satisfied customers in Orleans and here in Sante Fe—so we should be all right to begin with. I must conceal our packages in the summer-house, and tomorrow night, when the frenzy was at its customary height, we'd foregather at midnight by the back gate and be off. There was no reason, really, why we shouldn't have bowled off publicly, but the less pother the better. I'm always ready, as a rule, to turn the knife in anyone's wound, but I had a soft spot for Susie—and recollections of the brisk way she'd corrected John Charity Spring's exercises for him. I'd no wish to have the porters setting about me on behalf of a woman scorned.

Next day I bought a very pretty Arab gelding for myself, and a mule for Cleonie, left them in a livery stable south of the Plaza, and busied myself for the rest of the day with the final arrangements; by late afternoon I had our packages stowed in the summer-house, along with my rifle and six-shooter. Then, for old times sake, I surprised Susie at her toilet, and let her work her evil will of me as we'd used to in Orleans; she blubbered, even, afterwards, and my last memory is of her sitting there in her corset, sighing heavily and exclaiming at her reflection, with her glass of port beside her. I'll have a drink in the Cider Cellars for you, thinks I, and closed the door.

It was a slow night in the gaming-room, but all hands to the pumps in the bedrooms by the sound of it; at a few minutes to twelve I got up and sauntered through the grounds to the summer-house, and for some reason my heart was beating fifty to the dozen. I got my hat, and slipped my revolver into its holster; there was a rustle through the pines and the patter of feet, and Cleonie was beside me, a cloak over her head, held at her throat, her eyes shining in that lovely face pale in the darkness. She threw her arms round me, fairly sobbing with excitement, and I kissed her with some ardour and gave them a loving squeeze—goodness, it was all there, though, and as I'd done at every assignation with her, I shivered in anticipation.

From the distant house came the strains of music, and the faint sound of laughter; I cautioned her to wait and slipped out through the back gate to see that all was clear. It was an alley leading at one end to a street which ran to the Plaza; up there were lights and folk and traffic passing by, but down here all was in dark shadow. Something rustled under the wall behind me, and I whirled and froze in my tracks, my hand fumbling for the butt of my pistol but checked by sheer terror as a figure moved out from the wall, lean and lithe as a cat—and I gasped as the light fell on the tight-stretched skin of a painted face, with eyes like coals, and above, the double feathers of a Navajo Indian.

Before I could move there were two others, twin spectres on either side of me, naked to the waist, but I hadn't had time even to think of screaming when a voice whispered behind me, and I turned with a sob of relief to see the little priest. He held out a leather satchel to me.

"Two thousand dollars, as agreed. Where is she?"

I was so stricken I could only nod at the gate, and then I found my voice: "Indians, for Christ's sake!"

"Did you not say this afternoon that men would be needed to carry her off in silence?" He gestured to the Navajos, and they slipped silently through the gate; there was a muffled gasp, and a small clatter as though a chair had been disturbed, and then they were in the alley again, one of them carrying Cleonie's squirming figure over his shoulder while a second brave held her ankles and the leader kept a heavy blanket close-wrapped round her head. He grunted at the priest, and the three melted noiselessly into the dark while I held the wall and babbled at the priest.

"My God, those brutes gave me a turn! I thought you'd bring your own people . . ."

"I told you today, since you insisted, that my patron was Jose Cuchillo Blanco—Jose White Knife. What more natural than that he should send his own bravos to take her? Why—does the sight of them alarm you, on her behalf? Let me point out that you have had several hours to reflect on it, and on her fate as the wife of a Navajo chief."

"I wasn't expecting those painted horrors to be lurking in the dark, that's all!" says I, pretty warm. "Look here, though—will he really marry her, d'you think?"

"After their fashion. Does it matter? For two thousand dollars; perhaps you should count them. Oh, and the receipt, if you please." So help me the little bastard had a document, and a pencil. "In case the sale should ever be questioned. It is improbable; the wife of White Knife is not likely to be seen in Santa Fe again—or indeed, anywhere."

I scribbled a signature: B. M. Comber, R.N., retired. "Well, now, padre, I hope he takes decent care of her, that's all. I mean, it's only because you're a man of the cloth . . . Tell me," says I, for I was agog with curiosity, "I didn't care to ask earlier . . . but ain't it a trifle out of the way for a priest to be procuring women for savages?"

He folded the receipt. "We have many missions in the Del Norte valley; many villages whose people look to us for help. Cuchillo Blanco knows this—how should he not, he whose bands have left red bloody ruin in the settlements these years past? He comes to Santa Fe; he hears of the beautiful white women whose bodies are for sale; he desires white women—"

"Now, I told you—she ain't white, strictly speaking. Part Frog, part nigger—"

"She will be white to him. However . . . he fears that there will be reluctance to sell to an Indian, so he sends word to us: buy me such a woman, and the missions and settlements will be spared . . . for a season. Shall I hesitate to buy him a woman who gives herself to anyone for hire, when by doing so I can save the lives—perhaps the souls— of scores of men, women, and children? If it is a sin, I shall answer to God for it." I saw his eyes glitter in the dark. "And you, señor, with your two thousand dollars. How will *you* answer to God for this—what souls will you tell Him that *you* have saved?"

"You never know, padre," says I. "Maybe she'll convert your Navajo chief to Christianity."

I picked up my gear from the summer-house when he'd gone, and went quickly down through the crowded Plaza to the livery stable, where I slung my few traps over the mule, stowed the heavy purse of eagles in my money-belt, and rode out on the Albuquerque trail. I won't say I didn't regret Cleonie's absence—clever lass, fine mount, charming conversationalist, but too saucy by half, and she'd never have earned us two thousand dollars between Santa Fe and El Paso, not in a month of Sundays.

*   *   *

From Santa Fe to Algodones on the river the trail was dotted that night with emigrant camp-fires, and I passed their clusters of wagons as I rode, first through cultivated land and then through scrubby mesa. The Del Norte was smaller than I expected—you think of the Rio Grande as something huge, to compare with the Mississippi, which it may be farther down for all I know; this wasn't much larger than the Thames, muddy brown and flowing between banks of cottonwood, with ugly black crags looming up away on the southern horizon. I pushed on through the next night to Albuquerque, a big village swollen by the caravans and by the huts of the Mexican and American miners who worked the nearby gold-field.

Here I sold the mule, and considered crossing to the west bank. There were wagons and tents clustered all round the ford, and crowds of people making tremendous work of floating their vehicles and goods across on rafts and flatboats; the river hereabouts was quite swift, and about a quarter of a mile across through sandbars and quicksands. I watched one schooner being poled precariously across the currents, and then the whole thing pitched slowly into the river, while fellows roared and struggled in the water and hauled on lines and got in each other's way, and all was

161

confusion. The west bank seemed no better than the east, anyway, so I held on south along the wagon-road, where there was plenty of traffic in both directions.

That was when I discovered a new pleasure in life—riding in the American west. I'd spent enough time in the saddle on the plains, you might think, but this was different; here I was alone, and could take my own time. In other parts of the world one always seems to be in a great hurry, tearing from one spot to the other at a gallop, but out yonder, perhaps because distances are so great, time don't seem to matter; you can jog along, breathing fresh air and enjoying the scenery and your own thoughts about women and home and hunting and booze and money and what may lie over the next hill. It's easy and pleasant and first-rate in every way, and at night you can build your own fire and roll up in a blanket, or join some other fellows who are sure to make you welcome, and share a meal with you and a yarn over coffee or something sensible from a flask. This is in settled country, you understand.

The Del Norte seemed to be settled enough, for all Harrison's alarming talk, and if it ain't the finest scenery in the continent it was new to me. It's not a valley as we in England know the word: the river runs through its cottonwood fringe past numerous Mexican villages full of stray dogs and loafers in sombreros, all of 'em either asleep or preparing to lie down. Someone must work the place, though, for there are plenty of cultivated fields beyond the cottonwoods, with here and there a rancheria or hacienda, some of them quite fine, and beyond them again the scrubby plain stretching away on either side, with a dark barrier of mountains to the east, and little else to take the eye except one great black wedge of rock to the left which I had in view all through one day's ride. Not Buckinghamshire, but it'll do; any landscape without Indians suited me just them.

Six days down from Santa Fe I came to the ford at Socorro, where there was a fair concourse of emigrants. A few miles farther down, the Del Norte makes a great belly to the west, and it seemed to me from the map that time could be saved by making due south away from the river and behind the Cristobal mountains to rejoin it at Donna Ana. I mentioned this to a Dragoon despatch rider with whom I breakfasted at Socorro, and he shook hands solemnly and said should he write to my family?

"You take that road if you've a mind to," says he facetiously. "It's got this to be said for it, it's nice and flat. Other'n that, I'd think hard before I'd recommend it. Course, mebbe you *like* the notion of a hundred and twenty-five miles of rock and sand and dust and dead bones—plenty of *them* along the old wagon trail. No water, though, unless you happen to find a rain pool at the Laguna or Point of Rocks—which you won't, this time of year. But you won't mind, because the Apaches'll have skinned you by then, anyway, or rather, they won't, because before that you'll have died of thirst. That," says this wag, "is why it's called the Jornada del Muerto—the Dead Man's Journey. There's only one way across it—and that's to fill your mount with water till he leaks, take at least two canteens, start at three in the morning, and go like hell. Because if you don't make it in under twenty-four hours . . . you don't make it. Staying with the river, are you? That's your sort, old fellow—good day to you."[32]

So I crossed the river, like most of the emigrants, and kept to the trail along its west bank; some of them struck out due west, God knows where to. There was less traffic now, and by the time I came to Fra Cristobal I was riding more or less alone. I passed the occasional hamlet and small party of emigrants, but by afternoon of the second day after leaving Socorro it was becoming damned bleak; I pushed on with a great sinister black rock looming across the river to my left, scrubby bushes and hills to the right, and devil a sign of life ahead.

For the first time since Santa Fe I began to feel a chill down my spine; the priest's tales of savage bands who roamed this country filled my mind, with visions of ravaged villages and burned-out wagons; I began to fancy hidden watchers among the rocks and bushes, and whenever a fragment of tumbleweed rolled across my path I had the vapours. Far off a prairie dog yowled, and the wind made a

163

ghostly rustle through the cottonwoods. Dusk came down, my spirits sank with it, and then it was dark, and the chill of the night air sank into my bones.

There was nothing for it but to stop where I was, curl up under a bush, and wait for morning. Not for the life of me was I going to light a fire in that desolation—and on the heels of the thought I caught a glimpse, far off through the gloom, of what might have been a spark of light. I gulped, and slowly went on, leading my horse; the chances were that it was emigrants or hunters . . . then again, perhaps not. It was a light, sure enough; a camp-fire, and a big one. I stood irresolute, and then from the dark ahead a voice made me leap three feet.

"*Ola! Que quiere usted? Quien es usted?*"

I fairly shuddered with relief. "*Amigo! No tiras! Soy forastero!*"

A shape loomed up a few yards ahead, and I saw it was a Mexican in a poncho, rifle at the ready. "*Venga*," says he, so I came forward, and he fell in behind as I led my horse into a clearing under the cottonwoods, where the great fire blazed, with what looked like an antelope roasting over it. There were groups of men seated around smaller fires, some of whom glanced in my direction—buckskin hunters, Mexicans, two or three Indians in shirts, but mostly rough traders or hunters, so far as I could see. Close by the main fire stood a group of three, headed by a burly fellow with feathers in his hat and two pistols belted over his frock-coat; when he turned I saw he had a forked beard and a great red birth-mark over half his face—a Sunday school-teacher, devil a doubt.

"Who're you?" grunts he, in English, and for some reason or other I replied: "Flashman—I'm an Englishman. Going to El Paso."

The cold eyes surveyed me indifferently. "You're late on the road. There's *mole* in the pan, there—'less you want to wait for the buck." And he turned back to the fire, ignoring my thanks.

I hitched my horse with the others, got out my dixie, and was helping myself to stew and tortillas when one of his

164

companions, a tall Mexican in a serape, says: "You go alone to El Paso? It's not safe, amigo; there are Mescaleros in the Jornada, and Jicarilla bands between here and Donna Ana."

"Which way are you going yourselves, then?" says I, and the Mex hesitated and shrugged. Fork-Beard turned for another look at me.

"Chihuahua," says he. "In a week, maybe. Doin' us some huntin' in the Heeley forest. You want to ride with us?" He paused, and then added: "My name's Gallantin—John Gallantin."

It meant nothing to me, but I had a notion it was supposed to. They were watching me warily, and I had to remind myself that in this country men seldom took each other on easy trust. They were a rough crew, but that in itself was not out of the way; they seemed friendly disposed, and if there were Apaches on the loose, as the Mexican said, I'd be a sight safer along with this well-heeled party, even if it took a few days longer.

The Mexican laughed, and winked at me. "Safer to arrive—how you say?—than not get there?"

That wink gave me a momentary qualm for the cargo of dollars in my money-belt, but I was in no case to refuse. "Much obliged to you, Mr Gallantin; I'll ride along with you."

He nodded, and asked had I plenty of charges for my revolver and Colt rifle, whereafter I sat down by one of the smaller fires and gave my attention to the grub, taking stock of the company as I ate. No, they were more like hunters than bandits, at that; some sober citizens among 'em, mostly American, although as much Spanish as English was being spoken. But it was English, with a nice soft brogue, that broke in upon my thoughts.

"I'd ha' sworn the last time I saw you the name was Comber. Flashman, is it? And where have I heard that before, now?" says Grattan Nugent-Hare.

10

Since I had my mouth full, it wouldn't have done to speak, but for a moment I had difficulty swallowing. There he stood, large as life, pulling at his nose, and then he snapped his fingers.

"Eleventh Hussars! That duel . . . at Canterbury, was it? And then Afghanistan, seven–eight years back. You're *that* Flashman?"

My indiscretion could hardly matter down here, so I admitted it, and he gave that slow foxy grin, but with a harder eye than I remembered; there was nothing lazy about the set of him, either.

"Well, well . . . wonders never cease. Didn't I know ye were cavalry? Travelling incog, too. And what might you be doing down this way, so far from Santa Fe—not looking for me, I hope?"

Until that moment I'd absolutely forgotten that this rascal had two thousand of my—well, of Susie's—dollars in his poke. Plainly, this called for tact.

"Far from it," says I. "Have you spent it yet?"

He took a sharp breath, and his hand moved on his belt. "Let's say it's cached in a safe place," says he softly. "And there it'll stay. But ye haven't answered my question: what's your purpose here? Don't tell me ye've left that old strumpet?"

"What's it to you if I have?"

"Faith, ye might have given me warning, and I'd ha' stayed on, so I would." The grin was decidedly unpleasant now. "She'll be needing a man about the place."

I chewed, and looked him up and down, but said nothing, which stung as it was meant to. He gave a bark of a laugh. "Aye, look how ye like," says he. "It's not that kind of look she'd be giving me, at all—or did, while I rogered her fat

166

bottom off all the way from Council Grove. Didn't guess that, did you?—while you were taking the tail of every black wench in sight, more shame to you!" He sat down beside me, well pleased with what he supposed was his bombshell. "Fair mortified at your infidelity, so she was—and her such a fine, hearty woman. Ah, well, she paid you back by making a cuckold of you."

I'd never liked or trusted friend Grattan above half even when he was being civil; now I found him downright detestable. Not, oddly enough, because he'd kept Susie warm—for I didn't doubt his story, and it didn't diminish my affection for her a bit. The randy trot, paying me back in my own coin! And why not?—she'd always known well enough that I was like the tobyman who couldn't be satisfied by one woman any more than a miser could by one guinea, and that I'd stray sooner rather than later. She was another of the same herself. And it was gratifying to realise that she'd been prepared to keep me on, knowing I was unfaithful, and never say a word; quite a compliment. Dear Susie . . . no, my dislike of Grattan was for his own sweet sake, nothing else.

"Ye don't seem to mind?", says he.

"Why should I? She's a lustful bitch, and has to have somebody. I daresay she preferred you to one of the teamsters. Not much, though, or she'd have given you for the asking what you had to steal in the end. I think," says I, rising, "I'll have some coffee."

He was on his feet when I came back, but the foxy grin was absent and the voice less soft than usual. "I don't care for the word 'steal', d'ye know? Especially from a man that's ashamed to use his own name."

"Then stay out of his way," says I, sipping. "He can stand it."

"Can he so? Well, and he'd better stay out of mine," says he nastily. "And if he has any clever ideas about a certain sum of money, he'd best forget 'em, d'ye see? I've seen you in action, my Afghan hero, and I'm not a bit impressed." He tapped his Colt butt.

I weighed him up. "Tell me, Grattan," says I. "Did Susie ever cry over you?"

"What's that? Why the devil should she?" asks he suspiciously.

"Why, indeed?" says I, and ignored him, and after a moment he swaggered off, but continued to keep an eye on me. He couldn't believe my arrival had nothing to do with his theft, and certainly it was an odd chance that had brought us together again; no doubt he too was on the run for Mexico. I'd have set his doubts at rest if he'd been less offensive about Susie, but he'd proved himself a cheap creature, without style. Chainy Tenth, what would you? I kept my eye on him, too, and when we bedded down I changed my place after an hour—and in the morning saw that so had he.

We were away before dawn, and I saw that the group was about forty strong and well able to look after itself, riding two and two, with point and flank scouts. In the afternoon Gallantin sent two Indians ahead to find a camp-site; they came back at the gallop, and conferred with Gallantin and the tall Mexican, constantly pointing ahead; I was too far back to hear, but the way the word "'Pash!" rippled down the column, and men began to look to their priming and tighten their girths, said all that was necessary. We went on at the canter, until we smelled smoke, and then in a big clearing among the woods we came on a burning hacienda, a splendid place it must have been, but now a blackened ruin with the flames still licking on its charred walls, and a dense pall of smoke overhead.

There were bodies huddled about the place, and a few slaughtered beasts, but no one gave them even a look; the party scattered on Gallantin's orders, hunting among the outbuildings and stables, and the Indians circled about the limits, their eyes on the ground. Presently there were shouts, and I went with three or four others to where a couple of our buckskin men were kneeling beside a trough, supporting the body of a small, white-haired woman; they'd found her crouched under a blanket in an outhouse, but even when they'd given her water, she could only gaze about in a stupified way—and then she began to sing, in an awful cracked voice, and laughed crazily, so they laid her down on the blanket and resumed their search.

I went with the tall Mexican—and found more than I wanted to. Behind the hacienda were other smaller houses, all of them smouldering wrecks, and among them more bodies, scalped and mutilated. They were all peons, so far as I could bear to look at them, with flies buzzing thick about them; the Mexican stooped over one.

"Dead less than an hour," says he. "A few minutes earlier, by the guts of God, and we would have had them!" He grimaced. "See there."

I looked, and stood horrified. Only a few yards away, by a high adobe wall, was a row of trees, and from their branches hung at least a dozen bodies, naked, and so hideously mutilated that your first thought was of carcases slung in a butcher's shop, streaked with blood. They were all hung by the heels, about a foot above the ground, and beneath each one a fire was still smouldering, directly under the heads—if you can call 'em heads after they've burst open.

"They stayed long enough fer fun, anyway," says one of the buckskin men, and spat. Then he turned away with a shrug, and said something to his partner, and they both laughed.

That was the most horrible thing of all—not the hanging bodies, or the scalped corpses, or the vile stench, but the fact that none of Gallantin's followers *paid the slightest heed*. No one bothered with a body, except the Mexican when he pronounced on the dead peon; for the rest they just hunted among the ruins, and whatever they were bent on, it had nothing to do with the two score or more poor devils who'd been murdered and tortured in that ghastly shambles. I've served with some hard cases, but never with any who didn't betray horror or disgust or pity or at least *interest* at such beastly sights. But not this bunch of ruffians.

Then there was a yell from the other side of the hacienda, and everyone gathered where Gallantin and the Indians were examining a ball of horse dung in the dust. There was a great buzz of talk as an Indian and a bearded trapper poked and sniffed, and then the trapper cries: "Gramma!" and held up a peck of ordure for inspection. I didn't know then that these Indians and frontiersmen could tell from the age and composition of droppings just where a horse has come from, and who owns it, and what his grandfather had for luncheon two weeks ago, damned near. (Maize seeds in the crap mean Mexicans, and barley Americans, in case you're interested.)

Another Indian was crawling about, examining the ground, and presently comes up to Gallantin and says: "Mimbreno."

"Copper Mines band, for sure," says Gallantin. "How many?" The Indian opened and closed his hands nine times, rapidly. "Ninety ponies, eh? Maybe two hours off by now, but I doubt it. Headin' west. Hey, Ilario—that smoke t'other day. Could be a camp, huh? Ninety ponies, could be a couple o' hundred 'Pash."

"That's forty, fifty thousand dollars," says someone, and there were yells and laughs and cries of hooraw, boys, while they brandished their pieces and slapped each other on the back.

"Hey, Jack—that's better'n beaver, I rackon!"

"Better'n a plug a plew o' black fox, ye mean!"

"That's your style! Mimbreno ha'r's the prime crop this year!"

I'm not hearing right, thinks I, or else they're crazy. I couldn't make out why they were suddenly in such spirits; what was there in this ghastly place to be satisfied about, let alone delighted? And I wasn't alone, as it turned out; Ilario, the tall Mexican, roared to us all to saddle up, and when we came back to the group about Gallantin, all became suddenly, and shockingly, clear.

Two fellows, one a plain, bearded emigrant sort whom I'd noted as a sober file the previous night, and the other a youngster of about twenty, were in hot argument with Gallantin; I came in towards the finish, when the sober chap was shaking his fist and crying, no, damned if he would, so there. Gallantin, hunched in his saddle, glared at him in fury and flung out a hand to point at the burned-out hacienda.

"Don't you give a dam 'bout that, then? You don't car' that them red snakes butcher an' burn our folks? You one

170

o' these bastard Injun-lovers, seem-like! Hey, boys; hyar's a feller sweet on th' Pashes!"

There was a growl from the assembled riders, but the sober card shouted above it. "I give a damn, too! But I ain't no scalp hunter! There's a law fer them redsticks, an' I rackon th' Army can deal with 'em—" This was drowned in a roar of derision, Gallantin's eye rolled with rage, and he fairly spat his reply.

"Th' Army, by Christ! A sight o' good th' Army done this place! You ain't no scalp-hunter, says you! Then what the hell you jine wi' us fer?"

"We didn't know what you wuz!" cries the youth.

"You thunk we wuz some ole ladies' knittin' party, by the holy?"

"Come on, Lafe," says the sober card in disgust. "Let 'em git their blood-money ifn they wants." He swung into his saddle, and the young fellow followed suit. "Scalp-hunters!" growls the other, and swung his mount away.

"Whar th' hell you think you goin'?" bawls Gallantin, in a huge fury.

"Away from you," snaps the youth, and followed his partner.

"Come back hyar! You ain't goin' ter put the sojers after us, by God!" And he would have spurred after them, I believe, but Ilario snapped his fingers at one of the Indians, and quicker than light the brute whipped out his hatchet, and flung it after the departing pair. It hit the youth square in the back with a sickening smack; he screamed, and pitched from the saddle with that awful thing buried in his spine, and as his partner wheeled Ilario shot him twice. The sober chap rolled slowly past his horse's head and fell beside the other; his horse whinnied and bolted; Ilario spun the smoking pistol in his hand, and Gallantin cursed horribly at the two fallen men. The youth was flopping about, with awful gasps, then he was still. No one moved.

"They'd ha' put the sojers on us," says Gallantin. "Waal, thar they be! Any other chile o' thar mind?"

I knew one who was—not to notice, though, and if any others shared my doubts they kept quiet about it. It had happened with such fell speed, and now it was done there was only stony indifference on the bearded, savage faces of the band. Not all were indifferent, though; the Indian retrieved his hatchet, and called an inquiry to Ilario, who nodded. The Indian drew his knife, stooped over the youth, grunted with disgust, and stepped instead to the corpse of the older man. He knelt, seized the hair, made one swift circle with his point, and dragged off the scalp with brutal force. He stuffed the awful bloody thing into his belt, and then one of the hunters, a huge, pock-marked ruffian, slipped from his saddle.

"This coon don't see three hunner' dollars goin' ter waste!" cries he, and no one said a word while he scalped the dead youth. "Rackon it's good as Mimbreno ha'r, boys!" He grinned round, bloody knife in one hand and dripping scalp in the other.

"Good as squaw's ha'r, mebbe," cries another. "Kinder fine, Bill!" A few of the others laughed, and I noticed Grattan was wearing that foxy half-grin as he sat and tugged at his long nose. Myself, I reflected that here was another good anecdote for the next church social, and studied to look unconcerned. What else was there to do?

For like it or not, I was fairly stuck, and while I had much food for thought as we headed westward into the evening sun, there could be only one conclusion. Here I was, by the most awful freak of chance, among a band of those scalp-hunters of whom young Harrison had spoken, but whom I had supposed no longer existed now that American law governed the land; it was flattery of a kind, I supposed, that Gallantin had looked me over and thought me worth recruiting—I recalled our brief conversation of last night, and the way he had spoken his name; he wasn't to know that he was addressing perhaps the one man in New Mexico to whom it meant nothing. I'd ride along with him, I'd said in my innocence, and there was nothing else for it. Even without the fearful example of those two scalped deserters, I'd never have dared to quit, in a countryside alive apparently with the kind of fiends who had wrought the destruction of the hacienda. It was an irony that I was too terrified to

172

appreciate, that my one hope lay in the company of these foul brutes who were carrying me mile by mile closer to battle, murder, and sudden death which I could only hope would not be mine.

We rode the sun down, and pushed on into steep country of hills covered with pine and cedar, with only the briefest of halts while Gallantin and Ilario conversed with our Indians. Mile after mile we went, through that fragrant maze, and the order came back to eat from our saddle-bags as we rode, for Gallantin had the scent and knew exactly where he wanted to go. God knows how many miles it was, or how he and the others were so sure of the way; I can night-foray as well as most by the stars, but in those dense bottoms and ravines, or along those precipitous hillsides, thick with trees, I lost all sense of direction. But I know we rode fourteen hours from the hacienda, and I was beginning to believe my Arab must founder under me when a halt was called.

But even then it was only to take to the woods on foot, groping through the night with your hand at one man's belt while another held you behind, trying for dear life not to thrash about like a mad bear in a cane-break, gripping your rifle and gritting your teeth against the pain of saddle-sore buttocks. I became aware that the sky was getting lighter, and Ilario, who led my line, urged us on with whispers; once he stopped and pointed, and over the bushy ridge ahead was a dim reddish glow that was not of the dawn. Oh, Jesus, thinks I, now for it, as we pressed forward slowly up the slope, testing each step before we took it, no longer in touch but each for himself with Ilario ahead. Then it was down on our bellies and crawl; the dark was thin enough to see the man either side and Ilario in front, as he motioned us forward. We reached the summit of the ridge, and lay screened among the bushes, drenched in sweat and like to drop—but in no danger, I assure you, of dozing off.

To explain, as I understood the thing later: Gallantin had identified the marauders as Mimbreno Apaches of the Santa Rita Copper Mines, which lay some distance to the south. He had suspected the presence of a camp of them in this fastness of the Gila forest, a sort of temporary base to which this particular band had moved, no doubt for game; Apaches, you must know, are almost entirely nomadic, and will move on after a week or a few months, as they feel inclined. They build no permanent houses; their home, as they say, is their fireplace. Gallantin had further calculated that after their successful attack on the hacienda, they would return to camp, there to whoop it up in celebration and gorge and booze on *tizwin* and cactus-juice, and keep the girls in stitches with accounts of how their flayed victims had wriggled over the fires. By dawn he reckoned they would be well under—and here it was dawn, the rays striking down through the trees into the little valley, and on the heights about Gallantin and Co. were ready to go into business. (I wondered if Lieutenant Harrison knew that the going rate for Apache hair was now $300 a pelt. Better than beaver, indeed.)

Beneath us was a narrow, rocky defile, with a brook running through it, broadening into a goodish stream at a point where the defile itself opened out briefly into a level space of about an acre before it closed again to a rocky gorge. On the level space was the Indian village, and behind it rocks rose almost sheer for seventy feet to a forested lip. On our side, the slope down was steep, and studded with bushes; the ends of the defile were thick-wooded clefts. A splendid lurking-place, in fact, provided it was never found; Gallantin had found it, and so it had become a death-trap. If the Apaches had posted sentries, I suppose they had been dealt with—but I doubt if they had. Flown with triumph, confident of their remote security, they wouldn't see the need.

I half-expected that we would rush the place at dawn (and wasn't relishing a mêlée in the valley-bottom) and indeed that is what would have happened if the village had been in an open place with avenues of escape. What I had overlooked was that this wasn't a military or punitive expedition: it was hunting. The one aim was to kill the quarry and take its pelt, at sixty quid the time. If your game can scatter, you must pounce and take it by surprise; when it's fish in a barrel, your best road is to sit safe on the edge and destroy

174

it at leisure. (I tried to explain this once in an article to *The Field* entitled "The Human Quarry as Big Game, and the Case for and against Preserving", in which I laboured the point that to scalp-hunters the Apaches were no different from bear or wolf or antelope—of course they hated the brutes, but they ain't too sweet on wolf or lion, either, and a hunter's hate tends to be in proportion to his fear of the quarry. Oh, there were some to whom the lust of slaughter was sweeter than the scalp-price—folk who'd had families murdered and tortured and enslaved by these savages, or those, like myself that day, who perfectly enjoyed paying back what had been done at the hacienda—but for most it was a matter of business and profit. I cited the case I've described to you in which the hunters scalped two of their own kind, and pointed out that there were those in New Mexico at that time who claimed that Gallantin's practice of selling any hair he could get—Mexican, American, friendly Indian, and the like—was ethically unsound; it gave scalp-hunting a bad name, they said. *The Field* didn't print my piece; limited interest, you may say, but I hold that it's a matter worth serious discussion, and would have provoked a fine correspondence.)

So we waited, as the light grew until we could easily see the sprawl of wickiups on the level ground beyond the stream—they're big skin igloos with willow frames, perhaps twenty feet across, and can hold a family with ease, with a hole on top to let out smoke and stink. The whole place was filthy with refuse, and a few curs were prowling among it; here and there a human being was to be seen—a couple of braves sprawled and presumably drunk in the open; an old woman kindling a fire; a boy playing at the stream. Down near the gorge end was a rough corral in which were about a hundred ponies. Ilario passed whispered word of the range: a hundred and twenty yards. I looked to my caps, eased out my pistol, and examined my revolving rifle, head well down in the rough grass of the crest. There were about fifteen of us spread along it, five yards apart; the remainder of our band were evenly divided among the trees at either end of the defile. Nothing could get in or out. Nothing did.

The place began to stir, and I got my first look at the famous Apaches—the Sheeshinday, "Men of the Woods", or as they are widely and simply known, "the enemy". I'd had an impression that they were small, but not so. These, being Mimbreno of the Copper Mines, were not among the largest; even so, they were sturdy, well-made brutes, ugly as sin, and lithe and easy in their movements. Their hair was long and undressed, and while some wore it bound in a scarf, most were bare-headed except for a brow-circlet; a few were in shirts and leggings, many wore only the breech-clout. The women, in tunics, were buxom peasants— no tall, willowy jungle princesses here; their voices, shrill and sharp, floated across the stream as they fetched water or busied themselves at the fires, with the kidneys and kedgeree, no doubt. A few braves sauntered down to the corral, others sat outside the wickiups to yawn and gossip, and one or two began to paint, an operation which seemed to call for much care, and criticism from bystanders.

There must have been more than a hundred and fifty in view when one fellow in fringed leggings and a blanket stood forth and told the others to fall in, at which most of the men drifted in his direction to listen—the hunter next to me snapped his fingers softly and nodded, cocking his piece; I passed the signal on, and lay with my heart thumping. At a whispered word I pushed the rifle cautiously forward, covering a stout savage on the edge of the main group, my foresight just above his rump; I won't pretend I had a vision of those bodies at the hacienda, or any nonsense of that sort—he was a target, and any soldier, from the saintly Gordon downwards, would tell you the same . . . crack!

The shot came from the gorge, and the whole rim of the valley exploded in fire and smoke. I squeezed off, and saw my savage leap and topple sideways; around him they were falling, and the whole camp boiled with dust and re-echoed with screams and the boom of shots as we poured our fire into them point-blank; I missed a tall fellow, but spun another round as he bolted towards the corral, and then I was firing steadily into the brown.

It was deadlier than a Gatling, for here each man was a

marksman, and there were forty of us with six-shot rifles, except for one or two long-gun eccentrics who never missed anyway. A Sharp's fires six to the minute, and a Colt rifle considerably faster. Within two minutes there wasn't a live male Indian to be seen, and the ground was littered with bodies, none of 'em wounded, for any that kicked became instantly the target for half a dozen rifles. About a dozen had reached the corral, and came out like bats along the stream, but they got no distance; a few more dashed frantically through the water towards our position, and were cut down before they'd got half way up the hill. The slaughter was all but complete.

There remained the wickiups, and now our own Indians emerged at either end of the defile, with burning arrows which they shot methodically into the skins. There were shrieks from within as the lodges began to burn, and out dashed the females, with here and there a brave among them; the men were picked off while the women screamed and milled about like ants; one or two may have been hit as they ran blindly among the flaming wickiups, or cowered at the foot of the cliff behind. Round the lip of the valley hung a great wreath of powder smoke as our fire ceased; now there was no sound except the dry crackle of the burning wickiups, and the muted wails of terrified women and children.

Parties of hunters broke from the trees at either end of the defile, and Ilario stood up and waved us down the hill. We went quiet and careful, without whoop or halloo, because there had been no victory, and hunters don't yell and caper when they've downed their quarry. There were one or two shots, as victims were made certain, and a few shouted commands; for the rest we splashed in silence through the stream to the corpse-strewn camp, where Gallantin was waiting.

Guards were posted on the women and horses, and then out came the knives as they prepared to do what they had come to do. I shan't horrify you with more detail than I must, but one or two points should be recorded for history's sake. One was made by a buckskin hunter who was divesting a corpse of all the skin and hair above its ears, at which his mate, neatly removing the top-knot from another head, remarked that the first chap was being unnecessarily thorough, surely, to which the buckskin man replied that the Chihuahua authorities liked to see a *full* scalp.

"Ye see, some sonsabitches," says he as he panted and sawed away, "has bin takin' *two* scalps offn wun haid, so the Mexes is grown chary o' *leetle* scalps. Yew want yore full money, yew tek th' hull shebang! Come *hup*, ye bastard! Thar, now!"

Another thing I noted was that all scalps went into a common pile, which a popular novelist would no doubt describe as "reeking"—heaven knows why. They don't reek; en masse they look like a cheap and greasy black rug. Gallantin stood by and kept careful count as they were salted; there were a hundred and twenty-eight all told.

You may wonder if I took a scalp. The answer is no. For one thing, I wouldn't touch an Indian's hair on a bet, and for another, it's a skilled job. It did cross my mind, though, as something *to have done*, if you follow me—as I wrote for *The Field*, it's a nice point which trophy on your wall does you greater credit, the head of a pretty, gentle impala, or a switch of hair marked "Mimbreno Apache, Gila forest, '49". I even wandered across the stream to one of the bodies that had fallen on the hillside, and considered it a moment, and then came away quickly. He must have been all of eight years old.

That was the point at which I was sickened, I confess— by that and the cold, brisk efficiency with which the scalpers worked. There were a few crazy ones who obviously enjoyed it—I was intrigued to see Grattan red to the wrists, with a wild look in his eye—but for most of them it was no more than chopping wood. And if you cry out on them, as you should—well, be thankful that you weren't born along the Del Norte, and the matter never arose for you.

As for the massacre itself, I've been on t'other end too often to worry overmuch. The scalping was beastly, but I couldn't regret the dead Apaches, any more than Nana's people regretted us at Cawnpore. And if you've marched in the Kabul retreat, or fled from Isandhlwana, or scaled the Alma—well, the sight of six score Indians piled up without any tops to their heads may not be pretty, but when you reflect on what deserving cases they were, you don't waste much pity on them.

I won't say I was at my cheeriest, though, or that I ate much at noon, and I was quite happy to be one of a party that Galantin sent out to circle the valley for Indian sign. There wasn't any—which is the worst sign of all, let me tell you—and we came back at evening to find the camp cleared up, with a great fire going, and the real devil's work about to begin.

You will remember that the women had been rounded up, more or less unharmed, and if I'd thought about them at all I dare say I'd have concluded that they would be spared, give or take a quiet rape or so. In fact, I discovered that the habit of Gallantin's gang of charmers was to while away the night with them, and *then* slaughter and scalp them the next day—along with the children. If you doubt me, consult Mr Dunn's scholarly work*, among a score of others, and note that the *proyecto* made distinctions of age and sex only by price.

I was eating my stew like a good lad, and washing it down with more corn beer than was good for me, when Ilario came over to where I and a couple of others were sitting; he carried a leather bag, which he shook and proffered; not thinking, I reached in like the others, and came out with a white pebble; theirs were black, at which they cussed roundly, and Ilario grinned and jerked his thumb.

"*Felicitaciones*, amigo! You first!" cries he, and wondering I followed him over to where the main party were seated round the great fire, with Gallantin in the place of honour; three hunters were ranged before him, grins on their ugly faces as their mates chaffed them and they answered with lewd boasts and gestures. Then I saw the four Indian women

*J. P. Dunn's famous *Massacres of the Mountains*, 1886.

off to one side, and understood; presumably they were the pick of the crop, for all were young, and presentable as squaws can be in dirty buckskin and an agony of fear.

"He the last?" cries Gallantin, and if you had seen that blotched, fork-bearded face, and the crowd leering and haw-hawing either side of him, you'd ask no better models for Satan and his infernal crew. They'd been brisk and disciplined enough in action, but now they'd been at the *tizwin* and cactus juice, and the true beastliness was on the surface as they waited eager for their sport.

"Now, then, Ilario, look alive!" shouts Gallantin, and Ilario faced us with his back to the squaws. "Who shall have her?" Gallantin was pointing at one of the girls, unseen by Ilario, who grinned and kept everyone in suspense before indicating a squat, bearded fellow next to me.

The brute whooped and rushed to grab his prize—and to my disgust he set about her then and there, in front of everyone! How they yelled and cheered, those charmers; I can see their bestial, grinning faces still, and the bearded man on top of the struggling squaw, his backside going like a fiddler's elbow. Gallantin yelled above the din for the second girl, and again Ilario named a man; this one at least had the decency to haul her away, half-fainting as she was, to some private place, pursued by the groans of that mob of devils. Then it was the third girl, and this time Ilario pointed to me.

"Goddam!" yelled the ape beside me. "I wanted that 'un!" and they cat-called with delight at his disappointment. "Hooraw, Jem—don't ye wish ye cud! Haw-haw, she's yore sort, though." And as he made off with the last wench, they egged me on to be at the third one. "Go on, hoss—lay aboard! Whut—he's th' Englishman? I say, ole feller, give 'er th' Union Jack, haw-haw!"

If she'd been Cleopatra, I wouldn't have wanted her, not then. I'd never felt less like venery in my life, not in that ghastly place, after the sights I'd seen, and with that obscene mob about me; even apart from that, she did not prepossess—which shows how wrong you can be. As I looked across at her, I saw only an Indian girl in a grubby fringed tunic, with long braids of hair round a chubby, dust-stained face; the only thing different about her was that where the others had cowered and trembled, she was straight as a ramrod and looked dead ahead; if she was frightened, it didn't show.

"Go on!" roars Gallantin. "What ails ye, man? Go git 'er!" And he seized her by the shoulder and thrust her forward at my feet. Nice point of etiquette—I didn't know what to do, in that company, as they roared drunken encouragement and vile instruction, and the bearded man and his victim heaved and gasped on the ground a couple of yards away. Turned on my heel, possibly, or said "Your bird"; my girl scrambled to her feet, eyes wide now and fists clenched, and for no good reason that I can think of, I shook my head at her as I stood irresolute. The mob bayed and bellowed, and then a well-known voice sang out:

"He can't! The great soft Limey bugger! Well, here's one'll deputise for him, so he will!" And Grattan Nugent-Hare stood forth, a trifle unsteady on his feet, flushed with *tizwin*, and a triumphant sneer on his face as he reached for the girl.

Now, I ain't proud, and I'll run from a fight as fast as any; if it had been another man I don't doubt I'd have swallowed the insult and slunk off. But this was the detestable Grattan, who'd bulled Susie unbeknownst, and had a nasty long nose, and gave himself airs—and was three parts foxed, anyway, by the look of him. He was unprepared, too, as he grabbed the girl by the wrist—and my temper boiled over. I lashed out with all my strength and caught him full in the face; he went back like a stone from a sling, into the circle of watchers, who whooped with glee—and then he was on his feet like a cat, his nose spurting blood, mad rage in his eyes and a hatchet in his hand.

There wasn't time to run. I ducked his murderous stroke and sprang away, and Gallantin yelled: "Hyar, boyee!", jerked out his Bowie, and flipped it towards me. I fumbled and grabbed it, diving aside as Grattan swiped at me again. His hatchet head nicked the very edge of my left hand, and enraged by pain and terror, I hacked at his face; a Bowie is not a knife, by the way, but a two-foot pointed cleaver, and if I'd got home it would have been brains for supper, but he caught my wrist. In a frenzy of panic I flung my weight at him and down we went, Flashy on top, but drunk or not, he was agile as a lizard and wriggled out from under, letting drive with that razor-sharp axe as we regained our feet. It whisked so close above my head I believe it touched my hair, but before he could swing again I had my left hand on his throat and would have been well set to disembowel him if he hadn't seized my wrist again. I was bellowing with rage and funk, throwing up my left elbow to hamper his axe-hand; strong as he may have been, he was no match for Flash in brute coward strength, and I bore him back in a great staggering run and with one almighty heave pitched him headlong into the fire.

There was a terrific yell from the onlookers as he rolled out, sparks flying and his shirt smouldering. I'd have run then, but seeing him helpless I leaped on him, stabbing the earth by mistake in my eagerness. He hacked and clawed, and as we grappled on our knees I butted him hard in the face; it jolted him sideways, but he surged up at me again, axe raised, and I just managed to block his arm as he let drive. The jar of our forearms knocked me back; he hurled himself on top of me, and gave a horrible shriek of agony; his face was only inches from mine, mouth wide and eyes glaring—and then I felt his body go limp and realised that my right hand was being drenched with something warm. It was gripping the Bowie, and the blade had impaled Nugent-Hare as he fell on me.

I flung him off, and as I scrambled up he rolled over and lay with the hilt protruding from his midriff. For a moment I was rooted with shock; there lay the corpse, and just beyond it was the bearded fellow still on top of his squaw, his eyes round in fear and amazement. That was how quickly it had happened: a mere few seconds of fevered hacking and struggling, with no respite for truce or flight, and Nugent-Hare was in a pool of blood, his eyes sightless in the fire-glare, with that awful thing in his body.

There was dead silence as I stood in a daze, my right

hand dripping blood. I stared round at the faces—astonished, curious, frozen in grins, or just plain interested. Gallantin came forward, stooped, and there was an involuntary gasp from the watchers as he retrieved the knife. He glanced from me to the girl, who stood petrified, her hands to her mouth. Gallantin nodded.

"Waal, hoss," says he to me, conversational-like, "I reckon you earned her for the night."

That was all. No outcry, no protest, no other observation even. By their lights it had been fair, and that was that. (I put it to a good silk, years later, and he said a civilised court would have given me two years for manslaughter.) At the time, I was numb; he wasn't the first I'd killed hand-to-hand, by any means—there'd been Iqbal's nigger at Mogala, a Hova guard in Madagascar, and dear old de Gautet dipping his toe in the water at the Jotunschlucht, but they'd been with my eyes open, so to speak, not in a mad, sudden brawl that was over, thank God, before it had well begun.

Stupified as I was, some instinct must have told me not to refuse Gallantin's invitation a second time—it's a good rule, as I hope I've demonstrated, that when scalp-hunters offer you a squaw, you should take her away quick and quiet, and if you don't fancy her, then teach her the two times table, or "Tintern Abbey", or how to tie a sheepshank. I think I may have taken her wrist, and no doubt my aspect conquered resistance, for next thing I knew I was leaning against a tree in the grove beyond the corral, being sick, while she stood like a graven image and watched me. When I'd recovered I sat down and looked at her, not carnally you understand, but bemused-like. It was middling dim, away from the fires, and I beckoned her so that I could see her face; she came, and I examined her.

She was plump-cheeked, as I've said, and under the grime by no means ill-favoured. Rather a hooked little nose, small sullen mouth, and slanted eyes under a broad brow; she didn't smell unpleasant, either, although her tunic was filthy and torn. What was under it looked passable enough, too, but I was too shaken and fagged out to care. She looked down at me wide-eyed, but not fearful—and then she did

183

an extraordinary thing. She suddenly dropped to her knees, took one of my hands between both of hers, stared at me closely, and said: "*Gracias.*"

I was quite taken aback. "*Entiende Español?*", and she nodded and said: "*Si.*" Then after a moment she looked back towards the firelight and shivered, and when she turned her face again there were tears in her eyes and her mouth was open and tremulous. "*Muchas gracias!*" she sobbed, and dropped her head on my knees and clung to my legs and had a fine bawl to herself.

Well, one likes to be appreciated, so I patted her head and murmured some commonplace, at which she raised her face and looked at me dumbly; then she heaved a great sniffing sigh, but rather spoiled the effect by turning aside to spit copiously. She mopped at her tears, and continued to watch me, very grave, so to cheer her up I tapped her cheek and gave her the polite smile I reserve for females on whom I have no designs. She smiled back timidly, showing rather pretty teeth; it occurred to me that when washed and combed and stripped she'd be perfectly presentable, and since I was feeling rather more settled now I placed a hand gently on her shoulder. Her eyes widened a fraction, but no more, so I gave her my impish grin and very slowly slid my hand inside her tunic neck, so that she had every opportunity to start or shudder. She didn't; her eyes were as solemn as ever, but her lips parted on a little gasp, and she kneeled upright as I took hold—by Jove, it was A1 material, and quite restored me. I squeezed and stroked her lightly, asking myself was she all for it or merely steeling herself for the inevitable; I *do* prefer 'em willing, so I kissed her lightly and asked: "*Con su permiso?*"

She started at that, quite bewildered for a moment; then her eyes lowered, and I'll swear she stifled a smile, for she glanced at me sidelong and gave that little lift of the chin that's the coquette's salute from Tunbridge Wells to Pago Pago, as she murmured: "*Como quiera usted.*"

I pulled her on to my knee, and kissed her properly—and if you've been told that Indians don't know how, it's a lie. And I was just slipping her tunic from her shoulders when an odd movement in the distant firelight caught my eye through the thin branches which partly shielded us.

A man appeared to be dancing beside the fire—and then I saw it was not a dance but an agonised stagger, as he clutched at something protruding from his neck. His scream echoed through the trees, to be drowned in a crash of gunfire and whistle of shafts, figures leaped up around the fire, men shouted and ran and fell in confusion, and my pearl of the forest was hurled aside as I sprang to my feet. From the woods all about sounded blood-freezing whoops, shots boomed and echoed along the valley, bodies were rushing through the thickets. All this in a second; I could see Gallantin by the fire, rifle raised, and then he and the whole scene before me slowly turned upside down and slid from view; my body shook and a numbness in my head turned to a blinding pain as I fell forward into darkness.

11

There's no question that a public school education is an advantage. It may not make you a scholar or a gentleman or a Christian, but it does teach you to survive and prosper—and one other invaluable thing: style. I've noted that Grattan-Hare didn't have it, and you know what happened to him. I, on the other hand, have always had style by the cart-load, and it saved my life in the Gila forest in '49, no error.

Thus: any other of Gallantin's band, given possession of my Apache lass, would have gone at her bull at a gate. I, once I'd decided on reflection that I might as well rattle her as not, set about it with a deal of finesse—chiefly, I admit, because it's better sport that way. But I knew how to *go about it*, that's the point, patiently and smoothly and with . . . style.

You must understand the effect of this, of Flashy imposing his winning ways on that fortunate native wench. There she was, a helpless prisoner in the hands of the most abominable ruffians in North America, who had butchered her menfolk before her eyes and were about to subject her to repeated rape, possible torture, and certain death. Up jumps this strapping chap with splendid whiskers, who not only kills out of hand the cad who is molesting her, but thereafter treats her kindly, pets her patiently, and absolutely asks permission to squeeze her boobies. She is astonished, nay gratified, and, since she's a randly little minx at bottom, ready to succumb with pleasure. All thanks to style, as inculcated by Dr Arnold, though I wouldn't expect him to claim credit for it.

And mark the sequel. When other of her tribesmen, having got wind of the massacre, attack the scalp-hunters by night, she is alarmed for her protector. If he joins in the scrap—the last thing I'd have done, but she wasn't to know that—harm may come to him, so being a lass of spirit she ensures his neutrality by clouting him behind the ear with a rock. Then, when her tribesmen have wiped out or captured most of the marauders (Gallantin and a few others alone escaped)[33] she is at pains to preserve her saviour from the general vengeance. Had he been a man without style, she'd have been the first to set about him with a red-hot knife.

Mind you, luck was on my side, too. Had *she* been any common Indian wench, it would have been Flashy, b. 1822, d. 1849, R.I.P. and not even a line in the *Gazette*, for her rescuers wouldn't have heeded her for an instant; I'd have been just another white scalp-hunter on whom to practise their abominations. But since she happened to be Sonsee-array, the Morning-Star-Takes-Away-Clouds-Woman, fourth and dearest daughter of Mangas Colorado, the great Red Sleeves, chief of the Mimbreno, lord of the Gila, and scourge of plain, forest and mountain from the Llanos Estacados to the Big-Canyon-Dug-by-God, and since she was also famous for having more beads and trinkets than any other female since time began, and for never having worked in her young life—well, even a Bronco brave with blood in his eye takes notice, and decides to humour her.

So they contented themselves with stripping and hanging my unconscious carcase upside down from the cottonwoods, along with those of a dozen other scalp-hunters who'd been unlucky enough to survive the attack. They then built fires under us in the approved fashion, but at Sonsee-array's insistence refrained from lighting mine until she had stated her case to the great man. Meanwhile they beguiled the time by slowly removing the skins from my fellow-unfortunates, a process in which she and the other squaws gleefully joined. Mercifully, I was dead to the world.

When I came to I was blind, with a thunderstorm drumming in my skull, and my whole body in torment; to make matters worse, a voice nearby was alternately babbling for mercy in Spanish and screeching in agony—that, though I didn't know it, was Ilario being flayed alive on the next tree.

The screams died away to a whimper, with an awful distant chorus of cries and groans and hellish laughter; closer at hand voices were talking in a mixture of Spanish and some language I didn't understand.

I struggled to force my eyes open, trying to get to my feet but not able to find ground anywhere—that's what it's like to come awake when you're hanging upside down. I was floating, it seemed, while my feet were being torn away; then my eyes opened, I could smell smoke and blood, and before me were human figures the wrong way up—and then I realised where I was, and the ghastly sight of those bodies at the hacienda flashed across my mind, and I tried to scream, but couldn't.

"*Porque no?*" were the first words I made out. "Why not?", in a double bass croak so deep it was difficult to believe it came from a human being (I'm not so sure, from my later acquaintance with him, that it did). A woman's voice answered, high and fierce, mostly in Spanish, but there were men's voices trying to interrupt her, and in shouting them down she sometimes lapsed into the unknown tongue which I guessed must be Apache.

"Because he was good to me! When the others, like that dog-dirt there—" there was a horrid smack, and yells of laughter as she took a swipe at the unhappy Ilario "—would have raped and killed me—*he* fought for me, and slew a man, and used me gently! Are you all deaf? He is not evil, like these others!"

"He has white eyes!" shouts some curmudgeon. "Why should he be spared?"

"Because I say so! Because *he* saved me while you cowards were asleep, or hiding, or . . . or defecating under a bush! *I* say he shall not die! I ask my father for his life! And his eyes are *not* white—they are dark!"

"He is *pinda-lickoyee*—the enemy! He is Americano, scalp-taker, butcher of children! Look at the bodies of our people, mutilated by these beasts—"

"*He* did not do it—if he had, why should he help me?"

"Huh!" sulkily, and knowing grunts. "All men help *you*!

Evil men as well as good—you know the art of getting help."

"Liar! Pig! Bastard! Ugly lump of rotten buffalo dung—"

"*Basta!*" It was the bass voice again. "If he doesn't die, what will you do with him? Make him a slave?"

That seemed to be a facer for her; she wasn't sure, and there were sceptical grunts and sneers, which drove her wild. In a passion she cried that she was a chief's daughter and would please herself. The sense of the meeting seemed to be, oh, hoity-toity miss, and the leader of the opposition said no doubt she would want to marry the white-eyed villain . . . you understand that I give you the gist of the conversation, so well as I heard and understood it.

"And if I chose to, what then?" cries madam. "He is braver and more beautiful than any of you! You stink! Black Knife stinks! El Chico stinks! The Yawner stinks! And you, Vasco—you stink worst of all!"

"Do we all stink, then, except this creature? Does your own father stink?" The bass voice sounded closer, and through blurred eyes I made out two massive legs beneath a hide kilt, and huge booted feet. "He is big, even for an Americano. Big as a Striped Arrow*."

"Not as big as you, father," says she, sweet and tactful. "Nor as strong. But he is bigger and stronger and fiercer and faster and prettier than Vasco. But then—a Digger's arse is prettier than that!"

I must have fainted, for that's all I remember until a strange period of half-consciousness in which I was aware of women's voices muttering, and hands working on my body with what I suppose was grease or ointment, and being given a drink, and the pain ebbing from my head. At one time I was in a wickiup, and a dirty old crone was spooning some mush of meat and corn into me; again, I was being carried on a stretcher, with open sky and branches passing overhead. But it was all confused with evil dreams of hanging upside down among flames, and then I was plunged

*Cheyenne.

head-foremost into the icy depths under Jotunberg with Rudi Starnberg's wild laugh ringing in my ears. Women's faces swam up through the water towards me—Elspeth blonde and lovely and smiling, Lola sleepy-eyed with lips pursed in mockery, Cleonie pale and beautiful and very close as she hummed softly: "Oh-ho-ho, avec mes sabots!", and as her mouth closed on mine it was Susie who teased and fondled and smothered me in flesh, which would have been capital if we had not been upside-down with fellows arguing in Spanish, among them Arnold who said that *all* scalp-hunters at Rugby knew perfectly well that a gerund*ive* was a pass*ive* adjec*tive*, and Charity Spring shouted that here was one who didn't, this graceless son-of-a-bitch hung by the heels with his fat whore, and he must die, at which Arnold shook his head and his voice echoed far away: "I fear, captain, that we have failed . . .", and Susie's plump, jolly face receded, her skin darkened, the bright green eyes dissolved into new eyes that were black in shadow and cinnamon as the light caught them, set between slanting lids that were almost Oriental. Lovely eyes, like dark liquid jewels that moved slowly and intently, absorbing what they saw; whoever you are, I thought, you don't need to talk . . .

. . . the chubby-faced Indian girl stood above me, looking solemnly down; I was lying in a wickiup, under a blanket, and the horror of memory rushed back and hit me in the ribs with a boot belonging to one of the ugliest devils I've ever seen, who snarled as he kicked: a young Apache in hide kilt and leggings, with a dirty jacket about his shoulders and a band round the lank hair that framed a face from the Chamber of Horrors. Even for an Apache it was wicked—coal-black vicious eyes, hook nose, a mouth that was just a cruel slit and wasn't improved when he laughed with a great gape that showed all his ugly teeth.

"Get up, *perro*! Dog! Gringo! *Pinda-lickoyee*!"

If you'd told me then that this monster would one day be the most dreaded hostile Indian who ever was, terror of half a continent—I'd have believed you; if you'd told me he would be my closest Indian friend—I wouldn't. Yet both

190

were true, and still are; he's an old, done man nowadays, and when we met last year I had to help him about, but mothers still frighten their children with his name along the Del Norte, and as for friendship, I suppose one scoundrel takes to another, and we're the only ones left over from that time, anyway. But at our first meeting he scared the innards out of me, and I was deuced glad when the girl cried out before he could kick me again.

"Stop, Yawner! Don't touch him!"

"Why not? It feels good," snarls my beauty, with another great gape, but he left off and stepped back, which was a double relief, for he stank like a goat in an organ-loft. I thought I'd best obey nevertheless, and struggled up, weak and dizzy as I was, for I realised that any hope I might have in my fearful plight depended on this girl I'd rescued . . . it must have been she who had spoken up for me when I was hanging helpless . . . now she was interceding again, and with authority. Decidedly she deserved all the fawning courtesy I could show her. So I struggled painfully upright, gasping with my aches and holding unsteadily to the blanket for modesty's sake while I muttered obsequiously, muchas, muchas gracias, senorita. The Yawner growled like an angry dog, but she nodded and continued to inspect me in silence for several minutes, those splendid eyes curious and speculating, as though I were something in a shop and she was trying to make up her mind. I stood unsteady and sweating, trying to look amiable, and took stock of her in turn.

Seen in daylight, she wasn't unattractive. The chubby face, now that it was washed and polished, was round and firm as a ripe apple, with sulky, provocative lips. In figure she was sturdy rather than slim, a muscular little half-pint under her puppy-fat, for she couldn't have been over sixteen. She was royally dressed by Apache standards, in a fine beaded doeskin tunic, fringed below the knee, which must have taken a dozen squaws a week to chew; her moccasins had bright geometric patterns, a lace scarf was bound about her brows, and there was enough silver and beadwork round her neck to start a bazaar. She was utter Indian, but there was a cool, almost damn-you air that didn't sort with

191

the busty little figure and savage finery, an impersonal poise in the way she looked me up and down that would have suited a hacienda better than a wickiup—if I'd known that her mother was pure Spanish *hidalga* with a name three feet long, I might have understood.

Suddenly she frowned. "You have much ugly hair on your face. Will you cut it off?"

Startled, I said I would, certainly, ma'am, and the Yawner spat and muttered that given his way he'd cut off more than that; he was giving blood-chilling particulars, but she snapped him into silence, took a last long look at me from those slanted pools, and then asked with perfect composure:

"Do you like me, *pinda-lickoyee*?"

Now, I hadn't more than a half-notion of what this queer inspection was about, but it was a stone certainty that this young lady's good opinion was all that stood between me and a frightful death. Ignoring the Yawner's snort at her question, I fairly babbled my admiration, leering eagerly no doubt, and she clapped her hands.

"*Bueno!*" cries she, and laughed, with a triumphant toss of her head at the Yawner, accompanied by a gesture and an Apache word which I doubt was ladylike. She gave me one last hot appraising stare before sweeping out, and the Yawner let go a great fart by way of comment, and jerked his thumb at my clothes, which had been thrown in a corner. He watched malevolently as I pulled on shirt and pants and struggled with my boots; I ached with stiffness, but my dizziness was passing, and I ventured to ask him who the señorita might be. He grunted as though he grudged the words.

"Sonsee-array. Child of the Red Sleeves."

"Who's he?"

His black eyes stared with disbelief and mistrust. "What kind of *pinda-lickoyee* are you? You don't know of Mangas Colorado? Bah! You're a liar!"

"Never heard of him. What does his daughter want with me?"

"That is for her to say." He gave another of his gapes of laughter. "Huh! You should have dropped your blanket,

192

white-eye! *Vaya!*" And he shoved me out of the wickiup.

There was a motley crowd of women and children outside in the brilliant sunlight, and they set up a great yell of execration at sight of me, waving sticks and spitting, but the Yawner drew a sling from his belt and lashed at them with the thongs to make way. I followed him through the cluster of wickiups and across a level space towards a few ruined buildings and a great crumbling triangular fort before which another crowd was assembled. How far we were from the valley of the massacre I couldn't tell; this was quite different country, with low scrubby hills round the sandy flat, and one great hill looming over the scene; it looked like a permanent camp.[34]

There must have been a couple of hundred Apaches grouped in a great half-circle before the fort, and if you think you've seen ugly customers in Africa or Asia, believe me, there are worse. I've seen Fly River head-hunters who ain't exactly Oscar Wilde, and not many understudies for Irving among the Uzbeks and Udloko Zulus—but they're merely awful to look at. For an ugliness that comes from the soul, and envelops the stranger in a wave of menace and evil cruelty, commend me to a gathering of Gila Apaches. Or rather, don't. To have those vicious eyes turned on you from those flat, spiteful brute faces, is to know what hate truly means; you'll never wonder again why other Indians call them simply "the enemy".

They watched me come in silence, until the Yawner stopped me before a group seated under the fort wall. There were six of them, presumably elders, since in contrast to the crowd they all wore shirts and kilts and leather caps or scarves. But there was only one of them to look at.

He might have been fifty, and was undoubtedly the biggest man I've ever seen. I'm two inches over six feet, and he topped me by half a head, but it was his sheer bulk that took your breath away. From shoulder to shoulder he was three and a half feet wide—and I know that because I once saw him hold a cavalry sabre horizontal across his chest, and it didn't protrude either side. His arms were as thick as my legs, and bulged under his deerskin shirt; the knees

193

beneath his kilt were like milestones. His head was to scale, and hideous, with black snake eyes that bored out from beneath the brim of his flat hat with its eagle feather. I've felt my bowels dissolve in the presence of a few ogres in my time, but none more awe-inspiring than this celebrated Mangas Colorado; he was truly terrific. He surveyed me for a moment, and glanced aside, and I saw that my girl and two other young females were there, kneeling on a spread blanket before the crowd. She was looking bothered but determined.

Now, what I didn't know was that a heated debate had been in progress, the subject being: what shall we do with old Flashy? The overwhelming opinion had been that I should be slung up by the heels forthwith and given the skin treatment I'd have had days ago but for the unseemly intervention of young Sonsee-array; the only dissenting voices had been those of the lady herself, her girl-friends (who being common women counted for nothing), and her doting father (who being Mangas Colorado counted for everything). But it was widely recognised that he was only humouring her because he was a fond old widower with three married daughters, and she was all he had left, presumably, to fetch his slippers, preside at tea, and torture visitors; his indulgence had limits, however, and he had told her pretty sharp that it was high time she stated her intentions where this *pinda-lickoyee* was concerned. Was it true that she wanted to marry the brute, foreign white-eye and scalp-hunter that he was? (Cries of "No, no!" and "Shame!") Let him remind her that she had turned down half the eligible bachelors in the tribe . . . however, if this *gringo* was what she wanted, let her say so, and Mangas would either give his blessing or signal the band to strike up the cottonwood polka. (Hear, hear, and sustained applause.)

At this point Sonsee-array, accompanied by the Yawner in case the prisoner proved violent, had flounced off for a final look at me, which I have described. She had then gone back to Papa and announced that she wanted to marry the boy. (Sensation.) Friends and relatives had now urged the unsuitability of the match; Sonsee-array had retorted that there were precedents for marrying *pinda-lickoyee*, including her own father, and it was untrue, as certain disappointed suitors (cries of "Oh!" and "Name them!") had urged, that her intended was a scalp-hunting enemy; her good friend Alopay, daughter of Nopposo and wife to the celebrated Yawner, had been a captive with her and could testify that the adored object had taken no scalps. (Uproar, stilled by the arrival of the body in the case, with the Yawner at his elbow.)

If I'd known all this, and the interesting facts that Indians have no colour bar and that Apache girls are given a pretty free choice of husbands, I might have breathed easier, but I doubt it; no one was ever easy in the presence of Red Sleeves. He glared at me like a constipated basilisk, and the organ bass croaked in Spanish.

"What's your name, Americano?"

"Flashman. I'm not Americano. Inglese."

"Flaz'man? Inglese?" The black eyes flickered. "Then why are you not in the Snow Woman's country? Why here?"

It took me a moment to figure that the Snow Woman must be our gracious Queen, so called doubtless in allusion to Canada. I've heard Indians call her some odd names: Great Woman, Great White Mother, Grandmother latterly, and even the Old Woman of General Grant, by certain Sioux who held that she and Grant were man and wife, but she'd shown him the door, which I rather liked.

I said I was here as a trader, and there was an angry roar. Mangas Colorado leaned forward. "You trade in Mimbreno scalps to the Mexicanos!" he croaked.

"That's not true!" I said, as bold as I dared. "I was a prisoner of the villains who attacked your people. I took no scalps."

Although this, unknown to me, had been vouched for by Sonsee-array and her girl-friends, the mob still hooted disbelief; Mangas stilled them with a raised hand and rasped:

"Scalp-hunter or not, you were with the enemy. Why should you live?"

A damned nasty question coming from a face like that, but before I could think of several good answers, my little Pocohontas was on her feet, fists clenched and eyes blazing, like a puppy snapping at a mastiff.

"Because he is my chosen man! Because he fought for me, and saved me, and was kind to me!" She looked from her father to me, and there were absolute tears on her cheeks. "Because he is a man after my father's heart, and I will have him or no one!"

Well, this was news to me, of course, although her conduct in the wickiup had suggested that she had some such arrangement in mind. And if it seemed short notice for so much enthusiasm on her part, well, I *had* protected her, in a way—and there seemed to be a movement for marrying Flashy among North American women that year, anyway. Hope surged up in me—to be checked as dear old Dad climbed to his enormous feet and lumbered forward for a closer look at me. It was like being approached by one of those Easter Island stone faces; he loomed over me, and his breath was like old boots burning. Fine bloodshot eyes he had, too.

"What do you say, *pinda-lickoyee*?" says he, and there was baleful suspicion in every line of that horrible face. "You have known her but a few hours; what can she be to you?"

If he'd been a civilised prospective father-in-law, I dare say I'd have hemmed and hawed, lyrical-like, and referred him to my banker; as it was, a wrong word—or too fulsome a protestation of devotion—and it would be under the greenwood tree who loves to swing with me. So I forced myself to look manly and simple, with a steady glance at Sonsee-array, and answered by adapting into Spanish a phrase that Dick Wootton had used to the Cheyenne.

"My heart is in the sky when I look at her," says I, and she fairly shrieked with delight and beat her little fists on her knees, while the crowd rumbled and Mangas never blinked an eyelid.

"So you say." It was like gravel under a door. "But what do we know of you, save that you are *pinda-lickoyee*? How do we know you are a fit man for her?"

196

There didn't seem much point in telling him I'd been to Rugby under Arnold, or that I'd taken five wickets for 12 against the England XI, so I pitched on what I hoped would be a popular line by telling him I'd served with the Snow Woman's soldiers in lands far away, and had counted coup against Utes and Kiowas (which was true, even if I hadn't wanted to). He listened, and Sonsee-array preened at the silent crowd, and then one young buck, naked except for boots and breech-clout, but with silver ornaments slung round his neck, swaggered forward and began a harangue in Apache. I was to learn that this was Vasco, the jilted admirer on whose appearance and aroma Sonsee-array had commented; by tribal standards he was wealthy (six horses, a dozen slaves, that sort of thing), and quite the leading light. I suppose he was sick as mud that a despised white-eye looked like succeeding where he had failed, and while I understood no word, it was obvious he wasn't appearing as prisoner's friend; when he'd done bawling the odds he hurled his hatchet into the ground at my feet. There was no doubt what that meant, in any language; the crowd fell silent as death, and every eye was on me.

Now, you know what I think of mortal combat. I've run from more than I can count, and lived never to regret it, and this lean ten stone of quivering, fighting fury, obviously nimble as a weasel and built like a champion middleweight, was the last man I wanted to try conclusions with—well, I'd been ill. But with Mangas's blood-flecked eyes on me, I could guess what refusal would mean—no, this was a case for judicious bluff with my heart pounding under a bold front. So I glanced at the axe, at the furious Vasco, at Mangas, and shrugged.

"Must I?" says I. "I've killed a better man than this for her already. And afterwards—how many others do I have to kill?"

There was a creaking snort from behind me: the Yawner was laughing—I wasn't to know that her disappointed beaux had been legion. There were a few grins even among the crowd, but not from my lady; she was forward in a trice, demanding to know who was Vasco to put in his oar, and why should I, who had counted coup and killed for her, be at the trouble of chastising an upstart who had barely made his fourth war-party?[35] She fairly shrieked and spat at him, and the mob buzzed—by no means unsympathetically, I noted; the Yawner grunted that any fool could fight, and a few heads nodded in agreement. The Apaches, you see, being matchless warriors, tend to take courage for granted, especially in big, burly fellows who look as much like a Tartar as I do (more fool they), and weren't impressed by Vasco's challenge; rather bad form in a jealous lover, they thought it. But Mangas's snake eyes never left my face, and I realised in chill horror that I must go on bluffing, and quickly—and run the risk that my bluff would be called, if the plan that was forming in my mind went adrift. So before anyone else could speak I picked up the hatchet, looked at it, and says to Mangas, very offhand:

"Do I have choice of weapons?"

This brought more hubbub, with Sonsee-array protesting, Vasco yelling savage agreement, and the mob roaring eagerly. Mangas nodded, so I asked for a lance and my pony.

It was a desperate, horrible gamble—but I knew that if it came to a fight in the end, it was my only hope. I was still shaky from my illness, and even at my best I couldn't have lived with Vasco in a contest with knives or hatchets. But I was a trained lancer, and guessed that he wasn't—they use 'em overhead, two-handed, and have no notion of proper management. But with luck and good acting, it need never come to that; by playing the cool, professional hand, I could win without a battle.

While they were getting the lances and ponies, and a frantic Sonsee-array was shrilly damning Daddy's eyes for permitting this criminal folly, and he was growling that she'd brought it on herself, and the commonalty were settling down to enjoy the show, I turned to the Yawner and asked him quietly if he could find me three wooden pegs, about so by so. He stared at me, but went off, and presently they brought out my little Arab, apparently none the worse for having been in their hands, and a lance. It was shorter and lighter than cavalry issue, but with a sharp well-set head.

Vasco was already aboard a pony, shaking a lance in the air and yelling to the crowd—no doubt assuring them what mincemeat he was going to make of the *pinda-lickoyee*. They yelled and cheered, and he whooped and cantered about, hurling abuse in my direction.

I didn't heed him. I busied myself talking to the Arab, petting him and blowing in his nostrils for luck, and threw away the Indian saddle they had given him; without stirrups, I knew I'd be safer bareback. His bridle, which was the merest crude strap, would just have to serve. I took my time, and ignored the impatience of the crowd, while Mangas stood brooding and silent—and here came the Yawner, with three pegs in his hand.

I took them, and without a word or a look walked away and set them in the ground, about twenty paces apart, while the mob stared and shouted in astonishment, and Vasco trotted up, screaming at me. Still I paid no attention, but walked back to my pony, picked up the lance, turned to Mangas, and spoke my piece so that everyone should hear; while I was quaking inwardly, I flattered myself I'd kept a steady, careless front; I looked him in the eye, and hoped to God I was right, and that they'd never heard of tent-pegging.

"I don't want to fight your brave, Mangas Colorado," says I, "because he's a young man and a fool, and I'll prove nothing by killing him that I haven't proved already, in defence of your daughter. But if you say I must kill him . . . then I will. First, though, I'm going to show you something—and when you've seen it, you can tell me whether I need to kill him or not."

Then I turned away, and damnably stiff and bruised as I was, vaulted on to the Arab's back. I trotted him about for a moment or two, plucked the lance from the Yawner's hand, and cantered away fifty yards or so before turning to come in on the pegs at a gallop. My heart was in my mouth, for while I'd been a dab hand in India, I knew I must be rusty as the deuce from lack of practice, to say nothing of my cracked head and groggy condition—and if I failed or made a fool of myself, I was a dead man.

But it was neck or nothing now—there were the pegs, tiny white studs on the red earth, with the squat colossal form of Mangas close by them, Sonsee-array just behind him, and the watching multitude beyond. The Arab's hooves were drumming like pistons as I bore in, bringing down the point to cover the first peg as it rushed towards me . . . I leaned out and down and prayed—and my point missed it by a whisker, but here was the second almost under our hooves, and this time I made no mistake; the bright steel cut into the peg like cheese and I wheeled away in a great circle, the spitted peg flourished high for all to see. What a howl went up as I cantered towards Mangas Colorado, dipped my point in salute, and stuck the spiked butt of the lance in the earth before him. I was a trifle breathless, but nodded cool as I knew how.

"Now I'll fight your brave, Mangas Colorado, if you say so," I told him. "But before I do—let me see that he's a worthy opponent. There are the little pegs—let him try."

Not a muscle moved in that awful lined face, while there was uproar from the watchers; Vasco curvetted about, howling and shaking his lance—protesting, I dare say, that pig-sticking wasn't his game. Sonsee-array screamed abuse at him, with obscene gestures, the Yawner gaped with laughter till his jaw cracked—and Mangas Colorado's snake eyes went from me to the spitted peg and back again. Then, after what seemed an age, he glanced at Vasco, grunted, and jerked his thumb at the remaining pegs. The assembly bayed approval, Sonsee-array jumped with glee, and I settled back to enjoy the fun.

It was better than I could have hoped for. Tent-pegging ain't as hard as it looks, but you have to know the knack, and it was quite beyond Vasco. He ran half a dozen courses and missed by a mile every time, to renewed catcalls which made him so wild that at the last try he speared the ground, snapped the shaft, and came out of the saddle like a hot rivet. His pals screeched for joy and even the women hooted, and he fairly capered with rage, which made them laugh all the more.

That was what I'd been after from the start—to make him

look so ridiculous that his challenge to a man who was obviously more expert than he would be scoffed out of court. It had worked; even Mangas's mouth twitched in a hideous grin, while the Yawner gaped and slapped his thighs. Vasco stamped and screamed in rage—and then his eye lighted on me; he shook his fist, sprang to his pony's back, and made straight for me, yelling bloody murder, drawing his hatchet as he came.

It was so sudden that he nearly had me. One moment I was sitting my pony at rest, the next Vasco was charging in, hurling the tomahawk ahead of him. His aim was wild, but the whirling haft of the weapon hit my Arab on the muzzle, and as I tried to turn him to avoid being ridden down he reared with the pain, and I came to earth with sickening force. For two or three seconds I lay jarred out of my wits, as Vasco swept past, reined his mustang back on its haunches, and snatched the lance that I had left upright in the ground. Sprawled and helpless as his beast reared almost on top of me, its hooves flailing, I tried to roll away; he raised the lance to let drive, screaming his hate; I heard Sonsee-array's shriek and Mangas's bass bellow of rage— and something cracked like a whip, there was a hiss in the air overhead, a sickening thud, and Vasco's head snapped back as though he had been shot, the lance dropping from his hands. As he toppled from the saddle I had a glimpse of that contorted face, with a bloody hole where one eye should have been—and here was the Yawner, coiling up the thongs of the sling that had driven a pellet into Vasco's brain.

There was an instant's hush, and then uproar, with every-one surging forward for a look, and Vasco's pals to the fore, clamouring at Mangas for vengeance on the Yawner, who spat and sneered, with one hand on his knife. "The *pinda-lickoyee* was in my charge!" he snarled. "He was ready to fight—but this coward would have killed him unarmed!" Which I thought damned sound, and Mangas evidently agreed, for he quieted them with a tremendous bellow, stooped over the corpse, and then told them to take it away.

"The Yawner was right," growls he. "This one died like

a fool and no warrior." His glance seemed to challenge that ring of savage faces, but none dared dissent, and while Vasco's remains were removed, the great ghoul turned his attention back to me for a long moment, and then snapped to Sonsee-array, who came quickly forward to his side. He rumbled at her in Apache, indicating me, and she bowed her head submissively; for an awful moment my heart stopped, and then he beckoned me forward, favoured me with another gargoyle stare—and reached out to lay his hand on my shoulder.

It was like being tapped with a pitchfork, but I didn't mind that; I could have cried with sheer relief. Sonsee-array was beside me, her hand slipping into mine, the sullen faces round us were indifferent rather than hostile, the Yawner shrugged—and Mangas Colorado gave us a final curt nod and stalked away. Just the same, I couldn't help thinking that old Morrison hadn't been such a bad father-in-law.

12

Possibly because I've spent so much time as the unwilling guest of various barbarians around the world, I've learned to mistrust romances in which the white hero wins the awestruck regard of the silly savages by sporting a monocle or predicting a convenient eclipse, whereafter they worship him as a god, or make him a blood brother, and in no time he's teaching 'em close order drill and crop rotation and generally running the whole show. In my experience, they know all about eclipses, and a monocle isn't likely to impress an aborigine who wears a bone through his nose.[36] So don't imagine that my tent-pegging had impressed the Apaches overmuch; it hadn't. I was alive because Sonsee-array fancied me and was grateful—and also because she was just the kind of minx to enjoy flouting tribal convention by marrying a foreigner. I'd come creditably out of the Vasco business—nobody mourned him, apparently—and Mangas had given me the nod, so that was that. But no one made me a blood brother, thank God, or I'd probably have caught hydrophobia, and as for worship—nobody gets that from those fellows.

They were prepared to accept me, but not with open arms, and I was in no doubt that my life still hung by a hair, on Sonsee-array's whim and Mangas's indulgence. So I must try to shut my mind to the hideous pickle I was in, recover from the shock to my nervous system, and play up to them for all I was worth while I found out where the devil I was, where safety lay, and plotted my escape. If I'd known that it would take me six months, I believe I'd have died of despair. In the meantime, it was some slight reassurance to find that however unreal and terrifying my plight might seem to me, the tribe were ready to take it for granted, and even be quite hospitable about it, white-eye though I was.

For example, the Yawner made me free of the family pot and a blanket in the wickiup which he shared with his wife Alopay, their infant, and her relatives; it stank like the nation and was foul, but Alopay was a buxom, handsome wench who was prepared to treat me kindly for Sonsee-array's sake, and the Yawner himself was more friendly now that he'd saved my life—have you noticed, the man who does a good turn is often more inclined to be amiable than the chap who's received it? He'd evidently been appointed my bear-leader because although he wasn't a true Mimbreno, he was related to Mangas, and trusted by the chief; he was as much jailer as mentor, which was one reason it took me such a deuce of a time to get out of Apacheria.

Having taken me on, though, he was prepared to make a go of it, and that same evening he inducted me into a peculiar Apache institution which, while revolting, is about the most clubbable function I've ever struck. After we had supped, he took me along to a singular adobe building near the fort, like a great beehive with a tiny door in one side; there were about forty male Apaches there, all stark naked, laughing and chattering, with Mangas among them. No one gave me a second glance, so I followed the Yawner's example and stripped, and then we crawled inside, one after the other, into the most foetid, suffocating heat I'd ever experienced.

It was black as Egypt's night, and I had to creep over nude bodies that grunted and heaved and snarled what I imagine was "Mind where you're putting your feet, damn you!"; I was choking with the stench and dripping with sweat as I flopped on that pile of humanity, and more crowded in on top until I was jammed in the middle of a great heap of gasping, writhing Apaches; I felt I must faint with the pressure and atrocious heat and stink. I could barely breathe, and then it seemed that warm oil was being poured over us from above—but it was simply reeking sweat, trickling down from the mass of bodies overhead.

They loved it; I could hear them chuckling and sighing in that dreadful sodden oven that was boiling us alive; I hadn't even breath enough to protest; it was as much as I could do to keep my face clear of the rank body beneath me and drag in great laboured gasps of what I suppose was air. For half an hour we lay in that choking blackness, drenched and boiled to the point of collapse, and then they began to crawl out again, and I dragged my stupefied body into the open more dead than alive.

That was my introduction to the Apache sweatbath,[37] one of the most nauseating experiences of my life—and an hour later, I don't know when I've felt so splendidly refreshed. But what astonished me most, when it sank in, was how they had included me in the party as a matter of course; I felt almost as though I'd been elected to the Apache Club— which in other respects proved to be about as civilised as White's, with fewer bores than the Reform, and a kitchen slightly better than the Athenaeum's.

I had a further taste of Apache culture on the following day, when with the rest of the community I attended the great wailing funeral procession for the deceased Vasco, and for the victims of Gallantin's massacre, whose bodies had been brought down from the valley in the hills. That was a spooky business, for there were two or three of my own bagging on those litters, each corpse with its face painted and scalp replaced (I wondered who'd matched 'em all up) and its weapons carried before. They buried them under rock piles near the big hill they call Ben Moor (and that gave me a jolt, if you like, for you know what big hill is in Gaelic—Ben Mhor. God knows if there's a tribe of Scotch Apaches; I shouldn't be surprised—those tartan buggers get everywhere). They lit purification fires after the burial, and marked the place with a cross, if you please, which I suppose they learned from the dagoes.

Speaking of scalps, I discovered that the Mimbrenos had no special zeal for tonsuring their enemies, but they brought back a few from those of Gallantin's band they'd killed, and the women dressed and stretched them on little frames, to brighten up the parlour, I dare say. One scalp was pale and sandy, and I guessed it was Nugent-Hare's.

Meanwhile, no time was lost in bringing me up to scratch. After the funeral, the Yawner told me I must take my pony to Sonsee-array's wickiup and leave it there—so I did, watched by the whole village, and madam ignored it. "What now?" says I, and he explained that when she fed and watered the beast and returned it, I had been formally accepted. She wouldn't do it at once, for that would show unmaidenly eagerness, but possibly on the second or third day; if she delayed to the fourth day, she was a proper little tease.

D'you know, the saucy bitch waited until the fourth evening?—and a fine lather I was in by then, for fear she'd changed her mind, in which case God knows what might have happened to me. But just before dusk there was a great laughter and commotion, and through the wickiups she came, astride my Arab, looking as proud and pleased as Punch, with a crowd of squaws and children in tow, and even a few menfolk. She was in full fig of beaded tunic and lace scarf, but now she was also wearing the long white leggings with tiny silver bells down the seams, which showed she was marriageable; she dropped the Arab's bridle into my hand with a most condescending smile, everyone cheered and stamped, and for the first time I found Apache faces grinning at me, which is a frightening sight.

There was even more grinning later, for Mangas held an enormous jollification on corn-beer and pine-bark spirit and a fearsome cactus tipple called *mescal*; they don't mind mixing their drinks, those fellows, and got beastly foxed, although I went as easy as I could. Mangas punished the *tizwin* something fearful, and presently, when the others had toppled sideways or were hiccoughing against each other telling obscene Apache stories, he jerked his head at me, collared a flask, and led the way, stumbling and cursing freely, to the old ruined fort. He took a long pull at the flask, swayed a bit, and belched horribly; aha, thinks I, now for the fatherly talk and a broad hint about letting the bride get some sleep on honeymoon. But it wasn't that; what followed was one of the strangest conversations I've ever had in my life, and I set it down because it was my introduction to that queer mixture of logic and lunacy that is typical of Indian thought. The fact that we were both tight as tadpoles made it all the more revealing, really, and if he had some wild notions, he was still a damned shrewd file, the Red Sleeves. What with the booze and his guttural Spanish, he wasn't always easy to follow, but I record him fairly; I can still see that shambling bulk, his blanket hitched close against the night cold, like an unsteady Sphinx in the moonlight, clutching his bottle, and croaking basso profundo:

Mangas: The Mexicanos built this fort when they still had chiefs over the great water. The Americanos build many such . . . is it true that even Santa Fe is a mere wickiup beside the towns of the *pinda-lickoyee* where the sun rises?

Flashy: Indeed, yes. In my country are towns so great that a man can hardly walk through them between sunrise and sunset. You ought to see St Paul's.

Mangas: You're lying, of course. You boast as young men do, and you're drunk. But the *pinda-lickoyee* people are many in number—as many as the trees in the Gila forest, I'm told.

Flashy: Oh, indubitably. Perfect swarms of them.

Mangas: Perhaps ten thousand?

Flashy (unaware that ten thousand is as far as an Apache can count, but not disposed to argue): Ah . . . yes, just about.

Mangas: Huh! And now, since the Americanos beat the Mexicanos in war, many of these white-eyes have come through our country, going to a place where they seek the *pesh klitso**, the *oro-hay*. Their pony soldiers say that all this country is now Americano, because they took it from the Mexicanos. But the Mexicanos never had it, so how can it be taken from them?

Flashy: Eh? Ah, well . . . politics ain't my line, you know. But the Mexicanos *claimed* this land, so I suppose the Americanos—

*Gold; literally "yellow iron".

207

Mangas (fortissimo): It was never Mexicano land! *We* let them dig here, at Santa Rita, for the *kla-klitso**, until they turned on us treacherously, and we destroyed them—ah, that was a rare slaughter! And *we* let them live on the Del Norte, where we raid and burn them as we please! Soft, fat, stupid Mexicano pigs! What rule had they over us or the land? None! And now the Americanos treat the land as though it were theirs—because they fought a little war in Mexico! Huh! They say—a chief of their pony soldiers told me this—that we must obey them, and heed their law!

Flashy: Did he, though? Impudent bastard!

Mangas: He came to me after we Mimbreno rode a raid into Sonora with Hashkeela of the Coyoteros, who is husband to my second daughter—she is not so fair as Sonsee-array, by the way. You like Sonsee-array, don't you, *pinda-lickoyee* Flaz'man? You truly love my little gazelle?

Flashy: Mad about her . . . I can't wait.

Mangas (with a great sigh and belch): It is good. She is a delightful child—wilful, but of a spirit! That is from me; her beauty is her mother's—she was a Mexicano lady, you understand, taken on a raid into Coahuila, ah! so many years ago! I saw her among the captives, lovely as a frightened deer, and I thought: that is my woman, now and forever. I forgot the loot, the cattle, even the killing—only one thought possessed me, in that moment—

Flashy: I know what you mean.

Mangas: I took her! I shall never forget it. Uuurrgh! Then we rode home. Already I had two wives of our people; their families were enraged that I brought a new foreign wife—I had to fight my brothers-in-law, naked, knife to knife! I defied the law—for her! I ripped out their bowels—for her! I tore out their hearts with my fingers—for her! I was red to the shoulders with their blood! Do they not call me the Red Sleeves—Mangas Colorado? Uuurrghh!

Flashy (faintly): Absolutely! Bravo, Mangas—may I call you Mangas?

---

*Presumably copper, since this was mined at Santa Rita. *Kla-klitso*, literally, is "night-iron".

Mangas: When my little dove, my dear Sonsee-array, told me how *you* had fought for *her*—how you sank your knife in the belly of the *pinda-lickoyee* scalp-hunter, and tore and twisted his vitals, and drank his blood—I thought, there is one with the spirit of Mangas Colorado! (Gripping my shoulder, tears in his eyes.) Did you not exult as the steel went home—for her?

Flashy: By George, yes! That'll teach you, I thought—

Mangas: But you did not take his heart or scalp?

Flashy: Well, no . . . I was thinking about looking after her, you see, and—

Mangas: And afterwards . . . you did not uuurrghh! with her?

Flashy (quite shocked): Heavens, no! Oh, I mean, I was in a perfect sweat for her, of course—but she was tired, don't you know . . . and . . . and distressed, naturally . . .

Mangas (doubtfully): Her mother was tired and distressed—but I had only one thought . . . (Shakes head) But you *pinda-lickoyee* have different natures, I know . . . you are colder—

Flashy: Northern climate.

Mangas (taking another swig): What was I saying when you began to talk of women? Ah, yes . . . my raid with Hashkeela six moons ago, when we slaughtered in Sonora, and took much loot and many slaves. And afterwards this Americano fool—this pony soldier—came and told me it was wrong! He told *me*, Mangas Colorado, that it was wrong!

Flashy: He never!

Mangas: "Why, fool," I told him, "these Mexicanos are your enemies—have you not fought them?" "Yes," says he, "but now they have yielded under our protection, at peace. So we cannot suffer them to be raided." "Look, fool," I told him, "when you fought them, did you ask our permission?" "No," says he. "Then why should we ask yours?" I said.

Flashy: Dam' good!

Mangas: It was then he said it was his law, and we must heed it. I said: "We Mimbreno do not ask you to obey our law; why, then, do you ask us to obey yours?" He could not answer except to say that it was his great chief's word, and we must—which is no reason. Now, was he a fool, or did he speak with a double tongue? You are *pinda-lickoyee*, you know their minds. Tell me.

Flashy: May I borrow your flask? Thanks. Well, you see, he was just saying what his great chief told him to say—obeying orders. That's how they work, you know.

Mangas: Then he and his chief are fools. If I gave such an order to an Apache, without good reason, he would laugh at me.

Flashy: I'll bet he wouldn't.

Mangas: Huh?

Flashy: Sorry. Wind.

Mangas: Why should the Americanos try to force their law on us? They cannot want our country; it has little *oro-hay*, and the rocks and desert are no good for their farmers. Why can they not leave us alone? We never harmed them until they harmed us—why should we, with the Mexicanos to live off? At first I thought it was because they feared us, the warrior Apache, and would have us quiet. But other tribes—Arapaho, Cheyenne, Shoshoni—have been quiet, and still the *pinda-lickoyee* force law on them. Why?

Flashy: I don't know, Mangas Colorado.

Mangas: You know. So do I. It is because their spirit tells them to spread their law to all people, and they believe their spirit is better than ours. Whoever believes that is wrong and foolish. It is such a spirit as was in the world in the beginning, when it was rich and wicked, and God destroyed it with a great flood. But when He saw that the trees and birds and hills and great plains had perished with the people, His heart was on the ground, and He made it anew. And He made the Apache His people, and gave us His way, which is our way.

Flashy: Mmh, yes. I see. But (greatly daring) He made the *pinda-lickoyee*, too, didn't he?

Mangas: Yes, but He made them fools, to be destroyed. He gave them their evil spirit, so that they should blunder among us—perhaps He designed them for our prey. I do not know. But we shall destroy them, if they come against us, the whole race of *pinda-lickoyee*, even all ten thousand. They do not know how to fight—they ride or walk in little lines, and we draw them into the rocks and they die at our leisure. They are no match for us. (Suddenly) Why were you among the Americanos?

Flashy (taken aback): I . . . told you . . . I was a trader . . . I . . .

Mangas (grinning sly and wicked): An Inglese trader—among the Americanos? Strange . . . for you hate each other, because you once ruled their land, and they were your slaves, and rose against you, and you have fought wars against them. This I know—for are there not still chiefs among the Dacotah of the north who carry *pesh-klitso* pictures of the Snow Woman's ancestors, given to their fathers long ago, when your people ruled?[38] Huh! I think you were among the Americanos because you had angered the Snow Woman, and she drove you out, because she saw the spirit of the snake in your eyes, and knew that you do not speak with a straight tongue. (Fixes terrified Flashy with a glare, then shrugs) It does not matter; sometimes I have a forked tongue myself. Only remember—when you speak to Sonsee-array, let it be with a straight tongue.

Flashy (petrified): Rather!

Mangas: Ugh. Good. You will be wise to do so, for I have favoured you, and you will be one of the people, and your heart will be opened. When we fight the Americanos, you will be glad, for you are their enemy as we are. Perhaps one day I shall send you to the Snow Woman, even as the *pinda-lickoyee* of Texas sent messengers to her, with offers of friendship. Fear not—the anger she bears you will go out of her heart when she knows you come from Mangas Colorado, huh?

Flashy: Oh, like a shot. She'll be delighted.

Mangas: She must be a strange woman, to rule over men. Is she as beautiful as Sonsee-array?

Flashy (tactfully): Oh, dear me, no! About the same build, but nothing like as pretty. No woman is.

We were sitting among the ruins by now, and at this point

he toppled slowly backwards and lay with his huge legs in the air, singing plaintively. God, he was drunk! But I must have been drunker, for presently he carried me home in one hand (I weighed about fourteen stone then) and dropped me into my wickiup—through the roof, not the door, unfortunately. But if my final memories of that celebration was confused, I'm clear about what he said earlier, and if it sounds like drunkard's babble, just remark some of the things that supposedly simple savage knew—along with all his fanciful notions.

He'd heard of Spanish and British colonial rule, and of the American wars of '76 and 1812; he'd even somehow got wind of Britain's negotiations with the old Texas Republic before it joined the States in '46. At the same time he'd no idea of what Spain or Britain or the United States or even Texas really *were*—dammit, he thought the whole white race was only ten thousand strong, and obviously imagined Queen Victoria living in a wickiup somewhere over the hills. He probably thought the American troops he'd seen were some sort of tribal war party whom the 'Pash could wipe up whenever they chose. And yet, he could already read with uncanny wisdom the minds of a white race he hardly knew. "Their spirit tells them to spread their law . . . they believe their spirit is better than ours." Poor old Red Sleeves; wasn't he right, just?

No, he wasn't an ordinary man.[39] I knew him over several months, and can say he had the highest type of that lucid Indian mind which can put the civilised logician to shame, yet whose very simplicity of wisdom has been the redskin's downfall. He was a fine psychologist—you'll note he had weighed me for a rascal and fugitive on short acquaintance—an astute politician, and a bloody, cruel, treacherous barbarian who'd have been a disgrace to the Stone Age. If that seems contradictory—well, Indians are contrary critters, and Apaches more than most. Mangas Colorado taught me that, and gave me my first insight into the Indian mind, which is such a singular mechanism, and so at odds with ours, that I must try to tell you about it here.

Speaking of Apaches in particular, you must understand

212

that to them deceit is a virtue, lying a fine art, theft and murder a way of life, and torture a delightful recreation. Aha, says you, here's old Flashy airing his prejudices, repeating ancient lies. By no means—I'm telling you what I learned at first hand—and remember, I'm a villain myself, who knows the real article when he sees it, and the 'Pash are the only folk I've struck who truly believe that villainy is admirable; they haven't been brought up, you see, in a Christian religion that makes much of conscience and guilt. They reverence what we think of as evil; the bigger a rascal a man is, the more they respect him, which is why the likes of Mangas—whose duplicity and cunning were far more valued in the tribe than his fighting skill—and the Yawner, became great among them. This twisted morality is almost impossible for white folk to understand; they look for excuses, and say the poor savage don't know right from wrong. Jack Cremony[40] had the best answer to that: if you think an Apache can't tell right from wrong—wrong him, and see what happens.

At the same time these Apaches, of whom there may be a few thousands at most,[41] who live in some of the poorest land in the world, in the most primitive state, who are savage by nature, foul in habit, degraded of appearance (although some of their women are deuced handsome), who are backward and inferior in every outward respect, are nevertheless the most arrogant and self-satisfied people on God's earth. Their conceit makes the Chinese look modest; they don't merely pretend or *think* they're superior—they *know* it, like Lord Cardigan. The hatred which they feel towards all other folk springs from no sense of jealousy or fear or unworthiness; on the contrary, they truly despise white civilisation and want none of it, because they know absolutely that their own prehistoric ways are better. They hold the world in contempt, as prey to be lived off. (In some respects, you see, they're not unlike Britons or Americans.)

Now, this ingrained redskin conceit (for other tribes had it, too, if not as extremely as the 'Pash) is something the American government has never understood, and probably never will, and it's been at the root of the whole Indian question. I don't blame Washington—what civilised white, with his electric and gas light and huge cities and flying machines and centuries of art and literature and progress, could believe that this smelly, wicked, illiterate savage who looks like a cross between a Mongol and an ape *absolutely thinks he is superior to them?* It flies in the face of civilised reason—but not of Indian reason. They know they're better—and no demonstration or comparison will change their minds, you see, because their whole system of thought and philosophy is upside down from ours. You could take my old pal the Yawner and show him Paris or London, and it still wouldn't convince him. He'd say: "Huh, you can build great things and we cannot—but are they worth building? You can fly—but who needs to fly? I'd rather have my wickiup." And it wouldn't be sour grapes—the proud, stubborn, dear old bastard *would* rather have that wretched, stinking, flea-ridden hovel—lord, I itch just to think of it (but I've been less hospitably used, mind you, and felt less honoured, in some ducal mansions).

You see, it's been the great illusion of our civilisation that when the poor heathen saw our steamships and elections and drains and bottled beer, he'd realise what a benighted ass he'd been and come into the fold. But he don't. Oh, he'll take what he fancies, and can use (cheap booze and rifles, for example), but not on that account will he think we're better. He knows different.

You begin to understand, perhaps, the impossibility of red man and white man ever understanding each other—not that it would have made a damned bit of difference if they had, or altered the Yankees' Indian policy, except possibly in the direction of wiping up such intractable bastards even faster than they did. They knew they were going to have to dispossess the redskins, but being good Christian humbugs they kept trying to bully and cajole them into accepting the theft gracefully—which ain't quite the best position from which to make treaties with unreliable savages who are accustomed to rob rather than be robbed, and who don't understand what government and responsibility and authority mean, anyway. You can't treat sensibly with a chief whose braves don't feel obliged to obey him; contrariwise, if you're an Indian (worse luck) there's no point in treating with a government which is eventually going to pinch your hunting-grounds to accommodate the white migration it can't control. And it doesn't help when the two sides regard each other respectively as greedy, brutal white thieves and beastly, treacherous red vermin. I'm not saying either was wrong.

The Indian's tragedy was that being a spoiled and arrogant savage who wouldn't lie down, and a brave and expert fighter who happened to be quite useless at war, he could only be suppressed with a brutality that often matched his own. It was the reservation or the grave; there was no other way.

My little anthropologist would say it was all the white man's fault for intruding; no doubt, but by that logic Ur of the Chaldees would be a damned crowded place by now.

*   *   *

The morning after Mangas's *tizwin* party I was rousted out at dawn by a foul-tempered Yawner, who took me miles off into the hills, both with our heads splitting, to prepare for my honeymoon. We must find a pretty, secluded spot, he snarled, and build a bower for my bride's reception; we lit on a little pine grove by a brook, and there we built a wickiup—or rather, he did, while I got in the way and made helpful suggestions, and he damned the day he'd ever seen me—and stored it with food and blankets and cooking gear. When it was done he glared at it, and then muttered that it would be none the worse for a bit of garden; he'd made one for Alopay, apparently, and she'd thought highly of it.

So now I sweated, carefully transplanting flowers from the surrounding woods, while the Yawner squinted and frowned and stood back considering; when I'd bedded them around the wickiup to his satisfaction, he came to give them a final pat and smooth, growling at me to go easy with the water. We got it looking mighty pretty between us, and when I said Sonsee-array would be sure to like it, he shrugged and grunted, and we found ourselves grinning at each other across the flower-bed—odd, that's how I remember him, not as the old man I saw last year, but as the ugly, bow-legged young brave, all Apache from boots to headband, so serious as he arranged the blooms just so, cleaning the earth from his knife and looking sour and pleased among his flowers. A strange memory, in the light of history—but then he's still the Yawner to me, for all that the world has learned to call him Geronimo.[42]

The wedding took place two days later, on the open space before the old fort at Santa Rita, and if my memories of the ceremony itself are fairly vague, it's perhaps because the preliminaries were so singular. A great fire was lit before the old fort, and while the tribe watched from a distance, all the virgins trooped out giggling in their best dresses and sat round it in a great circle. Then the drummers started as darkness fell, and presently out shuffled the dancers, young bucks and boys, dressed in the most fantastic costumes, capering about the flames—the only time, by the way, that I've ever seen Indians dancing round a fire in the approved style. First came the spirit seekers, in coloured kilts with Aztec patterns and the long Apache leggings; they were all masked, and on their heads they bore peculiar frames decorated with coloured points and feathers and half-moons which swayed as they danced and chanted. They were fully-armed, and shook their stone-clubs and lances to drive away devils while they asked God (Montezuma, I believe) for a blessing on Sonsee-array and, presumably, me.

It was a slow, rhythmic, rather graceful dance, except for the little boys, whose task seemed to be to mock and tease the older men, which they did with great glee, to the delight of all. Then the drumming changed, to a more hollow, urgent note, and all the girls jumped up in mock terror, staring about, and cowering as out of the darkness raced the buffalo-dancers, in coloured, fearsome masks surmounted by animal heads—scalps of bison and wolf and deer and mountain-lion. As they leaped and whooped about the fire, all the virgins screamed and ran for their lives, but after a while, as the drumming grew faster and faster, they began to drift timidly back, until they too were joining in the dance, circling and shuffling among the buffalo-men in the fire-glow. All very proper, mind you, no lascivious nonsense or anything like that.

Then the drums stopped abruptly, the dance ceased, and the first spirit-dancer took his stance before the fire and began to chant. The Yawner tapped me on the shoulder—I was in my buckskins, by the way, with a garland round my neck—and he and another young brave called Quick Killer conducted me forward to stand before the spirit-chief. We waited while he droned away, and presently out of the darkness comes Mangas, leading Sonsee-array in a beautiful long white robe, all quilled and beaded, with her hair in two braids to her waist. She stood silent by me, and Mangas by the spirit-chief, whose headdress barely topped the Mimbreno giant. Silence fell . . . and here's a strange thing. You know how my imagination works, and how at the hitching-rail with Susie I reviewed my past alliances—Elspeth and Irma and Madam Baboon of Madagascar . . . well, this time I had no such visions. It may be that having Mangas Colorado looming over you, looking like something off the gutters at Notre Dame, concentrates the mind wonderfully; but also, it didn't seem to be a very *religious* ceremony, somehow, and I didn't seem to have much part of it. What was said was in Apache, with no responses or anything for poor old Flash, although Sonsee-array answered three or four times when the spirit-chief addressed her, as did the Yawner, grunting at my elbow. I suppose he was my proxy, since I didn't speak the lingo, and while it's a nice thought in old age that Geronimo was your best man—well, there was something dashed perfunctory about the whole thing. I don't even know at what point we became man and wife; no clasp of hands, or exchange of tokens, or embracing the bride, just a final wail from the spirit-chief and a great yell from the assembly, and then off to the wedding-feast.

There, I admit, they do it in style. That feast lasted three days, all round the fire, stuffing down the sweet roasted agave leaves from the mescal-pits, and baked meats, corn bread, chile, pumpkins and all the rest, with vast quantities

217

of a special wedding brew to wash it down. And d'you know, they don't let you near your bride in all that time— we sat on opposite sides of the fire, in a great circle of relatives and friends with the lesser mortals pressed behind (I suppose we must have left off feasting from time to time to sleep or relieve ourselves, but I swear I don't remember it) and she never looked in my direction once! Myself, I think they're damned cunning, the Apaches; you may know that in Turkey at wedding feasts they have a plump and voluptuous female who writhes about half-naked in front of the groom to put him in trim for the wedding-night; it's my belief that the Mimbreno are far subtler than that. Maybe there's something in the drink, maybe it's the repetition of the dancing that goes on during the feast, with those bucks in their animal heads chasing (but never catching) the young females, who flee continually (but never quite out of reach); perhaps it's just the three days' delay in getting down to business—whatever it may be, I found myself eyeing that white figure through the flames, and starting to sweat something frightsome.

I know she was no great beauty—not to compare with Elspeth or Lola or Cleonie or the Silk One or Susie or Narreeman or Fetnab or Lakshmibai or Lily Langtry or Valla or Cassy or Irma or the Empress Tzu'si or that big German wench off the Haymarket whose name escapes me (by Jove, I can't complain, at the end of the day, can I?)— but by the time the third evening was reached if you had asked me my carnal ideal of womanhood I'd have described it as just over five feet tall, sturdy and nimble, wearing a beaded tunic and white doeskin leggings, with a round chubby face, sulky lips, and great slanting black eyes that looked everywhere but at me. God, but she was pleased with herself, that smug, dumpy, nose-in-the-air wench, and I must have been about to burst when the Yawner tapped me on the shoulder and jerked his head, and when I got up and panted my way out of the firelight, no one paid the least notice.

Possibly I was drunk with liquor as well as lust, for I don't remember much except riding into the night with the

Yawner alongside and the shadowy form of Quick Killer ahead; the nightwind did nothing to cool my ardour either, for it seemed to grow with each passing mile through the wooded hills, and by the time we dismounted, and they and the ponies had faded tactfully into the darkness, I could have tackled the entire fair sex—provided they were all short and muscular and apple-cheeked. Through the trees I could see the twinkle of a fire, and I blundered towards it, disrobing unsteadily and staggering as I got my pants off, and there was the little wickiup, and no doubt the flowers were flapping about somewhere, but I didn't pause to look.

She was reclining on a blanket at the door of the wickiup, on one elbow, that sturdy little brown body a-gleam in the fireglow as though it had been oiled, and not a stitch on except for the patterned head-band above the cinammon eyes that gleamed like hot coals, and the tight white leggings that came up to her hips. She didn't smile, either; just gave me that sullen stare and stretched one leg while she stroked a hand down the seam of tiny bells, making them tinkle softly. My stars, I thought, it's been worth it, coming to America—and that's when I remember the pine-needles under my knees, and the smell of wood-smoke and musk, and deliberately taking my time as I stroked and squeezed every inch of that hard, supple young body, for I was damned if I was going to give her the satisfaction of having me roar all over her like a wild bull. I'd been teased and sweated by her and her blasted tribal rituals too long for that, so I held off and played with her until the sulky pout left her lips, and those glorious eyes opened wide as she forgot she was an Apache princess and became my trembling captive of the scalp-hunters' camp again, and she began to gasp and squirm and reach out for me, with little moans of *querido* and hoarse Apache endearments which I'm sure from her actions were highly indelicate—and she suddenly flung herself up at me, grappling like a wrestler, and positively yowled as she clung with her arms round my neck and her bells pealing all over the place.

"Now, that's a good little Indian maid," says I, and stopped her entreaties with my mouth, while I went to work in earnest, but very slowly, Susie-fashion, which was a marvel of delightful self-restraint, and I'm sure did her a power of good. For as the warm dawn came up, and I was drowsing happily under the blanket and deciding there were worse places to be than the Gila forest, there were those little lips at my ear, and those hard breasts against me, and the tiny whisper: "Make my bells ring again, *pinda-lickoyee*." So we rang the changes for breakfast.

13

There's nothing like teaching a new bride old tricks, and by the time our forest idyll was over I flatter myself Sonsee-array was a happier and wiser woman. Ten days was enough of it, though, for she was an avid little beast who preferred quantity to quality—unlike Elspeth, for example, whose beguiling innocence masked the most lecherously inventive mind of the last century, and whose conduct on our honeymoon would have caused the good citizens of nearby Troon to burn her at the stake, if they'd known. No, young Sonsee-array was more like Duchess Irma, who on discovering a good thing couldn't get enough of it, but where rogering had melted Irma's imperious nature to the point where she was prepared to await her lord's pleasure, my spirited Apache knew no such restraint. When she wanted her bells rung, she said so—she was tough, too, and discovered a great fondness for committing the capital act standing up under a waterfall in our stream; no wonder I've got rheumatism today, but it's worth it for the memory of that wet brown body lying back in my supporting arms while the water cascaded down over her upturned face, with me grinding away up to my knees in the shallows.

For the rest, she was an affectionate, cheerful little soul, so long as she got her own way—for she was damnably spoiled, and immensely vain of her Spanish blood, regarding the true-bred Mimbrenos with great condescension, even her terrible father. I remember the contempt with which she spoke of his habit of calling her by the pet-name of Takes-Away-Clouds-Woman, which she said was just what you might expect of a sentimental old savage, instead of by her proper name, Morning Star, which she thought much more fitting for an Apache princess.

"But it suits you," says I, stroking away at her leggings.

"You take away *my* clouds, I can tell you. Besides, I like your fanciful Indian names—what's mine, by the way, apart from white-eye?"

"Don't you know? Why, ever since you rode with your lance at the pegs, everyone calls you by a fine name: White-Rider-Goes-So-Fast-He-Destroys-the-Wind-with-His-Speed."

It sounded not bad, if a bit of a mouthful. "They can't call me all that every time," says I.

"Of course not, foolish one—they shorten it. He-Who-Breaks-the-Wind, or just Wind Breaker." She was in dead earnest, too. "Why, don't you like it?"

"Couldn't be better," says I. Just my luck to get one of their names that contracts to something frightful when translated. I knew an Oglala once whose full name was Brave-Pursues-Enemies-So-Fiercely-He-Has-No-Time-To-Change-His-Clothes—that came out as Stinking Drawers, and I can give you chapter and verse if you doubt it. I said I'd rather she chose me a pet name.

"Let me think," says she, nestling. "A name . . . you should win it by some great and wonderful deed." She giggled, and her hand strayed mischievously. "I know . . . it should be Man-Who-Rings-Her-Bells-Makes-Her-Heart-Melt." Her mouth trembled and her lids narrowed. "Ah, yes . . .! Win your new name . . . please . . . now, Wind Breaker!" I reckon I did, too, so far as she was conerned—but the Yawner was still calling me Wind Breaker last year, damn him.

Sonsee-array and I returned to the Copper Mines just as the community was moving into winter quarters in the hills, and if you wonder why I hadn't taken advantage of our solitary state on honeymoon to make a break for freedom—well, I still didn't know where I was, even, and although we'd been undisturbed, I'd had a shrewd idea that the Yawner and Quick Killer were never far away. Now, to make matters worse, the tribe moved about thirty miles south-west, farther than ever from the Del Norte and safety, into a mountainous forest where if I'd been fool enough to run I'd have been lost and recaptured in no time.

So there was nothing for it but to settle down, with a heavy heart, and wait through those awful months, telling myself that the chance of escape must come in the spring. When I thought back to the snug billet I'd abandoned at Susie's in Santa Fe, and the foul luck that had led me to Gallantin and this nightmare, I could have wept—but at least I was still whole, and no worse off than I'd been in Madagascar, and I'd got out of that, in the end. Now, as then, I forced myself to remember that there was a world outside this stinking collection of native huts and neolithic brutes, a world with Elspeth in it, and white faces, and beds and houses and clean linen and honest food and drink and civilised whores. I must just wait and watch, keep my Arab up to strength, learn everything I could, and when the time came, ride like the devil, leaving the latest Mrs Flashman and her charming relatives forever.

The more I saw of them that winter, the more I grew to detest them; in case you suppose from the recent tender passages that marriage and kinship had made me at all "soft" on Apaches, let me put you right. I became fairly well acquinted with Mangas Colorado, perforce, and quite friendly with the Yawner, while Sonsee-array was a charming and energetic bedmate—but they were monsters, all of them, and I include my dear little wife. Loving and even captivating she could be, with her pretty ways and fluent Spanish and a few civilised habits (like washing regularly) picked up from her unfortunate mother, but at heart she was as vicious and degraded an Apache as any of them. I shan't forget the night when she was snuggled up telling me Indian legends, like The Boy Who Could Not Go West, and some reference to a villain's sticky end reminded her of the fate of those members of Gallantin's band who'd been taken prisoner. There'd been fifteen of them, and the Mimbreno Ladies Sewing Circle had held a contest to see who could keep a victim alive longest under torture; the other women's patients, Sonsee-array told me proudly, had all expired after a few hours, but she had kept that poor devil Ilario lingering in unspeakable agony for two solid days—she described it in gruesome detail, chuckling drowsily, while I lay listening with the sweat icy on my skin. Having known Narreeman and good Queen Ranavalona and Gezo's Amazons, I had no illusions about the fair sex's talent for tickling up the helpless male—but this was the sweet child of sixteen whom I'd married and sported with in sylvan glades like Phyllis and Corydon! I tupped her with no great ardour that night, I can tell you.

But it was of a piece with all that I knew, and was still to learn that winter, of the Apache: they truly enjoy cruelty, for its own sake—and incidentally they are a living contradiction of the old fable (although it happens to be true in my own case) that a bully who delights in inflicting pain is invariably a coward. For if they have a virtue—in most folk's eyes, anyway—it is courage; you never saw a scared Apache yet. It's been their downfall; unlike the other tribes, they never knew when to quit against the pony soldiers; my old pal Yawner fought on until there was only a tattered remnant of his band left to be herded on to the reservation (which, be it noted, was more mercy than ever he'd shown to a beaten foe; if Apache custom had been applied to the 'Pash, there wouldn't be one left).

They knew how to fight, too, after their fashion, far better than the Plains Tribes; given numbers, they might be holding out in Arizona yet, for bar the Pathans they were the best guerrillas ever I saw. They train their boys from infancy in every art of woodcraft and ambush and decoy (and theft), which is the way they love to make war, rather than in open battle. That winter in the Gila hills I saw lads of six and seven made to run up and down mountains, lie doggo for hours, spend nights half-naked in the snow, track each other through the brush, run off horses, and exercise constantly with club and knife, axe and lance, sling and bow. Damned good they are, too, but best of all—they could vanish into thin air.

The Yawner himself showed me this, one day when I'd admired his skill in stalking a deer; he said it was nothing, and if I wanted to see how good he was, let me turn my back and count my fingers ten times. So I did, and when I looked round the little bastard had simply disappeared—this on a bare plain without a scrap of cover for half a mile. He absolutely wasn't there—until he stood up at my elbow, with his huge gaping grin, and showed me the shallow trench he had scraped *in silence and in less than two minutes*, within a few yards of me; he'd pulled tufts of grass and earth over his body, and although I'd looked directly at the spot, I'd seen nothing. No one ever believes that story, but I've watched as many as twenty 'Pash at a time vanish in that way, and there are U.S. Army scouts who'll vouch for it.[43] It's one of the first lessons they teach their boys; it was after seeing it that I began to suspect that they might give the Yanks a run for their money—and they did, didn't they?

Apart from these warlike activities, I learned many curious things about them that winter—their love of sports, such as running and swimming, horse-racing, and shooting or throwing lances at rolling hoops; the women have a game much like hockey, at which Sonsee-array excelled, but the great pastime is dice, for all Apaches are inveterate gamblers. They're also highly superstitious—an Apache will never speak his name (I'm told the Chiricahua never speak to their mothers-in-law, either, sensible chaps), or hunt a bear, and they think rattlesnakes are inhabited by lost souls; they regard fish as unclean meat, never drink milk, can't multiply or divide—although some of them can count higher than any other Indians I met—and speak a language which I never mastered. That was partly because most of them spoke Spanish, more or less, but also because it's damned complicated, with five times as many vowel sounds as we have, and the 'Pash, unlike most Indians, are the worst mutterers you ever heard, and nineteen to the dozen at that.[44] But the main reason I never learned Apache was that I disliked them and everything about them too much to want to.

From all this you'll gather that it was a damned long winter, and made no easier by the fact that a male Apache does nothing in all that time except a little light hunting; for the rest he loafs, eats, sleeps, drinks, and thinks up devilment for the spring, so that in addition to being miserable

225

and fearful, I was also bored—when you find yourself glad even of Mangas Colorado to talk to, by God you're in a bad way. The only worthwhile amusement was teaching Sonsee-array new positions—for there was no question of so much as looking at another female, even if I'd dared or wanted to; they're fearfully hot against adultery, you see, and punish it by clipping the errant female's nose off—what they do to the man I was careful not to inquire.

But one thing that interminable season of waiting certainly did accomplish: they got used to me, and by the time the snow melted in the lower valleys I doubt if it occurred even to the shrewd, suspicious Mangas that I might be preparing to slip my cable. I'd been a model, if reserved, son-in-law, Sonsee-array was clearly infatuated, and what *pinda-lickoyee*, honoured by admission to the Mimbreno and marriage to the Morning Star, would be so half-witted as to want to return to his own people? At any rate, when the first big war-party was formed to open the season with a descent on the Del Norte, it was simply assumed that I would take my part; Mangas even returned to me the revolver I'd lost when I was captured, and Sonsee-array herself painted the white stripe across my nose from ear to ear and gloated at the thought of the booty I'd bring home: jewellery was what she wanted, but silk or lace would be acceptable, too, and a couple of Mexican boys as domestic slaves—I can't think why she didn't ask for girls.

"And some new bells, for my moccasins," says she, with that slow pouting smile that was the only thing that had made life endurable through that awful winter. "To make her heart melt." D'you know, it was ridiculous, but as I took my arm from round her waist, mounted the Arab, and looked down into those lovely cinnamon eyes for what I hoped to God would be the last time, I felt a pang? There were great tears in them, and I don't care—it may be as hellish a place as that camp was, with those painted ape-men jabbering as they swung aboard their ponies, the women clustered round the hovels, the place foul and stinking with the winter's filth, the dogs yapping among the piles of refuse, the acrid smoke of the morning fires catching at your throat, and the horror of that captivity burned into your mind, but when your woman sees you away, and cries over your departure, and reaches up to catch your hand and press it to her cheek, and you look back and see the little white figure among the pines, waving you out of sight . . . well, I thought, I've ridden worse, waterfalls or not, and the next buck that gets you is going to be a lucky man, for you're the best-trained red romp in North America.

There were perhaps a hundred of us setting out from the hill camp that day, including all the principal men of the tribe, Mangas himself, Delgadito, Black Knife, Iron Eyes, Ponce, the Yawner, and Quick Killer; every horse in the valley had been pressed into service, for the Apaches were by no means so flush of horse-flesh then as they became later, and about a quarter of our command were afoot. The medicine men inspected us to make sure we had our talismans and medicine cords, and that the younger fellows had their scratching-tubes; then they threw pollen at the sun, chanting, and off we went, in five groups as we left the hills, which is the Apache style on the warpath, the separate bands scouring the country and converging on the main objective.[45] My heart leaped as I heard Mangas shouting in their dialect to the infantry groups as they branched off north-east across the plain, and I caught the name "Fra Cristobal". For that lay north on the Del Norte, not far south of Socorro, and if I couldn't win to safety between here and there—well, there would be something far wrong. Needless to say, there was.

From the hills our five groups fanned out across the mesa which stretched away endlessly towards the east; I was in the centre group, with Mangas and Delgadito; I wasn't sorry that the Yawner and Quick Killer went with one of the south-east bands, for they were the last chaps I wanted on my tail when the time came to cut stick. We rode due east, with the sun like a pale luminous ball in the misty morning, and made good time at a brisk trot; we must have covered forty miles that first day, and I was pleased that my Arab showed no signs of fatigue. We saw not a living soul on the plain, but in mid-afternoon I had the shock of my life, for

227

ahead of us on the horizon there came into view the outline of what could only be a city, and such a city as I couldn't believe existed in this wilderness. Great buildings reared up out of the mesa in symmetrical array; brown adobe by the look of them, but far larger than anything even in Santa Fe. It was bewildering, but my companions paid no heed to it, riding on in their usual sullen silence on either side of me, and it was only when we got to within a mile or so that I realised these weren't buildings at all, but enormous square and oblong rocks, for all the world as though some giant had set them down like a child's building bricks in the middle of nowhere. We passed within half a mile of them, and they looked so neatly arranged, and reminded me so much of an enormous Stonehenge, that I suppose they must be the work of some savage sun-worshippers, though how they transported those massive stones I couldn't image.[46]

We camped that night in a shallow river-bottom filled with cottonwoods, and rode on next day through broken country which began to incline slowly downwards; my excitement rose, for I guessed we must be approaching the Del Norte valley. Sure enough, in the late afternoon we came out of low hills, and there below us in the fading light of sunset lay the familiar fringe of cottonwoods, with here and there a gleam of water amongst them, and low scraggy bluffs beyond. Just over the river smoke was rising from a fair-sized village, all peaceful in the last rays of the afternoon sun. As we dismounted, my heart was thumping fit to burst as I realised that if this was our quarry, I'd never get a better chance to break.

We were in a little gully, and while we stripped off our shirts and oiled ourselves, and renewed our paint—it's mad, isn't it, a civilised white man decorating himself like a savage, but after six months among these beasts I never thought twice about it—Mangas told Delgadito what was to be done. We would ford the river with the last of the light, descend on the village, burn and pillage it, especially of any horses and mules it might contain, and withdraw to our present position for the night; we didn't want prisoners, since tomorrow we would be riding north, wiping up any small settlements that lay in our path along the river, making for the rendezvous where we would meet the walking bands.

Mangas was not to lead us against the village in person. In many ways he was a man after my own heart, for he never ventured his skin unless he had to, but no one thought twice about it, his valour was so well-established—and how many civilised generals do you know who scrimmage alongside their soldiery? While Delgadito, a slim, evil-faced villain who looked more Spaniard than Apache, gave us our tactical directions, Mangas loafed among us inspecting; I can still see that huge, stooped untidy figure in the gloaming as he stopped before me, the black eyes glinting beneath his hat-brim, and feel his coarse thumb as he wiped a smear of paint from my cheek and patted my shoulder, and smell the rank odour that I associate forever with the word Apache.

"Softly across the ford, then scatter and ride straight in," growls Delgadito. "First kill, then plunder, then burn—all except Iron Eyes, Wind Breaker, and Cavallo, who ride round for the far side and secure the corral." Very neat and professional, thinks I. "Right, Mimbreno? Let's go!"

I've ridden in some odd company in my time—Light Brigade at Balaclava, Ilderim's Pathan irregulars, Yakub Beg's Khokand horde under Fort Raim, to say nothing of Custer and that maniac J. E. B. Stuart—but that descent of the Apaches across the Del Norte must have been the strangest of all. Picture if you will that score of primitives with their painted faces and head-bands and ragged kilts and boots, fairly bristling with lances and hatchets, and in their midst the tall figure of the English gentlemen, flower of the 11th Hussars, with the white stripe across his face, his hair rank to his shoulders, his buckskins stinking to rival the Fleet Ditch, lance in fist and knife on hip—you'd never think he'd played at Lord's or chatted with the Queen or been rebuked by Dr Arnold for dirty finger-nails (well, yes, you might) or been congratulated by my Lord Cardigan on his brilliant turnout. "Haw-Haw, Fwashman wides uncommon well, don't he, Jones?"—and there was his pride and joy, as foul an aborigine as any of them, picking his way through the shallows and sand-flats, and breaking with a whoop and a scream as the first yell of alarm rose from the village, the shots rang out, and the savage band charged into the mass of huts with Delgadito at their head.

I swerved after Iron Eyes under the cottonwoods behind the village—and my eyes were already straining ahead towards the low bluffs beyond. If I could drop out of sight in the confusion, and make my way through the dusk, it might be hours before they realised I'd gone, and by that time I'd be flying north along the east bank of the Del Norte—by God, and I wouldn't stop till I reached Socorro at least . . .

There was a shriek from my left; Cavallo had reined up and was letting fly with his bow at an elderly Mexican who had emerged from one of the huts and was standing flat-footed as the arrow took him in the chest; he toppled back, clawing at it, and a woman ran to him from the doorway, an infant clasped on her hip. She stopped with an unearthly scream at the sight of Cavallo, and the evil bastard whooped with glee and rode her down; he leaned from the saddle to seize her by the hair and slashed her across the throat with his knife, and as the infant rolled free from the dying woman's grasp, he let her go and turned the bloody knife in his hand, managing his mount to get a clear throw at the helpless, squalling little bundle. Without thinking I jerked out my Colt and let blaze at him; the knife fell as he reeled in the saddle; he was staring at me in blank astonishment as he clutched his belly, and I thrust my pistol towards his ugly painted face and blew it to pieces.

It was all over in a second, and I was staring round in alarm for Iron Eyes, but he had vanished into the shadows ahead; my shots would be lost in the hideous uproar from beyond the huts, where those fiends were at their red work; shrieks of agony mingled with the whoops and reports, and a ruddy glare from a lighted thatch was already rising to light the shadows around me. I wheeled my Arab and urged her into the concealment of the bushes beyond the cottonwoods—in the nick of time, for here were two Mexicans appearing from between the huts, one of them crying out in horror as he saw the slain woman, the other letting fly with his ancient musket at Iron Eyes, who came at the gallop out of the dark. The shot missed him, and the Mexican went down before his lance thrust; as the second dago rose from the woman's corpse and hurled himself at Iron Eyes, I thought, now's your time, my boy, while they're well occupied. In all that mêlée, no one was going to miss old Flashy for the moment; I slid from the saddle, took the Arab's nose, and led her through the bushes to the far side, where I remounted and made haste towards a gully that opened in the bluff not a furlong away.

The bushes and trees screened me behind; over my shoulder I could see the glow of burning buildings, and envisage the horror that was taking place, but as I gained the gully the awful din of conflict was cut off, and I was coursing up the narrow ravine towards the dimly-seen mesa ahead. Five minutes and I was out on the flat, but there were bluffs ahead, and I veered off eastward, since to flank them on the river side might bring me too close for comfort to the eyes of my comrades.

I was free! After six months with those hellish brutes I was riding clear, and within a day—two days at most—of safety among my own kind. However fast Mangas and his mob of friends moved up the west bank, I must be flying ahead of them; I could have yelled with delight as I pressed ahead at a steady hand gallop, feeling the game little Arab surge along beneath me. Dark was coming down, and stars were showing clear in the purple vault overhead, but I was determined to put a good twenty miles between me and possible pursuit before I halted. They must miss me by tomorrow, and knowing their skill in tracking, I didn't doubt that they would pick up the Arab's trail eventually, but by then I would have a day's law of them; I might even have found a large enough settlement to count myself safe.

I took a sight on the North Star as I rode; so long as I made straight for it I should do well enough, and be able to turn in towards the river when I felt it safe to do so. It was too dark to see much on either side, but the going was hard and level, and I trusted the Arab's footwork. I was still trembling from the shock and elation of escape, and my mouth was dry, so I took a swig from the little canteen at my belt—I must make for water as soon as it was light, but I had some jerked beef in my pouch, and the Arab would be well enough with rough grazing.

For two hours I rode steadily on, and then slowed as the moon rose, to take my bearings. To my right was nothing; on the left a range of hills rose in the distance, which gave me a jar for a moment—the river ought to be that way, surely . . . but perhaps those hills lay beyond it; that must be the explanation . . . it was impossible to judge distance in that uncertain light. But as the moon came up I was able to see as clear as day, and what I saw puzzled me. Instead of the usual rough mesa, I was on a dead flat plain, with a few sparse bushes here and there; the ground, when I tested it, was more like sandy rock than the usual crumbly red earth of the Del Norte valley.

Off to my right a prairie dog howled dismally; it had turned bitterly cold, and I unstrapped my blanket before riding on, my spirits unaccountably lower than they had been. I couldn't figure where I was at all—but so long as I kept north I must be all right. It looked a fairly waterless desolation, though, and when I saw a point of rocks off to my left I made for it, in the hope of finding a stream, but no luck. The rocks were spooky in the moon shadows, and looked a likely lurking-place for snakes or poisonous lizards, so I turned away sharp, and to my relief found myself on a well-defined wagon road leading dead north. There were distinct ruts, and I pushed on in better heart, hoping to come on to less desolate country soon; but as I rode I realised that the scant bushes on either side had petered out, and there wasn't a sign of growth or grass as far as I could see in the silvery radiance. Even the occasional yelp of the coyote was absent now. I halted and listened. Nothing but an immense, empty silence surrounded me, and an icy fear that was not of the freezing night took hold of me. This was not canny; it was as though I were in some dead world— and at that moment the Arab's hoof struck something that rang sharp and hollow. It wasn't a rock, so I climbed down and groped under her hooves; my hand fell on a light, hollow object, I picked it up—and screamed an oath as it

232

fell from my shaking hand. Grinning up at me from the white floor of the desert was a human skull.

I squatted there trembling, and in sudden revulsion kicked the ghastly thing aside. It rattled off the road, and came to rest beside a pile of white sticks which I realised with a thrill of horror was the skeleton of some large beast—an ox or a horse which must have died beside the wagon-tracks. As I stared fearfully ahead I saw in the fading moonlight that there were other similar piles here and there . . . skeletons of men and animals beside a deserted road in the middle of a great waterless plain of rock and sand. It rushed in on me with frightening certainty; I knew where I was, all right. There was only one place in the whole of this cursed land of New Mexico that it could be—by some dreadful mischance I had strayed into the Jornada del Muerto—the terrible Journey of the Dead Man.

For a moment panic seized me, and then I took hold, and tried to remember what the soldier had said that morning south of Socorro: "A hundred and twenty-five miles of rock and sand . . . no water, unless you happen to find a rain pool . . . only one way across—fill your mount with water, take at least two canteens, start at three in the morning and go like hell, because if you don't make it in twenty-four hours, you don't make it."

I was in the saddle before I had finished recollecting, for my one hope was to push on at my uttermost speed while the cool night lasted. How far had I come? Perhaps twenty miles—one hundred to go . . . but unless I found water I was a dead man. Could the Arab carry my weight for another five hours—say, thirty miles, which would see me almost halfway on my journey? If he could, and I found water at—where was it? Laguna?—we should get through, but if I pushed him too hard, and he foundered . . . But I daren't dawdle now. I paused long enough to pour the last couple of inches of water from my canteen over his tongue, and then pressed ahead through the freezing night, while the moon sank and I was riding almost blind with no sound but the echoing hoofbeats over that trackless plain, and the Pole Star over the Arab's ears.

By resting at intervals, I kept him going for close to six hours, and then gave him two hours with my blanket over him to keep out the chill—his health was a damned sight more important than mine just then. The cold was sharp enough to be truly painful, and we were beginning to suffer damnably from thirst; the poor brute nuzzled and snuffled at me, trying to bite the canteen; I led him ahead for a while, and suddenly he began to chafe and heave, neighing feverishly, and knowing the signs I mounted and let him have his head. He fairly flew along, for the best part of another hour; I felt that we were descending a slight incline, and as the first dawn came over the Jornada I saw ahead through the mist the undoubted glitter of water pools. My tongue was too dry to holla for joy; I fairly flung out of the saddle and threw myself face down at the first pool—and to my horror the Arab sped on, clattering through the mist, while I sank down between consternation and thirst—thirst won, I thrust my face into the pool—and started back with a croak of horror. It was pure brine.

If I have grey hairs, is it any wonder? If I have any hair at all, it's a miracle, for I swear that in that dreadful moment I started tearing at the stuff, staggering to my feet, ploughing ahead, trying to rave to the bloody pony to stop, wherever he was, and unable to produce more than a rasping sob from my parched throat. I ran in blind panic, stumbling through the mist, knowing that I was a dying man already, without water, without a horse, and lost in that arid desert; twice I fell on the sandy rock, and twice I rose, blubbering, but at my third collapse I simply lay and pounded the ground with my fists until they were raw, and I could only writhe and whimper in despair.

Something touched the back of my neck—something wet and cold, and I rolled over with a gasp of fear to find the Arab nuzzling at me. By God, his muzzle was soaking! I stared ahead—there were other pools—one of them must be fresh, then! I lurched up and ran to the nearest, but the clever little brute trotted on to stand by a farther pool, so I followed, and a moment later I was face down in clear, delicious water, letting it pour until it almost choked me, rolling in the stuff while the little Arab came for another swig, dipping daintily like the gentlemen he was. I fairly hugged him, and then saw to it that he drank until he was fit to burst.

We rested for a couple of hours, and I wished to God I had just one good waterskin instead of the pathetic little pottle at my belt. Such as it was, I filled it, and we rode up out of that long shallow depression in the warm dawn; ahead stretched that fearful desert, with never a scrub or vestige of grass on it. To the right lay grim barren mountains, with rocky spurs running down to the plain, and to my left front more hills in the far distance—surely they must be the Cristobal range by the Del Norte? I pointed the Arab's head towards them; if we pushed on hard now, we might reach them even through the worst heat of the day. We set off at a gallop, I turned in the saddle for a last look-see behind— and reined in, staring back in consternation.

Far off on the south-western horizon a little column of dust was rising . . . ten miles? Fifteen? However far, it meant only one thing: horsemen. And the only horsemen who would be riding north in the Jornada del Muerto must be Apaches.

They had spotted my trail, then, within a few hours of my evasion, for I didn't doubt for a moment that it was Mangas's band, hell-bent to avenge the mortal insult dealt to their chief and his daughter, their raiding forgotten for the moment. Well, they could ride themselves blue in the face, for there wasn't one of their cattle fit to live in a race with my little Arab . . . provided he didn't go lame, or founder in the heat, or step on a loose stone . . .

I watched the cloud grow imperceptibly larger, and turned the Arab away from the Cristobal hills, heading just east of north to give them a direct stern chase in which they would have no chance to head me off. Time enough, when I'd distanced them, to make for the Del Norte.

For four hours we went at the run, while I watched the pursuing dust-cloud dwindle and finally vanish, but not on that account did I slacken our pace, for I knew they were still there, reading my trail, and it was only when the heat

235

of the day began to scorch us unbearably, and I became aware that I was almost dead from sheer weariness and hunger and thirst, that I drew rein at the first grass that we had sighted since entering that hellish plain. It was poor fodder, but the little Arab fairly laid his lugs back, and didn't I envy him?

I gave him the last of the water, telling myself that we must come on a stream in an hour or two, for the Jornada desert was petering out into mesa studded with sage and greasewood, and there were dimly-seen hills on the northern horizon; I trotted on, turning at every mile to stare through the shimmering heat haze southwards, but there was no movement in that burning emptiness. Then it began to blow from the west, a fierce, hot wind that grew to a furnace heat, sending the tumbleweed bouncing by and whirling up sand-spouts twenty feet high; we staggered on through that blinding, stinging hail for more than an hour in an agony of thirst and exhaustion, and just when I was beginning to despair of ever reaching water, we came on a wide river-bed with a little trickle coursing through its bottom. In the dust-storm I'd have passed it by, but the little Arab nosed it out, whinnying with excitement, and in a moment we were both gulping down that cool delicious nectar, wallowing in it to our hearts' content.

You mayn't think it's possible to get drunk on water, but you'd be wrong, for I reckon that's just what I did, gorging myself with it to the point where my brain became fuddled, so that in my lassitude common sense and caution took wing, and I crawled under the lee of the bank out of the wind, and lapsed into a sodden sleep.

The Arab saved me. I came to wondering where the devil I might be, and what the noise was; recollection returned as I gazed round the empty river bottom. The wind had dropped, but it must have been only a lull in the storm, for the sky was grey and lowering, and there was that uncanny stillness that you can almost feel. The Arab neighed again, stamping excitedly, and I was just scrambling to my feet when from far away down the water-course came a faint answering whinny. I threw myself at the Arab's head, clamping his nostrils and hugging his muzzle; I strained my ears, and sure enough, from somewhere beyond the bend of the dry bed came the sound of hooves. With an oath I seized the bridle and stumbled up towards the lip of the bank, heedless of the clatter of stones; we gained the flat, but it was empty both sides—nothing but low scrub and rank grass, with rising ground a mile or two ahead, and tree-clad foothills beyond.

All this in a glimpse as I swung into the saddle, dug in my heels and went hell-for-leather—and only in the nick of time. Three strides we'd taken when something whizzed like a huge hornet overhead, there was a blood-chilling shriek from behind, and as I turned my head, there they were, surging over the lip of the bank a hundred yards to my left—a dozen of those dreaded figures with their scarved heads and flying hair, bows and lances flourished, whooping like fiends as they bore after me.

Another half-minute in the river-bottom and they'd have had me—even now, as I put my head down and the Arab went like a rat up a drainpipe, it was going to be a damned close thing. A sling-stone buzzed past me (someone less skilled than the Yawner, thank God), but we were flying now, and in a minute we were out of range, drumming across the mesa with that chorus of savage yells waking the echoes behind. I stole another glance; there were four of them bunched together, close enough for me to make out Iron Eyes at their head, and the rest strung out behind; they screamed and urged on their ponies, but they'd been riding continuously, I guessed, for hours, while the Arab was fresh as paint; barring a slip, we must draw steadily away from them—I forced myself to keep my eyes forrard, intent on the ground ten yards in front of the Arab's ears; I picked my course through the low bushes, watching the forested gullies of the foothills coming closer, stealing another backward look—they were a furlong adrift now. That was the moment when the bridle snapped.

One moment it was whole, the next it was trailing loose in my hands. I believe I screamed aloud, and then I had my fists wrapped in the Arab's mane, holding on for dear life, crouching down as a gunshot cracked out behind—there was precious little chance they'd hit me, but now as I raised my head, an infinitely worse peril loomed before me. Out on the flat I had little to fear, but once into those rocky ravines and forested slopes my Arab's speed would count for nothing; I must keep to the open, for my life—but even as I prepared to swerve I saw to my horror that already I'd come too far; there were tongues of forest reaching down to the plain on both my flanks, I was heading into the mouth of a valley, it was too late to turn aside, and nothing for it but to race deeper into the trap, with the triumphant screams of the Apaches rising behind me.

Sobbing with panic, I thundered on, past rocky gullies on either side, past birch and pine thickets, the walls of the valley steadily closing in, and my Arab forced to slacken pace on the rough going. Shots cracked behind me, I heard the deadly swish of an arrow; my pony was stumbling among the loose stones, I jerked my revolver loose and glanced back—Jesus! the leader was a bare fifty yards away, quirting his mustang like fury, with another three strung out behind him. The Arab gathered himself and cleared a stream, slithering on that infernal shale as he landed; somehow he kept his balance, I urged him on—

A numbing pain shot through my right shoulder and something struck me a glancing blow on the face; I glimpsed a feathered shaft spinning away as we blundered through a screen of low bushes; I reeled in my saddle, dizzy with pain, as we raced between low red bluffs topped with thick forest, round a bend in the valley, out on to a broad expanse of loose stones bordering a shallow stream—and beyond reared a great tangle of rock and forest with no way through. The Arab slid and stumbled helplessly on the stones, I knew the Apache must be right on my heels, his war-screech rang in my ears, I was losing my hold, slipping sideways with one arm useless, and in that awful instant I had a glimpse of a man in buckskin standing on a rock not twenty yards ahead, in the act of whipping a musket to his shoulder. A puff of smoke, the crash of a shot, and I was pitching headlong into the stream.

238

I came out of it like a leaping salmon, floundering round to face the Apache—his riderless mustang was clattering away, and the Indian himself was writhing on the stones in his death agony; I saw him heave and shudder into stillness—but when I looked round the buckskin man was no longer there. The rock was empty, there wasn't a sign of life among the trees and bushes fringing the gully—had I dreamed him? No, there was a wisp of smoke in the still air, there was the dead Apache—and round the bend, whooping in hellish triumph at sight of me, came Iron Eyes with two other screaming devils hard on his heels. He flung himself from his pony and raced towards the stream, lance in hand.

Instinctively I pawed at my holster—my revolver was gone! I scrambled wildly up the far bank, clawing my way towards the bushes, and fell headlong; Iron Eyes was yelling with glee as he reached the stream . . .

"Don't stir a finger," said a quiet voice from nowhere. "Just rest right there."

There was no time to be amazed—for the painted red devil was bounding over the stream, brandishing his lance.

*"Ah-hee, pinda-lickoyee dasaygo! Dee-da tatsan!"** he screeched, and paused for an instant to gloat as I sprawled helpless, his head thrown back in cruel glee—something flickered in the air between us, he gave a choking gasp and staggered back into the water, dropping the lance and plucking at the horn-handled knife protruding from beneath his chin. The two other braves, halfway to the stream, checked appalled as he flopped into the shallows, bleeding his life out—and to add to our amazement, shots were ringing out in a volley from beyond the bend in the valley, shouts of command were mingling with war-whoops, and on my disbelieving ears fell the undoubted clarion note of a bugle.

If I was stricken dumb, the Apaches weren't; they yelled with rage or fear, and whirled about like victims in blind man's buff in search of the unseen attacker—and it was uncanny, for one moment the trees to my left had been

*"White-eyed man, you are about to die!"

empty, and then there was a small, sturdy man in faded yellow buckskin standing out in the open, leisurely almost, with a hatchet in his hand and an expression of mild interest on his placid, clean-shaven face.

He glanced at me, and then said something quietly in Apache, and the two braves gaped and then screamed defiance. The small chap shook his head and pointed down the valley; there was another crashing volley, followed by screams and the neighing of horses and the crack of single shots; even in my pain and bewilderment I concluded that some stout lads were decreasing the Mimbreno population most handily—and the nearest Apache rolled his eyes, yelled bloody murder, and he and his mate came at me like tigers, hatchets foremost.

I never saw the buckskin man move, but suddenly he was in their path and the murderous axe-heads clanged as they struck and parried and struck again faster than the eye could follow. I looked to see him cut down in seconds by those agile fighting demons, but if they were fast as cats the little chap was like quicksilver, cutting, ducking, leaping aside, darting in again as though he were on springs—I've seen men of their hands, but never one to cap him for speed, and he wasn't just holding his ground, but driving them back, his hatchet everywhere at once like polished lightning, and the two of them desperately trying to fend him off. Suddenly he sprang back, lowered his hatchet, and addressed them again in Apache—and now came pounding of feet, American voices hollering, and round the bend in the valley men in stained blue coats and dragoon hats were running towards us, led by a big black-whiskered cove in plaid trousers and feathered hat, brandishing a revolver.

One Apache made a bound for the forest and was cut down by a volley from the dragoons; the other hurled himself again at the buckskin man and was met by a cut that sent him reeling back with a gashed shoulder; the whiskered man's revolver boomed, the savage dropped—and to my amazement the small buckskin man shook his head and frowned.

"There was no necessity to shoot him," says he, in that same gentle voice that had spoken to me from thin air. "I had hoped to talk to him."

"Did you now?" roars Whiskers; he was a great, red-faced jolly-looking file. "Listen here, Nestor—you were talking to him just fine, in the language he understood best." He surveyed the four dead Indians in and around the stream. "Fact, you seem to have been having one hell of a conversation." He caught sight of me. "Who in the name of God Almighty is that?"

"Fellow they were chasing," says the buckskin man.

"I'll be damned! Why, he's got Injun paint on his face! And a damned Apache-looking haircut, too!"

"He's white, though. Hair on his chin. Wounded, too."

I was glad someone had mentioned that, for my arm was running like a tap, and if there's one thing that makes me giddy it's the sight of my own blood. What with that, the pain of my wound, the terror of the chase and of the bloody slaughter I had witnessed, I was about all in, but now they were all round me, grimed white faces staring curiosity and concern as they gave me Christian spirits—first down my throat, then on my wound, which made me yelp—and patched me up, asking no questions. A trooper gave me some beef and hard-tack, and I munched weakly, marvelling at the miracle that had brought them to my rescue—especially the supernatural appearance of the gently-spoken little fighting fury in buckskin; there he was now, squatted by the stream, carefully washing and drying the knife that had felled Iron Eyes.

It was the big jolly chap, whose name was Maxwell, who explained what had happened; they had been lying in wait for some Jicarilla horse-thieves who were believed to be making south for the Jornada, when they had seen me coming lickety-split with the Mimbrenos behind me. The little buckskin man, Nestor, knowing the ground, had guessed precisely where my flight must end, and while the soldiers had neatly ambushed the main body of my pursuers, that buckskin angel had just been in time to deal with the vanguard—one musket-shot, and then his knife and hatchet against three Bronco braves; God forbid, I remember thinking, that I should ever get on *his* wrong side.

But I was taking it in like a man in a dream, hardly able to believe that I was here, safe at last, among friends, and the vile ordeal of months, my escape and flight, the final horror of Iron Eyes rushing to finish me—they were all past, and I was safe, and absolutely crying with relief and shock—not sobbing, you understand, but just with tears rolling down my cheeks.

"Easy does it, now," says Maxwell. "We'll get those wet duds off you, and you can sleep a piece, and then we'll hear your side of it—and, say, if you feel like trading in that pony of yours, maybe we can talk about that, too . . ."

He was smiling, but suddenly I couldn't keep my eyes open; great waves of dizziness were engulfing me, my shoulder was throbbing like an engine, and I knew I was going to chalk out. The small buckskin man had come to stand beside Maxwell, looking down at me with the same mild concern he'd shown when he was facing the Apaches; I'd never seen such gentle eyes—almost like a woman's. Perhaps I was wandering in my mind; I know as I looked at that placid, kindly face, I mumbled something, and Maxwell caught it, and his laughter was the last thing I heard before I slid under.

"Magician, you say?" The cheery red face winked and faded. "Mister, you ain't the first that's said that . . ."

14

Maxwell claimed later that the arrow which wounded me must have been poisoned, and indeed there are some who say that the 'Pashes doctor their shafts with rattlesnake venom and putrid meat and the like. I don't believe it myself; I never heard of it among the Mimbreno, and besides, any arrow which has been handled by an Apache, or even been within a mile of him, doesn't *need* poisoning. No, I reckon they were just good old-fashioned wickiup germs that got into my system through that shoulder wound, and blew my arm up to twice its normal size, so that I babbled in delirium all the way to Las Vegas.

Why they took me there, instead of to Santa Fe which was only half the distance, remains a mystery. Apparently I started to rave and turn purple a few hours after my rescue, and since Maxwell, having whetted his appetite on the Mimbrenos, was still keen to come to grips with his Jicarilla horse-thieves, I was placed in the care of a couple of troopers with orders to get me to a medico with all speed; they carted me off on a litter borne by friendly Indians (I wouldn't have thought there were any in that neck of the woods, but there you are), and Las Vegas was where they finished up, with the patient singing "The Saucy Arethusa" and crying out for women, so they tell me. There, presently, I awoke, in Barclay's fort, as weak as a moth and fit for nothing but gruel.

I wasn't sorry to be there, though. In Santa Fe I might easily have had an embarassing encounter with my last wife but one, and for all I knew that greasy little Jesuit might have blown the gaff about my selling Cleonie to the Navajos. So I was content to recuperate under the care of Alick Barclay, a cheery Scot (which is almost as rare as a friendly Indian), and reflect on the sober fact that during eighteen months in the United States of America I had been laid out four times, married twice, shot twice (both from behind), blown up, chased for my life more often that I cared to remember, met some of the most appalling people, and . . . dammit, it wasn't worth it; sooner or later this bloody country was going to prove fatal. I was still stuck in the middle of it, no nearer to home than when I started, and the prospect of a safe passage out distinctly bleak. And all because I'd squeezed Fanny Duberly's tits at Roundway Down and played vingt-et-un for ha'pennies with the likes of D'Israeli. But it was all part of the great web of destiny, every bit of it, as you'll see; God moves in a mysterious way, and I just wish He wouldn't insist on carting me along with Him.

I'd been at Las Vegas a week when Maxwell rolled up, in great fettle; they'd not only intercepted the Jicarillas and killed five of them, but had also recovered the stolen horses, and he was now on his way back to his place at Rayado, up by Taos. He pooh-poohed my thanks jovially—I was sitting up in my cot in Barclay's back-parlour looking pale and interesting—and was all agog to know who I was, for there hadn't been time to introduce myself before I'd keeled over, and how I'd come to be booming up from the Jornada with paint on my face and a war-party at my heels. I was just preparing to launch into a carefully-prepared tale, leaving out such uncomfortable details as scalp-hunting and being Mangas Colorado's son-in-law, when who should slip in but the small man in buckskin.

You'll think me fanciful, but on the spot I decided that the yarn I'd been about to spin had better be more truthful than not. I can lie to anyone, pretty well, and usually do, but there are some birds it's safest not to try to deceive—as often as not they're stainless characters who could have been thorough-paced rascals if only they'd felt inclined, and consequently can spot villainy a mile off: Lincoln was like that, and Chinese Gordon, and my late Lord Wellington. And this quiet, harmless-looking little frontiersman. I don't know what it was about him; he was the most unobtrusive, diffident cove in the world, but there was something in the patient, gentle eyes that told you lying would be a waste of time, for this was not an ordinary man. You may say that having already seen him at his business, I knew how deceptive were his soft voice and modest bearing; well, I sensed the hidden force of him now, even before I'd made the faux-pas of addressing him as Mr Nestor—which was the name I'd heard in the valley—and Maxwell had slapped his thigh in merriment and introduced him: Christopher Carson.

I stared just the same, for I don't suppose there was a more famous man in America at that time. Everyone had heard of Kit Carson, the foremost guide, scout, and Indian fighter on the frontier, the "Napoleon of the Plains"—and most folk on first seeing him found it hard to believe that this shy, unassuming little fellow was the great hero they'd been told about. I didn't—and my instinct told me to stick to the plain truth.

It was as well I did, too. I told them my real name, since it was one I hadn't used in America (except among the 'Pash) and that I'd been on my way to Mexico when I'd fallen in with Gallantin and found myself in a scalp-hunting raid before I knew it; I made no bones about how Sonsee-array had protected me, or how I'd absconded at the first opportunity—Maxwell whistled and exclaimed as though he didn't believe half of it, but when I'd done Carson nodded thoughtfully and says:

"Figures. Heard there was an English scalp-hunter wintering with the Mimbreno, married to Red Sleeves' girl—thought it was just Injun talk till you rode up that valley with paint on your face. Then I knew you must be the man." The mild eyes considered me. "You were right to make tracks. I wouldn't care to have Mangas for my father-in-law."

I cried amen to that, inwardly thanking God that I hadn't strayed from the truth—plainly this little wiseacre had his finger on many unseen pulses. "But I hope, gentlemen," says I, "that I've made it plain that I'm no scalp-hunter, nor ever have been."

Maxwell laughed and shrugged it aside as of no consequence, but Carson thought for a moment (which was a great habit of his) and then said simply: "You must ha' made it plain to Mangas Colorado," as though that were the real point—which it was, when you came to think about it.

Still, says Maxwell judicially, I'd be best advised, the way things had fallen out, not to venture down the Del Norte again for a spell; if I was looking for a port of embarkation, why not San Francisco, and he'd give me any help he could along the way—d'you know, I suspect he absolutely felt he owed me something for having put him in the way of Apaches to slaughter, but I may have been underestimating his natural generosity. He was one of your self-made, cheery, open-handed sorts, and obviously a person of immense consequence in these parts, so when he talked of finding me a place on one of the Rocky Mountain caravans, or with a party of good Mountain Men travelling to California, I was all for it. Carson, who'd been sitting silent, spoke up again, diffident as always.

"I'll be going north in a week or two. If you're ready to travel then, you're kindly welcome to ride along."

"There you are!" cries Maxwell jovially. "That's better than a railroad train to San Francisco, if there was such a thing!" I protested that Carson had done so much for me already that I didn't like to trespass further on his favour; he said, on the contrary, he'd be obliged—which struck me as excessive politeness until he added, with one of his rare smiles (for he rarely grinned above a glimmer, and I never heard him laugh aloud): "Mangas Colarado's a powerful big Injun, and I don't know that much about him. I'd value your opinion."

So that was how I came to ride north with Kit Carson in the spring of '50, whereby I came safe to England eventually—and into such deadly peril, years later, as I've seldom faced in my life. But that was something I couldn't foresee, thank God, when a week later we made the two-day ride north to Rayado, a pleasant little valley in the hills where Maxwell and Carson had made their homes. They were an oddly-assorted pair, those two—Maxwell, the jovial companion, frontier aristocrat, and shrewd speculator who saw where the real wealth of the west was to be found, and built his modest farm at Rayado into the largest private estate in the history of the whole wide world; and Carson, the little gentle whirlwind whose eyes were forever straying to the crest of the next hill, who loved the wild like a poet, and asked no greater possession than a few acres for his beasts and a modest house for his wife and son. Between ourselves, I didn't care for him all that much; for one thing, he had greatness, in his way, and I don't cotton to that; for another, although he was always amiable and considerate, I guessed he was leery of me. He knew a rogue when he saw one— and we rogues know when we've been seen.

For all that, he couldn't have been more hospitable. We were two or three weeks at his house, which was like a tiny Bent's Fort, completely walled in round a central garden and courtyard, but with pleasant rooms comfortably furnished with a great profusion of buffalo rugs and Spanish furniture. His wife, Josefa, was a remarkably handsome Mexican lady of family, and his baby son, Charlie, was a seasoned ruffian of twelve months who took to me at once, as children usually do, recognising in me a nature as unscrupulous as their own. I played "This is the way the farmer rides", and "Roundabout mouse" with the little monster until we were both dizzy, knowing that this was the best way to win his parents' good opinion, and Carson was obviously well pleased.

It was a wonderful restoration after all I'd been through, for the grub was the finest, the air was good, and Maxwell, who had a much larger house close by, with a large staff of servants, had us over frequently to dinner. He was a splendid host, with a fund of stories and good talk, in which Josefa and I joined, while Kit would sit quietly, listening with that faint smile, and only occasionally answering a question, always to the point. I doubt if that man ever said an unnecessary word.

He was sensitive, though, in ways you'd never have suspected. One night I remember he produced a tattered novelette and showed it to me—and if anyone tells you he was illiterate, it isn't true. Whether he could write, I don't know, but he read from that novel—and it was about himself, full of lurid adventures in which he triumphed over hordes of savages, killed grizzly bears with his Bowie, and had hairbreadth escapes from forest fires and blizzards and heaven knows what. I asked, was any of it true, and he said: "Bits of it, but just by accident. I never met the fellow who wrote it."

I imagined his reading it was just a brag, to show how famous he was, but then he told me where he'd come by the book. The previous autumn, he'd been one of a rescue party chasing a band of Jicarillas who had wiped out a small caravan and carried off a Mrs White and her baby; Carson's folk hadn't been able to save her life, or the baby's, although they'd hammered the redsticks handsomely, and afterwards, in the dead woman's effects, he had come across the novelette. It troubled him.

"If she had read this book," says he very seriously, "with all these tall tales about me, then when she was carried off and knew I was coming in pursuit, her hopes must have been high that I would perform some miracle and rescue her and her child. Would you think that?"

I said I supposed she might. What then?

"I failed her," says he, and there were absolute tears in his eyes. "She trusted in me. How bitter her disappointment must have been. My heart is on the ground when I think of that poor lady and her little one, praying for a rescue that I was powerless to perform."

That was the way he talked, I may say, when he was in what he thought of as educated company. Well, I supposed I was meant to console him, but damned if I knew what to say; I racked my brains trying to think what some true-blue hypocrite like Arnold would have coughed up, and was inspired.

"You didn't write that book, Kit," says ministering angel Flashy, "so t'wasn't your fault if she had false hopes. And if she did—well, as one who's been in mortal danger of popping his clogs before now, I can tell you it's a sight better to *hope* you're going to escape than to *know* you're

248

going to die." Which is very true, by the way. "Why, a few years ago, my wife was kidnapped by beastly Borneo pirates, and she said later that she was kept alive by her belief that I would save her."

"And you did?" says he, very attentive.

The temptation to make a brave tale of it was strong, but once again, with those gentle eyes on me, I found myself telling the truth—much more of this little bastard's company and I'd finish up a Christian. "Ah . . . well, yes, in a manner of speaking. I got her out of it, all right . . . but to be fair, she saved us both, in the end." I told him briefly how we'd hidden in that garden in Antananarivo, and Elspeth hadn't so much as squeaked when a searcher's boot had cracked her finger.*

He shook his head in admiration, and says: "Your wife's a gallant lady. I'd admire to meet her." There was a questioning look in his eyes which I thought odd, and slightly uncomfortable, so I changed the subject.

"Anyway, the point about Mrs White is that it's better to die in hope than in despair, don't you see?"

He considered this for about five minutes, and then said: "Perhaps so. It's kind of you to say that. Thank you." Another pause. "Is your wife back in England?"

I said she was, and he nodded and gave me that mild, direct look that I was beginning to find decidedly uncomfortable. "Then we must see you get safe back to her soon," says he. "She will be grieving at your absence."

I wasn't so sure of that myself, but I was mighty glad when in the first week of May—on my twenty-eighth birthday, in fact—we fared north out of Rayado: Carson, a hunter named Goodwin, myself, and a few Mexican *arrieros* to manage the herd of mules that my companions were taking up to Fort Laramie to sell to the immigrant caravans; from there, Goodwin was heading for California, so I would be sure of a safe convoy to the coast.

That journey north took the best part of a month, for it's all of five hundred miles to Laramie, even as Carson rode—

*See *Flashman's Lady*

which was almost as straight as the crow flies—up through the Sangre de Cristo by Pike's peak and the South Park, over the high plains to Fort St Vrain, and through the Wyoming Black Hills to Laramie on the North Platte. It was one of the most splendid trips I ever made, for the scenery is lovely beyond description: I think of that marvellous fastness they call the Eagle's Nest, like a great bowl on the roof of the world, where the air is so clear and pure you want to drink it; the great silent forests, the towering white ramparts of the Rockies far away to the west, the prairie flowers in vast carpets of colour as far as the eye could see, the silver cascades in the deep woods—it was a wild and wondrous land then, untouched by civilisation, a splendid silent solitude that seemed to go on forever.

Best of all, it was safe—not because there weren't savage tribes and dangerous beasts, but because of the small, stocky figure riding ahead in his faded yellow fringed shirt and fur cap, apparently drinking in the view, but in fact recognising every tuft and tree and mountain peak, sniffing the wind, noting each track and trace and sign; and at nightfall, strolling out of sight and circling the camp before returning, with a placid nod, to settle into his blanket. It occurred to me then that I'd sooner have Carson by himself in this country than the entire Household Brigade; he *knew* it all, you see, and even asleep he was a more alert sentry than you or I wide awake. I remember one night round the fire, he suddenly lifted his head and remarked that we'd see buffalo tomorrow; we did; and again, riding up a forest trail, he paused and observed that Caleb was up ahead—sure enough, *a mile* farther on, we spotted an enormous grizzly ambling off among the thickets. How he sensed these things he didn't seem to know himself; he could foretell weather accurately for two days beforehand, and absolutely *smell* a human presence up to about fifty yards.[47]

You may ask if a month in the wilds with that great scout taught me much of woodcraft and mountain lore; I can reply with confidence that by the time we reached Fort Laramie, I could deduce by the sight of a broken twig that someone had stepped on it, and when I saw a great pile of dung on the prairie I knew at once that a buffalo had let drive. Beyond that, my ability to read sign was limited, but by talking with Carson and a Sans Arc guide who rode with us, I polished up my Siouxan and became quite fluent, and few of my languages have proved more vital than that one, for it was the *lingua franca* from Mexico to Canada, and from the Missouri to the Divide, and is so beautiful that I even continued to study it in England. And I guess he taught me a lot about the West without my realising it, for his knowledge was profound, although with remarkable areas of ignorance about the world outside: he had no idea where Japan was, and he'd never heard of Mohammed or geometry; on the other hand, he startled me by quoting at length a poem by some Scotch pessimist, part of which was absolutely in Latin;[48] he'd learned it as a child. I guess that like Sherlock Holmes he knew what he needed to know; he fairly turned me inside out on Mangas Colorado and the Mimbreno, for although he already knew plenty about Apaches, he was avid for any scrap, however trivial, that might add to this store; he even sought my opinion on such minutiae as their consumption of *mescal,* and the possible meaning of the masks worn in the wedding dance; I had to repeat, three or four times, the conversation with Mangas which I've recorded earlier in this memoir, and he would smile and nod agreement.

"Smart Injun," was his verdict. "Sees a long way, and clear. They'll go, as the buffalo go, which it will, with all the new folks coming west. I won't grieve too much for the 'Pash; they have bad hearts, and I wouldn't trust a one of 'em. Or the Utes. But I can be right sorry for the Plains folk; the world will eat them up. Not in my time, though."

I observed that the land was so vast, and the Indians so few, that even when it was settled there must surely be abundant space for the tribes; he smiled and shook his head, and said something which has stayed in my head ever since, for it was the plain truth years ahead of its time.

"An Injun needs a powerful heap of room to live in. More than a million white folks."

In later years I heard many, soldiers mostly, say that Kit

Carson was "soft" on Indians, and it's true, although he probably killed more of them than the cholera, in self-defence or in retribution for raid and murder. The truth is that like most Mountain Men, he was soft on everyone, if dealing amiably and fairly can be called soft; he knew that even the Plains tribes were dishonest and cruel and perverse, just as children are, and so he regarded them, watchfully but with a good deal more affection than they deserved, for my money.

There was no question that they liked him, and those who didn't still admired and respected him. We must have encountered a score of different bands on their spring hunts, and as we drew closer to Fort Laramie their villages and travelling camps became more frequent, for the fort was the very hub of the Plains and Rockies, as Bent's had been farther south, a great station for the immigrant trains, and the market where the northern tribes brought their robes and pelts to trade for civilised goods and booze.

I thought I'd seen Plains Indians on the way out from Independence, but they were nothing to the numbers and variety we encountered now; I carry in my mind a series of brilliant pictures from that time—a band of Pawnee hunters, bare-chested and with long trouser-like leggings of blue or red, their skulls shaved bald save for the bristling fringe of scalp-lock like a cock's comb; Crows in gaudy shirts with war-bonnets so long they trailed to their ponies' flanks; an Arapaho medicine man, his hair woven in fantastic plaits that stuck out from his head like horns, his arms bleeding with self-inflicted wounds as he walked in a trance, followed by a group waving long beribboned sticks as they chanted an incantation; Blackfeet warriors with lances strung with coloured feathers, little targes on their arms, skin caps on their heads, and as many as twenty strings of beads about their necks, for all the world like hawk-nosed dowagers sporting their pearls; Shoshoni, whom I remember for their ugly faces, and their great bearskin robes with the muzzles still attached as hoods; Foxes, with huge beaded earrings and weird designs painted on their backs and breasts; and everywhere, it seemed, swarms of Sioux in all their various clans, which Carson seemed to recognise at sight; one big band of them rode with us for the best part of a day, and a nervous business I found it, with as many as a hundred of the tall, copper-coloured brutes surrounding us, their faces streaked with paint beneath the short-feathered crowns, stripped to their breech-clouts in the sweltering summer sun, guns at their saddle-bows and lances at rest; they bore a name which was to become fearsome on the North Plains: Oglala. But best of all I have a memory of a long line of braves, wrapped in blankets, feathers slanting down from their long braided hair, riding slowly along a skyline at sunset, looking neither right nor left, dignified as grandees on their way to audience at the Escurial—my old acquaintances, the Cheyenne.

None of 'em offered us the slightest offence—though whether they'd have been as amiable if Carson hadn't been along, I don't care to think, for I gathered from him that there was a great discontent beginning to brew among them. They'd been trading about Laramie for years, peaceful enough, but after the cholera of the previous summer, which they blamed, rightly enough, on the immigrants, they were casting dark looks at the trains that came pouring westward in this summer of '50. Before 1849 there had been wagons enough on the trails, but nothing to the multitude that now followed the gold strike. I've been told that more than 100,000 pioneers crossed the plains in '50; from what I saw myself at Laramie and westward it was just a continuous procession—and I would say that was the year the Plains tribes realised for the first time that here was the rising of a white tide that was going to engulf their land—and their life.

You see, before '49, if you were a Crow or an Arapaho or a Cheyenne, you might sit on a ridge and watch the schooners crawl across the empty prairie, one at a time, perhaps only a solitary train in a week. You might trade with it, or take a slap at it for devilment, to run off a few horses, but mostly you'd leave it alone, since it was doing no harm, apart from reducing the grazing along the North Platte or the Arkansas, and thinning the game a little. But the Indian just had to turn his back and ride a few miles to be in clear country which the caravans never touched, the bison herds ran free, and game abounded. There was still plenty for everyone.

It was different after '49. A hundred thousand folk need a power of meat and wood and fodder; they must forage wide on either side of the trail, in what to them is virgin country, and wreak havoc among the buffalo and smaller game; they must strip the grazing to its roots—and it ain't in human nature for them to think, in all that vastness, what it may mean for those few figures sitting on the ridge over yonder (who are thieving, dangerous rascals anyway). But if *you* are those figures, Crow or Arapaho or Cheyenne, watching the torrent that was once a trickle, seeing it despoil the Plains on which you depend for life, and guess that it's going to get bigger by the year, and that what was once a novelty is now a menace—what d'you do? Precisely what the squire in his Leicestershire acres, or his New England meadow, would do if crowds of noisy, selfish foreigners began to trek through ruining the place. Remonstrate—and when that don't work, because the intruders can't see what damage they're doing, and don't care anyway—what d'you do then? I'll tell you; Leicestershire squire, New England farmer, Cheyenne Dog-Soldier or Kiowa Horse-Cap, you see that there's only one thing for it: you put your paint on.

But in that summer of '50 the tribes were still just at the fretting stage, wondering if they might not have to do something serious about this invasion eventually; when they hammered a caravan occasionally, it was more for fun that policy. As I've said, they were friendly enough to our party, and the last day before we reached Laramie a party of Sioux even invited us to share the feast they were making after a successful buffalo hunt; we'd passed them in the morning as they were skinning the carcases and lighting their fires, and Carson, who stopped off to talk with them, came up presently and says with his quiet smile:

"Injun back there claims to recognise you. Says you shared a hump with him last summer over to Council Grove, and he'd like to repay the hospitality. Spotted Tail—know him?"

I remembered that evil-looking trio who had made themselves free of our meat the day I'd shot my first buffalo with Wootton. With Carson on hand I didn't mind renewing the acquaintance, and sure enough it was the same six-foot handsome spectre with the coonskin headgear, bloody to the elbows among the slaughtered game but grinning all over his wicked hawk face; he shook my hand and growled greetings, and presently we sat round, our half-dozen among twenty Brulé warriors, gorging ourselves on the freshly-roasted meat. I sat by Spotted Tail, exchanging civilities in my newly-acquired Siouxan—Wootton had never named me to him, evidently, and I was ill-advised enough to tell him my Apache handle of Wind Breaker, which he said solemnly was a brave and creditable one. I expressed my appreciation of the grub in Sioux and English, and since it was a new phrase to him he took pains to repeat it several times, croaking with laughter: "Joll-ee good! Joll-ee good!"

He had his nephew with him on the hunt, a pale, bright-eyed skinny little shaver who couldn't have been above five or six years old, and was unique among all the Indians I ever saw, for his hair was almost fair. He sat very quiet among the feasters, and looked askance whenever anyone caught his eye. I found him watching me once and winked at him; he started like a rabbit, but a minute later our eyes met and he tried to wink back, shyly, but couldn't close one eye without shutting the other, and when I laughed and winked again he giggled and covered his face. Spotted Tail growled at him to be still and mind what he was about, and the child whispered something which made his neighbours roar with laughter, at which Spotted Tail snapped at him threateningly. I asked what the boy had said, and Spotted Tail told me, glowering at the infant:

"Forgive the impudence of my sister's graceless son. He asks if the big white man is sick, that he cannot keep one eye open."

"Tell him that winking is a great medicine," says I, "which will be useful to him when he grows older and meets girls,

255

and if he can learn how to do it I'll give him a ride on my pony."

They all guffawed again at this, and some of the Brulé braves called out to the boy, making fun of him—but when we came to take our leave, bursting with buffalo meat, there the little devil was, standing at my pony's head, with one eye clamped desperately shut and the other one watering with his effort to keep it open. Spotted Tail would have cuffed him, for while they are uncommonly indulgent of children, they have a fine sense of courtesy to guests, but I picked him up and planted him on my saddle, and the little tyke sat there like a pea on a drum, scared stiff but determined not to show it. I led him about a little, and he clung tight, squeaking with excitement to go faster, so I swung up behind and gave him a canter; I can still hear his shrill laughter, and see his fair hair blowing as we swept along. When he was all out of breath I passed him down to Spotted Tail and asked his name; Spotted Tail tossed him in the air and caught him, squealing.

"Little Curly White Hair," says he, slapping the infant's rump.

"Well, he'll be a great horseman and warrior some day," says I, and as we took our leave the imp perched on his uncle's shoulder and waved after us, his little voice piping in the wind.

"You made a friend there," says Carson.

"Who, the kid?"

"No, Spotted Tail. He values that boy—the father's a big medicine man among the Oglala. Come to that, Spotted Tail's a pretty big man among the Brulé, in all the Sioux councils. Handy friend to have, if ever you chance back this way."

Since I had no intention of ever setting foot in that awful wilderness again, I didn't pay much mind—but of course he was right, as usual. If I hadn't pleased Spotted Tail that day, by playing with the kid . . . who knows? I might have been spared a heap of trouble—or I might be dead by now. You can never tell where small boys are concerned; they may grow up to be your best friend—and your worst enemy.

We came to Fort Laramie next day, through a sea of prairie schooners and immigrant tents and Army horse lines and Indian lodges, all clustered for a couple of miles round the great adobe stockade by the Platte;[49] there were caravans coming in and caravans leaving, traders white and Indian hawking their wares, dragoons drilling beneath the walls, and such a Babel as I hadn't seen since Santa Fe or Independence. When word spread that Carson had arrived, there was such a press of folk to see the great man that it was only with difficulty that we got our mules to the corral, and while Goodwin began the bargaining with teamsters from the trains, Kit and I went off to the post kitchen, ostensibly to see about grub, but in fact so that Carson could get out of the public eye—he hated to be stared at, especially because, as he told me in a rare burst of confidence, people were so disappointed because he wasn't twenty feet tall.

We had an amusing illustration of that as we sat outside the kitchen, drinking coffee and talking to one or two of Carson's mountain acquaintances; there was a great press of folk about, and through them comes this big, grizzled Arkansas hayseed, bawling:

"I hear Kit Carson's hereabouts! Lemme see him—I want to shake his hand! I do that! Whar's he at, then?"

I heard Carson sigh, as someone pointed him out, and then the hayseed comes stumping across, frowning, and stands in front of him, scratching his head in bewilderment.

"Mister," says he, doubtfully. "You Kit Carson?"

Carson looked up at him with his customary mild expression and nodded. The hayseed stared dumbfounded.

"The Kit Carson? The . . . the scout, an' all?"

Kit just looked at him, embarrassed, almost apologetic in fact, and the hayseed shook his head.

"I don't believe it! You . . . you ain't tellin' me yore *him!* No, mister—you ain't Kit Carson for me!"

Kit sighed again, and then glanced at me. Now, while he was in his usual old buckskins, I was in the full prairie fig that Maxwell had given me, fringed beaded jacket and breeches and wideawake hat, with a Colt on my rump and a Bowie in my boot, and as you know I'm six feet odd and stalwart with it; you never saw such an image of a prairie hero in your life. Carson smiled, looked at the Arkansas boy, and gave an almost imperceptible nod in my direction. The hayseed swung round to me, and a huge beam of joy broke over his ruddy countenance as he looked me up and down.

"Now, that's more like it!" cries he, and I found my hand crushed in his huge grip. "Say, have I bin waitin' to see you, Kit! My, wait till I tell the folks 'bout this—why, sir, it's an honner! 'Deed it is! Kit Carson! So, now—thank'ee kindly, an' God bless you!"

There were absolute tears in the great clown's eyes as he turned away, glanced at Carson, growls: "Kit Carson? Huh!", tipped his hat to me with another broad grin, and strode off. The mountain boys held on to each other laughing, and I wasn't any too pleased, but Carson gave me his slantendicular smile and shrugged. "You look a heap more like me than I do, Harry," says he. He was right of course; I did.

I'd no cause to complain, though, of the pains he took to secure me a safe passage to the coast: Goodwin was travelling up to the Yellowstone before heading west, but knowing I wanted to lose no time, Carson put it about that a friend of his wanted to work his way to the coast as a hunter—and such was the magic of his name that the wagon-captains whose trains were resting at Laramie fairly fought for my services. Fifty dollars a month, I was offered, and all found, which was no small thing since the cash I'd raised on Cleonie had vanished mysteriously among the Apaches, and I hadn't a bean towards my sea-passage. Carson chose a big, well-found train of sixty schooners, and put in a special word for me.

"Harry Flashman's a good man on the trail," says he. "Been down among the 'Pash, and in the British Army. Good shot." The wagon-captain damned near pumped my hand off, and I heard him bragging to his mates that he'd got "one o' Kit Carson's boys".

Now, when I added this to all the favours Carson had

done me, I found it middling odd. Granted he was a generous, open-handed ass who'd rather do anyone a good turn than not; still, I guessed for all his kindness that he'd never cottoned to me, let alone liked me, so why was he being so deuced considerate?

I'm always leery of favours which I don't deserve, so when Carson left Laramie a day or so before my caravan was due to start, I rode out a few miles with him on his way, and fished for an explanation at parting. I thanked him again for saving my life, entertaining me at Rayado, convoying me north, and recommending me, and hinted that on that last score at least he'd been saying more than he really knew.

"No," says he, after some reflection. "I saw you shoot pretty good on the way north. You ride like a Cumanche, too."

"Even so," says I, "you've been more than generous—to a complete stranger."

He went into another of his pensive broods, his eyes on the trail ahead where his *arrieros* were riding down to the woods; we were alone on the little ridge. At last he says:

"You're going back to your wife in England. That lady in Santa Fe—she wouldn't be your wife."

I nearly fell out of my saddle. How the hell had he heard about Susie? I gaped at him, and regained my wits. "Good lord, no! That's a . . . a woman I met in the East—we were companions, don't you know . . . er . . . who . . . told you about her?"

"Dick Wootton," says he, perfectly mild. "I saw him in Santa Fe after we picked you up—while you were sick, at Vegas. He chanced to mention how he'd come west with an English fellow named Comber, last summer; from Dick's description, this fellow sounded pretty like you. So I was astonished when I saw you at Vegas and you told me you were called Flashman. Different name, you see."

"Ah . . . well, you see . . . it's a long story—"

"I'm not asking," says he gently, still looking down the trail. "Just telling. Dick told me this Comber fellow ran away from his wife—that was what Dick called her—in Santa Fe. But I didn't mention you to Dick. Not my business."

"Well, by Jove, Kit, I'm most obliged to you—but honestly, I can explain—"

"Don't have to." He frowned at the distance, and sighed. "Dick said he figured—I'm telling you just what he said—that this fellow Comber might be on the run; Dick had a feeling there was a price on his head back east, maybe. Wasn't sure, of course . . . just a feeling, you understand."

My blood was suddenly frozen, and my laugh must have sounded like a death-knell. "Good God!" cries I. "What an extraordinary notion, to be sure! Why should he think . . . I mean . . . whoever this chap was . . . well, there are other Englishmen . . . " It was no use: I tailed off lamely as the mild eyes turned to consider me, and his voice was quiet as ever.

"Dick told me this Comber was a good wagon-captain . . . kind of green, in some ways, but he got the train through. Spoke with a straight tongue to the sick Cheyenne, too. Did pretty well at Bent's when the Big Lodge blew up." He paused. "Dick said, whatever this Comber was, or had done . . . he liked him." Another long pause. "I value Dick's opinion."

I've had some strange testimonials in my time, including the Victoria Cross, a pardon from Abraham Lincoln, Sale's ludicrous report from Jallalabad, Wellington's handshake, the thanks of Parliament, a pat on the back from Rajah Brooke, and ecstatic sobs from all sorts of women—but I'm rather partial to the memory of Kit Carson telling me what a white man I was. God, he was gullible—no, he wasn't either, for he'd figured me for a scoundrel, right enough; his only mistake was in accepting the simpleton Wootton's estimate that I was a *brave* scoundrel. That was enough for little Kit; it didn't matter what else I'd done . . . running out on women, using assumed names, committing God knew what crimes back East. I'd got the train through.

It's a remarkable thing (and I've traded on it all my life) that a single redeeming quality in a black sheep wins greater

260

esteem than all the virtues in honest men—especially if the quality is courage. I'm lucky, because while I don't have it, I *look* as though I do, and worthy souls like Carson and Wootton never suspect that I'm running around with my bowels squirting, ready to decamp, squeal, or betray as occasion demands. And in their kindly ignorance, they give me a helping hand, as Carson had done—he'd also given me a damned nasty start for a moment; my nerves were still tingling.

"Ah, well," says I, trying to sound hearty. "He's a good chap, is Uncle Dick."

"Wah!" says he, and had another consider to himself. "Safe home, then." A final pause. "If you chance back thisaway, give me a hollo."

"I shan't be coming back," says I, and by George, I meant it.

He nodded, lifted a hand slightly, and turned his pony down the trail. I watched him out of sight, the small buckskin figure fading into the trees, and while I felt nothing but relief at the time (for the Kit Carsons of this world and I don't ride easy together) what sticks in my mind now is how easy and natural it was to part and go your ways on the old frontier, without ceremony or farewell. It was almost a superstition, I suppose: no one ever said good-bye.

* * *

Two days later our caravan started west for the South Pass, and I rode out that morning in a great contentment, as though I were coming to the end of a long trek—which was odd, with more than a thousand miles of prairie and salt desert and Rocky Mountain to cross to the coast, and long sea-leagues beyond that to England. But you know how it is—sometimes you know that a chapter is closing, as surely as though you were shutting a door behind you. As I swung aboard the little Arab, and heard the cry of "All set!" echoing down the wagon line, and heard the whips crack and the teamsters yell and the wheels groan forward—I knew I was nearing the end of that frightful journey which had begun when John Charity Spring strode into my hotel room at Poole and started raving in Latin; a journey that had carried me to the wilds of Dahomey and skirmishes with great black-titted females, through chases and sea-battles to New Orleans and desperate flights and escapes on the Mississippi, from brothels to plantations to slave-marts to that homely front-hall where I'd quaked and bled while an ugly, gangling young lawyer stuck his chin out and braved my ruffianly pursuers; and since then I'd rogered my way ouf of the law's clutches, across the prairies to the terrors of Bent's Fort and the Del Norte and the Dead Man's Journey . . . but it was all past and done with, and soon I would be taking ship for home. And Elspeth and soft beds and green fields and strolls down the Haymarket and white whores for a change and cricket and rides in the Park and hunting and decent cigars and conversation and everything that makes life worth living. By gum, I'd earned it.

And as for their damned redskins and prairie wagons and buckskins and bear's grease and painted faces and buffalo grass and sweat-baths and plug-a-plew and war-whoops and Mountain Men—well, they could keep 'em all for me.

They did.

The Seventy-Sixer

15

◀◀◀━━━━━▶━━━━━◀ It's only when you've grown old that you
begin to see that life doesn't run in a straight line; that you
can never be sure a chapter is finished, and that half a
century may lie between cause and final effect. Why, I met
Lola Montez and Bismarck in '42, bedding one and belittling
t'other, and thought that was that—and five years later they
popped up to give me the scare of my life. And I thought
I'd seen the last of Tiger Jack Moran after Rorke's Drift—
but, damme, *he* came back to haunt my old age and almost
had me indicted for murder. No, you never can tell when
the past is going to catch up, especially a past as dirty as
mine.

So it was with the old West. I left it on a summer's day
in '50, vowing never to return, and twenty-five years later,
when the old memories had faded, back it came with a
vengeance—and that word is well-chosen, as you'll see.

I blame Elspeth entirely. Having the brain of a backward
hen, it had taken her until middle age to discover the delights of luxurious globe-trotting, and since by then old
Morrison's ill-gotten pile had swollen prodigiously, she was
able to indulge her wanderlust to the full. As often as not
I went along, for after thirty years of travelling rough I
didn't mind being wafted about in style, from steamer stateroom to hotel Pullman, and stopping at the best pubs on
the way; another reason was that I didn't trust the little
trollop an inch, for Elspeth at fifty was every bit as beddable
as she'd been at sixteen, and had lost none of her ardour.
The Bond Street salons and swarms of effete Frog hairdressers kept that corn-gold hair as lustrous as ever, her
milky-pink complexion bloomed like a country girl's, and if
she'd added a stone to her figure it was all to the good and
well-placed. In fact, she continued to draw men like flies to

a jam-pot, and while in thirty years I'd never absolutely caught her *in flagrante*, there were a dozen at least I suspected her of slapping the mattress with, including that pop-eyed lecher Cardigan and H.R.H. Bertie the Bounder. So I wasn't having her panting with Alpine guides and sweaty gondoliers while I idled at home on half-pay; I preferred to keep her in trim myself and discourage foreign attentions. I loved her, you see.

Most of her jaunts were close to home, at first—Black Forest, Pyrenees, Italian lakes, the Holy Land and Pyramids, and endless piles of Greek rubble dignified by antiquity, for which she had a remarkable appetite, sketching away execrably under a parasol and misquoting Byron while her maid scampered back to the hotel for fresh crayons and I loafed impatiently, wishing I might slip down to the native quarter for some vicious amusement among the local wildlife. And then one winter's day early in '75 she remarked idly that I'd never shown her North America.

"Neither I have," says I. "Well, there's a lot of it, you know. Difficult to take in, and it's a long way."

"I should *so* love to visit it," says she, with that faraway imbecile expression that comes of studying engravings in the *Illustrated London News*, "to venture forth into the New World with its scenic grandeurs and huntsmen in picturesque garb, and the unspoiled savages and the cowboys with their coyotes and lariats," she babbled on, sighing, "and the Tremont Hotel of Boston is said to be *quite* superior, while the Society of New England is reputed *most* select, and there are all those battle-fields with peculiar names where you were so brave which I *long* to have you show me. The price of passage is also extremely reasonable and—"

"Hold on, though," says I, for I could see the cricket season vanishing. "It's farther than you've ventured before, you know—except for Singapore and Borneo—and you didn't care for *that*. Or Madagascar. Well, America's pretty wild, too."

"Why, I cared extremely for Borneo and Madagascar, Harry! The voyage was ever so jolly, and the climate agreed with me perfectly."

"And being kidnapped by pirates, and chased for our lives by enormous niggers—you enjoyed those, did you?"

"Some of the people were disagreeable, true, but others were most amiable," says she, and I knew from her complacent sigh that she was fondly recalling all the randy villains who'd ogled her in her sarong. "Besides," she went on, glowing, "*that* was an *adventure*—do you know, I never was so happy as when we fled through the forest, you and I—and you fought for me, and were so strong, and took such good care of me, and . . . and . . ." Her great blue eyes filled with tears, and she pressed my hand, and I felt a sudden odd yearning for her, which was rapidly dispelled as she went on: "In any event, America cannot be as barbarous as Madagascar, and since you have the acquaintance of the President and other persons of consequence, we are sure to have the *entrée*, especially with our money. Oh, Harry, my heart is *set* on it, and it will be *such* fun! Please say you'll take me!"

Since she had already bought the tickets, that was how we came to be at Phil Sheridan's wedding in Chicago a few months later, and there, with a startling coincidence, began the bewildering chain of events which completed the story that I have told you in this memoir so far. (At least, I hope to God it's complete at last.) Not all that happened in '49 has a bearing on what I'm about to tell, for life's like that, but much of it did. I can safely say that had it not been for my odyssey which began in Orleans and ended at Fort Laramie in '50, the history of the West would have been different. George Custer might still be boring 'em stiff at the Century Club, Reno wouldn't have drunk himself to death, a host of Indians and cavalrymen would probably have lived longer, and I'd have been spared a supreme terror as well as a . . . no, I shan't call it a heartbreak, for my old pump is too calloused an article to break. But it can feel a twist, even now, when I look back and see that lone rider silhouetted against the skyline at sunset, with the faint eerie whistle of *Garryowen* drifting down the wind, and when I had rubbed the mist from my eyes, it was gone.

It was sheer chance we were at Sheridan's wedding. Despite my loved one's expressed enthusiasm for scenic grandeur and huntsmen in picturesque garb, she'd been content to spend the first months poodle-faking with the smart set in Boston and New York, wallowing at the Tremont and Delmonico's, and spending money like a rajah in Mayfair. Society, or what passes for it over there, had naturally opened its arms to the beauteous Lady Flashman and her distinguished husband, and we might have been racing and dining and water-partying yet if Little Phil hadn't got word of my presence, and insisted that we come to Chicago to see him jump off the cart-tail. I'd known him for a good sort in the Civil War, and met him again during the Franco-Prussian nonsense, so to Chicago we went.

I must digress briefly to remind you of the vast change that twenty-five years had wrought in my own fortunes. Back in '49, though a popular hero in England, I'd been a nameless fugitive in the States; now, in 1875, I was Sir Harry Flashman, V.C., K.C.B., with all the supposed heroics of the Crimea, Mutiny, and China behind me, to say nothing of distinguished service to the Union in the Civil War. No one had been too clear what that service was, since it had seen me engaged on both sides, but I'd come out of it with their Medal of Honour and immense, if mysterious, credit, and the only man who knew the whole truth had got a bullet in the back at Ford's Theatre, so he wasn't telling. Neither was I—although I will some day, all about Jeb Stuart, and Libby Prison, and my mission for Lincoln (God rest him for a genial blackmailer), and my renewed bouts with the elfin Mrs Mandeville, among others. But that ain't to the point just now; all that signifies is that I'd gained the acquaintance of such notables as Grant (now President) and Sherman and Sheridan—as well as such lesser lights as young Custer, whom I'd met briefly and informally, and Wild Bill Hickok, whom I'd known well (but the story of my deputy marshal's badge must wait for another day, too).

So now you see Flashy in his splendid prime at fifty-three, distinguished foreign visitor, old comrade and respected military man, with just a touch of grey in the whiskers but no belly to speak of, straight as a lance and a picture of cavalier gallantry as I stoop to salute the blushing cheek of the new Mrs Sheridan at the wedding reception in her father's garden.[50] Little Phil, grinning all over and still looking as though he'd fallen in the river and let his uniform dry on him, led me off to talk to Sherman, whom I'd known for a competent savage, and the buffoon Pope, whose career had consisted of losing battles and claiming he'd won. They were with a big, abrupt cove, whiskered like a Junker, named Crook.

"And how the thunder do I keep 'em out of the Black Hills?" he was demanding. "There are ten thousand miners there already, hungry for gold, and I'm meant to say, 'Now, boys, you just leave the nuggets be, and run along home directly.' They'll listen, won't they?" he snorted, and then Sheridan was presenting me. I expressed interest in what Crook had been saying, and was enlightened.

It seemed that a few years earlier Washington had made a treaty with the Sioux Indians granting them permanent possession of the Black Hills of Dacotah, which the Sioux regarded as their Valhalla; no white settlers were to come in without Sioux permission, but now that gold had been found in the hills (by a scientific expedition sent out under Custer, in fact) the miners were swarming in, the redskins were protesting, and Crook had been told to get the intruders out, p.d.q.

"You may imagine, sir," he told me sourly, "how a hard-case prospector will respond when I tell him that he, a free-born American, can't go where he damned well pleases on American soil. Even if I do persuade or drive him out, he'll slip back in again. Can't blame him, sir; the gold's there, and you can't keep a dog from its dinner."

"Treaty or no treaty," says Pope solemnly.

"Treaty, nothing!" snaps Sherman; he was the same ugly, black-avised bargee who you remember observed that war is hell, and then proved it; I was interested to see that ten years hadn't mellowed him. "That's all I hear from the soapy politicians and Bible-punching hypocrites in Washington, and the virtuous old women who get up funds for the relief of our 'red brothers'—how our wicked government violates treaties! But not a word about Indian violations, no, sirree! We guaranteed 'em the Black Hills, sure—and they guaranteed us to keep the peace. How do they keep their bargain?—by ripping up the tracks, scalping settlers, and tearing six kinds of hell out of each other after every sun dance! How many of 'em have settled on the reservations, tell me that!"

Pope wagged his fat head and said he understood that some thousands had come in to the agencies, and settled down quietly.

"You don't say!" cries Sherman scornfully. "Seen the Indian Office figures, have you? Out of fifty-three thousand Sioux, *forty-six thousand* are 'wild and scarcely tractable'—those are the very words, sir. Oh, they'll come *in* to the agencies, and collect the provisions we're fool enough to hand out to them, and the clothes and blankets and rifles—you bet they'll have the rifles! For hunting, naturally." He prepared to spit, and remembered he was at a wedding. "Hunting white settlers and soldiers, I dare say. Know how many thousands of new rifles—Winchester and Remington repeaters, too—were shipped up the Missouri by Indian traders last year? How many million cartridges? No, you don't know, because Washington daren't say. And the benevolent government permits it, to hostiles who've no least notion of settling on reservations, or turning to farming, or accepting the education offered 'em by a bunch of old women in pants back East who'd never dare put their noses west of St Louis. Is it any wonder the Sioux think we're soft, and grow more insolent by the day?" He let out a great snort of disgust. "Oh, the hell with it, I need a drink."[51]

He stumped off, and Crook shook his head. "He's right on one thing: it makes no sense to arm the tribes while we keep our own troops short of proper equipment. Someone is going to have to pay for that policy sooner or later, I fear—probably someone in a blue coat earning $13 a month to guard his country's frontier."

It sounded very much like the usual soldiers' talk about politicians—except that Sherman and Sheridan at least weren't usual soldiers. Sherman was commander-in-chief of the U.S. Army, and Little Phil commanded the Missouri Division, which meant the whole Plains country to the Rockies. I didn't doubt they were well informed on the Indian question, and I knew the government was notoriously corrupt and inefficient, although Grant himself was said to be straight enough. Innocently I said I supposed the business of supplying the Indians was a very lucrative one; Pope choked on his drink, Sheridan shot me a glance, but Crook looked me straight in the eye.

"That's the devil of it—a trader can get $100 in buffalo skins for one repeater, and twenty cents a cartridge. But that's small beer to the profits of contractors who supply the agencies with rotten meat and mouldy flour, or agents who cook their books and grow fat at the Indians' expense."

"Come now, George," cries Pope, "not all agents are rascals."

"No, some of 'em are just incompetent," says Crook. "Either way, the Indian goes hungry, so I guess I can't blame him if he prefers not to rely on the agencies—except for weapons."

"Forty-six thousand hostiles, well-armed?" says I. "That's about twice the size of the U.S. Army, isn't it?"

"Gentlemen, we have a British spy in our midst!" says Sheridan, laughing. "Yes, that's about right—but not all of those Indians are truly hostile, whatever Sherman thinks. Only a handful, in fact. The rest simply don't want to live on agencies and reservations. The few real wild spirits—Crazy Horse, Sitting Bull, and the like—don't amount to more than a few thousand braves. There's no danger of a general outbreak, if that's what you're thinking. No danger of that at all."

And now came Elspeth tripping radiantly to reprove me for not presenting the famous General Crook—of whom she'd never heard, of course, but the little flirt knew a fine figure of a man when she saw one. So now Crook beamed and made a chest and bowed and called her "my lady" and absolutely behaved like a faithful sheepdog while I admired her performance with a jaundiced eye, and the talk murmured on under the trees in the drowsy summer afternoon;

I did the polite with the prettiest bridesmaid at the punch-bowl, and forgot all about Indians.

It came back a few hours later, though, when the coincidence happened. Until Sheridan's wedding I hadn't thought about redskins for years, and now, the very same day, the old West laid its horny hand softly on my shoulder for the second time.

Elspeth and I were going in to dinner at the Grand Pacific, and I had turned into their big public lavatory to comb my whiskers or adjust my galluses; I was barely aware of a largish man who was examining his chin closely in a mirror and grunting to himself, and I was just buttoning up and preparing to leave when the humming ended in a rasping growl of surprise.

"*Inyun*! Joll-ee good! *Washechuska** Wind Breaker! *Hoecah!*"[52]

I bore up sharp, for I don't suppose I'd heard Siouxan spoken in more than twenty years—and then I stood amazed. My companion had turned from the mirror, tweezers in hand, and was regarding me in delighted surprise. I gaped, for I couldn't credit it; there stood a figure in evening trousers and coat, starched front and all—and above it the bronzed hawk face of a full-blooded Plains Indian brave, with a streak of paint just below the parting of his glossy black hair, which hung to his waist in long braided tails, one adorned with a red eagle's feather. Well, I'd known American hotels were odd, but this beat all. The apparition advanced, beaming.

"You remember? At Fort Laramie, the year after the Great Sickness? You, me, Carson the Thrower-of-Ropes? *Han?*"†

Suddenly the years fell away, and I was back in the hollow where Wootton and I skinned the buffalo, and that awful visitation . . . the painted face with the coonskin hanging from its cap . . . and the feast with the Brulé at Laramie

---

*Englishman. *Inyun* and *hoecah* are exclamations of surprise and disbelief.
†Yes?

. . . "joll-ee good! joll-ee good!" . . . and the same black devil's eyes glinting at me. By some freak of memory it was his Indian name that I remembered first.

"Sintay Galeska! Good God, can it be you?"

He nodded vigorously. "The Spotted Tail. *Hinteh*,* how long has it been? You have grown well, Wind Breaker— with a little frost in your hair." He pointed to the grey in my whiskers, chuckling.

I was still taken all aback—as you would be if you'd met the King of the Cannibal Isles rushing naked round the South Seas, and twenty years later he tooled up to you in the Savoy in full evening fig, and began assailing you in broken English and a native tongue you'd all but forgotten. Why, the last time I'd seen him he'd been in breech-clout and war-bonnet, all smeared with buffalo blood . . . now he was rumbling on in Sioux, and I was struggling to identify those sonorous vowels, dredging words from the back of my mind.

"Hold on a moment . . . er, *anoptah*!† You're Spotted Tail, the Brulé? The . . . the killer of Pawnees?" And instinctively my hand went up to crook a finger at my brow, which is sign-talk for Pawnee, the Wolf-Folk—heaven knew where that memory had come from, after so long. He crowed approvingly, nodding. "But . . . but what the devil are you doing . . . here, I mean?"

"Here? Grand Pacific?" He shrugged massively. "It not so good. Palmer House better—bully girl-servants, joll-ee pretty. But got no rooms, so my people and I come here. Huh!"

This was a ridiculous dream, obviously. "I mean, what are you doing . . . far from your lodge? In the city—in those clothes?"

"Ho!" I could have sworn his eyes twinkled. "The white man's robes, very proper. I have been to the tipi of the Great Father in Washington. For pow-wow on high matters. Now we return to the place of my people—at my agency,

---

*Incredible!
†Stop!

273

the agency of Spotted Tail, on the White River. Two suns, in the iron horse. *How-how*! Wait." And he thrust his great head at the mirror again, breathed gustily, tweaked a hair from his chin, and pocketed his tweezers. As he straightened his coat I saw with alarm that he had a revolver in his arm-pit and a scalping-knife in an embroidered scabbard thrust in his pants waistband.

"*How*! We eat now, together. Horse's doovers and large snow puddings that make the tongue dead. Joll-ee good!" He grinned again and laid a huge paw on my shoulder. "My heart is as the lark to see again a friend from my youth, who remembers the time when the buffalo covered the plains like a blanket. *Hunhe*!* Come to grub!"

Still recovering as I was, I was suspecting that Mr Spotted Tail, chief of the Brulé Sioux, was something of a joker. My gift of language has always been good enough to enable me to turn my mind instantly to any tongue I've ever learned, no matter how long ago, so that within a minute of our meeting I was *thinking* in Siouxan. And while I knew how picturesque it was, with its splendid metaphors, I sensed that he was using them ironically as often as not. He didn't have to talk to me about "the tipi of the Great Father", or "snow puddings that make the tongue dead"; he could just as easily have said "White House" or "ice-cream"—he knew the names of Chicago's hotels well enough, and had a smattering of English. But he was smart as paint, and I guessed it suited him to play the romantic stage-Indian when he came east on the "iron horse" to "pow-wow".

But I couldn't get over our strange meeting, and as we walked to the dining-room I demanded to know what he'd been doing, and where he'd learned English—not that he had much.

"In prison," says he calmly. "At Fort Leavenworth, after we slew Grattan's pony-soldiers and the *Isantanka*† put me in irons. *Yun*!‡ And when the great pow-wows began be-

*Regret.
†Americans.
‡An exclamation of pain.

tween my people and the chiefs of the *Isanhanska*,* they took us to Washington to talk of treaties. *Heh-heh*!† How they bit through our ears! Now I live at the agency with my people, the Burned Thighs, and they try to make us scratch the ground with iron spikes." He shook with laughter. "And you, Wind Breaker? You have been beyond the big water all these years among the *Washechuska*? Tell me of . . ." He stopped abruptly, staring, and then like a big cat slid aside behind a potted palm, peering ahead over its fronds. "*Hinte! Hoecah! Wah!*"

I turned to see what had astonished him, and understood. My dear wife, who is nothing if not patient, was waiting on a couch by the dining-room doors, fanning herself idly, and innocently ignoring the admiring glances of gentlemen passing through. She was wearing something blue from Paris, as I recall, which left her mostly bare to the waist, and to impress the colonials she had decorated her upper works with the diamond necklace presented to her by the Grand Duke Alexis, a lecherous Russian lout of our acquaintance. I'm proud to say that she was a sight to gladden the heart; Spotted Tail was grunting deep and pointing like a gun-dog.

"*Hopa*! *Ees*,‡ *hopa*!§ That," says he reverently, "is a woman!"

"I believe you're right," says I. "My wife, don't you know? Come along. My dear, may I present an old associate, Mr Spotted Tail, of the Sioux. Not the Berkshire Sioux, you understand, the Brulés . . . my wife, Lady Flashman." He took her hand like a stricken grandee, bowing over it from his imposing height until his braids met. He implanted a smacking kiss you could have heard in Baltimore on her glove, murmuring: "Oh, lady, so pleased, so beautiful, just bully!" and his black eyes positively burned as he straightened up. "*Wihopawin*‖—*wah*! *Hopa*! *Hopa*!" My fair one

---

*Long Knives (cavalry soldiers).
†Alas!
‡A strong affirmative.
§Beautiful! See also Note 52.
‖Beautiful woman.

gave him her most wide-eyed, guileless smile, which I knew for a sure sign that she was willing to be dragged into the long grass at a moment's notice, and said in her shyest little voice that she was enchanted. He shot his cuff, thrust out an arm like a tree-trunk, delicately placed her glove on it, and stalked with her into the dining-room, crying "*Bes!*"* for the head-waiter. I followed on, marvelling; I wouldn't have missed this for the salvation of mankind.

He even had a table reserved, with his followers already installed: a couple of young braves dressed civilised like himself, and a third with a coloured blanket over his shoulders, so it was hard to tell whether he was in faultless dinner rig underneath or not—he wore no shoes, though. But what took me aback was that there were two squaws (both wives of the chief's) in fringed tunics, the whole party seated poker-faced at a large round table, heedless of the whisperings and amused glances of the civilised folk at neighbouring tables.

There were only two spare seats, so Spotted Tail simply heaved the blanket-clad chap to the floor, seated Elspeth next to himself with great ceremony, waved me to a seat on his other hand, pushed the menu aside, and barked: "Horse's doovers!" These proved to be *hors d'oeuvres*, and when he had gallantly helped Elspeth by jabbing a huge finger at each plate in turn and grunting "Huh?", he took the entire tray before himself and engulfed the lot in about two minutes—*using a knife and fork*, if you'll believe it.

I suppose I ate, but I confess I was too fascinated to pay much heed. It was startling enough that a great hotel admitted Indians, until I realised that they were used to these occasional delegations passing to and from Washington, and not only tolerated them but made much of them for policy's sake; also, they were a raree show for the other diners. I overheard covert whispers: "Why, they eat just like civilised people!" and "Isn't that chief a card, though? Wouldn't think to look at him he's taken a hundred scalps, would you?" and "Well, they sure don't look like savage Sie-oxes

*Attention!

to me—I think it's a great sell!" Drop in on them sometime in *their* dining-room and you'll learn different, thinks I to myself.

But it was true: bar the outlandish contrast of the men's braids and painted faces to their formal suits, and the women's colourful buckskins, they weren't at all unlike the other diners. Better-mannered, perhaps; they used the cutlery properly, didn't gorge or belch (thinking back to Mangas Colorado, or Spotted Tail himself tearing a bloody buffalo hump in his fingers, I could only wonder), sat with perfect composure waiting for the courses, and preserved almost total silence during the meal. Ne'er mind what they looked like, they had dignity by the bucket.[53] They didn't stink, either, which astonished me—Spotted Tail, next to me, had evidently discovered cologne among other wonders of civilisation.

Unlike his fellows, he talked, so far as anyone can, to Elspeth. Another woman might have been bemused or shocked at finding herself dining with a painted savage, but my darling has never had but one rule: if it is male, between fourteen and eighty, and isn't hump-backed or cross-eyed, charm it—which oddly enough she contrives to do by chattering incessantly and looking intent. Well, it means the chap can devote himself to looking at *her*, which Spotted Tail did most ardently; I realised with a qualm that with the paint and blood absent, he was a deuced fine-looking man, far handsomer even than most Sioux, and although he couldn't understand one word in twenty of what she said he nodded and smiled most appreciatively. Once I heard him say: "You, lady, you *not Washechuska* . . . Eeng-leesh? *Hopidan*!* You . . . Scot-teesh? Scotch—ah!" He considered this, and when the waiter presently whispered to her, "French mustard, ma'am? English mustard?", Spotted Tail threw back his great Sioux head, glared, and demanded: "For love-lee lady . . . why no Scotch mustard?"

That sent her into trills of laughter, and Spotted Tail beamed and patted her arm; aye, thinks I, we must look out

*Exclamation of amazement.

here. The young squaw beyond Elspeth evidently thought so too, for with an artless curiosity she leaned forward and began to finger Elspeth's necklace and earrings, murmuring with admiration. Women being what they are, in a moment they were comparing beads and materials; Spotted Tail sighed and turned to me, so I asked him what had become of his small nephew, the Fair-Haired Boy. He sat back in astonishment.

"Little Curly? You don't know? *Inyun!*" He shook his head at my ignorance. "The whole world knows him! He is a big Indian—maybe biggest war chief of all. He has great medicine, and his word runs from the Pahasappa to the Big Horn hills, all through Powder River country. His lance touches the clouds, that little horseman of yours. You haven't heard of Tashunka Witko of the Oglala?" He repeated it in English. "Crazy Horse."

I said I'd heard his name for the first time that afternoon— and recalled in wonder the laughing mite I'd carried on my saddle. Well, I'd said in jest that he'd be a great man some day; now, I said, the *Isantanka* chiefs spoke of him as a maverick, the most hostile of Indians.[54]

"Ho-ho!" cries Spotted Tail angrily, which is the Sioux equivalent of "Damn their eyes!" or strong disapproval. "*Hiya!** He is a wild warrior—he counted coup on Fetterman and whipped the Long Knives at Lodge Trail Ridge. He is a fighter who hates Americans and has taken many soldier scalps, and they fear him because he makes no treaties and fights for his land and people. But his heart is good and his tongue is straight. *Hiya!* I am proud of Little Curly, as a kinsman and a Lacotah.† *Wah!*"

"But you don't fight the Americans any more; you make treaties for the Burned Thighs, I suppose, since you live on an agency. You even go softly to talk to the Great Father in his tipi," says I, to bait him, but he just gave me a long slow smile.

"Look you, Wind Breaker, I have seen fifty winters and

*No!
†Sioux.

three. My war-shirt bears more scalps of Pawnee and Crow and Shoshoni and *Isantanka* soldiers than any other in the Sioux nation. Four times I counted coup on Long Knives in the Fight of Bear-That-Scatters under Fort Laramie. Is it enough? It is enough. I have seen the white man's world now, the fire-canoes and iron horses, the great tipis that touch the clouds, the lodge where fair young maidens guard the Great Father's gold, the cities where the people are like ants." He grinned in embarrassment. "Once I thought they sent the same white people after us from city to city, to make us think they were more numerous than they are; now I know that in New York every day more people come from far lands than would make up the whole Lacotah nation. Can Spotted Tail's lance and hatchet hold back all these? No. They fill the land, they sweep away the buffalo, they plant seed on the prairie where I ran as a young boy, they make roads and railways over the hunting-grounds. Now they will take the Black Hills, the *Pahasappa*, and there will be no free land left to the Indian." He broke off to roar "Joll-ee good! Pudden!" as the waiter set about a gallon of ice-cream before him, which he sank as smart as you like and waved for a second helping.

"No, we cannot stop it," he went on. "To fight is useless. This I know, and make the best terms I can for my own folk, because I see beyond these winters to the time when all the land is the white man's, and my children must be part of it or wither to nothing. Now others do not see as I do: Crazy Horse and Little Big Man, Black Moon, Gall, and Sitting Bull, perhaps old Red Cloud. They would fight to the last tuft of buffalo grass. They are wrong, and if they go out to battle with the Long Knives I will stay in my lodge, not because my heart is weak but because I am wise. But my heart is Lacotah," and he put back his great head and I saw the gleam in the black eyes, "and for those that take the last war-path I shall say: *Heya-kie*, it is a good day to die."

He said it matter-of-fact, without bluster or self-pity, and there's no doubt he was right—but then, he was probably the greatest of the Sioux leaders, certainly the cleverest—

and as he'd pointed out, quite the most distinguished in war. If the Sioux had heeded him, they'd have been a sight better off today.[55]

After dinner he insisted that we accompany him to the theatre, taking Elspeth's hand and positively pleading with her through me as interpreter. I translated those compliments which were fit for her ears, with the result that presently we were bowling off in a cab, with Spotted Tail up beside the driver in a tile hat, roaring at him to go faster. The squaws and blanket chap were left behind, and Elspeth and I shared the inside of the cab with the other two, fine young bucks named Jack Moccasin and Young Frank Standing Bear, who sat with their arms folded in grave silence. Elspeth confided to me that Standing Bear was quite *distinguished*-looking, and had an air of true nobility.

I might have guessed what entertainment Spotted Tail favoured. It proved to be the lowest kind of music-hall down in the Loop district—what they call burlesque nowadays—with sawdust on the floor, a great bar down one side of the hall doing a roaring trade, pit and gallery crowded with raucous toughs and their flash tarts, an atmosphere blue with smoke and a programme to match. Capital stuff altogether, comedians in loud coats and red noses singing filthy songs, and fat-thighed sluts in spangles and feathers shaking their bums at the orchestra. Elspeth, wearing her most fatuously ingenuous expression, affected not to understand a word—only I knew, when the chief buffoon regaled us with jokes that would have shocked a drunk marine, that behind her fan she was struggling to contain an un-Presbyterian mirth which was in danger of bursting her stays. During the Tableaux ("Scenes from the Sultan's Seraglio," "Forbidden Paris," and "The African Slave Girl's Dream of Innocence") she fanned herself languidly and examined the chandelier. Spotted Tail sat wooden-faced and motionless during most of the show, except for a deep internal growling throughout the Tableaux, but when the conjurer came on he bellowed approval, winded me with an elbow in the ribs, and fairly pounded his fists at every trick. Each vanishing card, emergent rabbit, and multiplying handkerchief was greeted with roars of "*Inyun! Hoecah! Hopidan! Wah!*", and when the buxom assistant finally stepped unharmed from a casket that had been thrust through with swords and riddled with pistol balls, the great chief of the Brulé Sioux arose from his seat, arms aloft, and bawled his applause to the ceiling.

That conjurer, he told me as we left the theatre, was the greatest medicine man in the world. *Wah!* he was gifted beyond all other mortals; the Great Father himself was a child beside him—indeed, why was that medicine man not made President? So flown was Spotted Tail that he banished Jack Moccasin to the box of the cab on the way home, so that he could sit with us and describe each trick in awestruck detail—at least, he described it to me and Young Frank Standing Bear, while Elspeth listened in polite incomprehension. For the rest, said Spotted Tail, it had been a pretty rotten show—except for the Tableaux; there had been one girl with red hair whom he would have gladly taken to his tipi, and the black beauties in the Slave's Dream had reminded him of the girls he had seen in my wagons back in '49—I hadn't guessed, had I, he added with a sly grin, that he and his braves had stalked our caravan for two days in the hope of stealing one, but Blue-Eye Wootton had been too watchful. *Heh-heh!*

I was thankful that Elspeth didn't understand Siouxan; so far as she knew I'd crossed the Plains with a company of farmers and Baptists who said prayers night and morning. I was also pleased to learn that Spotted Tail was leaving next day; I didn't tell Elspeth that he had compared her favourably, and in indelicate detail, with the female performers at the theatre, but there was no mistaking the enthusiasm with which he pressed her hand on parting—or the fact that the vain little baggage went slightly pink, lowering her eyes demurely and positively purring. The deuce with this, thinks I, there'll be no more noble savages on this trip. And then:

"Harry," says she, when we were in our room, "what does *hopa* mean?"

"Beautiful," says I, middling sour. "And *wihopawin*, in •

case you didn't catch it, is a woman of surpassing loveliness."

"Gracious me, the things men say! Can you unhook me at the back, dearest? Well, I must say I think it was rather forward of your Mr Spotted Tail to pay me such compliments, although I've no doubt he meant no disrespect. He's very gallant, for a barbarian, don't you think? Quite *distingué*, really—although his taste in entertainment is *shockingly* low."

"He's *distingué*, all right," says I, unhooking moodily. "Mostly for murder and robbery with violence. He's killed more men than the cholera. Women, too, I shouldn't wonder."

"Thank you so much, my love. Oh, such relief! But, you know, Harry, while I allow that it is highly distasteful, I don't see that it truly signifies if he has killed people or not. So have you—I've seen you—and so have any *number* of our military acquaintances, why, probably even that nice American general with the large beard whom we met to-day—"

"Crook," says I, reclining wearily.

"Yes, well, I daresay that in the course of his duties General Crook may well have taken human life . . . although he has such kind eyes . . . Harry," says she earnestly, surveying herself in the delectable buff before the pier glass, turning this way and that with her hands on her hips, "do *you* think I'm *hopa*?"

"Come over here," says I, taking notice, "and I'll show you."

"I believe I have increased slightly about the hips, and . . . elsewhere. Do you think it can be a consequence of the American cuisine—these rich puddings—"

"Don't talk about 'em, just bring 'em here, there's a girl. And if you want to lose weight, you know—a foolish whim, in my view—I can give you a capital massage, like the Turkish bath people. Here, I'll show you!"

"Do you think it would be efficacious? If so, I should be most obliged to you, Harry, for I have read that it is beneficial, and I think I should not care to be *too* plump . . .

Oh, you designing wretch! What deceit! No, now, desist this minute, for I see you are not really interested in reducing me at all—"

"Ain't I though? Come along, now, nothing like healthy exercise!"

"Exercise indeed! You are a shameless monster, to beguile me so . . . and at my age too! It is too bad, and you are a wicked tease . . . but . . . I'm gratified if you think I'm *hopa*. Mm-mh!. . . what was the other word . . . wippo-something?"

"*Wihopawin*—and no error! My God! Just shut up, will you?"

"They are such musical words—gently, dearest—are they not? They make me think of the brooding solitude of deep eternal forests, with stately Chingachgook beside the council fire . . . the fragrance of the peace-pipe and the cry of the elk among snow-clad peaks . . . Harry, my sweet, you are so *vigorous* that I am quite breathless, and fear for my digestion, perhaps if I go on top?. . . Well, now that we have met Mr Spotted Tail and his friends I am more resolved than ever to see the native Indians in their natural surroundings, just like the 'Deerslayer' and . . ."

"Could we leave Fenimore Cooper for the moment, you babbling beauty?" says I, gasping as we changed over. "Oh! Ah! Elspeth, I love you, you adorable houri! Please, for heaven's sake—"

". . . to observe them with their papooses and wigwams I'm sure would be highly edifying and instructive, for I believe they have many singular customs and ceremonies not to be seen elsewhere," continued the lovely idiot, squirming in a way that any respectable matron would have forgotten years before, "and I am certain that Mr Tail would render us . . . yes, my hero, in a moment . . . every assistance, and it would be such a romantic journey, which you know so well, and it would be so selfish of you not to take me . . . and you are not selfish, I'm sure . . . I hope not . . . *are* you, Harry . . .?"

"No! Oh, God! Anything! I'll . . . I'll think about it! Please . . .!"

"Oh, thank you, kindest of husbands! Dear me, I believe I am about to swoon . . . now, when I count to three . . . one . . . two . . . you will take me, dearest Harry, won't you? . . . two-and-a-half . . ."

As I said before, it was all her fault.

16

◀◀◀━━━━▶━━━━━━◀ Naturally I did my best to wriggle out of it next day, since the artful baggage had taken such unfair advantage of me, first provoking my jealousy and then my ardour, stirring her rump before the mirror—did I think she was *hopa*, forsooth—and extracting a half-promise when she had me *in extremis*. And she called *me* designing! And all because she had taken a passion for that damned Sioux, what with his feral charm and her nursery dreams of noble savages, forgotten while she'd had the social circus of Boston to distract her butterfly brain. They had revived under his smouldering regard, and I guessed she was having delicious shivers at the thought of him sweeping her off at his saddlebow and having his wicked will of her by the shores of Gitchee-Gummee. She'd been just the same with that fat greaser Suleiman Usman, who had filled her head with twaddle about being his White Jungle Queen—well, I wasn't risking that again. The trouble with Elspeth, you see, is that while I doubt if she really wants to be abducted and ravished by hairy primitives—well, not exactly—she's such a congenital flirt that she sometimes gets more than she bargains for.

So I wasn't going to have her making a Western jaunt an excuse for renewing fond acquaintance with Master Spotted Tail, who'd have her in the bushes quicker than knife. But when I said that on reflection I'd decided that a trip West would be too taxing for her, there were tears and sobs of "But you promised . . .", so in the end I gave way, secretly determining that whatever route we took would run well clear of his agency. Given that, I didn't mind indulging her girlish fantasies with a brief tour of the wilds in a transcontinental Pullman; she could have her fill of Vast Plains and Brooding Forests from the window of a private hotel car, and never mind Chingachgook; we might stop off at some tame Indian village (one sniff of that would cure her notions), and perhaps a cattle-ranch or gold-mine. It could all be done in luxurious comfort and perfect safety.

You see, it was all changed since my early days. The map was being filled in; the great wilderness had its railroads and stage lines now, its forts and towns and ranches and mines. It was still wild, in parts—some of it even virtually unexplored—but there wasn't a true frontier any more, in the sense of a north-south line dividing civilisation from outer darkness.

If you look at the map you'll see what I mean. The train and the steamboat had forged the links across the continent and up and down, leaving only the spaces in between. The most important of these, for my story, was the great stretch of the High Plains in what is now Montana, Wyoming, and the Dacotahs; to east and north it was bounded by the Missouri river, along which the steamboats carried the Western traffic to the foot of the Rockies, and to the south by the railroad from Omaha to Cheyenne and the Great Salt Lake. These were the arteries of civilisation, along which you could travel as swiftly and safely (with luck, anyway) as from London to Aberdeen.

It was the land they enclosed that was the trouble, for while the boats and trains might run round its limits, there wasn't much going through it, not in a hurry. This was the last stamping-ground of the Sioux, the biggest and toughest Indian confederacy in North America, a greater thorn in Washington's side than even my old friends the Apaches of the south-west. Fifty thousand Sioux, Sherman had reckoned, and their allies the Northern Cheyenne, first cousins to those stone-faced giants I'd met on the Arkansas. In those days the Sioux had been lords of the prairie from the Santa Fe Trail to the British border, from Kansas to the Rockies, tolerating the wagon-trains (give or take a raid now and then) and rubbing along quietly enough with the few troops that the Americans sent into the West.

All that had changed. The ever-advancing settlements, the bypassing of their country by rail and river, had forced the Plains Tribes back from the limits of civilisation around them, into their heartland, bewildered and angry. They'd broken out in Minnesota in '62, and been put down; when the government tried to put the Bozeman Road slap through their territory, Red Cloud had taken the war-path and fought them to a standstill; but although the road was given up and the forts abolished, their victory probably did the Sioux more harm than good, since it convinced the wilder spirits that the Yanks could be stopped by force. They didn't see it was a struggle they must lose in the end, and so for twenty-five years the scrappy, unorganised warfare had smouldered on, with every now and then a real dust-up to stoke the growing hatred and mistrust on both sides. Crazy Horse had hammered Fetterman, Spotted Tail and Co. had lifted eighty cavalry scalps almost in Laramie's backyard; on the American side the Cromwellian lunatic Chivington had butchered the Arapaho and Cheyenne at Sand Creek, and Custer on the Washita had descended on Black Kettle's village with his flutes tootling *Garryowen* and left more than a hundred corpses in the snow. These were the solo pieces, so to speak, but always there was the accompaniment of burned settlements, derailed trains, and ambushed wagons, and punitive expeditions, dispossessions, and tribal evictions.

Naturally, each side blamed the other for bad faith and treachery and refusal to see reason—the Indian version of Washita, for example, was that Custer wantonly attacked a peaceful village, but one of his troopers told me he'd seen freshly-taken white scalps in the Indian lodges. Choose who you will to believe.

The wiser Sioux leaders, like Spotted Tail and Red Cloud, saw how it must end and made peace, but that solved nothing while the real Ishmaels like Sitting Bull and Crazy Horse remained beyond the pale. And even the treaty Indians broke out from time to time, for the agents who were meant to supply them cheated them blind as often as not, Washington neglected them, and life on a reservation or agency was a poor thing compared to roaming their ancestral plains and robbing when they felt like it.

By 1875, though, it looked as though the thing must peter out at last; hunters and sportsmen had swept the buffalo off the prairie at a rate of a million a year, until they were all but extinct—and the Indian without buffalo is worse off than the Irish without the potato, for it's clothing and lodging to him as well as food. Plainly even the wildest hostiles would have to chuck it and settle down soon; the discovery of gold in the Black Hills, which would inevitably mean the loss to the tribes of yet another stretch of territory, must only hasten the process, for it would leave them little except the barely-explored fastness south of the Yellowstone called the Power River country, and with game so scarce they would have to call it a day or starve. That was the general view, so far as I could gather, and with it went the opinion that I'd heard from Sheridan: however it ended, there wouldn't be a war. An ugly incident or two here and there, perhaps—regrettable, but probably inevitable with such people—but no real trouble. No, sir.

Which was most comforting to me, as I considered how to satisfy my darling's hunger to see the Wild West; yes, the railroad would carry us well clear of the dangerous Sioux country—and Spotted Tail, incidentally. But before we set out, we must journey to Washington, for Elspeth's social navvying in Boston had secured us an invitation to visit the capital—Washington in summer, God help me—and my lady was confident that we would be summoned to the White House, "for the President is your old *comrade-in-arms*, and it would be very curious if he were to overlook the presence of such a *distinguished* visitor as a Knight of the Bath". I told her she didn't know Sam Grant. As it turned out, her ignorance was nothing compared with mine.

Washington, a dismal swamp at the best of times, was sweaty and feverish, and so were its inhabitants, with Grant's presidency soon to enter its final year and the whole foul political crew in a ferment of caballing and mischief. Any gang of politicos is like the eighth circle of Hell, but the American breed is specially awful because they take it seriously and believe it matters; wherever you went, to dinner or an excursion or to pay a call, or even take a stroll, you were deafened with their infernal prosing—I daren't go to the privy without making sure some seedy heeler wasn't lying in wait to get me to join a caucus. For being British didn't help—they would just check an instant, beady eyes uncertain, and then demand to know what London would think of Hayes or Tilden, and how was the Turkish crisis going? (This at a time when Grace was making triple centuries in England, and I not there.)[56]

We met Grant, though, and a portentous encounter it proved. It was at some dinner given by a Senator, and Burden, the military attache from our Embassy, whom I knew slightly, was there. Grant was the same burly, surly bargee I remembered, more like a city storekeeper than the first-rate soldier he'd been and the disillusioned President he was. He looked dead tired, but the glances he shot from under those knit brows were still sharp; he gave a wary start at sight of me—it's remarkable how many people do—and then asked guardedly how I did. I truckled in my manly way, while he watched me as though he thought I was there to pinch the silver.

"You look pretty well," says he grudgingly, and I told him so did he.

"No I don't," he snapped. "No man could look well who has endured the Presidency."

I said something soothing about the cares of state. "Not a bit of it," barks he. "It's this infernal hand-shaking. Do you realise how frequently the office demands that the incumbent's fingers shall be mauled and his arm jerked from its socket? No human constitution can stand it, I tell you! Pump-pump-pump, it's all they damned well do. Ought to be abolished". Still happy old Sam, I could see. He growled and asked cautiously if I was staying long, and when I told him of our projected trip across the Plains he chewed his beard moodily and said I was lucky, at least the damned Indians didn't shake hands.[57]

Our appetites sharpened by these brilliant exchanges, we went in to dinner, which was foul, what with their political gas and heavy food. Between them they must have numbed my brain, and by damnable chance it was before the ladies had withdrawn that a Senator of unusual stupidity and flatulence, called Allison, happened to mention his impending departure for the West, whither he was bound with a government commission to treat with the Indians about the Black Hills. I didn't pay much heed, until a phrase he used touched a chord in my memory, and I made an unguarded remark—my only excuse is that I was trying to escape the egregious stream of chatter from the Congressional harpy seated next to me.

"I make no doubt that our negotiations will have reached a fruitful conclusion by October, Mr President," Allison was saying ponderously, "and that we shall be enabled to proceed to formal treaty no later than November—or, as I believe our Indian friends so picturesquely describe it, 'The Moon When the Horns are Broken Off'." He chuckled facetiously, and as my neighbour drew breath for another spate of drivel, I hastily addressed Allison without thinking.

"That's correct only if you're talking to a Santee Sioux, Senator," says I, and I swear for once I wasn't trying to be smart. "If he happens to be a Teton Sioux, then 'The Moon When the Horns are Broken Off' is December."

One of those remarks, I agree, which will stop any conversation in its tracks. Allison stared, and a silence fell, broken by Grant's rasping question. "What's that, Flashman? Do you happen to be an authority on the Indian calendar?"

Before I could turn the question, the prattling dunderhead I married was interposing brightly. "Oh, but Harry knows ever so much about Red Indians, Mr President! He travelled extensively anong them in his youth, you know, and became *thoroughly* acquainted with many of their prominent men. Why, only lately, in Chicago, we met a most *unusual* person, a chief among the Stews, wasn't he Harry?—anyway, a most *imposing* figure, although *quite* unpredictable, a Mr Spotted Tail, and what do you think? He and Harry proved to be *old friends* from the past, and it was the most *amusing* thing to hear them conversing at dinner in those *outlandish* sounds, and moving their hands in those graceful signs—oh, Harry, do show them!" How I've kept my hands from her throat for seventy years, God knows.

"Spotted Tail?" says Allison. "Why, that's a singular

thing—of course, he recently returned from Washington. I take it to be the same man—the leader of the Brulé Siouxes? Well, he is to be a principal spokesman for the Indians at our conference."

"You speak Siouxan?" says Grant to me, quite sharp.

"My husband speaks many languages," says Elspeth proudly, smiling at me. "Don't you, my love? Why, it can make me quite dizzy to hear him—"

"I never knew you'd been out West," says Grant, frowning. "How did you come to know Spotted Tail?"

There was nothing for it but to tell him, as briefly as I could, and for once I didn't make a modest-brag about it; I could have kicked Elspeth's dainty backside, for I suspected no good would come of this. They were all attention—you don't meet many dinner guests, I suppose, who've commanded a wagon-train and learned the lingo from Wootton and Carson, and they probably didn't believe half of it.

"Quite remarkable," says Grant. "You don't happen to know Spotted Tail's nephew—Chief Crazy Horse?"

Any damage had been done by now, so I couldn't resist the temptation of saying that I'd put him on his first pony. (That I'm *sure* they disbelieved. Odd, ain't it?) I added that since he'd been only six years old I could hardly claim to know him well. Grant only grunted, and no more was said until the women had taken themselves off and the cigars were going. Then:

"You said you and Lady Flashman were going West, didn't you?"

"Purely for pleasure," says I.

"Uh-huh." He chewed his cigar a moment. "I doubt if anyone on Senator Allison's commission knows Spotted Tail all that well. I've met him a few times . . . shrewd fellow. Terry's your military representative, isn't he?" he asked Allison. "He doesn't know Indians at close quarters, exactly—and I'm positive he doesn't speak Siouxan." He studied me in a damned disconcerting way. "You wouldn't care to lend Allison your assistance, I suppose? It wouldn't take you much out of your way."

"Mr President," says I hurriedly, "I'm hardly an authority

on the Indian question, and since I'm not an American citizen—"

"I'm not suggesting you serve on the commission," growls he. "But I know something about your gifts of persuasion and negotiation, don't I?—and if Allison's going to get anywhere in this infernal business, it's going to take a power of informal and delicate dealing. He'll need all the help he can get, and while he'll have no lack of expert counsel, it can't hurt to have the added assistance of a soldier of rank and diplomatic experience—" sardonic little bastard! "—who not only knows Indians, especially Spotted Tail himself, but can also understand what the other side is saying before the interpreters frazzle it up. You concur, Senator?"

"Why, indeed, Mr President," says Allison gravely. "I'm persuaded that Colonel Flashman's ah . . . unusual qualifications would be . . . ah, invaluable." I guessed he didn't care much for it. "If he can be prevailed upon, that is, to assist informally . . ."

"I'm sure he can," says Grant firmly. "As to being a British citizen, it's nothing to the point," he went on to me. "It didn't matter in the war, did it? Besides, I'm sure Burden here will agree," and he nodded to our Embassy wallah, "that an Indian solution is almost as much in England's interest as in ours. The Sioux could be a damned nuisance in Canada—they don't respect national boundaries, those fellows—so I don't doubt Her Majesty would be happy to lend us your friendly assistance."

Burden didn't hesitate, rot him. "I think I can say that we should welcome the opportunity of having Colonel Flashman accompany the commission as an observer, Mr President," says he carefully. "As you point out, our respective interests converge in this matter."

"I'm glad to hear you say so," says Grant. "Well, Flashman?"

That was Grant all over. It was a tiny thing; my presence could hardly weigh in the balance—but Sam as a commander had never neglected the least possible advantage, and even one more voice in Spotted Tail's ear might conceivably help. I didn't know then, I confess, just how damned important

Spotted Tail was. Grant was looking at me, lighting another cigar.

"What d'you say? No Medal of Honour in it this time, I'm afraid, but I'd esteem it a personal favour."

I knew who else would, too—I could hear her in the distant drawing-room, regaling the other ladies with "Caller Herrin' " at the piano. Let me decline—and how the devil could I refuse Grant a personal favour?—and I'd never hear the end of it. What, deny her the chance to languish at "Mr Spotted Tail"? Well, perhaps when she saw him in his "natural surroundings" she'd be less enthusiastic for noble savages. Aye, perhaps. I'd watch the red bastard like a hawk.

"Happy to be of service, Mr President," says I.

* * *

As it turned out, I wasn't—of service, I mean—but I take no blame for that. Solomon himself couldn't have saved the Camp Robinson discussions with the Sioux from being a fiasco, not unless he'd gagged Allison to begin with. There is some natural law that ensures that whenever civilisation talks to the heathen, it is through the person of the most obstinate, short-sighted, arrogant, tactless clown available. You recall McNaghten at Kabul, perhaps? Well, Allison could have been his prize pupil.

To his blinkered eyes the problem looked simple enough. Despite General Crook's efforts (and having heard him in Chicago I didn't imagine they'd been too strenuous) white miners had continued to pour into the Black Hills that summer; gold camps like Custer City already had populations of thousands, and more arriving daily. The Sioux, rightly viewing this as a shameless violation of their treaty, were getting angrier and uglier by the minute. So, faced on one hand by a possible Sioux rising, and on the other by the *fait accompli* of the mining camps, Washington reached the conclusion you'd expect: treaty or no, the Sioux would have to give way. Allison's task was to persuade them to surrender the hills in return for compensation, and that, to him, meant fixing a price and telling 'em to take it or leave it. He didn't doubt they would take it; after all, he was a Senator, and they were a parcel of silly savages who couldn't read and write; he would lecture them, and they would be astonished at his eloquence, pocket the cash without argument, and go away. It didn't seem to weigh with him that to the Sioux the Black Hills were rather like Mecca to the Muslims, or that having no comprehension of land ownership, the idea of selling them was as ludicrous as selling the wind or the sky. Nor did he suspect that, even if their religious and philosophic scruples could be overcome, their notions of price and value had developed since the days of beads and looking-glasses.

Camp Robinson, where he was to meet the Sioux chiefs, was a fairly new military post out beyond the settlements, not far south of the Black Hills; close by it was the Red Cloud Agency where the old Oglala chief lived with his followers, and a day's march away was Camp Sheridan, near the agency of Spotted Tail and his Brulés. These were the "peaceful" Sioux, who had come in to the agencies in return for annuities and other government benefits such as rations, clothes, weapons and schools; it was the fond hope that eventually they'd take to farming. Since they were well-behaved and powerful chiefs, the government chose to regard them as spokesmen for the whole Sioux nation, conveniently forgetting that most of the tribes were roaming wild in the Powder River country farther west, under the likes of Sitting Bull and Crazy Horse, "but if *they* are so intractable and foolish as not to meet us, on their own heads be it," says Allison smugly. "We can talk only to those who will talk to us, and if the hostiles will not share our deliberations, they cannot complain if the treaty is not to their satisfaction. We can only reach it and trust that reason will prevail with them after the event." An optimist, you see.

Even before we set out, the omens were bad. The peaceful agency tribes were fractious because in the hard winter just past they'd been kept short of the necessaries government should have been providing—one of the reasons Spotted Tail had been east in June was to complain. In his absence his younger braves had worked themselves into a

294

frenzy at the annual sun dance and gone off for a slap at the Black Hills miners (and at their old foes the Pawnees, just for devilment); there had been a nasty brush between the Brulés and Custer's 7th Cavalry, and when Spotted Tail returned it had taken all his influence and skill to bring his bucks to heel.

To show willing, Washington had held an inquiry on the agencies, and found the Indians' complaints well grounded; they'd been swindled and deprived, but in spite of the findings no official or contractor was punished, although the agent at Red Cloud had been removed. So you can judge how content the agency Sioux were by the time our commission rolled out by rail and coach to Camp Robinson late that summer, Allison full of pomp and consequence, deep in discussions with his fellow-commissioners, while I lent an unofficial ear, and Elspeth in the hotel car cried out with excitement every time we passed a creek or a tree.

She got something to marvel at, though, on the last stage into Camp Robinson. It's far out on the prairie, nestling among pretty groves beneath a range of buttes, and in all directions the grassy plain was covered with Indian villages as far as you could see; every Sioux in America seemed to have converged on the fort, and as our coach lurched by with its escort of cavalry outriders, Elspeth was all eyes and ears while Collins, the secretary to the commission, pointed out the various tribes—Brulé, Sans Arc, Oglala, Minneconju, Hunkpapa, and the rest. Mostly they just stared as we went by, silent figures in their blankets by the tipis and smoky fires, but once a party of Cheyenne Dog Soldiers rode alongside us, and Elspeth fairly clapped her hands and squeaked to see them cantering so stately, stalwart warriors in braids and full paint, shaking their lances in salute and chanting: "*How! Hi-yik-yik! How!*"

"Oh, brave!" cries she ecstatically. "*How! How* to you! Oh, Harry, how proud and splendid they look! Why, I declare they are so many Hiawathas! Ah, but how solemn they all look! I never saw so many melancholy faces—are they always so sad, Mr Collins?"

I wasn't feeling too brisk myself; I'd supposed we'd be

meeting the chiefs and a few supporters, but there were thousands of Sioux here if there was one, and that's a sight too many.

"It takes three-quarters of the male population to make any agreement binding," Collins told me, "so the more who attend the better. It's what Red Cloud and Spotted Tail say that counts, of course, but we must have the democratic consent of the people, too."

"Is Allison intending to canvass that multitude?" says I, incredulous. "Dear God, does he know how long it takes an Indian to decide to get up in the morning?"

The fort itself was a fairly spartan affair of wooden houses and barracks, but Anson Mills, the commandant from Camp Sheridan, was on hand with his wife to make us welcome, and Elspeth was far too excited to mind the absence of city comforts.

The Mills gave a dinner of welcome that night, to which they had invited the chiefs for an informal foregathering; to my surprise Elspeth dressed in her plainest gown, without jewellery and her hair severely bunned, explaining to me that it would never do for her to outshine Mrs Mills, the hostess, "and anyway, I know you are sensible of our position, my dear, for we are not *official* here, and it does not do for us to put ourselves forward". This was uncommon sense for her; she knew that I was really a camp-follower of the commission whom they might find useful, but I'd borne no part beyond listening to some of their discussions, answering a question or two from Allison, and talking a bit of shop with General Terry, the military representative. He was a tall, sprightly, courteous fellow who'd been a lawyer (Yale man, apparently) before the Civil War turned him into a soldier; I found him quick and a good deal more open-minded than most Yankee military chiefs. The other leading lights of the commision were Collins and a clergyman.

The chiefs came to dinner in style, six of them all in buckskins and feathers, led by the famous Oglala, Red Cloud, a grim savage with a face you could have used to split kindling. Other names I remember were Standing Elk

296

and White Thunder, and towering over the rest, splendid in snowy tunic and single eagle feather, the well-known Tableaux-fancier and patron of Loop burlesque theatres. His black eyes widened momentarily at sight of me; then he was bowing and growling to Elspeth, who gave him a limp hand and her coolest smile, which alarmed me more than if she'd languished at him.

The dinner was a frost. From the first it was evident that the chiefs were thoroughly disgruntled, and at odds among themselves; I was seated between Red Cloud and Standing Elk, so that advantage could be taken of my linguistic genius; Red Cloud gave me one suspicious glare, and replied in monosyllables to the amiabilities and polite inquiries which Allison and the others addressed to him through me. You could feel the suspicion and hostility coming from them like a fog, and by the time desserts were served it was like being at a Welsh funeral. The chiefs were silent, Allison was aloof and huffy and the clergyman distressed, Mills was trying to look bland, and his wife, poor soul, was in a fearsome flutter, her hand shaking on the cloth in embarrassment. For once I thanked God for Elspeth's artless prattle, directed ceaselessly at everyone in turn, and never taking silence for an answer. But only from Spotted Tail among the Indians did she get any response, and even that was formal courtesy; his mind was too busy elsewhere even for flirting.

All the gloom didn't prevent our guests from punishing the victuals like starving wolves, I may say; Red Cloud's longest conversational flight was to remark that they were a sight better than the rubbish his people had been getting from the agency, which I translated to Mrs Mills as a compliment to the cook. And when we rose, White Thunder, who'd been even more voracious than the rest, went round the table scraping the contents of every plate into a bag; he was even lifting some of the spoons until Spotted Tail growled something at him which I didn't catch. As they took their departure the Brulé chief seemed to stare particularly at me, so once they were out, and Allison was exploding in pique at what he called "their cross-grained and sullen demeanour, upon my word, like the spoiled children they are!", I took a slow saunter out to the verandah. Sure enough, there was Spotted Tail, a huge pale figure in the summer dusk; his fellow-chiefs were already down on the parade, studiously looking the other way while the grooms brought their ponies. He didn't beat about.

"Why are you sitting with the *Isantanka*, Wind Breaker? What is this matter to do with the *Wasetchuska* Mother?"

"Nothing," says I. "I'm here because I know you and speak your tongue."

"They think I will listen to you? That you will grease their words so that I and my brothers will swallow them easily?" He wasn't the genial companion of Chicago now; his tone was on the brink of anger. I answered matter-of-fact.

"They think that because I'm a soldier chief in my own country, I can help to open their minds fairly to you. And because I know something of you and your folk, I can open your minds fairly to them. I understand high matters, which an ordinary interpreter might not, and I will speak for both sides with a straight tongue." He must know how much that mattered, and how many bitter misunderstandings had arisen through incompetent interpreters.

He watched me slantendicular and then put back his head. *"Wah-ah. Bes!* Then tell them this for a beginning. Since I came from Washington I have been in the Black Hills. There is much gold there, and now I have seen it. So we will not give up the hills, and we will not allow them to be taken from us."

Well, that was damned blunt, before the talks had even started. No courteous preliminaries or hints or soundings; he'd never have said anything so flat to the commission, but he could drop it in my ear as an intermediary. It flitted across my mind—had wily Sam Grant foreseen something like this? Presumably it was what I was here for, and I felt a gratifying tingle at being on the inside of affairs (there's an oily politician in the best of us, you see) and at the same time an apprehension as I realised that whatever I said might weigh heavy in the scale. God, what a chance for mischief! But I didn't indulge it; I gave back bluntness for bluntness, because it seemed best.

"The hills have been taken from you already, haven't they?" says I. "You've seen how many miners are up there. And you've said yourself that the lance and hatchet of Spotted Tail can't stop them."

I saw him stiffen, and then he says quietly: "There are other lances."

"Whose? Sitting Bull's? My little horseman's—Crazy Horse? That won't answer, and you know it. Look here, Sintay Galeska, this is nothing to me," says I, and it was true. For once in my life I had no axe to grind; I didn't give a blue light who had the Black Hills, since there was nothing in it for me either way. Tell you the truth I was feeling a most unaccustomed thing, a glow of virtue, as well as the pleasure of observing a drama in which I had no personal stake. I didn't have to be patient of diplomatic niceties. If Allison had known what I was about to say, he'd have had apoplexy; for that matter I don't suppose Red Cloud and his boys would have cared for it either. But when all the pussy-footing and lying and hypocrisy don't matter to you, you can go straight to business and enjoy yourself.

"These talks are a sham," I continued, "and you know it. The Black Hills are gone, and you'll never get 'em back. This lot won't leave you a rag to your back if you resist them. So isn't it time to get the best bargain you can? And make those mad bastards up in Powder River country understand that they'd better settle for it, or they'll get worse? I'm not saying it's right or fair; that don't count. I'm just saying it's common sense. And you know it, too."

If it was straighter talk than he cared for, he still couldn't deny it or say I spoke with a double tongue. He knew it was true.

"They'll pay, you know," says I. "How much, I can't tell you. Certainly not what the hills are worth in gold value— but then you wouldn't expect 'em to, would you? No, you'll just have—"

"Ho-ho!" It came out in a bark, the warning-note of the

Sioux when he's heard something he doesn't like. But his voice was quiet enough when he said: "You speak for the *Isantanka*; they seek to put fear into our hearts, so that we will be cowed into taking whatever they offer—"

"Look," says I, "if I was speaking for them, would I have admitted that they won't pay what the hills are worth? No; I'd have told you the price they'll offer is a fair one. I'm telling you the truth because I know you see it as clear as I do. Of course they'll cheat you; they always have. Don't you see—the Sioux aren't going to win, either in a bargain or in a fight? So you must just get as much as you can, while you can. Don't let these talks fail; get the best price you can squeeze out of them, and try to get Sitting Bull and the other hostiles to like it. If you don't, you'll wind up poor or dead."

He studied me poker-faced, stroking one of his long braids, and I wondered if he was hating me and all that he thought I stood for—hating me all the more, perhaps, because I knew as well as he did the bitter truth he was facing, that he must twist the Yankee purse to the last dollar for his people's sake, and that at the same time he would be betraying them and the ideals they held sacred. It's a damnable thing, the pride of a nation, especially when it's coupled with the kind of mystic frenzy that they had about their precious Black Hills. Or pretended they had. At last he says:

"Will you tell the *Isantanka* all that has passed between you and me here?"

"If you want me to," says I. "But I think it better I should tell them that Chief Spotted Tail is worried because his fellow-chiefs don't want to sell the hills. I'll tell them they would be best advised to offer a good price, and to take into account what it would cost in white blood and white money if the Sioux were pushed into fighting because the price isn't high enough."

"What price," says he, "do you think would satisfy the Sioux?"

"I don't know, and I don't care, and I won't try to guess. That's for you to decide. But I'd want it in gold, on the

300

barrel-head, and I wouldn't budge an inch for anything less. I wouldn't hand over my guns, that's certain."

It was then, I think, that he began to believe if not necessarily to trust me. As why shouldn't he, since I'd been telling truth straighter than I could ever remember? At any rate, he finally nodded, and said he would wait and see what was said publicly tomorrow. Almost as an afterthought, as he was about to go, he says conversationally:

"Why did your golden lady hide her beauty tonight? She wore no shining stones, and her milk-white flesh she covered in poor cloth. Have you been beating her, that she hides the bruises, or is she displeased and withdraws the loveliness that gives such joy to men?"

I explained, pretty cool, that she had left her fine dresses back east, as being unsuitable for the frontier, and he gave one of his astonishing rumbles, like a bull in a brothel. "Then my heart is sad," growls he, "for the more one sees of her the better. My heart sings when I look on her. She shines. I would like to see all of her shining! *Yun!* I would like to . . ." and to my rage and scandal he absolutely said it, smacking his lips, and me her husband, too. Mind you, I suppose it was meant as a compliment. "Joll-ee good! *Han, hopa!* Joll-ee good!" And he stalked off, leaving me dumbfounded.

The commission were all attention when I reported what he'd said (about the Black Hills, I mean); my own side of the conversation I kept to myself. I said I believed he was ready to settle, if the bargain could be made to look respectable; he could probably sway Red Cloud, and between them they could surely convince three-quarters of the Indians who had come to listen. That would still leave the absent hostiles, but if the offer was good enough even they might find it hard to hold out.

Terry and Collins looked pleased, but the clerical wallah made a lip. "However generous the offer, we are asking them to surrender land which they esteem holy. And while we may justly abhor their superstitious frenzy, I ask myself if they will abjure it for . . . well, pieces of silver." He blinked earnestly and Allison gave a patronising smile.

"With all respect, reverend, I'm not aware that their so-called religious fervour has any real spiritual depth. Their mode of life hardly suggests it, and I am not convinced that their concern for the Black Hills would be quite so great if there were no gold there. No, gentlemen," says he complacently, "I've no doubt the Colonel is right, and that they will sell, and as to the price, we shall have to see. A savage whose notions of time and space are so peculiar that he cannot comprehend that a day's journey on the railroad carries him farther than a day's journey by pony, may have an equally eccentric view of real estate values. *Pro pelle cutem* I'm sure they understand: a skin for the worth of a skin, but whether they encompass the higher finance we shall discover."

He did, too, the following day, when Spotted Tail got up in full council and blandly announced the price of the Black Hills: forty million dollars. I didn't believe my ears, and watched with interest as I translated, for it's not every day that you see a senatorial commission kicked in its collective belly. D'you know, they never blinked—and my suspicious hackles rose on the spot. There was a deal of huffing and consideration before Allison replied at judicious length, but all his palaver couldn't conceal his point, which was that the government were prepared to offer only *six million*, and over several years at that. There was much nonsense about renting and leasing, in which Spotted Tail showed politely satirical interest, but now that he'd seen the dismal colour of their money it was so much waste of time; he concluded that they had best put it in writing, and stalked out. Red Cloud, by the way, hadn't bothered to attend.

Allison wasn't disturbed; let him conduct matters privately with the chiefs, and they'd see reason, all right. For the life of me I'm not sure whether he believed it or not, but it was nothing to me, and while they all caballed for the next few days I indulged Elspeth by squiring her round the Indian encampments. Since sightseeing is to her what liquor is to a drunkard, she didn't seem to notice the stink and squalor, but exclaimed at the *variety* and *colour* of the *bar-*

baric scene, took a heroic interest in the domestic arrangements, waxed sentimental at the *docile resignation* of the squaws pounding corn and cooking their abominable messes, became quite excited at the sight of the young bucks playing lacrosse, and went into ecstasies over "the bonny wee papooses". For their part, the Sioux took an equal interest in her, and a curious procession we made as we strolled back to camp arm-in-arm with a gaggle of curious squaws and loafers and children at our heels, and one impudent urchin insisting on carrying Elspeth's parasol.

One day we spent at Camp Sheridan, driving across at Spotted Tail's invitation; he sent Standing Bear, the young brave we'd met in Chicago, to escort us, and I noted with a jaundiced eye that here was another gallant from the same school as his chief. Not only was he as handsome a redskin as ever I saw, three inches over six feet and built like an acrobat, his attentions to Elspeth were of the most courtly, and I knew from the way he held himself as he rode alongside that he fancied himself most damnably, all noble profile and grave immobility.

Spotted Tail welcomed us outside the fine frame house which the army had set aside for his use at Camp Sheridan, but after showing us round its empty rooms with a proprietorial pride, he explained gravely that he didn't live here, but in a tipi close by. The advantage of this was that when the tipi got foul he could move it to a clean stretch of ground some yards away (like the Mad Hatter at the tea-party), a thing he could hardly have done with a two-storey house. What, clean the floors? He shook his head; his squaws wouldn't know how.

To Elspeth's delight he invited us to sit by him at his levee, where he heard complaints, settled disputes, and dispensed hospitality out of the extra rations the agency allowed him for the purpose. When we dined, though, it was on the traditional Plains Indians fricassee from the communal pot; Elspeth picked away, smiling gamely, and I hadn't the heart to tell her it was mostly boiled dog. She didn't flirt with him more than outrageous, and he was on his best dignified behaviour. When I asked him how the treaty talks were going, he simply shrugged, and I wondered was he preparing to concede and look pleasant.

Yes, says Allison when I tackled him later, it was all as good as settled. He was preparing the commission's formal offer, to be delivered before the assembled tribes, and he had every confidence that Red Cloud and Spotted Tail would accept it, six million and all. Well, thinks I, I'll believe it when I hear it.

Sure enough, it was on the morning of the assembly that we got the first whiff of mischief. At Red Cloud's request the meeting was to take place out on the open prairie, some miles from the fort, where the Indian thousands could congregate conveniently, and we had already piled into the ambulance, with Anson Mills's two cavalry troops flank and rear, and Elspeth and Mrs Mills waving from the verandah, when there was a shout from across the parade, and here came a party of mounted Indians, armed and in full paint, cantering two and two and led by a stalwart Oglala, Young-Man-Afraid-of-His-Horses, whom I'd seen in Red Cloud's entourage. As he rode up to Anson Mills, I noticed young Standing Bear in war-bonnet and leggings, with lance and carbine, at the head of one of the lines; I beckoned him to the tailboard and asked him what was up.

"*How*," says he. "Chief Sintay Galeska sends word that you and the *Isantanka* chiefs should stay in the soldiers' camp today."

"What's that? But we have to go out to the meeting."

"He thinks it better you should talk here than there."

I didn't like the sound of this, and neither did the others when I told them. We asked why, and Standing Bear shook his handsome head and said it was the chief's advice, that was all; he added that if we insisted on going, he and Young-Man-Afraid had been ordered to ride with the cavalry as an additional escort.

That was enough for me. Didn't I remember riding out from the cantonments on just such an occasion to parley with Akbar Khan? I said as much to Terry, who agreed it was disquieting, the perceptive chap. "But we cannot stay in camp," says he. "Why, we should lose face."

I observed that it might be preferable to losing our hair, but he pooh-poohed that, and Allison, after some waffling, backed him up. "It is a strange message, to be sure," says he doubtfully, "but if Chief Spotted Tail were uneasy I am persuaded he would have come himself. In any event, not to keep the meeting would show a lack of faith which would be fatal to our whole negotiation. No, we must go—why, what harm can come to a government commission?"

I could have told him, and added that he could go without Flashy, for one. But it wouldn't have done, in front of Yankees, and with Elspeth watching, so I kept uneasily mum, and presently we were jolting out of camp, with the fat clergyman beside me sweating and twitching; I noticed Collins's hand stray under his jacket, and wished I'd thought to come heeled myself.

My nerves were not steadied by the sight that greeted us at the little grove which was the meeting place. Every Sioux in the world seemed to be there; beyond the tarpaulin canopy where we were to sit they squatted in row on endless row, brown painted faces grim and unmoving, war-bonnets and eagle feathers stirring in the breeze; every knoll and slope for a quarter of a mile was covered with them. The whole vast concourse was deathly silent; there wasn't a cough or grunt, let alone a welcoming "How!" from all those thousands; as we took our seats the only sounds were the flapping of the canopy overhead, the stamp and jingle of Mills's troopers, and the nervous rumblings of one set of bowels at least.

Mills ranged his troopers in line either side of our seats, while Young-Man-Afraid and Standing Bear sat their ponies out to the left, their mounted braves behind them, facing the great mass of waiting Sioux; I noticed Standing Bear make a little sign to Spotted Tail, who was seated with Red Cloud and the other chiefs in the front rank of our audience. Spotted Tail caught my eye and nodded, presumably in reassurance, which I needed, rather; sitting on my ridiculous camp-stool on the flank of the commission, looking at that mob, reminded me of being in the platform party on Speech Day when you've forgotten your address about Duty and Playing the Game, and the audience are already starting to snigger and pick their noses. Only this crowd weren't sniggering.

Allison got to his feet and cleared his throat, shooting nervous glances at the silent red assembly twenty yards off, and at that moment I noticed movement on the outer wings of the crowd. Mounted warriors were cantering in towards us, either side; they swept wide to outflank the canopy, and trotted in behind Mills's two lines of troopers. I screwed round to watch, my hair on end, as the two long files of painted braves, lances and guns at the ready, took station behind our cavalry—by God, they were marking 'em, man for man! Ten feet behind each trooper there was now a mounted Sioux, and there was no doubting the menacing significance of that. Allison stammered over the first few words of his address, and ploughed on, and I was preparing to translate aloud when a harsh voice cut in before me—a half-breed among the Indians was translating. So they'd brought their own interpreter with them; that might be significant, too.

There was a flurry of hooves to the left; Young-Man-Afraid and Standing Bear were moving their riders—*in behind* the lines of Sioux who were marking our troopers, so that they in turn were covered man for man! It was like some huge game of human chess, and damned unnerving if you were in the middle of the board; now there were three lines of silent horsemen either side of us, and the Sioux riders were neatly sandwiched in the middle; they didn't like it, and turned muttering in their saddles. Standing Bear grinned and made a derisive gesture at them, and then edged his pony close to where I was sitting. I felt a sudden warm surge of relief; with that hawk profile and lance at rest against his muscular arm, he looked a confident likely lad to have at your elbow. Terry, beside me, glanced round coolly at the troopers and the Indians and whispered: "*Quis* *custodiet ipos custodes?''** John Charity Spring would have been all for him.

Allison was in full spate now, and my fears returned as I realised that what he was saying wasn't even tactful, let alone conciliatory. Instead of arguing persuasively that white occupation of the Black Hills would really be in the Sioux's interest, since they could make a thumping profit out of it, or something of that sort, he was taking a most minatory line, like Arnold lecturing the fags. The government must control the hills, and that was that; compensation would be paid, and if it became necessary to occupy more land in the Powder River country, a price would be settled for that too. I listened appalled; if the fool had wanted to put their backs up, he couldn't have done it better—and not for the first time the suspicion crossed my mind: were they *trying* to provoke the Indians, to ensure that no treaty was reached, so that they'd have an excuse for disciplining 'em once for all? If so, he'd picked a bloody clever time to light the train, hadn't he, with several thousand Sioux getting shorter-tempered by the minute? For they were stirring now, and angry grunts and shouts of "*Ho-ho!*" were coming from around the arena; Allison raised his voice stubbornly, I heard the figure of six million mentioned again, and then he turned and plumped down in his seat, red-faced with oratory and determination.

One thing was clear: he hadn't made it any easier for Red Cloud and Spotted Tail to accept with dignity. Red Cloud was getting to his feet, his face a grim mask; as he raised a hand to the assembly and faced the commission, silence fell again; he pushed back the trailing gorgeous wings of his war-bonnet and fixed us with his gleaming black eyes.

No one will ever know what he was going to say, for at that moment there was an outcry from the back of the crowd, and it was like some huge brown page turning as every head went round to look. There was a thunder of hooves in the distance, and through a gap in the low hills to

*Who shall guard the guardians?

307

the right came pouring a bright cavalcade of Indians, armed riders who whooped and yikked as they galloped towards us; the whole assembly was on its feet shouting, as they swept up to the clear space on our right flank, a surging, feathered horde two hundred strong, milling and waving their clubs and lances while one of their number trotted his pony forward in front of the commission.

He was a sight to take the eye even in that wild gathering, a lithe, brilliant figure who carried himself like an emperor. He was naked except for a short war-bonnet and breech-clout, his face and chest glistening with ochre and vermillion, at his waist were strapped two long-barrelled Colts, a stone axe hung from his decorated saddle-blanket, and he carried a feathered lance. Standing Bear stirred and grunted as I looked anxious inquiry.

"Little Big Man," says he. "The right arm of Tashunka Witko Crazy Horse," and I began to sweat in earnest. These must be Oglala Bad Faces, the wildest of the wild bands from the Powder. The hostiles had come to the council at last.

I gabbled it in a whisper to Terry and Allison; the stout cleric goggled and Collins's hand twitched again at his lapel. We waited breathless while Little Big Man checked his pony close by Red Cloud; he looked all round the assembly and then deliberately wheeled his pony so that his back was to us. I can still see that slim painted body and feathered head, the lance upraised; then he hurled it quivering into the turf at Red Cloud's feet and his voice rang out:

"I will kill the first Lacotah chief who talks of selling the Black Hills!"

There was uproar, and I had to shout my translation in Terry's ear. Mills was barking to his troopers to hold their line, but Young-Man-Afraid and half a dozen of his braves were round Little Big Man in a second, hustling him back towards his fellows, all yelling at once; the assembly were in tumult, but they weren't breaking ranks, thank God; Spotted Tail was on his feet, arms raised, bellowing for order. Standing Bear tugged at my sleeve, and as I turned to follow his pointing finger I swore in amazement.

Behind where we sat was the ambulance, its horses cropping quietly at the grass and its driver standing on his box to watch the confusion—and cantering out of the trees towards the ambulance, a solitary rider, daintily side-saddle, waving her crop gaily as she saw me. I was out from under the canopy like a startled stoat, running towards her in rage and alarm; what the hell was she doing, I shouted, as I grasped her bridle.

"Why, I have come to see the great pow-wow!" cries the blonde lunatic. "My, what a splendid sight! What are they calling out for? Oh, see, there is Mr Spotted Tail! But I declare, Harry, I never knew there were so many—"

"Damn your folly, you should be in the camp, you—you mindless biddy!" I reached up and swung her by main force from the saddle.

"Harry, what are you doing? Oh, be careful—my dress! Whatever are you so agitated for?—and you must *not* curse in that dreadful way! Gracious me, I have only come to see the sight, and I think it was mean of you not to have brought me anyway—oh, look, look at those ones there with the horns and teeth on their heads—are they not grotesque? And the horsemen yonder—was ever anything so grand? Such colours—oh, I would not have missed it for anything!"

I was almost gibbering as I bundled her into the ambulance. "Get in there and sit still! For God's sake, woman, don't you know that this is dangerous? No, I cannot explain—sit there, and wait till I come, blast it! Keep her ladyship there!" I snarled at the startled driver, and ran back, followed by female bleats.

The space before the canopy was alive with jostling, shouting Indians; the vortex was the group round Little Big Man, arguing fiercely; the commission were on their feet, nonplussed, and Mills was whispering urgently to Terry. The great assembly was dissolving, some milling down towards us, others mounting their ponies. I saw weapons brandished as the whooping and yelling grew louder; here was Spotted Tail, his huge buckskinned figure thrusting through the throng as he shouted to Young-Man-Afraid; now he was under the canopy, addressing Mills.

"Put them into the ambulance, now! Away, at once, and make for the camp!"

Allison, mouth open, was about to deliver himself, but Spotted Tail seized his arm and almost ran him to the ambulance, while the troopers closed round us, keeping back the shouting crowd of Sioux riders. There was an undignified scramble into the ambulance, the clergyman dropping his spectacles and Allison his papers; you could feel the panic starting to spread like a wave; oh, Jesus, any minute now and the devils would be breaking loose; it was on a knife-edge—and Standing Bear was pushing me, not towards the ambulance, but to a riderless pony. That suited me: if hell was going to pop, I'd sooner take my chance in the saddle than in a crowded, lumbering wagon that would be the focus for their fury. Christ, Elspeth was in the ambulance!

There was nothing to be done about that; with Standing Bear knee to knee I urged my beast up against the canvas cover as the ambulance rolled away. We were surrounded by a phalanx of Mills's bluecoats, with Young-Man-Afraid and his braves among them. Thank God Mills was cool, and every sabre was in its sheath. All round was a disordered, threatening mob of Indians, yelling taunts, but the ambulance was moving well now, its horses at the trot; it trundled under the trees and out on to the trail to camp, towards the big buttes, and I swallowed my fear and looked about me.

The prairie either side was thick with mounted braves, whooping and singing; I caught some of the words, about how they would make the Powder Country tremble beneath any invader, so that his bowels would loosen with fear; the lightning about the Black Hills would flash and blind him. The more din they made, the better I liked it, for it sounded like drunken exultation; they were seeing the *Isantanka* chiefs scuttling for safety, and with luck that would content them. But a false move by Mills or his men, an accidental shot on either side, or a spurt of blood-lust in just one of that galloping host, and in a twinkling it would be massacre.

We were running briskly for the camp now, and Mills's men were in good order around us. Beyond them I watched the Sioux; there was one evil son-of-a-bitch in a horned headdress flourishing a hatchet and proposing that they should kill all the white men and burn their lodges; suddenly he wheeled between the troopers and rode screeching for the ambulance—and I saw one of the coolest, smartest tricks I remember. Standing Bear raced forward to head him off, and I yelped with terror, for I knew if he cut him down the whole mob would pour in on us. But as he came up beside the whooping Sioux, he simply reached out and caught the other's wrist, laughing.

"D'you want to kill something, great warrior?" he shouted. "Very good, kill away! See that colt yonder—let's see if you can kill that!"

There was a colt running loose among the riders; the fellow in the horned cap looked at it, rolled his eyes at Standing Bear, and with a great howl galloped away, drawing his pistol, letting fly at the colt. There were excited hoots as others took off after him. Standing Bear shrugged and shook his head as he fell back alongside me; I was cold with sweat, for I knew that only his quick thinking had saved us.[58]

The Sioux fell away after that, and we rolled on to the camp in safety, Mills sensibly holding one troop behind as rearguard while the other took the ambulance ahead. I stayed with him, since it always looks well to come in with the last detachment, scowling back towards the danger; it was safe enough now, and I knew that Elspeth was all right with the commission. Mills was thorough; he pulled up a mile from camp and we waited an hour while Young-Man-Afraid's chaps scouted back; they reported that the Sioux were dispersing to their tipis, and Little Big Man's hostiles had withdrawn. All was quiet after the sudden brief excitement, but I guessed it had been a damned near thing.

I finally rode in with the troop, rehearsing the rebuke I would visit on my half-witted wife. Of all the cake-headed tricks, riding out alone to watch the great pow-wow, indeed! Even she ought to have known that although it had been quiet enough about camp, it was folly for a woman to ride alone in wild country; if the meeting had boiled into real violence it would have been all up with her.

She wasn't in our quarters, Mrs Mills hadn't seen her, and I was making for Terry's billet to inquire when I saw the ambulance driver, a bog Irish private, puffing his cutty by the stables. I hailed him, and he stared like a baffled baboon.

"Her leddyship, sorr? Now, an' Oi hivn't seen hem nor hair of her since ye putt her in me cart."

"You mean since you brought her back?"

"Oi didn't bring her back," says he, and the icy shock stopped me in my tracks. "Shure an' didn't she hop out agin to see the show, jest after ye'd sated her down? I thought she was wid yourself, Colonel sorr, or the t'other gintle-men—"

"You bloody fool!" I was absolutely swaying. "D'you mean she's still back yonder?"

He gabbled at me, and then I was running for the stables in such panic as even I have seldom known. She was out there, among that savage, wicked horde—Christ, what might not happen in their present mood? The thoughtless, blind, stupid little—and on my unbelieving ears fell a sound that brought me whirling round with such a flood of relief that I almost cried out.

"Harry! Harry, dearest! Coo-ee!"

She was riding across the parade, touching her pony to hasten it to me, smiling brilliantly and not a thing out of place except her hat, which she had taken off so that her hair blew free about her face. I stood shaking with reaction as she slipped from the saddle and pecked me on the cheek. Instinctively I clamped her to me, shuddering.

"Why did you all hurry away so quickly? I thought I had been quite deserted," cries she laughing, and then opening her eyes wide in mock alarm. "All alone and defenceless among wild Indians! It gave me quite a start, I can tell you!"

"You . . . you got out of the ambulance . . . after I told you—"

"Well, I should just think so! I wanted to see what was happening. Was it not thrilling? All of them running to and fro, and making those whooping cries and shaking their feathers? Why were they in such a commotion? I hoped," she added wistfully, "that they might do a war dance, or some such thing, but they didn't—and then I noticed that you were all gone, and I was quite alone. I called out after the ambulance, but no one heard me."

"Elspeth," says I weakly. "You must never, never do such a thing again. You might have been killed . . . when I found you weren't here, I—"

"Why, my love, you are all a-tremble! You haven't been fretting about me, surely? I was perfectly well, you know, for when a number of them saw me and brought their ponies about me, grunting in that strange way, and of course I couldn't make it out, I was not in the least alarmed . . . well, not more than a wee bit . . ."

She wouldn't be, either. I've known brave folk in my time: Broadfoot and Gordon, Brooke and Garibaldi, aye, and Custer, but for cold courage Elspeth, Lady Flashman, née Morrison, could match them all together. I could picture her in her flowered green riding dress and ribboned straw hat, perfectly composed while a score of painted savages ringed her, glowering. I choked as I held her, and asked what had happened.

"Well, one of them, very fierce-looking—he had two pistols and was painted all red and yellow—" for God's sake, it must have been Little Big Man himself "—he came and snapped at me, shaking his fist; he sounded most irritable. I said 'Good morning', and he shouted at me, but presently he got down and was quite civil."

"Why on earth—"

"I smiled at him," says she, as though that explained it—which it probably did.

"—and he made the others stand back, and then he nodded at me, rather abruptly, and conducted me to Mr Spotted Tail. Then, of course, everything was right as could be."

My alarm, my agonised relief, my sudden welling of affection, died in an instant. I swung round on her, but she was prattling on, one hand round my waist while she tidied her hair with the other.

"And he seemed so *glad* to see me, and tried to speak in English—ever so badly, and made us both laugh! Then he sent the others away, and managed to tell me that there had been some confusion, and we should wait a little and he would have me sent back to the camp. So that was all right, you see, and I'm sorry if it caused you any anxiety, dear one, but there was no occasion."

Wasn't there, though? She'd been with Spotted Tail an hour and better, with the others away, and not a civilised soul in sight . . . I knew what *he* was, the horny savage, and that she'd been pouting and ogling at him . . . All my old, well-founded suspicions came racing back—that first day, thirty-odd years ago, when she swore she was in the Park, and wasn't, and frolicking half-naked with Cardigan while I lay blotto in the wardrobe, and cuddling with that fat snake Usman, and . . . oh, heaven knew how many others. I fought for speech.

"What did he do with . . . I mean, what did you . . I mean . . . dammit, what happened?"

"Oh, he showed me to such a pretty little grove, with a tent, where I should be comfortable while he went to business with his friends. But presently he came back and we chatted ever so comfortably. Well," she laughed gaily, "he *tried* to chat, but it was *so* difficult, with his funny English— why, almost all he knows is 'Joll-ee good!' "

Was she taunting me with mock-innocent hints, the damned minx? I can never tell, you see. I craned my neck as we walked—hell's teeth, there was loose grass sticking to the back of her gown, almost to the collar—there was even a shred in her hair! D'you get that with chatting? I gave a muffled curse and ground my teeth, and was about to explode in righteous accusation when she glanced up at me with those wondrous blue eyes, and for the hundredth time I knew that no one who could smile with that child-like simplicity could possibly be false . . . could she? And the fact that she'd patently been rolling in grass, positively wallowing in the stuff with her hair down? Eh? And Spotted Tail had had the cheek to tell me he was slavering for her . . . and they'd been alone for an hour in such a pretty little grove . . . Jesus, it must be the talk of the tipis by now!

"And then, after a little while, he bade me good-bye ever

so courteously, and two of his young men conducted me home."

What the devil was I to say? I'd no positive evidence (just plain certainty), and if I accused her, or even voiced suspicion, there would be indignation and floods of tears and reproach . . . I'd been through it all before. Was I misjudging her by my own rotten standards? No, I wasn't either—I *knew* she was a trollop, and her wide-eyed girlishness was a deliberate mockery. Wasn't it? No, blast it, it wouldn't do, I'd have it out here and now—"

"Oh, please, Harry, don't look so angry! I did not mean to cause you distress. Were you truly anxious for me?"

"Elspeth," I began thunderously.

"Oh, you *were* anxious, and I am a thoughtless wretch! And I am *selfish*, too, because I cannot be altogether sorry since it has shown me yet again how you care for me. Say you are not angry?" And she gave me a little squeeze as we walked along.

"Elspeth," says I. "Now . . . I . . . ah . . ." And, as always, I thought what the devil, if I'm wrong, and have been misjudging her all these years, and she's as chaste as morning dew—so much the better. If she's not—and I'll be bound she's not—what's an Indian more or less?

"I am truly penitent, you see, and it was perfectly all right, because Mr Spotted Tail took such excellent care of me. Was it not fortunate that he was there, in your absence?" She laughed and sighed happily. " 'Joll-ee good!' "

17

◄◄◄———►———◄ If, as I strongly suspect, that turbulent afternoon's work was a pleasant consummation for Lady Flashman and Chief Spotted Tail, it wasn't for anyone else. The Black Hills treaty died then and there, slain by Senator Allison and Little Big Man. There followed another meeting at Camp Robinson—which I didn't attend because I'd have exploded in his presence—at which Spotted Tail announced the Sioux's formal rejection of the offer; Allison warned him that the government would go ahead anyway, and fix the price at six million without agreement, but the most they could get from him was a promise to send word of the offer to Sitting Bull and Crazy Horse, and if they accepted it then he and Red Cloud would give it their blessing. Which was so much eyewash, since everyone knew the hostiles wouldn't accept. Standing Bear was to be the ambassador to the hostile chiefs, since he was apparently a protégé of Sitting Bull's and well thought of by him.

"So nothing remains," says Allison resentfully afterwards, "but for this commission to bear the bitter fruit of failure back to Washington. All your care and arduous labour, gentlemen, for which I thank you, have been in vain." He was fuming with inward rage at being rebuffed by mere aborigines, and him a Senator, too; for the first and only time I saw his pompous mask drop. "These red rascals," he burst out, "who wax fat on government bounty, have set us at defiance—defiance, I say! Well, the sooner they're whipped into line, by cracky, the better!"

I've wondered since how much either side really wanted a treaty. I believe Red Cloud and Spotted Tail were ready for any terms that even *looked* honourable, and if Allison had been more tactful and offered a half-decent price, they might have won over enough Sioux to make the opposition of the hostile chiefs unimportant. I don't know. What I can say is that the Indians went away from Camp Robinson in bitter fury, and while Allison was personally piqued I'm not certain he was altogether surprised, or that Washington minded too much. I've wondered even if the commission wasn't simply a means of proving how stubborn the Indians were, and putting 'em in the wrong; perhaps of testing their mettle, too. If so, it failed disastrously, for it led Washington and the Army to draw a fatally wrong conclusion: after Camp Robinson it became accepted gospel that whatever happened, the Sioux wouldn't fight. I confess, having seen the way they *didn't* cut loose at the grove, it was a conclusion I shared.

So now, with all the treaty nonsense out of the way, the government set about bringing them to heel, ordering them to come in to the agencies before February of 1876. The message didn't reach them all until Christmas, which meant it was next to impossible for them to comply, with the Powder country deep in snow. Shades of old Macaulay's Glencoe, if you like—an ultimatum to wild tribes delivered late and in dead of winter, culminating in massacre. Whether the intentions of the U.S. Government were any more honourable than William III's I can't say, but they achieved the same result, in a way.

However, I wasn't giving much thought to Indians that winter. Elspeth and I had concluded our western tour with a rail journey through the Rockies, a week's hunting in Colorado, and then back to New York before the snow. I received a handsome testimonial from the Indian Bureau, and notes from Grant and Fish* thanking me for my services, which I thought pretty civil since the whole thing had been a fiasco—only a cynic like me would wonder if that's *why* they thanked me. In any event, I was ready to wend our way home to England, and we would have done if it hadn't been for the blasted Centennial.

1876 being the hundredth anniversary of the glorious moment when the Yankee colonists exchanged a government

*Hamilton Fish, Secretary of State.

of incompetent British scoundrels for one of ambitious American sharps, it had been decided to celebrate with a grand exposition at Philadelphia—you know the sort of thing, a great emporium crammed with engines and cocoa and ghastly bric-a-brac which the niggers have no further use for, all embellished with flags and vulgar statuary. Our princely muffin the late Albert had set the tone with the Crystal Palace jamboree of 1851, since when you hadn't been able to stir abroad without tripping over Palaces of Industry and Oriental Pavilions, and now the Yankees were taking it up on the grand scale. Elspeth was all for it; she suffered from the common Scotch mania for improvement and progress through machinery and tracts, and had been on one of the Crystal Palace ladies' committees, so when she fell in with a gaggle of females who were arranging the women's pavilion at Philadelphia, it was just nuts to her. She was in the thick of their councils in no time—republican women, you know, love a Lady to distraction—and there could be no question of our going home until after the opening in May.

I didn't mind too much, since New York was jolly enough, and Elspeth was happy to divide her time between Park Avenue and Philadelphia, where preparations were in full cry, with Chinks and dagoes hammering away, for the whole world was exhibiting its Brummagem rubbish, and great halls were being built to house it. I even attended one of Elspeth's committee teas, and as a traveller of vast experience my views were ardently sought by the organising trots; I assured them that they must insist on the Turks bringing a troupe of their famous contortionist dancers, a sorority akin to the ancient Vestal Virgins; the religious and cultural significance of their muscular movements was of singular interest, I said, and could not fail to edify the masses.[59]

Mostly, though, we were in and about the smart set, and New York society being as small as such worlds are, the encounter which I had just after Christmas was probably inevitable. It happened in one of those infernal patent circular hotel doors; I was going in as another chap was coming out, and he halted halfway, staring at me through the glass.

Then he tried to reverse, which can't be done, and then he thrust ahead at such a rate that I was carried past and finished where he had been, and he tried to reverse again. I rapped my cane on the glass.

"Open the damned door, sir!" cries I. "It's not a merry-go-round."

He laughed, and round we went again. I stood in the lobby as he tumbled out, grinning, a tall, lean cove with a moustache and goatee and a rakish air that I didn't fancy above half.

"I don't believe it!" cries he eagerly. "Aren't you Flashman?"

"So I am," says I warily, wondering if he was married. "Why?"

"Well, you can't have forgotten me!" says he, piqued-like. "It isn't every day, surely, that you almost chop a fellow's head off!"

It was the voice, full of sharp conceit, that I remembered, not the face. "Custer! George Custer. Well, I'll be damned!"

"Whatever brings you to New York?" cries he, pumping my fist. "Why, it must be ten years—say, though, more than that since our encounter at Audie! But this is quite capital, old fellow! I should have known those whiskers anywhere—the very picture of a dashing hussar, eh? What's your rank now?"

"Colonel," says I, and since it seemed a deuced odd question, though typical of him, I added: "What's yours?"

"Ha! Well may you ask!" says he. "*Half*-colonel, and on sufferance at that. But with *your* opportunities, which we are denied, I'd have thought you'd have your brigade at the least, by now. But there," cries he bitterly, "you're a fighting soldier, so you'd be the last they'd promote. All services are alike, my boy."

Here was one with a bee in his bonnet, I saw, and could guess why. In the war, you see, he'd been the boy general—I'm not sure he wasn't the youngest in the Union Army—but like all the others he'd had to come down the ladder after the peace, and like a fool he was letting it rankle. I'd heard talk of him in the West, of course, for he'd been active against the Indians, and that he'd come under a cloud for dabbling in politics. Grant, they said, detested him.

"But see here," he went on, "I've been itching to see you for ever so long, and wishing I'd looked you out after the war. You see, I never knew then, that you'd been in the Light Brigade!" I was mystified. "Balaclava! The noble Six Hundred!" cries he, and shot if he wasn't regarding me with admiration. "But I hadn't the least notion, you see! Well, that's something I shall want to hear all about, I can tell you, now that chance has brought us together again."

"Ah, well, yes," says I uncertainly. "I see . . ."

"Look here," says he, sporting his ticker, "it's the most confounded bore, but I have to call on my publisher . . . oh, yes, I'm more of a writer than a fighter these days, thanks to the Stuffed Gods of Washington." He grimaced and took my hand again. "But you'll dine with me, this evening? Is your wife in New York? Capital! Then we'd better say Delmonico's—Libby will be head over heels to meet you, and we'll make a party. Fight our battles o'er again, eh? First-rate!"

I wasn't sure it was, as I watched him striding off through the falling snow. Aside from the Audie skirmish, Appomattox, and an exchange of courtesies in Washington, I'd hardly known him except by reputation as a reckless firebrand who absolutely enjoyed warfare, and would have been better suited to the Age of Chivalry, when he'd have broken the Holy Grail in his hurry to get at it. And while I'd met scores of old acquaintances in America, for some reason running into Custer recalled my meeting with Spotted Tail, with its uncomfortable consequences.

We dined at Delmonico's, though, with him and wife, a bonny, prim woman who worshipped him, and his brother Tom, a handsomer edition of the Custer family who got on famously with Elspeth, each being an accomplished flirt. Custer was all high spirits and presented me to his wife with:

"Now, here, Libby, is the English gentleman who almost made a widow of you before you were married. What d'you think of that? Sir Harry Flashman, Victoria Cross and

320

Knight of the Bath—" he'd been at the List, by the sound of it "—also formerly of the Army of the Confederacy, with whom I crossed sabres at Audie, didn't I, old fellow?" The truth of it was that he'd been laying about him like a drunk Cossack among our Johnnie cavalry, and I'd taken one cut at him in self-defence as I fled for safety to the rebel lines, but if he wanted to remember it as a knightly tourney, let him. "Ah, brave days!" cries he, clapping me on the shoulder, and over the soup he regaled us with sentimental fustian about the brotherhood of the sword, now sheathed in respect and good fellowship.

He was all enthusiasm for Balaclava, demanding the most precise account, and vowing over and over that he wished he'd been there, which shows you he should have been in some sort of institution. Though when I think of it, the Charge was ready-made for the likes of him; he and Lew Nolan would have made a pair. When I'd done, he shook his head wistfully, sighed, regarded his glass (lemonade, if you please), and murmured:

"'When shall their glory fade?' C'était magnifique!—and never mind what some fool of a Frenchman said about it's not being war! What does he think war is, without loyalty and heroism and the challenge of impossible odds? And you," says he, fixing me with a misty eye, "were there. D'you know, I have one of your old troopers in my 7th Cavalry? You know him, my dear—Butler. Splendid soldier, best sergeant I've got. Well, sir," he smiled nobly at me and lifted his glass, "I've waited a long time to propose this toast—the Light Brigade!"

I nodded modestly, and remarked that the last time I'd heard it drunk had been by Liprandi's Russian staff after Balaclava, and d'you know, Custer absolutely blubbed on the spot. On lemonade, too.

"Ah, but you British are lucky!" cries he, after he'd mopped himself and they'd brought him a fresh salad. "When I reflect on the contrasting prospects of an aspiring English subaltern and his American cousin, my heart could break. For the one—Africa, India, the Orient—why, half the world's his oyster, where he can look forward to active service, advancement, glory! For the other, *he*'ll be lucky if he sees a skirmish against Indians—and precious thanks he'll get for that!—and thirty years of weary drudgery in some desert outpost where he can expect to end his days as a forgotten captain entering returns."

"Come now," says I, "there's plenty of drudgery in our outposts, too. As to glory—you've had the biggest war since the Peninsula, and no man came out of it with brighter laurels than you did." Which was true, although I was saying it to sweeten Libby Custer, who'd shown no marked enthusiasm for me on hearing how I'd almost cut off her hero in his prime. She beamed at me now, and laid a fond hand on Custer's arm.

"That is true, Autie," says she, and he gave her a noble sigh.

"And where has it led me, my dear? Fort Abe Lincoln, to be sure, under the displeasure of my chiefs. Compare my position with Sir Harry's splendid record—Indian Mutiny, Crimea, Afghanistan, China, the lord knows where else, and our own war besides. Why, his Queen has knighted him! Don't think, old fellow," says he, earnestly, "that I grudge you the honours you've won. But I envy you—your past, aye, and your future."

"Luck of the service," says I, and because I was bored with his croaking I added: "Anyway, *I've* never been a general, and I've got only one American Medal of Honour, you know."

This was Flashy at his most artistic, you'll agree, when I tell you that I knew perfectly well that Custer had no Medal of Honour, but his brother Tom had *two*. I guessed nothing would gall him more than having to correct my apparent mistake, which he did, stiffly, while Tom studied the cutlery and I was all apologies, feigning embarrassment.

"They send 'em up with the rations, anyway," says I, lamely, and Elspeth, who is the most well-meaning pourer of oil on troubled flames I know, launched into a denunciation of the way Jealous Authority invariably overlooked the Claims of the Most Deserving, "for my own gallant *countrymen*, Lord Clyde and Sir Hugh Rose, were never awarded the Victoria Cross, you know, and I believe there were letters in the *Herald* and *Scotsman* about it, and Harry was only given his at the last minute, isn't that so, my love? And I am sure, General Custer," went on the amazing little blatherskite with awestruck admiration, "that if you knew the *esteem* in which your name and fame are held in military circles outside America, you would not exchange it for anything."

Not a word of truth in it, but d'you know, Custer blossomed like a flower; he had an astonishing vanity, and his carping about his lot had more of honest fury than self-pity in it. He knew he was a good soldier—and he was, you know, when he was in his right mind. I've seen more horse-soldiering than most, and if my life depended on how a mounted brigade was handled, I'd as soon see George Custer in command as anyone I know. His critics, who never saw him at Gettysburg and Yellow Tavern, base their case on one piece of arrant folly and bad luck, when he let his ambition get the better of him. But he was good, and felt with some justice that the knives had been out for him. I reflected, watching him that night, how the best soldiers in war are so often ill-suited to peacetime service; he'd been a damned pest, they said, at West Point, and since the war he'd been collecting no end of black marks—there was one ugly tale of his leaving a detachment to its fate on the frontier, and another of his shooting deserters; he'd been court-martialled and suspended, and only reinstated because Sheridan knew there wasn't an Indian fighter to touch him. Certainly he hadn't reached the heights he thought he'd deserved, thanks to his own orneriness, bad luck, and the malignant Stuffed Gods of Washington, as he called them.

The discontent showed, too. He was still in his middle thirties, and I swear without vanity he looked as old as I did at fifty-three. One reason I'd been slow to recognise him was that the brilliant young cavalier I'd seen bearing down on us at Audie, long gold curls streaming from beneath his ridiculous ribboned straw hat, had changed into a worn, restless, middle-aged man with an almost feverish glint in his eye; his skin was dry, the hair was lank and faded, and the tendons in his neck stuck out when he leaned forward in animated talk. I wondered—and I ain't being clever afterwards—how long he would last.

We saw a good deal of the Custers that winter, for although he wasn't the kind I'm used to seek out—being Puritan straight, no booze, baccy, or naughty cuss-words, and full of soldier talk—it's difficult to resist a man who treats you as though you were a military oracle, and can't get enough of your conversation. He was beglamoured by my reputation, you see, not knowing it was a fraud, and had a great thirst for my campaign yarns. He'd read the first volume of my *Dawns and Departures*, and was full of it; I *must* read his own memoirs of the frontier which he was preparing for the press. So I did, and said it was the finest thing I'd struck, beat Xenophon into a cocket hat; the blighter fairly glowed.

Our womenfolk dealt well, too, and Tom was a cheery soul who kept Elspeth amused with his jokes (I'd run the rule over him and decided he was harmless). So we five dined frequently, and visited the theatre, of which Custer was a great patron; he was a friend of Barrett the actor, who was butchering Shakespeare at Booth's, and would sit with his eyes glued to the stage muttering "Friends, Romans, countrymen" under his breath.

That should have made me leery; I'm all for a decent play myself, but when you see someone transported from reality by them, watch out. I shan't easily forget the night we saw some sentimental abomination about a soldier going off to the wars; when the moment came when his wife buckled on his sword for him, I heard sniffing and supposed it was Libby or Elspeth piping her eye. Then the sniff became a baritone groan, and when I looked, so help me it was Custer himself, with his hand to his brow, bedewing his britches with manly tears. Libby and Elspeth began to bawl, too, possibly in sympathy, and had to be helped out, and they all had a fine caterwaul in the corridor, with Libby holding Custer's arm and whispering, "Oh, Autie, it makes me so fearful for you!" Deuced ominous, you may think, and a waste of five circle tickets to boot. At least with Spotted Tail you got your money's worth.

It was in February that Custer announced that he and Libby would have to leave New York for Fort Lincoln, the outpost far up the Missouri where his regiment was quartered; when I observed that I didn't see how he could even exercise cavalry until the snow got properly away, he admitted flat out that they were going because they couldn't afford to stay in New York any longer: his pockets were to let. Since I knew it would give offence, I toyed with the idea of inviting them to stay with us, but thought better of it; he might have accepted.

"The sooner I am back the better, in any event," says he. "I must be thoroughly prepared for the spring; I *must* be. It may be the last chance, you see." I noticed he was looking more on edge than usual, so I asked him, last chance of what? We were in the Century Club, as I remember; he took a turn up and down, and then sat abruptly, facing me.

"The last chance I'll ever see of a campaign," says he, and drummed his fingers on his knee. "The fact is that once this question of the hostile Sioux is settled, as it must be this year, there's going to be precious little left for the U.S. Army to do—certainly nothing that could be dignified by the name of 'campaign'. The Sioux," says he grimly, "are the last worthwhile enemy we've got—unlike you we don't have an empire full of obliging foes, alas! It follows that any senior officer aspiring to general rank had better make his name while the fighting lasts—"

"Hold hard, though," says I. "It's common knowledge that the Sioux *won't* fight, isn't it? Why, the Indian Office was quoted in the papers t'other day, doubting if five hundred hostile Indians would ever be gathered together in America again."

"They'll fight all right!" cries he. "They're bound to. You haven't heard the latest news: Crazy Horse and Sitting Bull have defied the government's ultimatum to come in to the agencies by the end of January—there are thousands of 'em camped up on the Powder this minute who'll never come in! That's tantamount to a declaration of war—and when that war begins this spring I and the 7th Cavalry are going to be in the van, my boy! Which means that the Stuffed Gods of Washington, who have done me down at every turn and would dearly love to retire me to Camp Goodbye to count horseshoes, will have to think again!" He grinned as though he could taste triumph already. "Yes, sir—the American people will be reminded that George A. Custer is too good a bargain to be put on the back shelf. My one fervent prayer," added this pious vampire fiercely, "is that Crazy Horse doesn't catch any fatal illness before the spring grass grows."

"You're sure he'll fight, then?"

"If he don't, he's not the man I think he is. By gad," cries he with unusual fervour, "I would, if it was my land and buffalo! So would you." He smiled at me, knowing-like, and then glanced about conspiratorially, lowering his voice. "In fact, when we ride west in May, I'll be taking whoever I choose in my command party, and if some distinguished visiting officer cared to accompany me as a guest, why . . ." He winked, an appalling sight since his eye was bright with excitement. "What about it? Fancy a slap at the redskins, do you? Heaven knows you must have soldiered against everyone else!"

That's the trouble with my derring-do reputation—bloodthirsty asses like Custer think I can't wait to cry "Ha-ha!" among the trumpets. I'd as soon have walked naked to Africa to join the Foreign Legion. But you have to play up; I made my eyes gleam and chewed my lip like a man sore tempted.

"Get thee behind me, Custer," I chuckled, and ruefully shook my head. "No-o . . . I doubt if Horse Guards would approve of my chasing Indians—not that I'd care a button for that, but . . . Dammit, I'd give a leg to go along with you—"

"Well then?" cries he, all a-quiver.

"But there's the old girl, you see. She's waved me off to war so many times, brave little soul . . . oh, I can leave her

326

when duty calls, but . . ." I sighed, manly wistful. "But not for fun, George, d'you see? Decent of you to ask, though."

"I understand," says he solemnly. "Yes, our women have the harder part, do they not?" I could have told him they didn't; Elspeth had led a life of reckless and probably wanton pleasure while I was being chased half round the world by homicidal niggers. "Well," says he, "if you should change your mind, just remember, there's always a good horse and a good gun—aye, and a good friend—waiting for you at Fort Lincoln." He shook my hand.

"George," says I earnestly, "I shan't forget that." I don't forget holes in the road or places I owe money, either.

"God bless you, old fellow," says he, and off he went, much to my relief, for he'd given me a turn by suggesting active service, the dangerous, inconsiderate bastard. 'Tain't lucky. I hoped I'd seen the last of him, but several weeks later, sometime in April, when Elspeth was off in the final throes of her Philadelphia preparations, I came home one night to find a note asking me to call on him at the Brevoort. I'd supposed him far out on the prairie, inspecting ammunition and fly-buttons, and here was his card with the remarkable scrawl: "If ever I needed a friend, it is now! Don't fail me!!"

Plainly he was in a fine state of frenzy, so I tooled round to the Brevoort next morning, anticipating sport, only to find he was at his publisher's. Aha, thinks I, that's it: they've thrown him and his beastly book into the gutter, or want him to pay for the illustrations; still, Custer as an unhinged author might be diverting, so I waited, and presently he arrived like a whirlwind, crying out at sight of me and bustling me to his room. I asked if they'd set his book in Norwegian by mistake, and he stared at me; he looked fit for murder.

"Nothing to do with my book! I merely saw my publisher in passing—indeed, I'm only in New York because if I had stayed in that . . . that sink of conspiracy in Washington a moment longer, I believe I'd have run mad!"

"What's the row in Washington? I thought you were out in Fort Lincoln."

"So I was, and so I should be! It's a conspiracy, I tell you! A foul, despicable plot by that scoundrel who masquerades as President—"

"Sam Grant? Come now, George," says I, "he's a surly brute, we agree, and his taste in cigars is awful—but he ain't a plotter."

"What do you know about it?" snaps he. "Oh, forgive me, old friend! I am so distraught by this—this web they've spun about me—"

"What web? Now look here, you take a deep breath, or put your head in the basin there, and tell it plain, will you?"

He let out a great heaving sigh, and suddenly smiled and clasped my hand. Gad, he was a dramatic creature, though. "Good old Flash!" he cries. "The imperturbable Englishman. You're right, I must take hold. Well, then . . ."

He'd been at Fort Lincoln, preparing for his precious Sioux campaign, when he'd suddenly been summoned to Washington to give evidence against Belknap, the Secretary for War, no less, who was in a great scandal because of bribes his wife was said to have taken from some post trader or Indian agent (I wasn't clear on the details). Custer, not wanting to leave his regiment so soon before taking the field, had asked to be excused, but the jacks-in-office had insisted, so off he'd gone and given his evidence which, by his account, wasn't worth a snuff anyway. The mischief was that Belknap was a great crony of Grant's, and Grant was furious at Custer for having given evidence at all.

The whole thing stank of politics, and I guessed I wasn't hearing the half of it. All the world knew Grant's administration was rotten to the core, and I'd heard hints that Custer himself had political ambitions of no mean order. But what mattered just then was that he'd put Grant in a towering rage.[60]

"He means to break me!" cries Custer. "I know his vindictive spirit. By his orders I am kept in Washington, like a dog on a lead, at a time when my regiment needs me as never before! It's my belief Grant intends I shall not return to the West—that his jealous spite is such that he will deny me the chance to take the field! You doubt it? You don't know Washington, that's plain, or the toads and curs that infest it! As though I cared a rap for Belknap and his dirty dealings! If Grant would see me I would tell him so—that all I want is to do my duty in the field! But he refuses me an audience!"

I let him rave, and then asked what he wanted of me. He spun round like a jack-in-the-box.

"You know Grant," says he fiercely. "He respects you, and he is bound to listen to you! You are his old friend and comrade—if you were to urge him to let me go, he could not ignore it. Will you? You know what this campaign means to me!"

I didn't know whether to laugh more at his brazen cheek or his folly in supposing that Grant would pay the least heed to me. I started to say so, but he brushed it violently aside.

"Grant will listen to you, I say! Don't you see, you *must* carry weight? You're neutral, and free of all political interest—and you have the seal of the greatest American who ever lived! Didn't Lincoln say: 'When all other trusts fail, turn to Flashman'? Besides, Grant appointed you to the Indian Commission, didn't he? He cannot refuse you a hearing. You must speak up for me. If you don't, I can't think who will—and I'll be finished, on the brink of glorious success!"

"But look here," says I, "there are far better advocates, you know. Sherman, and Sheridan, your friends—"

"Sheridan's in Chicago. Sherman? I don't for the life of me know where he stands. By heaven, if Robert Lee were alive, I'd ask *him*—he'd stand up for me!" He stood working his fists, his face desperate. "You're my best hope—my only one! I beg of you not to fail me!"

The man was plainly barmy. If I carried weight in Washington it was news to me, and bearding Sam Grant on this crackpot's behalf wasn't my idea of a jolly afternoon. On the other hand, it was flattering to be asked, and it might be fun to help stir up what sounded like an uncommon dirty kettle of fish . . . and to see what effect my unorthodox approach might have on Grant—not for Custer's sake, but for my own private amusement. I was at a loose end in New

York, anyway. So I hemmed a bit, and finally said, very well, I'd come to Washington to oblige him, not that it would do the least good, mind . . .

"You are the noblest soul alive!" cries he, with tears in his eyes, and swept me down to luncheon, during which he talked like a Gatling about what I should say to Grant, and his own sterling qualities, and the iniquities of the administration. Not that I heeded much of it—my attention had been caught elsewhere.

It was her voice at first, high and sharp and Yankee, at the dining-room door: "Yep. A table by the window. Oh-kay." And then her figure, as she rustled smartly past in the waiter's wake; fashionable women in the '70s dressed so tight they could barely sit down,[61] and hers was the perfect hourglass shape—a waist I could gladly have spanned with my two hands, but for her upper and lower works you'd have needed the help of the lifeboat crew. Unusually tall, close on six feet from the feathered cap on her piled blue-black hair to the modish calf-boots, and a most arresting profile as she turned to take her seat. Commanding was the word for the straight nose and brow and the full, almost fleshy, mouth and chin, but the complexion was that dusky rose high colour you see on beautiful Italians, and I felt the steam rise under my collar as I drank her in. Then she turned her face full to the room—and arresting wasn't the word.

Her right eye was covered with a patch of embroidered purple silk with a ribbon across brow and temple, matching her dress. Don't misunderstand me; I don't fancy 'em one-legged or hunch-backed or with six toes, and after the first shock you realised that the patch was of no more account than an earring or beauty spot; nothing could distract from the magnetic beauty of that full-lipped arrogant face with its superb colouring—indeed, the incongruous note was her harsh nasal voice carrying sharply as she gave her order: "Mahk turrel soup, feelay Brev'urt medium rayr, Old Injun pudding. Spa warrer. Yep." Well, she probably needed plenty of nourishment to keep that Amazonian figure up to the mark. Italian-American, probably; the ripe splendour of the Mediterranean with the brash hardness of the Yankee. Ripe was the word, too; she'd be about forty, which made that slim waist all the more remarkable—Lord God, what must she look like stripped? And in that happy contemplation I forgot her eye-patch altogether, which just shows you. My last glimpse of her as we left the dining-room, she was smoking a long cigarette and trickling the smoke from her shapely nostrils as she sat boldly erect scanning the room with her cool dark eye. Ah, well, thinks I regretfully, ships that pass, and don't even speak each other, never mind boarding.

From that exotic vision to the surly bearded presence of Ulysses S. Grant was a most damnable translation, I can tell you. I had endured Custer's rantings on the way down—release from Washinton and return to his command were what I was expected to achieve—and while it seemed to me that my uncalled-for Limey interference could only make matters worse, well, I didn't mind that. I was quite enjoying the prospect of playing bluff, honest Harry at the White House, creating what mischief I could. When Ingalls, the Quartermaster-General, heard what we'd come for, he said bluntly that Grant would have me kicked into the street, and I said I'd take my chance of that, and would he kindly send in my card? He clucked like an old hen, but presently I was ushered into the big airy room, and Grant was shaking hands with fair cordiality for him. He thanked me again for Camp Robinson, inquired after Elspeth, snarled at the thought that he was going to have to open the Philadelphia exhibition, and asked what he could do for me. Knowing my man, I went straight in.

"Custer, Mr President."

"What's that?" His cordiality vanished, and his burly shoulders stiffened. "Has he been at you?"

"He asked me to see you, since he can't. As a friend of his—"

"Have you come here to intercede for him? Is that it?"

"I don't know, sir," says I. "Is intercession necessary?"

He took a breath, and his jaw came out like a cannon. "Now see here, Flashman—the affairs of Colonel Custer with this office are no concern of yours, and I am astonished, sir, and most displeased, that you should presume to intrude in them. Poking your goddam nose—I will hear no representations from you, sir! As an officer of a . . . another country, you should know very well that you have no standing in this. Confound it! None whatsoever. I am gravely angered, sir!"

I let him boil. "May I remind you with the greatest respect, Mr President," says I gently, "that I hold the rank of major, retired, United States Army, and also the Congressional Medal of Honour? If those do not entitle me to address the Commander-in-Chief on behalf of a brother-officer—then, sir, I can only offer my profound apologies for having disturbed you, and bid you a very good day."

I stood up as I said it, perfectly composed, bowed slightly, and turned towards the door. If the little bugger had let me go I was prepared to turn on the threshold and roar in a voice they could hear in Maryland: "I deeply regret, sir, that I have found here only the President of the United States; I had hoped to find Ulysses S. Grant!" But I knew Sam; before I'd gone two steps he barked:

"Come back here!" So I did, while he stood hunched, glowering at me. "Very good—*major*," says he at last. "Let's have it."

"Thank'ee, General." I knew my line now, I thought. "It's like this, sir: Custer believes, justly or not, that he has been denied a fair hearing. He also believes he's being held in Washington to prevent his taking part in the campaign."

I paused, and he looked at me flint-faced. "Well, sir?"

"If that's true, General, I'd say he's entitled to know why, and that he's sufficiently senior to hear it from you in person. That's all, Mr President."

The brevity of it startled him, as I'd known it would. He stuck forward his bullet head, frowning. "That's all you have to say? No other . . . plea on his behalf?"

"Not my biznay, sir. There may be political reasons I don't know about. And I'm no longer your military adviser."

"You never were!" he barked. "Not that that ever stopped you from advancing your opinions." He stumped to the windows and peered out, growling; apparently he didn't care for the view. "Oh, come on!" he snapped suddenly. "You don't fool me! What have you got to say for this damned jackanapes? I may tell you," he faced round abruptly, "that I've already had appeals from Sherman and Phil Sheridan, urging his professional competence, distinguished service, and all the rest of it. They also conceded, what they couldn't dam' well deny," he added with satisfaction, "that he's a meddlesome mountebank who's too big for his britches, and gave me sentimental slop about the shame of not allowing him to ride forth at the head of his regiment. Well, sir, they failed to convince me." He eyed me almost triumphantly. "I am not inclined, either on professional or personal grounds, to entrust Colonel George A. Custer with an important command. Well—major?"

I couldn't credit he hadn't been swayed, at least a little, by Sherman and Sheridan, otherwise he wouldn't be wasting time talking to me. My guess was they'd pushed him to the edge, and another touch would do it, if properly applied.

"Well, Mr President," says I, "I've no doubt you're right."

"Damned right I'm right." He frowned. "What's that mean? Don't you agree with Sherman and Sheridan?"

"Well, sir," says I doubtfully, "I gather you don't agree with them yourself . . ."

"What I agree or don't agree with is not to the point," says he testily. "You're here to badger me on this fellow's behalf, aren't you? Well, get on with it! I'm listening."

"Mr President, I submitted only that if he's to lose his command he should be told so, and not kept kicking his heels in your anteroom—"

"I'm not seeing him, so now! And that's flat!"

"Well, beyond that, sir, it's not for me to press my views."

"That's a day I'll live to see!" scoffs he. "I know you—you're like all the rest. You think I'm being unjust, don't you? That I'm putting personal and political considerations—of which, by the way, you know nothing—above the good of the service? You want to tell me George Custer's the finest thing since Murat—"

"Hardly that, sir," says I, and quietly gave him both barrels. "I wouldn't give him charge of an escort, myself."

I'm possibly the only man who's ever seen Ulysses S. Grant with his eyes wide open. His mouth, too.

"The hell you say! What are you talking about—escort? What's the matter with you?" He stared at me, suspiciously. "I thought you were a friend of his?"

"Indeed, sir. I hope that wouldn't prejudice me, though."

"Prejudice?" He looked nonplussed. "Now see here, let's get this straight. I'm not denying that Custer's a competent cavalry commander—"

"Jeb Stuart gave him the right about at Yellow Tavern," I mused. "But then, Stuart was exceptional, we know—"

"The hell with Stuart! What's that to the matter? I don't understand you, Flashman. I am not disputing Custer's professional merits, within limits. I'm aware of them—no man better . . . Escort, indeed! What did you mean by that, sir?"

"Well, perhaps that was coming it a bit raw," I admitted. "I've always thought, though, that George was a trifle excitable . . . headstrong, you know . . . inclined to play to the gallery . . ."

"He's given proof enough of that!" says Grant warmly. "Which is one reason I intend to send out a man who won't use the campaign as an excuse for gallivanting theatrically to impress the public for his own ambitious reasons."

"Ah, well, that's not my province, you see. I can only talk as a soldier, Mr President, and if I have . . . well, any reservations about old George—I daresay that having come up with the Light Brigade and Jeb Stuart I tend to—"

"You and Jeb Stuart! 'Jine the cavalree!'" He snorted and gave me another of his suspicious squints. "See here—have you got it in for Custer?"

"Certainly not, sir!" I was bluff indignation at once, and tried a contemptuous snort of my own. "And I'm absolutely not one of those cheap fogies who can't forget he came foot of the class at West Point—"

"I should hope not! We know what that's worth." He shook his head and glowered a bit. "I came twenty-first out of thirty-nine myself. Yeah. First in horsemanship, though."

"I never knew that," says I, all interest.

"Yes, sir." He looked me up and down with a sour grin. "You dandy boys with lancer figures think you're the only ones can ride, don't you?" He hesitated, but being Sam, not for long. "Care for a drink?"

He poured them out, and we imbibed, and after he'd got the taste of it and ruminated, he came back to the matter in hand, shaking his head. "No, I'd be the last man to belittle Custer as a soldier. Escort! I like that! But as to seeing him—no, Flashman, I can't do it. 'Twould only make bad worse. I know what you mean about excitable, you see. Impassioned appeals to me as an old brother-in-arms—I won't have that." He gulped his drink and sighed. "I don't know. We'll say no more about it, then."

Taking this for dismissal, I was ready to be off, well satisfied with having thoroughly muddied the waters, and he saw me to the door, affably enough. Then a thought seemed to strike him, and he coughed uncertainly, glancing at me sidelong. Suddenly he came out with it, peering under his brows.

"Tell me . . . something I've often wondered, but never cared to ask. Would you be . . . that is, were you . . . the Flashman in *Tom Brown's Schooldays*?"

I'm used to it by now, and vary my reply according to the inquirer. "Oh, yes, don't you know," says I. "That's me."

"Oh." He blinked. "Yes, I see . . . well." He didn't know which way to look. "Uh-huh. But . . . was it true? What he says, I mean . . . about you?"

I considered this. "Oh, yes, I'd say so. Every word of it." I chuckled reminiscently. "Great days they were."

He scratched his beard and muttered, "I'll be damned!" and then shook my hand, rather uncomfortably, and stumped off, with an anxious glance or two over his shoulder.[62] I strolled out, and Custer leaped from ambush, demanding news.

"He thinks you're a damned good cavalryman," says I, "but he won't see you."

"But my reinstatement? I may leave Washington?"

"No go there, either, I'm afraid. He don't hold it against you that you came last at the Point, by the way."

"What?" He was fairly hopping. "You . . . you could not move him at all? He concedes me nothing? In heaven's name, what did you say? Didn't you urge my—"

"Now, calm yourself. I've done you a better day's work than you know, if I'm any judge. Sherman and Sheridan have been at him, too. So just rest easy, and it'll come right, you'll see."

"How can I rest easy? If you have failed me . . . oh, you must have bungled it!" cries this grateful specimen. "Ah, this is too much! The corrupt, mean-spirited villain! I am to be kept like a lackey at his door, am I? Well, if he thinks that, he doesn't know his man! I defy him!"

And he stormed off in a passion, vowing to catch the next train west, and Grant could make of it what he liked. I ambled back to the hotel, whistling, and found a note at the porter's cabin; Grant wanting me to autograph his copy of *Tom Brown*, no doubt. But it wasn't. A very clerkly hand:

"The Directors of the Upper Missouri Development Corporation present their compliments to Sir Harry Flashman, etc., and request the privilege of a conference in Room 26/28 of this hotel at 3 o'clock, to discuss a Proposal which they are confident will be of mutual advantage."

I'd had 'em before, at home, fly-by-night company sharps hoping to enlist a well-known public man (if you'll forgive me) in some swindle or other, and prepared to grease the palm according. I'd not have thought I was prominent enough over here, though, and was about to crumple it up when I noted that these merchants were at least flush enough to engage a suite of rooms. No harm in investigating, so at the appointed hour I rapped the timber of Number 26, and was admitted by a sober nondescript who conducted me to the inner door and said the company president was expecting me.

I went in, and the company president rose from behind a desk covered with papers and held out a hand in welcome. The company president was wearing crimson velvet today, and as before, the eyepatch and ribbon were to match.

* * *

"Good of you to be so prompt, Sir Harry." Her handshake was firm and brisk, like her voice. "Yep. Pray be seated. A cigarette?" She had one smoking in a copper tray, and while I lighted another she sat down with a graceful rustle and appraised me with that single dark eye. "Forgive me. I'd expected you to be older. Yep. The letters after your name, and all."

If there's one thing I can tolerate it's a voluptuous beauty who expected me to be older. I was still recovering from my surprise, and blessing my luck. At point-blank she was even more overpowering than I'd have imagined; the elegant severity of the dress which covered her from ankle to chin emphasised her figure in a most distracting way. It was abundantly plain that her shape was her own, and certainly no corset—they were thrusting across the desk of their own free will, and the temptation to seize one and cry "How's that?" was strong. No encouragement, though, from that commandingly handsome dark face with the crimson strip cutting obliquely across brow and cheek; the fleshy mouth and chin were all business, and the smile coldly formal. The high colour of her skin, I noticed, was artfully applied, but she wore no perfume or jewellery, and her hands were strong and capable. In a word, she looked like a belly-dancer who's gone in for banking.

I said I believed I'd seen her lunching at the Brevoort, in New York, and she nodded curtly and disposed of it in her harsh nasal voice.

"Yep, correct. You were engaged, so I didn't intrude. I meant to speak with you later, but they said you'd left for Washington. I had business here, so I figured to kill two birds with one stone. Oh-kay," she drawled, and folded her hands on the table. "Business. I understand you have the acquaintance of Chancellor Prince von Bismarck."

That was a facer. For one thing, "acquaintance" wasn't how I'd have described that German ruffian who'd dragged me into his diabolical Strackenz plot and tried to murder me*, and how did she—

"You allude to him in your book—" She tapped a volume on the table "—in a way that suggests you've met him. *Dawns and Departures*. Most interesting. I take it you do know him?"

"Fairly well," says I, on my guard. "At one time we were . . . ah, close associates. Haven't seen him for some years, though." Twenty-eight, to be exact. I'd kept count, thankfully.

"That's very good. Yep. The Upper Missouri Development Corporation, of which I am president and principal shareholder—pardon me, is something amusing you?" Her single eye was like a flint. "Perhaps you think it's unusual for a woman to be head of a large corporation?"

In fact I'd been musing cheerfully on the words "upper" and "development", but I couldn't tell her that. "No, I was remembering how I introduced Prince Bismarck to boxing— I do beg your pardon. As to your position, I know several ladies who preside over quite large enterprises, including the Queens of England and Madagascar, the Empress of China, and the late Ranee of an Indian kingdom. You remind me of her very much; she was extraordinarily beautiful."

She didn't bat an eyelid. "Our company," she went straight on, "owns extensive lands on the Missouri river—it mayn't be familiar to you? Oh-kay—the area in question is located around a steamboat landing recently renamed Bismarck, after your friend the Chancellor, although I guess he doesn't know it."[63] She drew on her cigarette. "We intend to take advannage of that coincidence to attract German settlers and financial interests to the region. Yep. Vast sums

---

*See *Royal Flash*.

will be involved, and a personal endorsement—maybe even a visit—by the German Chancellor would be invaluable to us. Oh-kay?"

"My dear lady! You don't expect Bismarck to come to America? He's fairly well occupied, you know."

"Obviously that's highly unlikely." She said it dismissively. "But an endorsement—even an expression of interest and good will on his part—is certainly not. Naturally we'll canvass the German government. But a personal approach, from one who knows him well, would be far more likely to enlist his personal sympathy, wouldn't you say? Just his signature, on a letter approving the plan, would be worth many thousands of dollars to us."

"You're suggesting," says I, "that I should ask Otto Bismarck to give his blessing to your scheme?"

"Yep. Corr-ect."

Well, I'd heard of Yankee enterprise, but this beat the band. Mind you, it wasn't crazy. A respectable scheme, brought to Bismarck's attention, might well win a kind word from him, and trust the Americans to know how to turn that sort of thing into hard cash. The beautiful thought was Flashy writing: "My dear Otto, I wonder if you remember the jolly times we had in Schonhausen with Rudi and the rats, when you made me impersonate that poxy prince . . ." Could I blackmail him, perhaps? Perish the thought. But I could smell profit in her scheme, money and . . . I was watching her inhale deeply. By Jove, yes, money was the least of it. She stroked her cheek with the hand holding the cigarette and watched me speculatively. Was there a glimmer of more than commercial interest in that fine dark eye? We'd see.

"I'd have to know a good deal about your scheme before—"

"Yep. We'd want you to visit the town of Bismarck, as well as examining our plans in detail. A few weeks would—"

"Bismarck!" I exclaimed. "Wait—isn't that the place—yes, on the Missouri—close by an army post called Fort Abraham Lincoln? Why, it's right out on the frontier!"

"Corr-ect. Why, d'you know it?"

"No, but a friend of mine—in fact, the man you saw lunching with me at the Brevoort—commands at Fort Lincoln. Well, that's an extraordinary thing! Why, I was with him only today—"

"Is that so? I was about to say that when you'd been shown the area, and had the plans explained, you would be able to write Prince Bismarck—or visit him if you thought it advisable. The corporation would meet all expenses, naturally, in addition to—"

"Who'd show me the area? Yourself, personally?"

"—in addition to a fee of fifteen thousand dollars. Yep." She crushed out her cigarette. "Myself. Personally."

"In that case," says I gallantly, "I should find it impossible to refuse." She looked at me woodenly and put another cigarette between her full lips, lighting it herself before I could bound to assist.

"Of course," says I, "I can't promise that Bismarck will—"

"We would pay five thousand of the fee on despatch of your personal letter to the Chancellor, drafted in consultation with us," says she crisply, and blew out her match. "The balance would be dependent on his reply—five thousand if he replies but declines, ten thousand if he approves. According to the warmth of that approval, a bonus might be paid."

A business-like bitch if ever there was one; cold as a dead Eskimo, rapping out her terms and looking like the Borgias' governess. I told her it all sounded perfectly satisfactory.

"Oh-kay." She struck a bell on her desk, and spoke past me as the door opened. "Reserve a first-class sleeping berth for Sir Harry Flashman, V.C., K.C.B., to Bismarck and return." The door closed. "There's a hotel there, but I wouldn't put a dawg in it. Can you arrange to stay with your military friend? If not, we'll rent the best rooms available. You can? Oh-kay."

She put down her cigarette, rose, and went to an escritoire against the wall. I watched the tall, shapely figure lustfully, considering the curls that nestled around her ears, and the entrancing profile under the lustrous piled hair. It's my experience that a woman with a shape like that will invariably use it for the purpose which Nature intended. She might be a proper little Scrooge, with her cold efficiency and twanging voice and impersonal stare, but she didn't dress in that style, and paint in that artful way, to help balance the books. If I couldn't charm her supine, it was time to retire. As I got up she turned and came towards me with that smooth stride, holding out an envelope towards me.

"It's the corporation's policy," says she, "to pay a retainer in advance." At a yard's distance I realised she was barely three inches shorter than I.

"Quite unnecessary, my dear," says I pleasantly. "By the way, you still have the advantage of me, Miss . . . or Mrs . . .?"

"Candy. Mrs Arthur B. Candy." She continued to hold out the envelope. "We'd prefer that you took it."

"And I'd prefer that I didn't. Arthur," says I, "has a sweet tooth," and before she could stir I had my hands on that willowy waist. She quivered—and stood still. I drew her swiftly against me, mouth to mouth, feeling the glorious benefits and working to get her lips apart; suddenly they opened, her tongue flickered against mine, she writhed against me for five delicious seconds, and as I changed my grip to the half-Flashman—one hand on her right tit, t'other clasping her left buttock, and stand back, referee—she slipped smoothly from my embrace.

"Yep," says she, and without the least appearance of hurry she was behind her desk again, seating herself and making a minute adjustment to her eyepatch ribbon. "Ar-thur Candy", she went on calmly, "never existed. But in working hours, the initial B. stands for business." Her hand rested beside her bell, "Oh-kay?"

"Business is so fatiguing, you know. Don't you think you ought to lie down? All work and no play—"

"I have a full sked-yool for the next ten days," she went on briskly, consulting her calendar. "Yep. I intend to be in Bismarck around the third week of May. That gives you ample time to travel out at your convenience. When I arrive I'll check with Coulson's, the steamboat people, and we can meet at their office."

"I've a much better notion. Suppose we travel out together?"

"That's quite impossible, I'm afraid. I have appointments."

"I'm sure you have," says I, sitting on the corner of her desk à la Rudi Starnberg, although I don't recall his knocking a tray of pins to the floor. "But, d'you know, Mrs Candy, there's a good deal I ought to know about your corporation beforehand, I think. After all—"

"You can check with the New York City Bank as to our standing, if that bothers you. And there's the retainer." She gestured with her cigarette. I picked up the envelope—a sheaf of greenbacks, in hundreds—and dropped it back on her desk.

"The only thing that bothers me, as you are well aware," says I, "is the corporation president. Will she do me the honour of dining with me this evening? Please?"

"Thank you, Sir Harry, but I'm engaged this evening."

"Tomorrow, then?"

"Tomorrow I leave for Cincinnati." She stood up and held out her hand. "May I say on behalf of the corporation that we're both pleased and honoured that you are joining us in this enterprise?" She said it with calm formality, eye steady, the full mouth firm and expressionless. "Also that I am wearing a boot with a sharp toe and a pointed heel, and I'd like my hand back. Thank you." She struck the bell, and her bloody watchdog appeared. "I'll probably arrive at Bismarck by steamboat—the corporation has an interest in the company, so if your friend can put you up till then, perhaps we can arrange accommodation aboard afterwards." Her smile was admirably polite and impersonal. "They're extremely comfortable, and it will be so much pleasanter if we travel by water. Easier to see the country, too. Yep. You're sure you won't take the retainer? Oh-kay. Good afternoon, Sir Harry."

And there I was in the corridor, considering various things. Chiefly, that I admired Mrs Candy's style—the hard, no-nonsense aloofness, punctuated by a brief impassioned lechery, was one I'd encountered occasionally, but I'd never

342

known it better done. Why, though? Her proposal was rum, but plausible—even reasonable. There'd been a cool thou. at least in that envelope, and my sensitive nose hadn't smelled swindle—it would have been all the way to the sofa and break the springs if she was crooked, which was one reason I'd tested her with a grapple. No, my guess was that she was a lusty bundle who kept a tight rein on her appetite during office hours, just as she'd said, but would let rip once the shop was shut. For the rest, her scheme made sense: Otto's blessing would be worth a fortune to her (not that she'd ever get it through me), and even if I didn't make more than the first payment out of it, playing with the corporation president on a steamboat cruise would be ample compensation—for her, too, lucky Mrs Candy. And Elspeth would be fast in Philadelphia for another month anyway.

The one fishbone in my throat was the queer chance that I'd be going to Bismarck, next door to George Custer's fort. It's the sort of coincidence I don't trust an inch, but I was damned if I could see a catch. He'd sworn he was going to defy Grant and leave town tomorrow, so why shouldn't I go west with him?—I might even pretend that I was taking him up on his invitation to join his ghastly campaign, supposing the silly ass was allowed to have one. It might be an amusing trip to Bismarck with him, too . . .

By God, but it was all suspiciously pat! The wild notion that Custer had set Mrs Candy on to lure me west so that he could drag me along in pursuit of the Sioux crossed my mind, and I found I was grinning. No, that didn't answer—not having seen the exotic Mrs Candy. Not puritan George.

18

◄◄◄━━━➤━━━━━◄ The rail trip west was a fine mixture of boredom and high diversion. Custer was in a hysteric turmoil, what between his rage at Grant and his own recklessness in leaving Washington without permission. He was like a small boy smashing his toys in a bawling tantrum while watching with fearful fascination to see what Papa will do. He was all over me again, excusing his ill-temper at the White House as mere frenzy of disappointment; I was the truest of friends, rallying to his side when all others had forsaken him, I was a tower of strength and comfort—what, I would come west with him, even? Oh, this was nobility! Enobarbus couldn't have done better. Let him wring my hand again.

"As for that rattlesnake Grant," cries he, as we climbed aboard at the depot, me chivvying the porter and Custer waving his cane with his hat on three hairs, "let him prevent me if he dares! I have a voice, and the public have ears. Conductor, I am General George A. Custer and I have reservations. We'll see if his spite outruns his sense of self-preservation. First in horesmanship, does he say? A fine crowd of cripples they must have had at the Point that year!"

I had two days of this, all the way to Chicago; he was like a pea on a drum one minute and gnawing his knuckles in silent gloom the next. The Stuffed Gods would get him if they could, he was sure of it, and became almost lachrymose; then he would brighten as he recalled the news that only a few weeks back General Crook, making the first tentative move against the Sioux hostiles from the south, had blundered into the camp of Crazy Horse himself, and after a mismanaged action which accomplished nothing but

344

the destruction of the Indians' tipis, with scant loss on either side, had retired discomfited to Fort Fetterman.

"Imagine it!" gloats Custer, bright with scorn. "The arch-hostile in their grasp, and they let him slip! They burn a few lodges, kill an old squaw and a couple of children, capture the Indians' ponies—which they promptly lose again next day—and Crook counts it a victory. Ye gods, it doth amaze me! Crazy Horse must be helpless with laughter. And Grant thinks he can do without *me* on the frontier?" He laughed bitterly. "Crook—because he's scrambled after a few Apache renegades they think he's an Indian fighter. Well, he knows now what real hostiles are! Perhaps our perspicacious President does, too, and will have to swallow his gall and put me back where I belong."

I asked him mildly how he'd set about it, and he scowled. "Even if Grant sees sense, I'll still not have full command—no, that's for your genteel friend General Terry, who has never fought an Indian in his life—an impressive qualification, is it not?" He waved a dismissive hand. "Fortunately, the dispositions are so simple a child could direct them—Terry and I will march to the Yellowstone and strike into the Powder country from the north; old Gibbon's infantry column will advance from the west; and Crook, supposing he had collected himself before Christmas, will come up from the south—all converging, you see, so that Crazy Horse and Sitting Bull and all their hands will be ringed in, at bay." He smiled complacently, and winked. "And I, *bien entendu*, have charge of the cavalry, who move rather faster than anyone else." Then his face fell again. "Unless that rascal in Washington hobbles me at the last. But he can't, Flashman, I tell you! He can't!"

But he could. There was an embarrassed staff-walloper on the platform at Chicago to convoy our hero to General Sheridan forthwith, and from little Phil we learned that Sherman had sent word that the Sioux expedition was definitely to proceed *without* Custer. The resultant explosion of grief and rage shook the furniture, with me tactfully silent and enjoying every minute of it, and Sheridan looking more like an unhappy tramp than ever. Custer went wild; as heaven was his witness, he'd call Grant out, or sue him, or have him impeached, and in the meantime he was going on to Fort Lincoln if he had to swim through blood all the way. Sheridan observed bluntly that he could go to hell if he wanted, but if he hoped to see service on the way, he'd better think of a means of making his peace with Grant.

"How can I" bawls Custer, "when he will not see me?"

"Neither would I, in your present condition," says Sheridan. "I tell you straight, you'd better take hold, and stop acting like some damned opera singer. You're your own worst enemy, George. I'll telegraph Sherman again, but you'd better put your case to Terry, and if he wants you badly enough, maybe Grant'll listen."

Custer rolled an eye at me, as much as to say: "You see how I am used!", and I shepherded him on to the train to St Paul, all agog for Act II. It was like *East Lynn* overplayed, for Custer had apparently decided that the best way to approach the mild and courtly Terry was as a good man wronged; it would have broken your heart to see him clasping Terry's hand, tears in his eyes, swearing that if he were not permitted "to hazard myself in honour's cause, at the head of the regiment which has followed me so faithfully and far", it would bring down his grey hairs in sorrow to the knacker's yard, and there'd be nothing for it but to clap a pistol in his mouth and call in the decorators. He described, with outflung arm, how I had abased myself to Grant on his behalf, "beseeching" if you please, and when he actually went down on the carpet and fairly grovelled, Terry didn't know where to look.

"Do you think he'll do himself a mischief?" Terry asked me when the suppliant had retired, and I said, on the whole, no, but if he didn't get his way, Grant would be well advised to stay out of Ford's Theatre if Custer was in town.

"It is deeply distressing," says Terry. "I wish he wouldn't take on so; it isn't becoming. You've seen Grant, though—what d'you think? Will he be swayed if I speak on Custer's behalf?"

"If you don't, you'll be about the only man in the Army

who hasn't," says I. "But you'll carry more weight than all the rest—it's your expedition, and I'd hate to be the Commander-in-Chief who denied you your choice of senior men. Suppose he refused to give you Custer, and the expedition went wrong—say the cavalry were mismanaged by his replacement? The Democrats could make hay of that, I should think. No, if you ask for Custer, Sam daren't risk a refusal." And to increase the fun I added: "Custer knows it, too."

He stiffened at that. "I'll not be made a cat's paw!" Then he frowned. "Is it true, d'you think, that Custer has . . . hopes of high office? I've heard rumours . . . "

"That he'd take a stab at the White House? Shouldn't wonder—you Americans have a habit of promoting your military heroes, haven't you? Washington, Jackson, Grant —back home we did it with Wellington, and bloody near had a revolution. Before my time, of course. However, that don't help you. The point is: d'you want Custer along?"

"It is difficult not to be moved by his plea," he mused; he was a proper soft head prefect, this one. "And if this unhappy Belknap business had not arisen, there'd have been no question of Custer's removal. No—I believe it would lie heavy on my conscience if I didn't exert myself on his behalf."

Conscience, you see? Note that; it's a bigger foe of mankind than gunpowder.

Between us we concocted an appeal to Grant—me suggesting the more abject and crawling phrases which I knew would drive Custer to apoplexy, and Terry striking them out. Then I took it to Custer for his signature; he tore his hair and swore he'd die before he'd "truckle to that miscreant Grant".

"You put your John Hancock on that, my boy," says I, "or it's all up with you. Let me tell you, it would have been a sight more humiliating for you if Terry had had the writing of it; I had the deuce of a job persuading him to appeal to Grant at all. If you refuse this, I'll not answer for the consequences: Terry's about ready to wash his hands of you."

"You can't mean it?" cries he in panic, and scribbled his signature, insisting that I was his truest friend, etc. It went over the wire, and with Terry and Sherman and Sheridan and Uncle Tom Cobleigh and all besieging him, Grant finally gave way, and the word came back: Custer could go with his regiment. Why, God knows; if I'd been in Grant's shoes I'd have cashiered the bastard, just for spite.

Custer's behaviour after this was a revelation, even to me. I guess he remembered what an ass he'd made of himself to Terry, for he thanked him pretty curtly, and when we were on the train to Bismarck he confided to me that Terry would have been a fool to act otherwise. "There would have been mutiny in the 7th if I had not been restored," says he smugly. "Then where would Lawyer Terry have been? If he's done anyone a kindness, it is himself, not me." And he'd been weeping on the fellow's boot-laces, so help me. I was beginning to wonder if Custer wasn't perhaps some by-blow of the Flashman family.

This suspicion was dispelled when we reached Fort Lincoln, about a week after leaving Washington, for I hadn't been at the place a day before I realised that Custer lacked one quality which I and my kindred have by the bucket: popularity. I don't know how much his troopers cared for him, but his officers clearly disliked him. I don't say it was on professional grounds; I believe most of them respected him as a soldier, but as a man they'd have had a hard job tolerating him. This was a new slant to me; you see, he'd toadied me on account of my fame and success, and ever since the Belknap business he'd been in such a high-flown state that his character couldn't be judged; now, in his own mess, I saw the fellow's bounce and arrogance in full flight, and knew that whatever else it might be, the 7th wasn't a happy ship.

His senior officers, you see, were fellows of long service and good name who'd held higher ranks in the war than they did now, and it's no fun for a good man who's been a colonel, and knows how a colonel should behave, to take snuff from a demoted general. His top major, Reno, who seemed a dapper, quiet, clever sort of chap, concealed any animosity he may have felt, but the dominant spirit in the mess, a big burly bargee with prematurely white hair and a schoolboy's eyes and grin, called Benteen, seemed ready to lock horns with Custer as soon as look at him. I saw it within a minute of meeting him: he pumped my hand jovially and wanted to talk cricket with me—which I thought deuced strange in an American, but it seemed he'd played as a boy and was a keen hand.[64] Custer listened with a jaundiced air as we discussed those mysteries which are Greek to the uninitiated, and finally observed that it sounded a dull enough pastime, at which Benteen says: "Well, then, colonel, what game shall we talk about? Kiss-in-the-ring or blind man's buff?" and Custer gave him a glare and took me off to meet Keogh, a jolly black Irishman who had family connections with the British Army— and that didn't suit Custer either, evidently; I was *his* lion, I suppose, and to be welcomed as such. Again, there was Moylan, up from the ranks and with sergeant's mess written all over him, which didn't stop Custer from mentioning the fact in presenting me.

Then there was a large Custer faction at the fort: his brother Tom, whom I knew, and another brother, Boston, who was a civilian but had some commissary post or other, and Calhoun, Custer's brother-in-law, who seemed a good sort—but in my experience, let too much family into a regiment and you let in trouble; it must make for a house divided. Don't mistake me: I don't blame the unhappy officers' mess for what happened later, any more than I blame the Balaclava fiasco on the fact that Lucan and Cardigan detested each other. Both disasters would have happened if Custer's 7th had been all loving and loyal, and Lucan and Cardigan sworn chums. I'm just reporting what I saw.

The fort itself was a dismal enough place, on flat land west of the river, with baldhead prairie stretching away forever and coyotes waking the dead at night. Bismarck, an ugly settlement where the Northern Pacific railroad stopped, was about four miles down on the east bank; I took a prowl through it, and thanked God I wasn't staying there, for while it was bustling enough and like to spread and prosper, it was still rough and ready, with streets awash with mud and slush, touts and roughs and sharps abounding, and the grog-shops and whore-houses open day and night. I hired a trap and drove out of town, and while I'm no farmer, it looked to me as though the Upper Missouri Corporation might be on a good thing—rail and river convenient, good soil by the millions of empty acres, and nothing missing except thousands of contented kraut-eaters to be enslaved to the company store.

Not the kind of spot that would hold me for long, though, and it was only the thought of the delectable Mrs Candy that made life at Fort Lincoln tolerable in the two weeks I was there—gad, the discomforts I'll endure for the sake of a fresh skirt. But I was looking forward to this one with unusual zest; your melting ones ain't in it with the cool teasers when it comes to the bit. In the meantime, Libby Custer and the other wives were at pains to make me at home, Benteen scented my soldier's interest and showed me about the post, and I formed my impression of this famous 7th Cavalry of which no doubt you've heard so much.

For the time and the place they weren't bad—not to compare with Johnny Reb cavalry or Cardigan's Lights or Scarlett's Heavies or the Union horse in the Civil War, or Sikhs or Punjabis either, but then these were all soldiers *at war,* most of the time, and the 7th weren't. I've heard tell since that they were the finest unit of horse in the American Army at the time, and it may be so; I've also heard that they were a drunken, brutal parcel of rascals and drunkards and misfits, and that's a downright lie. They had their bad hats, but no more than any other regiment. They were hellish young, though; I watched Calhoun's troop at exercise, smart enough and rode well, but so many fresh faces I never did see. I've been told since that a third of 'em had never faced an enemy. That's nothing: I doubt if one man in ten of the Light Brigade had heard a shot in anger before we landed in Calamity Bay, and *they* proved themselves the best that ever rode to battle anywhere. The 7th Cavalry would have been as crack a regiment as you could wish, given a campaign to teach them their trade. They were good boys, and let nobody tell you different. And Jeb Stuart or Cromwell himself couldn't have done a whit better than they did when the time came.

I have to give Custer the credit for that. In the ten days at the fort he drove them hard, and his officers likewise. If there was a loose shoe or a galled back or a trooper who didn't know his flank man, it wasn't the colonel's fault. He fussed over that regiment like a boy with a new bride; he couldn't do enough for it, or let it alone. At the same time he was deep in discussion with Terry, who was now on hand; there was great heave and ho everywhere, with inspections and issue of rations and farriers and armourers going demented and messengers flying and the telegraph office open night and day; how the dickens Custer had energy enough for his evening's jollity I can't fathom.

For he was like a schoolboy on holiday as the time to march drew near, even behaving affably to Benteen and Moylan, holding parties at his house, getting up impromptu theatricals one night, I remember, in which I had to play Judge Puffenstuff in a comic breach of promise suit, holding all the prettiest young wives in contempt for giggling and sentencing Tom Custer to transportation for flirting. There were charades and games every evening, and much singing round the piano—I can see it so plain still; little Reed, who was Custer's nephew, turning the sheets for Libby, and Terry with his eyes shut, rendering "My Old Kentucky Home" and "My love is like a red, red rose" in his fine tenor, and Custer bright-eyed as he leaned on a chair, smiling fondly at Libby, and her quick loving glance at him from the music, and Keogh quite overcome with sentiment and drink, muttering "Oh, Jayzus, Ginneral, it's a darlin' gift of song, a darlin' gift", and the young folk holding hands while the firelight flickered on the wooden walls and the buffalo head over the mantel. And then Calhoun taps his foot, and Libby laughed at Custer and struck a rousing chord, and they all brisked up, and Custer himself led them off in his cracked baritone until the rafters rang and feet stamped and the glasses swung in rhythm as they roared out in chorus:

We'll beat the bailiffs out of fun,
We'll make the mayor and sheriffs run,
We are the boys no man dare dun,
    If he regards a whole skin!
In place of spa we'll drink down ale,
And pay no reckoning on the nail,
No man for debt shall go to jail,
    While he can Garryowen hail![65]

They didn't notice I wasn't singing; I was remembering the remnants of the Light Brigade in that grisly hospital shed by Yalta, croaking out those self-same words in their pathetic pride at having done what no horse-soldiers had ever done before. I thought of the pale fierce faces and the horrid wounds, and the unspeakable hell we'd come through, and the ghastly cost—and I wondered if it was a lucky song to sing, that's all.

Custer couldn't get enough of it; I remember he was whistling it the last night before Terry's force marched out, when I popped into his study to say good-night. He was packing his valise—with a volume of Napier's *Peninsular War,* among other things, I remember—and says to me in high fettle:

"I can't prevail on you to ride along with us, then? I'm taking Boss and Autie Reed, you know, and the newspaper fellow—they're all civilians. Your Bismarck bagmen can wait till we get back, surely?" I'd told him about the Upper Missouri affair, in strict confidence—and without mentioning the sex of the corporation president. Libby and he wouldn't have liked it, and word might have reached Elspeth's ears.

"Stop teasing a fellow, George," says I, very bluff. "You know I'd be there like a shot if 'tweren't for the better half. Anyway, you don't want a real cavalryman along; I'd just show you up."

"Oho! Sauce!" cries he merrily. "I was only asking you 'cos I thought you'd be useful for remounts."

"Much more of that, and I'll offer my services to Crazy Horse," says I. "Get a bit of own back for Yorktown, or wherever it was." Hearty stuff, you see, and delighted him no end.

"I'll look for you in the first war-party!" cries he, and then became all solemn. "Seriously, though—I can't thank you enough, old boy. I don't know what turned Grant, but . . . well, I couldn't have had a better man to speak up for me, I know that." He clasped my hand with manly fervour. "I only wish I could repay you."

"Well, now, if you should see Little Big Man, kick his backside for me."

"I'll do better than that!" cries he as I went out. "I'll fetch you his scalp!"[66]

I felt duty bound to crawl out and see them off in the morning, raw and misty as it was; there's no sight more inspiring or heart-warming than troops marching out to battle when you ain't going with them. Custer was prancing about at the head of the 7th as they marched past by column of platoons, with the garrison kids stumping alongside playing soldiers; the troopers dismounted for farewells at the married lines, and then the embracing and boo-hooing was broken by the roar of commands, Libby and her sister, who were riding out the first few miles, took post beside Custer, Terry and his staff assumed expressions of resolution, the word was "Mount!" and "Forward-o!", and as Reno and Benteen led off in double column we had another burst of *Garryowen* and *Yellow Ribbon*.

They looked well as they trotted by, the harness jingling, each blue rider with his brace of pistols and carbine—no sabres, I noticed—the guidons fluttering and everyone waving to them; the band crashed into *The Girl I Left Behind Me*, which was the signal for more female caterwauling, drowned by the prompt action of the distinguished-looking British civilian with the fine whiskers, standing erect by the main gate, who raised his hat and called for three rousing cheers and a tiger for these gallant fellows. Everyone hurrahed, and out they rode to the empty plain, the Ree scouts in their blankets and feathers trotting alongside, and then three companies of infantry, the platoon of Gatling guns, the wagons and mules churning up the dust, the piping of the music fading into the distance, the rising sun glinting here and there on the far column lining across the prairie, and in Fort Lincoln the silent crowd who had watched 'em go dispersed in little knots about the barracks, with only a murmur and shuffle in the stillness of the morning.

The next ten days were hellish. I was staying in the Custer house, and Libby and Margaret went about like two of the Three Fates, pale and listless with thoughts about their absent men; once I surprised Libby in Custer's study, her head on his desk beside his portrait, sobbing her heart out, but I managed to retreat unobserved. Much of this and I'd have taken to drink, and still no word from that elegant slut Candy—had it been some elaborate hoax, I wondered, and took to going down to the Bismarck wharf each day for news of the boats. You may say, come now, Flash, what's all this bother about one skirt—you've known a few in your time, we believe, and must have learned by now that they're all the same in the dark, surely? True enough, says I, as a rule—but every so often a real prime one comes by, like Lola or Cassy or Cleonie or the Empress Tzu'hsi or Lily Langtry, and nothing else will do. It's a pure passion, you know, just like the moon-struck youth who can't eat or sleep for dreaming about his sweetheart; the only real difference is that while his bliss is to bask calf-like in her fond regard, I want to roger her red in the face. D'you see? Anyway, call me susceptible if you will, but after three weeks of Fort Lincoln I hungered for the president of the Upper Missouri Development Corporation as the zealot yearns for paradise.

She came at last on the 27th, on the heels of a telegraph: "Arriving Far West steamer. Kindly meet. Candy." I was on hand as the stern-wheeler edged into the wharf with her whistle screaming, and there on the top deck was the tall figure, one elegant gloved hand on the rail, her face shaded by a broad feathered hat. The lines came ashore, the wheel churned to a stop, and I shouldered through the press as the plank came down and mounted the ladder to where she stood with a steel-eyed grey-moustached bird in a pilot cap. She was in bronze today, with tippet and feather and eyepatch according; she greeted me with her slight impersonal smile and the same cold Yankee rasp.

"Good morning. Captain Marsh—Sir Harry Flashman. The captain has been good enough to reserve you a forward cabin, away from the wheel. I hope that's convenient. Yep. Have you brought your bags? No? Perhaps, captain, they can be brought abroad." Her cool eye turned back to me. "We have a great deal to discuss before we sail, so the less time we lose the better. I've set out my papers in the forward part of the main saloon, captain; I'd be obliged if you'd give orders that we're not to be disturbed. Oh-kay. This way, Sir Harry, please."

These steamboat skippers take sass from no one, and I was intrigued that Marsh smiled politely and retired. Mrs Candy swept into the long main saloon, which was empty, and led the way to the forrard end, behind a partition curtain, where a large map and notebooks lay ready spread on the table. She shrugged aside her tippet with her back to me, removed her hat, and peeled off her gloves in a careful way that deserved musical accompaniment. I eyed the trim waist and swan-like neck and licked my lips.

"I hope your stay hasn't been dull," says she indifferently, without glancing round. "You'll have seen the town and country around, I guess. Yep. As you'll see on the map here, the sections we're chiefly interested in . . ."

I stepped close behind her, took a breast in either hand and squeezed ardently.

". . . lie mostly on the south bank of the river between here and Fort Buford, in Dacotah Territory. We don't control it all yet, but discussions with the government are going ahead . . ."

I fondled greedily and they quivered like jellies, but her voice didn't.

". . . and after we've settled our differences with the Northern Pacific, we should have acquired the choicest areas north of their railroad, which will be pushed clear across to the Yellowstone in the next year or two. Oh-kay. In the meantime . . ."

I was nuzzling her neck now and rolling 'em to and fro.

". . . the steamer will take us upriver; it's under charter to the Army at present, carrying stores for this expedition of theirs, but I've arranged with Coulson's directors for us to travel aboard as there's plenty of cabin space . . ."

Keeping one hand at work, I slipped the other to her waist and turned her round.

". . . and in a few days you'll be able to see all you need of the country and decide what to write to Prince Bismarck. Oh-kay."

The dark eye was cool as a fish's back, and the full mouth steady. She might have been addressing her shareholders—which in a sense she was.

"Damn the country, damn Bismarck, and damn you," says I, taking hold of both of 'em again.

"Why damn me, Sir Harry? The way you carry on—" she glanced down at my clutching hands "—I thought you liked me." She turned her head, took a cigarette from the table, and put it between her lips. "Go right ahead if you want to," she added, as she struck a match and brought it up between my hands to light the cigarette, rock steady. "I don't mind; you do it very well, but then I guess you've had a lot of practice. Yep." She blew smoke carefully to one side. "So have I."

"But you're much to cool to show it, eh?" says I, stroking artfully.

"Whatever for? I'm doing fine right here . . . a little more on the left, would you? Yeh-ep." She inhaled rather sharply on her infernal fag. "Oh-kay. I think that's enough for now, though, don't you? These windows have no curtains, in case you didn't notice." Before I knew it she had slipped her bosom aside and stepped neatly round the table. "I hope you were paying some attention to what I was showing you on the map—"

"Come here, you exquisite president," says I, fairly hoarse, but she moved a chair deftly between us, holding me at bay.

"No. Let's get it straight . . . Colonel. I guess we can stop being formal and drop that silly 'sir'? Yep. What I said about B for business—that's a fact. I've broken my rule

356

twice now with you—first time to sweeten you, just now because if I hadn't you'd have got powerful, and I'd have had to bust your toe—"

"Gammon! You enjoyed every minute of it!"

"I'm the corporation president. Oh-kay. But I don't break my rule again—and neither do you. Business hours, we do business, because I've got a heap of money tied up in this thing, and that comes first, and anybody forgets it—the depot's right down the road. Yep. Out of business hours, we do . . . what we please. Oh-kay."

She moved the chair back to the table and stood straight, not haughty or insolent but matter-of-fact and composed. I clapped politely and grinned at her.

"And what pleases madam the president?"

She drew impatiently on her cigarette. "This is wasting time. Oh-kay. I like business and I like money, but I didn't come all this way to show you the Dacotah Territory; I coulda sent a hired hand to do that. When this Bismarck project came up, and someone mentioned your name, I didn't know you from Adam, but you sounded like what we needed. Business, oh-kay? Then when I saw you at the Brev'urt," she tapped ash from her cigarette and considered me, "I thought exactly what you thought when you saw me. Yep." She turned away to seat herself at the table and began to look through her papers.

"Indeed? And what did I think, pray?"

She leaned forward to study the map. "You thought, that's a real bully looker with a patch over her eye; I'd sure like to put her to bed." She indicated the chair opposite. "Let's get to work, shall we?"

It's one of the secrets of my success with women that however contrary, cool, chilly or downright perverse their airs, I'll always humour 'em—when it's worth it. It just maddens them, for one thing. All her tough efficient front didn't fool me; she was on heat most of the time, I should judge, and while she'd probably had more men than Messalina, she was terrified for fear that her allure would fail her (the eyepatch troubled her, no doubt)—so being female, she had to pretend to be all self-assurance and keep your

357

distance, my lad, till I say jump. Kindly old Dr Flashy knows the symptoms—and the cure. So now I let her rattle on about surveys and options and mortgages and share issues and grants, admiring her profile and waiting for business to close down for the day.

We were interrupted at luncheon by the arrival on board of Libby Custer and the garrison wives—Libby knew, of course, that I was going off on private business, but when she saw the shape that business took, she sucked in her breath mighty sharp. I learned later that Libby's purpose aboard was to coax Marsh to take her upriver so that she could be reunited with her loving husband when *Far West* reached the expedition's supply camp on the Yellowstone; Marsh wouldn't have it, though, pointing out that his boat was in Army service now, and couldn't take passengers. What about this Candy woman, says Libby, and Marsh had told her that was different altogether, since he'd had explicit instructions from his owners. So poor Libby went ashore in some huff, having bidden me a distinctly chill farewell.

What interested me was the pull that La Candy obviously had; I quizzed Marsh gently about it, and he said he guessed she drew a powerful lot of water in the commercial world, being on very close terms with at least one of his directors. How close, he added drily, he couldn't say.

We sailed upriver next day after one of the most damnably frustrating nights of my life. Having been held at a distance by my delectable associate all day, I was nicely on the boil by bedtime—and stab me if the *Far West* didn't continue loading the whole night, which meant that the forward saloon beyond the curtain became an orderly room for military clerks and the like, and since our cabins opened on to it, there was no opportunity for me to creep in next door. I lay grinding my teeth and listening to the thump of bales and porters hollering, in the knowledge that all that fine flesh was lying neglected a mere three feet away through my cabin wall. Next morning she was all business with a B again, and we spent ever such jolly hours on deck as the *Far West* thrashed upstream, and she pointed out interesting lumps of prairie which we identified on the map. But at least we now had the boat pretty well to ourselves; Marsh and his officers berthed aft, as did the only other passenger, a young journalist who was going up to report the campaign.

I dutifully kept my hands to myself all day—not without effort, when we bent together over the map and it was all within temptingly easy reach; it was almost enough to make me risk a broken toe. I knew she was getting feverish, too, by the way she drew breath and kept moving her hand on her hip. Good business, thinks I, let the randy baggage sweat, but I was taken aback when she shut her notebook abruptly, glanced at the little gold watch pinned to her dress, and announced:

"Six o'clock. Yep. That'll do for today."

I remarked carelessly that it was an hour till dinner, and she stood up and crushed out her cigarette. She was wearing her crimson rig, with the velvet eyepatch, and seemed to breathe a little unsteadily as she said in her nasal drawl:

"I'm not hungry. Are you?"

"Marsh and the others may think it odd if we don't put in an appearance."

"Who cares what they think—they're the help," says she curtly. "Oh-kay . . . my cabin or yours?"

I've had some coy invitations in my time, but gallant as ever I begged her to state her preference.

"Yours," says she, and waited to be ushered in. As she passed me I slipped a finger on her pulse; the patient was satisfactorily agitated. I asked didn't she want to change into something less formal, and she moistened her full lips and took a deep breath.

"No," says she, "I want to watch you watching me while I undress."

And a very artistic work she made of it, too, spinning it out over half an hour, a lace and a button at a time, never taking her dark eye off me as I sat entranced—and not once did she fumble or show the least loss of composure, although I knew she was inwardly a-tremble with excitement as she gratified herself by making us both wait.

"You've done this before," says I, in a nonchalant croak.

"Yep."

"Tell me, Mrs Candy," I asked. "Do you ever smile?"

She made a minute adjustment at the mirror to her red velvet eyepatch, which now constituted her entire clothing, and turned to face me.

"This is no laughing matter," says she, and I shan't attempt to describe the impression she made as she stood there, drawn up to her full magnificent height, one hand poised lightly on that incredibly slender waist, the other at her side. I gloated all over her for a full minute; I've seen as fine, but never better, and my ears were fairly roaring with the tightness of my collar as I got to my feet—whereupon she sat down on her stool, crossed her legs, lighted a cigarette, inhaled luxuriously, and leaned an elbow on her dressing-table.

"Oh-kay," says she briskly. "Your turn."

*　*　*

In justice I must record that when Mrs Arthur Candy, president of the Upper Missouri Development Corporation, finally applied herself to the task at hand, she more than lived up to anticipation. Mind you, she continued to take her time; Susie Willinck I had always supposed to be the arch-protractor of the capital act, but she was greased lightning to this one. It must have been another hour before I persuaded her on to the bed—she was too tall to manhandle easily, you see—and even then she went to work with a slow deliberation which would have induced dementia if she hadn't been so wonderously good at it so often. It was a pale ghost named Flashman who eventually waved her a feeble good-night as she carefully gathered up her attire and departed, with a whispered "Yep. Oh-kay" as the door closed.

I wondered weakly if I'd ever know the like. Yes, a thousand times, but surely never with such a cool unhurried efficiency. It became clear why she wouldn't play during the day—there'd never have been a stroke of work done, and she'd have had a corpse on her hands by tea-time. Well, it promised to be a most satisfactory cruise, and with the distant throb of the paddle-wheel to lull me I was drifting off to sleep when another noise, muffled but closer at hand, began to pull me slowly back to consciousness. I listened drowsily, the hairs on my neck beginning to rise—but no, I must be mistaken. It must be some murmur of the boat, and not what I'd thought it was at first: the sound, faintly through the panels from Mrs Candy's cabin, of deep sobbing.

19

◄◄◄━━━━━━◄ If you care to examine the log of the *Far West* you will find an exact account of her voyagings on the Missouri and Yellowstone in the days that followed, but for my purpose the barest facts will do. A glance at the map will show you how it was—she was bringing the forage and gear for Terry's column which had struck due west from Fort Lincoln across the Dacotah Territory for the mouth of the Powder River; advancing to meet them from the west along the Yellowstone were old Gibbon and his walkaheaps, and they were to join forces and push down into the wild country between the Big Horn and the Powder to find the hostile bands who were in there somewhere—no one had much notion where, for it was territory that only a few bold scouts and trappers had ever penetrated. Crook with a third column was traipsing about somewhere to the south, out of touch with Terry, but as Custer had told me, the hostiles would be effectively hemmed in by the three forces.

Now you'll wonder if I was wise to be fornicating carelessly on a boat that was going so near to the scene of operations, but it didn't look like that at all from the warm embrace of Mrs Candy, or from the hurricane deck of the *Far West* as she thrashed up the Missouri to Fort Buford, and then into the beautiful grove-lined valley of the Yellowstone. For one thing there wasn't going to be any fighting worth the name beyond a skirmish or two if some of the hostile bands proved recalcitrant, and that would be far to the south of the Yellowstone, with a large and efficient army in between. In fact, it was quite jolly to be on the fringe of the action, so to speak, in the perfect safety of a comfortable steamboat, where one could loaf and stuff and yarn with Marsh and the boys, and gorge oneself with Candy after dark, if you'll pardon the pun, and lie snug and cosy listening to the churning of the great wheel. The Yellowstone is one of the finest river valleys I know, with its woodlands and islands and quiet inlets and clear rippling waters; sometimes you might think yourself on the Thames—and an hour later you're steaming between grand red bluffs as unlike England as anything could be.

It was a prime holiday altogether, and the president of the corporation improved with every performance, although she still remained as impersonal as ever during the day. I'd supposed that after Fort Buford she might unbend a little; after all, by then I'd absorbed all there was to know of her Bismarck scheme, and seen the kind of country to be settled; I'd even drafted (with a straight face) a letter to Otto explaining the thing and inviting his approval—God alone knew what he'd make of it if it ever reached him, with my monicker on it. Mrs Candy commended it briskly and said she'd submit it to her directors, and I thought, first-rate, now we can get to know each other socially as well as carnally. But not a bit of it; it was still B for business from breakfast till dinner, with her making notes and sketches of the Yellowstone country like a good little land speculator, and anyone seeing us on deck or in the saloon would have taken us for fellow-passengers who were formally polite and no more.

I didn't much mind; there was even a strange excitement in knowing that this sharp, no-nonsense Yankee business-woman, all efficiency and assurance, could turn into the most wanton of concubines when the blinds were drawn. I say concubine because she was by no means a lover; she'd talk civilly enough, without much interest, between bouts, but there was none of the intimacy you find in a mistress or even a high-quality whore. How much she enjoyed our couplings was hard to say; how much does a hopeless drunk-kard enjoy drinking? There was a hungry compulsion that drove her, always in that intense, deliberate way, like an inexorable beautiful machine. Ideal from my point of view, but then I'm a sensual brute, and I dare say if she'd been warm or loving I'd have tired of her sooner; as it was the cold passion with which she gave and took her pleasure demanded nothing but stamina.

With the other men on board she was politely discouraging; one or two of the Army officers whom we took aboard for short stages were disposed to be gallant, and short shrift she gave then—one, I'm sure, had her heel stamped on his instep, for I saw him follow her on to the foredeck one evening, only to return red-faced and hobbling visibly.

Marsh and his mate, Campbell, must have known how it stood with Candy and me, but tactfully said nothing. Marsh was a splendid sort, a capital pilot and skipper and tough as they came, I guessed, but with a fund of yarns and partial to a convivial glass or a hand at euchre.

It was about ten days out of Bismarck that we came to the Powder mouth, where a great military camp was taking shape. With the arrival of Terry's advance guard, and Gibbon only a few days' march away, there was tremendous work and bustle; the *Far West* was back and forth ferrying troops and stores and equipment; her steerage was a bedlam of men and gear, while our deck was invaded by all manner of staff-wallopers in search of comfort; Terry held his meetings in the saloon; messengers went galloping pell-mell along the banks; a forest of tents and lean-tos sprang up in the meadows; the woods rang and hummed with the noise of men and horses, rumours of Indian movement far to the south were discussed and as quickly discounted; no one knew what the blazes was happening—indeed, it was like the beginning of any campaign I'd ever seen.[67]

Terry seemed pleased, if surprised, to see me, and preserved his amiable urbanity when I presented him to Mrs Candy; his staff men eyed her with lascivious respect and me with envy. Marsh had explained our presence, and since *Far West* could carry far more passengers than there were staff, no objections could be raised. Indeed, Terry made no bones about talking shop with me; we'd got on well at Camp Robinson, and I sensed that he was anxious about his new responsibilities; he'd never campaigned against Indians, and regarding me as an authority on the Sioux, poor soul, and knowing I'd smelled powder on the frontier, he canvassed me in his quiet, cautious way. Not about his duties, you understand, but on whether Spotted Tail might have talked sense to the hostiles during the winter, and the possibility of defections to the agencies. Something else was troubling him, too.

"George Custer hasn't shaved since we left Abe Lincoln," he confided. "A small thing enough, but it worries me. I've never known him so melancholy and restless. I begin to wonder if I was wise in urging Grant to let him come."

"Nerves," says I. "Get the doctor to give him a purge. George is like a cat on hot bricks about this campaign, and a fortnight's trekking over empty prairie won't have improved his temper. Give him work and you'll see a difference."

He made a lip. "I've a notion, between ourselves, that secretly he resents my authority. I only hope he'll behave sensibly and not . . . not imagine he can be a law unto himself, d'you know?"

I asked what he'd heard, and he said nothing, really, beyond a feeling that Custer regarded Terry's job as the transport and supply of the 7th Cavalry, who could be left to take care of the soldiering on their own. I assured Terry that all cavalry commanders talked that way, and cited my old *bête noire* Cardigan, who had resented the least interference from his superiors.

"He was the man who led your light cavalry at Balaclava, wasn't he?" says Terry thoughtfully, and after that he seemed rather withdrawn, and presently went to bed with a hot toddy.

I raised an eyebrow myself when the boy general arrived a few days later, all brave in fringed buckskin and red scarf over his uniform, but with a face like a two-day corpse. He came striding up the gangplank barking orders to his galloper, slapping his gloves impatiently against his legs, brightened momentarily at sight of me, and went straight into a nervous fret because Libby wasn't aboard.

"Why didn't you bring her?" he demanded pettishly. "Who said she should not come?" He was bright-eyed with strain and hollow-cheeked under his four-week beard; his hair had been close-cropped and he looked even leaner and more worn than in Washington. "It's too bad! As if I hadn't had checks enough!" I told him Terry was in the saloon, and he snorted and strode off to berate Marsh for leaving Libby behind.

From then on the *Far West* was like a hotel-cum-orderly-room. Staff men were working in the saloon all day, and several chaps from the 7th, including Tom and Boston Custer, as well as Terry's party, occupied berths. Mrs Candy kept a good deal to her cabin, but I had to endure any number of digs and sallies from the fellows; I told 'em they were a young Army yet, and hadn't learned about campaign equipment. Her presence gave Custer another excuse to abuse Marsh over Libby; he didn't berth aboard, but had his tent pitched on the bank. "Our buckskin Achilles," grunts Benteen, grinning at me over his pipe.

Now, as the expedition moved leisurely up the Yellowstone, I was enjoying life hugely. I could watch the martial activity ashore, hobnob with the boys in the saloon, play poker in the evenings, drink hearty, pile into Mrs Candy by night (Terry, bless him, allowed no late carousing, and all were snug down by midnight), listen to the professional gossip—and reflect contentedly that for once it was nothing to do with me. When the columns swung south into the blue, I'd be left safely behind to loaf and roger in these idyllic surroundings. I can't recall when I've been in better fettle.

For now the grip was coming as the columns converged. At the mouth of the Tongue we halted, under the high bluffs to the north, with the troops camped on an old *to-ronto** on the south bank, where there were many Sioux burial platforms, mostly broken and derelict, but some quite new, and the troops thought it great sport to scatter them to bits. I remarked in Terry's hearing that it was bad medicine—for one thing, his Ree and Crow scouts wouldn't like

*By this word Flashman presumably means an Indian meeting-place. The area is now the site of Miles City, Montana.

it—and he ordered it stopped. If you wonder why I put in my oar, I'll answer that I've soldiered far and hard enough to learn one invariable rule, superstition or not: never monkey with the local gods. It don't pay.

And now the expedition began to buzz with definite news at last of hostiles far to the south. Reno had been off on a scout, and had found an abandoned camp ground where there had been several hundred tipis, as well as a heavy trail heading west towards the Big Horn Mountains. Custer was in great excitement at this. "The hunt is up!" says he, and was off with the 7th to meet Reno at the Rosebud mouth. *Far West* was there ahead of him, and I was on the hurricane deck, watching his long blue column jingling down under the trees to bivouac, when I found Mrs Candy at my elbow. Making chat, I asked her what she thought of Custer.

"They say he has good political connections," says she indifferently. "Yep. I wouldn't do business with him."

"Oh? Why ever not?"

"In business you have to be able to rely on people—not to say trust them, just to know how they'll act. Oh-kay. I wouldn't rely on him. He's crazy."

"Good Lord, what makes you say that?"

"He likes killing Indians, doesn't he?" She shrugged. "That's what I hear. I suppose he means to kill a lot of them, up there." She gestured idly towards the low brown bluffs to the south. Her costume today was of some pale material, and the eyepatch contrasted vividly with that rich dusky-rose complexion which had taken on a most becoming tint from the Yellowstone sunshine.

I said, well, he was a soldier—so was I, for that matter, and she turned her cold appraising eye on me.

"Killing for a living. Yep. I suppose your conscience gets used to it."

"Just as it does in business, I imagine."

"Business? It depends what kind of deals you make. Yep." And as bustle broke out below, with bugles sounding and Marsh bawling orders to warp the *Far West* to the south bank, she turned away in bored fashion and went down to her cabin.

That was June 21, and in the evening Terry issued marching orders to his commanders at one of the strangest staff conferences ever I saw. Since it was a vital moment in the Sioux campaign, and every survivor has recorded his recollections of it—not just who said what, but who *understood* what, or didn't, or sneezed, or scratched his backside—I must do the same. For I was there, as who the devil wasn't, except perhaps the ship's cook and the cat; when Terry summoned the senior men, the journalist fellow stood his ground in the saloon, and Mrs Candy continued to leaf idly through a magazine in her seat at the forrard end, within easy earshot, so I found myself a lounging place against the bulkhead where I could overlook the map on the main table.

Terry, spruce and affable, sat in the centre, smiling round with his short-sighted blue eyes; beside him was Gibbon, fine-featured and trim-bearded—I found myself thinking how many eminent soldiers are strikingly handsome men, as who should know better than I? Custer sat at one end of the table, gloomy and watchful, his fingers drumming softly. Others present were Marsh and Campbell of the ship, Reno, young Bradley the scout officer, old Grasshopper Jim Brisbin of the 2nd Cavalry, Lonesome Charley Reynolds, Custer's chief scout, with his arm in a sling, and a dozen or so others I've forgotten. A steward was serving coffee, and I recall Terry remarking how he'd tried to give up sugar, but couldn't, and his spoon tinkling in the cup as we waited.

"Well, gentlemen," says he, "tomorrow we take the field in earnest. Major Reno and Mr Bradley have carried out separate reconnaissances, and we have reason to believe that hostile bands have moved west to cross Rosebud creek in the direction of the Big Horn hills. The best estimate suggests that not more than eight hundred or a thousand braves are to be reckoned with; perhaps three thousand Indians all told. Now, we dispose above a thousand cavalry and six hundred infantry, in addition to General Crook's force of thirteen hundred to the south, so—"

"Pardon, general." It was young Bradley, a keen-looking

hand. "Those three thousand hostiles—aren't those agency figures calculated during the winter?"

Terry said, yes, but they could be relied on. Bradley feared they might be low, since many Indians might have left the agencies with the arrival of spring. "I've seen sign of about two-three thousand myself up there, you see sir," says he apologetically, "and I doubt if they're the only hostiles in the Powder River country."

"Me likewise, gen'l." This was Reynolds, Custer's scout, an innocent-looking youth who was talked of as a latter-day Carson. "Agency figures don't signify. There could be twice their reck'nin' up yonder, easy."

"Well, they are the only figures we have to go on." says Terry. "Shall we say possibly five thousand? It won't hurt to err on the safe side."

"Five thousand *braves*," insists Reynolds. "Ne'er mind women and young."

"You don't know that," says Gibbon.

"I don't *not* know it, Colonel," says Reynolds doggedly, and there were chuckles. Custer spoke up sharply.

"Five thousand or ten, Charley, it makes no difference, since they will be in divers bands, and we are more than a match for them if they were all together."

With that settled, Terry went on to say that he and Gibbon would march up the Big Horn to intercept the Indian force whose trail Reno had seen heading that way; with Crook advancing from the south, the hostiles would be caught front and rear. Meanwhile, Custer and his cavalry would have passed up the Rosebud to cut off the hostiles if they tried to slip out of the trap. Q.E.D. and any questions?

"Where's Crook?" asks someone.

"So far as we know," answers Terry, "somewhere in the region of the headwaters of Rosebud creek or Little Bighorn River. Which, unfortunately," he added, peering at the map, "are not clearly indicated here. About there, wouldn't you say, Brisbin?" Grasshopper Jim nodded and made vague crosses on the map, and everyone took a squint. "His exact position is not of too much import," continued Terry, "since he too has his scouts and will be closing on the same quarry as ourselves."

(What none of us knew, of course, was that while Crook was indeed around the head of the Rosebud, he wasn't feeling too happy about it, since four days earlier Crazy Horse had bushwhacked him and fought him to a standstill. But why should any of us suspect such a thing? These were the Indians who weren't going to fight, you'll remember.)

"Ideally our force and General Crook's would converge on the hostiles simultaneously," says Terry, "but in the absence of communications, that is too much to hope for."

Custer lifted his head. "I'm to prevent any escape of hostiles to the east, sir." His voice was casual. "If they're around the Big Horn, it's certain my cavalry will be there before Colonel Gibbon's infantry . . ."

Terry nodded, lifting a finger. "Precisely. I was coming to that. If you find the Indian trail leading towards the Big Horn, you should pass it by and go south towards the Big Horn itself; thus you will be in position south of the hostiles while Colonel Gibbon approaches from the north, and it should be possible for you to act together. It may be that you will encounter Crook en route—so much the better. But in any event our endeavour must be to act in concert so far as can be. It may prove impossible, since our objective is not a fixed one—we can't be certain where the hostiles will be found."

One thing was clear: Terry wanted no action against the Sioux until Gibbon was in position. But equally clearly, he had to allow his commanders some discretion, since in such an uncertain operation no one could foresee what emergencies (or opportunities) might arise. Everyone in the cabin understood that—but there was one man there with a special interest in forcing Terry to say it aloud.

"If I encounter hostiles," says Custer slowly, "before Colonel Gibbon has come up . . ." He left it there, leaning forward as though to examine the map, and it seemed to me he was avoiding Terry's eye and waiting for him to complete the sentence. And Terry, will-he, nill-he, spoke the fatal words, so amiably, so reasonably. I think back to that moment—Custer apparently intent on the map, Gibbon half-turned towards Terry, who was sitting back in his chair, choosing his words—and compare it with another moment: Lucan's face red with indignation under Causeway Heights, and Lew Nolan fairly bouncing in his saddle with impatience. "There, my lord, are the guns! There's your enemy!" There had been fury and passion, here was calm and polite discussion—but they both led to the same end, bloody catastrophe.

"You must use your own judgement, of course," says Terry, nodding. "It's not possible to give *definite* instructions, but you know my intentions; conform to them unless you see sufficient reason to depart from them."

In other words, please yourself. That's what Terry was saying—what he was bound to say—and Custer could throw it in the teeth of any court-martial. Terry was having to trust to Custer's common sense, and he knew as well as I did what a questionable commodity that might be. But he couldn't put *that* into words; a Sam Grant or a Colin Campbell could have said, "See here, Custer, you know what I want—and I know what you want, and how you'll interpret my orders to suit yourself, and claim afterwards I justified you. Very good, we understand each other—and if you play the fool, by God I'll break you!" But Terry, the gentle, kindly Terry, couldn't say that—and really, was there the need? It was just a simple operation against a few hostile bands, after all.

Custer said nothing more; he'd got what he wanted, and now he was studiously watching Brisbin pushing pins into the map to mark the Rosebud route and joining them with a blue pencil. Gibbon, with a glance at Custer, said something about there being no need for a precipitate attack— unless it was necessary, of course, and Terry interrupted.

"I hope there will be no need of any such thing as an attack. Our object is to bring these people under control to the agencies—to capture, not to conquer." Custer was sketching idly with a pencil now, chin in hand, but he roused himself when Gibbon offered to lend him some troops of the 2nd Cavalry.

"Thank you, Colonel, but any force of hostiles that is too big for the 7th will be too big for the 7th and four troops," which was as silly a remark as I've ever heard. No, he didn't want the Gatlings, either, since they might impede his march. Terry didn't press him; I guessed the last thing he wanted was Custer loose about the place with machine-guns.

There was more talk, but that in essence was the famous *Far West* conference, and no one was in much doubt what it amounted to. I heard young Bradley's aside as the senior men departed: "Well, guess who's going to get there first and win the laurels. Who, the 7th Cavalry? No, you don't say!"[68]

My own view, confirmed when I loafed out on deck and heard Custer down at his tent, firing off orders to his troop commanders and sounding deuced peevish about it: ". . . I tell you, Moylan, I know better than you what a pack mule can carry, and I'll have fifteen days' rations and 50 reserve rounds per carbine. Yes, in addition to the hundred rounds for each man, and 25 for the pistols, mind . . . Well, Captain Benteen, you are responsible for your own company; the extra forage is only a suggestion. But remember that we may have to follw the trail for two weeks, no matter how far it takes us, so you'd better take extra salt. We may have to live on horse meat before we're through!"

I saw him stamp into his tent as the others dismissed, and mooched down for a look-see. He was alone, chewing at a pen, but at sight of me he grinned.

"Well, are you coming along after all?" His eyes were exultant now. "This is going to be a 7th Cavalry battle, my boy! Gatlings, indeed! I have more respect for Crazy Horse than that, I hope!"

I declined again, and he teased me, but in a nervous, restless way that showed his mind was anywhere but here. I knew he'd held himself in at the conference, but now that the rein was off there was an almost furtive quality about his excitement. It wasn't quite canny, and presently I wished him luck, and left him calling high-pitched for Keogh and Yates almost before I was out of the tent. Back on board there was a great poker school under way in the saloon, which lasted until daybreak, so I made the most of the fellows' company while they were still there (and picked up a copper or two), neglecting Mrs Candy with the thought that there would be ample time for her in the quiet days ahead.

Custer was off at first light, the long blue and brown squadrons moving slowly out of bivouac in the misty dawn. The Rosebud is little more than a brook where it joins the Yellowstone, running between green banks with a hedgerow down one side—again I could have imagined it was an English meadow as the troops wheeled up the little stream. Custer, fussing over the pack-train, paused to shake Terry's hand and receive a clap on the back from Gibbon, who told him to mind and leave some redskins for the rest of the column. "Don't be too greedy, George!" cries he, and Custer snapped a reply at him and rode off. I heard Terry say something about eagerness, and Gibbon shrugged and said: "At that, we'd look regular fools if they were to escape after all this. Three columns to round up a few stray Sioux and Cheyenne!"

That was their preoccupation, you see—not Custer, but the possibility that the expedition might wear itself out chasing hostiles who wouldn't fight or surrender, but simply melt away into the desolation of the Big Horn.

Far West was to move down to the Big Horn mouth now, to ferry Gibbon's infantry across, and it would be the following night that we moored in a wooded reach, under the loom of a huge bluff that reared up along the southern shore.[69] It was a perfect balmy evening, the boat was quiet now with only Terry's staff men aboard, and I was smoking a cheroot at the maindeck rail, considering what drill I'd go through with Mrs Candy that night, when here she came from the saloon, very stately in her crimson, with a white silk scarf over her head and shoulders. We talked idly about the possibility that Marsh would be taking *Far West* back east for fresh supplies shortly, and I found myself regretting that soon our business-honeymoon would be over.

I'm like that, you see; I get fond of women, and while I'd been happy just to stallion away by night and be spared any cloying intimacy during the day, still it's plesant when a tough piece like this one begins to show interest in your more spiritual qualities. For in the past day or so it had seemed to me that Mrs Candy had been thawing a little; she'd been readier to talk about matters other than business—the weather, for example, and she'd even asked me a question or two about England. Now, at the rail, she admired the rising moon with modified rapture ("That's beautiful. Yep"), drew my attention to what she called the trees and all, and took me quite aback by laying a hand on my arm. I thought she was indicating that it was time for another protracted thrash in my cabin, but she sighed and said:

"It's such a lovely night, I guess I'd like a stroll. Oh-kay?"

We descended to the steerage and the main plank to the bank, where the crew had set up a temporary forge, now deserted, and presently we were pacing slowly under the trees, and I was describing nights in India and China, while she murmured an occasional "Mm-h?" or "Don't say?", leaning easily on my arm; it was quite delightful. The air was warm, the groves were dim in shadow, with moonlight in the glades, and the river lapped gently at the reeds. We walked a furlong or so, and paused under the spreading branches; I looked at her face framed in the white scarf, the dark line of the patch across her eye, and for the first time felt a tremor of pity for that disfigurement. She was such a magnificent creature, it was a damned shame, and I took her in my arms and kissed her fondly out of sheer affection— well, for a moment, anyway, before my better nature prevailed and I began to grapple her bottom. She fended me off gently, and slipped the scarf from her head, swinging it in her hand as we walked on.

"You're a strange man," says she, which is a sure sign that they want something. "You've been so many places, seen so many things. Yep. Lots of women in your life, I guess."

Modestly I admitted that I had seldom been solitary for long, and said that I supposed neither had she.

"Sure. I've known a lot of men. Too many." She shrugged. "Guess I'll go on knowing a lot more. Too many more. Yep." I said she didn't sound overjoyed at the prospect.

"Why should I? Men are trash, pretty much. Yep. All they want is to use women in bed." She paced slowly, glancing up at the purple sky. "And money. Women and money, and they spend them both as selfishly as they know how. Oh-kay."

"Well, thank-ee, ma'am. Women have purer motives, I suppose?"

"Some women—sometimes. Some women are soft, and fool themselves that one of these days they'll meet a man who doesn't just want to spend them. They're wrong." She stopped, and to my astonishment I saw there was a tear coursing down from her left eye. Suddenly I remembered the sound of sobbing from her cabin the first night, and caught her hand.

"Heaven's above! Whatever's the matter?"

"It's nothing." She pulled her hand free and turned sharply to face me. "You're not any different, are you?"

"What's wrong? Good Lord, look here, if I've misunderstood—"

"Oh, no," says she, composing herself. "You've understood, all right. You understood from the minute I walked by at the Brev'urt. Yep. You understood: 'Gee, that's worth mounting. Yes, sir, that's prime—I could use that.' "

"Of course I did," I agreed, slightly bewildered. "So did you, didn't you?"

She ignored the question. "That's the way you always look at women, isn't it? The face—is it beautiful? If it's disfigured—does that matter? The rest—the waist and hips and breasts and legs—they're what matter, isn't that so? Oh-kay. And will she? And if she does, what will it cost me? Can I get it for free? What's it worth?"

The contempt in her tone nettled and amazed me—and I thought she'd been melting. "Well, since I've just had dinner, I'd rather you didn't tell me how a lecherous female assesses *her* lovers, but my experience leads me to believe it's in exactly the same way! In your own case, your interest in me hasn't been precisely sentimental—"

"How would you know?"

This was too much. "Oh, come now! You haven't been a charming little ray of sunshine, exactly, have you? Provided I kept you happy in the night watches—which from your conduct I believe I did . . . What the devil," I demanded, "is all this about? Am I at fault because I haven't serenaded under your porthole, or given proofs of undying devotion? Don't tell me that you . . . well, that wasn't part of our bargain, surely?"

She was looking askance, and dammit, there were the tears again; she was absolutely weeping—and from under her patch, too. Interesting, that. But God help me if I understand women. "Mind you," I lied, consoling-like; "I won't say I haven't . . .." But she lifted a hand.

"No. Don't give me that. Oh-kay." She took a deep breath. "You're certainly right. Yep. I'm being a fool."

I'd not have believed it—not of her. The most unlikely females have gone moony over me, but I'd never have credited that this one had any thought beyond pork and beans. God knew, she hadn't let on—until now, anyway, if that's what she *was* doing . . .

"Most of all I'm a fool for wasting time," she said quietly. "I never thought I would—not with you. But just for a moment there I felt a grief . . . that I had thought long dead. A grief for someone else, someone I loved dearly, long ago. Oh, yes, I've been in love. But it ended . . . on just such a night as this, warm and soft and beautiful . . ."

The hairs prickled on my neck suddenly. This wasn't Mrs Candy talking; the voice, as well as the words, were different. The nasal Yankee twang had disappeared.

". . . a night when I was happier than I had ever been, because the man I loved had promised to take me out of slavery, and I was hastening to him, with joy in my heart, in a garden in Santa Fe . . ."

For several heart-beats it meant nothing, and then it hit me like a blow. But whereas I'd have acted instantly at a

376

physical assault (probably by flight), the implication of what she said, when I grasped it, so shocked my mind that I stood numb, incapable of movement even when she lifted the scarf abruptly and I saw that she was looking beyond me, and heard the rush of running feet suddenly upon me, and knew that here was terrible, deadly danger. By then it was too late.

Sinewy hands were at my throat and wrists, rank greased bodies were all about me, nightmare painted faces glared in the moonlight, and as I stretched my mouth to scream a handful of cloth was thrust into it and a binder whipped round my face. I heaved in panic, choking on my buried scream, as rawhide bit into my wrists; it was done in a twinkling and I was helpless, held by a half-naked brave on either side while two others, steel in their hands, hovered alert—my eyes rolled in terror back to her, not believing this monstrous, impossible thing, because it was . . . impossible.

She had not moved. She stood tall and straight in the moonlight, the scarf at her side; then she reached up and took the patch from her face, and I saw that the eye beneath it was sound and bright. She cupped it a moment with her hand, and then she shook her head and came a step closer, her face almost against mine.

"Yes, look well," she said. "Cleonie."

She was lying, she must be; it could not be true. Cleonie was . . . where, after twenty-five years? And she had been middling tall, and slender, while this woman was near six feet and statuesque, and had a bold, full face with heavy lips and chin—and Cleonie had been a negress! I stared, refusing to believe, while the bright dark eyes bored into mine, and then I caught beneath the full flesh of middle age a fleeting glimpse of the sweet nun-like face of long ago; saw how the dusky high colour might be no more than cosmetic covering on a skin that time had darkened from the pale cream of the octoroon; how that damnable patch had disguised the shape of her face . . . but the voice, the manner, the whole being of the woman was so utterly unlike the girl I had . . . had . . . And as the memory of what I had done rushed back, she whispered softly: "*En passant par la Lorraine, avec mes sabots . . .*", and the bile of terror came up behind my gag.

"You recognise me now? The girl you were going to take to Mexico? I probably had no need of this—" and she held up the patch. "After all, what should a woman look like who has endured twenty-five years of slavery in the hands of the Navajo? She should be dead—unless she's unlucky enough to be alive, when she should be a wrinkled, withered hag, a verminous shell of a living thing—" her voice was choking "—a poor mad ghost crippled by beatings and star-vation and terror of the hell she has been through!" Her eyes were blazing like coals, and her hand came up, nails crooked as though to rake my face; there were tears running down her cheeks again, tears of rage and hate. "You bastard! You filthy, degraded, cowardly, evil, cruel, cruel . . . cruel . . . cruel . . .!" It wailed away in a shuddering gasp, and her clawed hand went over her own face to stifle the great sobs that shook her. The fit passed, and she wiped her cheeks and lifted her face again. "That is what she should look like," she whispered. "An old, miserable skel-eton. Not at all like the splendid Mrs Candy! No, if you ever gave a thought to what Cleonie must have become, you couldn't have imagined anything like Mrs Candy. And you would hardly recognise in her the child of eighteen you sold for two thousand dollars to the priest of Santa Fe."

So he'd blabbed, the lousy little Judas! I might have known—but no, it *was* impossible, it *was* a nightmare. This could not be . . . *must* not be, Cleonie . . .

"But I had to be sure. Oh, I had to be sure! So . . ." She slipped the eyepatch on again. "Mrs Candy, you see. And Mr Comber—that was the name, was it not? How often I wondered—waited and hated, and wondered—what had be-come of him. And after twenty-five years I learned that he was Sir Harry Flashman, English gentleman. I didn't believe it . . . until I came to New York to see for myself. Then I knew . . . for you haven't changed, no, no! Still the same handsome, arrogant, swaggering foulness who used me and lied to me and betrayed me . . . You haven't changed. But

378

then, you haven't been a prisoner of savages, a tortured, degraded slave. Not yet."

One of the Sioux grunted, pointing—there, through the trees were the steamboat lights, and a distant voice, and I couldn't utter a sound! She spoke again, in fluent Siouxan.

"No danger. No one saw us. No one will see me go back."

I writhed in their grip, trying to plead with my eyes, to beg her to remove that beastly gag so that I could explain—Christ, I'd swear truth out of America, if only she'd let me—she must! I bulged my eyes in dumb entreaty, and she shook her head.

"No. I have the truth, you see. And nothing you could say could alter it. We both know how you betrayed and sold a girl who loved and trusted you—oh, yes, she loved you! If she had not—" her eye was fierce with angry tears again, and her voice trembled "—it would not have hurt . . . so much. And I could never have hated as I do now, if I had not . . . loved, once, you see." She steadied and went on:

"I could have had you killed in New York, for fifty dollars. But it would have been too easy. Yep." The vibrant Creole voice which had whispered like velvet and shaken with passion, was gone, and in its place the nasal Yankee of Mrs Candy, cold and flat as a mortuary slab, and all the more frightening because it was without emotion. She might have been discussing some new sexual activity, or the Bismarck project—Jesus, Bismarck and the letter and the corporation . . . my brain whirled with it all, and her voice cut through it like a knife.

"I'm not going to waste time. Just enough to let you know how I come to be here—so that when I go back to the boat, and you go . . . where you're going, you'll be able to appreciate the justice of it. Oh-kay." She broke abruptly into Siouxan. " Set his back against that tree. The light on his face."

They threw me brutally against the tree and held me. She came in front of me, and I began to blubber in panic, for in that merciless beautiful face I could see Narreeman in the dungeon, Ranavalona staring down from her balcony, the Amazon women when they caught that poor bastard on the

Dahomey creek . . . oh, God, was she going to set about me? I couldn't bear it, I'd go mad . . .

"You needn't cry yet," said the passionless voice. "Later. Listen. You sold me to a Navajo animal. I'll not describe what he did to me. I'll just say you're the only man I've hated more. For two years I belonged to him, and if I hadn't been a trained whore, knowing how degraded men can be, I'd have gone mad or killed myself. Then he died, and I was sold to Ute slavers,[70] who took me north—and amused themselves with me on the way—and sold me among the Blackfeet. There I went through another hell, until the Cheyenne raided our village, and I was taken as part of the loot, and sold to the Sioux in the Black Hills country. Oh-kay."

I was in such a drench of fear that I couldn't think of much, but it did occur to me that she hadn't had a much worse time of it than in Susie's brothel, surely. It wasn't as if she'd been kidnapped from a convent. She leaned closer.

"Do you know what I found among the Sioux? No, how should you? I found kindness. I don't say they're any better than Navajo or Ute or Blackfeet—only that the man who bought me was a *man*, who was good to me, and cared for me, and treated me as an honourable woman. Even you may understand what that means. I was twenty-one, and had been used and abused and beaten and raped by hundreds of men—white, Spanish, Mexican, Indian—and a Sioux savage who lived in a filthy tent and could eat raw meat—he treated me like an honourable woman. He wouldn't have understood the word, and I doubt if you do, but to him I was a lady. Yep. His name was Broken-Moon-Goes-Alone. I was his faithful wife for two years, although I didn't love him. And when I asked him to let me go back to what I called 'my own people', he agreed. That was the kind of man he was: he knew I wasn't happy, so he took me to Fort Laramie, and sold some robes for fifty dollars—and gave it all to me. All he said was: 'If you come back some day, Walking Willow, my tipi and my heart will both be open.' I never went back as his wife, but I visited some, till he died. And, as you see, I have good friends among the Sioux." So these smelly swine gripping me were presumably her bloody cousins-in-law.

"Oh-kay. Then I started in where I'd have started in Mexico if you hadn't betrayed me. I whored—and as no one knows better than you, I'm good at it. I had my own stable before I was thirty, and by the time the war ended I owned the biggest brothel in Denver. Yep, I still do, and have shares in several other businesses, some of them respectable. But they don't include the Upper Missouri Corporation—that was invented for your benefit. Oh, there's a genuine Bismarck scheme, yep, but I have no part in it. But I knew that this . . ." She placed her hands on her hips and swayed her body slightly ". . . would be the real bait to get Mr Comber where I've been wanting him for the past twenty-five years."

She replaced her scarf round her head, and glanced aside to the distant lights of the *Far West*—so close, but for me it might as well have been in New Zealand. Couldn't any of the fools aboard her see, or guess, or intervene to save me from whatever horror was in store? For it was coming now, and I'd have no chance to plead or lie or grovel; she was determined not to give me the chance, the callous, cold-blooded slut.

"You sold me to the Indians," she said quietly. "You did the foulest, cruellest thing—for two thousand dollars. I'm not getting a cent for you, but I wouldn't take a million to spare you one instant of what's going to happen to you. You sent me to death, or a lifetime of suffering, and it wasn't your fault I survived. So now you go the way I went. These savages are my friends, and they know the wrong you did me. You know what they do to white men prisoners at the best of times, and with your friend General Custer preparing to butcher them, the times couldn't be much worse. Oh-kay. Your suffering won't last as long as mine did, but I'm sure it'll seem a lot longer. I hope so."

I was struggling frantically, with those painted devils hanging on to me, but she seemed not to notice. She drew her scarf closer about her shoulders, and shivered a little, looking towards the boat. Her voice sounded tired.

"I'm going back to the boat now. They'll miss you to-morrow, and I'll insist on a search, but Captain Marsh won't dare neglect his duty to the expedition for long. And I'll be able to sleep alone again. When I was a young girl, new in the trade, I sometimes used to cry out against God: 'Was this what You made me for? Is this what You meant for me, God?' At its worst it was better than the last few weeks, when I played the whore to get you here." She glanced at me incuriously. "Strange to think I once did it for love . . . the only man I ever loved. You shouldn't have done that to me in Santa Fe."

She turned and walked away beneath the trees, the tall graceful figure receding quickly into the shadows. The Sioux dragged me away from the tree and ran me into the woods, away from the river.

20

◀◀━━━■━▶━━━━◀ I still say that if it hadn't been for that damned gag, I'd have been back on the *Far West* before midnight, rogering her speechless. And she knew it, too, and must have arranged for my abductors to muzzle me first go off, so that I'd never get a word in edgeways to sweetheart her. You see, however much they loathe you, whatever you've done, the old spark never quite dies—why, for all her hate, she'd blubbered at the mere recollection of our youthful passion, and for all she said, our weeks on the boat could only have reminded her of what she'd been missing. No, she knew damned well that if once she listened to my blandishments she'd be rolling over with her paws in the air, so like old Queen Bess with the much-maligned Essex chap, she daren't take the risk. Pity, but there it was.

But I confess these speculations weren't in my mind just then, as they dragged me through the dark woods, hammering me when I stumbled, and thrust me astride a pony. Then it was off up a gentle slope, with those four monsters round me; I was near suffocating with the gag, which didn't assist thought as I tried to grapple with the impossibility of what had happened.

Yet I knew it wasn't impossible. Mrs Candy *was* Cleonie, come back like Nemesis; once the patch was off, and she'd whispered that snatch of her French riding song, in her old voice, I'd have known her beyond doubt. I couldn't marvel at not recognising her earlier, even at the closest quarters; she'd grown, for one thing, filled out admirably, and the brash, hard Mrs Candy was as different from the dove-like Creole as could be, in speech and manner—aye, and nature. I suppose that's what twenty-five years of being bulled by redskins and whoring on the frontier and acquiring bordellos does to you. Not surprising, really. Even so, she'd played it brilliantly, hadn't she just? Keeping me at arm's length, the Bismarck nonsense, galloping me westward to the very spot where she could deal me out poetic justice, the spiteful bitch. What simpler than to send word to her Sioux friends (doubtless with a handsome fee) and have them scout the boat along the Yellowstone, ready at her signal to pounce on the unsuspecting victim and shanghai him into the hills to stick burning splinters in his tenderer parts? Neat, but not gaudy—simplicity itself compared to some of the plots that have been hatched all over me by the likes of Lola and Lincoln and Otto Bismarck and Ignatieff and . . . God, I've had some rotten luck.

What I couldn't fathom, though, was how the devil she'd discovered that the much-respected Flashy of '76 was the long-lost B. M. Comber of '49. She'd *heard*, she said—but from whom? Who was there still who'd known me as Comber in the earlies, had recognised me now, and tipped her the wink? Spotted Tail—why, he'd never heard the name Comber in his life; I'd been Wind Breaker to him from '50, and what should he and Mrs Candy know of each other? Susie, Maxwell, Wootton and the like I could dismiss; I hadn't seen them or they me in quarter of a century, supposing they were still alive. Carson was dead; no one in the Army knew about Comber. Lincoln was dead. But I was a fool to be thinking of folk *I* remembered—there must be hundreds I'd forgotten who might still remember *me*, and seeing Flashy promenading down Broadway would exclaim "Comber, bigod!" Old Navy men, perhaps a returned emigrant from the wagon train, a Cincinnati invalid, someone out west, like a Laramie hunter or trader. Susie's whores, by thunder! They'd know me, and if Cleonie was anything to go by, the graduates of Mrs Willinck's academy might be running half the knocking-shops in America by now—aye, and corresponding with the other old girls, devil a doubt . . . "Dearest Cleonie, you'll never guess who called in for a rattle at our shop the other day! 'Twas such a start! Tall, English, distinguished, fine whiskers . . . give up?" How many of the bawdy-houses I'd frequented had black madames? Difficult . . . but that would be it, like as not.

These were random thoughts, you understand, floating up through stupefied terror from time to time. The point was that four damnably hostile Sioux were bearing me into the wilderness with murderous intent, and if there was one thing I'd learned in a lifetime of hellish fixes, it was the need to thrust panic aside and keep cool if there was to be the slimmest chance of winning clear.

Once we had skirted the high bluff and reached the rough upland, they headed south-west by the stars. It might be they'd go a safe distance and then set to roasting me over a slow fire, but I doubted it; they were riding steady, so it looked like a longish trek across the northern Powder country towards the Big Horn Mountains; that was where the Sioux were mostly hanging their hats these days. Somewhere far off to my left, up the Rosebud, Custer would be starting his long swing south and west to roughly the same destination. I was pinning no hopes on him, though—the last man you want riding to the rescue is G.A.C., for there'll be blood on the carpet for certain, and the more I thought, the more my hope grew of emerging from this pickle peaceful-like. After all, Mrs Candy wasn't the only one with chums among the Sioux—I spoke the lingo, I could cite Spotted Tail as a bosom pal, and even if he was far away there must be hostiles who'd remember me from Camp Robinson and who might think twice about dismembering a U.S. treaty commissioner just to please the former squaw of Broken-Moon-Goes-Alone. Certainly they'd not be well disposed to anyone white just now, and given a prisoner they're more likely to take a long thoughtful look at his innards than not. But again, I might buy my way clear, or get a chance to play my real trump card—somewhere up ahead, and the nearest thing to God between Canada and the Platte, was Tashunka Witko Crazy Horse, and while I hadn't seen him since he was six, he wouldn't let them snip pieces off a man who'd practically dandled him on his knee, surely?

I put these points to my captors at our dawn halt, when they had to remove my gag to let me drink and eat some jerked meat and corn-mush; I suggested that the cleverest thing they could do would be to return me to the fire-canoe on the Yellowstone, where I'd see they got safe-conduct and all the dollars they wanted from Many-Stars-Soldier Terry.

They listened in ominous silence, four grim blanketed figures with the paint smeared and faded on their ugly faces, and not a flicker of expression except pure malice. Then their leader, one Jacket, started to lambast me with his quirt, and the others joined in with sticks and feet, thrashing me until I yelled for mercy, and didn't get it. When they were tired, and I was black and blue, Jacket stuffed the gag back brutally, kicked me again for luck, and stooped over me, his evil grinning face next to mine.

"You have two tongues—you are not American, although you sat with the liars at White River. You are the *Washe-chuska* Wind Breaker, who sold my brother's woman, Walking Willow, to the Navajo who shamed her. You are going to die—*kakeshya*!*" He launched into a description that can give me nightmares even now, and took another hack at me. "Spotted Tail! A woman and a coward! We'll send him a gift of your —, since he seems to have lost his own!"

The others howled with glee at that, and threw me on to the pony with more blows and taunts. And now I knew real fear, as I realised that I was tasting the temper of the hostile Sioux, the merciless desperate savages who stood beyond the law, who were not going to be rounded up on to the agencies, who loathed everything white and despised Spotted Tail as a traitor, and who were preparing, with all the hate and fury Custer could have wished, to meet whatever the Americans might send against them. One white captive wasn't going to buy or bully his way out of their clutches; torturing him to death would be a momentary amusement on the way to better things.

All day we rode south-west over the bare country east of the Big Horn; even allowing for my jaundiced eye, it was neither a grand nor memorable prospect, just endless low hills and ridges of yellow grass, with a few trees here and there, and the outline of mountains far in the distance. A

*Torture.

few vivid pictures stay in my mind: a buffalo skeleton picked clean in a gully, a hawk that lingered above us for hours in the blazing afternoon, a party of Sans Arc Sioux who crossed our trail and yelled exultant news of a great victory over the Grey Fox Crook to the south—not a word of Custer, though, which seemed odd, for he must be well up the Rosebud by now. Then on, over those endless sparse hollows and hills, with the grasses blowing in the wind, while my body ached with ill-usage and weariness, and my unaccustomed backside must have rivalled the setting sun. My thoughts—well, I don't care to dwell on them; I remembered the fate of Gallantin's scalp-hunters, and Sonsee-array laughing merrily over the details.

We lay that night in a gully, and every joint in my ageing body was on fire when we rode on next morning. Ahead of us there were bluffs now, and in the gullies we met occasional parties of Indians, hunters and women with burdens, and a few boys running half-naked in the bright sunshine, playing with their bows, their voices piping in the clear air. I caught a glimpse of a river down below us to the left, and presently we reached the top of the bluffs, my guards were whooping and calling to each other in delight, and as my pony jolted to a halt I raised my tired head and saw such a sight as no white man had ever seen in the New World. I was the first, and only a few saw it later, and most of them didn't see it for long.

Directly below us the placid river wound in great loops between fine groves of trees in a broad valley bottom. On our side the valley was enclosed by the bluffs on which we stood, although to our right the bluffs became a ridge, running away for a couple of miles into the hazy distance. From the bluffs to the river the ground fell pretty steeply, but from the crest of the long ridge the slope was much more gentle, a few hundred yards of hillside down to the river with a few gullies and dry courses here and there. It's like any other hillside, very peaceful and quite pretty, all clothed in pale yellow grass like thin short wheat, with a few bright flowers and thistles. All ordinary enough, but I suppose there are a few old Indians who think of it now as others may think of Waterloo or Hastings or Bannockburn. They call it the Greasy Grass.

But I barely noticed it that morning, for on the opposite bank of the river was a spectacle to stop the breath. Anyone from my time has seen Indian villages—a few score lodges, sometimes a few hundred perhaps covering the space of a cricket field. But here in splendid panorama was a town of tipis that must have covered close on ten square miles; as far as I could see the bank was a forest of lodges, set in great tribal circles from the thick woods upstream to our left to the more open land farther down opposite the Greasy Grass slope, and from the groves by the water's edge back to a low table-land in the distance, where a great pony herd grazed.

It was the largest assembly of Red Indians in history,[71] and while I couldn't know that, I was sufficiently awes-truck—were these the few dispersed bands of hostiles I'd heard lightly spoken of, the fag-end of the once-mighty Sioux confederacy which Terry and Gibbon had been afraid might melt away and escape, the thousand or two who weren't worth bringing up the Gatlings for? I saw Custer's face turned in impatience to Lonesome Charley Reynolds: "We are more than a match for them if they were all to-gether." Well, they were all together with a vengeance; there must be ten thousand of the red buggers down there if there was one—who the devil could they all be? I didn't know, but all America knows now: Hunkpapa, Sans Arc, Brulé, Oglala, Minneconju, the whole great roll-call of the Dacotah nation, with Arapaho, Blackfeet, Stony, Shoshoni and other lesser detachments from half the tribes of the North Plains and Shining Mountains—and not forgetting my old acquaintances, the Cheyenne. Never forget the Cheyenne. But five or ten thousand, Charley, it made no differ-ence—everyone knew they weren't going to fight. Not they—not Sitting Bull or Crazy Horse or Two Moon or Brave Bear or Lame White Man or Bobtail Horse or White Bull or Calf or Roan Horse or a few thousand others. Especially not the ugly little gentleman whom I'd put up for membership of the United Service Club if I had my way,

388

since he was the best soldier who ever wore paint and feathers, damn him. His name was Gall.

Well, there they were, all nice and quiet in the morning sun, with the smoke haze hanging over the vast expanse of tipis, and the women and kids down at the water's edge, washing or playing, but I didn't have long to look at it, for Jacket led us on to a ravine that ran down from the bluffs opposite the centre of the great camp; only later did I learn that it's called Medicine Tail Coulee, and that the river, which is hardly deep enough to drown in and half a stone's throw across, was the Little Bighorn.

The ford from the coulee to the camp was only a few inches of water above a stony bed; we splashed over and under the cottonwoods on the far bank, where women and children came running to see, but Jacket pushed ahead to the first line of tipis beyond a flat open space where fires burned and dogs prowled among the litter, and we dismounted before a big lodge with a few braves lounging outside. The stink of Indian and woodsmoke was strong inside as well as out; Jacket thrust me into the dim interior and cut my wrist cords, but only so that he could tie my numbed hands to the ends of a short wooden yoke which his pals laid across my shoulders. He thrust me down into the rubbish on the tipi floor and shouted, and a girl came in.

"This one," growls Jacket, "is a dirty lump of white buffalo dung who is to die by inches when the One-Who-Catches has seen him. Has he come yet?"

"No, Jacket," says the girl. "He was in the south, where the fighting was with the Grey Fox seven days ago. Perhaps he will come soon."

"Until he does, this one must speak to nobody. Take the gag from his mouth now and give him such scraps as the dogs have left. If he speaks," says he, glaring at me, "I will cut off his lips." And he drew his knife and threw it point first into the earth beside my foot. His pals crowed, and beyond them I could see curious faces peeping through the tipi flap, come to see the interesting foreigner, no doubt.

The girl fetched a bowl of water and a platter of corn and

389

meat, knelt by me, and removed the gag from my burning mouth. But for two or three short intervals, it had been there for the best part of thirty-six hours, and I couldn't have spoken if my life depended on it; I gulped the water greedily as she put the bowl to my lips, and when Jacket growled to stop she went on pouring without so much as a glance at him, until I'd sucked the last drop dry. As she spooned the food into me I took a look at her, and noted dully that she was pretty enough for an Indian, with a wide mouth and tip-tilted nose which suggested that some Frog voyageur had wintered among the Sioux fifteen years back. She was very deft and dainty in her spooning, and Jacket got quite impatient, pushing her aside before I was finished and shoving the gag back as roughly as he knew how. He bound it in place with a rawhide strip and soaked the knot, the vicious swine, just to make sure no one could untie it.

"Keep him that way till I come again," says he, and kicked me two or three times before swaggering out with his pals, leaving me in a state of collapse on the scabby buffalo rug against the tipi side. The girl collected her dishes and went out, without telling me to ring if I wanted anything.

I was in despair—and rage at my own stupidity. In my folly, I had destroyed my best chance, by pitching my tale prematurely to Jacket, offering him bribes, urging acquaintance with Crazy Horse, and so on. I couldn't have done worse, for Jacket, either out of brotherly affection for Cleonie, or for what she'd paid him, wanted me dead and damned, and was going to make good and sure that I had no second chance of stating my case to less partial Sioux who might have been disposed to listen. I was to be kept gagged and helpless until this mysterious person whom Jacket had mentioned—who was it, the One-Who-Catches?—came to have a look at me, and then presumably I'd be toted out to be strung up and played with for the amusement of the populace, none of whom would know who I was, or care, for that matter. God, that implacable bitch Cleonie-Candy had done for me with a vengeance—she and her stinking relatives.

I lay palpitating in the dim lodge, wondering if when next they fed me I'd get a chance to yell for help—and what good it might do if I did—and what were the chances of Terry and Gibbon's little army arriving, and what might happen then. This camp, after all, was their target, if they could find it—but they must, for their scouts would see its smoke ten miles away, and there was bound to be a parley, for neither side could take the risk of precipitate attack. And if they parleyed . . . I felt my hopes rise. When had Gibbon figured to come up with the hostiles? The twenty-sixth . . . I forced my numb mind to calculate the days since we'd left Rosebud—this must be the twenty-fourth! If I could stay alive for forty-eight hours, and Gibbon's column got here, and I could get my mouth open to some half-friendly ear . . .

The tipi flap parted, and the girl came in again. She glanced at me, and then began pottering with some utensils in a corner. I scrambled to my feet, with that damned yoke galling my neck, and as she looked round I ducked my head in the direction of the water-pitcher and tried to look appealing. She glanced towards the flap, and then back at me; I can't say she looked sympathetic, for her face was strained and tired and her eyes empty, but after a moment she motioned me to sit down again, filled a bowl with water, and with some difficulty slipped free the rawhide strap that held the gag. She eased it out, and I gasped and sucked at that blessed water, easing the pain of my parched lips and tongue. I wished to God I looked more presentable, for now I saw she was decidedly comely, with her boyish figure in its dark green tunic, her slim hands and ankles, and that saucy little face that seemed so woebegone; given a shave and a comb and a change of linen I could have cheered her up in no time, but seeing my eyes on her she made a little sign for silence, glancing again towards the entrance. I spoke quietly; it came out in a croaking whisper.

"What's your name, kind girl with the pretty face?"

She gasped in surprise at hearing Sioux. "Walking Blanket Woman," says she, her eyes wide.

"Oglala?" She nodded. "You know the Chief Tashunka

Witko?" Again she nodded, and I could have kissed her as my spirits soared. "Listen, quickly. I am the *Washechuska* Wind Breaker, friend of your chief's uncle, Sintay Galeska of the Burned Thighs. This evil man Jacket intends to kill me, although I am a friend to your people—"

"*Washechuska*, what is that?" says she. "You are an *Isantanka* bad man, one of our enemies—"

"No, no! My tongue's straight! Go to your chief, quickly—"

"Your tongue is double!" I was startled at her fierceness, and the flash of sudden anger in her eyes. "You have done great wrong—Jacket told me! All *Isantanka* white men are our enemies!" And before I knew it she had stuffed the gag back into my potato trap, and was hauling the rawhide up into place, while I tried to jerk my head free. But she was strong for all her daintiness, and cursed me something fearful, with little sobs among the swear-words.

"I was a fool to pity you!" She gave the strip a final tug and then clouted me over the ear. She knelt in front of me, her little face grim as she choked back her tears. "Seven days ago your *Isanhonska* Long Knives killed my brother in the Grey Fox fight! That is the kind of friends your people are! I was a fool to give you water and let you open your snake's mouth! Why should I be sorry for you!" And, damme, she clocked me again and flounced away, clattering her pots and wiping her eyes.

Of all the infernal luck. Womanly sympathy one minute, and the next she was battering me because her ass of a brother had got himself killed against Crook. I struggled with my yoke and scrabbled my feet in what I hoped was a coaxing, reasonable way, but she never gave me another look, and presently went out again.

Well, that was another hope dashed—temporarily. If I was patient, her natural kindness might revive, brother or no; my powers of persuasion with the female sex are considerable, and even with my scrubby chin and dishevelled locks and tattered clobber—the remains of full evening dress, God help us, in a Sioux tipi—I knew I could charm this little looker, if she'd only listen. Ain't it odd? Twice in as many days I'd been prevented by speechlessness from exercising my arts on unfriendly females. It never rains but it pours.

I thought I'd get another chance when they fed me again—but they didn't. Jacket looked in once for a kick at me, but no suggestion of dinner, and I lay there miserably as evening came, and outside the drumming and chanting began—they were holding a scalp dance for the Rosebud fight, I believe, but I was barely conscious of the din, for despite the cramping agony of my yoke, and my other aches, I fell into an uneasy doze, half-filled with horrid pictures of one-eyed women and painted faces and captives bound to burning stakes who looked uncommon like me in Hussar uniform. A Saturday night it was, too.

It was bird-song that woke me, and sunlight through the tipi flap catching the corner of my eye, which was drowsily pleasant for a moment, until a harsh voice jarred me back to my plight. There were half a dozen Indians in the tipi, looking down at me with stony indifference; the one who was talking was Jacket, and he seemed to be exhibiting me.

". . . when the One-Who-Catches has seen him, he will go to the fire. It is the wish of my brother's wife, and mine, and our family's!" He spoke as though challenging contradiction, but he didn't get any. "Whoever he says he is, he deserves to die by *kakeshya*. Who says he is a friend of Spotted Tail's, anyway?"

"Who cares?" says another, a burly ruffian with his belly hanging over his waistband and shoulders like an ox. His face was huge and ugly, but not without a humour that I was in no state to appreciate. His leggings and jacket were red, and he carried a short war-bonnet in his hand. "Do what you like with him; he's white," says this callous brute. "Come on! Totanka Yotanka is back from the hill; he has been 'seeing'." He gave a grunting laugh. "Pity he can't 'see' some buffalo."

If I'd known then that the speaker was Gall, the Hunkpapa chief I mentioned earlier, I might have been impressed, but probably not, for there was only one of the

393

half-dozen who claimed attention. He alone had no war-bonnet or feathers, or anything but a coloured shirt; he was young and wiry, lean-faced and lank-haired and without paint—but with those eyes he didn't need any. For a moment I wondered if he was blind, or in a trance, for he gazed straight ahead unseeing; I doubted if he even knew where he was. His shirt was blue-sleeved and gold-collared, with a great yellow band on which was a red disc, and its sleeves and shoulders were fringed with more scalps than I'd care to count. When Jacket tapped his arm, he turned those staring blank eyes on me,[72] but without any change of expression; it made my skin crawl, and I was glad when they trooped out, Jacket taking another kick at me on the way—he liked kicking me, no error.

I got no breakfast that morning, either. Possibly on Jacket's instructions, possibly because she was still peeved at me, Walking Blanket Woman didn't look near for several hours, by which time I could hear all the bustle and stir of the great camp—voices and laughter and kids yelling and a bone-flute playing and dogs barking, and the smell of kettles, and me famished. Even when she arrived she was decidedly cool and wouldn't remove my gag; it was only by piteous eye-rolling and head-ducking that I got her to relent sufficiently to pour water over my gagged mouth, so that I could obtain some refreshment. She raised no objection when I humped my yoke over to the flap, and took a cautious peep at the outside world.

It must have been just after noon of Sunday, June 25th, 1876. I wondered if Elspeth was in church at Philadelphia, examining the hats and pretending attentive approval of the sermon. I could have wept at the thought, and how my foolish whore-mongering had brought me to this awful pass. God, what an idiot I'd been—and that bitch Candy would be bedding one of the stokers on the *Far West*, no doubt. Fine subjects for Sabbath meditation, you see—but they don't matter; what I did and saw that afternoon are what matter, and I'll relate it as clearly and truthfully as I can.

All was calm in that part of the village between my tipi and the river. There was a fairish crowd of Indians doing what Indians usually do—squatting and loafing, scratching and gossiping in groups, some of the bucks painting, the women cooking at the fires, the kids scampering. There was a slow general drift upstream—that, I'm told, is where Sitting Bull's camp circle of Hunkpapa was, with the other tribal groups strung out downstream, ending with the Cheyenne at the bottom limit, out of sight to my left as I peeped towards the river. Where exactly my tipi was I've never quite determined; all sorts of maps have been drawn of that camp, and I believe I must have been in a lodge of the Sans Arc circle, close by the river—but Walking Blanket Woman was an Oglala, so God knows. Certainly the ford was to my right front, perhaps a hundred yards off, and above the trees I had a fair view of Medicine Tail Coulee running up into the bluffs on the far shore.

Walking Blanket Woman spoke suddenly at my elbow. "Take a good look, white-face," says she, pretty sullen. "Soon *they* will be looking at *you*. The One-Who-Catches will come today, and you will be burned. Maybe other white snakes will be burned, too, if they come any closer."

And off she went, clattering her pots, leaving me to wonder what the devil she meant. Had Terry's force been sighted, perhaps? If Gibbon had force-marched, he could be here today. Custer and his blasted 7th must be roaming off in the blue somewhere, or he'd have been here already. If only I could ask questions!

> The hawk stoops, but in the grass
> The rabbit does not lift his head.
> He runs but does not see. The hunter
> Waits, and the quarry is unaware.
> They come, they come! from the rising sun.
> Will any meet them, the hunter with his bow
>   and long lance?

It was an old man singing in a high, keening wail, as he shuffled by, face upturned and eyes closed, dirty white hair hanging over his blanket. He had a pot from which he dabbed vermilion on his cheeks in spots as he sang; then from a medicine bag he shook dust on the ground either side. The people fell silent, watching him; even the kids stopped their row.

> Who are the braves with high hearts?
> Who sings? Who sings his death-song?
> Is it the young hunter, shading his eyes as he looks
>   to the east?
> But the sun is high now; it shines on both the hawk
>   and the quarry.

The thin voice died away, and a great stillness seemed to have fallen on the camp. I ain't being fanciful; it was like the silence after the last hymn in church. Out in the heat haze they were standing in silent groups—women, children, braves in their blankets or breech-clouts, some with their faces half-painted; they were looking upstream through the trees, but at nothing that I could see. Over the river the bluffs were empty, except for a few children playing on the Greasy Grass slope to the left; the woods around us were quiet, and no birds sang now. A dog yelped in the distance, a few ponies under the care of a stripling snuffled and stamped, the crackle of a fire fifty yards away was audible, and the soft murmur of the Little Bighorn meandering through its fringe of cottonwoods. I'll never forget that silence, as though a storm were coming, yet the sky was clear midsummer blue, with the least fleecy drift of high clouds.

Somewhere on the right, away towards the Hunkpapa circle, there was a soft mutter of sound, a rustle as of distant voices growing, and then a shout, and then more shouting, and the low throb of a drum. People began to move up that way, the braves first, the women more slowly, calling their children to them; voices were raised in question now, feet moved more quickly, stirring the dust. The hum of distant voices was a clamour, rippling down towards us as the word passed, indistinct but of growing urgency; crouched under my yoke just inside the tipi, I wondered what on earth it could be; Walking Blanket Woman pushed past me—and then from the trees up to the right there was a scatter of people, and I heard the yell:

"Pony-soldiers! Long Knives coming. Run, run quickly! Pony-soldiers!"

In a moment it was chaos. They ran like startled ants, braves shouting, women screaming, children rolling underfoot, all in utter disorder, while the yells from upstream increased, and then came the distant crack of a shot, and then a fusilade, and then the running rattle of irregular firing, and to my disbelieving ears, the faint note of a bugle, sounding the charge! At this the panic redoubled, they milled everywhere, with some of the braves yelling to try to restore order, and the mob of women and children surging past downstream. The men were trying to herd them away, and at the same time shouting to each other, and with mothers crying for their children and vice versa, and the wiser heads trying to give directions, it was bedlam. The crash of distant firing was continuous now, and to my right I could hear the whoops and war-cries of men running to join the fight, wherever it was.

One thing was sure—it wasn't Gibbon. If he came at all it would be from my left, downstream; this was all up at the southern end of the valley, and they were pony-soldiers. Christ, it could only be Custer! And seven hundred strong, against this enormous mass of hostiles! No—it might be Crook, hitting back after his reverse at the Rosebud; that was far more likely, and he had twice as many men as Custer. Perhaps it was both of them, two thousand sabres; the Sioux would have their hands full if that were so.

(It wasn't, of course. It was Reno, obeying orders, coming full tilt towards the Hunkpapa circle along the bank with a hundred-odd riders. And I called Raglan a fool!)

Across my front braves were hurrying upstream. One young buck was strapping on two six-guns as he ran, and a girl hurried after him with his eagle feather; he was shouting as she thrust it through his braid, and then he was away, and she standing on tiptoe with her knuckles to her mouth; two more braves I saw tumbling out of a tipi, one with a lance and his face painted half-red, half-black, and an old man and old woman hobbling behind them, the old fellow with an ancient musket which he was calling to the boys to take, but they never heard, and he stood there holding it forlornly; another old woman hurried by with a small boy, the bundle she was carrying burst open, and they both paused to scrabble in the dust until the kid shrieked and pulled the old girl aside as a thunder of hooves came from my left, and out from beneath the trees came as fine a sight (I speak as a cavalryman, you understand) as one could wish—a horde of feathered, painted braves, lances and rifles a-flourish, whooping like bedamned. Brulés and Minneconju, I think, but I'm no expert, and then there was another yell somewhere behind my tipi, and by humping out for a look I could see another mob of feathered friends making for the river, too—Oglala, I fancy, and everywhere there were braves on foot, with bows and rifles and hatchets and clubs, racing towards the sound of the firing, which was growing fiercer but, I thought, no nearer.

The Brulé riders were thundering by before me, shrieking their "Kye-kye-kye-yik!" and "Hoo'hay!", and if ever you hear that from a Sioux, get the hell out of his way, because he isn't asking you the time. The only worse noise he makes is "Hoon!" which is the equivalent of the Zulu "s'jee!" and signifies that he's sticking steel into someone. Out before my tipi was the old singer, waving his arms and bawling:

"Go! Go, Lacotahs! It's a good day to die!"

There's a kindred spirit, thinks I—*he* wasn't going. But the rest of them were, by gum, horse, foot, guns, bows, and every damned thing—these were the Sioux who weren't going to fight, you recall. They vanished among the trees upstream, and the women and kids were away down in t'other direction by now—which left the world to sunlight and to me, more or less. Suddenly there was hardly a soul in sight between me and the river; a few stragglers, one or two old men, the ancient singer who had stopped encouraging the lads and was making tracks to his tipi. Upstream the firing was banging away as loud as ever—but I didn't care for it. The boys in blue were making no headway at all; if anything, the crash of musketry was receding, which was damned discouraging.

Now, two things I must make clear. First, that I had not

merely been viewing the stirring scene, but considering keenly which way salvation lay, and deciding to lie low. I was wearing four feet of timber across my neck, you see, with my hands bound to it, to say nothing of being painfully gagged, and while my feet were free, I felt I'd be a trifle conspicuous if I lit out from cover—and where to, anyway? Secondly, my memory, while acute for what I hear and see and feel in the heat of battle, is usually at fault where time is concerned. I'm not alone in that—any soldier will tell you that five minutes fighting can seem like an hour, or t'other way round. From the sound of the first shot I would guess that perhaps twenty minutes had passed, and now the sound of firing was decidedly fainter, when across the clearing Walking Blanket Woman came running—she'd pushed past me and disappeared, you remember, and here she was again, excited as all get-out.

"They are killing your pony-soldiers! Ai-ee!" cries the bloodthirsty biddy. "They are driving them back on the river! Everywhere they kill them! *Ees*! Soon all will be dead!"

She was rummaging in a corner of the tipi, and damme if she didn't come up with a most ugly-looking hatchet and a long thin knife, which she tested on the ball of her thumb, grunting with satisfaction. Plainly she was going to join in the fun, no doubt to avenge her brother—and then she stopped and looked at me, and the light of battle died out of the saucy little face, and I could read her thoughts as clear as if she'd spoken.

"Drat!" she was thinking. "There's this great idiot to look after, and me all over of a heat to help cut up the remains! How tiresome! Oh, well, someone's got to mind the shop, I suppose—hold on, though! If I 'look after' him permanently, so to speak, I can go with a clear conscience . . . on the other hand, Jacket *will* be annoyed if he's cheated of his little *kakeshya*—haven't seen a good flaying and dismembering for ages myself, for that matter. But I *would* like to join the fun up yonder . . ."

It was such a winsome little face, too, but as the expressions chased one another across it my gorge rose. She was eyeing me doubtfully, thoughtfully, angrily, determinedly—and I was about to bolt headlong, yoke or not, when above the distant din of firing came another sound, so faint that for an instant I thought it was imagination, and yet it was quite close at hand, across the river.

She heard it too, and we both stood stock-still, straining our ears. It was just the tiniest murmur at first, and then the drift as of a musical pipe, far, far away. And while I'm well aware that the 7th Cavalry band was not present at Little Bighorn, I know what I heard, and all I can say is that some trooper had a penny whistle, and was blowing it. For there was no doubt—somewhere beyond the river, on the high bluffs a bare half-mile away, was sounding the music of *Garryowen*.

Walking Blanket Woman was beside me in an instant. We both stood staring over the trees. The bluffs were empty—and then on their crest there was a movement, and another a little behind, and then another, tiny objects just above the skyline, slowly coming into view—horsemen, and one of the foremost carrying a guidon, and then a file of troopers, and I could make out the shapes of fatigue hats—ten, twenty, thirty riders, and as they rode at the walk, the piping was clear now, and I found the words running through my head that the 8th Hussars had sung on the way to Alma:

> Our hearts so stout have got us fame,
> For soon 'tis known from whence we came,
> Where'er we go they dread the name
> Of Garryowen in glory.

The piping stopped, and I heard the shout of command faint over the trees. They had halted, and in the little knot of men round the guidon I caught a glint—field-glasses, sweeping the valley. Custer had come to Little Bighorn.

Perhaps I'm a better soldier than I care to think, for I know what I thought in that moment. My first concern should have been how the blazes to get across to them, but possibly because it was a long, steep way, and there was a young lady beside me at least toying with the notion of putting her knife-point to my ear and pushing, it seemed academic. And the instinctive order that I would have hollered across that river was: "Retire! And don't tarry on the way! Get out, you bloody fool, and get out fast while there's still time!"

He'd not have listened, though. Even as I watched I saw a tiny figure with hand raised, and a moment later the faint call of "Forward-o!" and they were coming on along the bluffs, and wheeling down into the coulee, and beyond the bluffs to their left was a sputter of shooting, and down the steep came a handful of Sioux at the run, and after them a party of Ree scouts, little puffs of smoke jetting after the fugitives. There were yells of alarm from far up the river, closer than the distant popping of the first fight, which had faded into the distance.

A bugle sounded on the bluffs, and the first troop was coming down the coulee—greys, and I thought I could make out Smith at their head. Had lunch with your wife and Libby Custer on the *Far West* recently, was the ridiculous thought that went through my mind. And behind them there came a sorrel troop—why, that would be Tom Custer, who'd wept at that ghastly play in New York. And there, by God, at the head of the column, was the great man himself; I could see the flash of the red scarf on his breast—and I almost burst my gag, willing him to stop and turn, for he was doing a Cardigan if ever a man did, and he couldn't see it. The clamour in the trees upsteam was rising now; I thought I could hear pony hooves, and from the left, along the water's edge, came a mounted brave, yelling in alarm, waving his rifle above his head, and after him two more—Cheyenne, as I live, all a-bristle with eagle feathers and white bars of paint.

The girl gasped beside me, and I turned to look at her, and she at me. And what I tell you is strictest true: I looked at her, with a question in my eyes—Flashy's eyes, you know, and I put every ounce of noble mute appeal into 'em that

I knew how, and that's considerable. God knows I'd been looking at women all my life, ardent, loving, lustful, worshipful, respectful, mocking, charming, and gallant as gadfrey, and while I've had a few clips on the ear and knees in the crotch, more often than not it has worked. I looked at her now, giving her the full benefit, the sweet little soul—and like all the rest, she succumbed. As I say, it's true, and here I am, and I can't explain it—perhaps it's the whiskers, or the six feet two and broad shoulders, or just my style. But she looked at me, and her lids lowered, and she glanced across the river where the troopers were riding down the coulee, and then back at me—this girl whose brother had been killed by my people only a few days back. I can't describe the look in her eyes—frowning, reluctant, hesitant, almost resigned; she couldn't help herself, you see, the dear child. Then she sighed, lifted the knife—and cut the thongs securing my hands to the yoke.

"Go on, then," says she. "You poor old man."

Well, I couldn't reply with my mouth full of gag, and by the time I'd torn it out she had gone, running off to the right with her hatchet and knife, God bless her.[73] And I was cool enough to drain a bowl of water and chafe my wrists while I took in the lie of the land, because if I was to win across to Custer in safety it was going to be a damned near-run thing, and I must settle my plan in shaved seconds and then go bull at a gate.

To the right my girl was nearing the trees, and there were a few Indians in sight, but a hell of a lot more behind by the sound of it, no doubt streaming down from the first fight to give the boy general a welcome. Three Cheyenne had appeared from the left—and knowing them, I doubted if they'd be the only ones. By God, Custer had picked a rare spot to make his entry. The three Cheyenne were close to the bank, perhaps fifty yards away on my left front, arguing busily with a couple of Indians on foot; they were pointing up towards the ford and doubtless remarking that the pony-soldiers would shortly be crossing it and charging through the heart of the village. At that moment, out from between the tipis on my right came the old singer, leading a pony and yelling his head off.

"Go! Go, Lacotahs! See where the Long Knives come! The sun is on the hawk and the quarry! Hoo'hay! It's a good day to die!"

If I'd been the Cheyenne I'd have spat in his eye—for one thing, they weren't Lacotahs, and no doubt sensitive. But now was my moment. I looked across the river; the 7th were fairly pouring down the coulee, so far as I could see, for the farther they got down, the more they were obscured by the trees on the banks. The bugle was shrilling, shots were cracking on my side of the river, the three Cheyenne were apparently fed up with arguing, for they were skirting up towards the ford—and my ancient with his led pony was hobbling in their direction, shouting to the two dismounted chaps to take his steed and good luck, boys. I took a deep breath and ran.

The old fool never knew I was there until I was on the pony's back. It might have been ten seconds, probably less, but time for me to realise that I was in such poor trim, what with my ordeal, aching limbs, too much tuck, booze, and cigars, and general evil living, that if he and I had run a race, the old bugger would have won, by yards. But he was looking ahead, yelling:

"Here! Calf, Bobtail Horse! Mad Wolf! Here's a pony! Climb aboard, one of you fellows, and smite the white-faces, and my blessing go with you!" Or words to that effect.

I hauled myself on to the beast, grabbed the mane, and dug in my heels. I know people were running somewhere to my right, the Cheyenne were trotting purposefully towards the ford, shots were flying all along the river banks—and dead ahead of me, under the cottonwoods, was the ford leading to the coulee. Behind me the dotard was yelling:

"Go on, Lacotah! Here is a brave heart! See how he flies to meet the Long Knives!"

Apparently under the impression that I was one of the lads. The three Cheyenne were moving well, too—four of us going hell-for-leather, more or less in line abreast, three in paint and feathers, waving lances and guns, and one in white tie and tails, somewhat out of crease. Possibly they, too, thought that I belonged to the elect, for they didn't so much as spare me a glance as we converged on the ford.

They were three good men, those—again I speak objectively—for they were going bald-headed against half a regiment, and they knew it. If the Indians put up statues, I reckon those three Cheyenne would be prime candidates, for if anyone turned the tide of Greasy Grass, they did. Mind you, I'm not saying that if Custer had got across the ford, he'd have had the battle won; I doubt it myself. He'd have got cut up either side, I reckon. But the first nails in his coffin were Roan Horse, Calf, and Bobtail Horse—and possibly my humble self—for it was our appearance at the ford, I think, that checked his advance. I don't know—except that when my pony hit the shallows, with the three Cheyenne close behind, I lifted up mine eyes to the hills and saw to my amazement that the troopers in the coulee were dismounting and letting fly with their carbines. Whether the three Cheyenne stopped or came on,[74] I don't know, for I wasn't looking; there were shots buzzing like bees overhead as I scrambled up the bank—and not twenty yards away a Ree scout and a trooper were covering me with their carbines, and I was bawling:

"Don't shoot! It's me! I'm white! Hold your fire!"

One did, t'other didn't, but he missed, thank God, and I was careering over the flat to the mouth of the coulee, hands raised and holding on with my aching knees, yelling to them not to shoot for any favour, and a knot of bewildered men were standing at gaze. There was E Troop's guidon, and as I half-fell from my pony, there was Custer himself, all red scarf and campaign hat, carbine in hand. For a second he stared speechless, as well he might; then he said "Good God!" quite distinctly, and I replied at the top of my voice:

"Get out of it! Get out—now! Up to the top and ride for it!"

Somehow he found his tongue, and as God's my witness the next thing he said was: "You're wearing evening clothes!'' and looked beyond me across the river, doubtless to see if other dinner guests were arriving. "How in—"

I seized him by the arm, preparing to yell some more until common sense told me that calm would serve better.

"George," says I, "you must get out quickly, you know. Now! Mount 'em up and retire, as fast as you can! Back up this draw and on to the bluffs—"

"What d'you mean?" cries he. "Retire? And where in creation have you come from? How the deuce—"

"Doesn't matter! I tell you, get this command away from here or you're all dead men! Look, George, there are more Indians than you've ever seen over yonder; they're beating the tar out of someone upriver, and they'll do the same for you if you stay here!"

"Why, that's Reno!" cries he. "Have you seen him?"

"No, for Christ's sake! I haven't been within a mile of him, but it's my belief he's beat! George, listen to me! You must get out now!"

Tom Custer was at my elbow. "How many hostiles over yonder?" snaps he.

"Thousands! Sioux, Cheyenne, God knows how many! Lord above, man, can't you see the size of the village?" And in fury I turned to look—sure enough, they were swarming up to the ford from both directions, mounted Cheyenne among the trees downriver, now hidden, now in sight, like trout darting through weed, but coming by hundreds, and from the trees upstream a steady rattle of musketry was coming; balls were whizzing overhead and whining up the coulee; there were shouts of command to open fire coming from above us.

"Mount!" roars Custer. "Smith—E Troop! Prepare to advance! Tom, with your troop, sir!" He turned to bellow up the coulee. "Captain Yates, we're going across! Bugler, sound!" He swung himself into his saddle, and behind was the creak and jingle and shouting as the troopers took their beasts from the holders, and a scout appeared at Custer's side, pointing across the river.

"He's right, Colonel! Didn't I say—we go in there, we don't come out!"[75]

It must have been obvious to anyone who wasn't stark mad. But Custer was red in the face and roaring; he swung his hat and yelled at me.

"Come on, Flash! Forward the Light Brigade, hey? Didn't I know you'd be in at the death?"

"Whose bloody death, you infernal idiot?" I yelled back, and grabbed at his leg. "George, for God's sake—"

"What are you about, sir?" cries he angrily. "I'll—" And at that moment he jerked back in his saddle, and I saw the splash of crimson on his sleeve even as his horse surged past me. He didn't tumble—he was too good a horseman for that—but he reined in, and at that moment one of the Ree scouts close by spun round and fell, blood spouting from his neck. Shots were kicking up the dust all about us, a horse screamed and went down, thrashing—by George, that had been a regular volley, at least thirty rifles together, which you don't expect from savages; across the river a perfect mob of them was closing on their ford, halting to bring up their pieces and bows for another fusilade, a scarlet-clad figure ahead of them, arms raised, to give the word. I flung myself flat as shots and arrows whizzed past, and came up to see Custer standing in his stirrups, blood running over his right hand.

"F Troop! Covering fire! Tom! Smith! Move out with your troops!" Thank God he'd seen sense; he was pointing up the hillside, away from the bluffs. "Retire out of range! Bugler, up to Captain Keogh, and I'll be obliged if he and Mr Calhoun will hold the crest yonder—you see it, on the top, there?—with their troops! Go!" He urged his beast up the coulee. "Yates, sweep that bank yonder!" He pointed across the water, but already Yates's troop was blazing away, and Smith and Tom Custer were urging their men over the northern bank of the coulee, upwards towards the Greasy Grass slope that lay between the crest and the river. I was among them, clawing my way up the coulee side on to the rough hilly ground in the middle of a hastening crowd of troopers, a few mounted, but mostly leading their beasts. I swung myself aboard one of the led ponies, arguing blasphemously with its owner as we jogged over the hillside;

shots were still buzzing past, and here was another draw across our front over which we scrambled. Drawing rein as the bugle blared again, I had a moment to collect myself and look round.

A bare hundred yards away, at the foot of the slope, the trees were alive with hostiles, firing raggedly up at us. There were three troops on the slope round about where I was; when I looked up the hill, there were I and L Troops skirmishing out in good order. Custer was sliding down from his pony, using one hand and his teeth to tie a handkercheif round his grazed wrist; I ran to him and jerked the ends tight.

"Good man!" he gasped, and looked about. I don't know if he saw what I already knew, although it was too late now. Take a squint at my map and you'll see it. He'd come the wrong way.

I ain't being clever, but if he'd done what I'd told him he might have saved most of his command—by withdrawing straight up Medicine Tail Coulee and making a stand on the high bluffs, where five troops could have held off an army. Or, if he'd retired flat out, Calhoun and Keogh could certainly have saved their troops. By coming across to the Greasy Grass slope he'd put his command out in the open, where the redsticks could skirmish up over good broken ground and our only hope was to achieve the hill at the far end of the crest and make good a position there. And we might have done it, too, if that red-jacketed bastard Gall hadn't been an Indian in a million—that is, an Indian with an eye for ground like Wellington. The little swine saw at once how we'd blundered, and exactly what he must do.

It's a simple, tactical thing, and for those of you who ain't sure what turning a flank means, it's a fair example. See on the map—we *had* to make for the hill marked X, with half the Sioux nation coming up from the ford at our heels. If they'd simply pursued us straight, we'd likely have reached it, but Gall saw that the crest between the bluffs and the hill was all-important, and as soon as we were out on the Greasy Grass slope he had his warriors pouring up the second coulee in droves, nicely under cover until they could

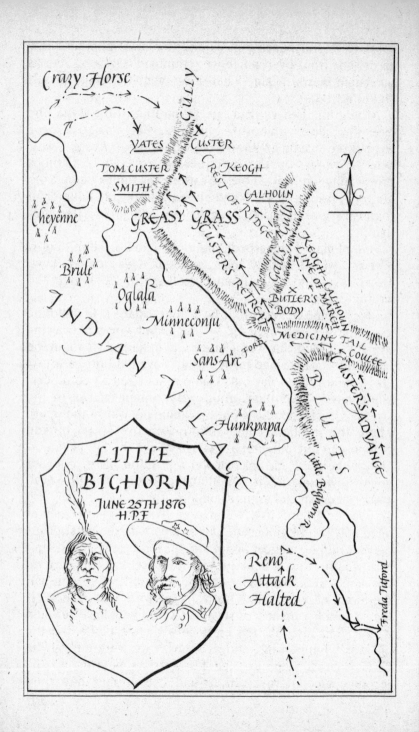

get high enough up to emerge all along the line of the second coulee, especially at the crest itself, where they could hit at I and L troops, and be well above Custer's three other troops making for the hill. Smart Indian, fighting the white man in the white man's way, and with overwhelming strength to make a go of it. In the meantime his skirmishers coming up on us from the river were pressing us too hard to give Custer time to regroup for any kind of counter-stroke. He couldn't charge downhill, for even if he'd scat-tered our pursuers he'd have been stopped by the river with Keogh's folk stranded; all he could do was retire to the hill with Keogh falling back the same way.

Our fellows were all dismounted, in three main groups across the slope, leading their horses and firing down at the Indians, who were swarming up through the folds and gul-lies, blazing away as they came. Curiously, I don't think we'd lost many men yet, but now troopers began to fall as the slugs and arrows came whistling out of the blue. And I saw the first example of something that was to happen horrid frequent on that slope in the next fifteen minutes—a trooper kneeling with his reins over his arm, raving obscenely as he dug frenziedly with his knife at a spent case jammed in his carbine. That's what happens: some factory expert don't test a weapon properly, and you pay for it out on the hill when the rim shears off and your gun's useless.

"Tell Smith to close up with E Troop!" yells Custer, and I saw the hostiles were up with Smith fifty yards below us

Flashman's map (opposite) of Little Bighorn is erratic in details – the course of the river, and the placing of the various tribal camp circles – but agrees with most authorities in showing Custer's advance along the bluffs, down Medicine Tail Coulee to a point near the ford, and then north up the Greasy Grass slope in an attempt to reach the hill marked X, where the remnants of his force were caught between the Indian charge from Gall's Gully and the encircling movement of Crazy Horse's cavalry. The underlined names (e.g. CUSTER) show where the various troops died with their commanders.

in a murderous struggle of pistols and lances, hatchets and carbine butts. To our own front they were surging up, ducking and firing, and we were retreating, firing back; I stumbled over a little gully through a clump of thistles, fell on my face—heard the rattle within a foot of my ear, and there was a snake gliding under my nose into the dusty grass; I never even thought about him.

"Give me a gun, for pity's sake!" I yelped, and Custer flung away his jammed carbine and threw me one of his Bulldog repeaters while he drew the other for himself. Christ, they were a bare ten yards off, shrieking painted faces and feathered heads racing towards me; I fired and one fell sprawling at my feet, guns were blasting all about me, Custer (he was cool, say that for him) was firing with one hand while with his wounded one he was thrusting a packet of cartridges at me. I saw the lens of his field-glasses splinter as a shot hit them; there were a dozen of us clawing our way backwards up out of a gully, firing frantically at the red mob pouring down the other bank. We broke and ran, in a confusion of yelling swearing men and rearing horses; below on the slope a body of kneeling troopers with their sorrels behind them—Tom Custer's people—were firing revolver volleys at our pursuers, and behind me as I flew were shrieks of agony blending with the war-whoops.

"Steady!" roars Custer. There he was, shoving rounds into his Bulldog and firing coolly, picking his men while the arrows whizzed round him. "Fall back in order! Close on C Troop!" Beside him a trooper with the guidon staggered, an arrow between his shoulders; Custer wrenched the staff from him and plunged uphill; I scrambled up beside him, swearing pathetically as I fumbled shells into my revolver—and for a moment the firing died, and Yates was beside me, yelling something I couldn't hear as I staggered to my feet.

We were in a long gully running from the hill-top to the trees far down by the river. The slopes below me were littered with bodies—the blue of troopers among the Indians, and lower still Indian attackers were bounding up the gully sides. The remnant of Smith's troop was reeling up the gully, turning and firing, loose horses among them, redskins

410

racing in to grapple at close quarters. I heard the hideous "Hoon! Hoon!" as the clubs and hatchets swung and the knives went home, and the crash of Army pistols firing point-blank. Around me were what was left of Yates's troop, staggering figures streaked with dust and blood; just down the slope Tom Custer's fellows were at grips with a horde of painted, shrieking braves, slashing and clubbing at each other hand to hand. I struggled out of the gully; in its bed a trooper was lying, screaming and plucking feebly at a lance buried in his side, two Indians dead beside him and a third still kicking. I looked back across the gully—and saw the final Death bearing down upon us.

Across the upper slopes of the Greasy Grass they came, hundreds of running, painted figures, and on a pony among them that crimson leader, waving them on for the kill. Tom Custer's tattered remnant was breaking clear of a tangled mêlée of blue-shirted and red half-naked fighters who still hacked and stabbed and shot at each other; somewhere on the crest I knew Keogh's people must be struggling with the right wing of that Indian charge sweeping across the slope. In less than a minute they would be on us; I turned sobbing to run for the hill-top, a bare hundred yards away—and even in that moment it crossed my mind: we've come a long way damned fast, for I'd no notion it was so close. We must have retreated a good mile from the ford where I'd ridden across with the Cheyenne just a moment ago.

Custer was on his feet, reloading, looking this way and that; his hat was gone, his hand was caked dried blood. There were about forty troopers round him, firing past me down the hill. As I came up to them an arrow-shower fell among us; there were screams and groans and raging blasphemy; Yates was on the ground, trying to staunch blood pumping from a wound in his thigh—artery gone, I saw. Custer bent over him.

"I'm sorry, old fellow," I heard him say. "I'm sorry. God bless all of you, and have you in His keeping."

There was a slow moment—one of those which you get in terrible times, as at the Balaclava battery, when everything seemed to happen at slow march, and the details are as clear and inevitable as day. Even the shots seemed slower and far-off. I saw Yates fall back, and put up a hand to his eyes like a man who's tired and ready for bed; Custer straightened up, breathing noisily, and cocked his Bulldog, and I thought, you don't need to do that, it's British-made and fires at one pressure; a trooper was crying out: "Oh, no, no, no, it's a damned shame!"; and the F Troop guidon fell over on a wounded sergeant, and he pawed at it, wondering what it was, and frowned, and tried to push its butt into the ground. On the crest behind them I saw a sudden tumult of movement, and thought, ah yes, those are mounted Sioux—by Jove, there are plenty of them, and tearing down like those Russians at Campbell's Highlanders. Lot of war-bonnets and lance-heads, and how hot the sun is, and me with no hat. Elspeth would have sent me indoors for one. Elspeth . . .

"Hoo'hay, Lacotah! It's a good day to die! Kye-ee-kye!"

"You bloody liars!" I screamed, and all was fast and furious again, with a hellish din of drumming hooves and screams and war-whoops and shots crashing like a dozen Gatlings all together, the mounted horde charging on one side, and as I wheeled to flee, the solid mass of red devils on foot racing in like mad things, clubs and knives raised, and before I knew it they were among us, and I went down in an inferno of dust and stamping feet and slashing weapons, with stinking bodies on top of me, and my right hand pumping the Bulldog trigger while I gibbered in expectation of the agony of my death-stroke. A moccasined foot smashed into my ribs, I rolled away and fired at a painted face—and it vanished, but whether I hit it or not God knows, for directly behind it Custer was falling, on hands and knees, and whether I'd hit *him*, God knows again. He rocked back on his heels, blood coming out of his mouth, and toppled over,[76] and I scrambled up and away, cannoning into a red body, hurling my empty Bulldog at a leaping Indian and closing with him; he had a sabre, of all things, and I closed my teeth in his wrist and heard him shriek as I got my hand on the hilt, and began laying about me blindly. Indians and troopers were struggling all around

412

me, a lance brushed before my face, I was aware of a rearing horse and its Indian rider grabbing for his club; I slashed him across the thigh and he pitched screaming from the saddle; I hurled myself at the beast's head and was dragged through the mass of yelling, stabbing, struggling men. Two clear yards and I hauled myself across its back, righting myself as an Indian stumbled under its hooves, and then I was urging the pony up and away from that horror, over grassy ground that was carpeted with still and writhing bodies, and beyond it little knots of men fighting, soldiers with clubbed carbines being overwhelmed by waves of Sioux— but there was a guidon, and a little cluster of blue shirts that still fired steadily. I rode for them roaring for help, and they scrambled aside to let me through, and I tumbled out of the saddle into Keogh's arms.

"Where's the General?" he yelled, and I could only shake my head and point dumbly towards the carnage behind me—but it wasn't visible, and I saw that somehow I'd ridden over the crest, on the far side from the river, and the crest itself was alive with Indians firing at us, rushing closer and firing again. Keogh yelled above the din:

"Sergeant Butler!" A ragged blue figure was beside him, gold chevrons smeared with blood and dust. "Ride out! See if you can find Major Reno! Tell him we're hemmed in and the General's dead!"

He shoved hard at Butler, who turned and slapped the neck of a bay horse that was lying among the troopers; it came up, whinnying, at his touch, and as Butler grabbed the reins he came face to face with me, and he must have seen me at Fort Lincoln, for he said:

"'Allo then, Colonel! Long way from 'Orse Guards, ain't we, though?" Then he was up and away, head down, going hell for leather at the advancing Sioux,[77] and thinks I, by God, it's that or nothing, and scrambled on my own beast as the red tide flooded in amongst us. It was like Scarlett's charge, a mass of men close-packed, contorted faces, white and red, all about me, carrying me and the horse whether we would or no, and there was no time to think or do anything but swing my sabre at every eagle feather in sight,

413

screaming wildly as the mass of men disintegrated and I dug in my heels and went in blind panic. As I fled I lifted my head and gazed on such a scene as even I can hardly match from all my memories of bloody catastrophe.

Until this moment, you'll agree, I'd had little time for careful thought or action. From the moment I'd crossed the ford and tried to reason with Custer, it had been one shot-torn nightmare of struggle up the slope away from those hordes of red fiends, followed by the chaos when our retreat had been caught in the death-grip between Gall's charge and the mounted assault (led, I'm told, by Crazy Horse in person) over the very hill to which we'd been struggling for safety. Now, with Keogh's troop being engulfed behind me, I was recrossing the crest overlooking the whole Greasy Grass slope to the river at its foot; I wasn't there above an instant, but I'll never forget it.

Below me the hillside was covered with dead and dying, and with little clusters where shots still rang out—a few desperate wretches taking as many Sioux with them as they could. There were hundreds of figures running, riding, and some just walking, across the slope, and they were all Indians. Most of them were hurrying across my front to the struggle still boiling just below the hilltop where Custer's group were dying. There may have been a score of them, I can't tell, standing and lying and sprawling in a disordered mass, the pistols and carbines cracking while the mounted wave of war-bonnets and eagle feathers rode round and through and over them, the clubs and lances rising and falling to the yells of "Hoon! Hoon!" while Gall's footmen grappled and stabbed and scalped at close quarters. There was no guidon flying, no ring of blue shoulder to shoulder, no buckskin figure with flowing locks and sabre (he was one of the still forms in that crawling mêlée); no, there was just a great hideous scrimmage of bodies, like a Big Side maul when the ball's well hidden—only here it was not "Off your side!" but "Hoon!" and the crash of shots and flash of steel. That was how the 7th Cavalry ended. *Bayete* 7th Cavalry.

Elsewhere it was already over. Far down to my left a mob of Indians were shooting and stabbing and mutilating over

414

a long cluster of blue forms—that would be Calhoun's troop. Straight ahead below me, to the right of the long gully, the cavalry dead lay thick where Yates and Tom Custer and Smith had died with their troops—but far down there was still a group mounted on sorrels, and I could see the puffs of smoke from their pistols.

All this I took in during one long horrified second—it couldn't have been longer or I wouldn't be here. I doubt if I even checked stride, for one glance behind showed a dozen mounted braves and a score running, and they all had Flashy in their sights. To the left and below the slope was thick with the bloodthirsty bastards—all you can do is see where the enemy are thinnest and go like hell. I swerved right in full career, for there was a break of perhaps ten yards in the mob surging up to join in the massacre of Custer's party. I went for it, sabre aloft, bawling: "I surrender! Don't shoot! I'm not an American! I'm British! Christ, I ain't even in uniform, blast you!", and if anyone had shown the least inclination to say: "Hold on, Lacotahs! Let's hear what he has to say", I might have checked and hoped. But all I got was a whizzing of arrows and balls as I tore through the gap, rode down two braves who sprang to bar my path, cut at and missed a mounted fellow with a club, and then I was thundering down the right side of the gully towards the group on their sorrels—and they weren't there! Nothing but bloody Indians hacking and stabbing and snatching at riderless beasts. I tried to swerve, aware of a mounted lancer coming up on my flank, a painted face beneath a buffalo helmet; he veered in behind me, I screamed as in imagination I felt the steel piercing my back, hands were clutching at my legs, painted faces leaping at my pony's head, my sabre was gone, an arrow zipped across the front of my coat, something caught the pony a blow near my right knee—and then I was through the press,[78] only a few Indians running across my front, when an arrow struck with a sickening thud into the pony's neck. As it reared I went headlong, rolling down a little gully side and fetching up against a dead cavalryman with his body torn open, half-disembowelled.

I lay sprawled on my back as two of those screaming brutes came leaping over the bank. They collided with each other and went down, and behind them the buffalo-cap lancer was sliding from his saddle, jumping over the other two, swinging up his hatchet. His left hand was at my throat, the frightful painted face was screaming a foot from mine. "Hoon!" he yelled, and his hatchet flashed down—into the ground beside my head. His breath was stinking against my face as he snarled:

"Lie still! Lie still! Don't move, whatever happens!"

Up went his hatchet—and again it missed my face by a whisker, and his left hand must have been busy with the dead trooper's innards, for a bloody mess was thrust into my face, and then he had a knife in his hand; it flashed before my eyes, there was a blinding pain on top of my skull, but I was too choked with horror, physical horror, to scream, and then he was on his feet, yelling exultantly:

"Another of them! Kye-ee! Go find your own, Lacotahs!"

I didn't see this, blinded with pain and human offal as I was, but I heard it. I lay frozen while they snarled at each other. There was blood running into my eyes, my scalp was a fire of agony—oh, I knew what had been done to me, all right. But why hadn't he killed me?

"Just lie still. I'm robbing your corpse," growled a voice close to my ear, and his hands were delving into my pockets, tearing at my coat, dragging my shirt half over my bloodied face—the laundry would certainly refuse my linen after to-day. Who the hell was he? I wanted to shriek with pain and fear, but had just wit enough not to.

"Easy does it," muttered the voice. "Scalping ain't fatal; it's just a nick. Have you any other wound? If you haven't, and understand what I'm saying, move the little finger of your right hand the least bit . . . good . . . and don't move another muscle—there are six of 'em within twenty yards, and I'm just muttering curses to myself, but if you start thrashing about, they may be curious. Lie still . . . lie still . . ."

I lay still. By God, I lay still, with my head splitting, while he emptied my pockets and suddenly shouted:

"Get away, you Minneconju thief! This one's mine!"

"That's not a pony-soldier!" snarled another voice. "What's that shining thing you've got?"

"Something too good for you, scabby-head!" cries my boy. "This is a white man's clicky-thing. See—it has a little splinter that moves round. Oh, you can have it if you like— but I'll keep his dollars!"

"It's alive, the clicky-thing!" cries the other. "See, it does move! *Hinteh! Hiya*, what do I want with it? Give me the dollars, eh, Brulé—go on!"

I heard a jingle of coins, and someone shuffling away, and all around me, through the waves of pain and fear, I could hear a ceaseless chorus of groans and screams and exultant yells, and one awful bubbling high-pitched shriek of agony—some poor bastard hadn't been killed outright. Occasional shots, wailing voices raised in chants, and all about my head flies buzzing, crawling on my head; I was matted with blood and stifling with filth, and the sun's heat was unbearable—but I lay still.

"He's gone," growled my unseen preserver. "Didn't want your watch—lie still, you fool!"

For I had jerked automatically as it dawned on me—to the Minneconju he'd spoken Siouxan, but all the words he'd addressed to me had been in *English*! Good English, too, with a soft, husky American accent. There it was again: "Keep lying still. I'm going to sit up on the bank above you and sing a song of triumph. For the destruction of all the pony-soldiers, d'you see? Right . . . there's no one here but us chickens at present, but it won't get dark for another four hours, I guess. Then we'll get you away. Can you play possum that long? Move your pinky if you can . . . that's the ticket. Now, take it easy."

I was past wondering; I didn't care. I was alive, with a friend close by, whoever he might be. For the rest, I still hadn't taken in the horror of it. Half a regiment of U.S. cavalry had been massacred, wiped out, in barely quarter of an hour.[79] Custer was dead. They were all dead. Except me.

"Don't go to sleep," said the voice. "And don't get

417

delirious, or I'll dot you a good one. Right, listen to this."

And he began to chant in Siouxan, about how he had slain six pony-soldiers that day, including a *Washechuska* English soldier-chief with a watch from Bond Street which was still going and the time was ten past five. Which beggared imagination, if you like. Then he went on about what a great warrior he was, and how many times he had counted coup, and I lay there with the flies eating me alive. Ne'er mind, worse things can happen.

I must have slept, in spite of his instruction, or more likely it was a long faint, for suddenly I was cold, and an arm was round my shoulders, easing me up, and water was being dashed in my face and a cloth was sponging away the caked blood. A bowl was held to my parched mouth, and the American voice was whispering:

"Gently, now . . . a sip at a time. Good. Now lie still a while till I get you smartened up."

I gulped it down, ice-cold, and managed to get my gummed eyelids opened. It was dusk, with stars beginning to show, and a chill wind blowing; beside me knelt the fellow in the buffalo-helmet, a fearsome sight and no prettier when he grinned, which he did when I croaked for information who he might be.

"Let's say a resurrectionist. Can you walk? All right, I'll carry you a piece, but then you'll have to sit a pony. First of all, let's get you looking like one of the winning team."

He dragged off my clothes, and somehow got me into a buckskin shirt and leggings. My head was aching fit to split, and wasn't improved when he insisted on putting his buffalo-cap on it. In the dim light I saw his long hair hung to his shoulders, and his face was bright with paint; American or half-breed, he'd taken pains with his make-up.

"Now, listen close," says he. "There are still braves and women around, collecting the dead." Sure enough, the evening was being broken by the high-pitched keening of the death-songs; against the night sky I could see figures moving to and fro, and there were pin-points of torch-light all over the slope. "All right, we're going downstream, to a ford farther along; that way we can skirt the village, and I'll get you to a place where you can lie up a spell. *Hoo'hay*, let's go."

I could just stumble, with him holding me. Then there was a pony, and he was helping me up; I reeled in the seat, with his arm about me, but although my head was bursting with pain I managed to balance, just. Then we moved slowly forward through the gathering night, down a slope and under cottonwoods; I could hear the river bubbling near. But I was like a man in a dream; time meant nothing, and I was only now and then aware that I was still astride a pony, that it was splashing through water, that we were mounting a slope. Twice I was falling from my seat when he caught me and held me upright. How long we rode I can't tell. I remember a moon in the sky, and a hand on my shoulder, and then I know I was lying down, and a deep voice was speaking in Siouxan, from very far away.

". . . put the grease on his head, and if it becomes angry send for me. No one will come, but if they do, and they are of our people, tell them he is to stay here. Tell them that this is my word. Tell them the One-Who-Catches has spoken . . ."

21

◄◄━━━► ━━━━◄ When you're past the fifty mark, you don't mend as quickly as you used to. For one thing, you don't want to; where once on a day you couldn't wait to be off your sick-bed and rampaging about, you're now content to lie still and let any handy ministering angels do their stuff. When I was a brat of a boy I went through hot hell in Afghanistan, had a fort collapse on me, and broke my thigh—and a few weeks later I was fit enough to gallop an Afghan wench with my leg in a splint and old Avitabile egging me on, and get beastly drunk afterwards. Not at fifty-three; if they'd paraded the Folies Bergère past me a month after Little Bighorn I'd have asked for bread and milk instead, and damned little of that in case it over-excited me.

I was in a delirium for the best part of a fortnight, they tell me, and near carried off by what sounds to have been pneumonia. When I came to, I was weak as a rat, and only able to move sufficiently to gulp down small mouthfuls of blood soup, which is capital stuff for a convalescent, but hard to come by unless you have a supply of fresh buffalo meat to hand. Apparently my hosts did—or I should say host, for there was only one of him, most of the time.

He was a 'breed called Joe Bright Deer, so he told me— and that was about all I could get out of him, at least where my miraculous rescue was concerned. Who the man was who'd pretended to kill me, and had genuinely scalped me (although pretty superficially, presumably to add verisimilitude for the benefit of Sioux bystanders), and had brought me here—wherever here was—he simply would not say, except that it hadn't been him. I pestered him about the last thing I remembered, asking who the One-Who-Catches might be, and he said that the One-Who-Catches had seen me, and would come again, possibly. In the meantime I could shut up, and have some more blood soup.

This took place in a cave, which was a fairly comfortable spot as caves go, with all the gear of a Mountain Man, buffalo robes, rawhide-and-wood furniture, and a good fire going. As I mended, Joe Bright Deer let me go as far as the cave-mouth for exercise, and I could see we were in hill country, with a good deal of conifer forest; somewhere in the Big Horn Mountains, I guessed. Outside the cave he wouldn't let me go, and since I was still fairly weak I didn't argue. Something told me I would find out all I wanted to know, if I sat tight long enough; in the meantime Joe was ready to talk about one subject in which I was tolerably interested, and that was the massacre I had survived.

Yes, Custer was dead, and every man who'd been on that slope with him. It seemed that he had gone up the Rosebud, but instead of skirting the Indian camp to the south, as Terry had instructed, had decided to take a slap at it himself, and to blazes with waiting for Gibbon. He'd split his force, sending Reno to charge into the camp with about 120 men from the south, while Custer himself took five troops round the flank to fall on the other end of the village. Well, I knew what had come of that, none better; in the meantime, Reno had managed to withdraw and hold out on a bluff until Terry and Gibbon arrived a day later. The Sioux, meanwhile, had decamped.

Everyone has had their say on this famous fiasco, and if you want mine, it's this. Custer was going to win an astonishing victory and refurbish his fame—very well. But having sent in Reno—a piece of arrant folly unless he was totally ignorant of the Indian strength—he then compounded his lunacy by launching his own attack even after he knew full well what that strength was. I saw that village from the bluffs, just as he did, and I'd not have attacked it with anything short of two regiments. It was just too damned big, and patently contained several thousand of the orneriest Indians in America. There are those who say Reno should have pushed harder, and others who say Custer could have charged through and met up with Reno—all my eye. He had one chance, and that was to hightail it the minute he got a good look at the village. But by then he'd put Reno in the stew, and *had* to go ahead. Mind you, George was such a fool of an optimist, and so obsessed with victory, that I daresay even at the ford he was still believing he had a chance. But the moment he was out on the slope he was done for, and he must have known it.

I'll say two other things. If the 7th had had decent carbines, they might have sickened the Sioux and been able to hole up on the hill, as Reno did. And that was Custer's fault, too. He should have tested those pieces before he went near the Powder country—tested 'em until they were red-hot, and he'd have seen them jam. T'other thing—Reno deserved the clean bill he got from the court-martial. I didn't know him, much, but Napoleon himself couldn't have done any better. If Custer had done half as well, there'd be a few old troopers still telling stretchers about how they survived the struggle up Greasy Grass hill.

Well, I've told you what I know about Custer, and you may judge for yourselves. He wasn't a bad soldier, though. Most commanders make a few mistakes, and no one hears about them. He made three in turn—sending in Reno, going in himself, and coming out the wrong way too late. As a result, he lost a pretty bloody skirmish—it wasn't a battle, really—but it shocked America, and he'll never live it down. For his troopers—well, if any of 'em ran, they didn't catch up with me. For the Sioux—it was their great day, for all it took thousands of them to knock over a few score. Gall gave them a victory, and Crazy Horse made siccar, as my wife would say.*

But that's by the way. A historic catastrophe it may have been, but to me it was the penultimate link in my American story, which was now drawing to a close twenty-six years after John Charity Spring had brought me over the Middle Passage. You may think it was the strangest of all my stories—but, d'you know, as I come to its final pages it seems

*See Appendix B: The Battle of the Little Bighorn.

perfectly logical; inevitable, almost. I might have known how it would be.

I'd enjoyed Joe's hospitality for the best part of a month, and was nearly whole again and feeling restless, and one evening as we were having a pipe at the fire, suddenly there was an Indian in the cave-mouth; I hadn't heard him come, but there he was, a splendid figure in black fringed leggings, with paint on his chest but none on his face, eagle feathers in his braids, and a pistol on his hip. He watched us in silence for a minute, and nodded to Joe. I'd seen him before, I knew, but it took me a moment to place him.

"One-Who-Catches," says Joe.

"No, he isn't, either!" I exclaimed. "I know you—you're Young Frank Standing Bear! I met you in Chicago with Spotted Tail—and then you and Young-Man-Afraid rode herd on us at Camp Robinson!" I regarded him in amazement. "Is Spotted Tail here?"

He shook his head. "The chief sits with his people at White River."

"But . . . he sent you? To me?"

He said nothing, and I stared from him to Joe in bewilderment. "But . . . what's all this nonsense about One-Who-Catches? If you're him, then I've been hearing about you ever since I was kidnapped by Jacket and taken to the lodges of the Sioux! What d'you want with me?" Another thought struck me. "And where's the man who brought me away from the Custer fight?"

He still said nothing, and then with one of those slow, graceful hand-motions he signalled Joe to leave the cave. He gestured me to sit, and sank down cross-legged opposite me, his hands on his knees. There wasn't a flicker of expression on the hawk face as the dark eyes studied me carefully; he seemed to be absorbing every hair of me, very thoughtful, and I didn't care for it a bit. Finally he says:

"I am Standing Bear, the grown-man name given me by the Hunkpapa Sioux. But as a child among the Brulés I was called the One-Who-Catches, the Clutcher, the Grabber, because I was greedy, and took what I wished." He said it without amusement. "The name Frank was given me by my parents, Broken-Moon-Goes-Alone and his wife the black white woman, Walking Willow."

The sonorous drone of the Siouxan words, the liquid movements of his hands as he followed the names in sign-language, lulled the meaning away from me for a moment. Then it struck home, and my hand began to tremble on my knee, even before he said the next words, his dark eyes intent on me.

"You knew my mother many years ago as Clay-o-nee, a slave-girl. You know her now as Mees-ez Can-dee."

"I don't believe you!" It was wrenched out of me. "Your tongue is forked! You're a Brulé—a full-blood Sioux if ever I saw one! You can't tell me you're her child! I don't believe it!"

"You sold her among the Navajo. How should I know that, if not from her? And why should she tell it to anyone but her own son, so that he might one day avenge her on the man who traded her for two thousand dollars?" It was as flat and emotionless as Mrs Candy herself; his fingers flicked like pistons as he spelled out the sum. "When I was a child, she told me how in the year of the great Cheyenne sickness, she had been in a wagon-train of black slave-women commanded by a man Comba, who betrayed and sold her to the Navajo at Santa Fe. Last year in Chicago, when Sintay Galeska Spotted Tail took us to the house-of-makes-plays-and-songs, he spoke to you of the days when you were young men, and how you had led a caravan of black slave-girls—also in the year of the great Cheyenne sickness. Then I knew that you, the *Washechuska* soldier-chief, were also Comba."

"Those black girls we watched tonight! Ees, they were as pretty as the black ones in your wagons, Wind Breaker! You remember them—the year the Cut-Arms were sick! Hunhe, what little beauties those were!"

I could see Spotted Tail's grinning face in the cab as we came back from the theatre—and all I'd been thankful for was that Elspeth didn't understand a word of it! This one had understood, though, and had kept the same stone face he was keeping now. But he'd passed the word to his mother in her Denver whorehouse that "Comba" was back. And she'd done the rest . . .

My mind whirled as I took it in. A chance in a million, that Standing Bear had been present at Chicago to hear Spotted Tail's randy recollections of twenty-five years before—but the rest of it fitted like an old shoe. I found myself staring at him—could he be the child of a Sioux and an octoroon? Yes; Cleonie herself had hardly been black to speak of—dammit, in her Mrs Candy guise I'd thought she was Italian. And she'd married this Broken-Bollocks fellow around '53, by her own account—well, Standing Bear was certainly somewhere in his early to middle twenties . . . oh, Christ, and he'd been treasuring up vengeance against me all these years. And now he had me.

"Now, look here, Standing Bear," says I. "I believe you. Your tongue is straight. But your mother is quite mistaken, you know—as I could have explained to her if she'd only let me. Good God above, *I* didn't sell her—I loved her truly and dearly, and was all set to take her to Mexico, but this wicked old woman who owned her, *she* sold your mother behind my back!" I shook my fist and went red in the face. "That spiteful old buffalo cow! I could have murdered her! To sell that dear, lovely girl whom I worshipped and hoped to marry—"

"Did the priest of Santa Fe speak with a forked tongue?" asks he quietly. "Why should he?"

"All priests speak with forked tongues," says I earnestly. "Every damned one of 'em. The snake-that-rattles speaks straighter—"

"And the wicked old woman?" The dark eyes were cold as ice. "When I was a little boy, my mother left the lodges of the Sioux—and went back to Santa Fe, and saw the wicked old woman. Mees-ez Soo-zee. The wicked old woman was kind to her, and helped her . . ." He leaned forward a little, and the words dropped like tombstones. "The wicked old woman told my mother how you had betrayed many women, and had stolen money, and done murder, and had a bad heart." His head shook, slowly. "Your tongue is forked. You know it. I know it. You sold my mother to the Navajo."

Oh, well, that disposed of that—worth a try, though. In the same steady voice he went on:

"When my mother learned from me last year that you had returned again from the Land of the Grandmother, she sought you out and trapped you, as one does the coyote, and had you taken on the Yellowstone by Jacket, brother of Broken-Moon-Goes-Alone, and he brought you prisoner to the Sioux lodges for delivery to me, so that you might die by *kakeshya* as my mother willed. I was away on the Rosebud, having fought the Grey Fox Crook, and I came back to Little Bighorn even as Yellow Hair's soldiers attacked. How you came to be in that battle I do not know, but I saw you there, and I saved you. I threw dust in the eyes of my brothers." He reached forward to point at my head. "I even took your scalp—a little—to deceive them. So that in their fighting-madness they should not kill you quickly. So that I should have you."

In the face of that awful implacable regard, the voice without emotion, I could say nothing—I could think plenty, though, and it was all dreadful. I'd been preserved from that carnage, so that I should suffer the unspeakably worse fate designed by that malignant slut Cleonie-Candy, a fate that this remorseless savage would take delight in inflicting. Better if I'd died with Custer, or blown my brains out . . . but wait, there was something here that made no sense—

"But . . . but he—you—the man who rescued me! He—he spoke English! Like an American!"

"And how the devil else should I speak it? I didn't have the advantage of a Rugby education, you know. Harvard had to be good enough for me."

I can't begin to describe the effect of hearing that pleasant, half-amused, half-impatient American voice issuing from the copper-red hawk face with its feathered braids; it was like having a Chinese mandarin suddenly bursting into "Boiled Beef and Carrots". I literally couldn't believe my ears; from the sonorous rolling tones of the Sioux he had slipped straight into the clipped voice of a well-educated, civilised man, without a muscle altering in his face. It was still a Brulé Sioux who sat regarding me stonily—until suddenly he burst out laughing, with his head thrown back, and then came abruptly to his feet, like a great cat uncoiling itself, and stood grinning fiercely down at me, his hands on his hips. No Indian in creation ever stood like that—but he wasn't an Indian any longer. Oh, it was still an Indian's face and body—but the voice, the expression, the gestures, the whole style of him . . . was of a white man.

"That's right—stare all you want to!" cries he. "Have a good look! By God, it would serve you right if I went through with it! If I carried out her wishes to the last burning inch! It would have served you right if I'd let them cut you up with Custer! I nearly did." He stood nodding grimly down at me; the grin had narrowed to a tight-lipped smile. "I nearly did. But it wouldn't have done. Would it?"

I'm not often at a loss for words, but now I sat dumb, understanding nothing, while my heart began to thump like a trip-hammer. I felt weak, and though I opened my mouth once or twice, no words came out. I could only stare at the tall painted savage with his braids and bucksins, the Burned Thigh brave with his hawk face and red skin. Then I managed to ask:

"Why didn't you?"

He moved slowly to stand in front of me. "You know why," says he. "You must know why." Suddenly he sank down swiftly in a crouch before me so that his face was on a level with mine, no more than a foot away. He was grinning again, but there was an odd look in the dark eyes—mockery, and wariness, and something I couldn't read. "You didn't know my mother when she went to you as Mrs Candy. Why should you, after twenty-five years? But this is different. Look at my face—as I've looked at yours. As I looked at it in Chicago and at Camp Robinson, and here tonight. Even if I hadn't my mother's word for it, just looking would be enough for me. But I have her word, too—that I was born in a Navajo village of New Mexico in spring of the year 1850."

427

It was as though I was hypnotised. It was nonsense, of course, but I looked anyway, and began to tremble again. For I did know the face. I understood why he had drawn my eye from the first, in Chicago, and again at Camp Robinson, and why I'd felt that strange comfort when he'd ranged up beside me on that hair-trigger day of the council with the agency Sioux. Oh, yes, I knew the face; I'd seen it most days of my life. The bold dark eyes with the slightly hooded lids, the aquiline nose when he turned in profile (I know my own side-view better than most, you see, because of the weeks I spent comparing it with Carl Gustaf's picture in the triple mirror at Schonhausen). Even the full mouth and the heavy jaw . . . he was a damned good-looking young devil, though, wasn't he, this Standing Bear? But I couldn't take it in—I'd been too numbed by this sort of shock, lately . . . Mrs Candy was Cleonie . . . this was her son . . . and now I was being expected to believe . . .

"Oh, come along, you silly old bastard!" cries he impatiently—and I knew it was true beyond a doubt. It would have taken a son of mine, at a moment like this, to talk to his father that way. But . . . no, it couldn't be true, although I knew it was. I searched for contradiction.

"You said . . . you said this Sioux fellow . . . what's his name? You said he was your father."

"That was Standing Bear who said that," says he in Siouxan. "Standing Bear the Brulé, the One-Who-Catches, to whom Broken-Moon-Goes-Alone *was* as a father." He broke into English again. "But I'm also Frank Grouard—or, properly speaking, Frank Flashman, son of Cleonie the slave-girl and the Englishman who sold her at Santa Fe."

"Grue-what?" says I, for no particular reason.

"Grouard. French—it was her father's name, so she gave it to me." He was watching me intently, with amusement and that other glint that I couldn't pin down. "Comes as a surprise, does it? From all I've heard about you—from Susie Willinck, too—I don't see why it should. You must have more bastards than Solomon." I don't shock easy, but that was like a blow in the face, coming from him. "And there's no miracle about it, you know. You and mother—" It shocked me, too, to hear him call her that, in that fashion, like a civilised son "—you were lovers in the summer and autumn of '49, and while I can't prove my birthday, she's sure of it. The Navajo don't keep parish records, either, but there are respectable citizens of Santa Fe, including one notary public, who'll testify that when she arrived there in '55, I had the appearance of a well-grown five-year-old. Well," says he, and grinned triumphantly. "How d'ye do . . . Papa?"

It's not easy, you know. He was right enough—I daresay I have by-blows all over the shop (India, mostly, and there's a Count Pencherjevsky in Russia whose paternity don't bear close scrutiny) and one of 'em was sure to come home to roost in the end. It takes the wind out of your sails, though, when he turns up as a Sioux brave with a Boston accent. For I was in no doubt now, you see—somehow it was less of a shock than "Mrs Candy" had given me, or the news that he was her son; it was almost as though I'd been expecting it. You may say he could have been the child of one of Susie's customers at Santa Fe, but I knew he wasn't. It was not a question of Cleonie's word, or his, or even the physical resemblance—which, in an instant, I'd recognised far more easily than Mrs Candy's to Cleonie. I simply *knew*; it was there, in him, his being and bearing and manner and . . . style. When he was being white, that is.

He was still squatting on his heels before me, watching me with that odd calculating grin, waiting. I don't know what I felt at all, but I know what I did.

"Well," says I, and put out my right hand warily. "How d'ye do . . . son?"

I don't know what he made of it, either. He took my hand, firm enough for a moment, but the shine in his eyes could have been anything—surprise, pleasure, emotion, amusement, anger, hatred even, but my guess is it was pure devilment. The young bastard (and I use the term with feeling) had had me on toast, sitting there solemnly playing his noble savage, keeping the old man agog, enjoying watching me squirm while he scared the hell out of me, turning the knife of fear and bewilderment in my innards, and keeping the really juicy surprise to the end. Oh, he'd had the time of his life. Good actor, too—aye, it all fitted, the skill in histrionics and dissimulation, the delight in twisting the victim's tail, the mockery, the cool damn-you cut of his jib, the callous way he talked of things other youngsters would have been ashamed of. Oh, he was Flashy's boy, no error—even if I hadn't sold his mama down the river, there'd have been no touching reunion between father and son. We ain't cut out for affection, much, our lot.

But that's not to say we aren't curious, and now that our formal introduction had taken place, so to speak, we compared notes, mostly his. He was itching to tell it, of course, knowing it must make my flesh creep, which was just nuts to him, being a Flashman—and the shock of that realisation, still sinking in, was enough to render me silent and attentive; if the 7th Cavalry had attacked our cave I doubt if I'd have noticed.

It was a remarkable tale, although not unique: scores of folk in the old West grew up half-civilised, half-Indian, as he had done. So far back as he could remember, he'd been Sioux of the Sioux till he was five, and when Cleonie had gone back to whoring in Santa Fe and Albuquerque, Susie Willinck had looked after him (which was a queer start, if you like), but he'd pined for the old life, and had been such a handful that they'd let him go back to Broken-Moon-Goes-Alone, who had died when Frank was about ten. Then Cleonie had put him to school, properly, at El Paso, and sent him east when he was thirteen, for by then she was well in the chips at Denver, and could afford him the best education going. He'd done uncommon well, and had gone on to Harvard, where he'd improved a talent for languages—which didn't surprise me—and then, to Cleonie's fury, had simply upped and gone back to the tribe, for three solid years.

All this, in the most matter-of-fact, offhand style, leaning against the table, arms folded on his painted chest, one foot elegantly over the other—a stance I recognised only too well. He'd known whose son he was, from infancy, and how his mother earned her keep, too. It was plainly all one to him; he seemed to have strangely little feeling for her, although he had gathered that it was only by a miracle that she'd kept him alive when he was born among the Navajo. And had done damned well by him since, it struck me.

"And you've been with the Sioux—you, an educated man—for the past three years?" I asked incredulously. I was still trying to hold them together in my mind—the Lacotah warrior who'd ridden to Little Bighorn and the young student who must have dined at the Oyster House and probably taken tea at Louisburg Square.

"Not altogether," says he carelessly. "I tired of it—I think. It was more home than anywhere, but . . . I'm two people, you see"—echoing the thought in my own mind. "Anyway, I 'came in' to the agency early last year—it was curiosity, mostly, I guess. That was only a few months before we met in Chicago. Being a Brulé, I drifted to Spotted Tail—I'm a full-blood Sioux to him, by the way; he doesn't even know I speak English. I've found it best to keep my two selves separate—mother and you are the only ones who've ever seen both of me. But Spotted Tail found me useful, and it was a lark going with him to Washington." He grinned at me. "Wasn't it, just? Here, though—my stepmother's a beauty, ain't she? Well, not my stepmother, I suppose—but whatever she is. She and Spotted Tail got on pretty well, I thought."

I didn't ponder on *that*, but asked why, if he'd come in to an agency, he now appeared to be living among the hostiles.

He smiled like a cat that's been in the birdcage. "Oh, that! Being on the agency was a bore, so after your commission made such a hash of the Camp Robinson treaty, I slipped across to Fort Fetterman as Frank Grouard and hired myself to Crook as a scout.* Been with him on and off ever since—I scouted for him on the Rosebud last month, you know; damnedest mess you ever saw." He laughed, and it was positively eerie to see that cruel, handsome face between the Indian braids crease into the knowing

---

*See Appendix A: The Mysterious Lives of Frank Grouard (1850–1905).

chuckle of a white man. "But the advantage is, I can slide out to the other side whenever I choose. It was because I was with Crook that I wasn't at Little Bighorn to receive you with due ceremony. As soon as I could get away from him, on the pretext of a long scout, I changed into Standing Bear again, and arrived in time for the fun of Greasy Grass. Lucky for you, wasn't it?"

Now, no one in his right mind would have believed this fantastic history—unless, of course, he had himself been a German prince and a Pathan *badmash* and a Dahomey slaver and an Apache brave and a Madagascar Sergeant-General, among other things, during his checkered career. So I believed him, and so can you, and for once you don't have to take my word for it, since much of what I've told you here about Frank Flashman, alias Grouard, alias Standing Bear, alias One-Who-Catches, alias the Grabber, is already public knowledge.

"I've a notion that Crook's people are getting wary of me, though," he went on coolly. "Not the Sioux—they know I scout for the Army, and think it a great jest. I suppose that shows which side I'm on, doesn't it?"

That was the question which brought us back to the vital matter which had been uppermost in my mind while I listened to his remarkable recital. As he lounged forward and tossed some chips on the fire I asked:

"If that's the case—then, what now?"

He squatted easily, blowing on the embers, and glanced up at me with his insolent smile.

"I'm not going to do you in, Papa, if that's what you mean."

"Ah. Well, I'm pleased to hear it. But I thought that was . . . the object of all this."

"Mother's notion, not mine," says he. "When I told her in Denver last year that I'd seen you in Chicago, she . . ." He paused. "I wondered if she'd gone a little mad. I'd always known that it was one of her fondest dreams that some day I'd be the one to pay you out for what you had done to her—sometimes I used to think it was the only use she had for me. Anyway, when I went to see her, she was like a crazy woman. She was always hard—cruel, even, but I'd never seen so much hate and spite in anyone—and I've lived half my life among the Sioux." He looked up at me curiously. "What was she like . . . when you first knew her?"

"Beautiful. Angelic, almost—to look at. Oh, but charming, bewitching, clever—quite calculating. Immensely vain."

He nodded cheerfully. "You're a yard-wide son-of-a-bitch, aren't you, Papa? Did you love her—at all?"

"No. I liked her, though."

"But you liked two thousand dollars better. Well," says this dutiful child, "I don't know that I liked her even that much. Certainly not enough, when I was little, to hate you the way she wanted me to. Why should I? You'd done nothing to *me*—hell, I didn't even know you! And Susie Willinck liked you."

"Good God!"

"Oh, sure. Susie used to laugh about you, and make you sound a jolly person. 'Proper young scamp, your old man was,' she used to say, and tell me I was another, a chip off the old block." He laughed, shaking his head. "I really liked Susie."

"So did I. Ah . . . how is she, d'you know?"

"She died four years back. She'd gotten married—" He stood up from the fire with his tongue in his cheek, "—again."

"I'm sorry—that she's dead, I mean." I was, too. I thought of that handsome happy face, the wanton lip and gaudy dresses, and . . . aye, well. Dear old Susie.

"Anyway, when I saw mother in Denver, it never even crossed her mind that I might not share her feelings about you. Later, when she'd laid her plans, and sent word—and two thousand dollars, you'll be interested to know—to Jacket and his people, she also sent word to me. I was to be the instrument of vengeance, if you please, and reveal my identity in your last painful moments." He shook his head in cynical wonder. "Honour bright, that's what she wanted. She's a Creole, all right—very passionate and dramatic, and a shade meaner than a sick grizzly." He shrugged. "Well,

433

then I *knew* she was crazy, and I wanted none of it. One reason I joined up with Crook was to be out of the way. Not that I bore you any good will," he added pleasantly, "and I won't say I'd have shed many tears if I'd arrived on Greasy Grass an hour later—but as it is . . ."

I was beginning to like this lad. "What'll your mother say?" I wondered.

"She won't know. She'll think you died in the fight. Not quite as fancy as she'd have liked, but I guess she'll be satisfied. How come you got into the battle, anyway—didn't Jacket have you hog-tied?"

I told him about Walking Blanket Woman, and he raised an eyebrow and looked at me for the first time with what might have been some respect, but probably wasn't. Yes, decidedly he had style, and watching him in the firelight it sent a tremor through me yet again to think that this splendid brave, with his paint and feathers so at odds with his *nil admirari* airs and crooked smile, was . . . who he was.

"You got me out, though," says I. "Why . . . Frank?"

He considered me with what I can describe only as impudent gravity. "Well, it seemed a sensible thing to do, on the spur of the moment. I had joined in, like a good little Sioux, hunting Long Knives—and suddenly there you were. Now that *was* a miracle, if you like, spotting you in all that—it was when we closed on the ridge, and that sergeant broke out, and you rode down the hill, so I followed on— you can ride some, though, can't you? I thought you were going to win clear, but I kept up, and when you went down . . ." He shrugged, and seeing me intent on him, grinned in pure mockery. "Well, now—what would you have done . . . if it had been your own dear Papa?"

I would get no change out of this one. So I must just play him at his own game—my own game. It took me a moment, so as not to choke or waver, but I managed it.

"Ah, well, now," says I, looking doubtful. "That's another matter, you see. You didn't know my guv'nor—your grandfather. You might have thought twice about him, you know." I nodded amiably, like the proud father I was. "Anyway . . . thank'ee, my boy."

434

"Filial duty, Papa," says he. "I wonder if Joe Bright Deer has anything for supper?"

* * *

It isn't every day you find a son, and if you ask me what I thought about it, I can't rightly tell you. It was just damned odd, that's all. I'd found myself stunned and disbelieving and convinced beyond doubt, all in a few moments, and after that, well, there he was—a walking contradiction, to be sure, but real for all that. I'd been shocked, almost repelled, by him, once or twice; I'd liked him, once or twice, and admired him, but mostly I'd just wondered at him. It was so strange to meet and talk to . . . *me*, if you follow. He acted like me, he thought like me, and take the paint and braids off him, and by God he looked like me: even the red skin was just weather, and I've been darker myself out east. If there was a difference, it was that I suspected (after Greasy Grass) he was brave, poor lad. I think he probably was; got that from Cleonie's side, no doubt. As to his deep nature, though, I can't tell; I doubt if he was as big a blackguard as I am, but then he was only half my age. And being so like me, he undoubtedly had the gift of concealing his character.

We set out from the cave two days later, the two of us. As Frank put it, having come this far he might as well see me to one of the Black Hills settlements, whence I could travel east; from the cave in the Big Horn foothills it was close on a week's ride. Crook was chasing hostiles somewhere, and Frank figured they'd be rounded up before winter, unless they made for the British border, which seemed likely. The Custer fiasco had evidently scared the Indians more than the Army, for they knew what the harvest would be, and the whisper was that only Crazy Horse was likely to fight it out. In the meantime, we went warily, Frank in his paint and me in buckskin, so that we'd be ready for either side.

It was a strange trip, that, across the High Plains; it has a sense of dreaming, as I look back on it. Considering our histories, our somewhat irregular kinship, how we'd met, and the initial difficulties of getting acquainted—which we'd managed pretty well, I thought, in our fashion—it was astonishing how easy we dealt. We were still taking stock, the first day or so at the cave—I'd catch him glancing sidelong as though to say, this big file with the whiskers, that's the guv'nor, God help us, and I'd think, well, I'll be damned, that's young Flashy. I probably found it odder than he did, since he'd known about my existence, at least, for more than twenty years. Yet sometimes it seemed as though we'd known each other all that time—and when we rode out it was a growing wonder and delight to see him, such a tall brave, so sure and easy, straight as a lance, and rode like a Cossack. I didn't look better myself at his age, by George I didn't.

We talked all the time, from sun-up till the fire burned low and the white wolves howled, and the days flew past. I can't think of all we said, but I know one of his first questions was whether he had any step-brothers or sisters, and I told him about my son Harry, the curate (now a bishop, and a praying one at that, heaven help the Church), and my daughter Jo, who was then eighteen and my alternate joy and despair—joy because she was as beautiful as a Flashy-Elspeth child could be, and despair for the same reason, young men being what they are. And one of my first questions was about his alter ego, Frank Grouard, and what did he purport to be, to Crook and other white folk.

"Back east I was French-American," says he, "but there were some Boston mamas who didn't care for that. So nowadays, when I cut my hair and put on a coat, I'm a Kanaka, son of a white father and Polynesian mother, born in the South Seas and brought to the States by Mormons, which is very respectable, and no one knows what a Kanaka is, anyway."

"They'll never swallow that," says I, "and the Boston mamas won't fancy Polynesian a bit, you know."

"They'll swallow it easier than if I tell 'em I'm half English soldier, half Haitian-French freed slave," says he smartly.

"As to Boston, it's what the daughters fancy that matters, not the mamas." I warmed to the lad more and more.

He, in turn, betrayed a flattering interest in me. Once he'd discovered that Flashy was the Saxon in the woodpile, he'd read up about me what little he could, and now asked many questions; I dare say he learned more about me in a week than anyone else has in a lifetime; I recall he was curious to know how I'd come by the nom de guerre of Beauchamp Millward Comber, so I told him—most of it. But I remember far better what he told me: about his childhood among the Sioux, about Broken-Moon-Goes-Alone, who seemed a decent, dull sort; about his days at Harvard; about what it had been like to be an Indian among white boys and men, and a white man among Indians (of which I knew something myself); about books he'd read, and music he liked, and plays he'd seen, all that kind of thing. But always he returned to the West, and talk of the tribes and hunters and the hills and the great plains, and I noted a strange thing. We spoke English all the time, in the same bantering, half-serious way that comes natural to me, and obviously came as easily to him, with wry comments and understatements—but when he talked about the West, it was in pretty plain English, with a phrase of Sioux here and there, and sometimes lapsing into the language altogether. I knew there was something there I couldn't touch, for it goes beyond blood, to country and the place where you were little. And when he talked of them there was something growing in my mind, but I didn't like to speak of it, for fear.

Until the last evening, when we'd ridden south and east all day towards the dark outline which is the Black Hills of Dacotah, the slopes of dark conifer which were so still and mysterious in those days. We rode into a long reach of prairie with tongues of woodland on either hand, in the summer gloaming, and Frank was whistling *Garryowen*, which might be odd in a Brulé warrior, but not in the American son of an English soldier. I was just casting about for a snug corner to camp when he reins up, and says:

"Well, d'you know, I think I should turn around here."

"What's that? Why, we're just going to camp! And what about Deadwood tomorrow? Good Lord, you can't just pop off now—it's far too late, for one thing, and we've had no supper."

"Well, I shan't be coming into Deadwood, anyway," says he. "I doubt if they're welcoming Sioux just now."

"Nonsense! Put your braids under your hat, if you like—or better still, cut 'em off—and who'll know the difference? A suit of buckskins—"

"No, I'd best be going now."

"But, dammit all, we haven't had any time to . . . well, to say goodbye, and so forth. And there are things I want to ask you, Frank, you know. Rather important things—"

"I know," says he. "Better not, really."

"You don't know what they are, yet! Now, see here, let's light a fire, and have some grub, and a smoke, and talk things over . . ." And I stopped, because in the dusk I could see he was shaking his head with the two eagle feathers, and when I reined closer I saw that half-smile with the look that I hadn't been able to fathom that first night in the cave.

"We'd better say goodbye now, Papa," says he.

I took hold of his rein. "Now, hold on, Frank," says I, and ordered my thoughts. "It's like this. I don't think we should say goodbye at all, d'you know what I mean? I think . . . look, I want you to come back with me." There, it was out now. "Back east, and then perhaps back to England. I . . . well, here's the way of it—there are things I can do for you, Frank; things that no one out here can do, if you understand me. Now, for example, if you wanted, I could get you into the Army. The British Army—or the American, if you'd rather. I know people, you see—like the President, and the Queen, you know. Well, you could make a simply splendid career as a soldier—"

"Fighting the Sioux for Uncle Sam?" says he lightly. "Or a half-caste officer in one of your exclusive cavalry regiments?"

"Half-caste be damned! You look no more like a half-caste than I do—and even if you did, it makes no odds. But it wouldn't have to be the Army, if you didn't care for it. Why, you could go to Oxford—or back to Harvard, perhaps—work at the languages, go into the diplomatic! Or anything you fancy—it would be nuts to a chap like you! I've got some standing, you see—and money." Elspeth's, but what the devil. "I want to help you . . . to get on, you know."

He touched his pony's mane. "Why? D'you think you owe it to me?"

"Yes, but that's not *why*! You saved my life, and I can't pay that back, but it ain't for that—"

"Is it because of what you did to my mother?"

"Good God, no! Look, my lad, I'll tell you something about me, which you may well have gathered already. I don't know what conscience means—or rather, I do, but I haven't got one, and I don't give a damn! Your mother—I played her a damned shabby trick, and we both know it. She tried to play me an even shabbier one in return—and it's only the grace of God and you that she didn't succeed. But it's nothing to do with any of that. You're my son." I found I was grinning hugely, with a great lump in my throat. "Such a son. And—there you are."

The light was fading fast, but I heard him chuckle. "Serve you right if I took you up on it. But it wouldn't do."

"In God's name, why not? If you didn't like it, you could chuck it, couldn't you? Look, my boy, you simply have to say what you'd like to do best—and we'll do it. Or rather, you will, and I'll help any way a father can—I mean, I know what strings to pull, and corners to cut, and palms to grease—and backs to stab—"

"D'you mean it? What I'd like to do best?"

"Absolutely! Anything at all."

"Well, Papa," says he, "the thing I'd like best is to ride back over the ridge there."

I sat for quite a little while after he'd said that, and then I said: "I see."

"No, you don't, either," says he dryly. "It's nothing to do with my mother—or with you. I said I didn't care for her much—don't care for anyone, specially. Except old Susie, bless her black heart. She was the nearest thing to a mother I've had. And God knows why, but I've no remarkable objection to my father." He laughed at me. "D'you know, after Greasy Grass, when I went down and the Sioux were breaking camp, I was wishing I could lay claim to you publicly. There were only two warriors they were talking about—apart from themselves, naturally: the soldier with the three stripes, and the rider with the long knife on the sorrel horse. What d'you think of that, now?"

God, the irony of it. And if I'd said I was screaming scared, neither he nor the Sioux would have listened for a second. The same old deception, the same old false appearance—but I was glad he believed it.

"So it's nothing personal, you see," says he, and turned his face to the Western sky, where the flame and gold and pale blue were fading as the day died. "It's just that over there is where I live."

"But Frank," says I, earnest and a shade hoarse. "Frank, boy, what's over there? Crook won't need scouts much longer, and you ain't going to rot on an agency, and there's nothing yonder you can do as Frank Grouard that you can't do far better and bigger—and richer—out in the wide world! Truly, you don't belong here, even if you think you do. You're half me and half your mother, and we ain't Westerners—"

"But I am," says he. "I'm not English or French or black. Or American. I'm Sioux."

I can see that stark profile now, the raised head with the feathers behind it, outlined dark against the evening light, and remember how my heart sank, and the emptiness within me as I made my last throw.

"You're nothing of the damned sort! There ain't a drop of Indian in you, whatever you feel . . . because of how you grew up. That's natural—but it'll pass, you know. And if you was Sioux to the backbone, don't you see?—the life you've talked about so much, this past week . . . well, in a few years it will have gone." I was leaning forward in my saddle, positively pleading at the dark figure. "Believe me, boy, I saw this country when hardly an axe or a wheel had

440

been laid on it. I rode with Carson from Taos to Laramie, and we never saw a house or a wagon or crossed a road or a rail the whole damned way! That was the year you were born—just yesterday! How long d'you think it'll take before it's all gone—vanished? Greasy Grass was the last kick of a dying buffalo—the Black Hills have gone, the Powder will follow, there'll be no more free plains any more, no game, no spring hunt, no . . ."

My voice trailed away, and I shivered in the cool night wind. He took up his reins.

"I know." His head was turned towards me, and I saw the crooked grin in the shadow. "I was at Greasy Grass, too, you know. And I'm glad—for your sake. But not just for your sake. Not by a damned sight."

Before I knew it he'd wheeled his pony and was off up the darkening slope, the hooves hollow on the turf.

"Frank!" I roared.

He checked at the crest and looked back. I felt such a desolation, then, but I couldn't move after him, or say what I wanted to say, with all the sudden pain and regret for lost years, and what had come of them. I called up to him.

"I'm sorry, son, about it all."

"Well, I'm not!" he called back, and laughed, and suddenly lifted his arms wide, either side. "Look, Papa!" He laughed again, and then he had ridden over the skyline and was gone.

I sat and looked at the empty ridge for a while, and then rode on, feeling pretty blue. I'd only known him a week, and he was a Sioux Indian to all intents, and when you thought of all the bother there had been about him, with every Deadly Sin, I suppose, for his godparents . . . but if you could have seen him! By jove, he looked well.

Still, it was quite a relief. Paternal piety's all very well, but it would have been a damned nuisance if he'd taken me up. I'd meant what I'd said, mind you, about starting him right and seeing him get on, but now he was gone and I could look at the thing cold, it was just as well. He'd probably have been a tricky, troublesome beggar, and Elspeth would have asked the most awkward questions, and once he'd cut his braids and put on a decent suit, the likeness would have been there for all the world . . . quite. I came all over of a sweat at the thought. Yes, undoubtedly it was just as well. Yet sometimes I hear that laugh still, and see that splendid figure on the ridge, arms raised, and I can feel such a pang for that son.

But life ain't a bed of roses, and you must just pluck the thorns out of your rump and get on.

* * *

I was in cheery fettle next day as I rode over the last winding miles of hill trail into Deadwood town. It was a regular antheap all the way in, with the miners crawling over the tree-clad slopes, and the ceaseless thump of picks and scrape of shovels and ring of axes, and ramshackle huts and shanties and sluice-boxes everywhere, with dirty bearded fellows in slouch hats and galluses cussing and burrowing, and claim signs all along—Sweetheart Mine, Crossbone Diggings, Damyereyes Gulch, and the like.

The town itself was bedlam; it was only four months old then, and wasn't much but a single street of log and frame buildings running the whole winding length of that narrow ravine, which can't have been more than a couple of furlongs wide from one steep forest slope to the other. But they'd lost no time: already they had a mayor and corporation, and a Grand Central Hotel, and a bath-house and stores and theatres and saloons and gaming-houses and dance-halls, with clerks and barbers and harlots and shopmen and traders and drink enough to float a ship, and everyone beavering away like billy-o and doing a roaring trade. "Boom!" they called it, and just to see it sent your spirits sky-high, it was so busy and jolly and full of fun, for everyone was riding high and spending free and about to make a fortune.

As I rode through the dust of the bustling street, the music was tinkling in the honky-tonks, the stores and saloons were full, the roughs and tarts chaffed at the swing-doors, and the sober citizens hurried by rosy with prosperity and optimism. They say you couldn't get a seat in the church of a Sunday, either, and "Greenland's Icy Mountains" and "Oh, Susanna!" were sung with toleration and good will next door to each other, and now and then somebody got shot, but in the main everyone was happy.[80]

There wasn't a dollar in sight, though—just gold-dust. It changed hands in little pokes; even at the bars they were paying for drinks with pinches, and there wasn't a counter or barrel-head in town without its scales and weights. Dust bought everything, and I had none, or a dollar either; I strode into the hotel and slapped down the gold hunter which the Minneconju had turned his nose up at, and the burly Teuton behind the desk looked at it, and me in my beard and buckskins, and sniffed suspiciously.

"Vare you git dat, den?"

Taking me for a road agent, you see, so I pointed out the inscription and assured him in my best Pall Mall drawl that I was the party referred to. He mumped a bit, but grudgingly allowed me thirty dollars on it, and I signed the register and ten minutes later was sound asleep in a hot tub, and all the grime and aches oozed away from me, and with them the turbulent memories of the *Far West* and Mrs Candy's patched eye, and Jacket and his braves, and the stinking stuffiness of the tipi, and Walking Blanket Woman with her knife at my cords, and the horrible bloody riot on that yellow hillside . . . copper bodies bounding up the slope . . . screams and shots and flash of steel . . . the rattler in the grass . . . Custer tossing me the Bulldog . . . " 'allo, then, Colonel. Long way from 'Orse Guards". . . the sorrel bounding beneath me . . . that painted face under the buffalo-cap . . . "Lie still, whatever happens!". . . the grave and handsome face splitting into its crooked grin . . . "How d'ye do—Papa?" . . . his hand in mine . . . Frank . . . Frank . . .

I woke up in the cold water, shivering, while someone pounded on the door and shouted was I going to stay in there the whole damned night?

A good steak put me to rights, and I was sitting bone-tired and content in their noisy dining-parlour, debating whether to buy a brandy at their crazy prices, and thinking happily that I'd be back in Philadelphia with Elspeth before the week was out, when someone swung my gold hunter on its chain before my eyes, and I stared up at a man I hadn't seen in ten years. Tall chap in a broadcloth coat and fancy weskit, long hair and even longer moustaches carefully combed, smiling down at me while he swung the watch; he burst out laughing as I jumped up and pumped his hand, and then we roared and exclaimed and slapped each other on the back and called for drink, and then we sat down and grinned at each other across the table.

"Well, Harry, my boy!" cries he. "And what the eternal hell are you doing here! I thought you were dead or in England or in jail!"

"Well, James," says I, "you weren't far wrong on the first two counts, but I ain't been in jail lately."

"I'll be damned!" he beamed, and pushed over the watch. "I just saw our good mine host fretting over this at the counter, wondering if it was brass after all, and when I took a squint—why, there it was 'Sir Harry Flashman' as ever was!" He slapped the table. "Old fellow, you look just fine!"

"So do you, and see how you like it! Here, though—he gave me thirty dollars on this watch, you know."

"Thirty? Why, the goddam German vulture pried fifty out of me! Say, I'll just have his fat hide for that—"

"Sit down, James," says I. "I'll send you a hundred for it when I get back east."

"You're going east? Why, you've just arrived! And where the hell have you been, and how are you, and what's your news, and damn your eyes, and so's your old man, and have a drink!" So we drank, and he swore again, laughing, and said I was a sight for sore eyes, and what the blazes brought me to Deadwood?

"It's a long, long story," says I, and he cried, well, we had all night, hadn't we, and shouted to the waiter for a full bottle, and keep 'em coming. "No, by thunder, we'll have champagne!" cries he. "If I'm drinking with a baronet, I want the best!"

"I'm not a baronet, I'm a knight."

"That's right, I forgot. A knight of the water closet—all right, the goddam bath!" roars he. "A long, dark, dirty knight! Now then—fire away!"

So I talked, and we drank, and I talked, and we drank, and I talked—because for some reason I was perfectly ready to tell the whole thing, from the beginning, when I'd knocked Bryant downstairs at Cleeve, to the moment when I rode into Deadwood. Deuced indiscreet, probably, but I was careless with content, and he was an old friend and a good egg, and I felt the better for the telling. He whistled and guffawed and exlaimed here and there, but mostly he just sat quiet, with those strangely melancholy eyes watching me, and the waiters kept it coming into the small hours, and steered other patrons clear of us, and roused the cook to bring us ham and eggs at four in the morning—nothing too good, you see, for Wild Bill Hickok and his guest.

When I'd done, he sat and stared and shook his head. "Flashy," says he, "I heard a few, but that beats all. I'd say you were *the* goddamnedst liar, but . . . here, let's see your head." He peered at the newly-healed wound on my scalp, and swore again. "Holy smoke, that's an Arapaho haircut, sure enough! Your own boy? By damn, that's thorough! That's . . . hell, I don't know what! And you were with Custer—no fooling?—in that massacre?"

"Don't spread it about," I begged. "I want to go home, nice and easy, and no questions, and have a good long rest. So forget it—and what are *you* doing, anyhow? Last I heard, you were in the theatre, with Cody."

So he told me what he'd been up to—on the stage, and here and there, a little peace-officering, a little gambling, drifting a good deal. But now he was married, with a wife back east, and he was in Deadwood to make a pile so that they could settle down. Mining or gambling, I asked, and he grinned ruefully and pulled back his coat, and I saw the two long repeaters reversed in the silk sash at his waist.

"If the cards don't start running smarter—and unless I can rustle up enough energy to try the diggings—I'll most likely have to put on a badge again."

Well, that was money for nothing, to him. He was the finest and fastest shot with a revolver I've ever seen (though I'd have paid money to see him from a safe distance against Jack Sebastian Moran). He wouldn't have to do a stroke as marshal; his name was enough. But he didn't look too content at the prospect; studying him, I saw he'd put on a touch of puffy weight over the years, and wondered if booze and loafing were closing in. He confessed that his eyes weren't what they had been, and he was ready to call it a day if he could take a small pile east from Deadwood.[81]

"I'll give it a few more weeks," says he, "and make tracks before fall. Hey, Tom, what's the date?" The waiter said it was August first if we were still in last night, but August second if we reckoned it was this morning. By jove, another couple of months and Elspeth would notice there was someone missing; I asked the waiter when the stage left for Cheyenne.

"You're not going out today?" grumbles Hickok. "Hell's bells, we haven't but had a drink yet! What's your hurry?" He wagged a finger. "You've been racketing around too much, that's your trouble; you're plumb excited and can't settle. Now, what you need is a good sleep, and a mighty breakfast in the evening, and then get tighter'n Dick's hatband, and there's the crackiest couple of little gals at the Bella Union, and we'll peel the roof off of this town—"

"And your father a clergyman, too," says I. "I'm sorry, James, but I'm all set. Look, why not come down to Cheyenne with me, and we'll ring the firebells before I catch the train east?"

But he wouldn't have it, the lazy devil, and we strolled out on to the porch of the hotel to look at the stars and see that the drunks were lying straight in the gutters. It was just coming to dawn, and I was dead beat.

"Too late to go to bed now," says Hickok.

I snatched a few hours' sleep, though, and piled down to the stage office just in time to catch the southbound. There was the usual crowd of roustabouts and loafers and boys to see the little coach pull out, piled high with boxes and bundles. There were only three other inside passengers, an elderly couple and a sleek little whisky drummer in check pants and mutton-chops; they were already in their places, and the driver was bawling: "All aboard! All aboard for Custer City, Camp Robinson, Laramie, an' Chey-enne!" as I ran down the side-street, with the kids whooping encouragement, and scrambled in. We set off north, and the little drummer explained that we would circle the block and then head south out of town.

"Goods to pick up at Finnegan's and Number Ten," he explained; we took on a case of his samples at Finnegan's, and rolled down the broad main street, which was busy with wagons and riders, to the Number Ten Saloon. Hickok had said it was a haunt of his; sure enough, he was taking a breather on the boardwalk as we pulled up; he had his coat off and his two guns in full view.

"Still time to come along, James!" I cried from the window, but he shook his head as he came across to shake hands.

"I've got Skipper Massey inside there," says he, "and I'm going to bluff, raise and call him from Hell to Houston—I beg your pardon, ma'am. Forgive my thoughtless speech," he added, raising his hat to the old lady. Very particular that way, was J. B. Hickok.

Much good it did her, for now the driver discovered a lynch-pin sprung, and his language poisoned the air. A boy was sent scurrying for a replacement and a hammer, and Hickok winked at me and called, "Don't take any wooden nickels, Flashy," as he sauntered back into the Number Ten. The driver thrust a crimson face in at the window, saying just ten minutes, folks, and we'll be on our way, and we sat patiently in the Deadwood stage watching the world go by.

"Beg pardon, sir," says the whisky drummer, leaning forward. "Did I detect a British accent?"

I said coolly that I believed it was.

"Well, that's delightful, sir!" He raised his tile and extended a paw. "Charmed to make your acquaintance, indeed! My name is Hoskins, sir, at your service . . ." He rummaged and thrust a card at me. "Traveller in fine wines, cordials, leecures, and high-class spirits." He beamed, and I thought, oh God, please let him get off at Custer City; it was hot, and I was dog-tired, and wanted peace.

"May I say welcome, sir, to the Great American West? Ah, you've been here before. Well, I trust your present trip is as enjoyable as the previous one."

(The seventh packet of the Flashman Papers ends here, without further comment or elaboration from its author, on August 2, 1876, the day on which Wild Bill Hickok was shot dead in the Number Ten Saloon, Deadwood.)

Appendix A:

The Mysterious Lives of Frank Grouard (1850–1905)

The most remarkable thing about Flashman's claim to be the father of Frank Grouard Standing Bear, the famous scout and mysterious figure of the American West, is how well it fits the known facts. That he should have had a son by Cleonie, and that son should have grown up among Indians, is in no way surprising, given the circumstances of Flashman's relations with Cleonie. Their child was not unique in this way; half-breed children raised as tribesmen were common enough (Custer himself is supposed to have had a son by a Cheyenne woman, although in the light of Custer's character this may be thought unlikely). Nor was it unknown for a man to be able to pass equally well as Indian or white; apart from Flashman himself, there are plenty of witnesses to testify that Frank Grouard did it, with a success that still baffles historians as much as it did his contemporaries. Or one might cite the case of James Beckworth, the mulatto who became an Indian chief, returned to the white side of the frontier, and then took to the wilds again.

However, to Grouard. There is no doubt that he scouted for Crook in the 1876 campaign, and was regarded as the best frontiersman with the American Army. But who exactly he was, or where he came from, was less certain, and the subject of much controversy. Some thought he was white, others that he was Indian; another theory was that he was half-Indian, half-Negro (which is interesting); yet another that he was the son of a French Creole (more interesting still). Grouard himself, after having refused many offers from journalists for his life-story, and having lost all his records in a fire at his home, finally dictated his story entirely from memory in 1891, to a newspaperman named de Barthe. It was a most curious tale.

Grouard said he was born at Paumotu, in the Friendly Islands, in 1850, the son of an American Mormon missionary and a Polynesian woman, that he was brought to the U.S. when he was two, lived with a family named Pratt in Utah, and ran away at 15. He became a teamster and mail-carrier, and was captured by Sioux in 1869. He was so dark that the Indians took him for one of themselves, and spared him; the name of Standing Bear was given him by Sitting Bull personally, because Grouard had been wearing a bearskin coat when captured. He was with the Sioux for six years, was a special favourite of Sitting Bull's, and knew Crazy Horse well. He became, naturally, fluent in Siouxan.

In the spring of 1875, Grouard decided to leave the Sioux. He came in to the Red Cloud Agency and (his own words) "stayed until the commissioners came to make the Black Hills treaty". He does not say that he went to Washington with Spotted Tail, but there is no reason why he should not have done so. After the failure of the treaty, he was sent as an ambassador on behalf of the whites to Sitting Bull and Crazy Horse, who rejected peace offers (and there are those who say they did this at Grouard's suggestion, and that his loyalties lay with the Sioux). In any event, Grouard says that he returned to the Red Cloud Agency, decided to become white, and enlisted with Crook. This he certainly did, and scouted for him in the March campaign on the Powder, and later on the Rosebud; it is worth noting that one of his fellow-scouts at this time became suspicious, and told Crook he suspected Grouard of plotting to lead the command to destruction.

So much for Grouard's own story thus far. His movements as a scout for Crook are sometimes well-documented, at other times not so. After the Rosebud battle (June 17) he appears to have been in and out of Crook's camp; he was certainly not with Crook on June 25 (the day of Little Bighorn) or for two days thereafter. When he did return to Crook it was with the news of Custer's disaster. For the next few weeks Grouard's movements are accounted for, but towards the end of July he fades away again.

Now, all this fits exactly with Flashman—but there is

more. According to de Barthe, Grouard's biographer, a story was current that Grouard had joined in the attack on Custer's force at Little Bighorn, but not with the intention of *defeating* Custer; on the contrary, Grouard had supposedly been trying to lure the Sioux to destruction against what he hoped was a superior American force, but the plan miscarried and the Sioux won.

At this point the imagination begins to reel slightly—but it is interesting that a rumour was going about that Frank Grouard, scout to Crook, had fought *with* the Indians at Little Bighorn.

On balance, Flashman's story of Grouard's early life is more plausible than the one Grouard told himself to de Barthe, and all the mystery and confusion surrounding Grouard in the '76 campaign go to support Flashman rather than not. After '76, Grouard scouted in government service, and Bourke and Finerty, reliable sources, agree with Crook that as a woodsman he stood alone. But no one was ever sure what to believe about him; the *Dictionary of American Biography* notes of his life-story that it is "fact . . . liberally intermixed with highly-wrought fiction".

Flashman students may be interested to know what Grouard looked like, in the light of Flashman's description. He was six feet tall, swarthily handsome, weighed about sixteen stone, had a large head with black hair, large expressive eyes, prominent cheekbones, a kindly humorous mouth, firm chin, and large nose (See J. de Barthe, *Life and Aventures of Frank Grouard*, ed. Edgar I. Stewart, 1958; Finerty; Bourke; J. P. Beckworth, *My Life and Adventures*, 1856; *Dictionary of American Biography*).

Appendix B:

The Battle of the Little Bighorn

Perhaps the reason why so much has been written about this famous action is that no one is sure what happened; there is nothing like ignorance for fuelling argument. Because until now there has been no account from a white survivor of the Custer part of the fight, the speculators have had a free rein, and what one eminent writer has called the Great American Faker and the Great American Liar have flourished. This is the more extraordinary when one considers that Little Bighorn was not (except to the participants and their families) an important battle; it settled nothing, it changed nothing; it was, as Flashman says, not really a battle at all, but a big skirmish.

And yet, Little Bighorn has an aura of its own. It is impossible to stand on the Monument hill, looking down towards the pretty river among the trees, or walk across the ridges and gullies of Greasy Grass slope, with the little white markers scattered here and there, showing where the men of the 7th Cavalry died, or look up from the foot of the hill at the silently eloquent cluster of stones where the last stand was made, or the distant ridge where Butler's marker stands solitary—it is impossible to look at all this, and listen to the river and grass blowing, without being deeply moved. Few battlefields are more haunted; perhaps this is because one can stand on it and (this is rare on old battlefields) see what happened, if not how. However they came, on whatever course, is unimportant; any soldier or civilian can envisage the retreat from the river and coulee to the ridge and hill, for here there are no complex manoeuvres or great distances to confuse the visitor—just a picture of two hundred men in blue shirts and a few in buckskin fighting their way across a sloping field, pursued and outflanked by overwhelming numbers of an enemy determined to fight them in their own way, man to man and hand to hand. Purists and propagandists alike dispute over terms needlessly; in the English language, it was indeed a massacre.

Flashman's account, in fact, is not one for the controversialists. Apart from his eyewitness detail, he does not help much to clear up the questions (most of them fairly trivial) which have raised such heat and fury over the past century. The Great Reno Debate is not affected in any matter of fact; only in his opinion does he touch on it, and supports the majority view.

What did happen, then, at Little Bighorn? So far as one can see, after studying as much of the evidence as one can reasonably digest, Custer split his command into three as he approached the (roughly) southern end of the valley where the Indian camp lay; he sent Benteen to the left, went himself along the right flank of the valley, and ordered Reno to charge into the valley itself; the idea was that while Reno was attacking (and possibly sweeping through) the camp from end to end, Custer would fall on it at a convenient point from the right flank, or possibly rear. A reasonable plan, in view of Custer's previous experience; reasonable, that is, on the assumption that he did not know the Indian strength.

Reno did not get far; he was checked, and eventually, with Benteen who had come up, established a position on the bluffs where they held out until the Indians withdrew. Custer, meanwhile, had seen the camp from above the valley, and determined to attack it. Here we enter the realm of uncertainty; looking from the bluffs today, and knowing how big the camp was, it strikes one that Custer was ambitious; his scout Boyer certainly thought so: "If we go in there, we won't come out", and a pretty little quarrel ensued before Custer followed his own judgment and went down towards the ford. How far he got, we do not know; the precise movements of his five troops, we do not know. These things do not really matter; we know where they ended up. In the event, Custer obviously mismanaged his last action; how far it was his *fault*—for not having got better information of the Indian strength, for failing to assess it

453

properly when the village was in sight, for exceeding the spirit if not the letter of Terry's orders—these are things we cannot fairly judge, without knowing what was in Custer's mind. And that we can only guess at. It *looks* as though he was unjustifiably reckless in deciding to go in with his five troops; with hindsight we know he was. But how it looked to him from the bluffs? He was there, and we were not.

Looked at from the Indian side, it was a competently, even brilliantly handled action. For a people unused to war or battle in the conventional sense, the Sioux and Cheyenne fought Greasy Grass in a manner which would have been approved by any sound military theorist. They turned back the initial attack, held it, saw the danger on their own flank, and enveloped this in turn. Reviewing it from their side (and this is personal opinion) it seems to me that Flashman is right to give the main credit to Gall, although Crazy Horse's circular movement was an inspired use of cavalry. Gall as the anvil and Crazy Horse as the hammer is a fair simile—but it was an extremely mobile anvil.

One other point it seems fair to make. Reno came under heavy and unjustified criticism, initially from Custer's hero-worshipping biographer Whittaker, later from others. He was subsequently cleared officially. And barely a week after the battle, four-fifths of the surviving rank and file of the 7th Cavalry petitioned Congress asking that Reno be promoted to fill the dead Custer's place. After that, what do critics matter?

The number of books and articles on Little Bighorn is literally uncountable. Those against which I have checked Flashman's story, not only of the battle, but of related subjects, number close on a hundred, so I am listing here those which readers may find of particular interest. Foremost must be a work which, though outstanding, is curiously hard to come by: Fred Dustin's *The Custer Tragedy* (1939); it and those two splendid works by Colonel W. A. Graham, *The Custer Myth* (1943) and *The Story of the Little Bighorn* (1926), are the three books which no one interested in the battle can do without. The research of these two authors has been prodigious; Colonel Graham's collection of letters, memoirs, and interviews, and Dustin's great bibliography, have been immensely helpful. Here, for example, one finds Gall's account of the battle, given to General Godfrey in curiously touching circumstances, as the two old enemies walked over the battlefield ten years later; here, too, Mrs Spotted Horn Bull's story, and Two Moon's, and Benteen's lively reminiscences, and Wooden Leg's story, and the Crow scouts', and the arguments of survivors and critics. Also: Whittaker, *Custer's Life*; E. S. Godfrey, *General G.A. Custer and the Battle of the Little Bighorn*, 1921; Bourke, *On the Border with Crook*; Miller, *Custer's Fall*; Vestal, *Sitting Bull*, 1972; E. I. Stewart, *Custer's Luck*, 1955; Miles, *Personal Recollections*; Dunn, *Massacres*; Finerty, *Warpath and Bivouac*; Hanson, *Missouri*; De Land's *Sioux Wars*; Custer's *My Life*, and Mrs Custer's *Boots and Saddles* and *Following the Guidon*; P. R. Trobriand, *Army Life in Dakota*, 1941; O. G. Libby, *Arikara Narrative of the Campaign of June 1876*, 1920; P. Lowe, *Five Years a Dragoon*, 1926; A. F. Mulford, *Fighting Indians in the U.S. 7th Cavalry*, 1879; Mrs O. B. Boyd, *Cavalry Life in Tent and Field*. But there are many others, and among them I should mention the late William Smith of Regina, Saskatchewan, former scout for the North-west (later Royal Canadian) Mounted Police, who served in the Indian wars, and whom I interviewed more than 30 years ago. And for those who want to know something of Little Bighorn that cannot be got from books, let them travel up the Yellowstone valley, past the Powder and Tongue to the mouth of Rosebud Creek, and then take the Lame Deer road, past the great modern mining works which Custer and Crazy Horse never dreamed of, and follow the Rosebud to Custer's camp-site, and so to the bluffs and the river, and walk across the Greasy Grass.

Notes

1. Helen Hunt Jackson, author of *A Century of Dishonour*, a champion of Indian rights, and a severe critic of American Indian policy. [p.18]

2. From this, and other internal evidence, it appears that this packet of the memoirs was written in 1909 and 1910. [p.21]

3. Pigs, i.e., police. An interesting example of how slang and cant repeat themselves across the centuries. The term is commonly thought of as a product of the 1960–70s, chiefly among protest groups; in fact it was current even before Flashman's time, but seems to have vanished from the vulgar vocabulary for over a hundred years. [p.52]

4. Hiram Young, a black, was the foremost wagon-maker and expert on prairie conveyances in Independence; Colonel Owens was one of the leading citizens. The stage run to Santa Fe began about this time, so it is quite possible that one of their new coaches was privately purchased for Susie's caravan, no doubt at a high price, for they were as luxurious as Owens described them. But travelling by them on the express run was anything but comfortable: Colonel Henry Inman, in *The Old Santa Fe Trail* (1896) writes with feeling of the non-stop journey, with horses changed every ten miles to keep up the high speed—this was at a later date, when the less troubled state of the plains enabled way-stations to be set up, and the journey from West-port to Santa Fe could be made in two weeks, weather and Indians permitting. The equipment of *four* revolvers and a repeating rifle, mentioned by Flashman, was standard for a stage-line guard. [p.67]

5. The bill in Colonel Owens' store was evidently a version of an advertisement which appeared in the *New York Herald* in December, 1848, advising emigrants on equipment for the gold-fields, including tombstones. [p.68]

6. Throughout Flashman's memoirs he never fails, when opportunity arises, to 'name-drop', and it is remarkable that he seems to have been unaware of the probable identity of the frontiersman in the Life Guards coat who examined him on Wootton's behalf. For it is almost certain that this was the celebrated scout Jim Bridger. At least we know that Bridger received from his friend Sir William Drummond Stewart, the sportsman and traveller, a gift of a Life Guards cuirass and helmet—there exists a sketch of Bridger wearing them. It seems reasonable that he may have received a coat as well, and still had it in 1849. Whether he was at Westport in late May or early June of 1849 cannot be established; it is said that he bought land there in 1848 and spent the next winter at the western fort which bore his name. But his movements in the months thereafter are uncertain;

about mid-June, 1849, he was apparently at Fort Bridger, for an emigrant named William Kelly records in his journal that he met the great scout there; it is possible that Bridger had been east in Westport earlier. Certainly Flashman's description of a tall, good-humoured, kind and patient man fits Bridger, so we may assume that Flashman met one of the legendary men of the West without knowing it. (See G. M. Dodge, *James Bridger,* 1905; J. Cecil Alter, *James Bridger,* 1925, and M. R. Porter and O. Davenport, *Scotsman in Buckskins,* 1963.) [p.73]

7. Flashman's judgment was entirely sound. Although less famous than the Carsons and Bridgers, Richens Lacy Wootton, familiarly known as "Uncle Dick", was unsurpassed among the trappers, scouts, and Indian fighters of his day. He spent a lifetime on the plains and in the mountains, and probably no one was more expert as a guide on the Santa Fe Trail. A genial, slightly eccentric character, he eventually conceived the idea of establishing a toll-gate on the Trail, where it crossed the Raton Pass on the Colorado-New Mexico border. He pioneered a road across the summit, and although he had occasional difficulties persuading travellers that a toll was reasonable ("with the Indians, I didn't care to have any controversy . . . whenever they came along, the toll-gate went up, and any other little thing I could do to hurry them on was done promptly and cheerfully") he seems to have made it pay. He lived to a great age, and is commemorated on a tablet set in the rock where the modern highway crosses the Raton summit. (See Inman, and *Uncle Dick Wootton,* by H. L. Conard, 1890.) [p.74]

8. "The earlies". So many correspondents have asked about Flashman's use of this expression in previous *Papers* that it seems worth a note. The only other literary allusion to it that I know is in Ethelreda Lewis's *Trader Horn,* where it signifies the 1870s on the Ivory Coast; my own father used it in talking about the history of settlement in East Africa, and it seems to have meant "early pioneer days", and been one of these pieces of Imperial slang which have long gone out of fashion. Flashman's use of it invariably refers to the first half of the last century, usually the 1840s. [p.74]

9. A rather cavalier description of one of the giants of New World exploration, Sir Alexander MacKenzie (1755–1820), who completed the first crossing of mainland North America in 1793. But what Flashman has to say of the misconceptions existing about the American West even in the middle of the last century, is true enough. Captain (later General) R. B. Marcy of the U.S. Army, who escorted emigrants from Fort Smith on the lower Arkansas to Santa Fe in 1849, wrote in his report that he had been given a "quite erroneous" notion of the country beforehand. "The best maps I could find" showed the great mountains and desert to which Flashman refers— in fact, they were not there, and Marcy remarked that he had never seen country where wagons could move so easily. (See Marcy's *Report on the Southern Route,* in vol XIV, 1849–50, Senate Documents, 1st Session, 31st Congress.)

As to what Flashman says of the unknown nature of the trans-Mississippi country in general, he can hardly be faulted. The Santa Fe and Oregon routes were already well-trodden, and trappers and traders from MacKenzie and Lewis and Clark onwards had penetrated to the remotest parts of the continent; American armies had marched south to Mexico and west to the Pacific via the southern routes; but to the emigrant for all practical purposes it was terra incognita. The editor has two maps, made by geographers of the highest repute between 1845 and 1853; they are by no means entirely reliable for the western territories; even Johnson and Ward's American Atlas of 1866 has a strange look beside the work of modern cartographers, and all three maps give a most striking impression of the emptiness of the country, with their vast white spaces marked only by rivers and mountains, and here and there a fort or settlement.

But then, it is difficult to grasp how suddenly western America happened. It is trite to say that in fifty years it was transformed from a wilderness into a settled countryside; consider rather that an infant could cross the plains by wagon train in the gold rush, and live to watch a programme about it on television; and somehow even that is not quite as sad as old Bronco Charlie Miller driving past filling-stations and movie theatres where once he had ridden for the Pony Express. [p.75]

10. Flashman's brief resumé of the Mexican-American war and the boundary changes needs a little enlargement. Until 1845, the U.S. western frontier ran (see map in end-papers) up the Sabine and Red Rivers bordering Texas, and then due north to the Arkansas, which it followed to the Rocky Mountains. Here the Continental Divide became the frontier up to the Canadian border at the 49th parallel.

In 1845 Texas was annexed, and in the following year Oregon became fully American by agreement with Britain. Following the Mexican War (1846–1848), Mexico ceded to the U.S. all territory north of the Rio Grande and Gila Rivers. This to all intents and purposes established the mainland frontiers of the U.S. as they are today; the only major change took place in 1853 when, by the Gadsden Purchase, the U.S. obtained the area between the Gila and the modern Mexican frontier. So in Flashman's time the Rio Grande and the Gila were the effective boundaries, for what this was worth; American administration of the ceded areas had barely begun, the frontiers were still uncertain, and it was not until the Boundary Commissions had completed their surveys in the early 1850s that the limits were determined. And, as he rightly says, New Mexico was still entirely Mexican in character. [p.76]

11. There are many authorities for the conduct of wagon-trains, and prairie pioneering in general; most of them are infinitely more detailed than Flashman, but his descriptions are well supported by other early writers. His account of Westport-Independence is highly accurate, down to such details as the cost of wagons and supplies, the pay of guards and riders, and the appearance of the varied multitude that thronged it in the spring and summer of 1849; the only point on

459

which he seems slightly hazy is the internal geography of the area which later became Kansas City, and he was overcharged for claret at St Louis. On the details of travel, too, he is sound in his description of caravan order and discipline, equipment, mule-loading, guard-setting, and the like. The best-known authority is Francis Parkman's *The Oregon Trail*, 1847, but others include Marcy's *The Prairie Traveller*, 1863; Josiah Gregg's *Commerce of the Prairies*, 1848; J. J. Webb's *Adventures in the Santa Fe Trade, 1844–47*, ed. Ralph P. Bieber; Lewis H. Garrard, *Wah-to-Yah and the Taos Trail*, 1850; and a personal favourite, G. F. Ruxton's *Adventures in New Mexico and in the Rocky Mountains*, 1847. Colonel Inman is excellent on the outfitting and equipment of trains on the Santa Fe route.   [p.83]

12. This cryptic remark must surely refer to the calling out of the militia in New York in May, 1849, to suppress rioting which followed the appearance of the actor Macready in *Macbeth* at the Astor Theatre—hardly the kind of social unrest Susie can have had in mind where the wagon guards were concerned, but her arch-conservative mind may have seen a parallel. The riots were extremely violent, twenty people being killed when the militia opened fire on a crowd. (See M. Minigerode, *The Fabulous Forties*, 1924.)   [p.83]

13. Among the Sioux, of whom the Brulé or Sichangu (Burned Thighs) were an important sect, the wearing and arrangement of head feathers were highly significant. An eagle feather denoted a scalp taken, a red-dotted feather an enemy killed (if the feather was notched, the enemy's throat had been cut). Since much importance was attached to counting coup (touching, but not necessarily killing, an enemy), feathers could also indicate the order in which a brave had laid hands on an enemy's body—notches on one side of a feather showed that he had been the third to touch the body; notches on both sides, the fourth; a stripped quill with a tuft, the fifth. A feather split down the quill indicated a wound stripe, as did a red hand symbol on a brave's robe; a black hand symbol stood for an enemy killed. Spotted Tail, the Brulé whom Flashman met (see also Note 55), was said to have counted coup 26 times; rumour also credited him with a hundred scalps, but this seems rather high, even for one of the greatest warriors of the Sioux nation. His name, originally Jumping Buffalo, is said to have been changed when, as a child, he was given a racoon tail by a white trapper, and attached it to his headdress; certainly he was wearing such a tail in the 1850s. (See *Spotted Tail's Folk*, a history of the Brulé Sioux, by George E. Hyde, 1961; *Handbook of American Indians*, by F. W. Hodge, 2 vols 1907–10, and the great encyclopedia of the Indian people, H. R. Schoolcraft's *Historical and Statistical Information Respecting . . . Indian Tribes of the U.S*, 6 vols, 1851–60. Also *Letters and Notes on the Manners and Customs and Conditions of the North American Indians*, 1841, by George Catlin, the most famous illustrator of Indians; his work has run to many editions, and is essential for anyone who wants to know what the early Indians looked like; *Our Wild Indians*, R. I. Dodge, 1883; *The Indian Races of North and South America*, C. Brownell, 1857.)

A minor point of interest is what Spotted Tail was doing so far east at this time; certainly the Sioux were hunting Pawnees that summer, and may have come as far as the Neosho. [p.86]

14. Sign language, so essential among nomadic tribesmen with no universal tongue, was perhaps more developed among North American Indians than among any other people. Nor was it a crude business of a few basic signs, but a highly-sophisticated visual system, in which the "speaker" could communicate quickly quite complicated facts and ideas. Some signs are probably well-known from the cinema—the flat hand, palm down, moved from the heart to the front, signifying "good", for instance; but a better idea of how much could be expressed in a simple gesture may be obtained from the following: the right hand, pointing forward with the edge down, meant a horse; if the thumb was raised, this signified a horse with a rider; a bay horse was indicated by touching the cheek, a black horse by indicating a black object nearby; a horse grazing was shown by dipping the fingers of the hand and moving them from side to side. Combine them all in one quick movement—and many authorities mention the speed and grace with which signs were exchanged—and you have a bay horse grazing, with or without a rider, in a split second, probably less time than it would take to say the same thing.(See G. Mallery, *Sign Language Among the N. American Indians,* 1st American Report, U.S. Bureau of Ethnology, 1879–80; Schoolcraft, Hodge.) Flashman mentions the Cheyenne sign; among others he must have seen that day would be the sign for Sioux (a throat-cutting motion); Pawnee (fingers cocked at the head to denote "Wolf People"); Arapaho (nose pinched—they were known as the Smellers); and Cumanche, the Snakes (waving motion of the hand). (See Marcy, *30 Years of Army Life on the Border,* 1886.) [p.86]

15. Ruxton gives a colourful description of a similar eating competition in his *Adventures.* [p.87]

16. The image and reputation of the American Indian have changed greatly in the last few decades; from being the cruel and treacherous villain of the Western scene, he has become its patriotic hero. Pendulums of fashionable thought have a tendency to swing violently, and it would be as wrong to discount the opinions of Wootton and his contemporaries as it would be to accept them without question. Undoubtedly the frontiersmen distrusted, and usually disliked, Indians: Kit Carson, who was more enlightened than most, is recorded as saying simply: "I wouldn't trust a one of them"; Jim Bridger spoke of "the mean and wicked Sioux", and Jim Baker, a sober and respected Mountain Man, gave the following opinion to R. B. Marcy:

"They are the most onsartenest varmints in creation, and I reckon tha'r not moren half human. You never see a human, arter you'd fed and treat him to the best fixins in your lodge, jes turn round and steal all your horses, or any other thing he could lay his hands on. No, not adzackly. He would feel kinder grateful, and ask you to spread a blanket in his lodge if you ever passed that-a-way. But the Injun don't care shucks for you. 'Tain't no use to talk about honour

461

with them. They ain't got no such thing. They mean varmints, and won't never behave themselves unless you give 'em an out-and-out licking. They can't understand white folks ways, and they won't learn 'em. If you treat 'em decent, they think you afeard."

An expert opinion—and what the Indians thought of Baker and his fellow-frontiersmen would be equally illuminating. We know what later Indian chiefs thought of the American Army and government, not without cause. Baker was probably right, in that Indian morals and sense of honour were different from those of the whites, and it was perhaps as difficult for a Sioux to understand white ideas of the inviolability of property as it was for a white man to appreciate, say, the point of counting coup on an enemy in battle, but not killing him. Best to say, along with Flashman, that the two sides had very different notions of proper behaviour, and leave it at that. But Wootton was right in one thing: it was not wise for a traveller to be off his guard, even with apparently friendly Indians; there is plenty of evidence that they were, to say the least, unpredictable—rather like Scottish Highlanders, in a way. (See Marcy, *Thirty Years*.)   [p.88]

17. "He kin slide!" in this context means "then there must be something wrong with him!" and is an example of what Flashman calls the "plug-a-plew" talk of the Mountain Men, from their catch-phrase referring to the poor price of skins (a plug of tobacco for a pelt). Readers of frontier travellers such as Ruxton, Marcy, Garrard, and Parkman, and of contemporary novelists like Mayne Reid and Ballantyne, will be familiar with the dialect; apart from its many cant phrases, it had its peculiarities of pronunciation—principally the reduction of the "ai" and "ee" vowels to "ah", as in bar (bear), thar (there) hyar (here), and har (hair). Presumably it was an exaggerated form of the dialects of the Border states whence came many of the Mountain Men; as with nearly all American dialects one can trace it back to its East Anglian-Puritan-West Country origins, to which the accents and vocabularies of Northern England, Scotland, and Ulster contributed in due course. To an outsider it must have sounded barbarous, and one suspects that the Mountain Men rather enjoyed using it for effect, and that most of them could speak good formal English when they chose, in whatever accent. Uncouth they might be in many ways, but recorded examples of their speech show a respect for grammar and construction, and purity of expression, that put most modern Americans and Britons to shame. In addition, many were skilled linguists, at least acquainted with Spanish and French as well as with Indian languages.   [p.88]

18. Invalids travelling the Plains for their health were not as rare as Flashman imagined; even in the early days the air of Colorado and New Mexico drew chest-sufferers west. A. B. Guthrie, Jr, notes in a recent edition of *Wah-to-Yah* that Garrard may have made his trip because of a weak constitution.   [p.89]

19. It has been suggested that this expression originated in the wagon-trains, where the captain (or as he was later sometimes called, the major) was elected by vote of all the men present, candidates standing

apart and their supporters tailing on behind them, the supposition being that as his "tail" grew a candidate had to run ahead to give it room. However this may be, the emigrant companies were frequently known by their captain's name, as well as by more picturesque designation; on May 26, 1849, there arrived in Santa Fe the Black River Company, the Western Rovers, and the New York Knickerbockers. (See *Marcy and the Gold-Seekers*, by Grant Foreman, 1931, an excellent work containing extracts from Marcy's report and writings, and from the letters of Forty-Niners.) [p.90]

20. Flashman's memory is playing him false. Whatever musical accompaniment Cleonie provided, it was certainly not "Swanee River"—better known as "Old Folks at Home"—since Stephen Foster did not write it until two years later; probably he is confusing it with some equally slow and melancholy song, perhaps a spiritual. His earlier mention of "Oh Susannah!", also by Foster, is correct; it was published in 1848, and taken up almost as a signature tune by the Forty-Niners, who parodied it with various verses, including those quoted by Flashman. [p.97]

21. Flashman uses *arriero* (mule-packer) and *savanero* (night-herder) indiscriminately when referring to his mule-men. [p.97]

22. The cholera epidemic of 1849 bore most severely on the Southern Cheyenne, who probably contracted it from an emigrant train on the Oregon Trail. About half the tribe died. (See David Lavender, *Bent's Fort*, 1954, and H. H. Bancroft's *History of Nevada, Colorado, and Wyoming, 1889*, volume XX in that great scholar's series on the Western States. Like Schoolcraft, Hodge, Parkman, and Catlin, his work is indispensable to anyone studying the history of the Far West.) [p.101]

23. "Poor bull" meant hard times, inferior eating—from the fact that bull buffalo meat was less appetising than cow meat, especially when the bull was in poor condition. "Fat cow", in Plains parlance, meant living off the best. [p.103]

24. The modern visitor to the Upper Arkansas, hearing talk of the "Picketwire" river, will search the map for it in vain. The early Spaniards called it Las Animas, but after the death of unshriven pioneers in the area, it was aptly renamed El Purgatorio. Voyageurs translated this into the French Purgatoire, which the sturdy Anglo-Saxon Americans insisted (and still do) on rendering as Picketwire, *pace* the cartographers, who retain the French spelling. [p.114]

25. Indian smoke-signalling was a code—a single puff meant that a party of strangers had been sighted; two puffs, that they were well-armed and able to resist attack. Nugent-Hare deduced correctly that the single puff, informing nearby tribesmen that the caravan was present but not formidable, would shortly bring down an attack. His immediate concern was to prevent the Indian scouts getting close enough to frighten the draught animals and so delay the train while the main attack assembled. [p.116]

26. Presumably Tom Fitzpatrick, a noted frontiersman who was

Indian agent for the country between the Arkansas and Platte rivers. [p.136]

27. Bent's Fort, the "Big Lodge", perhaps the most famous outpost in the American West, was founded by the three partners of Bent, St Vrain and Company—William and Charles Bent and Cerain St Vrain—in 1833–4, to take advantage of the trade opening up between the United States and Mexico along the Santa Fe Trail. It was the hub of the trail, and of the southern plains and Rockies, the great way station of the Santa Fe traders, Mountain Men, hunters, and Indians of the region, for William Bent, the "Little White Man", was a firm friend of the tribes, and married a Cheyenne wife. For well over a decade the fort flourished, and at its peak was as Flashman describes it—a great citadel on the prairie, with its fine rooms, stores, shops, smithy, wagon-park, billiard-room, and the rest; every Westerner of note was familiar with them. With the decline of the Santa Fe trade, the growing emigrant invasion, and the Mexicah War, the prosperity of the fort declined, and after the death of his brother Charles, killed in the Pueblo-Mexican rising at Taos in 1847, William abandoned the fort in August, 1849. Thereby hangs a mystery, although it may be thought now that Flashman's account has solved it at last.

It is supposed that William Bent, disappointed in his efforts to sell the fort to the U.S. Army for a good enough price, destroyed it by placing explosive charges and setting the place alight on August 21, 1849, having first removed all its supplies (*pace* Flashman). Another theory, generally discounted now, is that the fort was destroyed by Indians: Bancroft, in his *Colorado* (1889), refers to the destruction of Roubideau's Fort on the Green River and adds: "Bent's Fort was also captured subsequently and the inmates slaughtered. The absence of the owners alone prevented their sharing the fate of their employees." Flashman has the virtue of agreeing with both theories, up to a point; his story is certainly consistent with the view that Bent mined the fort with explosives and then withdrew (although how Flashman's caravan did not encounter him on his way down the Arkansas to Big Timbers is a mystery), and with the tradition of Indian attack, but not capture and slaughter. (The definitive work is Lavender's scholarly history [see Note 22] which rejects the Indian destruction story of Bancroft and others. See also Garrard; Ruxton; *Life of George Bent* (William's son) by George E. Hyde, 1967; and the U.S. National Park Service pamphlet, *Bent's Old Fort*, which provides an excellent plan and description of the buildings.)

There is, fortunately, a happy ending to the tragic story of Bent's. Recently it has been rebuilt at the original site, and restored to its old glory in appearance at least. Every detail, down to the trade goods and tools in the stores and shops—even the early Victorian billiard table—has been painstakingly recreated; it is a reconstruction which no enthusiast for the old West should miss. [p.137]

28. We can be grateful for a passing reference which definitely establishes a date. Colonel Washington's punitive expedition, which included

Pueblo and Mexican militia, left Santa Fe on August 16 and returned on September 26, so Flashman and Susie arrived in the city on September 27. Lieutenant Harrison is one of the officers mentioned in Major Steen's subsequent operations against the Apaches. [p.142]

29. Conditions in New Mexico were as Harrison said. The Indian agent at Santa Fe at this time, J. S. Calhoun, wrote in the week of Flashman's arrival that Apache, Navajo, and Cumanche raids were happening daily, and that it was unsafe to travel ten miles; four days later he was noting that the Indian trouble had increased and that "this whole country requires a thorough purging". He urged a policy of "enlightenment and restraint . . . at the point of the bayonet". (See Calhoun, *Official Correspondence*, 1915, edited by A. H. Abel. For conditions in Santa Fe and the territory, see Foreman; Webb; Inman; Marcy; Bancroft, *Arizona and New Mexico*, 1889; W. W. H. Davis, *El Gringo, or New Mexico and her People*, 1857. Also Lockwood and Cremony, see Note 30.) [p.143]

30. The payment of scalp-bounty dates back at least to colonial times, a fact which some Indian apologists have been quick to seize on as proof that scalping itself was introduced into North America by European settlers; such evidence as there is (and it invariably includes reference to the Visigoths, Abbe Domenech, and the celebrated passage on the Scythians in Book IV of Herodotus) strongly suggests that scalping was an indigenous North American Indian practice which needed no encouragement from white settlers—although they gave it when it suited them, as in the case of the *Proyecto de Guerra*. This provided for payment on the scale quoted by Lt. Harrison, plus any loot that might be taken from the Indians; in the 1840s the price sometimes rose as high as $300 per Apache scalp. ($250 was being paid in Arizona as late as 1866; in 1870 bounty was still being paid in Mexico.)

That scalp-hunting could be a highly profitable pursuit is undisputed. Several hundred Apache scalps are said to have been taken in the infamous operation referred to by Harrison, when Johnson (variously described as an Englishman and as an American) invited the Copper Mines Indians of Santa Rita to a feast, and opened fire on them with a hidden howitzer. Another notable scalp-hunter was James Kirker, a Scot who had been a prisoner of the Apaches and risen to the rank of chief, in which capacity he was such a nuisance that the Governor of Chihuahua put a price of $9000 on his head. Kirker, a man of resource, promptly made a deal with the Mexican authorities for the sale of Apache scalps, abandoned his tribe, and led against them a mixed band of 200 Americans, Mexicans, and Shawnee Indians. A graphic eyewitness account of Kirker's raids has been left by Captain James Hobbs, who describes his band as "a fearful set to behold" and notes that while the usual scalp bounty was $50, "we would fight certain Indian tribes for the fun of the thing." Chico Velasquez, referred to by Flashman, was also reputed to have driven the trade. (See *Massacres of the Mountains*, by J. P. Dunn, 1886; J. C. Cremony, *Life Among the Apaches*, 1868; *Wild*

465

Life in the Far West, by James Hobbs, 1873; F. C. Lockwood, *The Apache Indians*, 1938; and for a fictitious but vivid account of a bounty-hunting expedition by a contemporary author who knew the scenes he described at first-hand, *The Scalp-Hunters*, by Captain Thomas Mayne Reid, 1851. Reid (1818–83), an Irish adventurer, was by turns an actor, journalist, and soldier; he served in the U.S. Army during the Mexican War and distinguished himself at Chapultepec, where he was badly wounded. He became famous as a writer of adventure stories, and is to be regarded as a founder of the great Victorian tradition of schoolboy literature which included Ballantyne and Henty.) [p.144]

31. The law on slave-holding in New Mexico was in some confusion at this time. In September, 1849, a convention at Santa Fe of 19 elected delegates, under the acting governor, Lt-Col Beall, appointed a representative to Congress to obtain recognition as a territory; he was unsuccessful, but in May a convention at Santa Fe framed a constitution for New Mexico under which slavery was prohibited. Before this the Southern States had maintained the right of owners to hold slaves in the territory, whereas Northerners were insistent on prohibition. The position was complicated by New Mexico's recent transfer from Mexican rule (under which slavery had been abolished) to American military government. (See Bancroft.) [p.155]

32. The Jornada del Muerto was one of the most feared journeys in North America in Flashman's time, and is no picnic today, with its unpromising grit road which, on some maps only, is shown running between San Marcial and Hatch. The editor has experience only of its southern end, and recommends a vehicle more robust than the average car; he is not aware whether the northern end of the road even exists. Mayne Reid and Ruxton testify to the Jornada's dangers in the 1840s, as does the intrepid Cremony, who rode it several times—on one occasion covering the last 70 miles "at a run", pursued by Apaches. The modern traveller may reflect that the Jornada's name, so apt in the early days, was also horribly prophetic: if Ruxton and Reid and Cremony had been able to make the Dead Man's Journey exactly a century later, they would have seen on its eastern horizon the mushroom cloud of the first atomic bomb test. [p.163]

33. But not for long. Gallantin (also known as Glanton) had driven a thriving trade in scalps sold to the Chihuahua authorities, who were much puzzled that in spite of all his efforts, Apache raids seemed to be increasing, with Mexicans and friendly Indians being scalped in large numbers. Eventually it dawned on them that Gallantin himself was responsible, and was selling these "innocent" scalps as well as Apache ones. Gallantin was forced to flee in 1851, taking about two thousand stolen sheep with him through the Gila River country; here he was met by Yuma Indians whose chief Naked Horse protested friendship and, at the first opportunity, wiped out Gallantin and his entire party. (See Dunn, Cremony, Bancroft.) [p.187]

34. The Copper Mines of Santa Rita, once the stronghold of Mangas Colorado and the Mimbreno Apache, and scene of the infamous

Johnson massacre, would not be recognised by Flashman today. The triangular *presidio* and buildings of the Mexican occupation have gone, and in their place is a man-made excavation almost a mile across, showing strata of remarkably varied colours, for the copper which the Spaniards first sought centuries ago is still being mined by modern commercial methods. [p.193]

35. Among the Apache it was customary for young men to accompany four war-parties in subordinate positions, as look-outs and auxiliaries, before they were considered fully-fledged warriors. (See Note 45.) [p.198]

36. The reference to *King Solomon's Mines* is obvious; Captain Good's monocle and the prediction of the eclipse are justly famous. But long before Rider Haggard wrote his story, Captain Cremony (see Note 40) had described how a similar prediction was used to impose on the Apaches. While it is a device that could well occur to an imaginative writer, the possibility remains that Haggard had read Cremony, and borrowed a factual incident for fiction. [p.203]

37. The *ta-a-chi* or sweatbath of the Apaches was normally a great tent of blankets, in which heated rocks were placed; the bathers then packed inside in large numbers, and when they were near suffocation, emerged for a cold plunge. (See J. G. Bourke, *An Apache Campaign in the Sierra Madre*, 1886). [p.205]

38. Obviously Mangas Colorado had heard of the brass badges given by the British to friendly chiefs in the colonial days—a practice carried on in many parts of the world under the Empire. It is said that Sitting Bull himself possessed a badge of King George III, possibly inherited from an ancestor, and that when the Sioux sought refuge in Canada after Little Bighorn, he displayed it to Inspector Walsh of the North-west Mounted Police, exclaiming: "We are British Indians! Why did you give the country to the Americans?" [p.211]

39. Mangas (or Mangus) Colorado (1803?–1863), leader of the Santa Rita Copper Mines band of the Mimbreno Apaches, was one of the great Indian chiefs, certainly the most gifted of his nation, although less famous than his successors. Originally named Dasodaha (He-Only-Sits-There), he is supposed to have won the title of Red Sleeves by stealing a red shirt from a party of Americans; only Flashman suggests that it was in reference to his duel with his brothers-in-law—an encounter mentioned by Cremony. Although he was unusually large and powerful, there is some uncertainty as to how tall he was; some sources suggest as much as six feet six or seven, but Cremony, who knew him well a year or two after Flashman, settles for six feet, and John C. Reid, another eye-witness, simply says "Very large, powerful mould, villainous face" (*Reid's Tramp*, by John C. Reid, 1858). What is not in dispute is Mangas's intelligence and political ability; Cremony, although he despised his character and noted that he was not remarkable for personal bravery, thought him brilliant, statesmanlike, and influential beyond any other Indian of his time. As leader of the Mimbreno, Mangas showed great skill in unifying the Apache people, partly through marriage alliances; three of his

daughters by the beautiful Mexican lady became wives of the Coyotero, Chiricahua, and White Mountains clans; one of his sons-in-law was the celebrated Cochise. Of the fourth daughter, Sonsee-array (the Morning Star), there is no historical trace; since she did not marry an Apache chief, like her sisters, she presumably had no political importance.

While Mangas's character may well have been as deplorable as Cremony suggests, in justice to the chief he appears to have been initially well-disposed to the Americans, at least until the Johnson massacre of 1837. For this he took a swift and terrible revenge, killing various bands of American trappers, ambushing convoys to Santa Rita, and finally wiping out almost all the Copper Mines settlers when they tried to escape to Mexico. Thereafter he established himself at Santa Rita, offered help to General Kearny in the Mexican War (see W. H. Emory, *Notes of a Military Reconnaissance*, 1848), and had friendly relations with Commissioner Bartlett of the U.S. Boundary Commission, although they had occasional disputes over the status of Mexican captives in Apache hands. At this time (less than two years after Flashman met him) Mangas suffered an indignity which turned him bitterly against the white intruders—he was set upon and brutally flogged by a party of American miners, whether on suspicion of treachery or out of malice is not clear. Thereafter he waged occasional war against Americans and Mexicans alike, until 1863, when he was taken prisoner by treachery, provoked into resistance, and like many another Indian leader, "shot while trying to escape". (See also Bartlett, J. R., *Personal Narrative of Explorations*, 1854.) [p.212]

40. John Carey Cremony (1815–79) is worth a note to himself, not only because he was the first and most-quoted authority on the Apaches, but as one of those splendid Victorian extroverts who did so much to enliven the last century; in many ways, he was a man after Flashman's own heart, possessed of a bizarre sense of humour, and the hero of adventures so remarkable that they are quite probably true—confronting Cuchillo Negro pistol in hand, baffling the Apaches with his eclipse prediction, pursued across the Jornada with Indian arrows thudding into his serape, perhaps best of all fighting hand to hand with an Apache warrior—"my erratic and useless life passed in review before me . . . to be killed like a pig by an Apache seemed preeminently dreadful and contumelious." As a former journalist on the *Boston Globe*, he knew how to make the best of his stories, but as a scholar and observer of the Apaches during his two years as interpreter to the Bartlett Commission (1849–51) he deserves the highest respect. No one knew the Apaches better, as friend and enemy, and whoever studies or writes about them will go first, and last, to Captain Cremony. [p.213]

41. The Apache nation consisted of several tribes spread across New Mexico, Northern Mexico, and Eastern Arizona, the most prominent being the Mescaleros, Jicarillas, Chiricahuas, Gilenos, Mimbrenos, Mogollones, and Coyoteros, as well as the related Kiowas. Their

numbers have always been something of a mystery; Cremony put it as high as 25,000, which seems unlikely; William Bent, builder of the Fort and a sound judge on Indian affairs, was probably closer to the mark when he estimated a grand total of five to six thousand. (See Cremony, Schoolcraft, and Hodge.) See also Notes 44 and 45.

[p.213]

42. It is not remarkable that Flashman should have known Geronimo (1830?–1909), since at this time the great Apache, the grandson of a chief from another tribe, had settled among the Mimbreno following his marriage to Alopay. Known originally as Goyathlay (The-One-Who-Yawns), Geronimo was among the bitterest opponents of Mexico and the United States; his family had been killed by Mexicans, and he waged intermittent warfare in the south-west until Apache resistance was finally overcome by campaigns in the 1880s, conducted by Generals Crook and Nelson Miles. Geronimo was sent to Florida, but was allowed to spend his last days at Fort Sill, Oklahoma, where he became something of a tourist attraction. Since he was one of the most photographed of all Indians (once being snapped at the wheel of a car), there is ample confirmation of Flashman's description. (See Geronimo's *Autobiography*, edited by S. M. Barret, 1906; Bourke's *Apache Campaign* and *On the Border with Crook*, 1891; Dunn.) [p.216]

43. Cremony for one; he was shown the trick by Quick Killer, the brave whom Flashman mentions as a friend of the Yawner's. [p.225]

44. What Flashman has to say of the Apaches—their culture, habits, characters, their ceremonies relating to courtship, marriage, honeymoon, burial, and war—is born out by other contemporary authorities, especially Cremony. (See also Bourke, *The Medicine-Men of the Apache*, 9th Annual Report, U.S. Bureau of Ethmology, 1892), and his other works; Bartlett; Lockwood; Bancroft; Hodge; Schoolcraft; J. Ross Browne's *Adventures in the Apache Country*, 1863, and Robert Frazier's *The Apaches of the White Mountain Reservation*, 1885.) [p.225]

45. The pollen which the medicine men threw was *hoddentin*, to invoke the sun's blessing on the enterprise. It was much prized by Apache braves, who invariably carried it on the warpath with their cords and the talisman bags which contained such relics as twigs riven by lightning—a great medicine this, and not only among the Apaches: Scott refers to it in *The Lady of the Lake*, canto 3, stanza 4. The medicine cords, sometimes decorated with feathers and with a circlet to be laid on any wound or injury, were worn on the hip. The "scratching-tubes" were the most curious piece of war-party equipment; they were carried by the youngest men who had not yet made four war-paths, and who were forbidden either to scratch themselves with their fingers or let water touch their lips during the campaign. So they scratched themselves with a stick or with the tubes, which they also used for drinking. One thing which Flashman does not mention is the plucking of eyebrows and eyelashes, and one wonders how he managed for several months among people who practised depilation;

presumably they tolerated his shaving. (See Bourke, *Medicine Men;* Sir James Frazer, *The Golden Bough,* 1922.) [p.227]

46. This was undoubtably the City of Rocks, now a tourist attraction some way off the road between Silver City and Deming; from a distance the great mass of rocks looks remarkably like a town of modern buildings, but they are entirely a work of nature, although it is easy to understand Flashman's conclusion that they were man-made. [p.228]

47. Christopher "Kit" Carson (1809–68), guide, scout, Mountain Man and soldier, is one of the great Americans, and by all accounts, even when revisionists have combed his history for faults, seems to have been every bit as likeable as Flashman makes him sound. Only one or two points need to be made here, in relation to Flashman's account: 1) Carson pursued Apache horse-thieves south from Rayado in March, 1850, with a party of friends and dragoons, recaptured the horses, and killed five Indians. This fits precisely with Flashman's story, and only one question arises: either Carson's party went 200 miles south in their pursuit (which is unlikely, but not impossible), or else Flashman has misjudged time and distance again, and was chased farther north by Iron Eyes' band than his account suggests. The nature of the ground where Iron Eyes ran him to earth and Carson rescued him suggests the latter; his flight north may have taken a day longer than he says it did. 2) His description of Carson is accurate: the great scout was 40 at this time, clean-shaven, small and compact in build, soft-spoken, and with twinkling grey eyes, according to others who knew him. That he was illiterate seems doubtful; one biographer states flatly that he owned more than a hundred books and wrote a good clear hand; he certainly spoke French, Spanish, and several Indian dialects fluently, and does not appear to have spoken like an uneducated man. 3) Flashman says Charles Carson was a year old in the spring of 1850; historians give varying dates for the birth of the child, between 1849 and 1850. 4) Flashman's memory is playing him false about the name of the hunter who went with them to Laramie; he is variously described as Goodall and Goodel, but not Goodwin. For the rest, the account of the journey and its purpose fits with Carson's movements at this time; the story on pp. 244–6 is true, as is the story of Mrs White and the novelette on p. 248. 5) Carson was nick-named, among other things, the "Nestor of the Plains", and it is likely that Maxwell was using the name in jest. 6) Lucien Maxwell (1818–1875), a former Mountain Man and hunter, was a close friend of Carson's, but of much greater ambition and worldly ability; he seems to have been a charming rascal and an intrepid frontiersman, but although he did control one of the largest private empires ever known (the Maxwell Land Grant), he died comparatively poor. (*The Life and Adventures of Kit Carson,* by Dewitt C. Peters, 1859; *Kit Carson,* by Noel B. Gerson, 1965; *Dear Old Kit,* by H. L. Carter; *Kit Carson,* by Stanley Vestal; Inman, Lavender, Bancroft.) [p.250]

48. The poem is clearly William Dunbar's *Timor mortis conturbat me,*

470

and one must assume that Carson, who like many frontiersmen, including Bridger and Davy Crockett, was of Scottish descent, had learned it from his father, Lindsey Carson, or possibly from his grandparents; they were William Carson, a Scot who emigrated from Ulster, probably in the 1740's, and Eleanor McDuff of North Carolina. [p.251]

49. It is not clear exactly which fort Flashman means. The first Laramie fort, a wooden stockade called Fort William (and the subject of a well-known painting by A. J. Miller) was established in 1834 on the Laramie river; six or seven years later the adobe Fort Platte was built close by on the Platte river; then came Fort John, commonly called Fort Laramie, and replacing the original Fort William; it also was adobe-walled. The army took it over shortly after Flashman's visit, and additional buildings were added. So he is probably referring to Fort John. Today Fort Laramie is a beautiful spot, with the army buildings in excellent repair, but of the original forts of the Mountain Men and hunters there is no trace, and even their sites are uncertain. Visitors should note that the historic site of Fort Laramie is not to be confused with the modern village called Fort Laramie on the north bank of the Platte, and still less with the large town of Laramie farther south and nearer Cheyenne. (See *Fort Laramie,* by David L. Hieb, National Park Service Handbook Series, 1954.) [p.257]

50. The mariage of Philip Sheridan (1831–88), the famous Civil War general, to Irene Rucker, took place in Chicago, on June 3, 1875. General Sherman, head of the U.S. Army, was a guest, as were Generals Crook and Pope. (See *General George Crook, his Autobiography,* edited by M. F. Schmitt, 1946.) [p.269]

51. For the Indian Office figures, and the state of official opinion on the Indian question at this time, see *The Sioux Wars,* by C. E. De Land, S. Dakota Historical Collections, vol. xv. Figures for arms shipments up the Missouri may be found in Bourke's *Wild Life on the Plains* (1891) an expanded version of General Custer's *My Life on the Plains* (see below). [p.270]

52. The Siouxan words are given here as Flashman has written them in his manuscript, and are to be found in S. R. Rigg's *Dakota-English Dictionary,* 1890. Authorities seem to differ on certain words; for example, one finds both *Isanhanska* and *Millahanska* for "Long Knives", meaning cavalry; there are also different words for "white men", and I have had to assume that when Flashman writes *Isantanka* and *Washechuska,* he means American and English repectively. One or two words I have not troubled to footnote because their meanings are well-known—for example the *How!* of greeting, and the *Wah!* of agreement. (See also P. W. Grant's *Sioux Dictionary* and W. A. Burman's *The Sioux Language.)* [p.272]

53. This description of the Sioux's behaviour in a civilised environment heightens one's regard for Flashman as a scrupulous reporter, for it accords exactly with the account given by D. C. Poole, who spent eighteen months among the Sioux as agent at the Whetstone agency in 1870. Poole accompanied Spotted Tail and other Brulés to

Washington and New York, where the chief was especially taken with the young ladies working in the Mint, and with the performance of a theatrical conjurer. Poole, an excellent raconteur, has some good stories: his description of the earnest clergyman who believed the Indians were one of the Lost Tribes of Israel, and lectured them on the subject without realising that they spoke no English, is well worth reading. (D. C. Poole, *Among the Sioux of Dakota*, 1881.)   [p.277]

54. Crazy Horse, war chief of the Sioux, was born in or slightly before 1844, the son of an Oglala medicine man (also called Crazy Horse) and Spotted Tail's sister. A shy, reserved child, known as Curly or the Fair-Haired Boy because of his light colouring—which led some observers to suppose he was part-white—he seems to have been unusually visionary, even by Indian standards: he dreamed of himself on horseback with a red hawk feather in his hair and a pebble behind his ear, and great things were prophesied for him, which were fulfilled. As one of the leaders at Little Bighorn and the Rosebud, he achieved a reputation unequalled by any other fighting Indian. He surrendered to the army in 1877, and like Mangas Colorado, was killed while trying to escape. (See F. J. Dockstader, *Great North American Indians* and other works on the Sioux cited in these Notes.)   [p.278]

55. This seems to represent Spotted Tail's philosophy very fairly. A remarkable man, the Brulé chief was considered the Sioux nation's foremost warrior in the 1840s and 50s; he was credited early in his career with counting 26 coups, and by the end of his life had more than a hundred scalps on his war-shirt. Following the wipe-out of Lt Grattan and his troops by the Brulé under their chief Bear-that-Scatters in 1854, Spotted Tail and four other braves agreed to "give their lives for the good of the tribe", and surrendered, singing their death-songs. Spotted Tail was imprisoned at Fort Leavenworth, where he is said to have learned some English, and where his observations seem to have convinced him that it was futile to attempt resistance to the white man. Later, as chief of the Brulés, he was a resolute champion of peace and reconciliation and, says his biographer Hyde, obtained advantages for the Sioux by persuasion which their militant leaders failed to win by war: "He was probably the greatest Sioux chief of his period. . . (and) played his part better than any of the other Sioux leaders."

Spotted Tail was highly intelligent, good-natured, and strikingly handsome; the painting by H. Ulke, done in 1877, shows a bold, humorous face which might well have given Flashman cause for jealousy. Bishop Whipple called him "a picture of manly beauty, with piercing eyes". The chief was also something of a dry wit: dining at the White House, he remarked that the whites had fine tipis, and was assured by President Grant that if he settled down to agriculture, the Government would give him an excellent tipi; Spotted Tail's response was that if it was a tipi like the White House, he would think about farming. In 1877, it was partly through his efforts that

472

Crazy Horse was persuaded to surrender, and possibly because of this and his "non-hostile" policy in general Spotted Tail was murdered four years later by Crow Dog. (See Hyde, *Spotted Tail*; Dunn; Poole.) [p.280]

56. It is possible that Flashman heard the names of S. J. Tilden (Democrat) and R. B. Hayes (Republican) canvassed this far ahead of the 1876 election, but not for another fourteen months could he have been aware of W. G. Grace's prodigious innings: the Doctor's scores of 344 against Kent, 177 against Notts, and 318 not out against Yorkshire (all within six days), were not made until August of the following year. The contemplation of American politics has plainly clouded the author's memory. [p.289]

57. Ulysses S. Grant's dislike of hand-shaking was purely physical; at some functions, after his retirement, he asked to be excused it on the grounds that he found it positively painful. (See *From the Tanyard to the White House, the story of President Grant's life,* by William M. Thayer, 1886.) [p.289]

58. Anson Mills, who commanded the escort, has left a vivid account of the council in the grove, which lies about eight miles from the present Fort Robinson, Nebraska, not far from the road beyond the modern town of Crawford. Mills tallies closely with Flashman, and corroborates even the detail of Standing Bear's suggesting to a hostile Sioux that he should shoot a colt. The negotiations at Camp Robinson followed very much the line described by Flashman, although there are discrepancies about the timing of the various offers and their rejection. Anyone reading the histories of this period may be confused by the fact that both the Red Cloud and Spotted Tail agencies shifted to different locations over the years; at this time Red Cloud was close to the present Fort Robinson, while Spotted Tail and Camp Sheridan were about 15 miles due east of the modern town of Chadron. (See Anson Mills, *My Story*, 1918; R. W. Frazer, *Forts of the West*; Roger T. Grange, Jr, *Fort Robinson*, 1978; Hyde; De Land; Poole.) [p.311]

59. The great Philadelphia Centennial exhibition was opened on May 10, 1876, at Fairmount Park, by President Grant. The foreign contributions included a belly-dancer from Tunisia, but it is unlikely that she was sponsored by the ladies' committee, whose work was on an altogether more serious level. (See *Frank Leslie's Illustrated Historical Register of the Centennial Exposition,* reproduced in 1974 with an introduction by Richard Kenin.) [p.318]

60. This gossipy summary of the Belknap case is true enough in its essentials, but what is still not clear is Custer's motive in giving evidence at the time. He did have high political ambitions, and the corruption of the administration was no doubt a tempting target. But he was probably sincere in not wanting to leave his command to testify in person, for purely military reasons—and possibly also because he feared the consequences of embarrassing Grant at that particular moment. It was, perhaps, a question of timing—and Custer's sense of timing could be deplorably bad. (For details of Custer's

correspondence with the Clymer committee, who summoned him to Washington, see *A Complete Life of General George Armstrong Custer,* by Frederic Whittaker, 1876; Dunn.) [p.328]

61. Tight waists were a fashionable joke at this time. *Punch* has a cartoon of three ladies who have dressed for the evening on the understanding that they will not even have to climb the stairs. [p.330]

62. President Grant was an admirer of *Tom Brown's Schooldays* and its author, Thomas Hughes, the Radical M.P. and social reformer, who (like his book) became extremely popular in the United States—Hughes even helped to found a model community in Tennessee, which was christened Rugby, after his old school. During Grant's visit to England in 1877, Hughes proposed the former President's health at a private dinner at the Crystal Palace; Grant had been told that a speech from him was not expected, but he insisted on rising to express his gratification at hearing "my health proposed in such kind words by Tom Brown of Rugby". (See Thayer.) [p.336]

63. The name of Edwinton Landing was in fact changed to Bismarck in the hope that the German Chancellor might encourage financial help to the Northern Pacific railway, which was in difficulties. [p.338]

64. Captain Benteen's famous holograph letter about Little Bighorn does, in fact, contain an incidental reference to cricket, but Flashman's is the only evidence that he was an enthusiast. [p.349]

65. *Garryowen*, the stirring march forever associated with Custer's 7th Cavalry, dates from the late eighteenth century, when it was a drinking song of rich young roisterers in Limerick. It attained immediate popularity in the British Army and was played throughout the Napoleonic Wars, becoming the regimental march of the 18th Foot (The Royal Irish Regiment), and was a favourite in the Crimea; Fanny Duberly mentions it in connection with the Connaught Rangers (Devil's Own), and the 8th (Irish) Hussars who were part of the Light Brigade. When it crossed the Atlantic is uncertain, but it was known during the Civil War, and quite probably caught Custer's fancy at that time, despite the traditions that it was introduced later to the 7th either by the Irish Captain Keogh or the English Sergeant Butler. (See Lewis Winstock, *Songs and Music of the Redcoats, 1642–1902,* 1970; Walter Wood, *The Romance of Regimental Marches,* 1932.) [p.352]

66. As a guide to the character and psychological condition of George Armstrong Custer (1839–76), Flashman's account of him is interesting and, in the light of published information, convincing. Custer was only 37; he had served with distinction in the Civil War, achieved general rank when he was 23, had ten horses shot under him, and was spectacular in an age which did not lack for heroes. After the war his career was less happy; his impulsive temper led to his court martial and suspension in 1867, and although Sheridan had him reinstated, his name was not free from controversy even in victory, as when he defeated Black Kettle's Cheyenne on the Washita. That he was in an excitable state in the winter of 1875–6, and regarded the coming campaign as a last chance for distinction (and possible

political advancement), as Flashman suggests, seems highly probable. The last-minute check received when Grant almost removed him from the expedition can have done nothing for his stability; as one eminent commentator puts it, Custer took the field "smarting".

Flashman's record of Custer during the vital months before the campaign, while more personal than any other, accords with known facts. The general, a teetotal non-smoker who never swore, was highly emotional and easily moved to tears; the story of his weeping at the play *Ours*, at Wallack's Theatre, is authentic, and he was known to choke when reading aloud some moving passage; he liked party games and amateur theatricals, and would sometimes lie on a bearskin rug listening to Swiss zither music played by a soldier of the 7th. He was an energetic writer and avid reader, British military history being one of his favourite studies. Unpopular with his officers (Benteen seems particularly to have detested him), he obviously had an engaging personality when he chose; secretive in planning, occasionally devious, proud to a fault, he could be embarrassingly open: Flashman was only one of the friends to whom he confessed his penury in New York. He appears to have been close to desperation during the Grant-Belknap episode, whose course Flashman charts fairly accurately, although in much greater detail than has been available hitherto. From all this Custer may appear, to say the least, eccentric. If so, it should be remembered that he was not alone in his time; he was a Victorian man of action, and a not untypical one, and as a soldier he should not be judged solely by his last campaign or the events that led up to it. (See Whittaker; Dunn; *Boots and Saddles*, 1885, and *Following the Guidon*, 1890, by Mrs E. B. Custer, his widow; *My Life on the Plains*, by George A. Custer, 1876; and works cited later in these Notes and Appendix B.) [p.353]

67. For a detailed account of *Far West*'s voyage up the Missouri and Yellowstone rivers, including the movements of the military forces, see J. M. Hanson, *The Conquest of the Missouri*, 1909. [p.364]

68. There is no doubt that Terry wanted a combined operation (this was Marsh's opinion) but that he could not lay down hard and fast restrictions on Custer. It has to be remembered that a principal concern was to prevent the Sioux escaping, and a strict prohibition on independent action might have resulted in Custer's standing helplessly watching the hostiles melt away, simply because Gibbon had not appeared. No one envisaged the kind of situation that eventually faced Custer, because no one could guess that the number of hostiles had been badly underestimated. At the same time, there is no doubt that if Terry had been able to foresee the concentration of Sioux that was waiting on the Little Bighorn, he would surely have forbidden Custer to attack it single-handed. Terry's own report (curiously clumsily phrased for a lawyer) says in part ". . .that either of them which should be first engaged (Gibbon or Custer) might be a 'waiting fight'—give time for the other to come up". Lieutenant Bradley's aside is reflected in a note which he wrote after the *Far West* conference: "It is understood that Custer is at liberty to attack at once if

he deems it prudent. We have little hope of being in at the death and Custer will undoubtedly exert himself to get there first and win the laurels for himself and his regiment." Others thought so, too.

An often-quoted passage is the supposed last-minute instruction given verbally by Terry to Custer: "Use your own judgement, and do what you think best if you strike the trail; and whatever you do, Custer, hold on to your wounded." But whether Terry ever did say this is open to question. (See *The Field Diary of General A.H. Terry*, 1970; General Nelson Miles, *Personal Recollections*, 1897; Dunn; Hanson; Wittaker; and other Custer authorities cited below.) [p.372]

69. It is difficult to estimate times and distances from the sketchy details of the narrative, but this sounds like the big bluff overlooking the modern town of Forsyth. The Rosebud creek, referred to earlier, still looks rather like an English brook near its junction with the Yellowstone, and the hedgerow remains, but it is not an easy stream to find from the highway, and the marker which once showed Custer's campsite has disappeared. [p.373]

70. The Navajo were unusual in the high position they accorded to their women-folk, who could own property of their own; thus Cleonie presumably passed into the possession of her owner's widows, which might not have happened in another tribe. As a slave, her position must have been dreadful; Mayne Reid, who knew the Navajo, was in no doubt of their cruelty to captives, and their eagerness to capture white females. On the other hand, Hyde singles out the Navajo as a jovial and progressive people, not given to torture and more averse to warfare than their fellow-Indians, so there are, as usual, two sides to the question. [p.380]

71. Estimates of the number of Indians in the Little Bighorn encampment vary, but ten to twelve thousand is a popular figure. It was not by any means the largest assembly of Indians ever known, although other writers than Flashman have made this error; the largest gathering of so-called hostiles it may have been, but there were twice as many Indians present during the Camp Robinson council of the previous year. (See Anson Mills.) The size of the village itself has been variously estimated at from three to five miles long; bearing in mind that the Little Bighorn is an extremely winding river, and that its course varies slightly today from that of 1876, it seems unlikely that the distance from the Hunkpapa camp at the upstream end of the village to the Cheyenne at its other extremity was more than a bare three miles. [p.388]

72. There can be no doubt that this Indian was Crazy Horse. While the one unauthenticated photograph of him is too vague for comparison, Flashman's description tallies fairly well with others, and the design of the medicine shirt puts the wearer's identity beyond question; it corresponds exactly with the shirt belonging to Crazy Horse which was presented by Little Big Man to Captain John G. Bourke of the 3rd Cavalry, the well-known Indian authority and historian. (See Bourke, *Medicine-Men.*) [p.394]

73. Walking Blanket Woman, the Oglala girl, fought at Little Bighorn.

She rode in full war-dress, carrying the war-staff which her brother had borne on the Rosebud. (See *Custer's Fall*, by David Humphreys Miller, 1957.) [p.402]

74. This passage substantiates one of the most cherished traditions of Little Bighorn: that four Cheyenne warriors—Bobtail Horse, Calf, Roan Horse, and one *unidentified* brave—advanced to the river alone to oppose Custer's five troops. Some versions say they took cover behind a ridge, and were joined by a party of Sioux, who helped them to check Custer's advance by rifle fire. One theory is that Custer, unable to believe that four men would ride out against him unsupported, halted and dismounted because he expected a large force to be following the four. It is fairly certain that Custer did halt and dismount, for whatever reason, and there are those who believe that if he had continued to advance he would have won across the ford and possibly overrun the village before Crazy Horse and Gall, who had been fighting Reno upstream, had regrouped. Again, some versions have Custer actually reaching the river before being forced back; one belief is that he himself was killed there. These are matters of controversy; the one thing that now appears to have been settled is the identity of the fourth mysterious Cheyenne. [p.404]

75. This sounds like Boyer, one of the scouts, repeating the warning which he had given to Custer when the Indian camp was first sighted. [p.405]

76. This clarifies, if it does not settle, one of the controversies of Little Bighorn—where and how Custer himself died. Indian accounts of his death have been so varied as to be almost useless; he has been killed by many different hands, in several places, including the ford at the very start of the battle. If that were true, then his body must have been carried almost a mile to where it was found on the site of the "Last Stand" on the slope below the present Monument, which seems highly unlikely. Flashman's account suggests that he died on the spot where his body was found, and indeed where the greatest concentration of 7th Cavalry appear to have been killed in the final desperate struggle, with the remnants of Yates's, Tom Custer's, and Smith's three troops scattered down the north side of the long gully below. It is worth noting, though, that Flashman's recollections are (not unreasonably) somewhat confused; in what he calls the "slow moment" he saw Yates and Custer together; in the hand-to-hand combat that followed, the fight must have surged some distance uphill to the point where Custer died, since Custer's body and Yates's were found about three hundred yards apart. One point at least may be regarded as settled; however he died, Custer did not commit suicide. [p.412]

77. Sergeant Butler's body was discovered, alone and surrounded by spent cartridges, more than a mile from his own troop's last stand. This has been one of the mysteries of Little Bighorn. The explanation that he had been despatched, when all was obviously lost, to carry word of the disaster if not to get help, is one that must have occurred even without Flashman's corroboration. Butler was, after all, a trusted and experienced soldier, and no one in the regiment would

have been more likely to win through, a point acknowledged by the Sioux themselves. Sitting Bull, Gall, and many others paid tribute to the courage with which the 7th Cavalry fought its last action, and singled out some for special mention, but above all the rest they praised "the soldier with braid on his arms" as the bravest man at Greasy Grass. [p.413]

78. Flashman's ride clean across the battlefield, from the point where Keogh's troop fell until he must have been close to the river, might seem improbable if it were not corroborated by an unimpeachable source of which Flashman himself was probably never aware. In a magazine article published in 1898, the Cheyenne chief Two Moon, who played a leading part in the battle, and is regarded as one of the most reliable Indian witnesses, had this to say of the final moments of the struggle:

> "One man rides up and down the line—all the time shouting. He rode a sorrel horse . . . I don't know who he was. He was a very brave man . . . (a) bunch of men, maybe some forty, started towards the river. The man on the sorrel horse led them, shouting all the time. He wore buckskin shirt and had long black hair and moustache. He fought hard with a big knife . . ."

Except for the buckskin shirt (and Two Moon admits that the soldiers were white with dust, which might easily have misled him) this description fits Flashman exactly, even to the sound effects. And historians have been at a loss to identify the black-moustached rider until now, since his appearance does not tally with that of any known officer of the 7th. One theory is that he was a scout, and De Land considers the possibility that it was Boyer, but dismisses it on the ground that Boyer was clean-shaven. It is also worth noting Two Moon's statement that the man "fought hard with a big knife", by which he probably meant a sabre (the chief Gall also confirmed that one of the white men definitely used a sabre). Since the 7th Cavalry carried no sabres in the battle, but we know that at least one Sioux warrior did (having captured it from Crook's forces on the Rosebud), and since Flashman describes how he took a sabre from a Sioux, it seems safe to say that the identity of the mysterious rider with the black moustache has at last been established. As to the only other inconsistency between the versions of Flashman and Two Moon— that the moustached rider was at the head of a bunch of fugitives— nothing in Flashman's writing has ever suggested that, in the heat of flight, he paid much attention to any other unfortunates behind him. [p.415]

79. When the Custer part of the battle began, and how long it lasted, has never been satisfactorily settled. Reno went into action (the first shots heard by Flashman) apparently at about 3.15 p.m., and according to Sgt Martini, the last messenger from Custer on the bluffs, Custer first came under fire at about 3.20 (sooner than Flashman's estimate). It seems the fighting on the Greasy Grass was over by about 5 p.m., if not earlier, but it is impossible to tell how much time

Custer's force took to get out on to the slope, and how long the action there lasted. Not more than an hour, certainly, and probably a good deal less. General Edgerly, who as a subaltern was in the Reno part of the fight, is said to have estimated the Custer action at fifteen minutes, or thirty at the outside; Gall, who was in the action throughout, put it at half an hour, and a Cheyenne estimated twenty minutes. So Flashman may not be far out. Differing figures have also been given for the numbers of casualties. Custer lost about 200 dead on the hill, and Gall put the Indian dead at 43, which seems rather low, although his statement suggests that many others died of wounds. [p.417]

80. For a good description of Deadwood in its early days, see John F. Finerty, *Warpath and Bivouac*, 1890. In some ways, although it declined sadly after the mining-boom, and has since grown again, Deadwood is not very different today; solid masonry has replaced much of the log-and-frame and the town has extended greatly along the ravine since it is physically impossible to expand sideways—but there is still sawdust on the floor of the Number Ten Saloon, and the Deadwood Stage carries tourists for a moderate fee. But it is sad to see the Bella Union Theatre empty and boarded up. [p.443]

81. James Butler ("Wild Bill") Hickok (1837–76), peace-officer and gun-fighter, had deteriorated from the days when Mrs Custer observed: "Physically, he was a delight to look upon." A former Union soldier, frontier scout, and Indian fighter, he achieved celebrity between 1868 and 1871, as marshal of Hays City and Abilene (Flashman served as his deputy at some time during this period, but so far no record of this curious partnership had been found in *The Flashman Papers*). The first, and reputedly the best, of the notorious Western gunfighters, Hickok is believed to have killed 17 opponents, apart from Indian and Confederate enemies. A tall, handsome figure who is said to have modelled his expression (but not his clothing) on the late Prince Albert, Hickok was a pleasant, modest and well-spoken man, if Mrs Custer and Sir Henry Stanley, the explorer, are to be believed. [p.446]

A Note About the Author

George MacDonald Fraser was born in England,
schooled in Scotland, served in a Highland Regiment in India,
Africa and the Middle East, was a journalist, and now
lives with his family on the Isle of Man. He is the
author of *Flashman, Royal Flash, Flash for Freedom!*,
Flashman at the Charge, Flashman in the Great Game,
and *Flashman's Lady*—the first six books in The
Flashman Papers, which have won him critical acclaim as a
comic novelist of rare distinction—of
The Steel Bonnets, a history of the Scottish
Border reivers, of *Mr. American*, and of two
volumes of stories, *The General Danced at Dawn*
and *McAuslan in the Rough*.

A Note on the Type

The text of this book was set in a computer
version of Times Roman, designed by Stanley
Morison for *The Times* (London) and first
introduced by that newspaper in 1932.
Among typographers and designers of the twentieth
century, Stanley Morison has been a strong forming
influence as typographical adviser to the English Monotype
Corporation, as a director of two distinguished English
publishing houses, and as a writer of sensibility,
erudition, and keen practical sense.

Display type by Sara Reynolds